A Mercedes for

Soldier Boy

Fall of the Cities – Book IV

By
Vance Huxley

© 2018 Vance Huxley
Published by Entrada Publishing.
Printed in the United States of America.

TABLE OF CONTENTS

TABLE OF CONTENTS

DEDICATION

To my Noeline and to the Joy of my life

Acknowledgements

Thank you to my editor Sharon Umbaugh,
for turning my words into a book worth reading.

My thanks to Rachel at Entrada
for all her hard work and encouragement.

Chapter 1:
Shaken and Stirred

Four years after the Crash, when the Cabal's attempt at global domination fell in a maelstrom of violence and starvation, many of the survivors are still struggling to survive. Some countries, mainly in South America, have fallen under Cabal control, but chaos rules in most of the rest. Africa, the Middle East and the Indian sub-continent have been left to devour themselves as centuries of tribal and religious enmity become armed conflicts. In the UK there is a tenuous balance, where the Cabal have control of the government but their surplus population still lives, penned inside the ruins of the major cities. The enclosed populations have devolved into small, fortified city-states, many ruled by brutal dictators.

At the edges of the second largest city in the UK, a democratic enclave, called Orchard Close, has worked through all the stages from ragged refugees to fortified estate. Their enclave is led by Harold Miller, a military clerk who resigned from the Army to rescue his widowed sister and her kids. Harold, ably abetted by the other residents of a small block of flats, gathered together people with useful skills. The group moved to suitable housing, scavenged and stockpiled essentials, built defences and encouraged everyone to practice with their unfamiliar weapons. As a result, the group of thirty disparate civilians with no military training managed to survive the initial upheaval. After more training and taking in more refugees the determined group survived attacks by rioters, foiling two attempts to orchestrate their destruction and finally persuading the neighbours to leave them alone.

The surrounding gangs call Harold "Soldier Boy" and believe he is the gang boss, and an SAS sniper. Since very few survivors can shoot at all, even the gangsters, and firearms are in short supply, that makes them very cautious. In reality, the mixed group in Orchard Close have pooled their skills to create a stable community, led by an unofficial committee known as the Coven, who have no ambitions beyond survival. Spreading rumours bring more valuable refugees, such as people with medical and knitting skills. Harold believes there are others among the gangs, tradespeople who hide their skills to avoid semi-slavery. As a result, the neighbouring gangs need dental, plumbing and electrical work, gun repairs or knitted goods, and will trade ammunition, weapons, scavenged materials, and coupons that can be spent in the Marts. The concentration of skilled workers, and trading their skills and fresh garden produce, turn Orchard Close into a valuable local asset. Fighting off continual small raids also makes the residents dangerous in a minor way, dangerous enough for the neighbours to prefer Soldier Boy as an ally.

Their leader, Harold, isn't aware his enclave has caught the eye of the Cabal. He's only too aware he's caught the eye of at least one powerful gang boss, the General, who is bent on conquest. To stop that Harold has been negotiating alliances with a gang of heavy metal nutters, a bunch of sleazy ex-shop assistants, a sadistic ex-car thief, and a group of escaped female prisoners notorious for torturing and dismembering trespassing men. The General won't accept his first defeat; Harold expects another attempt. He is using the reprieve to try and train up his group of no-longer-peaceful citizens, so they can beat off the next horde of maniacs.

Across the UK, the remaining decent, honest enclaves come under increasing pressure as Cabal agents plot their destruction. Harold and Orchard Close don't know about them, but potential allies in their own city are already under attack. Some enclaves will not survive their own version of the Valentine's Day massacre, while others will be fundamentally changed.

* * *

Dudley Zoo:

Miles to the west, across a heavily patrolled motorway, but still in the same city as Orchard Close, a small group of armed youths moved up closer to their target. These wannabe gangsters weren't looking for conquest, just a chance to steal fresh meat and maybe a weapon or woman. Encouraged by alcohol and the information they'd been given by a stranger, a Cabal agent, the disorganised group moved up to the edge of the ruins around their target. "Are you sure the blowpipes are bullshit?"

Their self-appointed leader sneered. "You heard what that guy told us, it's all bullshit. Come on, blowpipes with poison darts, Zulus and a hunter with an elephant gun? Whoever came up with that had been smoking some really good shit." He gestured at the clean, unspoiled patch of woodland ahead, incongruous among the surrounding acres of derelict housing. "The gangs round here buy meat so the big animals are definitely in there. Zebras and deer and some pig things for starters, with only shop assistants to protect them. There's even charcoal for a barbecue if we cut those trees down."

As the gang advanced, a short series of high-pitched calls rang out, getting louder. The men paused until one saw the small creatures with white tufty ears darting through the trees. "Fucking monkeys. Shoot them with crossbows before they wake everyone up."

Too late. the clump of woodland came alive as a cloud of birds sporting bright, exotic plumage took flight, calling out in alarm and temporarily drowning out the monkeys. Once the advancing gangsters started shooting, the Marmosets quickly disappeared into the trees, but they had served their purpose. The group of young men moved into the woods, shooting at any sign of movement until one stopped and raised a rifle. "Fucking hell, look at that." He raised the rifle further and fired above a clump of low trees, then again. "Yeah! Oh shit." Those nearby looked across but quickly crouched down, because a hypodermic dart with a tuft of bright red on the end jutted from his thigh. The shocked rifleman turned to look at them before crumpling.

"Fuck, no!" Another stared down at the dart in his arm. He staggered a few steps before going down. A loud boom echoed. Something picked one of the men off his feet and hurled him backwards as blood spattered over the trees and bushes.

"Poison darts, oh fuck they're real!" A gangster turned to go but fell, clutching his leg. The rest froze for a moment, staring at the head of the thrown spear that had sliced his thigh wide open. They'd all seen the distinctive shape of a Zulu assegai on TV, before the Crash. Another crumpled with a hypodermic in his arm.

* * *

"Zulus! It's all true! Run, run, that fucking hunter is here as well. They'll kill us all!" The youths scattered and ran, but not before others went down under a hail of arrows, spears and crossbow bolts. A few of the wounded screamed or shouted for help, until spears flew from the undergrowth to silence them. As another youth crumpled with a dart in his back, his friend hesitated until a bullet from that big firearm smashed him into a tree. More youths dropped their weapons, staggering as arrows struck. Friends helped a few of them back towards the familiar safety of the ruins, but more shafts, darts and spears finished off the rest. Silent figures, decorated with greenery and wearing feathers in their hair, pursued the surviving youths through the undergrowth. Their spears and machetes ruthlessly killed any wounded. The slowest invader crumpled just before he left the trees, another of those small darts buried in his thigh.

A young woman wearing a green smock over her jeans and blouse, camouflaged with leafy twigs, rose from behind a rhododendron bush. She gestured with an ancient crossbow, her eyes full of unshed tears. "They've gone, Teddy, but they killed Gwendoline."

The man she spoke to, wearing a tiger-skin cloak with the paws crossed on his chest and the tiger's head as a hat, sighed. "It had to happen eventually, Imogen. She was just too tall." He lifted a thin tube with a small compressed air can attached. "I think I hit one at the edge of the trees. We'd best get his weapons first, before any of those yobs recover enough to try and retrieve them."

"But Gwendoline? I helped when she was born." The first sob broke through.

Teddy turned as Imogen dropped her crossbow to wrap her arms around him. He let the tube fall to swing on its sling, and held her tight while she cried. "I'm sorry Imogen, I really am." He stroked her back and then hugged her again. "Keep clear and the rest will see to the skinning and jointing. I'll let the canteen know you won't want any of Gwendoline. They'll make you something else."

"I don't want to see her, but I don't mind once she's in the stew. That's better than selling her for the rotten sods out there to eat." She looked up, her eyes red and puffy from crying. "Can I have a piece of skin, you know, something distinctive for memory?"

"As much as you want. Would you like a cape? Though you won't want her head on it." Teddy sighed, gesturing at the tiger skin he wore. "I only left Sangha's head on because Inga swore it would look better. I'm not so sure but the rest of his skin keeps the wind out."

Imogen reached up to stroke the tiger's head. "Sangha's head scares those horrible people out there, him and that dart gun." She hugged a bit tighter. "Sangha might have saved us right back at the beginning, when

Stephanie let him out. Those people with guns were terrified, so they all shot at him and the smaller cats instead of us. He gave us time to get the dart guns and the shock sticks." A hint of a smile crossed her face. "Then you and the other staff charged out, waving those spears and throwing the stock from the gift shop."

"We couldn't have kept him alive anyway, or any of the larger carnivores. We can't spare enough meat. Are you feeling better now, maybe up to helping me strip the ones I hit?" Teddy looked a bit guilty. "It still doesn't seem right, shooting them with animal tranquillisers when I know it will kill them."

"But you do it because they have guns and would kill us all, or worse. I don't know what we would have done without you, and Inga, and Takato and Stephanie. Takato and that elephant gun frighten them every bit as much as your hat." Imogen kissed him and his arms tightened as he kissed back, briefly.

Teddy pulled his head back, suddenly very worried. "I'm sorry, that was inappropriate."

Imogen giggled, then smiled through her tears. "Nobody cares any more about a manager kissing an under-keeper. I thought you fancied me but daren't push." She cuddled in and sighed. "Now I know, so you may as well give in."

"Really? Oh." A smile started, but before Teddy could say more a woman's voice cut in.

"Come on you two, let's strip the bodies. This lot weren't a real gang, just a bunch of yobs so we've only got a few wounded. Setting the Marmosets free was a brilliant idea, they make terrific perimeter alarms." The woman stopped talking, breaking into laughter instead. "About time you two stopped dancing round each other." Four more people, three carrying pseudo-Zulu assegais and shields and the fourth wielding a bow and a machete, came past the pair and headed into the trees. The fifth, wearing a multitude of exotic feathers in her brightly coloured dreadlocks, paused and looked back before following. "The last giraffe is dead, Teddy. One of the rotten sods shot Gwendoline, even though they'd never have got near enough to take the meat. We just haven't enough people to keep the bastards out of the woods."

"I know, Inga." Teddy looked down at the woman in his arms. "Imogen would like a piece of Gwendoline's hide to make a souvenir, a cape or skirt. She helped at the birth." Teddy and Imogen moved apart, a little self-consciously, then followed the rest through the woods to the north of the partially depopulated zoo.

"Do you think that policeman who came to see us was the real thing, Teddy? He had a police machine gun and uniform." Inga sounded hopeful, but a real policeman surviving the last three years seemed unlikely. "He could have taken them from a body?"

Teddy paused to think. "He had the right manner, if you know what I mean. We have to find a gang we trust enough to ask for help, otherwise the neighbours will eventually join forces and run over us to get at the animals. At least with this Precinct Nineteen, we can go through the canal tunnel to make contact, or a few of us will."

"I thought the film was Precinct Thirteen?"

"It was, Imogen. He reckons they got it wrong to start with, and now it's stuck." Teddy hugged her. "That actually helps me to trust them in a daft way."

"I'm willing to take a chance to get that machine gun in these trees, waiting for the next bunch of yobs." Inga stopped, looking down. "Here's one of yours, Teddy." They bent to strip the body, careful to remove the dart without damaging it. Behind, as the flag above the ruined castle unfurled in a gust of wind, the strengthening daylight clearly showed the black on white depiction of a tiger's face.

* * *

Sutton Park:

More alliances were being considered eight miles to the northeast of Dudley Zoo, still in the same city but across a motorway patrolled by armoured vehicles. The residents of Sutton Park, many of them ex-wildlife wardens or Park workers, already had a loose confederation. That had been enough to keep any of the surrounding gangs from more than occasionally rustling a few animals or fish from the extensive grasslands, woods and lakes. Like Dudley Zoo, the Park residents bred animals and fish. Since the Marts didn't sell fresh meat, protein that wasn't rabbit, rat or cat made Sutton Park a prime target for the surrounding gangs.

Now those gangs had realised an alliance might work for them as well. Three days after the successful defence of Dudley Zoo, the heavily armed representatives of eleven small gangs gathered to discuss the conquest of Sutton Park. While these gangs were less violent than some of those near

Orchard Close, none of them were either democratic or peaceful. Today they'd declared a truce and met at a neutral location to deal with a common enemy.

A gang boss known as Odin, an imposing figure wearing a long red cloak and a gold painted safety helmet, stood at the head of a big old dining table in a partially burned-out hotel. He smacked the table with a long-shafted lump hammer. "Stop arguing and shut the fuck up, you stupid bastards. If you don't want to join in, fuck off, but if you leave now you keep clear of the fucking park afterwards, right?"

"Elsewhat,Odin? Who died and made you God? Just because you call yourselves Vikings and use Viking God names means naught." The speaker, a burly black youth with close-cropped hair, glowered. He wore an old-style skinhead 'uniform' of rolled up jeans, Doc Marten boots, and a donkey jacket. "You're a jumped up shoplifter same as the rest of us."

"I've got twice as many men as you, Shiner, and if I've got four brain cells that's twice as many as you as well. I'm not fucking God. I'd just rather eat those cows and horses and fish than fight any of you lot for them."

"Yeah, go shine your boots and we'll eat your share." Several other voices agreed with the latest speaker, a young Asian woman with the hilt of a samurai-style sword jutting up behind her shoulder.

"As long as you ain't tryin' ter take over." Shiner sat again.

"No, but there's eleven gangs here and if we work together we all get to eat better. Right now, each of our gangs attacks on their own, but the residents combine, which costs us men and ammo. If my gang manage to snatch something, one of you twats jumps in to nick whatever we get. That means we're all losing men to each other, and getting fuck all for it." He raised a hand to several objections from an all-female gang and several women fighters. "Sorry Hangaku, Angel, we lose men or women. That bunch of gardeners and eco-nerds in the Park are laughing at us while they scoff their fish and chips or steaks. If all eleven of us combine, draw up a plan of the park and divide it now, we can go in mob-handed and take the lot."

"Including all the people. We want the ones who raise the animals and fish, who know what we can eat and can breed more. Otherwise we all get fish and steak for a week and then it's back to raiding each other and eating Mart shit. There'll be enough to go round if we're careful, so we want a proper treaty, peace between all of us." The fortyish man looked out of place because of his age and his suit. His followers of both sexes, a gang based in a partly burned-out college, were also dressed smartly, and many were well past their teens. Despite that, the plethora of well-made and well-used weapons all of them wore guaranteed that nobody underestimated the Hard School. If any of them had been genuine teachers at some time, it must have been at one of the rougher inner-city schools.

The Asian woman, Hangaku, turned to scowl at Shiner. "The Headmaster makes sense. No poaching, right? If enough of us sign up, we can chop any smartarse that gets out of line."

"Let's divvy the land up now and share the livestock after the fight, the two-legged sort as well." Odin unrolled a big sheet of paper, an old poster showing Sutton Park including the main landmarks and buildings. Around the park edges, the border with each of the gangs had been drawn on. He used his hammer to weigh down one corner and a couple of machetes and a knife were donated for the others. "They've got bigger fields than those twats on TV, the ones with the women that shoot." He grinned acknowledgement at a bleached blonde with a shotgun, they had some women here who could shoot.

"Can we talk to the residents before everyone rolls in and starts shooting?" The Headmaster shrugged at the jeers and comments about being scared of farmers. "We trade text books from our college for food so they'll listen to us. If they'll agree to a takeover without a fight, everyone gets their meat and we'll all save ammo."

Shiner spoke for several others. "Yeah, but that also warns them."

"Give us an hour, once everyone is ready. That's not long enough for them to set up anything effective." The Headmaster, the boss of the Hard School, stared the objectors down. "I don't give a shit how many of you lot die, but I'll be pissed if the fish expert or cow midwife gets killed in the crossfire."

"The Headmaster has a point, Odin. Some of these aren't exactly accurate." Hangaku, leader of the Yakuza, sneered at several of the noisiest gangsters. "We each keep whoever lives in our section, right?"

"Except the cow midwife and other experts, we share those." The Headmaster leant back in his chair after giving the rest one last sour look. "Or we'll end up fighting over that."

"As long as we get our share of the women." This speaker, dressed in jeans and a motorbike jacket, leered at the women present.

Hangaku put a hand up to her sword hilt. "Your blokes probably won't notice or care if they get a cow, Kurt. Better yet, I'll geld you all now so you don't have to bother."

Odin glowered and banged his fist on the table. "Cool it, Hangaku. You promised not to start trouble." The Asian woman subsided with a smirk as the eleven gangs settled down to wrangle over borders.

* * *

Mid-morning the following day, deep inside Sutton Park, one of the park residents looked out of a window as shots rang out. The woman's eyes opened in alarm as someone started banging on an iron bar. She turned to her husband. "That's the alarm, Wilf! They're coming. Oh shit, oh Christ, Wilf."

In the distance a bell clanged, another of the groups in the park calling for help. "Oh my God Chrissie, the trader was right, the others are being attacked as well. The council thought it was a con, to get us to surrender to that bloody Kurt and his Studs. Run like the clappers to the old railway station, the Hard School and the Yakuza are over that way." Wilf pointed out of the window, then reached down and picked up his bow. "Here they come. I'll try to slow the Studs up for a few minutes, then offer to surrender. The Trader from the Hard School said they want us alive." He opened the door but paused before leaving. "I really hope so."

Chrissie hesitated, but another flurry of shooting made up her mind. "Try to get away later, if you can. I'll ask to join the Yakuza. Love you." She kissed him quickly before running out of the back door, snatching up her coat as she went. Minutes counted now.

* * *

Across the two-thousand-four-hundred-acre park, variations on the scene played out again and again. Most residents only put up a token resistance, just to give their women and children time to run or hide. One group of park residents had more in common with Kurt and the Studs than their neighbours, but fought harder than rest. "No fucker takes us over, and definitely not some slant-eyed bitch." This man checked his handgun and scowled. "She'll free the women for starters, then either carve us up or give them fucking knives to do it themselves." His eyes passed over the six weeping women sat on the floor along one wall of the room. "I'll shoot these bitches before I let that happen."

"We can try to make it to the area the Studs are taking? Come on Slade, they might steal our women but won't mind us raiding for more." The skinny young man with a deep scar across his nose scowled at the women. "Better yet, why not leave these for the Yakuza and just run. Women will slow us up."

"Fuck off Nosy. You might be right about the women slowing us, but I'm not leaving them alive to tell tales." He raised his weapon and gunshots roared.

Nosy looked down at Slade's body, then at the shocked women. "It ain't that I care a shit about you, but that Yakuza bitch would hunt us down if it took ten years." He bent over Slade's body, stripping him of weapons and ammunition. "Tell that bitch Hangaku I don't want no trouble. I just want to join a different gang, right?" Several nodded mutely. Gunfire sounded outside, across the wetland. "Crap. I'm gone. Keep yer heads down, right?" Nosy crouched and headed out of the rear of the house, calling to several other gang members.

* * *

As the liberated women stared at Slade's still-bleeding body, across the park other residents were hoping to survive without any bloodshed. Beside a long, narrow lake, a man helped three women climb into a rowing boat. "Shiner and his men are a rough bunch, but once the fighting is over they shouldn't mess with the women. It's just that I'd rather you don't risk it, not for a few hours after they've won. Pull the boats up out of sight and hide in the trees over there. Watch for a signal." The middle-aged Asian man looked back over his shoulder, to where his friends were setting up a defence. "We'll wait until the Skins' women arrive. Shiner's missus won't let their blokes mess you about."

The last woman to board hugged him. "Don't fight too long Asif, all right? Don't make them mad at you."

"We won't have to if you get gone. As soon as all the boats are hidden, we'll stick up a white flag." Asif pushed the boat, and the women began to row as fast as possible. He turned away, heading through the cluster of buildings to the line of men with weapons.

An older man waved him towards one end of the line. "You're the last, Asif. Remember, we just need to pin them for a bit where none of them can see the lake." He fixed a couple of the younger men with a stern glare.

"Try to do it without killing, or even wounding if possible. It'll just make them worse."

A teenager reluctantly lowered his crossbow. "I've got it, Jer. Are we firing the meadow to slow them up?"

Several men, erstwhile wardens looking after the wildlife in the park, looked at each other. None looked keen, so Jer shook his head. "Not unless we have to. There's nesting birds in there."

"Fair enough." The wardens nodded agreement. Despite the Crash, none of them agreed with wanton destruction of habitat, and so far they'd managed to preserve most of the breeding areas. Luckily, the area around the park had included a good proportion of middle-class housing, rather than slums with gangs. Many of those inhabitants left one night through a gap in the Army cordon. Most of the rest went in a fleet of buses to demonstrate in the city centre. Neither group came back. Even the mob that eventually rampaged through the area had ignored the park, more interested in looting and burning houses and shops.

There had been a short honeymoon before the local gangs grew large enough to be a threat. That had been long enough to prepare, especially since the local criminals and delinquents were a bit more civilised than many shown on the TV. Now the gangs had combined, and a few park wardens weren't going to stop them.

*   *   *

By midday the firing died away, even where the park residents had decided to fight it out. In the old railway station, eight gang leaders met up as planned. Hangaku sheathed her sword after saluting the Headmaster. "You were right. We've got at least a score of women who don't belong here, running to get clear of the Studs or the other two."

A bleached blonde nodded. "We've all found extra people in our sections, mainly women and kids. Those three will demand we hand them over as part of the livestock. Have you all thought about what the Headmaster and Hangaku suggested?"

The Headmaster took his cue to repeat the message. "There's a nasty bastard called Conan over the other side of the city, across the motorway. He's building an empire, so unless someone stops him he'll head this way sooner or later. When that happens, the Studs or one of the other two gangs would sell us out. They're his sort of shithead, and there's only one cure." His hand rested on a pistol.

Odin nodded, as did Shiner, then Hangaku, and one after the other the rest followed suit. Angel, the bleached blonde, checked over her pump action shotgun. "You were right. It'll have to be done sooner or later. Best done now while we've got all our fighters together."

Hangaku smirked and reached up to tap her sword hilt. "You all know I've been looking for the chance to sort out Kurt, so this is going to be a real pleasure."

"Just remember, Hangaku, Shiner is on your side now." Laughter greeted the Headmaster's last comment as the eight gangs split into three groups and set off for their new targets.

* * *

The Studs were settling into their section of Sutton Park, unaware of the meeting in the railway station. "Hey, Kurt, I thought we were gonna get a shitload of fresh women?" The unshaven, acned youth in a leather jacket scratched his crotch. "I've got an itch and there ain't enough scratchers to go round."

"Try one of those sheep, Putz, or a cow." Kurt sneered at a middle-aged woman cowering in the corner of the room. "She ain't up to much, but you can have her after I've trained her up a bit. At least she's told me where the rest are. The bitches ran to the Yakuza or the Hard School." He turned to Putz with a grin. "They don't realise they're livestock under the agreement, so the slant-eyed bitch will have to hand them back. I wanna see her fucking face when the rest agree and she has to suck it up."

"What about the blokes? If they hadn't fought so fucking hard at the start we'd have caught more women. Three of our blokes were hit by those fucking arrows." Putz pulled out a knife. "We want to use a couple as an example, just to encourage the rest in the future."

"We wait until we see what we've got then yeah, we'll carve up a couple of the useless ones. That'll blood the new blokes as well, see if they've got the balls to join us." Kurt paused, because at least one didn't really need testing. "That Nosy seems to have brass ones. He shot his fucking boss and brought six men, all armed to the teeth."

The acned youth scowled as he sheathed the knife. "As long as that's not a habit, shooting the boss. Do the new ones get to share?"

"Only when the missing women get back. Until then it'll keep them hopeful." The gang boss turned back to the woman. "C'mon you, I need something scratched." Kurt waved towards the stairs, then slapped the woman when she didn't move. "That's your first lesson, bitch. Move it."

* * *

Putz never had to decide between sheep and a cow. A short time later a storm of gunfire erupted outside the front of the house, interrupting Kurt's teaching. He cuffed the woman at the side of the head. "Remember where we go to." The Studs' leader looked out of the bedroom window where four of his men lay on the track, bleeding out or dead. Motion caught his eye. Nosy and three of the new men were running away towards the nearest trees. "You bastards." Kurt ran down the stairs, drawing his gun as more shooting broke out. He stopped dead. "Fuck!"

"I always said you were armless." Hangaku stepped out from the side of the stairs, bloody sword ready for a second strike. Kurt clutched his wrist, blood trickling between his fingers as his handgun fell to the floor. She inspected him slowly, with a mocking smile. "Yup, armless and clueless." Three more Yakuzas came through the door, their blades dripping. They all wore big smiles. Behind them, two more Studs sprawled in pools of blood.

"The rest will carve you a new one. We had a deal." Kurt couldn't understand it. If Hangaku broke the agreement, the others would plough the bitch under. An icy trickle ran down his back as Kurt realised that didn't mean he'd live to see it.

"We made a new deal. The ones with some sort of bloody morals did anyway." Kurt turned at the voice, staring at a grinning Shiner. He opened his mouth to point out that Shiner didn't have morals, he was just pussy-whupped, then realised the usual jibes might be a bad idea.

Hangaku laughed at his expression, pointing her sword at Kurt's groin. "I intended carving you a new one, but you've still got your pants on."

"Kill the bloody animal." The naked woman at the top of the stairs, covered in small cuts and bruises that were still swelling, glared at Kurt. "Beat the bastard to death, give him some of his own training."

"I'll loan you a knife?" The Asian woman pulled a short blade and offered it.

"Or if you prefer beating?" Shiner offered his baseball bat, after using it to prod Kurt clear of the stairs. "Put your clothes on, and come down when you're ready. This arse isn't going anyplace."

The woman remembered she was naked, using her hands in a vain attempt at modesty. "He tore them off or cut them." She turned away from the stairs. "I'll find something."

As she went out of sight, Shiner prodded Kurt again. "Come on you, drop your belt and leave it. I reckon your girlfriend will want the knife. Let's go and see if any more of your mob survived."

Kurt stumbled outside in some sort of a daze. Three of his men knelt in the street, one clothed and two in underwear, but the five others in sight were sprawled out, unconscious or dead. As Kurt looked around, Nosy staggered into view, followed by a bleached blonde with a shotgun. She grinned at Hangaku and prodded her captive with her gun barrel. "You said this one got a pass so we saved him."

"You back-shooting fucker! You let them in." Kurt reeled, his hand going to his head as Shiner settled the bat back on his shoulder.

"Manners, Kurt. That was the first bit of your training, Skins style." Shiner sighed heavily, in mock exasperation. "He did nothing, you dumb fuck. Your blokes were all either at the women or complaining they hadn't got one. Half a dozen ten-year-olds could have taken the lot." The skinhead gang leader eyed up Nosy before turning at Hangaku. "What happens with him? He's part of your livestock under the agreement." A startled Nosy glanced apprehensively from one to the other.

"Slade and his mob had six women locked up, and he was going to bury the evidence. This bloke saved them so he gets one pass." Hangaku smiled happily, indicating the bleached blonde. "He can join Angel's Valkyries, or my Yakuza, or your mob. Then if he's a good boy, he's clear." She switched her gaze to Nosy. "Your choice."

Nosy flinched at the first two options before staring at Shiner, or at his clothes. "Do I have to wear that gear and shave my head?"

"Yeah, if you don't want the blokes to pick on you, or if you ever want a woman to come near you." Shiner glared, hefting the bat. "Their option, right?"

The scarred man shrugged. "It's a life, and better than the other options. What happens to these?" He looked at the four live Studs.

Hangaku smirked at the blonde, Angel, then at Shiner. "I reckon he should prove he means it." She nodded towards the clothed Stud kneeling in the street. "He'll do. Give your new man a machete, Shiner."

"In a minute, the locals get first crack." Shiner whistled, raising his voice. "Hey, bring all the ones we rescued." A crowd of cautious men with a few women came down the track from both directions, shepherded by members of the Skins, Valkyries and Yakuzas. Ahead of them staggered four battered Studs, one bleeding heavily.

Behind Kurt a door opened. He cringed as a voice spoke up. "I found this knife at the bottom of the stairs. Now I want my piece of that shithead." Five minutes later Kurt's erstwhile victim felt better, if a bit ill, as did several others in the crowd. Kurt and all his men were face down in the street.

"That's all the nasty shit done with, as long as you burn or bury the bodies. Any of your people who ran will be coming back, unhurt. Now if you all gather round we'll let you know which gang you belong to, and where the new boundaries are." Hangaku held out her hand for a Yakuza to pass her a map. "We've drawn a new version."

*　*　*

Conan:

Ten miles west of Hangaku, still inside the northwest borders of the ruined and largely depopulated city, a small, democratic enclave slept peacefully. They had guards, but some had been drugged so the inhabitants had no hint of the predator stalking them. A violent gangster known as Conan, encouraged and provided with information by Cabal agents, wanted to add them to his growing empire. Just upstream from the enclave's sleeping guards, a raft floated down the nearby canal, using only the current. Derelict housing and warehouses, silent and eerie in the half-light, lined the banks. To maintain the silence, the passengers fended off any obstacles using their hands, as did the dozen men on each of the other two rafts.

When the man at the front pointed, the raft swung in until willing hands caught hold of the timbers of a short pier. The heavily armed invaders swarmed ashore, careful not to let their weapons clink, some of them quickly tying and gagging the drugged guards. Conan, a heavily muscled, bearded man carrying an axe, pointed as the other rafts emptied, directing small groups of fighters towards their objectives.

A voice rose in alarm but the men crouched, waiting. Another voice shouted before gunfire echoed from the east, a diversionary attack beyond the walls of this small enclave. Shouting spread through the buildings as the residents roused, while anyone already awake ran to their walls to repulse the attack. Conan stood upright, raising his crude battle-axe. "Barbarians, take them!"

Conan ran towards a nearby house, his specific target. The door flew open as he approached, but he swung the axe and the man went down without a chance to lift his machete. Conan raised the pistol in his other hand, shooting a youth trying to load his crossbow. An older man ran down the stairs, swinging a baseball bat at the big axeman coming through the front door. Conan knocked it aside before pulling his opponent past to fall down the steps. As he thundered up onto the landing, a savage grin split his bearded face.

"No!" A woman screamed as Conan came through the bedroom door. The axeman blocked her knife thrust, clipping the woman with the butt of his pistol. She crumpled against the wall.

Within moments two of his men crowded in. Conan pointed to the two young women cowering at the far side of the room. "Take very good care of those, because one of them is the key to this place. The traitor wants her as his price for letting us in." He gestured to the crumpled woman. "Check her out. If she'll survive, tie her as well."

As Conan clattered down the stairs to re-join the fight, he heard screams behind him, while out in the streets pure chaos reigned. Sleepy, half-dressed residents staggered out of their homes to be faced by alert, fully armed opponents. Any carrying weapons were swiftly beaten to the ground or killed. On the barricades around the walls, the fighters realised too late they were caught between two forces. The attackers outside closed quickly, while others erupted from between the buildings inside the defences. Too many defenders died as they hesitated, reluctant to fire into the tangled mass containing friend as well as foe.

As dawn stained the sky, the victorious attackers worked their way back through the enclave, forcing all the residents out into the widest street. Wounded defenders, unless their names were on a list, were killed. The armed men quickly separated the better looking women from the males and children, questioned them and released about half. The rest waited, their wrists bound and their ankles hobbled by the short rope tied between them. The axeman looked over the cowed residents.

"I am Conan of the Barbarians, and now you all belong to my empire." Cries of protest sounded but clubs rose and fell, silencing them. "Forget the democracy bullshit. The Barbarians are a real gang, not a bunch of pussies and fairies. I've got five other enclaves and the only vote that counts is mine." A wide grin split his bearded face and he hooked a thumb at the bound women. "You can have one choice, a sort of vote? These women are for my troops, for their amusement. If you have a useful skill, you can trade your work for one of your women and save her. As long as you work hard and well for me, you keep the woman and my men will leave her alone." He stroked his bushy beard, running his eyes over the cowed inhabitants. "Choose carefully. If your daughter and wife are hobbled, you can only save one."

"What if the woman has a skill?" The speaker flinched from a raised baseball bat.

"Then she has been released. We already had a list of those. If she doesn't work hard enough, we can soon put her back in a hobble." A good few men came forward, claiming valuable expertise. Conan consulted a list and most were allowed to choose a woman, whereupon the gangsters untied her bonds and let her re-join the crowd. The rejected men could only watch in anguish. Once the applicants stopped coming, the axeman crooked a finger at the crowd. "Come out, Arthur. Your turn."

This man, Arthur, swaggered out from among the defeated residents, not at all cowed. The Barbarian leader led him down the line of women to those captured in the first house. He gestured to the pair, then handed the man a dog collar and a leash. "Your prize."

"Arthur? What does he mean?" The youngest woman glanced from Arthur to Conan. "This man killed Dad."

"Not really, Arthur killed him." Conan raised his voice so everyone could hear. "Your new boyfriend fed the guards on the riverside bowls of hot stew with a little something in it. They dozed off nicely, and never noticed us sneaking in behind your defences. Now he wants his pay." The Barbarian leader laughed at the crowd. "Your friend even gave me this list so I know all about you, who has what skills."

Arthur, the traitor, sneered at the young woman. "You won't tell me no next time I want a dance, bitch. Now you're going to do what I want, any time I want it." He stepped forward, raising the collar but the young woman fended him off with her bound hands. Conan seized her hair and held her head still while Arthur fastened the leather in place, pulled on the leash and slapped her, hard. "Come on bitch." He towed the stunned woman up the street, tugging to keep her stumbling as the hobbles tripped her. Armed men beat back a few protesters who tried to go beyond words.

Conan caught another woman by the arm when she tried to intervene. His eyes narrowed. With a grin he grabbed her long, auburn hair and twisted until he could see the livid bruise on her temple. "You survived." He tore her nightdress away. "Oh yes, you'll do nicely. I like a woman with some fire, especially one who can stand a bit of punishment." He looked up and down the street, at his own men. "Make sure our wounded have a friendly nurse, a pretty one. One Barbarian in four gets to choose a woman, while the rest make sure this lot behave. Cut cards, throw dice, I don't give a shit as long as three in four stays on duty. I'll be busy, so don't fight over choosing or I'll kill the fucker that started it." He started up the street, dragging the woman by her hair. "I've got a wildcat to tame."

* * *

The General:

Within days of the reorganisation of Sutton Park and Conan's conquest, the General, much closer to Orchard Close and Soldier Boy, paid a debt with someone else's blood. Eight miles south of Sutton Park, still in the city but across yet another heavily patrolled motorway, a small, peaceful enclave found themselves the targets of a hostile takeover. A horde of gangsters wielding machetes, axes or baseball bats crept up on an old department store. This enclave had only survived so long because of their proximity to the city centre exclusion zone. Less than a quarter of a mile lay between the building and the barbed wire and warning signs around the site of the riot, massacre and the Mayor's death. Anyone firing an automatic weapon, or any indiscriminate shots straying over the wire, would bring a helicopter gunship with napalm.

Four men stood on the roof of a burned-out block of flats, inspecting the department store and its defences from a safe distance. None of them had any intention of risking napalm. Two of the men, the Men in Black, or MiB, wore black suits and dark glasses. Both carried automatic weapons, but as status symbols. They rarely used them, preferring to hire out their superior weaponry. The other two wore Army-style uniforms, but only the General had gold braid on his peaked cap. All four had a lot more in common with the way Conan ruled his gang than with the Zookeepers, Orchard Close or even the gangs now in charge of Sutton Park. The General knew about the Zoo, vaguely, because a van came round now and then selling meat, but as yet he stayed focussed on the third of the city he wanted to rule.

One of the MiB raised binoculars, looking across the broken rooftops towards the target and the multi-storey car park next door. "No reaction yet. At least this plan is working better than the last time. We began to wonder if you really were a fucking General."

"Armchair General, Branson, but better than most." The man with gold braid scowled. "If I'd known who the fucking Geek Freeks had as their general, I'd have pulled back sooner. Probably straight after those catapults threw a lot further than expected."

The second suited man glanced back, surprised. "You know that little shit?"

"Too true I know him, Scrooge. We met in quite a few wargames tournaments and we were about evens. Wellington is a sneaky bastard. He specialised in sucking his opponent into traps but I still don't know how the bastard knew we were coming. Once I saw his ugly face on TV, looking up at the drone, I wasn't surprised about what happened." A smile spread across his face. "He's a lot uglier than last time I saw him. From the look of those scars, Wellington hasn't always done so well either."

"It's all right for you, you've got plenty of men to lose or at least you can recruit more. We can't afford to lose our automatics or the decent rifles." Branson, leader of the MiB, pointed beyond the target buildings. "We can't go back into the city centre for more. Even if we dodged the helicopter, any weapons in there now will be rusted or the Army will have picked them up."

"We lost four automatics and four fucking rifles, good ones." Scrooge kicked moodily at the gravel of the roof. "We also lost the men using them, all good shooters." His lip lifted in a snarl. "I want that black bitch, the one with that fucking rifle."

"We lost eleven shooters between good and good enough, and over a hundred and thirty men once the wounded finished dying. Another score and maybe more will never fight again so I reckon you did well." The other man in military gear spat into the gravel. "On top of that we lost a shitload of weapons, so maybe you should stop whinging. Fucking office ponces."

"Shut it Patton. We need their automatic weapons, they need my brain and your lunatics." Everyone turned to listen to the radio message. "Baker." The General lifted his binoculars. "They're nearly in place. Are the Bloodsuckers ready to fight again?"

"Yeah, getting chewed up just pissed the rest off. Those that have recovered enough are ready to go, and mad enough not to care I've taken their firearms away. The fucking lunatics can't be trusted not to empty a pistol towards the city centre just to show off." The big, heavily muscled commander of the lunatics grinned, putting a hand on his machete. "I've threatened to cut the nuts off any arse who sets fire to the place or smashes up loot. They can beat up who they like, and fuck who they fancy, but we want the people alive and fit to work once they've healed up." Patton laughed at the expressions on the two MiB. "They'll probably kill a couple by mistake. The survivors will be pleased when they find out they belong to you lot, and the Bloods are leaving. They'll be good little workers in case you invite the fucking maniacs back for a sleepover." All four men laughed, then stopped as the radio crackled again. "Alpha." They all raised their glasses to look at the target again.

Scrooge raised his voice to call out to the riflemen spaced along the edge of the roof. "Remember, no automatic fire or shooting high. We're too near the city centre and that helicopter gunship." Three of the riflemen lifted a hand in acknowledgement. More shooters lay or knelt on the roofs of two nearby office blocks, where they had a clear view of the target.

Puffs of smoke showed from the top of a car park and the store. The defenders had spotted the machete-wielding attackers as they closed in, and opened fire. Branson lowered his binoculars, briefly. "Mark the smoke, you lot."

One of the riflemen laughed. "Sucking. Eggs." A ripple of laughter ran through the rest. "Charlie" came over the radio and the General raised the mike to his lips.

"The General here. Shooters execute one, execute one." The rifles along this roof and nearby began to fire, deliberate aimed shots at the defending riflemen. "Gentlemen?" The General waved towards a small brick structure, the top of the stairway. "Just in case one of their rifles gets lucky." The four men retired behind the bricks, occasionally looking out with their glasses.

Within minutes, one of the riflemen called back to them. "Firing suppressed, sir."

"The General here. Alpha, Baker, Charlie execute two, execute two. Rifles, shoot any defenders with firearms but try to miss the friendlies." The General lowered the radio mike and relaxed. "This should be a nice, easy victory to get the Bloodsuckers back in the groove." He nodded towards the MiB. "The enclave is your payment for the lost weapons. We'll use your remaining weapons to take over two or three small gangs, to build up my soldiers again. Snipe the leaders, then a burst of automatic fire to convince the rest who the new boss should be."

Scrooge glanced at Branson, who nodded for him to speak up. "Then I suppose you'll be going after that Wellington again. Is that such a good idea?"

"Not straight away, not until I've got the new recruits trained up and all the Bloods fighting fit. Even then I'd like to deal with that Soldier Boy fucker first. It had to be him that convinced the RAF to interfere. More than that, those two blocks of disciplined fighters, the ones firing aimed shots even with handguns, have to be his. The TV pictures were really useful." His smirk died and the General turned to scowl in the general direction of Orchard Close. "I need a way through those walls around Orchard Close, if his fighters are that disciplined. Once we take him out, we've broken the whole alliance wide open. It'll leave smartarse Welly out on a limb with his nuts swinging in the breeze." His hand closed into a fist as if crushing something, or someone.

"Rockets might do it, break those walls." Branson shrugged at the sour look from the other MiB, Scrooge. "We told you about the SIMS but you wanted to go the other direction. Their missiles are nasty, but if you can get the Bloods in among the fighters, they'll fall apart. It's a commune, everybody and nobody in charge. The SIMS fighters are like Orchard Close, using women to make up the numbers." He paused, turning to look in the same direction as the General. "How will you get to Orchard Close first? We'll have to get across that water, then break through the GOFS or Geeks to get Soldier Boy."

"That's what I intended, but maybe not if we can get decent rockets. You leave that part to me. Rhys gave me some detailed information on that Orchard Close, about the skills and the women collected there. That's why I wanted them, even before that flash bastard stole my armour and rifle." The General stepped out of cover, raising his glasses to inspect the target buildings. "These twats should have knocked down more of the ruins nearby, made a proper killing ground. The Bloods are already inside. We may as well go down now because it'll be over by the time we get there. We'll tell the Bloods what good boys they are, grab some decent booze and maybe a woman, and celebrate." He turned to Branson. "Tomorrow you can tell me about these rockets. While the Bloods heal, I'll start thinking about those SIMS and that fucking Orchard Close. Some people pick truly stupid gang names. SIMS? A fucking orchard? Pink Panthers? Barbie Girls? Gods of fucking Fire and Steel? At least the Hot Rods are a bunch of car thieves."

* * *

The Professors:

Hangaku and the General weren't the only ones revising a map. Only four miles north of the General, almost halfway to Sutton Park and just south of a heavily patrolled motorway, a group of ex-university lecturers and students pored over an old map of the city. One of the students, a brawny young man, tapped two areas outlined in red that separated their own enclave from another outlined in green. "We should attack south, Prof, take out these two gangs. We've knocked back all our neighbours, but Mart runs are difficult because none of us can shoot. These SIMS are our sort of people but they beat back a gang that had automatics, so they must be better fighters."

"We are not predators, Chad. There will be no empire building. If we trade a little medical help, or a few seeds or plants, the two gangs may allow us through to trade." An older man, looking a lot like someone's slightly batty granddad in his well-worn robe, gave all the younger people a stern look. "Our job, the lecturers, is to teach you. We will also teach our neighbours, but the price will be a modicum of civilised behaviour. When this lunacy ends, our enclave will march out with our heads high, ready to re-establish civilisation again. You and the other students will finish your education before then, and be ready to help us."

"If it ever ends. Sorry Prof, but we wonder sometimes." This young woman looked guilty, glancing down. "We, the student council, just wanted to meet some decent people again, someone who isn't trying to rob or kill us." Behind the old man, Prof, some of the other lecturers exchanged glances. They'd all come to the conclusion this wouldn't end until everyone in the cities had died, but Prof wouldn't tell the students the bad news. Unfortunately these were bright young people, smart enough to suspect the truth.

Prof turned to a tall, willowy woman in a flowing dress. "Celeste, the gangs will talk to you because they consider you an easy mark. Try to arrange a convoy to these SIMS, or at least ask the gangs to trade us modern ammunition and hopefully more weapons. How are you doing with negotiating the latest Mart run?"

"Two gangs are competing to get medical help at the moment, so they are undercutting each other to give us safe passage. They have just been fighting each other so they have a lot of injuries. I've already told them we'll want hard liquor for anaesthetic. Then we can go easy on it, let the casualties suck up a bit of pain so we can keep some spirits for disinfectant." Celeste had lost much of her innocence since those first brutal days. "We may have to treat some from each gang to stop one of them feeling slighted. How are we for medical supplies?"

"We are growing more old-fashioned remedies, and some of the medieval wound dressings are better than expected. Adding essential oils from rosemary or lavender has given us anti-bacterial soap, and ashes make lye for scrubbing surfaces. We have trouble keeping the honey for medicinal use." This tutor smiled at the rolling eyes from some of the students. "There's comfrey growing wild and plenty of potted Aloe vera, and a dozen old wives' cures from weeds and bushes, but we save the best for our own people. All the new preparations are tested on gangsters, so a few casualties would be handy."

"Good enough." Prof turned back to Celine. "Offer each of them treatment, and try to get two Mart runs out of it. If not, insist on ammunition or propellant. Get them to bring bleach and disinfectant, and any useful drugs in original packaging. Especially bleach, we need it to make more explosives for the trebuchets to throw." He tapped the map, looking round the group. "We will not try to conquer, but we must be ready to defend our own. To avoid actual fighting, we will make our neighbours just a little bit dependent on us. Everyone try to think of what the gangs need and we can supply, but without making them greedy." He patted the burly young man on the shoulder. "Meanwhile, Chad, if you want to beat on a gangster or two you could invite them to a rugby match?" As Prof intended, the meeting broke up in smiles.

* * *

Orchard Close:
In one of the enclaves with an allegedly stupid name, eight miles slightly south of east from the General, Harold, aka Soldier Boy, held a meeting in his house. The old road sign at the end of the street explained the enclave name. It read "Orchard Close." Harold wore a puzzled expression that had nothing to do with redrawing maps; he knew next to nothing about all the other battles taking place in the same city. Unfortunately, the whole country knew about Orchard Close because his fighters had been featured in TV news reports, twice. Hopefully most gangs wouldn't have the faint-

est idea of which city held their enclave. Harold would have worried much more if he'd realised that the likes of the General had agents of the UK government surreptitiously feeding them information.

"Windmills?" He looked around the group meeting in his house, most of his best friends and advisors. Liz the artistic smith, Casper the heavily muscled gay bodyguard, Patty the knitting and crossbow queen, Emmy the six-foot Jamaican sharpshooter gardener, Finn the pistol-toting electrician and Sharyn, Harold's big sister and the head witch, all looked at the other person present. So did Harold. "Charlie? This is your idea?"

Charlie, a thirty-three-year old erstwhile washing machine repairman, squirmed under their scrutiny. "Sort of. I kept wondering about Glasgow, about why the inhabitants broke out of the cordon and went north into the mountains and snow. It made no sense even after their Marts closed down." Several others nodded. They'd wondered the same thing. "It's bad in the cities, we know that well enough even if we've still got our Marts to buy food from. Even so, hunger isn't a reason to leave shelter in winter. Especially since they all went north where there's no food anyway. Then I suddenly realised." He stopped, still unsure if this was a good idea, and looked around the circle of faces.

"Cripes, don't stop now." Patty grinned as she shook a fist in a mock threat. "Or I'll get bloody annoyed even if Harold doesn't."

Charlie took a deep breath, obviously nervous about how his listeners would take the next bit. "Electricity. One winter when I lived in the Lake District, a storm cut the power over a wide area. The news showed all these villages covered in snow. The Army and RAF flew in generators and lifted out the sick." Charlie shrugged again, trying to sound relaxed. He hadn't been here long, and even if Soldier Boy seemed a lot better than the other gang bosses, Charlie didn't know what would wind him up. Timewasters with theories but no proof might be enough. "It always struck me how pristine those villages looked, all the white roofs with no melted patches. They were too far from the main towns to have gas pipes, so without electricity the houses lost their heating."

Everyone else concentrated, trying to remember the recent TV footage of Glasgow. Casper gasped, turning to the rest. "Glasgow looked the same on the TV. There were a few columns of smoke where people must have been burning timber, but no other sign of heat anywhere. There should have been big patches, enclaves where the roofs were clear. Cripes, he's right. The nasty bastards, the government, cut off the electricity. In the middle of winter." The rest of them stared back at him, realisation dawning.

Patty recovered first, enough to speak. "Cripes, Harold. You said at the time you'd never lead us out of the city into a trap like that, but what if there's no option?" Silence fell for a moment, as they all remembered the TV showing explosions, marching back and forth over the column of gangsters and innocent refugees. The artillery onslaught hadn't stopped until darkness hid the swathes of still figures scattered in the snow.

"We won't have a choice if they cut the electricity. That's all we've got to keep us warm in winter." Emmy looked and sounded sombre. "We can manage for a bit without the Marts because we grow a lot of our food, but electricity is all we've got for cooking, heat and light. We won't be able to do what you said, make the bastards come into the ruins to try to root us out." All but one person here had come to the same conclusion. The government intended wiping out the trapped populations, everyone still inside the ruined cities across the UK. So far none of them could work out why.

Harold, Soldier Boy, ex-Army and allegedly an SAS sniper, realised one person didn't know. "Charlie, you keep your mouth shut about what we say here, okay? You'll only cause panic among the rest. We've made plans but the more who know them, the more who might open a careless mouth."

Charlie gulped, this wasn't the reaction he'd expected. "All right, Harold. Cripesing hell, why would the bast…cripes do that? Attack us?"

"Don't worry about saying damn and blast, bloody, sod or bastard, that sort of thing. Even if you make a mistake, residents don't get caned. That's for the visiting scroats, to keep them in line." Orchard Close fined visiting gangsters who were obscene. For a second offence, the men were stripped, then ran a gauntlet of women wielding garden canes. Any three time offenders became living targets for crossbow practice. Physically molesting a resident meant the offender being gelded, or tied to a lamp post for the crossbow practice. That had more impact than just killing the scroat.

Charlie smiled nervously. "Ah, right, it's just that a lot of us new arrivals aren't sure where the line is, so we play safe." His smile strengthened, reassured by the amused expressions on the others. "Our kids could grow up not actually knowing how to curse, how weird is that? We all use cripes to be safe, and a lot of our women are reassured by the non-swearing. The refugees who arrived before us said about using cripes. Why pick that?"

Harold pointed at the tall, slim figure with the smug smile. "Liz started it. We found it funny and copied her."

"She's the carrier." Patty held up her hands as if to fend off Liz. "I told you, it's an infection. Each new refugee catches the cripes from the one before."

"Too late to stop it now. Even the visiting gangsters use it now, just to be safe." Now Casper looked smug and several of the others nodded and chuckled.

Harold smiled briefly, then sobered. The rest did the same, their humour dying as they returned to the real problem. "The answer to the cripesing question is 'yes,' Charlie. We reckon the government will shut the cities down one by one, and kill us all. We've no idea why, but we did have a plan for when." His wry smile admitted the plan had just broken down. "The plan relied on having the cripes' electricity."

Charlie still looked cautious, unsure how the gang boss would react to his solution. "I'm not sure about the electric, it just made sense, in which case I might have a solution."

Harold looked around the others, noting their small nods of agreement. "We are absolutely sure now, even if I still can't work out why the Glasgow lot went north. Now how does that bring us to windmills?"

"Windmills can be used to create electricity." Charlie seemed more confident now. "I used to charge up a lorry battery like that, to run my CB radio at home."

"You mean like the wind farms? We can't build those." Harold glanced over at Finn, the electrician. "Can you fix up a super-sized meter bypass or something, Finn, in case we get turned off?"

"No chance. Remember the storm cutting the power? That happened outside the Army cordon, and that's what they'll do." Finn wasn't convinced by Charlie's solution. "Even with Charlie's little windmills we'll never find enough working car or lorry batteries to run everything. Maybe we can fix up heating with wood fired boilers?"

"What about the fumes, because all the roof timbers and floorboards are full of chemicals?" Liz shrugged at all the stares. "Hey, I'm a smith and paranoid about fumes, but that don't make me wrong."

"True, but we can put the boilers outside the houses and run the pipes and hot water inside. That'll burn a lot of timber, and we'll lose the cookers, blow heaters and electric blankets, but we won't freeze. I'm more worried about the laptops, pads and radios, we'll never recharge them with a few windmills." Finn wasn't the only one looking despondent now.

"We can cook on stoves in garages to avoid fumes. There might even be proper wood burning stoves out there in the ruins. The scavengers can collect plenty of wood from the ruins, rafters if need be. Bernie will have a kitten when we go back out there for the rest of the floors and the roof timbers." Patty smiled briefly. "I did tell him everything had a use." The smile developed into a definite smirk. "Mind you, I don't fancy going all hardy soldier with cold beds. I might have to tempt someone warm to share."

"We can generate enough electricity with windmills." Charlie still seemed confident.

"But that would take a wind farm." Harold paused, brow furrowed in thought. "Won't it?"

"Not much of one. A couple of those big things from an old wind farm would be enough, if we could get them, because there's usually some wind. If we stick smaller windmills up everywhere, and charge up everything when it's windy, I reckon we can manage. It's a pity there isn't a river or we could have a waterwheel." Caught up in his own enthusiasm, Charlie lost his caution completely even though most of those present still weren't convinced. "Wind will keep us going, even if we might not have electric lights all the time."

"We don't need a river for waterwheels, because you've just reminded me. A little fan in the downspouts works like a waterwheel, using rainwater or even the water from an upstairs bath or sink. There were commercial versions at one time." Finn looked much happier now. "I'll need more drainpipe connections, then the generators can go in them. We could put more in the irrigation pipes laid out into the fields, for when that water is flowing. If Charlie can help with building windmills, we might even keep the electric blankets working."

"Super. Scavenging for more bits of pipe. At least we won't have garden gnomes driving us out into mud to plant." Casper glanced at Emmy, in charge of the hundred plus acres of cultivation surrounding the walled enclave.

Emmy snickered, completely unworried. "I'll be busy in the warm greenhouses most of the time. Tammy still needs Mummy so I'll have to stay home to feed her." She sighed happily. "I'll think of you out there in the cold and wet, getting scratched by brambles and stung by nettles."

"You, you, smug momma." Liz glared at her. "I hate the cold, but not enough to get with child. Be warned, if I suffer, so will anyone working with me." She brightened, turning to Harold with a triumphant smile. "I should be excused to practice my dark arts in my lovely warm forge."

Oddly, the banter as the group worked through how to combat a loss of electricity took away the shock. Perhaps because this was a problem they could do something about.

* * *

Elsewhere in the UK, others were taking action to improve their lot. None would affect Harold or his friends, not immediately, but the ripples would spread and grow...

* * *

The Reivers:

Five hundred miles north of the Orchard Close, a minor flaw in the clearance of Glasgow was about to bite hard. A small band of Glaswegians, the pitifully few survivors of the massacre, had spent nearly two months hiding in the snow-covered mountains. Trained by a few experts, the fugitives left no tracks and minimised their heat traces, eating a mixture of food they'd carried with them and ambushed sheep. Now the food had run out, so the embittered survivors took the direct path to a solution. Beyond the foothills, where the Scottish Highlands finally became the eastern coastal plain, a signal light flickered rapidly in the dim light. Back nearer the hills, crouching in a ditch, a big bearded man swathed in plaid over his padded clothing turned to talk to his scruffy band. "So far so good. Remember everyone, we want food more than blood."

"Speak for yourself, Bruce. There's a big blood debt tae pay." The woman, dressed in the ragged remains of a snowsuit over her thick jacket, hefted a machete. "We all left family dead in the snow north of Glasgow."

"But first we eat, Maeve, because we have tae be alive to collect on that debt. There's nae other food left, and I'd like something different tae mutton." This man wore a raw sheepskin over his quilted jacket. His smile had no humour at all. "Though since they tried tae kill us all, I've no problem wi' shedding blood tae get fed."

The light flickered again. "That's the signal. We're a wee bit too far north, but let's show these Sassenach bastards why the borders still remember the Reivers." The burly man in plaid raised a claymore, one of a very few among the horde. Glancing around the group, his bearded face split in a big grin. "As Mel Gibson would hae it, Freedom!" The ragged band, half the survivors of the massacred population of Glasgow, swept silently out of the ditches and clumps of trees and across the strip of overgrown farmland. Behind them the Grampian mountain range loomed, white against the evening sky.

As they reached the sandbagged walls of a guard post, more bearded figures rose to meet them. The greeters waved crossbows and machetes in triumph as the horde finally cheered, having stayed silent just in case surprise was needed. The leader, Bruce, clambered over and approached another plaid-clad man with a beard. "Did they get a message off, Angus?"

The slimmer man straightened from stripping a fallen figure clad in a military-style uniform. "Nae chance, Bruce. These play soldiers have nae met the real thing before, I'll wager." His face split in a wolfish grin. "We could do wi' a few more real soldiers. I'd love tae get the Black Watch into these hills. Half the lads would desert if they found out what actually happened."

"The brass are nae that stupid. Now let's clear the other two guard posts, widen the gap. We've only got until the next shift change." The pair went inside the shelter to check the map. Minutes later the two military Land Rovers belonging to the guard post set off, both crammed full of fighters. Their targets were the smaller guard posts north and south of this one. The smaller groups of survivors waiting near each of those would loot them before joining the raid. Almost every person left at the first target crammed into the vehicles in the car park and set off east, heading for the unprotected, unsuspecting farms and food stores.

The last to leave, Angus and Bruce, left two men and a woman to monitor the radios and warn the Reivers of any alarm. Their unit, heavily armed fighters in looted uniforms, travelled in a lightly armoured Vector 6x6. The guard post's Foxhound, sporting a machine gun, escorted them towards the main north-south highway.

*　*　*

About thirty minutes later and fourteen miles away, sixteen heavily loaded lorries preceded by an armoured Land Rover slowed. Two military vehicles were parked across the road, blocking the way, and the machine gun on one aimed straight at the Land Rover. Either side, men in uniform aimed weaponry. The officer in the vehicle tapped a man on the shoulder. "Call it in."

The radio man pointed at the huge sign saying 'Radio Silence,' propped against the larger vehicle. "Maybe some of the scum have a radio, boss? I'd rather not annoy this lot, not with all that nasty shit aimed at us."

"Good point. I suppose that means I've got to get out in the cold." The paramilitary officer opened his door while the rest huddled deeper into their coats. "Spring in Scotland, fucking mid-winter anywhere else." A figure muffled up in Army weatherproofs came around the vehicles blocking the road, impatiently waving him forward. "Fucking prima donna," he muttered.

The figure waved him out of the wind, so the officer gratefully headed that way. As he reached shelter he sighed in relief, but a hand clapped over his mouth and something cold pricked his throat. "Hush now laddie, and ye might live." The officer froze, his eyes widening as the man he'd come to see pulled down his face protection to show a bushy beard.

"Aye, not a normal look in the Army, but shaving didnae seem so important up there in the snow over winter." The teeth showing in the beard weren't smiling. "I'm Bruce. Not the Bruce, even if these are as hard a bunch as ever came down frae the hills tae harry the lowlands. Now ye tell me who I have tae shoot so none of those send a message. If they do, I'll kill ye all."

"I wasn't there." The officer had suddenly realised where any hard bunch out of the mountains had to have come from. The Glaswegian accents coming from inside the vehicle were a big hint. "They were Specials, not normal paramilitaries, and regular Army artillery."

"Are there any Specials near here, laddie?" Despite his warm clothing, the officer shivered as he looked into the speaker's cold blue eyes. "Ah left ma Grace and three bairns cold in the snow back there. I'd like tae meet some o' the bastards put them there." Others growled and muttered, indicating just how much they wanted a chance at a Special.

The officer would have loved to point this lot towards the Specials and let the nasty sods kill each other, but he couldn't. "I don't know where they're based, none of us do. They're a nasty bunch and only came for Glasgow, then went back south. What are you going to do with us?" He didn't like the quiver in his voice but those eyes, and the others he met as armed figures turned to watch him, hadn't an ounce of pity. With a shock the officer realised some were women.

"Yon lorries are enough tae stock up a Mart. We're a wee bit short after the winter so we'll be driving them away." A trace of humour crossed the bearded face. "That's traditional for Reivers, driving the stock away. Now who do we have tae shoot?"

"Nobody, I swear. Look at my radio, its short-range so it'll only reach them, not a guard post. The radio in the Land Rover is the only one that will reach headquarters. The ones on the lorries might reach the nearest guard post." He stopped as several people shook their heads.

Bruce enlightened him. "The guard posts won't be listening, not now. Just in case somebody else is, we'd best shoot the men in the lorries."

"No, please. Check my radio." Hands roughly searched him. "I'll tell them all it's a Special Unit exercise, that the radio men are to shut their sets down." He took the offered radio, speaking very carefully and clearly. "All NCOs and drivers, this is an operation by the Specials. Shut down the radios because the scum have cracked the radio codes. Come forward one at a time to show your ID but keep your traps shut. Don't ask this lot stupid questions or wind them up. Each vehicle confirm by handheld, on this channel, when the transmitter is cold." He paused, thought of the look in those cold blue eyes, and emphasised the next bit. "Keep your big mouths shut and don't fuck up. These are the real thing, so you know what'll happen."

* * *

Ten minutes later the drivers, guards and radio operators sat huddled together in a ditch as their vehicles roared off into the distance. "At least they left us some clothes."

The officer cut in before the rest could start. "Because half of us have shat our pants, Thompson. Unfortunately, they took all the cold weather gear." He turned to the sergeant. "Fuck it, McTavish, we'll freeze to death before the next convoy comes this way."

"No we won't, sir. We'll march like hell towards the nearest guard post, about fifteen miles southwest." The sergeant glared at the muttered complaints from some men. It would be a brutal march in this weather, but moaning wouldn't help. "From what they said I'm guessing they'll have stripped that as well, but the buildings will break the wind. I'm hoping we find an old house or even a barn before that. We'll burn the furniture or the floorboards, whatever. That'll keep us warm until the RAF come looking and see the smoke." He turned to look up the now empty road. "Who were they? They didn't look like the usual street yobs that escape from the work camps."

The officer followed his gaze. "They aren't. Those are survivors from Glasgow. I told them a little porky so you all owe me your miserable lives. I said we weren't there, it was all down to the Specials." A round of swearing and blasphemy followed. "Now aren't you glad you weren't chatty? The leader is called Bruce, and his sidekick lost a wife and three kids and wants blood. I'll settle for getting frostbite and a bout of flu. Now come on, get moving." The line of men bent their heads against the wind and headed southwest.

*　*　*

The Cabal:

Two days later, the raid in Scotland sparked an emergency meeting of the UK cell of the Cabal, the global conspiracy that had triggered the current disaster. Safely tucked away in their clean, warm bunker deep beneath pristine, rolling Lincolnshire countryside, none of them felt any cold or wind. The atmosphere in the underground room, however, felt decidedly frosty and crackled with tension. Joshua, the spare, balding military liaison wearing an Army uniform, looked apologetic. "We had no idea some of them would break out of Glasgow properly outfitted to live in the mountains." He scowled at an innocuous man further round the large polished table. "Our intel seemed to miss that."

Owen, the aristocratic chairman and leader of the Cabal, looked at the same unassuming figure, their spymaster. "Well, Maurice? You claimed to have a source in every gang and enclave."

"Had." Maurice shrugged apologetically. "As expected, closing the food Marts around Glasgow caused utter confusion and bitter fighting among the scum. My people were caught up in that, some died while others were unable to report." He turned a little and clicked the control, bringing the wallscreen to life. The picture panned, showing a vast expanse of bodies in a valley, with snow still covering the hills either side. "To answer Joshua, even real arctic clothing didn't make any difference. The idea still worked out well enough, most of the escapees died during the artillery barrage. At least ninety-five percent died either there, or trying to break into Fastlane." He chuckled, but cut it short when nobody else smiled. "Even scum should have worked out a nuclear submarine base would be well defended."

The youngest man present objected. "The five percent are the problem.

How many is that? They hit our supply convoys up the east coast, but where did they go to in the interim? How did they survive the winter?" He switched to the Army liaison. "Joshua, you claimed the weather in the mountains had driven even the sheep to leave."

Another voice interrupted. "Losing a few supply convoys isn't the real problem. They also attacked some of the farming communities in the low-lands, killing or kidnapping people we actually need. These supposed refugees went on to kill the guards and free everyone in three work camps. The loss of transport, materials and manpower will cause serious disruption in our schedules. Worse, two of those missing have B passes, people who aren't full Cabal members but knew enough to guarantee them a pass out of the cities. They may tell the scum that at least some of the Crash was planned." Henry, the bearded farm manager, looked worried as well as angry because both A passes, those fully aware of the Cabal, and B passes, those who only knew their part of the master plan, were supposed to be kept safe. C passes, people who were particularly useful or relatives of A or B passes, didn't know about the Cabal or its plans. He turned to join Gerard in questioning Joshua. "Who are these attackers exactly, because that seemed like a military operation?"

Before Joshua could reply, Owen butted in. "Worse, with those liberated workers, their numbers have substantially increased. But first I have questions for Faraz." As the chairman switched his attention to the RAF liaison, so did the others. "Why didn't you spot all these escapees, and worse still, why can't you find them now?"

Faraz looked embarrassed and sounded defensive. "Joshua used artillery to kill the main mass, with no ground forces in contact." He glanced at Maurice and Joshua. "My instructions were clear. There must be no sign of air power on the TV, so the artillery opened up as night fell and we used drones without lights. The residual heat from an artillery bombardment, combined with the numbers of dead and dying, swamped the sensors. Even dead bodies retain some heat for hours. We reported people escaping into the hills. Some came back when the guns stopped but unfortunately, once night fell, we kept losing them against the background."

Owen looked around the table, and he wasn't the only one still unconvinced. "Why didn't you follow them as they left, or spot them between the escape and now?"

Faraz turned his hopeful gaze towards Joshua, who sighed in resignation before answering. "I've already gone through all this with Faraz.

Which of the scattered traces should they have followed? Many of the survivors ran but died later. Much less than five percent survived over the winter, perhaps as few as three hundred from the evidence. Those who returned probably stripped additional clothing and food from the bodies so yes, Maurice, I accept that arctic clothing didn't matter. Deep enough snow will have masked any sign of heat, and living like Eskimos would help them keep warm. A few small fires, well hidden, would be enough." Joshua hesitated, then pushed on. "Some of them are trained in arctic warfare, ex-military. This must all be kept from the armed forces at all costs."

"Aberdeen and Inverness already know." Ivy, the redheaded woman responsible for supplying the Marts, glared at Joshua. "Your Army cordons let an unknown number from the liberated work camps break back into the cities. The gangs are taunting the Mart guards about Reivers being loose in the Highlands. Hundreds of the freed prisoners apparently joined them." Her glare moved onto Maurice. "You won't empty either of those cities with the same trick. Worse, there's claims that Robert the Bruce is back."

Maurice laughed at her, shaking his head. "One of the leaders is actually called Bruce, that's all. The liberated scum are making something of nothing." His humour died again as he saw the expressions on the others. "There is no contact between those two cities and any other, and we are scotching the rumours where possible. Better still would be a clear shot at the bastard himself, and that bloody Angus. He's an ex-warrant officer from the Black Watch who lost a wife and three children, and is a very dangerous man."

"They are all dangerous now, every man and woman. They've spent nearly two months under the snow, learning from the experts, practicing with their weapons and honing their hatred. That Bruce made himself very clear. They are Reivers and intend putting the lowlands to fire and the sword. Blood feud, revenge for Glasgow." Joshua looked around the table, his expression and voice deadly serious as he tried to drive the situation home to men and women who'd never been cold or hungry. "I've stopped any communication between the Army units around those cities and other units, and they'll not be rotated out. If what they've heard gets to the rest of the Army, especially the Scots Guards or the Black Watch, they'll mutiny. We'd better get the Specials moved up somewhere nearby. If the wrong captive talks, and the wrong rumours get back to the scum, we'll need them to take out the Army units around the cities." He shrugged, his sour expression echoed by some of the others as realisation dawned. "The regular forces are already unhappy about conditions in the enclosures. We don't want any of them joining the rebels."

Now thoroughly alarmed, Gerard, the youngest man, turned on Faraz. "You could hunt these Reivers down. Use jets and helicopters and the night vision thingies to burn or shoot them."

"We can detect their heat while they are moving, but those escapees are in the Scottish Highlands." Gerard and Ivy continued to glare so Faraz continued. "Firstly, there are thousands of square miles to search, slowly enough so the pilot can identify and maybe shoot what he finds. Secondly, have you any idea how many sheep live there?"

"Sheep?"

"Sheep, Gerard, each of which is a warm spot that has to be identified, or we'll use up all our munitions on haggis fillings. Contrary to popular opinion, even last winter wasn't enough to make all the sheep come off the mountains." The RAF man glanced at Owen, the chairman, for support. "We may want to conserve the munitions for London or Europe. In addition, can we afford to use up that amount of avgas?"

With a scowl, Owen shook his head. "Not yet."

"I thought the corned beef had arrived. Doesn't that mean the Falklands refineries are producing?" Vanna, the tall slim Asian woman in charge of the military contractors, the paramilitaries, didn't look convinced. "At last."

"They are producing a little fuel, but we had to use up some reserves to send for the corned beef because the spam finally ran out." Owen turned his scowl on Ivy, responsible for processing local food. "From what you said it was that or no meat in the Marts, and we couldn't afford for all the population centres to get aroused at the same time. I thought the spam was made with any rubbish available?"

"Yes but we had to put some pork in with the fats, to give it a flavour so the scum didn't realise. We've even hunted out the wild boar so most of the last batches were rat and dog and yes, some sheep, including everything but the wool." Ivy's frown hadn't faded. "I pushed that corned beef straight out to the Marts to quieten everyone down, so I hope there'll be more?"

This time Owen sounded more confident. "Yes, there will be, along with some frozen beef for the civilised citizens. What about distribution? Gerard?"

The youngest Cabal member glanced at the figures in a file in front of him. After a brief but bitter exchange over how many ports were already available, and the number of troops tied up protecting them, the group conceded another wouldn't hurt. After another tussle over when the para-militaries would be finished in Glasgow, Joshua, Vanna and Gerard settled on Hull, providing that meant the troops could abandon Liverpool. Those docks were the most difficult to defend because the surrounding city held too many enclaves to be cleared yet.

A cultured woman's voice cut into the talk about numbers and timing. "One moment please. Nobody has given an answer on what is to be done about those Reivers or whatever they are in the Highlands. They have food, real weapons including automatics, and are properly organised. Forget the enclosures because they are actually enclosed, and we have enough ports to manage." Grace, the grey-haired aristocratic woman in charge of the work camps, turned to Joshua. "There is also the problem of rumours spreading through the armed forces. Well?"

"These Reivers have just gained an unknown number of recruits. I've warned you, we daren't use regulars to flush them out. As it is we'll have to move the Scottish troops south, just in case they find out. I'll replace them with English regiments, so there'll be no local connections." Joshua sighed heavily, obviously unhappy with the next part. "The Army units around Aberdeen and Inverness already know what happened, so they'll have to die as soon as the problem is resolved. The trouble is, any Army units we send to chase these Reivers will soon realise who they are. We should uti-lise your people, Vanna, the civilian contractors, perhaps all the Specials including those from your processing facilities? You keep saying they'll do the jobs the Army can't."

"Against irregulars trained by Army personnel, fighting on their home turf? Not a snowball's chance in hell." Vanna hesitated, reluctant to give Joshua more reasons to belittle her forces. "Worse still, didn't you just say that Angus made it clear his men would welcome a chance to kill Specials? This one is down to the Army, the professionals, as you so often point out."

The rotund man at the end of the table, silent until now, suddenly smiled. "Weren't we thinking of using rescued European troops in selected areas, or was that just their planes and warships?"

"Excellent idea, Boris. We did persuade a few European ground units to surrender, most of them along with the warships, but we'd need more of them. Use the reconnaissance info to compile a list of any remnants of national armies in Europe. We'll offer them a safe place for their families.

They can repay us by traipsing over the mountains hunting Reivers." Owen glanced at Joshua. "Will that work?"

"There'll be a hell of an attrition rate, but they can use the foreign airpower that came here when their airfields were overrun. That will stop rumours spreading among any British Forces." Joshua fell quiet but the rest waited. They could see him consulting papers and working something out. "No new clearances until next winter at least. I want enough regulars free to deal with the imported troops if they act up."

The chairman, Owen, had heard enough. "Agreed. Boris, use the survivors of European Cabal cells to recruit from the continent. The ex-government members will be recognised by their national armies, and may have enough authority left to give orders. Victor, will you arrange for the Navy to transport any recruits? Use the French warships that came over when Brest fell." The Navy man agreed without looking up, busy with his own files.

Maurice, the spymaster, lifted a lip in a sneer. "Give the Scots Guards London to guard. It'll take some of the vim out of the feisty bastards. Demanding to see the King? Who the hell do they think they are?"

"They are the British Army. That means the King is their commander, especially since we aren't actually a legal government. Heaven forbid the Army ever find that out." Owen gave a dismissive shrug and indicated Vanna. "That's why Vanna's Specials guard him, and the two younger Royals. We only allowed a few officers to see the King in his sickbed in Edinburgh Castle, too drugged to get ambitious. They were actually pleased to find out one of the Royal Family had survived. Typical that it has to be that red-haired wildcard, not someone we could control."

"We only need him to live a few more years, just until the young Royals reach twenty-one. We'll have one of them obedient by then." Grace brandished a page of figures. "A longer term worry is London itself. The residents are proving resilient."

"When the numbers are low enough, we can use firepower to process the rest. Vanna's contractors can be used for that." Owen switched to the bearded man. "I hope we finally have good news about food, Henry?"

Despite plenty of ideas on how to grow more, nobody could get around the basic problem. The Army believed the draconian measures were necessary because of the food and fuel shortage. That meant the areas where the Army could see the fields had to be farmed inefficiently, by hand, so the soldiers didn't realise the Cabal had enough fuel for tractors. On the plus side, the destruction or capture of the European fishing fleets meant the revitalised fishing ports were bringing in record catches.

* * *

Maurice, Vanna and Grace held back after the meeting for a quiet word with Owen, the chairman. They had plans afoot that the rest of the Cabal didn't need to know about. At the beginning, the vastly swollen ranks of hired paramilitaries had been little better than rabble. Sweeping the countryside for villagers and farmers, guarding Marts and convoys, and now clearing York and Glasgow, had honed some of them. These four had even managed to get them some armour and now discussed ways to transfer more, all part of their master plan to dispose of the professional Army entirely.

The other secret project involved training snipers by brainwashing some of the traumatised survivors of the clearances. Maurice, the spymaster, believed they could be turned into killing robots, programmed so they were otherwise mindless, but progress was slow and he needed more 'volunteers.' Once he perfected the technique, all of them had potential targets they daren't ask the Army snipers to kill.

* * *

London – Cyn Palace:
While the gangs in the smaller cities fought, the Cabal and Reivers faced off against each other and the Cabal squabbled and plotted, some of the beleaguered inhabitants of London had realised the futility of shooting each other.

One group of gangs would have been of particular interest to Soldier Boy, if he'd known Cyn Palace still stood and some of the inhabitants had survived this long. The leaders of the five gangs were meeting to try and make sure they survived a little longer, specifically by extending their previous agreements to share arable land. Without Marts, any cultivated land in London became a valuable commodity and the school playing fields behind Cyn Palace were a real prize.

"We need something a bit tighter than the first agreement. Everyone sending help when it's needed isn't fast enough." The speaker, a man wearing a clerical dog-collar, looked around the rest. "At the moment, if our patch of crops is raided, we call for help. By the time the rest get organised it's all over. We're losing men and food."

"Come on Preacher, the Imam and the Sinners aren't going to join the same gang as you." A tall, slim, white gang leader, Eli, indicated a shorter black man. "My gang and Kermit's might join the Sinners if it came to it, but none of us agree with how any of the others organise things."

"Well I'm not going to abandon Sin, am I, Eli?" The biggest man there, Sinner, put an arm around a smaller redheaded woman. She grinned and elbowed him. He glared at her without any real heat. "Since it's your idea, you explain it."

Sin smirked before turning to the other gangsters. "Not combined into one gang, but we can come part of the way. How about if we put twenty fighters from each gang together, as a sort of central force?" The woman indicated the Preacher, then the Imam. "Your people fight side by side when there's an attack. Can they do that every day, put up with unbelievers?"

"As long as your people accept that we are entitled to our beliefs. Then you are helping to feed the children of the faithful, so you are misguided but good people." The Imam's brief smile at Preacher acknowledged that none of them met pre-Crash definitions of good. "The last few years have tempered the more extreme believers, and left realists."

"What happens if some other religious nutter decide to attack?" Kermit, the black youth, scowled at both the religious leaders. "Will your people join them if they declare a bloody jihad, Imam, or will Preacher help that bunch up around St. Paul's Cathedral if they start another crusade? The first crusade is how they got control of the place."

The Imam curled his lip in a sneer. "The fanatics aren't true followers of any faith. They twist words to gain power. My people at least will be keener to kill them than they are to shoot you." His smile had a real edge to it as he looked around the others. "Which should come as a relief to all those present. I agree with Sin, not something I would normally say. Twenty fighters, fully armed. Where do they live?"

"Near the playing fields, the farm, in the old school buildings. They can work on the farm in between protecting the crops." Sin nudged Sinner and gave him a wickedly knowing look. "We should have arranged this before Valentine's Day, so they could have a party to settle in. Never mind, we'll have a warm welcome for the next assholes who try to raid the crops." Heads went together to sort out the practicalities.

* * *

Across the world, the unwanted surplus, the people who had no place in the Cabal's new world, struggled to survive. The original culling of the global population had now exceeded any of the Cabal's estimates. Even so, more must die because the new social order did not include categories such as unemployed, poorly educated, criminally violent, or some ethnic groups such as gypsies.

A growing number of the proposed victims in the UK suspected they were on the government's hit list. None had any idea their deaths had been ordained decades ago, before many of them had even been born. For now, many people, even those ruled by violent gangsters, concentrated on making their lives at least tolerable. The more ambitious gang bosses led their fighters in pursuit of power and wealth, and in doing so brought the Cabal a little nearer to total success.

Chapter 2:
Corned Beef Lunatics

Sin might be happier, down in London, but a fortnight after Valentine's, any hint of good feeling in Orchard Close had long since gone. "I hate shopping, especially when I traipse five miles and then can't get in." Casper scowled down the access road from the bypass. A big crowd outside the local Mart were being held back by mesh, barbed wire, fully manned guard towers and a repainted armoured car. Beyond those the squat grey shape of the Mart, with the doors still firmly closed, wasn't exactly inviting.

Alfie sighed and turned back, his shoulders slumping. "We've got no option but to go home, Casper. The nutters are out in force so there must be new computer games for sale. If we get in the way they'll kill us."

"We've got no option but to shop, Alfie." Harold, Soldier Boy, wasn't any happier, because Alfie's reaction should be the right one. "Myxomatosis has hit the wild rabbits, hard, and according to the Coven the captive ones can't supply enough protein. We also need spam for the fats, and there hasn't been any for a month." He inspected the blocks of young men waiting at the front of the crowd, each gang wearing something distinctive. The front ranks were all armed with machetes, with those at the rear carrying baseball bats or homemade clubs and knives. "When the gangs go for the games, we might get to the spam and out again while they're fighting. More dried chews would help, but the Coven reckon we'll all get sick without the spam."

"We can't get our weapons out, not where the Army can see us." Casper glanced back at the Army post guarding the bypass, scowling again. Only unarmed pedestrians were allowed along the Army-controlled bypass, so the iron bars were disguised as frames in the backpacks. "That lot down there don't have to come down the bypass, so they'll be armed to the teeth."

"But we've got the right people to deal with anything but gangsters."

The other four nodded. Casper, well over six feet of weight-lifter type muscle, and Alfie, only six-foot but similarly muscled, were all that stopped Henry from looking truly impressive. Those three made Harold and Billy, both almost six feet and strong fit men, look fairly average. "We'll head for the toilets, get the weapons out and shop quickly. If there's tins we can just shove the iron bars in the packs on the way back. The scanners will never pick them up." Harold pointed at the crowd. "We want to be just back of the gangs, three or four people back. Otherwise all the rest will pick the shelves clean anyway."

"Like the last time. There's less food on the shelves every time, Harold." Alfie squared his shoulders. "I don't fancy it but you're the Soldier Boy."

"If you get a bruise, Hazel or Veronica might kiss it better?" Casper sniggered, seizing an opportunity to tweak the youngster. "Which is it this week?"

Alfie blushed bright scarlet, suddenly looking much younger than his seventeen years. "It's not like that." He still didn't like admitting anything to do with Hazel where Harold could hear, despite Harold seeing them kissing several times. When the Crash left her a teenage orphan, Hazel found refuge with Harold's sister and 'adopted' Harold as a surrogate uncle. Now seventeen, she'd moved out but vacillated between still calling him Uncle Harold and accusing him of spying on her love life. "Come on or we'll be too late." Alfie started down the road.

"Wait up. Let those maniacs pick a spot first." A convoy of SUVs pulled up in a ring on the rubble near the Mart, the occupants pouring out of them to form a tight group. All the fighters were women, and those wearing blonde wigs regardless of their ethnicity warned everyone. The Barbie Girls were here. Because of their reputation, other gangs made way for the nutters to take a prime spot at the front of the crowd. "None of our treaties cover Mart visits, so we'll find a good place behind one of the less aggressive gangs. The GOFS are the best of our neighbours so they shouldn't give us grief." Harold smiled, trying to look confident. "Not if they want to buy more decent beer." The GOFS, Barbie Girls, Hot Rods and Geek Freeks were all theoretically allies of Orchard Close, but that didn't guarantee safety today.

The five men moved down to the back of the crowd, using their size and appearance to make their way through the shoppers. The ordinary citizens, residents who weren't fighters, parted without giving Harold any trouble but he stopped before reaching the GOFS. One glanced back, raising a hand in greeting. "Hey, Soldier Boy. I thought you didn't play computer games."

"Hi there Ogou. Some of us shop for food." Harold glanced each way to see who had noticed. His Soldier Boy rep came in handy sometimes, but some of this lot might try for a scalp while he was outnumbered and under-armed. Hopefully they were all more interested in new computer games.

"Cooee, Soldier Boy. Want a lift home?" The blond wig beneath the raised hand made that a no. Any man getting into a Barbie Girl vehicle ended up in Beth's, and never came home. "Ooh, it's Alfie. Can I get searched while we wait?" Two more women looked over and waved, laughing as Alfie blushed scarlet.

"Alfie needs to save his strength for the walk home. It keeps him fit." Harold smiled and waved back, hoping that Chandra wanted computer games more than trouble. The gods that Harold didn't believe in must have been feeling benevolent, because the electronic locks in the three double gates clicked open. With a roar the front ranks of the crowd pushed through, surging across the open yard towards the three sets of revolving steel doors.

Along the Mart roof the guards rose from behind their sandbags, some of them bringing up rifles rather than the usual shotguns firing non-lethal rounds. Worse, the bowser usually connected to the armoured car wasn't there. Instead, the slim barrel of a machine gun poked out of the turret alongside the water cannon. "Come on, keep up or we'll get trampled." Harold prayed none of the idiots ahead had brought a firearm or even a crossbow, because the Mart guards weren't known for restraint. All the joking of the early days had disappeared.

"Crap." Henry had just seen the reason for today's turnout.

"What is it?" Casper, with Henry, kept close by Harold while Alfie and Billy watched their backs. All four looked around for the problem.

Harold looked where Henry pointed. "The adverts on the Mart. There's a new TX-Box out today and a new upgrade to Urban Riot." Both were must-haves for any gang boss.

Casper glanced back, without much confidence. "It won't be the usual fighting over games, the gangs will kill for either of those. We can call it off?"

"We'll get trampled trying to get back now." Behind them a solid mass of people had the same idea as Harold, get to the food quickly. "We'll just stock up and run."

"Cripes, we'd better hurry." Casper moved faster as those directly ahead broke into a run.

"Quick, catch up." Harold set off, easily catching up because the initial rush slowed. Chants, screams and the clash of steel weapons announced the first gangs reaching the doors. While the five shoppers waited for the blockage to clear, they fended off others trying to get in front. Harold didn't want some idiot attracting attention from the nutters ahead. Behind him he heard grunts, as either Alfie or Billy punched or kicked the more persistent.

To either side a few fools ran past before reeling back, screaming, as gang fighters turned on them. At least the rearguards were using baseball bats or fists. A roar of triumph heralded the first through the doors, but the access choked again when too many tried to follow. Now some of the bodies reeling back or dropping spurted blood. The knives were out and the machete blades were swinging in earnest.

"Hold up." Harold paused to take a set of brass knuckles from a conveniently unconscious gangster and pocketed them. "For emergencies." Sharp cracks sounded from behind. Harold tensed, but there were no more. The guards had shot some poor bastard but only one or two. The Mart visits were getting more dangerous as the amount of food slowly lessened.

The crowd surged forward again as the surviving gang members spread out inside the Mart, aiming for their prizes. Once inside, Harold sidestepped away from the tangle of fallen, shoving past a couple of loners fighting over some poor bastard's trainers. With a sigh of relief, he headed towards the food aisles.

"Oh cripes, some nasty little pervert has changed the layout, again." Nobody could work out why that happened, unless the Mart employees enjoyed watching the shoppers mill about in confusion. Harold stopped, looking where Henry pointed and flinching. Today's confusion would be lethal, because the glittering boxes of gaming gear and the racks of games were right where the meat should be.

"We've got to get out of the way." Casper pointed to the opposite side of the doors. "Over there." Sure enough, the screaming and yelling at the back, around the usual games shelves, had started back towards the front. The machete wielding maniacs would arrive any moment, just in time to meet the poor suckers here for basic rations. The Mart version of customer care had gone from confusing their customers to trying to kill them.

The five of them tried to get across to the other side, away from the approaching mayhem, but hit a traffic jam. The unarmed shoppers had stopped just inside. Seeing their usual gangster bodyguards now bearing down on them, most tried to retreat, but more shoppers pushed in from behind. Meanwhile the screaming horde of gangsters lashed out at each other, and anyone else blocking the way to the gaming shelves. Those outside shoved harder to get inside as more gunshots rang out in the yard. It wasn't a massacre yet, but the place had only been open a few minutes.

Harold slid his hand into the pocket with the knuckles, barging his way across the flow. Just in front, a score of Trainspotters wearing anoraks assaulted a smaller group, so Harold pointed left. "There, go round them. Make for the toilets." Harold needed privacy, so the Mart cameras didn't spot how he smuggled weaponry past the Army.

"That's further in, Harold." Alfie glanced at the doors but more people pushed in, adding to the chaos. If anybody retreated, the guards might shoot them as they came out of the entrance.

Billy had already started off. "If the games are here, the meat should be back there anyway."

"Cripes Harold, the nutters are everywhere." Casper caught a swinging arm, slapping the man hard so he spun away. "Oh great, look." Harold and Alfie followed Casper's arm and saw the sign.

"Oh the nasty, stinking, perverted little creeps." Alfie avoided swearing but doing so would be hard today. The signs for flour and meat hung near the exits. May some God help anyone shopping there, when some barmy banger ran for the exit with whatever he'd grabbed. Queues always formed at the score of booths because only one person could go through at a time, but today they'd be death-traps. Gangsters who'd already fought for their prize wouldn't wait patiently in line. They'd kill to get out before someone stronger set on them.

"Toilets first, get the iron bars, then wait our chance. First lull in the lunatics, we dive into the meat shelves, fill the packs and come back this way. We'll leave after the fighting dies down." Harold glanced back at the scrum just inside the doors. "But definitely iron bars first, and soon." Gangs of men and youths were already hunting, catching and robbing smaller groups who had collected games or gaming boxes. That probably seemed safer than joining the melee by the shelves.

* * *

"You two, out, now." The two startled men having a pee finished quickly and left. Billy smashed the only camera that still might be functional while Casper blocked the doors. Unfortunately, the swing doors had no handles to hang on to. Harold passed his pack to Alfie. "You get the iron bars out, I'll stop anyone trying the door." He slipped the brass knuckles on.

"Here, in case you need a shield." Harold accepted Alfie's pack, one with a frame of aluminium tube. Once outside, as expected, the only ones coming towards the toilet were unarmed shoppers. The nutters were concentrating on fighting to get out, or so Harold thought, until a tight knot of fighters boiled out of the next aisle and into him. Harold staggered, trying to keep his feet as he was caught up in the tangled fighters. He stumbled and went down, almost losing the rucksack. Rolling clear of the feet, Harold brought the rucksack round over himself, just in time to stop someone caving his head in.

For a moment, Harold thought a gang had decided to collect his scalp, but the fight swept onwards. Some of the gangsters were taking an indirect route to the exit, but others had realised and set an ambush. The running fight boiled around Harold as the defenders tried to make a stand.

Someone dropped next to Harold, shook himself and sat back up. The oik looked at the rucksack and made a grab. "Cheeky git." Harold let go with one hand and elbowed him in the side of his head, hard enough to rattle the scroat's head on the shelving. Harold did it again on the side of his exposed neck and the bloke slithered to the floor. Keeping tight to the shelving while keeping the bag between him and the mayhem, Harold eased up onto his feet. Boots or maybe clubs hit the rucksack twice on the way up but canvas absorbed blows better than he would have. When his floor-wrestling partner grabbed Harold's leg, Harold leaned over and smacked the brass knuckles into the side of the thieving git's head. "Stay."

Harold looked for a way to get back to his friends but the remnants of the melee, a mixture of gangsters and innocents, were still fighting or being kicked or trodden on. As the fight shifted further towards the checkouts, Harold gratefully headed towards the toilet door. "Harry! Harry!" Another yell, more frantic this time, gave Harold a direction. He located the source, Pete, Tessa's younger brother, and the youth had found real trouble. Even if Tessa lived in a different enclave, so he didn't see much of her these days, Harold couldn't just abandon her brother to a nutter with a machete. Tessa had a young son by Harold's best friend in the Army, Stones, and before the Crash he'd spent more than one night sleeping on their couch.

Pete, wearing an old cycle helmet, used a battered wooden baseball bat to fend off another blow from the machete. Biting back a curse, Harold glanced back and forth. The main fighting concentrated on a small group with two big boxes, probably the new TX-Boxes, rather than the computer games scattered across the floor nearby. More pieces flew from Pete's splintered club as the machete landed again, but luckily the wielder relied on brute force. The blade could have easily lopped off a few fingers.

With two quick strides Harold reached over the top of the assailant's open-faced crash helmet, jerking back and down. He lifted a knee into the small of the youth's conveniently angled back, hard, yanking him over backwards and down with a high-pitched squeal. Harold stamped on the hand with the machete. It wasn't enough, so he leaned down, using the brass knuckles on the lad's exposed nose and mouth. Once, twice, three times, short solid jabs hard enough to break teeth but not the skull. The nutter dropped the machete, clutching at his ruined face. Harold glanced up again to check if anyone had noticed.

Not yet, Harold's latest victim curled up whimpering and bleeding, while Cheeky still seemed to be out cold. The last of the box-holders went down, so the victors would soon be looking for more victims or a way out. Pete lunged for the machete but Harold stamped on the blade. "Don't be a fool. Somebody will kill you for that. Or those," he continued as the youth tried to gather up the games. Behind them the battered gangster crawled away, leaving a trail of blood.

"They'll kill me if I don't bring something back, and some sort of weapon," Pete retorted. "I have to get the games. I owe Caddi big-time."

"Stupid bastard." Harold wouldn't be able to face Tessa if Caddi decided to kill her idiot brother, not if he could have prevented it. With a sigh, he turned his back to the fighting before picking up the machete, keeping it out of sight. "Take off the bloody helmet and stuff this down your jeans. That way you can walk out through the checkout with a few cans like any other civvie."

Pete looked down at the games. "But..." he began.

"Pick two." Harold picked several of the rest up off the floor. As Pete stuffed his games inside his jacket and stowed the machete, Harold covered the action with his body and the rucksack. Three of the victorious fighters, Ferdinands, pounced on the crawling gangster and then the unconscious man nearby. They killed and searched both before turning towards Harold. Harold held the games out to the nearest. His other hand, wearing the knuckles, poised to toss the rucksack and wade in. "Here, we don't play fighting games. We're here for groceries." Harold bent a little, scooting the games boxes along the floor before kicking the others in the same direction.

"No balls? Clever little boy." The Ferdinand grinned, picking them up. He stepped to the side to point a machete at Pete. "What's he got then?" Another two Ferdinands joined the group.

"Does someone need spanking, Harold?" The voice belonged to Casper, and came as a relief to Harold at least.

Harold straightened, grinning and holding his hand out to the side. He heard footsteps and an iron bar nearly a metre long slapped into his palm. He got a good grip. "Thanks Casper." Harold looked the nearest gangster straight in the eye. "Well, do you want spanking?" The youth's eyes widened. Harold knew he'd be seeing Casper, Henry, Billy and Alfie, all wielding similar bars.

"Leave it, you twat, it's Soldier Boy. I recognise that big bald bastard." The man, pulling on the gangster's arm, tugged harder. "They'll kill you." The gangster looked at the games he'd just been given, puzzled.

Harold sneered at him. "I told you, I don't play at fighting." He dropped the rucksack to show the bloody brass knuckles. "Well?"

"Fuck it, no chance." The Ferdinands turned, running towards the checkouts.

Harold glanced back to the rest. "Sorry Casper, he's in a hurry." All five laughed.

"I have to get out." Pete cringed as the five big men turned towards him. "The rest will expect me to bring the stuff out." The lad glanced down at his jacket. "At least I kept the best ones, but you know what you gave away? A bloody fortune."

"You have to be alive to spend it, stupid. In any case, I really don't play computer games." Harold hustled the youth further to the side. "Pick up your hat again. You can walk out nice and peaceful in a bit, when all the scrapping calms down. Have you got enough coupons for those games?" Pete nodded, but he looked decidedly shifty. "How come? Remember, I know your sister so no crap."

Pete swallowed hard, looking anywhere but straight at Harold. "I, well, er. Look, don't tell Tessa. Please?" The silly idiot looked more frightened than when someone had been trying to cut his fingers off. "I owe someone and this is how I have to pay. I borrowed some coupons...."

Harold didn't want to hear details because he already had enough troubles. "Caddi is your problem. Just get it sorted without involving Tessa because she's had enough crap already." Like a boyfriend left behind in Kuwait when the Army pulled out, well over three years ago, and a five-year-old kid. Even the MOD had stopped trying to pretend any of those blokes were coming home. "Grab a few cans or packets, try and make it look as if you really are shopping." Harold turned to the others. "We'll get what we can from the shopping list, then look at the clothing while we wait."

"You can get some new frillies, Casper." Alfie grinned at the big bald man.

"It's not my frillies you're interested in." Casper smirked as Alfie glanced at Harold and away.

As Alfie looked away from Harold, at the displays on the nearby shelves, his eyes fastened on a stack of tubs. "There's even some coffee again, though not much." The group took the lot. "D'you reckon the rumours are true, that the idiots in Glasgow burned their Mart because there were no teabags and coffee?"

"Bugatti reckons they'd been distilling booze from any rubbish they could, and went crazy." Pete flinched away as Casper and Henry turned towards him. Casper still wanted some personal payback from Bugatti, a local gangster. "That's what they're saying in the Mansion." Harold bit off a question about what Pete had been doing talking to Bugatti or visiting the headquarters of the Hot Rods, a neighbouring gang, because it wasn't his business.

"There's sugar as well today." Alfie stuffed bags into his pack. "This will be popular with, er, the girl club." He glared at Casper's snigger. Billy and Henry brightened, quickly collecting some sugar.

Harold smiled without letting Alfie see. "Shortages might be a real reason to riot. There must be a reason tea and coffee are still on the shelves when foreign imports have supposedly stopped." He pointed to the stack of small plastic tubs behind the Perspex door on a nearby shelf. "Be a real Uncle Casper and get some chocolate powder, will you, please?"

Casper picked up a tub, smiling. "For Daisy's cereal? One day she'll have to accept there never will be any more Coco Pops, though I'm not going to be the one to tell her."

Henry flinched dramatically. "Cripes, nor me." Alfie nodded heartfelt agreement, because even at six, Daisy could out-argue most of Orchard Close, or cry for England.

"Chocolate is another import." Casper glanced at Harold, puzzled.

"Are you skint? I'll get a couple for Sharyn. If she doesn't want them some-one else will be happy to pay." He picked two more tubs for Harold's sister. The others quickly calculated what they could afford before taking more tubs. As the only chocolate product, the powder would be very popular with more than the girl club, the unattached females.

Harold shook his head, pointing deeper into the Mart. "I'm buying clothes for the kids today, so I'll need all my spare coupons."

Alfie hesitated, calculating, then put a third tub of chocolate in his pack. "The girl club would burn the Mart if chocolate stopped altogether."

"Both the Coven and Barbies would help." Harold frowned at a thought. "Daisy might do it all on her own if she finds out Coco Pops are extinct."

The other four looked amused, because Daisy's reaction would be truly spectacular. "Cripes, yes."

"Back to real shopping. We're supposed to get spices." Alfie looked around hopefully, but with the shelves all changed round, he'd no idea where to start. Casper spotted the spices but that didn't help. "The names on the shelves don't match the list, but Liz and Patty threatened to skin me if we didn't bring some."

Harold peered at the list of flavours, then the shelf. "Sharyn is the head witch and she threatened to curse me, so I'm not taking the blame."

"Your sister might run the Coven, but Patty is their hit-woman and she gave me my instructions." Casper started putting random packets of spices in his pack. "I'm a fairy and Harold's a wimp so we'll blame you, Alfie, if these are wrong. You'll get hauled into the girl club to explain." Alfie start-ed to object, rethought the last bit and smiled. After all, at seventeen he didn't care if he was invited or hauled into the two big houses full of single women. The five of them quickly worked down the list, except for the meat and flour on the shelves by the exit.

*　*　*

Once they'd sorted out the Coven list, Harold headed for the clothing to pick up new T-shirts for young Wills and Daisy. As usual they also need-ed underwear; despite the food shortages the kids grew like weeds. All five men bought new boxers while the Mart had some in stock, while Alfie also chose a few packs of women's knickers, allegedly for resale. Henry started to tweak him, thought again and bought some as well.

Finally Casper tapped Harold's arm. "Now's our chance." The noise by the exits had died down so all six headed that way. Casper took the machete from Pete, just in case stray gangsters turned up. The five of them wanted to shop quickly, before the second string gangsters were finished with the games shelves. They'd only be beating on each other, not killing, but there were a lot of them. Harold stopped where the spam should be, when the Mart had any. "Pinch me, Casper. Cripes, punch me. Is that really corned beef?"

"Glory hallelujah." Henry picked up a can with true reverence. "Instead of spam?" He scowled, looking closer at the label. "It's the same price as spam. If they've just changed the labels I'll personally burn the damn Mart down."

"Worry later. Come on, take as much as we can carry while those idiots are still fighting over computer games." Harold turned to Pete. "Fill your pockets."

Pete looked down, shamefaced. "I've haven't many coupons of my own."

"Then carry some for us as payment for the protection. We want all we can stagger away with." Harold held out a can. "Come on, move it." The sounds of combat seemed to be moving this way again.

"Flour, there's plenty of flour as well." Alfie's smile faded as he looked from one stack to the other. "Do we take self-raising or plain, they've got both this time?"

"How would I know, it's a year since I've seen a choice. Just get as much of each sort as possible." Harold grinned even as he stuffed corned beef cans into his pack. "Pippa can make proper bread cobs to put the rabbit burgers in." Alfie started loading up with flour, smiling quietly at the thought. Billy threw a few more cans in his pack, then joined Alfie.

"This is about enough." Casper grunted as he lifted the pack and nudged Henry. "Be careful with yours. Mine's still got a frame inside to strengthen it." Harold gave Casper a warning glance. He didn't want Pete opening his mouth and telling the rival gangsters in the Mansion how Orchard Close hid their weapons. Everyone quickly stuffed their pockets with extra cans, before pulling back several aisles as the second wave of nutters arrived. The small group used the half hour before the sounds of strife died away again to go through the wizened potatoes, looking for any suitable for chitting. Emmy had complained too many had been used for food; she needed enough to plant this year's crop.

When Harold and his friends came back to the meat and flour aisles, they were filling with unarmed shoppers. These poor sods paid protection to the gangs for the privilege of living in their territory, so they kept well clear of five big men with iron bars and a machete. The men themselves were laughing about the reaction once the gangsters realised what they'd missed. The nutters wouldn't even be able to steal the corned beef from the ordinary shoppers, because by tomorrow most of the cans would be a tasty memory.

Harold's group topped off their packs with the dried meat sticks most people called dog chews, strongly flavoured but inedible unless cut up and stewed. While they wrangled over which flavours came closest to the descriptions, Harold kept an eye on the checkouts. "Come on, three aisles are clear." He glanced at Pete and beckoned. "Give me our cans and your stuff to take through."

Pete started handing over the corned beef but looked decidedly wary. "I ought to take the games through myself."

Harold shrugged, cramming the cans wherever they'd fit. "Okay. I'm going through with the machete first, in case there's trouble outside. Henry and Billy will go through the aisles either side. Alfie and Casper will wave their iron bars and watch our backs, then go through straight after us. You have no pack, so some scroat will assume you've got games and rob you."

Pete stared, shocked, until Harold saw realisation dawn. Gangsters like the ones he'd come with would do just that. "All right. I'll go out the no-shopping exit." He hesitated, his hand straying towards a pocket. "Can you carry my spare coupons because if I lose them C… someone will skin me."

"You're working directly for Caddi? You're a bloody idiot but yes, because Tessa wouldn't want you used as crossbow practice." Pete shuddered because Caddi, the Hot Rod gang boss, did consider that a normal punishment. The youth handed over three games and a fat roll of coupons, then headed for the mass exit. There Pete hesitated, waiting until he could go through with people he judged weren't stupid enough to shoplift. The Mart scanned everyone leaving that way in batches. One person shoplifting meant they were all arrested and sent to the work camps.

Harold also had a thick roll of coupons this time, because the Coven had given him part of their emergency fund. He split them between all five of them. "Here, coupons for the food. I've got extra to cover buying as much spam as possible, or corned beef as it happens, but don't flash them about." The Coven paid for basic food, but everyone bought their own luxuries such as chocolate, coffee and clothes.

"I'd say things about learning to suck eggs, but there aren't any eggs to learn with." Casper glanced after Pete, now heading into the exit, and smirked. "We could pay with Caddi's coupons?"

"If I didn't know Pete's sister I'd be tempted. That roll of coupons he brought for games is more than we've brought for food." Harold smiled blissfully, patting the roll Pete had handed over. "Now I know how rich he is, I'll jack up the prices for fixing Caddi's guns and Patty can charge more for knitting." They parted, laughing, to head down three separate narrow metal-walled corridors, each leading to a door and a checkout. After paying for the groceries with the Coven coupons, Harold used almost all his personal nest egg for his private shopping. He scowled as he peeled off the coupons from Caddi's roll to pay for Pete's games. Few carried the same name, yet every one already had the second thumbprint to make the coupon legal tender. Protection payments.

*   *   *

By the time Harold came out, Pete waited, twitching, almost hopping from one foot to the other. "They've gone!"

"Cripes, give me a chance! I've just got out of the doors. Who's gone? No, I don't want to know." Harold had no intention of getting dragged into strife with Caddi over whatever Pete had done. If it didn't concern Orchard Close, Harold didn't want to know. He'd rather get to the neutral territory of the bypass. Unfortunately, he had to wait for the others by the doors, so Pete bent his, Henry's and Billy's ears anyway. Pete had come with escorts to guard the games, but he'd lost them in the melee. They'd left, probably assuming Pete was dead. Caddi would be annoyed, but only over losing the coupons.

Pete daren't go home along the neutral road without guards, because desperate loners often lurked along the route. A youth not wearing gang colours and walking alone would be ambushed. He couldn't go any other way because a quarter-mile wide no-go zone, enforced by machine guns, lay between the Mart and Hot Rod border. Despite the whinging getting on his nerves, Harold had to smile. Emmy and Patty, and a crossbow bolt, were responsible for the no-go zone. The pair would be happy to know they were still causing Caddi's people some grief.

"You got yourself into the trouble, so you get out of it. I'm headed home and if you've got any sense you'll come with us on the by-pass. That way you can walk home from the other direction and won't need an escort. You'll have to come part way up there anyway, because your stuff is in my pack and I'm not stopping to look for it until I get to safer ground." As soon as Casper and Alfie came out, Harold set off with Pete in tow. "If it wasn't for Tessa I'd have walked away anyway. Thank her when you see her. How is she anyway?"

"Er, she's okay. I think?"

Harold let the disgust show in his voice. "Stupid burke, you've left home. Bet she doesn't know about any of this crap, does she?"

"No. Maybe." Pete sounded sullen now, but at least the whining stopped. Outside the Mart yard gates, Harold turned towards the bypass. The occasional sharp cracks of gunshots echoed from the entrance to TesdaMart, out of sight of the exits behind a brick wall. This last year the Mart guards had become more and more callous. They'd be shooting the badly wounded, so they could shift the bodies and close the doorways. As soon as the last shopper left, and the less seriously wounded had been thrown outside the fence, the Mart dispensers would be topped up and the floors cleared and washed down. They'd be ready for the afternoon opening as if nobody had died.

Pete roused from whatever he'd been mulling over. "Can I come back with you? You're right, I can make it from there on my own."

"As long as you go straight home." Harold glared at him. "If someone comes for you I'll hand you over. The treaty means I can't take runners from Caddi."

Pete smiled, the first real happiness Harold had seen from him. "Yeah, no problem. I'll let Tessa know I saw you." The youth's grin faded. "Oh Christ, what about the, er..." Pete gestured to the machete. "The Army don't allow weapons on the bypass, but I can't go back with nothing, no weapon. The bat wasn't mine."

"It was Caddi's, wasn't it, you stupid idiot?" Harold didn't wait for a reply. "Put the machete down your jeans again. I'll hide that hat in my pack. The Army won't be suspicious because you've got no gang tattoos or logos on your gear. They'll think you're an ordinary shopper. The wand will bleep so the soldiers will start searching for the metal, but they'll stop when they find corned beef." Harold called the other four across to hide what Pete would be doing, and explained. As Pete hid the machete he glared at the youth. "You go through alone and well ahead. You are not with us, get it? Remember, I'll come after you if you cause us any grief or nick any of those cans, right?"

"Yeah, no problem. Bloody hell, Tessa would kill for one of these." Pete looked hopeful.

"You got any of your own coupons at all?" The youth nodded cautiously. "You can take her one if you pay. She might even let you back in the house after whatever stupidity you've been up to." Harold would have given Tessa a free can, but daren't because she lived in Hot Rod territory. Caddi, the Hot Rods warlord, would love to find out he had a friend of Soldier Boy's under his thumb. That's why they'd only exchanged the occasional careful word at the Mart.

At the checkpoint, the wand bleeped but as soon as the first corned beef can came out the squaddie waved Pete through. Harold's group had their IDs checked, but they had obvious shopping and were waved through. "Next one. Come on, move it, move it, move it."

Harold frowned at the squaddie. "What's the rush?"

The squaddie glanced again at Harold's ID. "Soldier Boy, Orchard Close? Supply convoy coming through for the Mart. If you're within three hundred yards when it arrives, we'll shoot you."

"Cripes why? We're unarmed."

"Some animal got a suicide bomb past an Army checkpoint outside Leeds. He blew up a supply lorry. The scum were waiting, they swarmed over the wire and onto the road to steal the food. Fair warning, keep well away from the central reservation or the convoy guards might open up anyway. How's the blonde?"

Harold had to think for a second because the bit about being shot had thrown him. "Doll? She's on her feet again, and thank you." Harold meant that because not all squaddies would have warned him. Doll, a twenty-two-year old blonde, had been very badly wounded in the fighting when the local gangs combined to stop a horde from storming the local Mart. The TV pictures showing the blood from her lung wound trickling from her mouth had made her a local celebrity. Better yet, the Army squaddies loved the idea of a pretty blonde with guns, which had bought Orchard Close some tolerance. "Come on you four, move it. Trigger-happy convoy coming." Pete overheard the message and kept up until Harold explained properly, once they were three hundred yards away. When they heard the lorries coming, the six of them knelt, as far as they could from the other carriageway. They also turned their backs, putting their hands on their heads as the convoy roared past.

* * *

The trip home to Orchard Close took over an hour of solid marching, but Harold didn't stop. As he turned down the off-ramp he sighed in relief because home lay three hundred metres away, just outside the exclusion zone. As a squaddie let him through the Army checkpoint, a figure waved from the upstairs window of number one, a guardhouse, giving Harold the all-clear.

The steel plated gates squealed and creaked as they opened, but only because they had been made deliberately noisy and hard to move. Even with the locking bars removed, opening them would alert everyone nearby. Jeremy stood in the doorway of number two with a machete while Matti, his gartered wench, stood at an upstairs window with a crossbow. Fergie, a statuesque twenty-one year old woman, stood at a window in number one where the Army couldn't see her shotgun. They weren't expecting trouble; Orchard Close always guarded their gates like this.

"Hi Louie, are you teamed up with Fergie now?"

The young man with half an ear missing knew Harold meant for guard duty, but he laughed. "In my dreams, Harold."

Billy smirked, patting his pockets. "It's a pity you didn't come this time, because we brought corned beef."

"Hey you two, my favours can't be bought with corned beef." Fergie rolled her eyes upwards with a blissful expression. "Now chocolate, for that I might negotiate." Billy and Henry smirked, but neither spoke up.

Harold looked around, wondering why nobody had come to meet him. "I thought there'd be a few waiting to pounce, just in case we brought coffee or chocolate powder."

"Not this time Harold, we've got visitors. Caddi's bodyguard, Big Mack, is here with some Hot Rod scroat, looking for you. Most people are keeping clear in case there's trouble." Louie pointed up the road, deeper into Orchard Close. "I sent the Hot Rods up to the canteen in case Mack wanted stew." Everyone laughed because Caddi's giant bodyguard made a big fuss about how good the Orchard Close stew tasted. Home grown veg and home-reared rabbits were the not-so-secret but rare ingredients.

Harold lowered the rucksack, holding out a hand as Jeremy passed over his stick, the official posh one. He half-turned to watch Pete from the corner of an eye. "Is this anything to do with you?" Pete shook his head but that wasn't a very confident gesture. "Stay here then."

Harold took his time walking up the road. He used those few minutes to check the rest of Orchard Close, but saw no signs of trouble. Any residents in view were watching him, but none seemed nervous so the Hot Rods might have come for a beer and stew and to relax a bit. Mack acted as Caddi's bodyguard so Harold thought it more likely Caddi had sent a message, a polite message if it came with only two men. Twirling the stick, Harold strolled up the path towards the canteen. "Hello Mack, has Caddi turned you out to graze and get some exercise?"

"Eyup, 'Arry. No need, 'e lets me gallop up and down the cleared bit outside the wall now and then. Caddi wants to see you, says you might 'ave 'ad your feet in 'is trough, or some such." Mack looked towards the gate where Pete waited. "Looks like 'e might be right."

"Not really. Pete came back with me because his mates had gone off and left him. He's headed on home in a minute." Harold wasn't too worried about Mack, because Mack would do what he'd been told. He wouldn't cause trouble just for the hell of it. Harold didn't recognise the other gangster, strutting about with a sneer on his face, so perhaps Caddi had decided on another little test? Harold didn't mind too much, the type Caddi sent to challenge Soldier Boy needed a good beating anyway. He glanced up the path as Patty and Elizabeth came out of the door to meet him.

Patty looked pointedly at his empty hand. "Hello Harold. Where's your rucksack? Didn't you get any shopping?"

Before Harold could answer the Hot Rod youth with Mack turned to the two women. "About time the fucking women turned up. Which one gives the free blow jobs, or do I get to choose?" He started to reach out towards Patty but Mack stopped him.

"Leave it."

Mack spoke just as Harold snapped, "Watch your mouth." Harold raised his hand slightly to stop Patty, grateful she wasn't carrying her crossbow or machete, or Mack would have been carting a body back home.

The youth looked at Mack first, before turning to Harold. "Else what?"

Harold firmed up his grip on the walking stick, because any visitor knew better than to act like that. This scroat must be deliberately looking for trouble so Harold didn't answer directly, speaking to Mack first. "Is he just stupid, or has this dipstick done something to annoy Caddi and he wants the scroat spanked? Either way, he's just earned a fine at least."

"Dunno 'Arry. Caddi just said to bring 'im. 'E's new and just come in a couple of days ago, brought some grub an' blades an' a big mouth." The big man shrugged, a little smile on his face. "Caddi said ter bring 'im back, but didn't say 'e wasn't ter be 'urt." Mack paused, thinking for a moment. "Best if 'e's not dead. Caddi might take it wrong and I don't fancy carryin' 'im."

The Hot Rod scroat didn't appreciate being ignored. "Oi, I'm here, you two."

Mack glanced over. "Quiet Lada, the men are talkin'. Get to you in a bit." The big man deliberately turned away from the Hot Rod, grinning at Harold.

Ah, wonderful, Harold thought, Mack had just wound the little scroat up. Sure enough, the youth reacted. "Lada? I told you all, Firebird, bloody Firebird!"

"Nah, you'll get a proper name when you earn it. Until then it's Lada." Mack darted a glance at Harold, rolling his eyes a little. "Think yerself lucky, yer mate got Yugo."

"Well I'll fucking well earn a proper name, Firebird, right now!" The idiot seemed genuinely upset about his gang name. Behind him Patty had started back towards the canteen, probably for her crossbow, but now she stopped and the smile she produced had a lot of anticipation.

"Ooh, 'Arry, 'e's all annoyed and such. Might even cry." Mack dropped the humour. "I told yer the rules. Now yer got to pay a fine. If yer stupid enough to keep goin', Soldier Boy will spank yer and send yer 'ome without yer supper." Now Harold knew he'd been set up, but openly, so Caddi didn't mind his boy getting roughed up a bit.

"I'll have more than supper. We're the Hot Rods, and we take what we want. When I've finished with them two whores you can have seconds, but first I'm gonna fix this mother fu.... Oof!"

While speaking, the youth stepped forward, lifting his right leg high in an obviously practised move. As he did so the gangster drew a knife from his right boot, bringing the eight inches of bright and sharp up and back as his foot came forward and down. He meant to gut his opponent before the other man could draw a weapon, an old and amateur move these days. Worse still, Harold already had his weapon drawn.

Harold also stepped forward, slashing sideways with his walking stick to smack Lada's knee and knock the leg wide. As the youth threw out his knife arm to keep his balance Harold extended his own arm, front leg bent, and lunged in a passable imitation of a fencer. The tip of his stick buried itself in Lada's gut. The stance braced Harold so that Lada's gut stayed where it was as his leg, head and arms continued forward.

The gangster's upper body bent over with an oof of expelled air, so Harold took a second to get it dead right before cracking him on the wrist bone. Lada yelped as his knife tumbled onto the path, then lifted his head with a snarl, his other hand going up towards his neck. Harold pulled his stick back after the strike, but now took hold of it by the other end. As Lada's hand went behind his head the big brass boss on Harold's stick smacked the youth at the side of his head. Lada collapsed in a heap. "I wouldn't have done that if he'd quit after losing his knife." Harold prodded the recumbent figure with his stick but it didn't stir. "With luck he's not too badly concussed. If he is you'll have to leave him overnight." Patty looked hopeful, that would give her a chance for some payback.

"'E should be pleased you knocked him out, or 'e'd be caned good and proper for talking to Patty like that, and the language." Mack's smile widened to a grin as he saw the way Patty eyed the youth. "Never seen your version."

Harold picked up the knife. "Tell Caddi thanks, I haven't got one like this. I'd take the sheath as well but he's had his feet in it." Harold glanced down at the spreading stain on the path. "And I think he's just pissed in it."

Mack laughed, head back in real humour. "Ooh, 'e's gonna 'ave an 'ell of an 'eadache when 'e wakes up. Mind, after that smack I reckon we'll 'ave to wait a bit until 'e can walk." He glanced at the knife. "Fair do's 'Arry, yer took it fair and square. Lada"—he chuckled—"brought it with 'im, so it's yours. 'E 'ad an alli bat with 'im, an' gave it up at the gate with mine."

"We'll take the bat as a fine of course. Caddi's got plenty more." Harold knew any aluminium baseball bat belonged to Caddi, because no Hot Rod owned one personally. Even if Caddi had set this up, he'd still punish Lada for losing the weapon.

"Nice trick that. I've seen it before of course, but real smooth 'Arry. Mind, if yer tried it on me yer'd bust the stick." Big Mack slapped his muscled abdomen. "Bit more weight 'ere."

"Ah, but you wouldn't do something like that, not unless Caddi gave you the word or I went for Caddi." Harold knew that Mack's confidence in his strength and size precluded any dominance games. Though if he clashed with Harold, Mack didn't know the stick was steel tube, etched and painted to resemble wood so it might not go down quite as expected. "Nobody warned Lada, so I suppose I've just helped Caddi out by slapping down some lippy scroat. I should charge him. I'll get someone to stand watch, otherwise this idiot might say something fatal when he wakes up." Harold nodded towards the canteen door. "Fancy a brew and a bite to eat?"

"Wot you got? Got any beef-burgers?" Big Mack returned the smiles, he knew all about the jokes over his name.

"Yeah right, me and Ronald got this arrangement, see." They both laughed and both Patty and Elizabeth joined in. Ronald McDonald might still be serving up burgers in the fabled compounds full of rich bastards, but if someone offered a burger now it wouldn't contain beef. In most places it might contain rat or cat. Up to now Orchard Close stuck to rabbit, which is why they always had customers for their burgers and stew. "Hey, Patty, any stew on the go?"

She'd come back towards Harold, stepping on Lada's hand in passing and grinding her heel into it. Patty smiled, looking down at her foot. "That's because I won't get a chance to cane him." She deliberately spat on the comatose gangster, then kicked him in the nuts. "That's your Patty freebie, a scroat special." She turned to Harold and Mack, satisfied for now. "There's always something in the pot, though at this time of year it will be mystery stew. That's any veg we can scrounge up mixed with spices and chew sticks, with a bit of bunny thrown in. There's still bread but that's stale now, or a potato cake. Did you get any flour?"

"Yup, lots, and the spices this time. We also brought corned beef, lots of corned beef." A couple of the blokes coming up from the gate with Pete cheered. Five big men with big packs could carry over five hundred pounds, so there'd be enough for everyone.

Patty and Elizabeth both stared. "Really?" Mack stared as well.

Harold pulled a can out of his pocket, throwing it to Patty. "No spam, because the shelves were full of this. The scroats were busy fighting over games so we loaded up, as much as we could stagger home with. For now I'll settle for stew. It'll soften the bread. Come on Mack, stew and a beer." Harold stepped over Lada, heading for the door, followed by a smiling Mack. Elizabeth waited, adding her saliva and a kick to the nuts to Lada's still form before escorting Harold's pack inside.

Mack glanced at the women. "Sorry about the language, Patty. I told 'im to watch 'is mouth round you, but we don't 'ave any rules like that back in the Mansion. Yer know Caddi. The blokes can treat the women 'ow they like."

Patty wasn't even slightly mollified. "You manage to remember, Mack, and so do most of the other Hot Rods. Anyway, Lada was meant to start something with Harold, wasn't he?" She collected cans from Harold as he emptied his pockets, stacking them on a table where two of the kitchen helpers quickly scooped them up.

Mack sighed, looking longingly at the stew in the two bowls being filled from the steaming pot. "Caddi said if Lada started ter act up, I should wind 'im up and let 'im try. But only with 'Arry, 'e weren't ter start with anyone else." The big man hesitated. "Do I still get me stew?"

Patty didn't answer, looking to Harold for a decision. "Yeah, and the beer. It's home brew, not that canned stuff from the Mart. That's bloody expensive and it tastes awful." Harold started to smile, anticipating the reaction.

"Ooh, good. Your 'ome brew is all right. Not as strong as some, but real smooth. You should open a pub." They both laughed at the perennial joke. Some rumour or other always claimed that a pub still existed somewhere. If you knew the right people and the right passwords you could get superb beer, a packet of crisps and a game of darts.

*   *   *

While they ate their soup and drank their beer, Harold took the chance to catch up on the local gossip, and the current state of the gangs beyond Caddi. He might get better information from Mack because, being Caddi's bodyguard, he heard a lot of news that the ordinary gangsters and civvies didn't.

At first the gossip wasn't much. A few boundaries had shifted a little bit, but nothing to interest Harold until Mack chuckled. "There'll be work for you, 'Arry, gun work. Caddi just took two streets off the Murphies an' the guns we captured are a real mess. The Murphies ain't asked for a meetin', so I reckon there'll be more."

"A real war, Mack? Is Caddi feeling that confident?"

"'E took a good look at the gangs at the big fight, over at the Mart?" Mack paused and Harold nodded because he'd taken the same opportunity to assess the neighbours. "Caddi reckons the Ferdinands would be easier, but they ain't got much border with us. We could be caught in a pincer by the Murphies and Baggies." Harold nodded again because that made sense. "If the 'Ot Rods take over 'alf the Murphies patch, Caddi reckons 'e'll make peace if they want. Then 'e can start on the Ferdinands. If 'e does a deal with the Trainspotters to let 'em snip off a bit of both gangs, and the Baggies get a bit of Ferdinand territory, 'e reckons they'll stand for it."

"Ambitious all the same." Worrying as well, because that would nearly double the size of Caddi's gang. "What about the Barbie Girls? I heard rumours about them catching someone shoplifting, but the occasional visitors are being bashful and teasing." Harold grimaced, he needed to know what had happened but didn't expect to like it. "Not like them to keep quiet, but I'm pleased if they've done something gruesome."

"If, 'Arry? Of course they 'ave. The Barbies 'ave taken pictures of what's carved into the prisoners, an' passed 'em to other gangs wiv Bluetooth. Not Caddi, they don't talk to us so I've only seen wot they sent to the GOFS." Mack shook his head, glancing to make sure the women weren't too close. "Some prat tried to raid fer women, an' the Barbies caught three alive. They chained 'em ter lamp posts in daylight an' on the roof with a big light on 'em at night. Every Barbie took turns to carve something on 'em or kick 'em a bit." Despite the violence he must have seen as Caddi's bodyguard, Mack looked uneasy, so the pictures must have been gross. "Then they rented 'em out to the Pinkies, the queers. The Barbies put 'em in one of them big windows, an' invited witnesses from other gangs."

"Cripes. Thank all and any gods I'm not on their dance card. There's some news I'd rather hear about without full visuals." Harold frowned. "How come Caddi doesn't?"

"There was some bad business between them an' the 'Ot Rods early on. Best kept well apart." Mack glanced towards the kitchen, but the women were still out of earshot. "If yer want ter see 'em, the bodies are shrink wrapped an' tied to lamp posts well away from Beth's. They reckon it's your idea."

"That was a message early on, before we had borders, and I killed mine straight away."

"Yeah, an' you don't need summat like that now. Everyone knows about you an' that rifle so they don't want ter start shootin' trouble." Mack turned to look towards the door. "'Ow long do yer reckon 'e'll be, Lada? I ain't frightened of the dark but I want yer over there before then. So Caddi don't get nervous. 'E really does want ter talk to yer."

"You walked again?"

"No. I came with Roller so 'e can stay as 'ostage for yer, but 'e'll want ter keep 'is motor. I didn't think you'd mind the walk but Lada ain't up ter it. Especially after the Patty love-kick." Mack glanced round but there weren't any Hot Rods here, so he couldn't commandeer their car. "I'll ask the two up there at the island ter pass a message if I can borrer a radio. I'll get my truck sent 'ere. It'll save yer the diesel."

"Don't bother. I'll go in my pickup so I can come home if Caddi starts acting up." Harold finished his beer and stood. "I'll go and sort out this and that. If you want me, ask the kitchen to call me on the phone."

"That still does my 'ead in, 'Arry. Caddi managed to get a field phone thing set up to the gate, but not a proper exchange an' all that like you lot." Mack started chuckling. "You should set up a proper system, phone boxes across the city like BT did. It'd make a fortune."

"Until I tried to empty the coin boxes." Harold joined in with Mack's laughter, but then remembered he'd got another possible passenger here. "Will Pete come with us or walk home?"

"With us."

That confirmed the coupons and games definitely belonged to Caddi. At least Pete hadn't officially joined the Hot Rods or he would've had a better weapon. As long as Caddi settled for what Pete had brought back, Harold thought the youth should be okay. "I'll go and get my toothbrush just in case." Both smiled because even if he stopped over, Harold wouldn't need it. There'd be a brand new one supplied as part of Caddi's showing off.

Harold headed home to put on some clean and more or less new clothes, part of the gang boss pose. Soldier Boy had to wear good gear to get respect. He stopped at the serving hatch on the way out. "Patty, I'll be going to sort out some bother with Caddi, and might not be back tonight. Let everyone know please?"

"Not a problem, we'll sharpen the welcome mat for midnight visitors." Patty mimed aiming her crossbow and smirked. "I'll ask Liz for some special artwork." Harold laughed at the joke about the blacksmith's viciously ornate crossbow heads.

*   *   *

Once he got home, Harold gave Sharyn the remaining Coven coupons and let her know what he'd be doing. She promised to arrange a Casper-story for Daisy and Wills at bedtime, because it was already past midday so Harold probably wouldn't get back tonight. When Harold came in through the back door of the canteen Mack already stood by the front door, waiting. Harold could hear Lada complaining, loudly but carefully avoiding obscenities.

Casper had brought his rucksack up from the gate, and now he'd joined Matthew in keeping an eye on Lada. Considering the size of Casper and his outsized machete, Matthew's crossbow might be overkill. Lada shut up immediately when he saw Mack and Harold, warily watching them both. Mack grinned, looking around. "Told yer to watch yer mouth. It's the rules 'ere. Now shut it or Soldier Boy or one of 'is lot will insist on the canin' as well. I 'ope yer can walk cos I'm not carryin' yer, and I don't fancy yer chances if I leave yer 'ere."

That steadied the little git up, because there were several other scowling people nearby and two were holding crossbows. One wrong word and he'd get the caning at least. Lada grimaced, bent over, and emptied his stomach onto the lawn. Matthew scowled at him. "That's a shame because all the other gardens are veg plots. They could have done with the fertiliser."

Harold looked back when the door behind him opened again. Patty came out with a bucket in her hand, offering it to the retching youth. "Probably concussion. Still, duck your head in here, rinse your mouth and take a nice brisk walk. That should sort it out."

Everyone including Mack stared, surprised, because Patty hated all gangsters and she'd spat on Lada and kicked him not too long ago. Patty held out the bucket, smirking as Lada gripped the sides and bent forward. Her other hand came down on his head, forcing it right into the bucket for long moments before Lada came up spitting and spluttering and pawing at his eyes. She sneered at him. "I was going to chuck it on the veg garden, but I didn't want to waste clean water on a piece of crap." Patty tipped the rest over Lada's head before stalking off back into the house. Big Mack looked at Harold with a question in his eyes.

"It's the water from washing the pots, so a sort of grease and soap soup." Harold inspected the dripping gangster. "Lada should consider himself lucky. If Patty had been carrying her crossbow or machete when he opened his mouth, you'd have been carrying a corpse home."

"I know. Patty oughta join the Barbies, they'd luv 'er." Mack slapped Lada on the back then sniffed his hand. "Yer smell better, but don't walk too close. Yer boots are still full of piss, I reckon. Come on, let's get goin'. Caddi will want to 'ear this."

"My knife." Lada reached for his neck and looked round. "Knives?"

Casper held up a sheath on a cord, a six-inch-long, very slim sheath with a hilt nearly as long coming out of the top. "I found it down the back of sleepy's shirt when we checked him over. There might be something else in those boots but I'm not looking there, or inside his pants." Casper curled his lip. "I'm not that desperate." The watchers all knew about Casper being gay so the laughter grew.

Mack reached out, stopping Lada's abortive grab for the weapon. "No, yer lost yer stuff. Rules, remember? Some folk I know would've took yer clothes an' boots as well." Lada looked very wary, then flinched as the big man continued. "'Arry 'as kept yer bat an' Caddi won't be 'appy yer lost it. Now c'mon." Mack glanced at Harold and grinned. "Any chance of a drink so 'e don't keel over on the way 'ome? Without soap?"

"There's a barrel of rainwater by the gate, for the gardeners. Nobody's washed their hands in it yet, I think." As the trio left the canteen, Pete, looking worried now, followed them towards the gate. A subdued Lada stopped by the barrel to rinse and spit on the ground, carefully clear of anyone, then drink deeply. Mack collected his aluminium baseball bat and a machete before all four headed out through the gates. Lada wasn't moving very fast after being knocked out, though it might be his aching nuts that kept him hunched over as he walked.

Five Hot Rods emerged from the nearest ruins, nearly half a mile from the gates near the traffic island. When three drove down the approach road, Mack took them aside for a quick chat while Louie brought Harold's pickup round to the gate. The laughter that followed must have burned Lada's soul. One of them, Roller, went into Orchard Close as the hostage for Harold's visit to the Mansion. Meanwhile, Mack pointed to the rear of Harold's pickup truck. "Get in there Lada, where we don't 'ave ter smell yer." One of the Hot Rods helped Lada climb in because his hand had swollen up, either from Harold's stick or Patty's stamp. The youth sat shivering while Harold and Mack got into the front. Pete sat in the back of the crew cab with the two Hot Rod bodyguards.

* * *

Pete didn't want to talk on the journey, becoming more and more obviously nervous as they approached the Mansion. Mack didn't know or didn't want to discuss why Caddi wanted to see Harold, or what Pete had to do with it, which cut down on conversation. Harold took the opportunity to have a good look round as he drove.

The wasteland of rubble, ruins or abandoned houses and weeds continued for a mile and a half, half a mile past the Orchard Close borders. Three years after the last big riots, the sharp edges of paths and walls were blurring, and even houses that were still standing had weeds growing from inside their broken windows. The first break in the devastation was a small group of habitable houses surrounded by a low wall built of loose bricks. The inhabitants paid protection to the Hot Rods so they had a pair of guards outside the entrance, one with a crossbow and one with a small-calibre shotgun. Neither had hand guns, which caught Harold's attention.

The guards on housing usually had plenty of firearms, so Caddi must need all his for the war with the Murphies. Perhaps the takeover of the two streets wasn't as smooth as Mack had said, or maybe it wasn't completed? Either way, the strife shouldn't affect Harold this trip, because that border lay nearly four miles from Orchard Close.

Harold also took note of the increased use of nearby gardens for vegetables. Unlike Orchard Close, the other gangs hadn't planted up the cleared areas around their bases. They bought their food from the Marts, using the coupons they took from others as protection payments. Continual shortages at the Marts, and the gangs taking the best, meant the ordinary residents were taking matters into their own hands. When he mentioned the large garden to one side of the houses, Mack explained the new system. Some old parks and cleared areas had been planted up for the Hot Rods, tended by the nearby residents.

Thinking about that and Caddi's expansion kept Harold occupied until the Mansion came in view. Caddi had been improving his defences since the last time Harold visited. The approach to the only way in and out of the enclosed area now wound around concrete blocks, with two bricked pillboxes framing the steel faced gate. Only cars belonging to Caddi and his favoured few went through the gates.

Harold parked up outside, following Mack to a guardhouse. Mack confiscated weapons from Pete and Harold, putting Harold's into a locker. "'Ere yer go 'Arry, yer keep yer stick." Mack grinned. "I still don't see why yer keep that instead of a machete like yer entitled."

"Your boys have been spanked often enough for this to be a reminder."

Mack wore his weapons because after all, he was Caddi's bodyguard. The big man also kept Pete's machete and Lada's ex-knife. As they headed for Caddi's house, both Lada and Pete were clearly hoping for something to intervene. Lada looked even worse now, hunched over, limping, nursing his hand and still shivering. The youth hunched down even lower when a couple of gangsters looked out of a door at him, laughed, and went back in. That sort of news spread faster than light these days.

* * *

A maid in a micro-mini and tight T-shirt, but without the usual cane marks on her legs, opened the door. She led them down the hall, past the study and opened a door. Mack chuckled, standing back to let Harold through. "Through 'ere 'Arry. Not the study this time, so Caddi thinks this might be pleasure, not business."

Harold looked around because business had always been conducted in the study, so he'd never seen the rest of the house. Caddi lounged in what would have been the lounge at one time, in the largest of several leather easy chairs. Along one wall a huge glass fronted cabinet had been crammed with expensive luxuries, including some lovely looking cut glass. Caddi had no doubt stolen the best. The luxuries were rows of bottles, top brands, and many were still sealed, as well as real capsule coffee and named teas in labelled tins. Valuable salvage still turned up in cellars or ruined houses, but less often. It wouldn't be long before the price of Caddi's luxuries finally went out of the reach of all but the very top of the new tree.

The three automatic firearms chained to the wall were a definite boast, two Army rifles and an AK. Every gangster wanted an AK, because of the publicity about the Russian automatic rifles. Most other gang bosses would flaunt one if they could get one, even a broken one with no ammo. Not Caddi, he was smart enough to only use these weapons for a serious emergency, because the Army or RAF bombed or shelled anyone seen using either.

Bug, Charger, Chevy and Cooper, elite gang members, were already reclining in smaller armchairs. The new arrivals were all offered seats according to their status. As a gang boss, Harold had one of the largest armchairs opposite Caddi. Mack took one set back from the rest, where the bodyguard could watch them all.

Pete and Lada were seated very conspicuously on dining-type chairs against the wall, obviously the centre of attention. A call to bring some cloth for Lada to sit on, so the furnishings weren't messed up, caused a short delay. While the rest waited, another young woman, in another very short skirt and tight tee, slipped in and served tea and coffee. She did so with eyes carefully averted, leaving as soon as possible.

Harold avoided looking at the woman, part of a game between himself and Caddi. If Harold acknowledged her, Caddi would arrange for her to be in his bed naked, or offer herself, or anything else the warlord thought might embarrass them both. The pressure had increased over time in direct proportion to their clothing shrinking. Harold had a private mental bet that eventually the server would be kneeling and wearing just knickers and manacles, or maybe just the nervous smile.

"Harry, Harry, what have you been up to?" Caddi smiled, a completely insincere friendly smile. "Abusing one of my valued associates, and trying to poach my staff? Naughty, naughty Harry." Caddi knew Harold preferred being called Harold, which was why all his gang now used Harry. Hope flickered briefly on Lada's face, so the newcomer didn't know Caddi very well. Pete knew Caddi well enough to sit very still. "Stealing personal property, poaching staff and interfering in my transactions. Very bad." His voice gave the game away, the last complaint seemed to be what had got Caddi's back up.

Harold leaned back into the armchair, with his stick across his knees and a cup of coffee in his hand. "Why on earth would I interfere in your business, Caddi? You to yours, me to mine, because that's the treaty. As for poaching your staff, do you mean Pete?" Harold glanced at the youth in question. "It was lucky I was there or the Ferdinands would have your coupons. You should take better care of your grocery boys if you want them to come back in one piece."

"What about my valued associate and his personal property?" The tone of voice actually said 'this stupid dickhead,' and wasn't much concerned about the answer. Caddi always picked on the easiest or least important item first.

Harold obliged. "He broke the rules. I told him to stop and he braced me. He went for a hidden knife so I took it off the prat. That makes it mine. Mine twice because he shouldn't have brought a second one in." A round of sniggering followed from the elite. Everyone visiting Orchard Close tried to keep hold of an extra knife. "I kept the bat, of course, as a fine. I knew he'd pay you for it."

Caddi looked at Big Mack, who nodded and answered. "Yup. I warned Lada before we went in, an' agen when 'e swore an' started insultin' women. Then 'e threatened 'Arry an' pulled this." Mack showed everyone the knife. "'Arry poked 'im, clouted 'im, then we went an' 'ad some stew an' a beer 'til 'e woke up." Caddi gestured and Mack handed the knife over. "Good stew, an' their beer is the best round 'ere."

The rest of the sidekicks were hooting now. It sounded funnier somehow when told by Mack, and even Pete smiled a little. Caddi looked over at Lada, who didn't see the funny side at all. "Well now, and what did you call the ladies? How did you manage to annoy such an even-tempered man as our Harry?" Caddi's smile wasn't fooling Lada now.

"I said it were nice to see some, er, women cos I thought we could have some fun." Lada paused, swallowed hard and continued. "Then I said Big Mack could have seconds." Caddi raised an eyebrow at Mack.

"More or less. 'E were warned after the blow job and whores thing, an' 'e offered me seconds once 'e sorted 'Arry out. 'E went for 'Arry first."

"What about the disgusting state he's in?" Lada would be either broken or killing mad after this, because Caddi had decided to have fun.

"Heh." Mack sniggered. "One of the women 'e were talkin' to were Patty, which makes 'im lucky cos she didn't 'ave 'er crossbow. She gave 'im a kick in the nuts instead of a blow job and stomped on 'is 'and. 'E pissed 'imself. Elizabeth kicked 'is nuts as well. We didn't like the smell when 'e woke up so Patty stuffed 'is 'ead in 'er dirty dish-washin' water, then tipped it over 'im." The others had another roll about at Lada's expense, while he looked down at his hand in sudden comprehension and put the other hand protectively over his groin. "'E still stinks of piss."

"We all noticed that." Caddi put the knife down on the coffee table, with the hilt towards Harold. "This is a personal weapon, so he lost it and it's yours of course, Harry." The gang boss turned to Lada. "You are a jumped-up stupid little shit, who is lucky that Harry is particular about who he kills. I am not, so be warned. Now you owe me for one aluminium baseball bat"—Caddi paused one careful beat—"barely used, one careless owner." The laughter chorus dutifully struck up. "You lost it, so you pay. Unless you can make Harry give it back?"

Lada didn't answer or lift his gaze from the floor, even when Caddi gave him plenty of time. The gang boss curled his lip into a sneer, his smile long gone as his voice rose in volume. "On top of that, I now have to give you new clothes, and return the weapons you brought in with when you arrived. Unless I want you out there bare-assed naked, for the first ten-year-old with any fucking balls to stomp flat?" Specks of spittle flew as Caddi shouted the rest. "So perhaps you might want to try very hard to do something with them. Just to convince me that it's worth risking you losing the fucking lot again!"

A pale-faced Lada nodded, dumbstruck. Caddi jerked his head towards one of the laughter chorus, all glowering now. "Sort it, find him a shit job somewhere out of my sight. Get someone to spray that chair before the stink soaks in." A scowling Chevy followed Lada out, smacking him on the back of the head for no real reason. Caddi had just put on an act of course, or mostly. Lada had been sent to try something in Orchard Close. Having failed, the youth would pay in full, because the warlord would be genuinely angry about losing the bat.

*　*　*

Caddi turned to Pete as the door closed but didn't bother with the fake smile. "What are you doing running off to another gang with my shit?" He gestured to one of the seated men. "Bug, bring her in." Bugatti left, quickly.

"I didn't, honest. I was on my way here. I've got some games and the rest of your coupons, and a machete to replace the bat. I had to go that way cos I didn't have an escort." A sheen of sweat broke out on Pete's forehead.

Caddi's raised eyebrow went to Mack first, who indicated the machete before passing it across. The eyebrow moved on to Harold. Cripes, Harold thought, it's twenty questions without the questions. "I went shopping, for food." Harold's grimaced at the memory. "Nobody mentioned the TX-Box or new games. It was a battlefield out there."

"You would know, Soldier Boy." Caddi paused, waiting again, but the door opened and Bugatti came back in with a young woman. Both Harold and Pete spoke at the same time.

"Tessa!"

"Sis!"

Bug seated the young woman on a naughty chair, one of the dining types, but away from her younger brother. Pete looked at her with a mixture of horror and guilt. When Tessa raised her head at the voices, shock and a sliver of hope replaced the despair on her face.

"No introductions needed then. You should have a little background, Harry." Caddi nodded towards Pete. "This young man has been sampling our merchandise. Some of it was quite expensive." He turned his eyes to Tessa. "As I explained to you, your brother has tastes well above his means." Caddi leaned back, opening his arms. "We reached an accommodation where Pete agreed to carry out some tasks for me, and Tessa agreed to stand surety until he'd paid off the debt."

Pete understood Harold's disgusted look. "Not drugs, I don't take drugs. Honest! Tell him, Mr. Cadillac, please."

Harold raised an eyebrow himself at the 'Mr. Cadillac' and Caddi smiled slightly as he saw it. "True, our foolish young man has taken quite a fancy to a young lady, and has bought her some gifts. He has also improved his wardrobe, after Fantasia mentioned how drab his current garb seemed to be."

Harold sighed because conned by a pretty smile had to be one of the oldest scams in history. "She works for you?" Caddi nodded, with a smirk. Turning to Pete, Harold let his disgust show. "So you were stupid enough to get yourself in the shit. Why did you drag Tessa in?"

Pete hesitated, but Tessa answered for him. "He was in trouble, serious trouble, Harry, so I got him out of it. This gentleman insisted on payment, so I agreed to cover the amount until it was cleared. Pete promised to work it off." She didn't sound happy about the last bit.

"That all seems reasonable, so why is Tessa here now? Since Pete is working the debt off." Harold couldn't work it out yet, but from the smirk on Caddi's face, this would be nasty.

"But he isn't. Or wasn't. In fact he has run up another substantial amount. The unpaid interest on your debt"—Caddi glanced at Tessa—"has grown large enough that I must take action. I have a reputation to uphold." The last bit had no humour or mercy in it.

Pete squirmed at the looks from both Harold and his sister. "I had a good run at cards, at poker. I nearly had enough to clear it all but the run broke and I lost the lot. I just borrowed enough to get it started again. Then Fantasia needed coupons as well, you have no idea how bad it is for her. She needs them to buy herself out, so we can look after her parents because...."

The glares from Harold and Tessa moved until they met. They rolled their eyes before returning to Pete. "Oh, God, I've buggered it all up." He raised his face, "Fantasia isn't ever leaving, is she?" Caddi shook his head gently a couple of times.

"Not at any price you could afford, and now, young fella, your debts are due. The original one, the interest, the new debts and the interest on them. You were to pay a substantial part back today, but have failed to do so." Caddi indicated the machete. "A good weapon, but it doesn't even cover the interest on the second debt."

Hope flared in Pete's eyes. "But I got them, the games." The youth stopped and his eyes dropped. "Well, some of them." He looked up again. "The best ones!"

"Some of them, and a machete? I do believe we need another take on this. Harry?"

Harold sighed in resignation. What a complete screw up, and the stupid little prick walked right into it. Harold suddenly realised someone was missing. "Where's little Ed?" He meant Edward, Tessa's five-year-old son.

"He's safe. Caddi gave the neighbours the food out of my house, and asked them to look after him for a week. He's told them to spread the word that if anyone touches my house he'll"—her eyes dropped—"cut their dicks off." Tessa looked straight at Harold. "Will you check up on him? Please, as a favour?"

"'Course I will. Do you want me to take him home? To Orchard Close?" Harold frowned, because he still wasn't sure what Caddi had in mind. "How long are you supposed to be here anyway?"

Before she could answer, Caddi butted in. "Not yet, Harry. That depends on your answers and his, so can we get on with it?" No teasing from Caddi now, just business.

"Right, so, food shopping. I got in after the fight moved inside. Half the gangs in town were there! Then I find that some asshole moved all the aisles, and the horde are headed back. I got round or through, and found where they'd put the food, but didn't have chance to fill up my rucksack. We were too late and the fight rolled back over me. I got a bit of space." That earned both Caddi's eyebrows and a little smile. "But then someone yells my name. Harold."

Harold looked at Caddi so the gang boss registered the dig about proper names, even if Pete had actually called out Harry. He received another smile, no more sincere than the first. "It was Pete, with somebody chopping his wooden bat into toothpicks with that machete. The asshole wanted the games spread all over the floor. There were some Ferdinands nearby, busy relieving another gang of a couple of TX-boxes so they hadn't noticed. I stopped the asshole before the bat was completely gone."

That brought another insincere smile. Caddi would no doubt get the gory details from Pete. "I gave Pete the machete to replace the bat." Pete got the smile this time. "The rest of the Ferdinands were coming over by then, so Pete hid three games and I gave them the rest."

"You what?" A startled Bug stared from one to the other. "How many bloody games did you give away?"

"Enough to save any strife, since you weren't there to help and I don't play at fighting." Harold lifted his lip in a snarl. He'd had enough from Caddi and wasn't going to take it from anyone else. Given his supposed status, Harold was entitled to smack Bugatti's teeth in, and just now Harold felt the need to do so. The flare of alarm in Bugatti's eyes showed that he'd just realised the same.

"Calm down, Harry." Caddi looked Bug up and down. "You would have told them to stuff it and then?" He waited for the other's eyes to drop before finishing. "And then you would have died. Whereas Harry has brought Pete, my coupons, some games and a dinky new machete, as well as getting his groceries home." Caddi let out a theatrical sigh. "Which is why I keep pointing out that no amount of balls will work without some brain. How many times must Harry provide an example for you? At least this one is free, for you anyway, and you've still got your clothes." Caddi sniggered as he reminded Bug about being sent home in his underwear. Bug flushed as the warlord turned back to Harold. "Are you sure I can't give you a job, Harry?" Harold just looked back at him, ignoring the old request.

Caddi switched to Pete. "And you followed him home because? He has good stew and beer?" That came with a glance at Mack.

"No, because by the time we got out everyone had gone! They all pissed off and left me. I had to go round by the bypass, which comes off at Harold's place, and then we met Big Mack."

"You went through the Army checkpoint with that machete? Pull his, it's got bell's on." Caddi indicated Bug.

"Seriously, Harold sorted it."

"Did he?" Caddi had a speculative look now. He'd get it out of Pete but sod it, Harold shrugged. He'd let Caddi work for the information.

"'E did come in with 'Arry, and 'e 'ad the machete, and 'Arry 'ad 'is rucksack. Then Lada started so..." Mack stopped at a gesture.

"Now this is where you make me happy, Pete. Show me my coupons and my games."

Pete dug into his pockets, pushing the coupons and games onto the table. "All three are Urban Riot, and you only paid for two. I paid for one, against the debt."

Caddi smiled, properly at last. "Three. Well done, boy, well done. Shame about the rest. Right, your cut of the mark-up will cover your interest to date, and since you paid for one, a bit off the debt, and the machete pays off some more." Pete and Tessa started to relax.

Harold had actually listened to the words. "What about Tessa?"

"Oh, he has to pay the unsecured debt before anything comes off the secured one. It's how finance works. After all, secured means that if he doesn't pay up on time?" Caddi glanced at a calendar on the wall. A calendar which someone must have drawn for the flash bastard, because there weren't any sold or any printers now. "That's in three days, from nine a.m. this morning. If he doesn't clear the interest and the original debt, I will foreclose. Anything Pete earns in that time will go to clear the unsecured debt first, of course." Both Tessa and Pete had gone white, and Harold's face set.

"But how can I pay?" Tessa whispered, her face ashen. "I don't have anything, not even furniture because the house is rented from you. I can't pay." Tessa knew how she'd pay. Something like this had happened too many times to too many other young women in gang territories. She just hoped that it wouldn't happen this time.

"Of course you can, dear. You don't think I would accept security that I couldn't cash?" Pete looked horrified, finally realising what he'd done, while Caddi looked from one to the other with that little smile. "You don't see it? A good looking white woman in her mid-twenties. Not scarred, bruised or abused and not a drug addict or a whore. I'll get my money without any problem at all, and the interest, especially with the child to keep you obedient." Dead silence filled the room.

Caddi counted his coupons, while the other Hot Rods watched the expressions on Pete's and Tessa's faces now that the trap had been sprung. Tessa would probably be put to work here first, for just a select few, to make sure she was properly broken and trained. From their inspections, Bug, Cooper, and Chevy all liked that idea, a clean, obedient woman instead of the usual hopped-up or brutalised girl.

"How much?" Harold said the words before he'd made a conscious decision to speak up.

"For what?" Caddi frowned, he knew Harry didn't buy flesh, or play video games. Or everyone said not, however... Caddi's face cleared, because with luck this meant his information had been spot on. Soldier Boy's reaction had shown he really did know Tessa from before the Crash. Now it seemed he knew her well enough to try to save her. "The woman or the games?"

"Both." Harold's face set like granite. He could feel the urge to set into the lot but Mack sat behind his shoulder, and not by accident. That bloody guard, Samuel, would be looking through a loophole somewhere, aiming a shotgun at him as well. Caddi didn't take chances.

"On the open market these games are worth about ten times what they cost at the Mart, which would pay off the interest and a third of the debt." Caddi waved at the Urban Riot boxes. "But there won't be any left now."

"What about other games? Top ten, latest edition." Tessa stared at Harold, mystified, but at least the terror had ebbed a little. Harold dragged his eyes back to Caddi. The little bastard played with him, because everyone knew the shelves would be clear after the gangs finished. They wouldn't be re-stocked until the next update, too late, which was why the games were so valuable.

"Depends on the title but three would easily pay the debt, with the same for the interest. That's why I am closing the deal. The interest is now as much as the debt." Harold definitely had Caddi intrigued, wondering what Soldier Boy would offer to rescue the damsel.

"Just the debt. The interest is his because she only covered the debt." A little spark of hope had lit inside Harold. Three!

"No, no, it doesn't work like that Harry. How would I persuade the slippery little shit to pay?" But Caddi meant come on Harry, show me how desperate you are. He'd wanted to get to the smartarse since they first met, and this was pay dirt.

When he looked at Pete, the venom in Harold's eyes didn't need any faking. "He could secure it. There's a sale for young white ass, even male. After all, the Pinkies won't care about how stupid the head end is. They might prefer to use that end anyway. He's not a druggie, no scars or bruises, bloody hell he's probably a virgin. Pete won't run if he doesn't pay, because I will find him and bring him back. Do you believe me, Pete?" The youth's white face gulped, swallowed, and nodded with a quick jerk.

"My, my, he's more frightened of you than of me. That won't do. I will have to try harder." The tones were gentle, but they dragged Pete's eyes round and he gulped again. Caddi turned back to Harold. "Intriguing proposition. The thing is, that would work, and I might go for it, but you can't get them. There is no way to purchase three top ten games in two days. Or rather there is, but you'll pay street price, at least six or seven times the Mart price. If you've got that amount of coupons, just hand them over instead, and we'll settle up now." Caddi knew that Harold never had many spare coupons, and since Harold was the gang boss that meant

Orchard Close must be broke. Actually, Harold thought the Coven might have enough in the kitty, but those coupons were to feed everyone.

Harold reached out, offering his hand. "Three top ten games, mint condition, unopened, latest release, within forty-eight hours of now. Those will pay the original debt, and Pete's lily-white ass will be surety for the interest and his other debt. You will use him as cheap labour to pay it off. You will give him enough shit jobs, and enough time, so that he can pay it off if he tries really, really hard. Deal?" The hand hung there while Caddi deliberated.

Harold could see Caddi assessing, deciding that Harold couldn't do it and must be playing for time. Soldier Boy might be able to steal them, but then Caddi would know where from because of the uproar and he'd have Harold's nuts in a vice. Harold watched as Caddi decided to let the bait float, sucking him in to find out what else Soldier Boy would offer when he couldn't raise the price. Caddi had asked Harold to shoot a man more than once, but even for that the bastard wouldn't let Tessa go. He'd just cancel some interest.

"Deal." Caddi took the hand. Harold clamped down on his expression, not letting his elation show. The warlord smirked, putting on just a little bit of pressure. "Bug, put her back in her room, same rules. Nobody touches her, nobody gives her shit until the three days are up."

Harold stood up but he was looking at Tessa, not Caddi. "Just a minute." He put his hand inside his jacket, pulling at the stitches on the lining where they'd been loosened. Harold's hand went inside and brought out the boxes, scattering them on the table. "Three top ten games, latest edition, unopened, mint condition." Now Harold just hoped Caddi kept the deal. He might because most deals between gangs relied on the boss's word being good.

Just for a moment Harold saw a flash of surprise, then pure rage, cross Caddi's face. Both were quickly smothered by a tight-lipped smile, as Caddi snatched the games up and fanned them out. The graphics meant he didn't have to read the titles. "See Bug, balls and brains. Don't you cross our Harry, he'll eat you up. Good enough, Harry. You've got 'Iron Wheels VII – Balls of Steel,' 'Gorefest IV – Fangs for Nothing,' and 'Arachnoid III – Bite This!' You sneaky mother! Heh, you won't need coupons now, just bought yourself a woman, Soldier Boy. Thought you didn't believe in that, selling women and such? Finally got fed up of using your hand, or fell out with that queer, Casper?" The jovial patter fell from Caddi's lips, but Harold could see the rage still flaring behind the gang boss's eyes. He knew Caddi would push hard, looking for a pretext, a way to force Harold to break a rule before leaving. Something that allowed Caddi to kill him without breaking the treaty, or starting a sniper war with Emmy, Roy and Alfie.

Caddi would make a handsome profit on the games, while Pete would work his lily-white to the bone on the shittiest jobs Caddi could find to pay his debt. But the warlord had set his heart on more. Harold had almost seen the scenario flitting across his avaricious features. Harold had never let the bastard know he and Tessa were friends because Caddi would have used Tessa as a control, and ended up having Soldier Boy over a barrel. Either that or Caddi would have taken great pleasure in having Tessa serve the tea and coffee, in a G-string or something similar to wind Harold up. Eventually he'd have tired of the game, then either Harold would have done as he was told or Tessa would be rented out.

What Harold didn't realise was how much time and trouble Caddi had gone to, setting this up. The gang boss had known for months, trapping Pete and then Tessa just so he could get to Soldier Boy. Just for a moment it had worked even better than expected. He'd felt his grip tighten on the slippery shit, and now he'd wriggled free! For long moments, the gang boss hovered on the edge of breaking a deal, but word would get out.

Caddi finally bottled his anger, stood, and managed a real smile. "I suppose you want her stuff moved into your room tonight, or, well, she's only got a single bed but you could squeeze in there instead?"

Harold would rather leave, sharpish, but after this he daren't drive home in the dark. Caddi would arrange an ambush, because at night he could blame some roaming gang of scroats. "I would appreciate it if you would let her stay there tonight, but I'll sleep elsewhere. I'll take her home tomorrow." Harold glanced at Tessa but her eyes were down. The young woman had a faint blush on her cheeks.

She walked past with a quiet "Thank you Harold," following Bug out of the room.

Caddi bent over a safe in the corner, hiding the dials as he retrieved the loan agreements. It only took a few moments to transfer Tessa's remaining debt to Pete's, and burn Tessa's records. While Caddi stowed Pete's agreement, the youth raised his haunted gaze to Harold. "You just sold me."

"No. You sold your sister and then we bought her back. If you work very hard for Mr. Cadillac, you can pay your half and keep your body free and undamaged. It will be shitty work, but I'm sure you will try very hard to save your own ass. Much harder than you did to save your sister's." Pete dropped his eyes, because he had no real answer to that.

As Caddi straightened, Harold saw a sudden smile of anticipation. That had to mean payback started now. "Mack, find Pete something disgusting and low paid to start on will you?" Caddi smirked, which worried Harold more than a scowl would. "Send in Mercedes to keep Harry company. Ask herself to dress for a special guest who is stopping overnight. Let her know who, so she makes an effort. Oh, and tell chef that Harry and Mercedes will be joining us for dinner." Harold had been told that Mercedes killed people for Caddi, so this might be payback time.

"Sure thing, boss." Mack left with a subdued Pete.

Caddi patted his hands gently together. "Well played, Harry. I never saw it coming."

Harold sat back in his chair, feigning relaxation. "I didn't see this coming either. I just took the chance to grab a few games even if we don't play them. We could have traded them one at a time, for things we need in Orchard Close. I didn't know what they were worth, so I brought them to find out and maybe sell one. Still, you'll make a profit so it worked out well enough for you."

"Will your bird be pissed off that you gave them away for a woman? Bet there's one or two would have volunteered without you paying." Caddi might be having a dig or actually trying to find out who Harold's woman was. Harold disliked visiting for business, let alone socially, because of this sort of prying and tweaking.

"I bought them with my own coupons because I'd saved a few. Nobody knew." Harold coloured slightly. "That's not why I paid the debt." None of them would believe him. In the Hot Rods' world, Soldier Boy, as the gang boss, took any coupons he wanted from Orchard Close and would only buy a woman for sex.

Maybe Caddi realised the truth. "I know, Harry. You, my boy, are a dying breed, which might be best for the likes of me. If things get tight, I can find a couple of one-off jobs for a man with your training?" Harold didn't reply, but Caddi had cast out the bait again. The Hot Rods boss still hoped he'd get some use out of Soldier Boy, as a sniper. All the local gangs thought he could shoot the nuts off a gnat, while it was still flying.

E-Type, another Hot Rods lieutenant with a car name, arrived with a report about some damaged machetes and the conversation shifted to more general matters. Harold's coffee had a drop of brandy in it, and the rest were hitting the beer, when Mack stuck his head round the door. "Mercedes is here, boss."

Caddi waved 'come in' at Mack but he grinned at Harold. Harold got an itch that he couldn't quite locate. He turned to the door and forgot the itch, or maybe found her. Hellfire, but the girl scrubbed up well. Mercedes smiled at him. "Well hello there, Harry." Her voice gently stroked Harold's hindbrain, low enough to be sexy, high enough to be definitely female.

Chapter 3:

Cadillac's New Mercedes

Looking at her now, Harold could see how Mercedes got close to her victims. Mercedes dressed to kill, a thought best kept firmly in mind. No sign remained of the gaunt young woman Harold had seen last year, with her cuts and bruising still healing and her hair hacked short. She'd only just joined the Hot Rods, a young woman still bearing the marks of surviving out there with the animals for gods knew how long. Mercedes had already earned a reputation as the only Hot Rods woman who carried weapons, but nobody had realised how dangerous she could really be.

Slim but not scrawny, more pop pin-up than catwalk, Mercedes stood about five inches below Harold's six-foot. The heels on her boots brought them almost eye-to-eye, boots that caught his eyes when Harold stood up to say hello. No woman wore long, impractically high-heeled boots these days. Once caught, Harold's eyes stayed. The young woman's legs were probably only the standard length for her height, but her short black dress had a slit just far enough up her thigh to tease.

The combination meant her legs appeared to go on forever. Harold didn't usually check out women these days, especially at the Mansion. Now his eyes followed the boots upward, then the stockings and that hint of stocking top, without any conscious thought. His eyes kept going because the rest of the new Mercedes didn't disappoint. Unlike many gang women Mercedes wasn't busty, but she had enough of a figure to fill out her little black dress in all the right places.

Once Harold's eyes finally reached her face, the rest became almost irrelevant. Caddi treated Mercedes much better than wherever she'd been before. There were no bruises or dark rings of fatigue around her eyes; her cheeks were smooth and her skin clear. Mercedes hadn't used much make-up, just a bit of lippy to set off her wide, full lips. Looking at her face she could be anywhere from thirteen to thirty, although her body said more like sixteen to early twenties. Her mouth smiled, and said whatever age you fancy right now. Short, straight, jet-black hair, now stylishly cut and shining with health, framed her face and finished the picture. Almost.

All in all, Mercedes made a very appealing package, but the sort of men she met these days didn't look at a girl's eyes. That could be a fatal mistake with this girl. Her eyes were a deep brown and should have finished the picture, but they were dead. Harold could see no animation behind them, giving the lie to her smile, her voice, and the gentle sway of her hips as Mercedes walked over and tapped Harold on the chest.

She tipped her head the fraction necessary to look at his eyes. "Someone told me you were sleeping alone tonight, Harry." Mercedes smiled wider. "Big stud like yourself, that's just not right. Lucky you, I'm here now." She glanced across at the rest, all grinning at Harold. "Sorry boys."

Harold would have refused if offered an unwilling girl, one of the usual games Caddi played, but the warlord had flipped the usual setup. Mercedes periodically offered a visiting gang boss or lieutenant the chance to sleep in her bed. If they accepted, she had one proviso, any attempt to touch her in the night meant the man losing pieces of his anatomy. So far she had killed at least four men in the bed, while others had accepted the loss of status and refused. But some had accepted, stayed awake and very still, and survived.

Harold had his reputation as a fearless SAS bastard to keep up, so he couldn't back down. Sometimes only that reputation stopped the nutters from washing over Orchard Close and picking it clean. Smiling and accepting turned out to be easy, because Mercedes had developed into one hell of a package up close like this. "Cripes, Mercedes. If I'd known you were waiting, I'd have been here weeks ago. You only had to send word."

Mercedes almost purred. "I heard you didn't want me to visit. Now you say such nice things, Harry. Do you do nice things?"

Harold had once sent a message, after a couple of Hot Rods mentioned Mercedes collecting ears from rival gangs. If Caddi's assassin came within half a mile, he'd promised to shoot her. Looking like this he might not have recognised Mercedes, and anyway, this wasn't within half a mile of Orchard Close. "You only have to ask. You might be surprised." Too true, she had to ask. Harold didn't touch women without permission anyway, but Mercedes' eyes worried him. He'd seen eyes like that on squaddies who had survived something truly bloody nasty, by doing something truly bloody nasty to the other bloke or blokes. People with eyes like that were never quite right afterwards. Those who didn't break often had sudden attacks of rage, or nightmares, or both.

"Smooth talker, but not much of a welcome to go with it. You could at least put your hands on my waist, for starters. Don't you like me Harry?" Mercedes slid her hands up both sides of Harold's neck, clasping them behind his head and pulling her elbows in a little. The movement opened the scooped top of her dress, but Harold manfully resisted looking down. He wondered if he could have decided the daily betting on whether Mercedes had put on a bra or not. Mercedes noted his restraint and rewarded Harold with a small smile, one that still didn't reach her eyes.

Harold carefully slid his hands round her waist, resting them where it began to flare out towards her hips. "I don't know you well enough to decide, Mercedes." That won him another small smile.

"Tonight might help." Mercedes moved a little closer, but Harold carefully kept his hands from slipping down onto her ass. With a shock Harold realised he'd actually considered letting them, but not enough to bleed for. He didn't know the exact rules yet. Mercedes had a list of penalties for invading her personal space without permission; all included blood. Caddi, watching closely, looked like a cat regarding a particularly plump canary.

Harold had to get his head back into the game. "Since we are getting to know each other, why are you called Mercedes?" When Harold had asked Mack, the big bodyguard wouldn't or couldn't say. He'd told Harold to ask if he wanted to know. From the chuckles, this lot knew already.

"We are all in the Hot Rods so it had to be a car name. A Mercedes is the sweetest, smoothest, most sinfully luxurious ride you will ever have, and the wildest, if you really turn her loose." She paused, "Providing you are willing to pay the price." The whole room burst into laughter, and Harold joined in. The delivery had been perfect. Mercedes licked her lips as the hilarity died away. "Well Harry, are you willing to pay the price to ride a Mercedes?"

"I wish." Harold grinned, then softly sang the classic Janis Joplin line, "Oh Lord, won't you buy me a Mercedes Benz." This time Harold got the laugh, and he thought possibly the first genuine smile from the young woman.

Caddi chipped in, stirring the pot a little. "He might have made a bid, but Harry's just bought a woman. A very expensive one."

Mercedes wasn't smiling now when she looked at Harold. "Really?"

Not so much purr as snarl in her voice now.

"Paid off her debt, not bought her. There's a difference." For a moment Harold thought he saw a flicker in those dead eyes. He wondered if something human still hung on in there.

"Yeah, right," a voice muttered, but neither of them were paying attention.

"Such a generous act deserves a little reward, I think." Mercedes had her purr back. "Ask me to ask you to grab my ass, Harry."

"Harold."

Her eyebrows rose a little. "It matters? Hmm. Harry, or Harold? No." That little smile reappeared. "I think I know what would sound better. How about 'Arold?" Mercedes said the last word with a pseudo-French/Swiss accent.

"If it's you saying it." Harold realised he'd started flirting with her, which, with Mercedes, could be lethal.

"Well, 'Arold, are you going to ask me to ask you?"

Harold looked right into those dead brown eyes and smiled. "Mercedes, would you please ask me to grab your ass?" He paused briefly. "Or at least stroke it gently."

"No." The room erupted in laughter, while Harold relaxed because he'd passed the first test. Mercedes didn't laugh, she leant a little closer. "But you can put your hand on my dress, 'Arold. Right on top of where my ass is." The general hilarity stopped dead.

"Bloody hell, first base," someone exclaimed.

"Might be second, depends what's under the dress." The laughter started again but neither Harold nor Mercedes joined in. Harold glanced at Caddi, who had a decidedly speculative look and wasn't laughing either. Moments later Harold thought his hand, sliding gently down, could settle today's betting on whether Mercedes was commando.

Mercedes sniggered and wriggled her hips, just a tiny bit. "A little bit firmer, 'Arold, make me feel as if you're enjoying it." Harold decided that he'd already forfeited his hand if he'd been set up. He took a firm hold of the smooth curve, pulling her slightly towards him. After all, he enjoyed it.

"Mmm, better." Mercedes moved a little closer, gently pecking Harold on the cheek. "Now that feels as if you mean it."

Mean it? Harold needed a cold shower. That bit of movement left him stone cold certain there was nothing but girl under that dress. Now that dress had moved so close to him that a fag paper would have to wriggle through. Caddi saved Harold from finding a reply, slapping him on the shoulder. "Come on, Harry, sit down and let us all get an eyeful." As Harold started turning, Mercedes moved forward to slip a hand behind him, round his waist. She put her other hand behind herself, to slide Harold's hand across to the other cheek as they ended up side by side.

As she did, Mercedes murmured, "You don't want to lose that, do you?" Harold hoped she meant the grip on her ass, not his hand, which had just had a very interesting trip. So far, Mercedes seemed to be having fun so hopefully Harold wouldn't be donating body parts. Mercedes kept Harold's hand firmly in place as she perched on the arm of his chair, turning a little. She lifted her near leg far enough for the strip at the top of her stocking to show through the slit, stretching it over his legs. "I would sit on your lap, 'Arold, but you might lose control. You wouldn't want to eat dinner with stained jeans."

Harold had recovered a bit from those first few moments, and the effect on him. Now he went into the expected gang boss mode, his own less crude version. He smiled up at Mercedes. "Ah, but when you sit on my lap I'll take my jeans off first." Mercedes rewarded him with a slight raise of her eyebrows and a twitch of her lips, ignoring the exclamations from the spectators.

A couple of low whistles and "brave bastard" sounded from someone.

"When, 'Arold, not if?"

"I can hope. We're all entitled to hope a little." The flicker in her dead eyes definitely showed this time. Harold wondered what Mercedes hoped for.

"Maybe I should have gone to your place first. What would you have done if I'd turned up on your doorstep, 'Arold?" Mercedes licked her lips, slowly. The rest were waiting to see how Harold dodged this bullet. There wasn't much light entertainment these days.

"Run like hell." Everyone laughed, including Mercedes, easing Harold's mind a little. Harold hoped that dinner came soon because he would get this wrong sooner or later, and tonight would be bad enough without pissing her off first.

Bugatti managed a "too bloody true" through his laughter.

"Like a rabbit" came through the hilarity clearly enough to keep it going a bit.

When the laughter died down, Mercedes leaned forward, opening her neckline invitingly. Bug nearly put his neck out trying to get an eyeful.

"That would have been a mistake. Never run 'Arold. I'll just hunt you down, and when I've done, you know I'll have to kill you." Harold kept his eyes on hers. They'd started a private competition now, after he hadn't looked the first time, even if that gape beckoned temptingly. If Mercedes had gone commando, Harold would bet on braless as well.

"Is that to encourage me or put me off?" Harold grinned, a bit more on balance now. Unfortunately, the muscles in her ass kept flexing under his hand, just enough to continually threaten his concentration. That had to be deliberate.

"Why 'Arold, do you think I might be worth dying for? How sweet." Harold detected a bit of a challenge there.

"I must admit, just for a moment back there I seriously considered it." Harold paused a beat. "But then I realised I would want the memory. To keep me warm in the long cold days when I was too old to get it up any more." Harold won another genuine laugh from Mercedes as the others erupted.

Mercedes sat back up slowly, the muscles under Harold's hand sliding about pleasantly in his palm. She carefully smoothed non-existent wrinkles from the skirt where it stretched over her thigh. "Oh, it would keep you warm, 'Arold." She smiled, obviously pleased with the result of her teasing. Harold seemed to have passed her test because Mercedes started to gently tweak the others, though her muscles kept massaging Harold's hand now and then. Multi-tasking, Harold thought.

Another twenty minutes of gentle flirting and piss-taking all round followed, before a young woman in a white blouse and short, rather than micro, black skirt came into the room. She announced that dinner would be served in the dining room, asking them to take their seats. The smooth twist and turn that Mercedes executed to keep Harold's hand in place on her ass felt delightful, messing up Harold's concentration—again. She slid her own hand into the back pocket of Harold's jeans before giving his ass a squeeze. Harold looked at her but didn't need to ask. "I'm fed up of waiting for you to ask me to ask you." Harold began to wonder when Mercedes would lose interest in this part of the game. Presumably when she went to bed.

Harold nearly missed a step thinking about how easily Mercedes could get out of her clothes with his hand still there. He dragged his mind back out of her pants, if she was wearing any. Bloody hell, Harold wasn't playing cards or negotiating anything important with Mercedes in the room. Maybe Mercedes was the reason Caddi had a reputation as a dealer?

He usually managed to act indifferent to women, or at least avoid showing any real interest. Now he had definitely flirted, and had just given her ass a squeeze to return hers. It wasn't love or even infatuation. Mercedes just tweaked every button Harold had, and probably had the same effect on every male in the place. Even knowing the game, that Harold had been set up, some of the looks from the elite definitely had some envy in them. Caddi kept looking at Harold's hand on her ass, torn between speculation and anticipation. Harold had never heard of anyone getting hands-on before, now he wondered if different or new meant good or fatal?

Before they sat Mercedes sighed and retrieved her hand, before sliding Harold's hand off her dress. She patted it gently before sitting down next to Harold for the meal. "You'd better have this back, 'Arold. If you get creative I might spill my soup, and then you'd have to wipe my dress clean."

For a moment, Harold had thought Mercedes intended sitting on it, but she'd suspended the game for now. "If you'd left your hand I might have spilled something in my lap, which might have been even more fun." He looked right into her dead eyes. "If we'd both been careless?"

That little flicker appeared briefly before Mercedes sniggered. "Ooh, naughty Harold. There'll be plenty of opportunities for spilling and mopping later—in bed." Harold did his best to return the smile. It wasn't easy because he'd suddenly remembered that four men died in that bed. At least one gang boss, Paddy, bled out, according to the Hot Rods. That happened just before the Hot Rods attacked the Murphies, which seemed more than just convenient for Caddi. Harold shelved tonight, turning to the meal with a genuine smile because E-Type had told him about the chef. If Caddi still had the same one, the food would be absolutely superb.

*   *   *

The permanent and currently favourite women of the lieutenants joined their men at the table. Caddi didn't have a companion. Chevy's, Bug's and Cooper's women were young, pretty and seemed very nervous. Bug's woman glared at Mercedes, usually when she made another attempt to get Harold to cop an eyeful down her dress and Bug tried to see. The older woman with Charger looked his age, mid-thirties, and dismissed the show with a tolerant smile. E-Type's woman looked down when she saw Harold at the table, blushing very slightly. Caddi had once forced her to ask Harold to spank her. Spanky, as the others called her, soon joined in with the laughing and joking and seemed relaxed with E-Type.

In some ways this could have been a dinner party, thrown by a successful businessman for his top performers. There would probably have been a Mercedes equivalent there, but not the occasional casual references to violence or the language. The names of the elite were another thing that jarred—Caddi, Bug, Chevy, Charger, E-Type, and Cooper. Harold wondered if they ever thought of themselves as anything else these days. Harold still twitched at Soldier Boy, when people used that instead of his name.

Since Caddi usually acted civilised with Harold, the conversation stayed pleasant and relatively intelligent. That was as much of a treat as the meal, because real conversation rarely happened outside of Harold's friends in Orchard Close. In here, in private, Caddi seemed to be acting as a benevolent despot, some sort of Lord of the Manor instead of a cold-hearted homicidal gang boss. Better yet, he'd cut back on the obscene language and the rest took their cue from the boss.

Harold did his best to keep up with the conversation while they ate, as did Mercedes. She occasionally gave him an opportunity to look down her cleavage, smiling when Harold declined while Bug or others tried to look. Luckily the food distracted Harold all by itself. The meal had four courses of the kind of food usually talked about with the reverence given to legends of impossible pleasures. Harold had always thought the fancy sauces were some sort of posh affectation, but these enhanced the fish, veggies, and the meat, a real pork joint again. Caddi always seemed to find luxuries nobody else had.

The situation became more surreal when Caddi suggested, at the end of the meal, that the ladies retire while the men had their brandy and cigars. Harold wondered what books the gang boss had been reading. Mercedes leaned over invitingly. "I'm not a lady, 'Arold. Or maybe I am, but since I have a proper gang name I'm entitled to stay. By rights I should have my own companion for these meals. Would you like to volunteer?"

"But volunteer for what, Mercedes? After all, I have responsibilities elsewhere." Despite his dislike of her dead eyes, Harold found them the safest place to look until Mercedes moved back.

Her voice held a definite challenge. "I can't tempt you? I must try harder."

"But I'm a rough tough soldier, we're trained to resist." Harold kept up the gentle banter, actually enjoying himself. He'd realised that he could flirt with Mercedes without it meaning anything at all. Even Caddi couldn't use this as a way to hurt anyone, because Mercedes would never come near Orchard Close, or would do so as one of the Hot Rods' elite with a bodyguard and attitude. While they tweaked each other a little, the other women left, and the quiet girl and her clone cleared the table. The pair actually brought real cigars and brandy to go with the coffee. One went to close the curtains but Caddi shook his head, which caused some of those present to smile for some reason.

Harold had encountered enough problems when breaking his tobacco addiction to avoid resurrecting it, even if the smell of cigars tempted him. Various people grew pot, but tobacco cost much, much more. Mercedes recaptured Harold's hand, making sure everyone saw her pull it over and place it on her thigh. "I need to keep track of this, 'Arold, or who knows where it might turn up?" With the women gone, the pretence dropped and there were a few suggestions. "Just remember, my skirt isn't very long. You wouldn't want to accidentally touch my leg."

The loudest of the comments was "not bloody much he wouldn't." Opinion seemed divided between Harold wanting to touch anyway, or preferring his hand undamaged.

Nobody asked Harold but he replied anyway, to Mercedes. "I promise I will always keep careful track of where my hand touches, especially on you, Mercedes. That's if I actually get to touch you." Harold accompanied that with a very small squeeze. Her thigh muscles said hello. He sat forward a little. "Do I have to ask you to ask me?" Mercedes raised her eyebrows just a little, then smiled. She slid her hand into the back pocket of his jeans and squeezed a bit. Harold didn't have the muscle control to reply.

There wasn't much point Mercedes reminding Harold about the length of her skirt. When she moved a little, his fingers were suddenly only a few inches from the sleek length of stockinged leg coming from under the hem. After her little shuffle an inch of flesh showed through the slit in the dress, above the stocking and just below Harold's thumb even if nobody else knew. Harold wondered if Mercedes had decided to wind him up and get him killed, maybe as her cheese and biscuit surrogate after the meal. That wouldn't take much with how near his fingers were to her hem and that slit, which helped Harold get a mental grip; Mercedes had got to him—again.

Mercedes might be off the script given how curious Caddi seemed to be, a truly scary thought. As the muscles in her thigh took up where their sisters on her ass had left off, Caddi finally brought the conversation round to trade between him and Orchard Close. Harold had begun to wonder why Caddi had got him over here, because the warlord hadn't known Tessa was an old friend. For a moment he wondered if the nasty bastard had known, but he had to abandon that line of thought to keep up with both Mercedes and Caddi. Harold had his own multi-tasking to deal with, keeping track of Mercedes having fun with his hand, her occasional attempts to show him her cleavage, and the serious business from Caddi.

At first the dealing seemed straightforward. Caddi had a box of hand-held radios, all faulty or damaged, and wanted them fixed. Unfortunately, the surrounding gangs had a strict rota for access to important repairs such as radios and guns, and it wasn't Caddi's turn. After Caddi offered new batteries in their plastic wrap and a couple of rechargeables, Harold met him halfway. He admitted Trev had some spare time right now, but stressed that Caddi's gear would wait if other work came in.

Caddi must have been lining the next bit up because he immediately pounced. "I know your gun repairer has some spare time, because he's got nothing better to do than fondle our women." The gang boss took a long significant look at where the Orchard Close gun repairer's hand rested on Mercedes' thigh. "Lucky, really, because I've found a few guns." The gang boss grinned because that meant he'd killed or captured Murphy fighters, so he'd probably taken more territory.

"Just what could be better than fondling? Mind you, I'm not fondling anyone, yet, just stroking clothes." Harold smiled, wondering if the squeeze on his ass classed as a warning or encouragement. He squeezed her thigh as a thank you anyway.

"We'd better go through there so you can look at the guns. If you ask Mercedes to sit in your lap, maybe you'll get to fondle?" Caddi looked at Mercedes and alarm bells rang in Harold's head.

"He hasn't asked yet." Mercedes turned to Harold. "Well?"

"Later, because Caddi will tell you I don't do that sort of thing in public." Too true he didn't and Caddi wired every visitor's bedroom for sound and vision. Harold didn't expect an invite to stroke anything under her clothes anyway, ever.

"Come on you two. I want to see just how she gets your hand from there to her ass without cutting it off." Cooper looked at Harold, then his hand, and chortled. "If you cut it off, Mercedes, you can keep it and get a fondle whenever you like."

Mercedes thought for a moment, then smiled and stood with Harold's hand still on her leg. He managed to avoid getting over her hem or onto that slit—just. "Maybe I like the uncertainty, wondering where it will wander next? Watch and learn, boys." She took Harold's hand on a trip up the front of her thigh and round, right across her ass to the opposite side, without losing contact.

Caddi laughed and pointed. "This is a lot more fun than I'd thought. So is Soldier Boy's face, look at him." Harold knew he had to look somewhere between startled, relieved and cautious. He changed it into gang boss smug. At least Caddi seemed to be happy or intrigued rather than annoyed.

"Oh, he's not even started having fun yet." Amid the laughter Mercedes escorted Harold back to his armchair in the lounge. She sat back on the arm of Harold's chair but further up, far enough up to keep her hand in Harold's back pocket and wave her cleavage under his nose. "Hmm, just where should your hand go now?" Bug and Chevy made suggestions but Mercedes hesitated. Harold kept quiet because he'd already had a hand on her ass and leg, and had no idea of the rules. Mercedes pulled his arm round further so his hand rested on her opposite hip and round onto her thigh. "There, where I can keep an eye on it." That also meant Harold's arm hugged her, gently. Caddi looked intrigued, and he wasn't pretending now.

Mack interrupted, bringing in a large cardboard box. "Here's the radios, Caddi."

Harold leant over to look at them. Trev would be busy with that mess. "You never said they were that bad. They'll take work, time and spares."

"I know, expensive. Get him to use one broken radio to fix others and make as many as possible work. He can get that apprentice of his to help." Caddi smirked but Harold didn't react to the Hot Rods finding out about Trev's apprentice, Elise. The nervous teenager didn't need to know Caddi now had her on his kidnap list. "I'll give you more batteries, still in the shrink wrap, and maybe three or four more rechargeables if the job's done fast enough."

"I hear you." Harold did, those were both increasingly rare items, and valuable. Caddi wanted these radios in a hurry. "I suppose you'll want the guns in a hurry as well? Enough to part with real ammo or propellant?" His attention wavered as the thigh under his hand played with his palm, more than before. Harold realised his hand had moved almost too far when he leaned forward so he sat back, sliding his hand to safety. Mercedes pouted so he slid it back down her thigh a bit and she smiled. Her dead eyes flickered and her thigh muscles said hi. Harold hoped she eased off, because a night of this level of teasing and he'd make a mistake.

Caddi had carried on with his answer, oblivious. "Maybe. I've got some original rounds for a two-two rifle and a thirty-eight pistol?" Thirty-eight wasn't much good but Harold had two-two rifles, as Caddi well knew. The weapons for repair came out and the real bargaining started. Not precise prices, just a general idea for each based on the condition and damage. The captured guns were a long way from their original condition, showing that the Murphies knew less than the Hot Rods about maintaining them. The elegant engraving under the grime on the over and under shotgun showed it had been an expensive weapon, someone's pride and joy. The Murphies had abused and neglected it until the weapon stopped working.

In the end, Harold took the .38 rounds in part payment. They were originals, not reloads, and Harold thought Rob could adapt one of the shotguns to fire them. Once he'd agreed, however, he wondered if Mercedes had affected his judgement. Her gentle but unrelenting onslaught varied between muscle massage, and putting her cleavage where he could look down inside her dress. Halfway through the negotiations, Mercedes put both her legs right over Harold's, the slit in her dress giving him a perfect view of one stocking top. She kept moving enough to play peekaboo with the inch of bare flesh above it, a little game nobody but Harold could see.

*   *   *

At least Harold could gather up his tattered concentration when the negotiations ended. Caddi switched to waxing lyrical about Harold being lucky to have decent specialists. Harold had heard it all before, including the lists of faulty work and ruined kit. Right now, growing food came top of the complaints. This time E-Type seemed to be seriously trying to work out why. "You've got loads of gardening experts. How the hell did you manage that?"

Harold opened his mouth to answer, but hesitated a moment as Mercedes leant forward, blowing gently in his ear when he turned his head to avoid the view down her dress. All the men laughed while Mercedes looked triumphant. He made it the second try. "I reckon they were trying to leave the city and we were nearest when the Army turned them back." Harold also thought most people with useful skills kept quiet, so their local gang didn't recruit them without pay or options.

"You've got all the experts, not just the gardeners. Can your bloke fix Barbie Radio?" Caddi scowled at his lieutenant but Cooper shrugged. "They give us a lot of shit but the music was better than the BBC."

"How come the Barbies can't fix it? I know they stopped transmitting just after New Year, but surely they've got an engineer with that setup." Harold hoped so or they'd be trying to kidnap Trev, the usual Barbie Girl method of recruiting men. "There's no way Trev is going near them, not voluntarily."

"Hell no, they'd keep him. One of the GOFS heard the radio guy went nuts and completely fucked the transmitter." Cooper scowled, genuinely annoyed. "The Barbies killed the poor fucker and that probably wasn't pretty."

Harold thought death might have come as a relief, then moved his head to avoid checking if Mercedes had a bra, again. He glanced up at her with a little smile when she blew in his ear again, squeezing her leg in reply. As Harold looked at Caddi, everyone looked back, waiting. "What?" Harold tried to work out what he'd missed but he'd lost track for a moment or two. Mercedes gave a small triumphant laugh while the Hot Rod lieutenants looked at her, then at Harold, with smiles or outright laughter. Harold grinned at them all and rolled his eyes. "You lot should try it. My brain keeps migrating into my pants."

"I wish."

"Lucky bastard."

"Her pants you mean."

"What pants?"

Caddi just laughed, happy that Mercedes seemed to be getting to Soldier Boy. "You haven't heard about the Army pulling out? Surely your mates would pass the word, or did you fall out with the Army?" Everyone assumed that as ex-Army, the squaddies kept Harold posted on the current news. The news turned out to be a rumour, allegedly a very strong one, and several gangs were speculating on who would replace the soldiers. The consensus seemed to be Mart guards, with Bug wondering if the government might hire local gangs. Caddi liked that idea. He reckoned he might be able to get a real soldier as part of the deal, one who could fix his weapons.

"Oh, you might get a soldier, but I doubt you'd get another Soldier

Boy." Mercedes licked her lips, slowly. "If you don't need him anymore, can I keep him?"

The laughter broke the moment but Harold didn't like the look of Caddi when the idea of getting the contract, and Army weapons, had come up. "Make a bid," he told Mercedes and blew in her ear, which got him a cheer from the men and a long calculating look from Mercedes.

"I thought that's what I'm already doing." Harold almost inclined his head, acknowledging the point, then turned smoothly away as Mercedes leaned forward. Harold had a problem now. Did Mercedes want him to lose and take a look or not, because she wasn't teasing. One glance down right now and he'd probably see her belly button. Very tempting, but he had a long night ahead with just Mercedes and a knife. If Mercedes truly intended giving Harold an eyeful he would soon know. That thought scrambled Harold's concentration again.

Caddi always negotiated hard, but Mercedes added a whole new dimension. Harold hoped she'd been sent elsewhere the next time he visited the Mansion, maybe hunting Murphies if the war wasn't finished. According to the other Hot Rods, Mercedes had already killed three senior Murphies and several other gang members.

With a couple of drinks inside him, Caddi touched on the border war, Harold assumed a calculated touch. Nothing put clearly, but the descriptions of fights and gains made a picture. Caddi had definitely got into a war and not a skirmish. He also had a plan, to progress slowly by clipping off an estate here and a crossroads there. Caddi wanted to avoid anything heavily defended, while snapping up any careless gangsters or vulnerable occupied housing. That would strangle the income and trade of the Murphies, not a normal gang strategy. Harold's estimation of the Hot Rods as a threat went up a few notches.

* * *

The lack of anything except the two official TV channels until ten p.m., and the BBC radio, which closed down at the same time, had changed the habits of a nation. Everyone tended to go to bed earlier. Caddi finally grinned at Harold and stood up. "Fun's over, or for us at least. Now remember, Harry, don't do anything I wouldn't do. Mercedes, play nice, he's allowed to ask you to ask him. You never know Harry, she might." They all stood, waiting for the end of the show before heading to their barracks or back to their homes. As Harold stood, Mercedes removed his hand but leant very close.

"Full sound and vision, lover-boy, so keep your hands and mouth under control," she murmured in his ear. Mercedes continued, but louder. "Come on 'Arold, you wouldn't want to let it get cold, would you?" As the laughter died down Mercedes swept off towards the door, swaying gently and looking back over a shoulder. "I'll go up first, so that you can have a preview. Try not to trip over your tongue. Or dick."

Mercedes continued out and up the stairs, giving it a bit more wiggle for everyone present. Harold followed with about an even mix of anticipation and apprehension. He didn't know if survival would move him up or down on Caddi's shit list. Mercedes got it right about the effect of following her upstairs, even if Harold managed not to trip. Wondering why she'd warned him about sound and vision distracted him, but not much.

*   *   *

Mercedes wore her little smile as she let Harold inside her bedroom. A queen sized bed with a huge plump quilt dominated the room, while an expansive dresser covered in perfumes and makeup, and a couple of chairs, completed the furnishings. There were wardrobe doors along one wall and a door with a padlock at the opposite side. Seeing Harold glance that way, Mercedes curled a lip.

"I sprayed-painted the bathroom walls when I moved in so I'd spot any drilling, and put on a padlock. I promised to skin any bastard who ran in a wire or camera, even if Caddi had ordered them to do it. Caddi agreed I could. I only had to carve one up to make it stick. No home movies in there." Mercedes looked around the bedroom, making it clear that the same didn't apply in here which seemed odd. "Of course, the other side the agreement is that I can't take you or anyone else in there." Mercedes waved Harold through, after opening the combination padlock while blocking any view. "Go and brush your teeth or whatever, and I'll wait."

Harold used the loo, and took the chance of a quick shower before putting his clothes back on except for his boots and socks. He came back out to find Mercedes sorting through a selection of frilly nightwear. "What do you fancy, 'Arold? A bit of lace?" A very little bit, Harold thought. "No, so maybe some silk?" Mercedes held up two small scraps.

Harold's mouth nearly said yes and Mercedes could tell, judging by her laugh. Harold remained half convinced that Caddi had told her to push him over the edge and kill him. If he'd been one of the usual gang bosses, Harold would have made a grab by now. They weren't used to teasing, so maybe this was how Mercedes killed the others? "Wear whatever you usually do. Don't make a special effort for me." Harold kept his voice level and his face straight despite the big smile in response.

"Dangerous, 'Arold. Perhaps I don't usually wear anything?" For one moment Harold thought Mercedes meant that, and knew he was a dead man. He couldn't have ignored her naked in the bed all night, not the way Mercedes seemed to be getting under his skin. A relieved Harold remembered the cameras. No way did Mercedes give them a show every night. A big fluffy set of flannel pyjamas his brain prayed for, over the protests of his libido. Mercedes helped by moving on. "So this is the famous stick. What's the story because it doesn't seem to be up to the job? Most gang bosses have a good quality machete, but a stick?"

"A present from a friend after a bit of strife. Anyway, you shouldn't judge by appearances. You might get a surprise."

"Ha, yes. I can but hope, 'Arold. I've been told your stick can be surprisingly effective. Now I'm wondering if you've got any other surprises for me." Mercedes headed for the en-suite with that small smile back in place, leaving Harold sat in the chair by the bed. He entertained himself by trying to not think about a very sexy young woman, naked in the shower, while listening to it running. He also tried very hard not to imagine what Mercedes usually wore to bed.

It had been a long time since a sexy woman got anywhere close to him, so Harold's resistance was low. He usually avoided women in case they were targeted by the likes of Caddi. Harold realised he didn't have to worry about putting Mercedes in danger, she already lived in the pit with the snakes and tigers.

"Ready or not, I'm coming out." Harold stood up. The result turned out to be anti-climactic, because Mercedes had put on a large man's shirt. The bottom came lower than the dress had, just past her knees, and she held it overlapped at the throat and the waist. The shirt might have fitted Mack, but Harold thought it a stone certainty Mercedes wouldn't be wearing a shirt belonging to a Hot Rod. She leant against the door frame, smiling. "Well?"

Harold couldn't say the first thing he thought of. Mercedes looked about thirteen with her figure buried in the fabric, and her hands clasped like that. The tongue peeking from between her full lips, and those dead eyes, jarred with the rest. "Unexpected. I might even survive the night." Her mouth smiled wider as Mercedes sauntered across the room. Nope, definitely not thirteen.

"Nearly eighteen," she murmured, so someone had told Mercedes what the effect was. She glanced down, frowned and said, "Damn."

Harold was human. He looked down just as, with perfect timing, Mercedes opened the shirt wide until her hands were touching his shoulders. She leaned back, just a little. Without her boots the young woman now stood about five inches shorter than Harold, so she had to tip her head back to look him in the eyes with a real smile and whisper, "Gotcha." Well she had, because there wasn't much point looking away now. Mercedes didn't wear a bra or knickers and yes, Harold could see her belly button as well.

Mercedes leant forward just a bit, close enough to feel her breath, close enough for Harold to take a sharp breath. "The pool for the man who confirms that I'm going commando is substantial, I've been told. You could be a wealthy man, 'Arold."

When she closed the shirt before stepping back, Harold realised Mercedes made sure the cameras couldn't see the flash. The cameras definitely meant everyone would know that Soldier Boy had a perfect view. Harold had to clear his throat, and even then his voice sounded a bit rough. "Sod 'em. A bit of suspense is good for them."

Mercedes looked up from fastening the buttons. Her real smile flashed, and that something flickered in her dead eyes again before she swept her gaze up and round the room. "Eat your hearts out, boys." Mercedes rolled the sleeves up to her elbows, before putting out her arms and twirling. "Sexy enough, 'Arold?"

Harold cleared his throat again and this time his voice had almost returned to normal. "Mercedes, you could make a bin sack look sexy. As you bloody well know."

"Ooh, smooth." Mercedes stepped closer, her little smile back again. "Well you picked my night wear, so now I suppose I get to choose yours." She put her fingers on his chest before walking them down towards Harold's belt.

"Er. No?"

"Wrong answer. If I insist you can't say no, men never can." Her fingers started on the buckle, but stopped as she looked up with a wicked little grin. "You haven't gone commando, have you? Being a Soldier Boy and all that."

Harold laughed at the mischief in her voice. "No."

"Oh, what a pity. But then I might not have been able to resist, and then you would never get that memory." Mercedes finished with the belt, yanking the zip down hard.

"Careful!"

"Oh, I was very careful to avoid anything that might be needed. Just a minute, let me have a proper look." His jeans went down over Harold's hips and dropped to the floor. "Mmm, very nice. So are the boxers. New, are they?"

"Yes." Harold was being careful, because so far the young woman seemed playful. Way too bloody playful, but the steel had shown when Mercedes mentioned no memories. Harold kicked the jeans away before she knelt down to shift them, because a man could only stand so much. Mercedes pouted. She bloody knew. "How many?" Harold asked because he had to try and distract Mercedes, ease this up a bit.

Mercedes genuinely seemed puzzled. "How many what?"

"How many claimed the pool?" Harold needed to figure out if she'd given him the usual razzle or special treatment. He couldn't believe that Mercedes usually put on a show like this, not for every man brought in here. Unless she only did it for the ones she killed.

That little smile came back as Mercedes pecked him on the cheek. "Nobody else has ever qualified, Soldier Boy. Smile, you're a legend. I didn't want you lying awake all night wondering." Harold thought of pointing out that knowing wasn't going to help him sleep, but before he could react Mercedes tapped his shirt. "This definitely comes off. Shall I help?" Since Mercedes already had hold of the cloth, 'no' wasn't going to have any effect.

Harold tried to manage himself, but Mercedes insisted on helping and kept bumping her thin shirt against him as she did. She tossed the shirt into a corner. "I'll get you a fresh one if you survive the night," she promised, then indicated the bed. "After you, lover-boy, I want to watch your ass." Harold climbed in, conscious of her appraising his body, a fair return for the stairs. He had expected Mercedes to be indifferent to men, but the way she acted and eyed him up said different, so what happened now? Mercedes sauntered over to the bed, flipped back the covers and slipped in on the opposite side.

"Take a really good look, Soldier Boy." Mercedes showed Harold the big knife without a sheath that went under the covers as she pulled them up. "Anything that pokes, prods, tickles or lightly strokes me in the night, I keep." She wasn't teasing now. Mercedes turned on a table light, one of those that projected stars onto the walls and ceiling, and low muzak started up. She reached up to pull the cord, wriggling down the bed a little once the light went out.

Harold had turned on his side, away from Mercedes, because that had to be safest. Behind him she pulled the quilt up almost over his head, so probably over hers. "This is so they can't see me drool or suck my thumb"—a pause—"or anything." Mercedes shuffled up tight behind Harold and slid an arm over, spooning into his back. "Goodnight, sleep tight." Her soft voice breathed into his ear, followed by a silent laugh. Harold knew she'd laughed because her body vibrated against his back, and Mercedes would know as well.

Hell, Harold could sleep tomorrow. He knew Mercedes didn't usually snuggle and hug or no gangster would have survived, so she must be pushing again. But Harold wasn't the usual gangster, so despite the special treatment he could handle it. He would take the ragging in the morning, collect Tessa and get out. Tessa. That thought calmed Harold down, the hand resting on his six pack stayed mercifully still, and, surprisingly, Harold dozed.

* * *

Harold woke suddenly because Mercedes had moved behind him. Just a bit of wriggling but now Mercedes had her hands between them, working downwards. Harold barely had time to think of the buttons before her shirt came open. It must have because Harold could feel two warm points on his shoulder-blades, then every inch of her skin downwards including her thighs. He bit off a gasp when another of those silent laughs did interesting things to her skin and his, and again when her hand slid over again and dived towards his boxers! Harold grabbed her wrist. Mercedes wriggled, ruining any concentration Harold had left. "Sorry, I couldn't wait any longer." Her soft voice barely whispered, her warm breath tickling the nape of his neck.

"Mercedes?" Harold kept his voice low, but knew the sound and vision would probably pick it up. What the hell, he had to ask. "Are you going to kill me?"

Harold heard a bit of surprise in her reply. "No, 'Arold," she breathed.

Then louder, "Why, what would you do if I said yes?"

"Turn over and make it worthwhile?" Harold felt the shudder of laughter very personally and much too naked.

"After that, if you turn over I might not kill you until you get your ride." Mercedes dropped her voice to that breathy whisper. "Ssh, 'Arold, they can't hear me over the music, not with my head under here. The cameras can't see properly with the lights flickering, especially with this big lumpy quilt on." A silent giggle vibrated against him. "They can hear you so you'll have to suffer in silence. I thought we'd have a little fun, now I know you aren't the type to kiss and tell."

Her hand had been trying to get free while Mercedes spoke but now she stopped. "Relax and enjoy, lover-boy. In a minute anyway." Her hand slid over behind Harold, but came straight back. "Here," and when Harold raised his hand Mercedes pushed a hard object into it. The knife! "Put it under your pillow." As he did so her hand slid south again and Harold hadn't a chance of an intercept this time.

Harold shifted a bit. "Don't turn over. If you turn over they'll see, stupid." He could hardly hear her voice, muffled by the quilt and his back. "Come on, up a bit." Harold obediently lifted his hip and his boxers were out of the way. That friendly hand became even friendlier.

Harold smiled to himself. So madam wanted a little fun, did she? He slid his own arm and hand up, over and down his back until his fingertips touched warm skin. Mercedes didn't react and her hand never faltered, so Harold slid his hand down Mercedes' side and onto the swell of her naked hip. That brought a small gasp from behind him and a slow wriggle as Harold squeezed and stroked.

Her hand had stopped, but after an appreciative murmur tickled his neck Mercedes started being friendly again. "You need to try harder than that." Right, sauce for the goose. Harold slipped his hand down onto her belly and headed south. That should get a reaction.

Bloody hell, did it ever! Her hand tightened, and there was a short explosion of air onto his neck followed by "yesssss." Her whole body moved up a bit and pulled in tight, pinning Harold's hand between them while her knee came up onto his thigh. Mercedes sighed. "Oh yes, 'Arold, you have no idea how good that feels."

Harold tensed a little. What the hell? Mercedes must have felt it, because her hand eased a bit and she giggled. "What I would love to do," her soft voice murmured, "is to turn you over and see just what your hands can do. Then what the rest can do, and they could sell the videos on street corners for all I care." Even as Mercedes said it her leg came further over and she pushed against Harold's back, and his trapped hand.

Bitterness entered her soft tones, "But I have a deal." Shit, this was the famous deal, the one with Caddi that nobody could work out. "If I screw you, if I screw anyone, Caddi gets me until he is tired of banging me. After which, in spite of any promises, he will pass me round the rest." A sigh followed, no louder than the faint breathy voice. "This is breaking all the rules, but I am so tired of my own hands. Give me another memory, lover-boy." Mercedes backed off a fraction, enough so that Harold could move his hand, and her thigh rubbed along the top of Harold's. The rest of her stayed in contact all the way up his back but wriggled in a bit, while her hand went back to having fun.

Harold didn't even consider saying no. He wondered afterwards if his brain had quit by then, probably when she yanked his pants down. Enough conscious thought stayed for him to bite back his own moans, and groan, which didn't take long. It had been a while since anyone's hands had been on Harold as well. Her snigger felt wonderful, as did the writhing and soft moans, and the muffled noises preceding her long shudder. A quiet breathless voice tickled his neck. "Again, please, 'Arold."

Harold repeated the treatment and got a repeat reaction followed by a long, soft sigh. Mercedes gave another of those muffled giggles that were more sensation than sound. "I think I might have bitten a hole in the pillow case." Another giggle massaged Harold's back. "I don't let the perverts near my bedding so it won't matter."

Mercedes gave a slow writhe, settling in to spoon as close as possible against Harold. "If I ever do a runner, I'm coming to find you." A soft kiss caressed the back of Harold's shoulder, he felt the arm across his belly relax, and Harold did the same.

Harold woke again, later in the night or early morning, with a hot tongue on the back of his neck. "Your leetle friend is awake, 'Arold." True, but Mercedes was certainly making sure he stayed awake. "Once more, lover-boy. Slowly, gently, and with feeling." Mercedes pulled Harold's hand over behind him. He just knew they'd never get away with it again, not with cameras.

Her giggle short-circuited Harold's brain, while the hot breath on his shoulder went straight down Harold's spine to his leetle friend. "I always wake them up for more torment. That's if they sleep at all." Harold realised she meant the watchers were expecting some muttering, shuffling, and maybe a few noises. To hell with caution now anyway, because a gentleman should return a favour and Mercedes seemed insistent on doing Harold a definite favour.

This time Mercedes wasn't so urgent and demanding, and held on longer, but when the shuddering started Harold couldn't see how the quilt could hide it. The funny muffled noises went on longer but they were very muffled. They finally stopped, and a little later her breathing slowed as well. "Whew. Thank you, kind sir." Mercedes gave a gentle sigh. "I might have bitten through the pillow this time."

Mercedes sighed again, which felt really pleasant. "When this war of Caddi's is over, promise you'll visit again, 'Arold." Harold squeezed her hand, he wasn't allowed to talk. "Go to sleep now. Some asshole will bang on the door in the morning. We'll be expected at breakfast, you looking haggard and me looking smug." Another muffled giggle vibrated the warm sweaty flesh plastered to his back. "I can do the smug, no problem." Her lips kissed Harold's neck again. "Goodnight, lover-boy." This time Harold went off to sleep without any trouble.

*   *   *

Sure enough, someone banged on the door in the morning, with an injunction to pull it out and wipe it off because breakfast started in half an hour. Mercedes stretched luxuriously, peering down under the quilt, "To see if you've lost anything." Checking the buttons more likely, while Harold took advantage of the disturbance to ease his boxers up. Mercedes didn't play any games now. Enough light came through the curtains to negate any interference from the light show.

Mercedes bent sideways to put her knife back on the dressing table, her shirt tightening across her ass. Harold quickly stifled the impulse to spank it, or stroke it at least, cursing to himself and scowling for the camera to help him to hide the smile. Mercedes glanced over as Harold sat up and saw the scowl. "Why Harold, anyone would think you didn't enjoy your night?"

Sound and vision, sound and vision, Harold reminded himself, and get the hell out of here as soon as possible. "Why Mercedes, how could I not enjoy it? Every man for miles around dreams of spending the night in your bed." Harold flipped the covers up enough to get out.

"You'll be leaving your boxers behind, Harold. They aren't fit to wear, judging by the way you sweated all over my lovely sheets last night. Once they're clean I can keep them as a trophy since I didn't get anything else." Mercedes busily sprayed air freshener around. "You Soldier Boys should wash more often if you want to impress a girl." That also killed any passion in the air.

Harold resigned himself to going home commando, but Mercedes hadn't finished. "Phew, these sheets need washing. I'll get someone to sort it out while you shower, and she can bring you some new undies. Maybe." A pause. "Tempting thought, but since you are a guest it would be impolite to send you home without your shirt or panties." Mercedes raised her voice. "Hey, whoever. Get this man some clothes before I lose control, and send Eleanor." Another slow up and down look at Harold followed. "Now get in there and clean up, you filthy beast."

Harold forced the scowl to get stronger and stomped into the en-suite before stripping and throwing the boxers out the door. He enjoyed the shower, taking the time to use a disposable razor from the pack on the shelf above the sink. There were murmurings and movement outside before the door to the en-suite suddenly opened. Harold grabbed for the towel. "Spoil-sport. Here." A pair of boxers and a tee were tossed onto the floor before Mercedes turned away, laughing loudly. Harold dressed, finding fresh socks outside by his jeans and boots.

The sheets, pillowcases and quilt cover had gone, as had his tee and boxers. "All that sweat; I had to send my nightie as well." Mercedes wore a huge padded dressing gown, one the size of a small tent and plenty big enough to cover the shirt coming off. The watchers were probably chewing their monitors in frustration. Harold realised that the continual teasing had to be Mercedes' way of dealing with the tension. The tease in question gave him a speculative look and moved her hands fractionally. "Want to check?"

"I would love to conduct a leisurely private inspection, but until then the wonderful memory is burned into my brain with stunning clarity." That got a wide smile with an eye flicker so Mercedes had caught the 'private' part.

"Big words and compliments, all in one breath." Mercedes looked away, addressing the wall. "I hope you boys are learning." She managed a hip sway while crossing to the en-suite, despite wearing a tent. "Get your jeans on, or I'll be getting all hot and bothered." She took a final pop at him just before the door closed. "I won't be long. And to think that they always accuse us girls of taking too long to pamper ourselves." Harold gave the expected huff of annoyance, scowling at her retreating back. He felt really, really, relieved that Mercedes had taken a liking to him. It still seemed a bit like riding a tiger, fine until the tiger felt peckish.

Mercedes wasn't kidding, she showered and pampered in no time. She exited wearing a pair of jeans and a long-sleeved top that came right up to her throat. Both looked tight enough to threaten blood flow, except that the soft cloth wouldn't even be uncomfortable. Except, probably, to any blokes who looked at it too long. As Harold had, he realised, when Mercedes gave a satisfied smirk, posing to give him the full benefit. "Why, 'Arold, I do believe you are smitten."

"With a hammer. Between the eyes. Cripes, do you ever take pity on us blokes? Wear a set of baggy camos or a long loose dress?" Harold rolled his eyes. "Have you never heard of leaving a bit of mystery?"

"Blokes and modesty, or mystery? Let's see, what's wrong with that? Oh, yes, the blokes part. You all see me naked anyway, in your heads. Be honest, Harold, what do you see in your head when you look at me?" Mercedes said that in a teasing tone, but Harold heard a bloody edge in there.

"Sorry, you'll need to be twenty-one to see that." Harold turned to the door, suddenly very keen to get to breakfast. He didn't need imagination, not with that very clear memory. A laugh followed him out of the door. Mercedes seemed happy with her night's work.

*   *   *

There were eight people already sat round the breakfast table, including Tessa. She looked up and smiled as Harold came in, but her face set as Mercedes eased in behind him and slipped an arm through Harold's. "Ah, the love-birds." Caddi looked at Tessa and faked being taken aback. "Oh, you didn't know. Harold had to sleep somewhere, and Mercedes has this big double bed, so..." He shrugged.

Mercedes smiled sweetly at all of them. "Queen sized, because some men are bigger than others." She aimed Harold at a seat, taking the one next to him. The quiet girls flitted in and out. One put a breakfast plate in front of him, and Harold's eyes and nose caught up.

"Bacon!"

Caddi gave a huge smile, because he'd got the right reaction. "For special guests only. Now you know where the rumoured pigs went, Harry, but I can only slaughter one every three or four months so even I have to ration it." So, the gangster had more than one and must have a sow and boar, or access to a boar. "Only for special guests, and you are a very special guest, Harry." Harry tore his eyes from the plate. He managed to keep a hand from going for his stick when he registered the anticipation in Caddi's voice.

This anticipation wasn't a threat. Caddi pulled a huge pile of coupons, held together by a bit of string, off the nearby sideboard and placed them in front of Harold's plate. "A third of all knicker, commando and topless bets placed, and the ones about her bra since the last sighting of said item. After my ten percent of course. They belong to the man who can confirm all of them. You are a rich man, Harry, since everyone present is certain of what wasn't under that dress." Caddi looked at Mercedes. "And we know she didn't change anything but the dress." Caddi gave another glance, this time at Tessa. "You could buy another couple of women with this."

"Paid her debt, not bought." Harold aimed the reply at Tessa, who blushed as she met Harold's eyes.

"So she owes you, and how are you expecting to collect the interest?" Bug just had to open his mouth.

"No interest or repayment required for a gift, Bug. That's something friends do, make gifts." Harold held Bug's eyes now, as Tessa flushed again and looked down at her plate.

"Shut up, Bug, we have a serious bet to settle here." Caddi sat up straighter and the anticipation sharpened. "We know you got a full frontal. You do know that her room is wired for sound and vision?" Harold shrugged nonchalantly, Mercedes had actually told him. "So now you just have to confirm if the fair Mercedes went to bed without bra or without panties last night." Caddi licked his lips. "Or without either." All the men were looking at Mercedes, not Harold, while she looked straight at Harold with that little smile.

Harold smiled back at Mercedes. "A gentleman never tells." They all stared at Harold now. He continued quickly, before someone opened his gob and Harold started a fight. "Not if he ever intends using his nuts for anything other than cufflinks." After a short pause everyone burst out laughing. Caddi seemed to be just going along. Harold could see that speculative edge again and wondered how to deflect it. Bug, the gobby shite, did the job nicely.

"You're like the other pussies, bloody frightened of her. Big bad Soldier Boy is frightened of a bloody woman!"

Thank you Bug, Harold thought, leaning back a little with a big sod-you smile. Harold had seen the momentary warmth in her dead eyes at his answer, more than a flicker, and worth all the crap Harold would get. "Of course I am, you stupid dick. Anyone with two brain cells is scared of Mercedes. You are if you've got the balls to admit it." That would probably mean a fight after all, but Harold didn't mind slapping Bug down. Slapping Bugatti had been on his to-do list for a couple of years now, and would definitely deflect any other questions.

"But we already know, we could see there was nothing under that dress. She even let you put your fucking hand on it, and then gave you a full flash. What else did you get last night?" Bug actually went bug-eyed as Caddi sat smiling, letting him run.

"Aching balls and a headache, and a night spent sweating like a pig and hoping I didn't fall asleep and move the wrong thing to the wrong place. As for the hand, I half expected I wouldn't get it back!" Harold looked at Caddi, willing the suspicious little shit to believe him. "I honestly thought you'd told Mercedes to kill me, that your pet killer meant to push until she got an excuse."

Caddi relaxed, reverting to his trademark half-smile. "Yeah, we heard, Harry. What was it? Oh, yes. 'Mercedes, are you going to kill me?'—'What will you do about it?'—'Turn over and make it worthwhile?'—I nearly pissed myself laughing over that bit. See Bug, that's style." Caddi laughed properly this time.

The table fell about, and even Tessa smiled but still seemed puzzled. Harold laughed, partly from relief. Mercedes had spoken louder at that moment, but they still hadn't got her word perfect. She obviously knew what could be heard with her head under the quilt. Mercedes preened, accepting the implied compliment on her lethality and allure.

"Even so," Bug didn't want to give it up. "We all know she was commando. Come on boss, pay up! Some of us bet extra after seeing his hand on her ass."

"No. I can't pay out on the bets because the rules are clear. Confirmation has to come from a bloke we know had the clear opportunity to see." Caddi lapped it up. His Killer Queen had just had another layer added to her legend.

"Which nobody else did, Bug, even if you nearly broke your neck trying. Looks like Soldier Boy went one better again." E-Type had decided to do some winding up himself. It wouldn't take much, Bugatti had spent over two years being tweaked about Harold capturing him and stripping him to his boxers.

"Only because I've not been trying, not properly. Shit, I could settle it easy enough, and show you what a pussy Soldier Boy really is. All it needs is a hand on her ass now, because the bitch has done it again today!" Bug came half out of his chair.

Caddi smirked, and egged Bug on a little. "You have to put eyes on her ass, not hands on her jeans, Bug. That's if you reckon you can do what we all know Soldier Boy did, even if he's being bashful. Another free lesson in what a real man can do, Bug." The bastard knew his troops, leaning forward a bit in anticipation.

Bug finished standing. "Fine. Eyes on her ass. Just because you wankers let her walk around here with your dicks on a leash doesn't make her the Black Mamba or something." He started forward. "I'll just show you all."

Even as Bug started towards her, Mercedes came smoothly off her chair with a long slim blade in her hand. From her boot, Harold knew, even if nobody else saw it come out. Bug stopped, the blood starting to leave his face. "Bug," Mercedes purred. "I didn't ask, and you didn't even ask me to ask you. Didn't you learn from Soldier Boy? A girl likes to be asked."

His rush of blood had chilled, not just cooled, but Bug had already taken two steps from his chair. He had no way forward without bleeding, while retreat screwed his rep forever because Bug wore a knife. That meant he could theoretically keep coming, if he had the balls for a knife fight with Mercedes. It couldn't happen to a better bloke, Harold thought. He suddenly noticed the rest of the elite around the table, watching Bug as if the gangster was the next Christian going into the Coliseum. Breakfast and the Romans were waiting, eager for blood. Caddi leant back with a self-satisfied smirk.

Harold realised Caddi had prodded Bug just enough. Now the elite's disappointment about the commando bet had gone, and they might even get to see Bug killed as a bonus. Bug swallowed hard, his shoulders slumping as the gangster decided on derision rather than that blade. "Sorry, Mercedes. Will you ask me to look at your ass?" A round of hysterical laughter and piss-taking followed, because nobody ever bothered with that question.

"You can try if you like." Ooh, that wasn't permission, Mercedes had issued a challenge. "I didn't get the chance of a trophy last night because

Soldier Boy is a light sleeper. So Bug, do you want to try?"

"No, Mercedes." Bug turned towards the door.

"You should trim at least one ear, Mercedes." E-Type wore a huge grin. Bug classed as wounded prey in this jungle and the pack wanted a piece.

"Go on Boss, award her both ears and the tail." The rest hooted with laughter as Charger chipped in as well.

Cooper wasn't to be left out. "How many bits can you carve off a bug anyway, with all those extra legs...?"

"Bugatti, you little shit, Bugatti not Bug!" Bug whirled and glared at Cooper. Personally Harold thought that had to be as stupid as bracing Mercedes.

"Bug." The incensed ganger stopped because Caddi's voice held no humour at all. "I told you again and again, you need to engage your brain now and then. You chose Bugatti, knowing that I am called Caddi, and there's Chevy and Cooper. In time E-type will be ET." E-Type shrugged, looking more hopeful than worried. "But you chose a name that shortens to Bug." Caddi's voice hardened. "As you seem to have the brains of a bug you're stuck with it. Mack, go with him and make sure he doesn't do something that means I have to kill him. He might eventually learn enough to be useful."

"Okay, Boss. Oy, Bug, come 'ere." The subdued young man followed Mack's broad back out of the door, the big man stuffing the last of his bacon into his mouth as he left. Caddi moved the coupons back onto the dresser with a little shake of his head and a smile.

Mercedes reversed her knife, and as she sat down the point speared a slice of bacon. "Well, if all the excitement is over, I'm eating this while it's still warm. What about you, Soldier Boy, do you prefer it hot?" Oh, yes, back on script.

Harold looked her over. "I like piggy's ass hot and crispy. I really fancy something warm and smooth now and again, but not enough to bleed for it." Harold put a lot of emphasis on 'really' and joined in the relaxed laughter. The animals had been fed, even if actual blood hadn't flowed.

Caddi pushed Bug's plate across to Mercedes. "Your trophy." He looked round. "We can't waste it. In fact, anyone who wastes any of my pig will end up feeding it." From the looks, nobody could be certain if Caddi meant carrying a feed bucket or being in one, but there'd be no chance of waste anyway. Piggy rapidly became grease stain as everyone tucked into their delayed breakfast.

Mercedes still rubbed it in a little. She carefully divided Bug's bacon, putting half on Harold's plate. "To keep your strength up in case you visit again." The slightly speculative edge in Caddi's stare came back but Harold had decided that Mercedes did it deliberately, poking the tiger a bit. Maybe as payback for the hoops the bastard put her through. Harold hoped Mercedes didn't overdo it.

He set into his breakfast with relish. The bread had been fried in the bacon fat, but when people felt happy to get any food, all the fuss about what type was best for them soon died out. Tessa flushed a little when Harold caught her eye but then locked eyes, slid them deliberately to Mercedes and back to Harold, and an eyebrow twitched. Cripes, did Tessa think him and Mercedes were an item? Harold reconsidered as Tessa dropped her eyes again to give her breakfast the attention it deserved.

Mercedes and he were an item. Or as much of an item as the young woman would ever be with anyone while that deal stood, which made Harold a bit uncomfortable. Not the semi-sex, totally unexpected as that had been, but who with. Mercedes had turned out to be a lovely looking woman but something had broken, or been badly bent, inside her head. Those eyes still worried Harold. He wondered what would have happened if they had been face to face, and he'd looked into those dead eyes. He stifled a smile at the thought that perhaps her eyes weren't dead when Mercedes shuddered and chewed the pillow.

The meal progressed with gentle conversation about the day ahead. Harold suffered low-level teasing about needing nourishment, and having two women to satisfy. Mercedes spread her own version of happiness about, but without the previous night's edge. Tessa finally stopped giving Harold odd looks, or blushing at the comments about Harold's women.

Eventually Tessa went up to get her things. Caddi personally escorted Harold to the front door. "We'd better send you home, Harry, or I'll never get herself back to work. Anyway, you've got that one to sort out." Caddi waved towards the approaching Tessa. "Some radios will be ready in four days, right, and the quickest guns?" Caddi gave one of his insincere grins. "If you've got time between all the fondling."

"Our smith will check the charcoal first to see if it's the good stuff." Liz would be almost ecstatic about the charcoal because she never had enough. "We'll get as many as possible of each ready, but only if we can make them work properly. We don't turn out rubbish."

"I should hope not, the prices you charge. Cooper will escort you and

Tessa to her place so you can get her sorted out, but I'll send the repairs straight to your place. We don't want guns waiting about unprotected for who knows how long." Harold let it all slide off. Caddi wasn't even pushing hard, so the night had gone well for the nasty little sod. "After all, you might not have enough energy left to unload them."

"You'd send an escort anyway, Caddi, so this won't cost you a bean. Tell whoever to be very careful approaching Orchard Close. They might be a bit twitchy if I'm not along."

"ET will take the convoy." E-Type looked pleased at the shortening of his name, a promotion in the Hot Rods.

"Don't worry Harry. I give you my word there'll be no shit, and the men will remember their manners round your women." Harold didn't doubt that because there'd be shotguns covering the Hot Rods every minute they spent in Orchard Close. Even so, ET's verbal assurance actually meant something. If his men caused offence, the gangster would now be expected to answer a personal challenge from Soldier Boy. These rules kept evolving.

* * *

As Harold turned to leave, an arm hooked into his and tugged him close. "I'd better see you off, or you could turn up anywhere." Mercedes sniggered and hugged a little tighter. "You wouldn't like me when I'm startled. I can be quite sharp." Her other hand dropped just a little, towards her boot and the knife.

"You might like some sorts of surprises?" Harold and Mercedes followed Cooper, leading Mack, Chevy, ET and Tessa towards the vehicles.

"I've been surprised a few times, but only once did it turn into real pleasure. Maybe twice depending how you count?" The pressure from her arm let Harold know exactly what Mercedes meant, very privately while the Hot Rods joked about what the surprise might have been. They were all in a terrific mood today. So were the gangsters in view, word of last night had already spread.

A group of Hot Rods came out of a house near the gate. Harold tensed in case Caddi had decided to play games again, but not this time. They all started laughing, then pointed and a chant of 'comman-do' started up. "Cheeky sods." Her voice had no annoyance in it, and Mercedes followed the comment by blowing them a kiss and wiggling her ass a bit. The Hot

Rods turned away towards their canteen, still laughing.

Cooper headed for his car, a Mini Cooper of course. Tessa's meagre possessions went into Harold's pickup, which someone had brought in through the gates, before she climbed into the passenger seat. She kept very quiet, glancing around now and then as if waiting for something else, probably Caddi arriving to tell her hard luck he'd changed his mind. Harold's weapons, including Lada's big knife, also went into the pickup. All the lieutenants waited with expectant smiles. Harold braced himself but instead of a round of obscene suggestions about Tessa, Mercedes spoke up.

"Well, Soldier Boy, I hope you aren't going to rush off without saying goodbye? Sort of look and run?" She'd let go of his arm as Tessa settled in, so Harold had to turn to answer. Mercedes produced a magnificent pout.

Harold's didn't have to force his completely genuine smile. "Oh, I'm sure a lot of people look and run, Mercedes, even if some wait to take a longer look first."

"Yes, but I wondered if what you saw might stop you from running?" Harold suddenly wondered if Caddi had asked her to recruit Soldier Boy. The gang boss had found some tempting bait this time, because Mercedes had somehow wormed her way in under Harold's skin. A moment later Harold realised that Caddi wouldn't let anyone have Mercedes, not unless Caddi did first. That was a status thing. Cripes, Harold had considered it just for a few moments. The girl was good!

"I promise I won't shoot you or run away, even if you come and visit. If you invite me nicely, I might even come back here." Harold grinned and borrowed Caddi's trick, lifting one eyebrow.

"So ask me to ask you, 'Arold." Harold thought this smile might be genuine. It certainly looked more natural than any she had given with Caddi watching.

"Will you ask me to come back, Mercedes? Please? Or you can visit." Harold looked straight into those dead eyes. "Now I know you better, you can come over any time." There, Harold saw that flicker. Mercedes had hopefully remembered her whispered words, words that Harold thought came from her heart for once. 'If I ever do a runner, I'm coming to find you.'

"Come back nicely please, 'Arold. But only if I'm home." She sighed dramatically. "Caddi will be keeping me too busy for some time now, but I will remember your invite, 'Arold. Now say goodbye."

"Goodbye Mercedes." It couldn't be that easy.

Mercedes looked at the grinning men, then back at Harold. "No, no, no, 'Arold, that's not how to say goodbye. Now"—she took the hand she had 'claimed' last night—"what do you want me to ask you?"

"Will you ask me to put my hand on your ass, Mercedes? Please?" Harold put some real emphasis on the please, enough to get the blokes laughing again. A little something to let Caddi know Soldier Boy might be hooked.

"Ooh, naughty! Still living in hope, 'Arold?" More laughter from the men greeted that. "'Arold, will you put your hand on my jeans, right where they cover my ass?"

Harold ignored the murmurs from the men at a second partial yes, and got a good solid grip this time. He tugged slightly. "Like this?"

"You're learning." Mercedes smirked at the other men. "I might get him trained, eventually."

The muttered comments included "might get him killed" but Mercedes hadn't waited for their replies.

Her hands walked up Harold's arms and round the back of his neck. "You have been a good boy, 'Arold, so you deserve a reward." Mercedes licked her lips and for a moment Harold wondered just how far she intended pushing this. Maybe it was an adrenaline thing, the buzz, riding the thrill? Mercedes pulled his head forward and brushed Harold's lips, just. She glanced to the side, grinning. "Always leave them wanting a bit more. Works every time." Harold would confirm that any time he was asked.

She'd done it again, got him relaxed while she'd got much too close. Bloody treacherous, those hormones, they could get a man killed. Harold had reacted automatically to the kiss by squeezing her ass a little and pulling a bit. Mercedes let herself come forward until those firm, pert breasts were near enough for Harold to feel her body heat through his tee. "I might work harder for a bit more."

"But could I restrain myself to just a bit?" For a long couple of seconds Mercedes stayed close, before stepping back and sliding his hand off her ass. She turned smoothly away from the one on her waist and started back towards the Mansion. After a couple of steps, Mercedes turned enough to call, "Watch this space," and pat her ass, before wiggling it enough to make sure all the men did.

Cooper sighed, Mack laughed, and ET whistled quietly before calling the others' attention to Harold. "Hey, he looks as if he's been clouted with a bat."

"Christ Almighty, if she treated me like that you could hit me with a bat. It might be worth it." Cooper sounded as if he might mean it, so maybe Caddi wanted to get all the lieutenants hopeful and tie them tighter? That idea worked its way into Harold's mind and got him back on balance.

"Bloody 'ell, 'Arry. Never seen 'er do that." Mack had to be steered off that idea, that there was anything special going on.

"Oh, I think Caddi's got ideas for me and mine, and he's using very juicy bait." A round of agreement followed, either to the idea that Mercedes was bait, or juicy. Harold turned to the pickup with, "See you for a beer, Mack," followed by "Yeah, you scroungers as well" to stop the protests. Cooper gunned the engine, advertising to all that the car belonged to one of the elite. Harold took his chance to get the subject away from Mercedes. "How the hell do you lot get the diesel? Everyone keeps screaming it's all gone."

It worked because Chevy laughed. "Caddi's supposed to have grabbed a couple of tankers before the shit truly hit, and they're tucked away safe. Only maybe, because none of us know where, so the sneaky bastard probably shot whoever hid them. The rest of us? We used petrol while we could, then when it all spoiled we went onto the diesel. We'd got it all in cans by then, emptied every filling station and vehicle, and nobody else gets to use any." He looked at the pickup, then at Cooper's car. "Charger put diesel engines into our gang cars but even so, yours isn't up to a race."

"Don't worry about it. If I get lost, Tessa can put me right." Harold waved to get Cooper going and the car accelerated off down the road. With a sigh of relief, Harold followed at a more modest pace.

Chapter 4:
An Other Woman

Cooper went roaring through the streets doing some imitation of a rally driver. The pedestrians in the few inhabited areas scattered when they heard the car coming, because any motor vehicle had to mean one of their lords and masters was on their way. Cooper used main roads and only made six turns, so Harold did his best to keep the scroat in sight. He didn't want Cooper poking around in Tessa's house, or telling little Ed his Mum had been bought. Judging by the rubber Cooper left as he skidded round the corners, and the locked wheels and screeching halt before the gangster hopped out, Caddi must have a good supply of tyres.

Thinking of that, and trying to keep up, kept Harold from worrying about what Cooper would say when they arrived. Not only that, but he wasn't sure how Tessa would take his next suggestion. Cooper waited, smiling, as Harold pulled up. "We don't get the chance to race very often now." The driving had stripped as many years off Cooper as it had put on Harold. The madman had to be a fan of that TX-Box game, the one where players stole cars and raced them around a ruined city.

Harold shook his head. "Not exactly a race."

Tessa climbed out, looking around as if she had never expected to see home again. Harold looked around because he'd never seen where she lived. Tessa had moved here when conditions worsened just prior to the Crash, to look after her late Dad. She lived in one of the older council terrace blocks with brick chimneys, the ones that had been slated for demolition every few years then reprieved.

"Nearest we get to racing these days. We used to have competitions but there isn't enough diesel left now." Cooper paused before getting back into his car. "I'm coming back this way tomorrow. I'll escort you home if you're still here getting Tessa"—Cooper smirked—"sorted out. Use your radio if you want one of the others to escort you." The car shot off leaving two strips of rubber on the tarmac, the raucous tune from the air horn echoing as Cooper screeched around the corner and out of sight.

Tessa had a carefully blank look on her face, and her face looked a bit pink. That had to be the 'sorted out' dig. Harold put on his weaponry before picking up Tessa's bag. "I don't expect I'll still be here tomorrow." Silence. "I came because, well, it might be better if you moved into Orchard Close."

"Whatever you say, Harold." Harold looked sharply at the young woman. Tessa's set face and blush told him what she thought he meant.

"Cripes, no! You can live where you like, Tessa. It's just that it might be better if the two of you left here." Harold sighed and kept going because Tessa just didn't get it. "Safer for you because Caddi is permanently pissed off with me. I've been careful to never let on I know you, because the arse will use you to get at me. But if you want to stay?"

Now Tessa looked Harold in the eye. "Don't you like me, Harold?"

"Eh, what? Yes. You're a fine woman, and a good mother, but it wouldn't be right to expect you to, you know." Harold could flirt or talk dirty with Mercedes, but Tessa tied his tongue up. She was too nice. Normal.

Her face cleared. "Ah, that woman." Slut, the tone said. "Will she be moving in?"

The question might be serious but Harold couldn't help it, he laughed. "No, Mercedes is not the type, and she's not allowed to leave anyway. There's nothing like that between us." Harold hoped not, because that would be a real chance for Caddi to wind him up.

"Why not, you sure as hell want to." Ooh, that was sharp!

"Look, I only spent the one night in her bed, same as anyone else who allegedly gets treated. That's a test, a deadly game Caddi plays, and Mercedes plays it very well. She's killed four men that way." Harold wondered why he was defending himself. "There's nothing real about it."

"Not much." Yes, he could hear a definite edge in Tessa's voice. "So why didn't you tell them what she was wearing?" Tessa's tone changed, inquisitive now. "What was she wearing under her nightie?"

"It was a big shirt, not a nightie, big enough for Mack. Now why would I tell you, when I wouldn't tell that lot with all those coupons up for grabs?"

"Yes, why would you, Harold? Because I'm a woman?" Tessa snorted. "We're better at body language than blokes. You only look at the tits and ass."

"And her eyes." Not necessarily first, Harold privately confessed.

"Yes, but if that's true you're an exception. Maybe that's it? Anyway, she walked in there with you as if you'd been screwing her all night with her enthusiastic assistance!" Tessa laughed out loud. "Oh Harold, your face, but that confirms it. I don't care what the sound and vision saw and heard, you two had a lot more fun than anyone else thinks. I get it, it's not allowed, but you'll need to be a lot more careful in the future."

"How? What do you mean? We didn't." Harold took a breath. "Look, I swear to you, if I'd turned round she'd have killed me. It's the deal."

"Stop it. You did, well… something." Tessa shook her head at Harold's denial. "There was something in your faces when you looked at each other. Yes, Harold, in your eyes and even in those dead things of hers, and a something in your voices. Those stupid bastards wouldn't see it, but another woman…?" She glared at Harold in exasperation and shook her head again. "Bloody men."

"Shit. Could anyone else see?" Harold flinched at the thought of Caddi knowing. "Cripes, don't breathe a word, to anyone. He'll kill her, but only afterwards." He spat the last word out.

Tessa still looked unhappy, maybe at Mercedes' possible fate. "I won't tell. I owe you."

"No you don't, but I'll make you a deal. I'll answer the other question if you promise to keep your trap shut about all of it?" Harold was horrified, and scared shitless, as much for Mercedes as himself, which was all wrong considering how lethal she was.

"I won't tell anyway. You don't think I'd give that arsehole anything to use against anyone, especially you?" Tessa smiled properly at last. "But I would really like to know."

"Nothing. Ab-so-bloody-lutely nothing. I swear, I thought I was a dead man." Harold snorted. "And no, I didn't look at her eyes until afterwards." He caught Tessa's eyes. "I won't give that arsehole anything he can use either." Harold looked around. They were out in the street and not talking loudly, but there were faces peeking cautiously from some of the windows. Nobody would actually bother them because Harold had turned up in a motor, and carried a weapon openly. That put him at the top of the local hierarchy and untouchable, but the locals would listen if they could. "Now can we go indoors and discuss where you'll be living?"

Tessa's face blanked again. "Wherever you say. After all, you just bought me, and my son."

"Stop it. We'll talk inside." Harold grinned, trying to make it a joke. "All right, if I'm your master you're supposed to say 'yes Harold,' and lead me to the kitchen."

"Yes Harold." Deadpan, no humour. Tessa turned and headed for the house, pulling out a set of keys. Damn, Harold thought, that didn't work.

It took two cups of tea and some fairly heated conversation before Tessa accepted that Harold hadn't actually bought her, regardless of what everyone else assumed. Tessa considered herself in debt for whatever Harold had paid. According to the Hot Rod rules, rules she'd lived under for over three years, the debt meant she was, in effect, owned. Sometime during that stay with Caddi, Tessa had given up hope, and she didn't truly believe the nightmare had ended. Oddly, it was Mercedes who finally got the message through. Tessa kept harping on about the amount that Harold had paid to buy her.

"Did you see that pile of coupons on the table? The ones that were mine if I confirmed that Mercedes wasn't wearing panties? That was more coupons than those games were worth, easily enough to pay both of the debts and the interest." Harold watched it finally sink in.

"So why didn't you tell them?" Tessa still wasn't completely convinced.

"I told you. I wouldn't give the arseholes the satisfaction." Harold smiled at the memory. "And for the one smile."

"She was already smiling. She does it a lot, smiling."

"Not with her eyes."

A long silence followed while Tessa got her head round it all. "What do you intend doing about her? Will you pair do a runner one moonlit night? Romeo and Juliet with shotguns?" Tessa had a little half-smile now, much nicer than Caddi's version.

"Hell no!" Harold gave a short, uncomfortable laugh. "It's not romance. I don't know what it is. Some sort of animal attraction, or maybe it's the thrill of the forbidden? Mercedes has no real feelings left, not human ones, and I really, really don't know why she's picked on me for her latest toy. As in the mouse caught by the pussy cat toy." He shrugged as if it didn't matter. "It won't happen again anyway, because I survived the test. I doubt I'll see her at Orchard Close, and probably not at the Mansion. It won't be fun for Caddi anymore."

"Maybe you will, if only because she hasn't met someone with morals for a while? Anyone else she knows would have only paid that for a woman for one reason, and would have bragged to everyone about what he'd seen." Tessa gave Harold a long look. "Would you have paid that to get any woman out of the shit? Given it away like that and wanted nothing back?"

"No." Harold whispered because he felt ashamed, but Tessa deserved the truth. Orchard Close needed the coupons those games would have brought.

"So why for me?"

"Stones..."

The crash of the mug hitting the wall echoed as Tessa whirled, eyes wide and tears starting. "No it bloody wasn't! Me and Stones were together for three years, and he last went abroad four years ago! You haven't seen him for over three years, nobody has! Missing in action but the Army don't even pretend he's coming back." Tessa's voice dropped. "I don't expect him back. We weren't married or anything but Stones was fair, he put me and Eddie down as his dependants so we get the extra coupons. Everyone reckons that'll stop soon."

Tessa waved her hands at the house around them. "Being dependants didn't stop the bastards leaving us to live like this. The MOD kicked even the married ones out of quarters if their bloke didn't come back. They wanted the families of every soldier still in the country to be safe." Her voice firmed up. "It wasn't a love match, Harold, and even if it had been, you didn't do this for Stones."

"No." Damn. Bloody women.

"So why?"

"Dunno. You're too nice. I couldn't see you treated like that, passed around the favoured few." Harold blushed, the first time for ages. "He'd have brought you in and offered you to me when I visited, to wind me up because I always say no. I couldn't have that."

After a long pause, Tessa sat down. "Too nice," she said quietly. "I can live with that. You are a soft sod, Harold, so how did you get such a reputation as a hard man?" She shook her head, a slightly mocking smile on her lips. "I had the shock of my life when they all called you Soldier Boy. You never said a word in the Mart. Soldier Boy has got a hell of a reputation with the Hot Rods."

"I had to do a couple of hard things, for Sharyn and the kids. The nutters know about it, and that I was in the Army. They've seen me shoot, and"—Harold smiled happily—"they think I'm SAS or something."

Tessa spluttered for a moment. Her face showed true delight for the first time since Harold had seen the young woman in the Mansion. "They don't know? Oh, Harold, you brass-balled bastard. Oh, what I'd give to see that shithead's face when he finds out!"

Harold lost his smile. "If he does, pray you are many, many miles away in the next county, or country if possible. There are at least three gangs of homicidal lunatics, led by psychopaths, who are only being kept back by the legendary prowess of the SAS. If they find out I've made prats of them they'll tear Orchard Close apart brick by brick, then burn it down to make sure they got me. When word spreads, there are nasty bastards all over the city who would come to piss on the ashes. It's a pride and status thing, an insult to be washed away in blood."

Tessa had gone pale. "But someone has to know."

"Maybe, but there aren't many ex-squaddies hereabouts that might have known me. If you didn't actually see me, would you connect Harry the pay clerk with that nasty bastard Soldier Boy?" Harold knew there wasn't much left of that Harry, the soldier who was a clerk because he didn't like shooting at people. He'd turned into someone a lot more like Soldier Boy these days, even if his victims still came back at night to haunt him. "That's why I try to get everyone to call me Harold. If someone sees me that knows the truth I either get to them first or run. If I run, everyone who doesn't come with me will pay. If whoever it is doesn't know about the stick, that might give me an edge. Just enough to get a start." Harold looked Tessa in the eye. "So now, knowing that, would you like to come and live in Orchard Close, Tessa?"

Tessa looked back at him for long moments, then nodded. "Yes Harold, I think I'll risk having to run so that my son can grow up in Orchard Close. Soldier Boy is a better role model for Eddie than Caddi and his lot will ever be. Hah, if you run, we're coming with you." She managed a little smile at the next thought. "Your girlfriend might surprise you and give you a bit of warning. She might even come with us."

"I doubt Mercedes will live the year out because she's getting reckless. But oh, can you imagine Caddi if she did?" It wasn't Caddi Harold thought of, but Mercedes and that open shirt back in Orchard Close without the sound and vision. That worried Harold because the woman had got to him. Mercedes was supposed to do that, get to blokes, but knowing that should have allowed Harold to dismiss the show, the act.

* * *

With her future location settled, Tessa started fretting about Caddi changing his mind or deciding her son wasn't part of the deal. She went to collect Eddie so they could leave before any Hot Rods turned up. Eddie, nearly five now with dark hair and eyes like his mum, had sprouted up again since Harold last saw him. Those big round dark eyes peeked cautiously at Harold from behind mum's legs. Eddie knew Harold because they'd met in the Mart a few times, but the lad had already learned to be wary of men carrying weapons. Still, he seemed happy enough to be coming to live near 'Uncle Harold' and Wills and Daisy. Sharyn, another Army widow and single mum, had met Tessa before the Crash, so she already knew someone in Orchard Close.

Harold left the food with the erstwhile carers since there wasn't much, and the furniture belonged with the house. Tessa rounded up her clothes, bedding, ornaments, her kettle, clock, several mismatched mugs, screw top pop bottles, pots, pans, crockery and cutlery, what would once be called her goods and chattels. Despite her wanting to hurry, it took about an hour to make sure Tessa had taken everything she wanted. Not because of the amount, she just kept worrying she'd missed something. The whole lot went onto the back seat of the pickup, a pathetic collection. They could both remember when a move would involve vans and packing cases.

Harold finally shut the house door, leaving the keys inside as Caddi had told him to. He could have called for an escort from the Hot Rods but didn't want the crudity about Tessa in front of her or her son. Harold couldn't stop the gangsters harassing her, not here because Orchard Close rules didn't apply. As it was, the neighbours were all watching from windows and doorways, many with knowing or pitying looks. A few wished her luck, and Tessa answered those with a wide smile and cheerful voice which puzzled the others. It wasn't unknown for a woman to shack up with a gangster voluntarily, but they didn't usually want a woman with a child.

Harold relaxed as he drove, relieved to be talking to a woman without a dozen scroats listening for a mistake or the woman working on getting him to commit suicide. The few occupied streets cleared as if by magic when a motor approached, so he had a clear run.

On the way, Tessa explained how she'd been sucked in by Pete. Tessa had found her little brother on her doorstep, badly beaten but not badly enough to cripple him. Pete had been terrified of what he'd been threatened with next. Tessa had believed Pete about the girl, or had been persuaded because Pete believed, and didn't mind keeping her brother from getting beaten up again while earning the money. She'd thought Pete had learned his lesson.

Now Harold found out another little side-line. Caddi sometimes allowed girls to save themselves from the brothel, if they found someone who could afford the ransom. Those who could meet the price were usually a family that had managed to hide something valuable, from before the Crash, so Caddi probably took the girls because he'd got a hint. That had made the spiel from Fantasia at least believable, even if her name should have been a big hint. But Fantasia wasn't trying to buy herself out. She might even be working off a debt to keep her own ass her own, another way to recruit.

They dropped the subject of using debt to control people, because that's how Caddi had 'recruited' Tessa. Her brother ending up on Tessa's doorstep, beaten up badly enough to worry her, hadn't been a fluke. "What about Pete? Will he be all right now?" After all this, Tessa still worried about her little brother.

"The deal is that he gets enough crappy work to pay everything off, if he works hard." Harold smiled at the memory. "I told Pete he would be a lot keener with his own lily-white on the line. "

Tessa quietened for a couple of minutes, then smiled back at him. "How do you know mine's lily-white? I might sunbathe and then it would be tanned?" Yeah, right, Tessa had to be joking. Every remotely attractive woman kept clothes on in public these days. If she showed some skin and they heard about it, the gangsters wouldn't wait for a lass to sunbathe again to check.

Harold laughed and leaned back a little to glance at her backside. "Hmm, I might have to check out warm sunny places this summer. Just in case." Tessa laughed, and Harold thought she had finally relaxed. Maybe because she was able to make jokes like that and just get a laugh.

* * *

As they drove down the last stretch from the traffic island to Orchard Close, a young teenage girl came out, heading across the road to the old caravan park. She looked nervous, jerking her head from side to side and jumping at shadows, so as he came nearer Harold pulled up and called her over. "Why are you out here, Elise?" Harold kept his voice calm, because Elise often froze when spoken to directly.

Even so Elise almost whispered her answer. "Trev asked me to test this radio. I thought it would be okay because Trev told me to. I'm sorry."

Harold took the two-way radio from the girl. "No, don't apologise. It's not a problem. Go back in and tell Trev I'll get someone else to do it. We wouldn't want you to have an accident out in this rubble." Elise headed for the gates, almost running until she got there.

Tessa looked round. "What's the problem? It looks safe out here. What was she frightened of?" A fair question because long trenches full of dirt striped the wide area of tarmac beside the road, an area cleared of rubble. The one isolated, partially ruined house had a guard on it.

"Elise is frightened of shadows, bless her, and terrified at any hint of gangsters." Harold curled a lip, glancing back down the road before answering Tessa. "There are a couple of Caddi's blokes in the last of the ruined houses we just came past, because he likes to keep an eye on us. Technically that's neutral territory and the caravan park is ours, but if a young lass like that wandered too near? She should have had a four-legged bodyguard at least, a big mastiff." Harold's annoyance faded as he glanced towards the nearest guardhouse. "To be honest, if any scroat tried for her this near the walls they'd probably get a fatal migraine."

Tessa wasn't convinced. "What if you aren't here to shoot at them?"

She looked startled when Harold burst into laughter. "Wait until you meet Emmy, Roy and Alfie. They can all use a rifle and then there's Patty the crossbow queen. Caddi upped the crossbow practice for his men when he saw Patty use hers; she loves either head or groin shots."

Tessa looked suspicious, then relaxed when she realised Harold wasn't joking. "So what was that girl doing out here?"

"Elise? Good question. I can't see her volunteering to come out here, especially without her doggy guard. Since Trev sent her, let's test this radio and find out." Harold held the transmit down. "Trev?"

"Yes? Who's this? Where's Elise?"

"Coming back into the compound where she should have been all the time."

A long silence followed before Trev answered. "Harold?"

"Yes. Don't give Elise any crap. I just happened to come up the road while she was out here. Without Thandia?" Normally Elise didn't go anywhere without the mastiff.

"Er, no. Um, I told her to stay over towards the Army, and there wasn't time to get the dog's lead. There's someone with a crossbow as a lookout on that side and lookouts on the gate." Trev sounded defensive but not convinced he'd been wrong. There were lookouts on every side, but that wasn't an excuse. Harold thought a moment.

"Would you come out here if a couple of Barbie Girls were hanging about?" Harold held out the radio so Tessa could hear the answer.

"Cripes! No! Are there Barbies out there?" Trev sounded nearly ready to wet his pants at the thought.

Tessa looked about ready to laugh, but Harold kept his voice very serious. "No, but you know that Caddi's lads are out here, and that's the same to Elise. Don't you remember how she arrived?"

"Yes. Sorry. I didn't think." Trev didn't sound that sorry, but definitely sounded rattled. "But I need the radio tested at a distance."

Harold sighed loudly enough to be heard. "So you ask a bloke. I'll ask someone this time, but no more sending Elise outside the walls."

"Okay, I hear you. Sorry." Trev still seemed more interested in his test. "How soon will the test be?"

Harold frowned, because Trev just wasn't getting the message. "When someone else calls you? Which will be when I get around to asking someone?"

"Ah. Right." The radio went dead as Trev realised who he'd been chivvying, and maybe heard the frown in Harold's voice.

"Bloody hell, Caddi would love him. He'd be dead in a week."

"Caddi might be annoyed, but he'd put up with it to get Trev. Trev fixes radios." Harold gave a short laugh. "Trev should remember how he turned up. Bruised, limping, and hammering on the gate in the night begging for shelter."

"Why?"

"Nobody knows, but the thought of any Barbies nearby scares Trev shitless. Elise turned up in a similar way so Trev should understand her situation."

"Hammering on the gates?" Tessa looked after the lass in question. "She's not very old."

"Not hammering on the gates, but in a bad state and terrified of everything, especially scroats." They drove up towards the entrance where Harold beckoned to Casper, standing with the gate guards.

Casper came up to the truck with his Dobermann cross, Amber, bouncing around on her lead. As Tessa got out he inspected her with a little smile. "Hello Harold. Did you have a lovely time at Caddi's?" Casper's smile widened because he knew all about the usual windups.

Harold climbed out of the cab. "Hi Casper. You know Tessa. Tessa and

Eddie, that bouncy thing is a dog, honest. She's called Amber and likes treats. Any chance of a wheelbarrow for the gear on the back seat, Casper?" Harold looked back at the old caravan park. "How come Elise went out there on her own?"

Casper glowered at the three guards. "I've just been asking the same thing. Elise came up and swore that Trev had said she'd be all right because of the lookouts. I've just explained the difference between a bloke with a machete and Elise with a radio." The guards shuffled their feet a little, looking at the ground as Casper continued. "It won't happen again, because I'll have a chat with the rest as well." He raised his voice. "Is there a wheelbarrow in any of the gardens nearby?" One of the men set off to look.

"Thanks Casper. Don't be too hard on them, because they're fairly new here and won't know about Elise. At least they've volunteered to stand a watch." Harold gestured at the heap on the back seat of the vehicle. "Tessa is here with Eddie because Caddi's agreed she can join us in Orchard Close."

Casper smiled at the pair. "Hi Tessa, Hi Eddie." His smile faltered as he realised exactly what Harold had said. "Caddi's being generous? Did you sell him a pint of your blood or something?"

"You know me, I'm a silver-tongued devil at times." Harold had to get off how he persuaded Caddi because Tessa blushed. "I've organised some more work for Trev, and Caddi wants it done in a hurry."

"We know. Patty had her crossbow with her biggest needle in it earlier, when a pickup truck arrived full of Caddi's maniacs. They handed over a box full of radios and some charcoal, but had some work for you as well." Casper's eyes darted towards Tessa and away.

"Tessa knows about me and guns. Her bloke was Army so her and Sharyn can swap dirt and lies. I was thinking of that end terrace, the two bedroomed one that's just dried out?" Harold broke off to thank the guard for the barrow, and started moving Tessa's gear into it.

"It's dry, but not ready to live in." Casper glanced at the meagre possessions and then Tessa. "Where are you staying tonight? The girl club are already overcrowded, and they're a bit rowdy for a kid."

Harold paused a moment, thinking. "Probably with Sharyn, then Eddie can double up with Wills. I'll take her up there now."

"Okay, I'll get the rest sorted and your truck parked up. The repairs for you are outside your workshop with someone keeping an eye on them." Casper looked a bit harder at Tessa and then Harold. "E-Type seems to be promoted to ET now. He was laughing about women fighting over you?"

"Mercedes, Caddi's assassin? She's been playing, spreading a little happiness around, and I'm her new chew-toy. It's not a problem." Harold picked up the barrow handles. "I'll take these home for now."

The three continued through the gate with the barrow, but Tessa glanced back. "So is Casper your heir, the one who'll take over if necessary? He seems to have it all under control."

"Not Casper, but not because he couldn't. It's just that a lot of the gangsters, and some men and women here for that matter, wouldn't accept it. The likes of Caddi certainly wouldn't. I told you Casper is our resident gay, when you met him at the Mart." Harold laughed at Tessa's second, longer look back.

"I thought that must be a windup, especially when he said he was the Orchard Fairy." Tessa still didn't sound completely convinced. "He's not quite a stereotype gay, is he?"

"I know. A big, muscular bloke and he's not the flamboyant, pink pant-ie type. But if you want a safe pair of hands to put sun cream on your lily-white, Casper's your man."

"I might not want safe." The young woman had relaxed completely as they came through the gates. She seemed a lot more like the Tessa Harold remembered, the laughing girl hanging on Stones's arm and flirting with the other squaddies.

"Careful, I'm a big bad gang boss. You know what we're like at the merest hint of a lily-white."

This time Tessa laughed out loud, startling little Eddie for a moment. She stopped to inspect the building they were approaching, a substantial four bedroomed house at the end of the original Orchard Close. Harold pointed at the house. "Sharyn's in there. Go on in and get the character assassination over with before I get back. I'll bring the rest of your gear." Harold grinned at her and Eddie. "I've got Soldier Boy stuff to sort out."

"Cripes Harold, you don't have to go out and kidnap one." The tall, wiry woman at an upstairs window on the right, one of the girl club hous-es, glanced back behind her. "There's volunteers in here, I'm sure." Orchard Close's heavy metal fiend waved to Tessa. "I'm Liz, the blacksmith. Don't believe that boyish charm or that silver tongue until I've filled you in on the dirty secrets."

Harold seized the chance to wind her up, because Liz liked gossip al-most as much as rock music or beating on hot iron. "Tessa knows more secrets than you do, Liz. Anyway, she's got dirt and lies to swap with Sharyn first."

"Keep out of this, wimp, or I'll be down to beat on you." Liz inspected Tessa, definitely intrigued. "More secrets than me? I'll be waiting."

"Definitely a big bad gang boss." Tessa waved to Liz before turning to Harold. "Thank you Harold, for everything. I can take my gear from here, so you can go and soldier. Come on Eddie." Eddie had been gazing about open-eyed, but from behind his mum's skirt. "Nobody will hurt you, they're all Uncle Harold's soldiers round here." She picked up the barrow handles, setting off for the house with a big smile on her face.

*   *   *

Harold headed off to his gun workshop, where Patty stood guard over the wrapped firearms. "Patty, Caddi's getting greedy eyes over the other direction to us. I'm a bit worried about how big his gang is getting, and I've already signed up more or less any bloke who'll fight. Could you find a few lasses who will use a crossbow, as extra night guards?" Harold pointed to Patty's crossbow. "You're as good with that as any of the blokes and probably better than most. Especially at night?"

Patty looked suspicious at the dig about night vision, a reference to their private joke about Patty Bats, but then her face broke into a smile. "Probably better?" Harold laughed because Patty had to be the best shot with a crossbow here, and possibly in four gangs. She glanced down at the firearms. "So when do I get to learn to shoot one of those?"

"A rifle?" For the first time since Curtis had been injured, Harold seriously considered training another shooter. Patty had asked a couple of times, but Harold thought Emmy and possibly Holly had been targeted because they'd learned to shoot. He didn't want to make anyone else a target, especially a woman, because he already had enough shooters for the big rifles.

Two of them, Emmy and Roy, were lethal at any distance up to six hundred yards and dangerous for a lot further than that. Alfie's accuracy suffered because of his eyesight but he could kill a man at three hundred yards, well outside accurate crossbow range. Along with Harold, who'd learned to shoot in a rifle club long before joining the Army, those three were better than any of the neighbouring gangsters. Harold rethought that, and realised that some gangsters had been fighting long enough to be better than Alfie. Patty as an additional shooter, even with a two-two rifle, could be a big help. If some scroat targeted Patty she could look after herself with either a machete or a pistol.

Better still, Patty seemed a natural shot with a crossbow, so getting her past the basics should be easy. "Okay. Just one of the two-twos for now but that's a good starter rifle. You'll get all the basics and if there's trouble it won't be at long range." Harold smiled and patted a package beside the weapons, then pointed at a wrapped rifle. "I've just scored some extra ammo for those."

Patty curled her lip a little, unwrapping the weapon Harold pointed to just enough to recognise it. "That's a toy, isn't it? They had them in the fairgrounds. They've got no power which is why you shoot the scroats through the eyes."

Harold shook his head, smiling with anticipation. "Come back when the extra guards are sorted and talk. You might change your mind."

"Fair enough. Thanks Harold, I'll sort out a few likely lasses." Patty thought for a few moments. "There are plenty here who were caught and escaped, or escaped just in time. I can think of a dozen women and maybe more who won't hesitate to kill scroats. Where shall I send them?"

"A dozen? Bring them to see me if you find that many, and I'll look them over and decide." Patty nodded, leaving immediately to start canvassing the women. Harold thought about Patty and a rifle, and a dozen women wanting to fight. Perhaps he'd been a bit paranoid over putting women in danger, after realising the bastards had tried to kill Emmy. Nobody else had connected the dots, because they all assumed the bolt that hit Curtis had been aimed at Harold, not Emmy. He'd got worse after Doll nearly died in the Mart massacre just before Christmas. Stupid because he, of all people, knew women really were as dangerous as the men. He'd taught Emmy to shoot a rifle and Patty to use a crossbow, pistol and machete, and either were a match for any gangster.

As he stripped weapons and put them to soak to loosen the crud, Harold wondered what had sparked him to suddenly reassess. Maybe it was that at the Mansion it had never crossed Harold's mind to worry about Mercedes being in danger. Now he'd suddenly realised that Patty might be just as lethal, in her own way. Mercedes had been a shock, a short sharp shock, and thank all and any gods not one that would be repeated.

Harold decided that part of his new outlook could be Tessa. He'd been thinking about what she'd make of Orchard Close, and that meant him reassessing the place as an outsider. With the refugees from the General, and the occasional refugees turned away by the Army, Orchard Close had filled right up. Harold needed more lookouts. Not just lookouts, he could do with a few more people willing to pull the trigger if someone ever attacked the place. All the other gangs had brought a lot more fighters to the Mart fight.

Harold smiled quietly about one definite change, his home life. Tessa would team up with Sharyn and have no qualms about teasing him, because he wasn't Soldier Boy to her. Harry Miller counted as fair game for some winding up, ably aided and abetted by Sharyn. Then Liz, Emmy, Patty, Casper and half a dozen others would chip in with their own comments. Oddly enough, that actually cheered Harold up instead of being a worry. Maybe he'd needed a bit of a jolt.

*   *   *

Once the weapons had been stripped to soak, Harold went home. He'd barely come inside when Patty followed. "Those extra night guards you wanted, Harold. I've found some if you want to check them?"

"If I find them crossbows, will they shoot?" Harold stopped, holding up a hand in mute apology. "Sorry, I asked you to find those who would. I'll see you outside the gun room in what, half an hour?"

"That's plenty of time." Patty headed off to collect the potential recruits.

"Do we need more guards, little brother?" Sharyn looked at Patty's retreating back, a frown on her face. "Is there an extra threat I don't know about?"

"No, but we've grown and so have all the other gangs, or at least their fighter numbers have. They all had a lot more fighters at the last gathering, comments were made, and I don't want anyone getting greedy." Harold sighed at his big sister's expression, she knew he didn't like putting women in danger. "I've also decided I've been too paranoid about teaching women to fight in case they're targeted. After all, Patty is probably the most dangerous woman in four gangs, and more dangerous than most of the men."

"It's about time. After all, Emmy can probably outshoot any of them but you." Now Sharyn looked inquisitive. "Tessa reckons your new girlfriend is dangerous."

"Not a girlfriend. That was a tease, and also a setup by Caddi that has killed four men at least. There won't be a repeat. Where is Tessa anyway?" Harold glanced upstairs, keen to get off the subject of Mercedes. "Is she hiding up there?"

"Not hiding, idiot. She's putting her stuff away and settling little Eddie into Wills's room. Tessa will be sleeping here until her house is fit to live in." Sharyn frowned. "How come Caddi let her leave his territory and come and live here? I would have thought he'd have used her against you, once he found out she's a friend?"

"We made a wager and I won, so he had to let her go." Harold knew he looked smug, but that one had been a real win. "Not happily. That's why he tried to give Mercedes a chance to polish her Killer Queen crown." Even talking about Mercedes had to be better than telling Sharyn he'd bought Tessa to get her free, especially since Tessa hadn't mentioned it. "I'll tell you about the visit this evening."

"Yes, you can explain why you look so tired."

"No mystery, I don't sleep well when visiting Caddi." Especially this last time. "Now I'm off to interview recruits for what Tessa tells me is my army." Harold wondered if explaining later would be better or worse. Tessa would be there this evening.

*　*　*

Harold paused when he saw the crowd waiting for him. "Blimey Patty, you got the full dozen." He looked the women over and chatted to them, and they all seemed keen. Initially he had intended putting an extra person into each existing squad as volunteers turned up, but this worked better.

"So what do you want us to do for you?" Fergie grinned and struck a pose with her chest out. "Since it's not dance night so we're supposed to be good."

Harold grinned back at her, then Patty. "You do what your new squad leader says, she's a real demon." Harold paused for a moment. "A demon knitter I'm told."

Patty looked surprised, then unsure. "Really?" Everyone called her the demon knitter, but now she looked worried.

Harold shrugged, pretending it was no big deal. "We've more women than blokes anyway. The blokes are only in charge of the other three squads because the scroats don't give them as much trouble. It's a tossup if Matthew or Bess is in charge of their guardhouse, number six, and Emmy would have her own squad if it wasn't for breast feeding little Tammy." His smile grew because he knew how Patty would react. "This'll piss off the visitors so you'll get some crap from them?"

Patty's lip curled but the sneer had to fight to get past her smile. "Not much. They all know me." She compromised on a smirk and posed just a little, her hand on her machete. "The Barbies will love it. They'll probably figure I'm butch enough to try to recruit me." They both laughed because Harold knew Patty was heterosexual, even if she didn't practice much. "Hey, does that mean I'll get to keep this when we visit?" She patted her machete and they both laughed again, because Harold didn't take women to visit neighbouring gangs. Even if he did, the gangs would never accept a woman as one of the elite, allowed to keep a weapon in strange territory.

"Go and have a chat to Casper. I'll ring to let him know you're coming and why. He'll explain the system and introduce you officially to the leaders of the other squads." Patty straightened a bit. She already knew the men concerned, but that would be official confirmation of her new status. "Work out with the others where the sentry line can be shortened and thickened, and you can take over a section. Work out shifts with this lot so nobody is on lookout too long." Harold turned to the line of smiling faces and tried to look stern. "Can't have you using it as an excuse for lazing about all day."

Patty chuckled, and so did some of the women. "That's easy. I've got at least twice this many women complaining because you didn't want more sentries." Patty gestured at the dozen women. "Which makes these the first shift."

"Cripes. You can take over a full quarter of the boundary, day and night. That will be a big help. If anyone wants more crossbow practice, sort out time on the targets, will you, please?" Harold laughed at her expression. "Your job now since you recruited them. No good deed goes unpunished."

Patty recovered, throwing a very bad mock salute. "I'll survive. I can knit while I critique." She led her new squad off to find Casper, calling out "left, right, left, right" as they attempted to march and laugh at the same time. Harold stood a few moments, watching them go before going inside to phone Casper. Most women refugees were very subdued when they arrived. They were either abused, relieved to find safety, or just frightened, and definitely not looking for any confrontations. These women looked very keen, raring to go. Maybe they'd been ready to stand up for themselves for a while now. He would have to start new classes in machete fighting, but this time he didn't have to do it all. Given how lethal Patty had been in the last hand to hand fight, she could teach them the basics.

* * *

At dusk Harold made his usual tour of the Orchard Close perimeter wall, checking on the guards. Not a proper brick wall, the barrier filling the gaps between perimeter houses consisted of bricks from demolished ruins, stacked so they interlocked. The low points were already six feet high and three feet wide but they weren't finished. Casper had started building a three-foot-wide firing step along the inside. Harold scrubbed up in the washroom and swapped his boots for slip-ons, otherwise Sharyn would give him hell for tracking oil and mud inside. His stomach muttered appreciation at the lovely smell; the canteen had opened the corned beef.

Sharyn called out from the kitchen as Harold walked in. "Just in time, or we were going to eat yours. It's corned beef hash so we were definitely tempted." Tessa already sat at the table with Eddie, her five-year-old son, Daisy, Harold's nearly seven-year-old niece and his five-year-old nephew Wills. Someone must have let Sharyn know that Soldier Boy had gone to walk the walls. She'd collected tonight's special from the canteen for when he arrived home.

"It's a good job Caddi didn't hear that." Tessa looked across the table and sniggered. "The idiot would think you were getting soft."

"Softer," Sharyn chipped in. Harold rolled his eyes. This pair were going to have such a lot of fun. Sharyn hadn't had someone here to help her tease Harold for too long now, not since Holly died. Hazel had started to join in, just a little, but moved to the girl club when she turned sixteen.

He tried for a scowl. "I might turn nasty if I don't get some food?"

"You're always grumpy when you're tired. I heard that you had an energetic time, and didn't sleep very well?" Sharyn had a bit of a query in her voice.

Harold tried to sound offhand. "Mercedes needed a new chew toy, and it's me."

The wide eyes weren't even slightly shocked, just having fun. "Ooh, did she bite you? Where?"

Deciding that his big sister didn't need to know what Mercedes had bitten, the pillow, Harold sat down and relaxed. "Not yet. Hopefully never because I've been treated and survived. I'm starting to wonder if I made a mistake putting you two together, because this could be more dangerous."

"I'll need a knife in my boot like her, if I'm going to be…" Tessa stopped and glanced at Sharyn, then the kids.

Sharyn shook her head with a sad smile. "I told you, soft lad doesn't have a woman and you'll get your own place."

"What about tonight, Sharyn? Eddie is doubling up with Wills but there's only four rooms up there. You won't want me sharing your bed every night until the place is ready." Tessa stopped at the worried expression on Sharyn's face when she looked at Harold.

Harold took a deep breath. It was time to let go. "You can use the fourth bedroom, because nobody sleeps in there." He pointed at the study door. "That's my bedroom."

Sharyn looked startled. "Are you sure?" The fourth bedroom had been Holly and Harold's room. Hazel had slept in there for a while after Holly died, but only until she was sixteen. Harold never moved back in.

"Yes sis, I'm sure. I'll feel safer knowing Tessa is safely tucked away up there, instead of lurking out here on the sofa." That worked because both women smiled.

Tessa got in first. "I might sleepwalk, wander down and then, well, one door looks much like another?"

"Harold's door has four padlocks, a thumbprint reader, and probably a grenade strapped to the doorknob. Apart from when I take a hoover and a duster in there, no woman has passed through the doorway." Sharyn laughed, because that had been a bitter-sweet joke between them. Now, with the fourth bedroom in use, the sting had gone.

"But surely?" Tessa looked at the kids, busily eating but paying close attention. "Later."

"Maybe." Harold smiled, concentrating on his corned beef hash.

* * *

Later came after Harold had read a bedtime Wills-story, and then two Daisy-stories to make up for being away last night. When Tessa finally got her chance, it wasn't how Harold arranged his love life that bothered her most. Now she'd had time to think, Tessa had started worrying about how she paid her way. The Hot Rods charged anyone living in the area. They claimed rent for the housing, and an additional sum to protect residents from roaming gangsters. If the residents grew extra food, or employed their old skills to earn a few coupons, those were heavily 'taxed' as well.

It came as a big relief to find out there'd be no rent, just a fixed sum paid to the Coven, the committee that ran the finances in Orchard Close. That would cover Tessa's share of the balanced diet provided by the canteen, and services such as schooling for Eddie. Tessa, along with every other able-bodied person without a skill, would earn the rest of her food by working four hours a day gardening, scavenging, building walls or something similar. Those with specific skills paid ADT, Asshole Deterrent Tax, instead of working in the fields.

If anyone wanted something different to the day's menu, they had to buy it with their own coupons, the same as with clothing and luxuries such as coffee or chocolate powder. Harold had no idea of the actual sums, claiming he had enough problems already. After some discussion with Sharyn, Tessa looked relieved because she'd end up keeping a lot more of her coupons, the ones issued by the government instead of money. She'd be expected to pay for cleaning materials, and extra bedding and curtains for her new accommodation, but she'd be given time to pay. The Coven only charged enough to replace whatever was used, and didn't charge interest.

Tessa wanted to know exactly what ADT consisted of, quickly finding out it was Harold's main job. "All the tradespeople pay a cut of their profits, the ADT, Asshole Deterrent Tax. Rob charges extra if he goes to fix the toilets for the GOFS, for instance. I organise his security and Orchard Close takes a cut."

"It's like a military operation." Sharyn stopped and laughed. "It is a military operation I suppose. An old style one with hostages given and held against the safe return of the expert. Lots of grim types with machetes and scowls. The expert is allowed to take an armed man in with him so there's no quick snatch."

Harold pointed up at the light fitting. "The gangs put up with it, because they sometimes need a real professional. They have to come to Orchard Close to keep the lights burning."

"How come you've got so many experts?" Tessa looked up at the light, intrigued. "The guards were moaning about it before you visited, about how you had the only decent beer, knitting, stew and burgers."

"The stew is because we grow most of our veg, so we don't have to be mean with them, and we've got our giant bunnies. Our brewers are the real deal, we rescued them and all their gear just after the Crash. Harold reckons there are other tradespeople out there, but they keep quiet because the gangs treat them as slaves. That means the likes of Caddi have to pay us." Sharyn smirked, because she liked that part. "Here anyone with a skill keeps what they earn, apart from ADT to cover the security and the negotiating. Guess what, everyone here wants to learn a trade!"

"ADT also covers those on guard searching anyone coming in for weapons, and dealing with trouble." Harold scowled because the searching wasn't easy. "We take most weapons off the visitors, but they're allowed a knife. They don't start serious trouble, because a crossbow trumps a knife."

"Or a stick." Tessa turned to Sharyn. "Is it true? Do they really think soft lad is SAS?"

"Yes, but he's done a couple of things that mean he isn't soft lad any more. The sort of things we were all grateful for." Sharyn glanced at Harold's gently shaking head and dropped the subject. Tessa would get it out of Sharyn once they were alone, but Harold wasn't proud of some of the things he'd done to back the gangs off.

"Then you can tell me who or what a Coven is. Have we got witches here?" Tessa looked around, eyes wide with mischief. "Do I get to dance around nekkid in the moonlight?"

Harold shook his head. "No, you twerp. It's what I call the women who run the place. They make out the shopping lists, and organise the cooking and gardening, that sort of thing. Sharyn is the head witch." Harold smiled at his sister, teasing her for a change.

"He started the witch thing, then some idiot actually gave me a black cat called Grimalkin. The reason I'm head of the committee is because I'm Soldier Boy's sister. Most of the scroats that trade with us used to insist on dealing with me. They wouldn't respect a woman unless she had a big strong man waiting to leap in if trouble started. If he'd just get a woman..." She hesitated, darting a glance at Tessa. "Er. Not like that." Sharyn sighed, then suddenly smiled. "Not now. The gangsters have to deal with other witches like Emmy, Liz, June, Gayle the dentist and Susan, Rob's partner. Patty always sold her own knitting from day one."

"Patty never needed anyone to back her up, though she might not have time for the Coven now. She's got her own squad," Harold quickly explained.

Tessa didn't see a problem. "She's a woman so she can multi-task. So what else do you sell? I'd like to earn extra coupons because of Eddie, but I can't fix electrics and I'm hopeless at gardening or knitting. I'm used to being short, because Caddi took almost everything, but I'm not a fan. I kept very, very quiet about my extra Army coupons, or the arse would have taken them as well." Her voice sobered now, talking about life under the Hot Rods. "We daren't even grow too much veg, or the Hot Rods would come and take some."

Harold kept his voice cheery, trying to pull Tessa out of her memories. "Most of your coupons are yours now, including the Army ones, and you can earn more because our tradespeople are always after apprentices. You won't have a garden because it all belongs to Emmy's farm, which supplies us all." Harold laughed at the next bit. "There's jobs in the kitchen because our beer, burgers and stew really are famous. Big Mack does a great job of advertising."

"We let gangsters eat in the canteen if we've got enough surplus to sell, and even supply takeaway as long as they bring their own containers. I sometimes serve in there to keep them polite." Sharyn bared her teeth and tapped them. "There's other benefits to living here. Gayle is a dental trainee so she can give anaesthetics as well as fix teeth. We've got Lenny, who was a paramedic, and Patricia who was a trainee nurse, so medical care is free for residents. Lenny is a lot better than anyone except the Barbie doctor for gang fight wounds." This time her laugh had some malice. "The gangs pay his truly eye-watering prices because we let the patients go home again. Barbies don't."

As Sharyn paused, Harold picked it up. "Kerry always wants more embroidery and sewing trainees. Patty is the knitting demon, and has imps in training. She designs patterns, logos, even names into knitted jumpers and scarves. Balaclavas with camouflage patterns are popular so the gangs can play at being SAS." Everyone laughed, because all three knew the real thing. Harold gestured through towards the hall. "Bright colours like those are popular, now that the Marts only sell earth tones and puce green. We've got a room half full of different sorts of wool." He rolled his eyes. "It's a status thing for Caddi to wear a hand knitted Arran or Cable Knit jumper, or for Cooper to wear a bobble hat in Hot Rod colours. Bloody crazy."

Tessa looked a bit overwhelmed. "So you buy and sell anything?"

"No drugs!" Sharyn and Harold answered together.

Harold continued. "We won't sell people either, and prefer not to buy them. I've only bought two and they were youngsters. Soft lad, guilty as charged."

"It was Jilli's lucky day when those scroats offered to sell her." Sharyn scowled, but not at Tessa. "Jilli is fifteen now. She was a skinny thirteen back then, too skinny for horny gangsters. She sings like an angel, and can get a tune out of two pans and a taut washing line."

Harold nodded, because Sharyn wasn't exaggerating by much. "Close. Jilli will never have trouble earning her way, because there's no new or live music on the radio. Nor any rock, pop or protest now Barbie radio has stopped."

"That was mostly heavy rock anyway. Except Valentine's Day and now and then when they felt the lurve." The Barbie idea of lurve could include some odd choices.

"Jilli spent years at a music school and can play any tune she hears. If I could get the music and words, and blank CDs, we'd be paid real coupons for recordings. Her songs would fetch even more if I could get more than a guitar and maybe some music scores. The Barbies have got both, a shop full, allegedly." Harold chuckled, with just a little smug in it. "That's where the guitar came from. I insisted that was the payment when they needed electrical work."

"So why haven't they traded the rest?" A lot of people had asked Tessa's question about the goodies in Beth's, the shopping centre that became the Barbie stronghold. Rumoured goodies, because nobody but the Barbies ever came back out once they went inside.

"The bitches don't need anything enough." Sharyn scowled because she missed her music.

"Except to get Barbie Radio fixed. That's a big commercial transmitter so they need a real expert. Their bloke is dead, but I'm not letting Trev have a look. They'd never let him out again." Harold's rueful smile admitted the other problem. "That's if I could get him in there. He'd pass out first."

"What does it need?" Tessa shrugged, smiling a little. "Not technically, but couldn't they buy instructions?"

Now Harold scowled, because the answer annoyed him. "If any of the crazy bitches would slow up enough to ask, I'd try and find out. What they'd like is to steal Trev, so negotiations aren't easy."

"Bloody radio. Bastards." Sharyn meant the BBC now. The music on the BBC didn't include any protest songs, or even tunes considered slightly anti-establishment. Most pop and even many love songs apparently fell into the banned categories. "I swear there's nothing that was made after 1940. If then."

* * *

Eventually they finished their drinks and went to bed. Tessa paused on the stairs to inspect Harold's bedroom door. "I reckon I could open that, so you'd better sleep lightly." She grinned before heading upstairs to the spare bedroom.

Harold didn't get to sleep straight away, but not because he expected Tessa to break in, nor because he missed Mercedes and her hand roaming around the bed. The evening talk, with a new perspective on Orchard Close, had churned his thoughts up again. Harold had been sheltered from the worst effects pre-Crash, until the Army brought him home. The speed that all organisation collapsed, and the mindless violence, still baffled him.

The Marts bugged Harold. The TV said that civilisation had collapsed, all around the world, but the new clothes, electrical gear and computer games had to be made somewhere. Unless, which always gave Harold a chill, there really weren't many people left so the stockpiles were lasting. It didn't take much infrastructure to design new games and make lots of copies of them, or put bar codes and different labels on clothes and electrical items.

*   *   *

Harold's head went round and round until he finally slept. He slept too well and had to be woken up. That led to merciless teasing over breakfast about his sleepless night with Mercedes. Sharyn immediately took over sorting out her new ally's house, but it would be a few days before Tessa moved. As Harold had expected, a lot of others living in Orchard Close pitched in to help. They understood, because many had arrived with even less than Tessa.

Harold didn't have time to worry about fixing one house. Finn and Charlie now had a list and some sort of master plan for generating electricity. That meant scavenging plenty of pipe fittings, some other bits of plastic, and any copper wire of any thickness anyone could find. Harold organised parties for collecting, and teams to strip the covering from what would probably be miles of wire. After consulting with the electrical experts, Liz took drawings, wire and steel away to her forge.

Useless bits of electrical equipment, usually left out in the ruins, now had to be dismantled for a list of pieces. Quite a few components had to be explained, with examples or sketches where possible, since the names meant nothing to the scavengers. If in doubt the scavengers were to bring

the whole item. Fortunately, Orchard Close scavengers were used to working to a list now, trusting the experts to make something useful of whatever they brought back. The collecting and wire stripping would be a slow
process, because Emmy and her gnomes were into farming mode. Anyone
even pausing for a moment found themselves commandeered for working
in the fields.

Once he'd got the teams moving, Harold headed off to get on with his
own work, firearms repairs. Patty waited for him at the gun room. "With
that big heap of guns to fix, I knew you'd be coming here as soon as possible. Did you mean it about me learning to shoot a rifle?" She frowned,
thinking about that. "You haven't taught anyone since Holly died, have
you?"

"It's actually since we lost Curtis, except when I gave Roy some tips.
The crossbow bolt that hit Curtis should have hit Emmy. I reckon someone tried to thin out our shooters, and I didn't want to set anyone else
up as a target." Harold sighed, then fixed Patty with a stern look. "Don't
tell Emmy, she still thinks they were trying for me." He continued with a
wry smile. "Now, after seeing how the Hot Rods step around Mercedes, it
crossed my mind you are at least as dangerous. Or you could be if I get over
my hang-ups." Harold's smile became a chuckle as something occurred to
him. "You've even got similar rules about touching. So yes, you will learn
to shoot a rifle. The two-two."

Patty pouted, not her usual look. "I still think it's a toy gun, not dangerous until I can hit their eyes."

"I used to do that, but only because I didn't know how well the rounds
would penetrate. The new ones will make a hole in a skull up to a hundred
yards away, then rattle around in there like a pea in a can." Harold offered
her a two-two rifle. "Dangerous enough for you?"

"That's why you still carry it! We all wondered why you always have
that one of yours handy-like when there might be trouble. It doesn't look
up to the job and I know the scroats don't rate it." Patty had a gleam in her
eye as she took the rifle and inspected it. An underrated weapon that would
kill them at a hundred yards, she wanted some of that.

"That's the idea. Their two-twos won't do the same, so you keep very,
very quiet about ours." Harold didn't smile this time.

Patty sobered, quickly. "Done. When do I start?"

Harold pointed at the steel and wire contraption slung on her back.
"You already have, with that great big crossbow. Recoil or weight won't be a

problem after using that, while aiming a rifle is easier because it has sights. Unlike the crossbow there'll be no appreciable drop at fifty yards, so that'll take getting used to. What you need is practice at loading. The faster you can do that, the more times you shoot when the time comes. It'll be a lot faster than your crossbow."

"I don't care if mine is a bit slower than most." Patty reached back to tap her heavy, crude crossbow. "The original pre-Crash versions are lighter and faster than this but not as powerful, and I'm always terrified they'll finally break." She didn't add that hers was a relic, an early experiment the Geeks built too heavy. Patty kept it because of the sheer power, more than the perfected, lighter versions had.

Harold nodded in reply. "For one shot, up to fifty yards and using Liz's points, that crossbow is possibly more dangerous than a rifle. Even so, the Geeks rely on firearms to keep their neighbours at bay, not their crossbows or Tell's archers. Firearms hit faster and further and a lot more accurately." He bowed her inside. "Enter my lair, fair maid, though you already know your way. The workshop is too crowded so we'll have to go someplace else for you to learn the basics." He nudged her gently. "We could use the bedroom here? It'll be safe if I don't shower first?"

Despite smiling at the reference to one certain night, and a shared shower, Patty shook her head. "You'll be safe anyway, because I've got a new boyfriend." She stroked the rifle. "I'd rather keep the training private so nobody knows about him. Not until we kill the first totally surprised scroat."

Harold knew Patty liked surprising her victims. She always carried her handguns out of sight, so the gangsters thought she relied on her crossbow. "This part will be boring. Sit there for a few minutes while I make up five duds to practice loading and firing." As Harold worked he explained about the sights and Patty had a look through them. "I'll paint these rounds blue. While that dries we'll sort out the sling."

"Why?" Patty slung the rifle over her shoulder. "That's good enough."

Harold took the rifle off her. He put his arm through the sling and wrapped his wrist around to brace his hand against the rifle, holding it one-handed but locked in place. "This sling is right for me. Held like this you won't have to worry about the barrel wobbling all over. Come on, we'll need a bit of room so I'll adjust it for you in the bedroom."

"Where have I heard that before?" Despite the joking, Patty stayed absolutely serious about the rifle training part. After some experimentation the sling fitted her perfectly.

Harold moved on to showing her how to load and operate the weapon, slowly. After that he did so with his eyes closed, quickly pulling the trigger, reloading and pulling again through all five duds. "You have to learn to do that."

"With my eyes shut?" Patty frowned, looking at the blue rounds on the floor and back to the rifle. "Are you taking the piss? Like with apprentices?"

"No. If you're watching the scroats diving in and out of cover, or fighting in the dark, this part has to be totally automatic. No thought, all your concentration stays on the target." Harold moved on to the peep sight, explaining how that worked.

"Fair enough, but learning the eyes-closed thing will take hours. I'll be spending all my time in here." Patty looked round the small bedroom. "People might talk, especially since you've already got two women."

"Take the rifle home. I'd better not visit to see how you're getting on, or the rumour mill will have a field day." Harold steered clear of the two woman dig; the Orchard Close gossip mill seemed to be alive and well.

Patty laughed, stroking the rifle. "You are coming home with me, big boy. Well, not big, but I like your style, and I promise to be gentle." Her eyes went back to Harold. "When do I get to shoot something?"

"When I test one. You know the drill. I take them out into the rubble, usually at night, and only fire a few times so neither the Army or the neighbours get nosy." Patty pulled a little face because that could mean long, slow weeks to get any real practice. Harold pointed at the wrapped weapons. "I've just taken in all these repairs, and you've already seen that one of them is a two-two." Her face brightened with anticipation. "So the sooner you can load in the dark?"

"I'll nip home for a coat, because if I wear your dressing gown to hide this?" Her eyes widened, crinkling a little with humour. "If you teach Doll to shoot a rifle, she might not have my willpower once you're in that bedroom."

"Doll isn't up to either learning to shoot or bedrooms yet, so scat." Harold went back to repairs, breaking off to run through the training again when Patty called back wearing a long coat. Rifles and shotguns had to be kept hidden, or the Army would shoot the owner. When she'd gone, he thought about Doll, and Patty had a point. Not about the bedroom, but about teaching her to shoot a rifle. He could give Doll a squad for starters, then assess her for rifle training. The exuberant blonde did well in her machete training and had already killed up close and personal with both a pistol and a machete, which made her another obvious candidate. Now that he'd got past his hang-ups, Harold thought of several other women who only needed a bit more training to become lethal surprises.

Chapter 5:
Training and Tweaking

Four days after delivering the radios and firearms, ET arrived to see if any of them were repaired because Caddi wanted them quickly. Harold stared at what ET brought with him, perplexed. "You can't pay with those. Well, you can, but you'll not get much credit." The Hot Rods were bringing boxes full of empty bottles and containers with screw tops up from their vehicles. "Cripes, I didn't think you'd got that many to spare." The brewers in Orchard Close were always on the lookout for sealable bottles, because constant breakages and none for sale in the Marts had led to a real shortage.

"We want you to fill all the empties with beer, not buy them. There's a lot of them because we've nearly run out of home brew. Our last batch isn't fit to drink. Even these drunkards won't touch it." ET scowled but perked up again. "Your beer is the best around here, so having to buy it is a win."

"Too true. Berry Beer rules!" The gangster carrying a big box full of empty bottles grinned. The other two with him nodded, making jokes about what berries might be in the booze.

Harold smiled back. "You're in a good mood today?" ET was, he'd been laughing and cracking jokes with his men as they drew up.

ET let the others get a bit ahead. "I owe you a favour, Soldier Boy. Two actually. When you and Mercedes wound Bug up and chopped him down, I got promoted into the top group. I'm officially ET instead of E-Type now."

"Congratulations, I think. What's the second favour?"

"Ah, right." ET spoke more cautiously. "You know the girl Caddi forced into your bed? The one who offered to be spanked?" Harold needed the clarification; Caddi had put women in his bed more than once.

Harold scowled at him. "Yes. I noticed you'd taken her."

"Hey, I asked her, there's a difference. She's a lot happier than staying with Caddi or in the brothel. I look after her properly." ET smiled happily.

"That's the other favour, whatever you said to Caddi. He let her go after that because he didn't want to use her to wind you up again. That lot call her Spanky, but she just laughs at them. Better still, they all leave her alone."

"Hasn't she got a real name?" Harold suddenly felt a lot better because Caddi had got the message. All it had taken was suggesting the next person who tried to force a girl into Harold's bed could end up crippled.

"That's private. Christ, what does it matter?" ET sped up to catch the rest at the gate. The Hot Rod kept his machete under the evolving rules, but his men gave up everything but a knife after a quick search. The shotgun and crossbows up in the guardhouse windows reminded them to be good. "Can we get a beer while that lot is being filled?" ET nodded at the containers being carried away for filling. The brewery and beer stocks were kept well outside the area gangsters could visit.

"Have you got any stew on the go? With chips?" One of the Hot Rods looked towards the canteen. "Or a burger, a real rabbit burger? Caddi still reckons we haven't got enough rabbits to start eating them." Harold didn't have chance to answer.

"Is Doll there?" This gangster waved his phone, no doubt hoping for a picture.

"There's always stew or soup, and probably chips. Come on, we'll ask about burgers. Doll is resting at the moment." Doll would be practicing with her machete, building back her muscle and speed for if she ended up fighting Hot Rods. She wasn't happy about losing her fighting edge while recovering from being lungshot. Harold led them to the canteen where all four promptly ordered a beer. ET didn't pay for his first one, another perk of being promoted to a top ranked visitor. The three Hot Rods soldiers had stew, fresh bread and a plate of chips each. They flirted with the waitress and the women eating there but kept their language clean, restricting themselves to cheeky, barely suggestive. That didn't come easily to the young men, but they seemed to enjoy the challenge, or maybe the novelty.

Sharyn and Tessa served them today, both laughing at the comments. Tessa's clothing surprised Harold, because she had worn plain and baggy whenever he saw her at the Mart. Now Tessa wore a knee-length skirt, a pretty blouse, a bit of lippy and a big smile, and looked her real age of twenty-five instead of five or six years older. She seemed to have found her niche. Harold knew that Sharyn served gangsters because they all minded their manners around Soldier Boy's sister. He suddenly realised the Hot Rods were treating Tessa with the same caution. He fervently hoped she didn't realise she'd been tagged as Soldier Boy's woman.

Harold explained the work done on the gun and radio repairs, and the cost, privately, while waiting for the beer. By the time ET handed over the batteries, and counted out coupons to make up the balance, filled beer bottles were arriving back at the gate. Seth, Nigel and Berry, the brewers, didn't take long filling the bottles and containers, but eight people had to wheel them back to ET. A lot more coupons changed hands, but Harold ran every one through his scanner. The little gadget checked that the thumbprint printed on each one when the government bus issued them matched the ink thumbprint applied later. The system meant stolen coupons were worthless, only the original recipient's thumbprint could authorise them. These coupons were authorised by tenants paying Caddi for protection. "Hey, we won't cheat you."

"One of your gang tried it with Patty. We check everyone's now in case there's a duff thumbprint. I don't want to be dragged off to a work camp for using one at the Mart." Harold pointed at the scanner. "That's why the Marts sell these things, to stop someone setting up a rival. Rumour has it a couple of gang wars were settled like that." He stacked the coupons. "Spot on. You can borrow the barrows to help carry that lot down to your motors."

"That's handy." ET hesitated, looking hopeful. "We could use them to take some spuds down there as well?"

"Spuds?"

"Yeah, the frost got to ours so chips have been rationed. The fighters aren't happy." The three Hot Rods definitely looked happier at the mention of buying spuds. They'd all bought extra chips in the canteen.

"They're old potatoes because none of this year's crop is ready yet." Harold fought back a big grin. "Worse, all veggies are Emmy's children. You've got to persuade her you'll treat them right, then pay her prices." He wanted Emmy involved so he didn't sell spuds she needed for growing this years' crop.

"Hah, your veg are never cheap but they're better than the crap in the Mart. Half the spuds there are mouldy." The other Hot Rods echoed ET's scowl. "We did buy some, and I swear the rats had been at them. Your dogs and cats must be better guards than the blokes with rifles at the Marts."

"Maybe our guards know they've got to eat the veg, so they're a bit keener." Harold sent a request for Emmy to negotiate for potatoes, and for garden gnomes to collect them. He enjoyed the next bit because Emmy didn't let go of her veggies without persuasion, expensive persuasion.

While the gardeners filled the barrow and Emmy counted coupons, ET had more news. "Your visit must have fired Mercedes up. We reckon she's frustrated at not getting to kill you, because she's taken another three pairs of ears, sentry ears. She opened a gap and we were in before the Murphies woke up to it. We got another two streets for sod all fighting. Caddi might invite you over before the next push to get her fired up again." ET went down the access road with seven fixed radios and the repaired shotgun, still chuckling at the idea.

Harold wasn't chuckling, because Emmy wanted details about this Mercedes and how Harold had fired her up or frustrated her. From her expression, Emmy already had some gossip, but wanted sordid details to swap with Liz. She sobered when Harold explained the importance of two streets. They'd be two inhabited streets, so the area of ruins around them had also fallen to Caddi's men.

$$*\quad*\quad*$$

Despite Caddi wanting the rest of his guns as soon as possible, Harold set aside some time to teach machete fighting to the new recruits. The trainees included Bethany, Fergie and Tilly, who had already had some practice, as well as several young women he'd never seen much of before now. "We've joined Patty's new squad because of the perks." Fergie wore a big smirk. "We heard there's hand to hand involved, and were hoping you were instructing."

"Naughty. You already had extra personal training at Christmas." Harold turned to the rest. "This is deadly serious even if we're using wooden machetes and sticks. They'll raise a nasty bruise if you don't pay attention." He smiled at the apprehensive faces. "If you find someone to kiss the bruises better, that might include some hand to hand."

"Will we all learn to shoot? Patty says we're her apprentices but she only uses a crossbow. I want a pistol." Bethany pointed to her Gnome hat, folded to hide the first 'Gnome' so it only showed 'Sweet Gnome' again. "I'll need a new hat if I qualify, one saying Demon."

"Not Sweet Demon?" Harold didn't mention Patty usually carrying up to three hidden handguns.

"Yes!" Bethany high-fived the others. "Told you he'd call me Sweet."

"You'll call me something else soon, after the first practice." Harold lined everyone up, and started them on the exercises he'd developed from his first experimental lessons. Once the dozen women and two men had wooden machetes in one hand and a stick in the other, all the joking stopped. Every one of them wanted to be as dangerous as possible.

By the time they'd done, their enthusiasm had been dented a bit. "Ooh, when do I get to actually fight?" Bethany rubbed her arm where her muscles were complaining. "I can stand some pain if I'm dishing some out, but I haven't hit anyone yet. Worse still, Fergie had that private practice so she's better than us."

"You can try sparring with me next time, then you'll feel foolish and want to concentrate on exercises for a week. This makes you suppler, and works the right muscles. Cutting browse for the bunnies helps?" Harold smiled at the sceptical looks. "You and Tilly are Gnomes so you shouldn't mind the extra exercise."

"Since my sore muscles are sweet ones, how about some of that slow hand stuff we've heard rumours about?" Bethany grinned and waggled her eyebrows.

"Scat, or I'll tell Emmy you've been skiving instead of gnoming." Harold watched them going down the road in a laughing, jostling group. He wondered how many of them would be mentally capable of hacking a human being, because nobody could be certain until the moment arrived. He set off to find someone who was very capable of killing close-up, to teach her how to kill long-range.

Harold caught Patty on her way to check on her squad, or those currently on guard. "I'm going to test a rifle and an experimental weapon. If you go and get your two-two you can be my guard. We'll see if you can hit anything with it." Patty's eyes lit up, and she took off like a whippet to collect the weapon.

By the time Patty and her rifle arrived at the gun workshop, Harold had collected the other two weapons. "I'll be firing the repaired two-two, but you'll use that one and also watch my back."

"No problem." Patty hesitated, looking down at her rifle. "Except I've only got duds for loading practice?"

"That's why I brought you some real ammo. These are for close up." Harold gave her a box of rounds and two pouches to fit on her belt. "One pouch is to collect your empty brass, so I can reload it. Sew some loops into a belt sometime, to hold a few rounds for easier access. You'll be using those for practice firing as well." He passed her five rounds stuck in a drilled block of wood. "Keep these separate."

Patty looked at the five rounds with a little red dot on the end of the brass. "What's the red dot mean?"

"Migraines." Harold tapped his forehead and Patty smiled, a really evil one. "Aim between their eyes. Goodnight asshole because those have a hardened steel core. The rest are just lead but will work well enough close-up, in their chest or gut. If you get good enough, then you can be very dangerous with those at longer ranges."

Patty nodded eagerly. "How many shots do I get?"

"It depends on the repaired one. I'm more or less sure the sights are right now, but I'll probably have to adjust some more. I'll take a shot to check. If that tells me what I need to know, you take a couple with your rifle. You've been practicing with the sights?" Harold laughed at the look on Patty's face.

"Do fish swim? I've been seeing my dreams through peep sights. Little dot on a stick in the middle of the fuzzy circle, not wandering about, smack in the middle and still. It seems a bit more basic than the scopes on the scavenged crossbows, the modern ones?" Patty had moved onto one of her favourite gripes. "I have to admit it's a bloody sight better than what's on the new crossbows, even the Geek ones."

"I showed you the old targets from the rifle club. Even the two cross-bows with telescopic sights can't score bulls on those, but peep sights and that little rifle can. When you're done we'll test this as well." Harold showed her the other weapon.

Patty hurriedly inspected the single barrelled shotgun, almost hopping up and down with impatience. "What's different about this one then?"

"This is an experiment so we'll move elsewhere and risk another three shots. If it works then the less shots the better. There's a copper tube in there so .38 pistol rounds fit, and I don't want to wear it out." Harold re-alised Patty wasn't really paying attention, she wanted to go shooting. "I'll explain when we get back." Patty nodded and headed for the door.

*　*　*

Harold took them over the rubble to a ruin with a good view down a deserted road, out of sight of Orchard Close and the Army. The remaining walls would muffled the sound a bit and conceal some of the flash. The test showed the rifle needed more work, but not too much. Harold never made the guns he repaired for other gangs truly accurate. The weapon might be aimed at him one day.

Patty's first attempt went off into the ruins someplace, or maybe into orbit. "Cripes, cripes, cripes." Patty unwound the sling from her arm.

"Calm down. You can see the target?"

"Yes, but…."

"You can see that little stick and dot?" Harold spoke calmly and quietly, because he knew exactly what her problem was.

"Yes, but the bloody thing is jumping about! It must be because we're outdoors, or do real rounds weigh more or something?"

Harold laughed quietly and shook his head. "No. Your arm is jumping about like a demented frog because your nerves are making it twitch. Buck fever. The sheer excitement."

"It's all this sneaking about. That and I'm probably the third woman to learn how to shoot properly since the Crash." Patty looked and sounded dejected. "Maybe I'm just crap with a rifle."

"You didn't shoot your own foot or the instructor, and both have been done. Half the problem is we've snuck off with one ear open for a helicopter or some nutter, so we're both nervous. Calm down. I'll bet a lot of the Barbies have used a gun since setting up in Beth's, some of them for the first time." Harold put a hand on her shoulder and Patty jumped. "Sorry."

"It's all right. I think you just made the point about nerves. It's just that, well, it's a rifle! Three years ago I'd never seen one or heard one except on TV." Patty produced a magnificent sneer. "Barbies? None of them were ever trained, proper Army training, by an honest to God soldier. Cripes! Now I feel a complete prat."

"The Army didn't train me. I learned in a rifle club with one of these, a two-two. That's why I can shoot the thing in my sleep." Harold smiled at Patty's puzzled expression. "The Army had to break me of going for the bolt after every shot, but I could always hit the targets. It pissed off the instructors because I wouldn't go for sniper."

Curiosity replaced annoyance in Patty's voice. "Why not?"

"I didn't like the idea of killing people, especially without giving them a chance." Harold didn't usually tell anyone about it, but the talking was calming Patty down. She'd find this funny and relax even more.

"Are you taking the piss?" Patty sounded suspicious, which was fair. Harold kept telling the trainees to stick an arrow in the bastards from behind cover, in the back if possible.

"No. I had to reassess." Harold's sombre answer echoed memories of what he'd gone through to learn his lesson. "Not only that, but there seems to be a lot of people around these days who really do need killing."

"Too true there are." Patty tapped the rifle and nudged him. "Cheer up. This will help."

"Oh yes. Now, if you've calmed down a bit, wrap the sling round your arm again. Take it steady, make sure you do it properly." Patty did as she was told. "Now let go with your other hand." The rifle stayed rock steady, held firmly. "Perfect, which proves it isn't the wind or the bullet weight or anything else, just your nerves. Now imagine the rifle is your crossbow. That target is some gangster sneaking over the wall after Elise, or Jilli."

"Got it."

Harold saw the set of Patty's shoulders. "Gently, relax, you don't want the bastard to get away. Just get the dot settled in, on that white square right in the centre of his body mass. Take up the pressure and breathe gently and then, when you're ready, just…" The crack made Patty jump but the target jerked and twisted a bit.

"Gottim!" Patty gave a short nervous laugh. "It surprised me when the rifle went off!"

"It's supposed to, unless you know the rifle really, really well." Harold clapped her on the shoulder, gently. "Well done, you can shoot. Now there's just practice and confidence so you can do it further and further away. After that you learn about wind and uphill and leading a moving target, but this is the hard part."

"How much practice?"

Harold could hear the eagerness in her voice. "As much as we can. I'll take you out as my bodyguard some of the time, so you can take an occasional shot where nobody can see."

"Bodyguard?" A little smile played over Patty's lips, unsure if Harold was winding her up.

"You're lethal with that crossbow, and for one close-up shot, a Liz special is more dangerous than that rifle." Harold smiled happily at his next thought. "Just hearing about it will piss off the Hot Rods and the Geeks, while half the Barbies will be over to buy you a beer. Now come on, take another shot to prove it wasn't a fluke. We'll move after that, just in case someone is nosy."

Patty took her third shot, not answering until she was picking up her empty brass. "The Barbies will try to kidnap me if they find out I can shoot a rifle. They already make me some interesting offers if I'll wear fewer clothes and more weapons. Now let's go and look at my target."

She hopped about like a demented flea once she saw the target. Harold also inspected the two little holes, almost in the middle of the wooden square. Even shooting at more or less point blank range, they showed promise. Now he assessed Patty properly as a bodyguard, someone to help him in a tight spot.

Patty would definitely kill close-up in a fight with pistol or blade. Now she seemed to be a natural shooter, one of those people who had an eye for it. Harold had always thought Patty might also kill in cold blood. She'd stuck a crossbow bolt in a Mart guard who'd upset her, ambushed him even if it wasn't quite cold-blooded. Just now Patty had firmed up nicely when thinking of the target as a person, the opposite to the usual reaction.

A female bodyguard would be a definite statement about women's status in Orchard Close. Better yet, Patty looked slight, but all the practice with her heavy crossbow left her wiry and strong. The gangsters would underestimate her in a physical fight. With that in mind, Harold might experiment. If Liz could make one of the usual machetes slimmer, with a long point on the end, Harold could teach Patty a whole new way to kill a scroat.

Harold found a spot to test the adapted shotgun, moving carefully in case some asshole had been attracted by the shots. That didn't happen often these days, most of the roaming loners were dead. When he fired, the .38 sounded like a cannon. Patty whistled quietly at the size of the hole in the last of three interior doors stacked one behind the other. "Soft lead expands quickly," Harold explained. "It'll do that inside a person as well."

"How big a hole does this rifle make?" Patty would be remembering the neat little holes in her own target.

"The hardened ones split into a steel core and lead surround after they hit anything solid, bad news for the recipient. Just soft lead will expand a surprising amount, even in flesh. In a person they might hit a bone and break up as well. Then even if the target gets away?" Harold shrugged. "With the state of medicine now they'll probably die."

"Good. Wouldn't want to waste a round."

Harold took note. Patty might have too little hesitation about shooting, she might not wait for the kill shot. "If you have to shoot, then killing the target quickly stops them shooting back." Harold looked at the hole in the doors again. "That's good enough because this isn't a precision weapon." He reached out and tapped 'her' rifle. "So you'd better have another couple of shots. Remember, keep calm."

This time Patty had got the message and relaxed, but she tried to speed up the reload. Harold stopped the aspiring markswoman. "No. Slow and accurate kills one every shot. When you hit that square dead centre every time at fifty yards, we'll work on speed." She took a deep breath, let it go and settled properly, and again the white square jumped as she hit it.

Picking up the brass seemed to take a while, though it sometimes bounced in among loose bricks. As she straightened, Patty tried to sound casual, but Harold had seen her working up to the question long before she asked. "So when can we come out again?" She giggled, which had to be sheer adrenaline. "Will your new wench, Tessa, mind about us running off together?"

"You should talk to Sharyn and Tessa sometime about that."

"Why?" Patty suddenly sounded worried.

Harold decided now might not be a good idea. "It isn't a problem and they'll tell you why when we get back. We'll do it straight away because you're hyped just now. It's best if you get it off your chest to those two, because the rifle practice is a secret. Remember, we wouldn't want the scroats to find out until someone dies of surprise."

"Too true. Are we done then?" Patty put her empty brass in the little pouch and tapped the remaining rounds. "There's plenty of time for me to take a couple more shots someplace." Again she attempted nonchalance and innocence, and failed. "Since we're out here anyway?"

"I only let people take extra shots when there's a crowd that won't tempt a scroat." Harold shook his head at Patty's little sound of protest. "All right, just this once, because I don't want you to cry the first time."

Patty's next three shots at fifty yards would have hit the target's head. Considering she hadn't shot a rifle before, that impressed Harold. "Very good. We'll make a real shooter of you in time." For most of the way back Patty pushed for more real practice, despite the risk that too many shots would make someone curious. Her answer, to shoot the nosy sods as practice, would only cause more curiosity. She switched to going through every heartbeat of every shot, several times, explaining just how it felt. Harold let her rabbit on. Patty needed to get the adrenaline out of her system, so she didn't say the wrong thing where someone could hear her. Even so, once inside the walls Harold thought she might explode as she tried to keep quiet until they reached his house.

*　*　*

When he brought Patty in she immediately started telling Sharyn about the shooting, but Harold interrupted long enough to mention the wench part. Sharyn, still a little stunned by this bouncy version of a usually intense and serious Patty, phoned the guardhouse nearest Tessa. While they passed a message, Sharyn made drinks. Patty paced up and down impatiently until Tessa arrived, when some apprehension leaked into her excitement.

Once they knew what worried Patty, that Harold's wench might be jealous, Tessa and Sharyn fell about laughing. Harold got out of the house while they explained, taking a stroll around the walls. He arrived back to an intense discussion, because both Tessa and Sharyn were interested in Patty's shooting. Both women had lived with soldiers and heard plenty of discussions about guns and shooting, even if they'd never actually had a gun.

"Before you three settle into the serious character assassination, Patty has to learn to clean her rifle." Harold pointed towards the study.

Sharyn looked shocked. "Ooh, one whiff of gun smoke is all it takes. You're the first woman he's ever taken in there." Patty looked suspicious because both Sharyn and Tessa were laughing, while Harold had blushed just a bit.

"The weapons need cleaning, and there's cleaning gear in there even if it's my bedroom. Cripes, it's just off the lounge." Harold tried to scowl but could see the funny side. "Patty has to learn to keep her weapon clean. I don't want to go and open up the workshop just for three weapons that have barely been used."

"That's a new one, let me show you how to get my weapon clean. Don't worry that it's in my bedroom, my thoughts are pure." Tessa managed to finish before laughing again.

"I've got to admit it's a new one, new enough to fool me." Patty smirked, eyeing Harold up. "Maybe that's another reason to learn to shoot? There could be a queue if this gets out."

"Hey, this is a secret."

"So only a queue of three?" Patty tried to look shocked but couldn't stop laughing. "Unless you can clean three at a time."

"Excuse me, two. Sister here. Yeuk, the very thought of watching him with you innocents is nauseating, let alone joining in." Harold laughed as well, because Sharyn hadn't made jokes like that for a long time. He left the door open, allegedly to preserve Patty's reputation, which meant both Sharyn and Tessa watched. It wasn't long before they started asking questions. All three women found it funny that a lot of Harold's business came because the scroats didn't clean or oil their weapons properly. Afterwards Patty took 'her' rifle back home so she could practice reloading in the dark. Also, allegedly, in case she wanted to invite someone in to teach him about cleaning.

*   *   *

A week later Harold came back with a backpack full of wire from the scavengers, walking to save on diesel, and found official visitors waiting outside the gates. Five GOFS were sat in an SUV, watching the Hot Rods' pickup being loaded with beer while hops and malted barley were carried into Orchard Close. "I hope that lot have left some beer for us?" Ogou and the four GOFS soldiers didn't seem amused.

Gang lieutenants like Ogou rarely visited except on official business, but that would be sorted out in private so Harold didn't ask. "Don't worry, we never sell all the beer. We're Caddi's new off-license because his brewing is completely screwed up." That seemed to surprise Ogou, so Caddi had kept the loss of his brewer very quiet. Harold thought he knew why, Caddi would be looking for a replacement. "Part of the problem is that Caddi drowned his brewer in the last bad batch. I suggest keeping a special eye on your brewers until he finds a new one." Harold paused, looking from the GOFS to the Hot Rods around the pickup. "There's a good few Hot Rods spending their coupons in our canteen just now, so no trouble, all right?"

"You know us, just a bunch of lads visiting the pub for a beer." The GOFS soldiers laughed at the pub joke. Rumours still surfaced now and then about a real pub surviving someplace. "Well behaved lads, especially if Patty is serving. She actually puts a crossbow bolt with one of those fancy points on the counter." Ogou's shudder might not have been completely faked. "Has anyone ever survived one of those?"

"Nope. The limb has to come off to get our bolt back, so the victim bleeds out. It makes them good deterrents." Harold looked up the road at two approaching figures and pointed. "Leave a couple of seats empty, at the same table if you want to get lucky, because they're Barbies. I thought they weren't allowed across your territory?"

Ogou glanced back up the road at the approaching women. "Hah, good luck to anyone trying to stop them. At least they don't take the piss by driving through with the music blaring. A pity in a way, they've got the only decent music round here. I wish someone would fix Barbie Radio." He glanced at the other four GOFS, who were all watching the Barbies. "I'm sure there'll be two obviously empty spaces at our table."

Harold turned towards the gates, beckoning. "Come on, let's get you through the search so you can find a suitable spot. It could be a waste of time, some of the Barbies visit to chase Doll or Patty. I'll call Alfie for them, because the Barbies reckon he likes searching them." The Barbies insisted on Alfie searching, then wriggled about and complained about what he'd touched. Alfie usually ended up blushing bright scarlet.

Harold didn't send for Alfie because he'd just gone off duty so he'd be hanging out with Hazel again. Alfie would blush and stammer if Harold found them together, and then seventeen-year-old Hazel would blame Harold. The last time he'd walked round a corner and found them snogging, Hazel had accused him of deliberately spying on them. Instead, Harold headed for the canteen to make sure the Hot Rods behaved when the Barbies turned up.

* * *

Once inside Orchard Close, Harold didn't get as far as the canteen. "Hey, wimp, I need you in my lair." Liz put down her wheelbarrow and pointed to the load, bags of charcoal. "No, not because I'm sooty passion deprived, because of this. You can push it now because I'm only a frail woman. Come on, gee up." Liz glanced round nervously, she didn't like being in the public area with gangsters about.

Harold laughed because Liz had to be the strongest woman here, and stronger than many of the men. He picked up the barrow handles and headed for her forge. "You call me wimp then expect me to do the hard work? What's the problem with the charcoal, mouse?"

"Nothing, this is lovely clean chemical free charcoal and we've got oodles at the moment." Liz scowled, glancing round to make sure they were clear of any eavesdroppers. "Since we have, I want to try some tempering again. I had to stop when the alleged squirrels ate all the trees allegedly grown for charcoal, so the Mart stopped stocking the stuff." A year later, she still bridled about that particular item on the BBC news. "I made progress when you brought that extra after the Mart fight, but I'm getting low again."

"Can you try an experiment for me at the same time, pretty please?" Harold's attempt at an innocent smile bounced.

"Pretty? You?" Liz inspected him, very obviously. "A few more muscles, some soot and sweat, and maybe. This had better be more fun than those bullet middles. Those are fiddly and not even a bit artistic." She opened the door to her forge, an adapted garage. "In here please, driver."

Harold tipped the bags of charcoal with the rest. "We'll need your slate and chalk."

Liz sniffed derisively. "Typical, you need a diagram and it still won't be much fun. I'm warning you, this one had better be more artistic."

Harold chuckled because this would definitely be more artistic than the hardened steel cores for bullets. "How about turning a big butch machete into a slimmer, lighter, girly version. One with a longer, sharper point on the end, one that our fighters can stick in some unsuspecting big butch gangster when he tries to brain them?"

"Ooh, that might actually be a bit artistic." Liz brought her slate over to the bench as Harold perched on the end. "Maybe a couple of twee spikes on the back?"

"Perish the thought. We want to pull it back out after sticking the scroat, to stab another. I want a slimline machete so they can still slash. It'll be cheaper without artwork." Harold grinned at her scowl. Liz had made house signs and metal ornaments before the Crash, but the nearest she got to artistic these days was on crossbow heads.

"Spoilsport." Liz looked at him perched on her bench with a little smile. "You seem better, not quite as grim. Was your mystery night of passion that lively?"

"Mystery night of passion? I don't remember singing in the streets?"

"Low blow." Liz smirked, completely unrepentant. "So you had a spring rite night as well?"

"Not quite. Caddi played a trick, two tricks, and they turned on him. As a bonus, I prised an old friend free of the nasty scroat." Harold hesitated, but then asked, "I thought you'd got the dirt from Tessa?"

"Not a lot, or not about how she ended up walking away from that shite. Nor about why the Hot Rods treat her like an unexploded bomb.

Just that you got her out of trouble, so as usual you got it wrong. A bad boy is supposed to get women into trouble." Liz's smirk gave way to anticipation. "But she gave up lots of dirt from before the Crash, about pimply youths. She also made some interesting comments about your night-time entertainment?"

Harold refused that bait. "I just told you, Caddi lost a competition to see if he could get to me."

"His men seem too happy about that. There are broad hints you've got a Hot Rod girlfriend." Liz thumped Harold on the chest when he sat there with a bland smile. "Just be careful, all right?"

"Yes mummy. I won't see her again and I'm trying to forget anyway."

That set Liz off laughing. "Ooh, one of those nights. Cripes, she won't turn up all starry-eyed and simpering, will she?"

Harold's face cracked and he burst out laughing at the thought of Mercedes simpering. "Highly unlikely. Now can we sort out this new hand-held needle for Patty?"

"For Patty? Too true, because she'll definitely use it. A stabber will be easier for her than beating them to death with her crossbow." Liz sobered a little and sat next to Harold on the bench. "The more sharp things between me and Caddi the better. Patty's dead chuffed about the squad leader bit. Are you over your thing about women fighters as well?" Which meant that at least one person had caught on.

"Only if I can make them dangerous enough. I thought of giving Doll a squad as well, once she's back up to speed!" Harold waited for a reaction, because he trusted Liz to tell him if he'd got it wrong.

"She's getting fed up just convalescing. Make it sooner rather than later. Now come on, get scribbling before I nod off from boredom."

* * *

Liz didn't nod off. Within three days she had an experimental version, just to see if the theory worked. Harold waited a few days, because bringing her new squad up to speed took most of Patty's time. Despite her love affair with her rifle, Patty still encouraged her squad to practice with crossbows so the trainees spent all their spare time on that and machete muscle-strengthening exercises. Harold only took her away from her squad twice, as his bodyguard when they'd be travelling alone so she could get in some rifle practice. Patty took three shots with 'her' rifle each time and

Harold had been right, she was a natural. He'd intended having a serious talk about the new machete on those trips, but Patty still got too excited about shooting for any attempt at serious conversation.

A week after ET's visit, a small group of Hot Rods, led by Charger, visited Orchard Close to bulk purchase more beer. After they'd gone, Harold faced tentative questions from a couple of people. Tessa had served the gangsters in the canteen, once more dressed in a skirt and blouse. The questions were about a couple of Hot Rods saying Tessa looked happy with her new bloke. Harold fobbed the queries off, pleading ignorance. Once her house was ready, Tessa had moved to the other end of Orchard Close, so the residents hadn't put it together, yet.

When Harold mentioned Tessa volunteering for the canteen, Sharyn told him the lass enjoyed being able to dress in nice clothes again. According to Tessa the gangsters weren't any worse than squaddies after a few beers, or not in Orchard Close anyway. That impressed her, because she'd seen the Hot Rods at home, and it also gave her the chance to check up on her brother, Pete. Sharyn admitted to prying a bit but Tessa wouldn't tell her any more than she'd told Liz. She'd been in a lot of trouble with Caddi, but Harold had got her out of it and out of Hot Rod territory. Harold ignored the obvious hint for him to fill in the details.

The gun repairs were finished even if Caddi didn't know yet, so Harold spent time in the gardens and fields enjoying the spring sun. He could feel his spirits rising every day as spring meandered towards summer, as if he'd finally woken up from a long, unpleasant dream. The sheer number of people out in the fields, laughing and joking as they worked, were enough to banish the blues. There were a lot more workers than last year. The number of refugees who had trickled in became apparent, now they weren't tucked away hiding from the weather.

* * *

The slow, happy summer feeling lasted less than a week. Harold straightened from weeding as his radio buzzed. "Gate, Harold. We've got a big convoy of Hot Rods. Cripes, that's Caddi's car, the big posh thing."

"No problem Doll, he'll have come for his gear and more beer. Just in case it's more than that, warn the off-duty guards. Ask Emmy and Alfie to take their weapons to the guardhouses, Casper as well, please." Caddi hadn't visited for a while, which made Harold nervous. He wanted Casper there to slow Mack up if trouble started, hopefully long enough for some-one else to shoot the big man. As he went for his stick, machete and pistol, Harold tried to work out what had brought Caddi mob-handed.

Harold smiled when he arrived at the gate because someone had put his box out, the old one for looking over the barricade before it was a gate. He stepped up and Caddi might not be annoyed after all. Caddi's Cadil-lac SUV, a Jeep, Mack's minibus, two pickups and five quads made a big convoy, but Harold could only see fifteen people. The backs of the pickups were heaped with something under tarpaulins instead of armed men, so Harold relaxed. Caddi had come to trade.

Mercedes stood up from behind the Jeep driver and waved, smiling wide enough to be seen under her broad-brimmed hat. Harold's mouth stretched in an answering grin and he raised a hand in reply. Cripes, he hadn't thought about her in ages but she'd already got him grinning like an idiot. The Hot Rod boss cupped his hands to call. "I've brought some loot to trade instead of using all my hard-earned coupons. Can we borrow a few barrows, Harry?" Caddi also wore a smile, but his might not be real.

It took a moment for Harold to realise he'd assumed Mercedes wasn't faking her smile. Cripes again, she'd got to him even at this distance. "No problem. I'll go and get the trade goods." Shouting guns would be a bad idea with the Army listening. As Harold came off his box, Casper snig-gered from the nearby doorway.

"So that's the one the Hot Rods keep hinting about. I haven't seen you smile like that since... For too long."

"Just happy to see a smiling face. Warm your hands up Casper, there's a lot to search." Casper's laugh followed Harold up the street. None of the visitors would let Casper near them and the mere threat of a gay search usually quietened any stroppy gangster. Even before he reached his work-shop, Harold saw people with hand carts and barrows heading for the gate. The phones had been busy.

By the time Harold came back down the street, the gate guards had almost done with searching and disarming Caddi, Mack and eight Hot Rods. Mercedes came out of a guardhouse after being searched, followed by Patty. Both were laughing at something. Harold noticed that people were stopping work to stare, probably because Hot Rod women never vis-ited Orchard Close.

The Hot Rods came up the street in a group, but as they came nearer the rest held back for Mercedes to walk ahead. She wore a long coat as well as the hat but as she came clear of the group, Mercedes passed the hat to one of the Hot Rods. She slipped her coat off and tossed it to another. Harold laughed, because the Hot Rod youth looked offended for a moment, then proud as if he'd received some high honour. Harold forgot the youth when he got a good look at Mercedes.

More or less everyone's eyes widened as Mercedes strode up the road. Most Orchard Close residents had heard some sort of rumour about her reputation, or Harold's overnight visit, but few had seen her. None had seen a visiting woman, even a Barbie, dressed like this. Mercedes hadn't put on her minidress or even a short skirt, she wore a blouse with a pair of skimpy, skin tight, soft denim shorts.

Worse still for Harold's peace of mind, they came with those stockings that held themselves up with magic. The Orchard Close audience would be impressed that she would wear them openly around gangsters, but the Hot Rods knew that the strip of thigh between the stockings and shorts was amputation territory. The stockings themselves were serious injury territory, not much stocking because Mercedes wore over the knee, high-heeled boots.

As a gang boss, Caddi kept his machete while Mack had an alli baseball bat. The rest wore belt knives. Harold would bet money on a blade inside the boots Mercedes wore, and this time she wouldn't need to bend to get it. Mercedes saw him glance at her legs and smiled, though it didn't reach her eyes.

"Want to search me, 'Arold?"

"Love to, Mercedes, if you ask nicely and step into my private office?" Harold joined in the laughter from the Hot Rods, while most of the Orchard Close people were a bit puzzled. Not Patty or Casper, who had followed. They were stood, grinning, just behind the Hot Rods.

"Tempting, 'Arold, very tempting, so don't stop trying." She took a step closer. "I thought you said you'd run if I came for you?"

Harold kept his smile but watched her eyes. He wasn't sure he'd get any warning from them, because they were flat and dead again. He caught movement from the corner of his eye as people gathered around them, some from other gangs.

"There didn't seem much point in running. After all, you told me you'd hunt me down." Harold waited just a couple of beats before saying, "And I want to be facing you if I'm caught." Mack and Caddi laughed but what mattered to Harold was that those dead eyes flickered. Once again Harold wondered how much of the real Mercedes still survived in there. He also wondered why it mattered to him, and why he kept trying for the flicker.

Caddi watched the meeting with his little smile, while the Hot Rod fighters watched a denim-clad ass. So did several Orchard Close men, a couple of Geeks, and four GOFS who had come out of the canteen. Further up the street a Barbie kept well clear. Caddi spoke up. "I had to bring Mercedes, Harry. Herself reckons she needs to know just where you are, in case she can't wait any longer." The Hot Rods laughed and Harold saw another flicker in those dead eyes. He wondered if the time might be coming when Mercedes woke up and went crackers.

"Mercedes knows she's always welcome." Damn it, Harold found he meant that.

"She's out to get you, Harry. Our little Killer Queen is mad as hell that you got away. She took it out on the neighbours." Caddi looked tremendously pleased about that. "I thought that if the guns are ready it might be a good idea to wind her up again. Besides, Mercedes is such a good negotiator."

"Yes Caddi, but the rules are a little different here. Especially with the ladies present."

"Yeah, we know, the language will stay right. I've threatened to geld anyone who steps out of line, with a hammer. That won't stop Mercedes much, because she won't be bargaining with words." Caddi looked round and pretended to be surprised at seeing Tessa. "Oh dear, I hope you're not embarrassed by meeting Mercedes in front of your, what is she?"

"Friend, Caddi. I've got a good few here." Harold smiled amiably rather than breaking the bastard's teeth, which was what he deserved.

"He's been a good friend to me and Eddie, the best I've found since the Crash." Tessa showed a lot more defiance than the last time she'd met Caddi, and his eyes widened.

"To me as well, and a lot of others in here." Patty might not be sure what this was about, but she'd got her crossbow loaded. So had at least a dozen others, Harold realised, including five of Patty's squad. A general mutter from the audience agreed.

Caddi looked around him and back at Harold. "My, my, Harry, you've got a proper little army. Now can we get the weight off our feet, since we can't drive in here civilised like?" Not likely, four lengths of steel girder were concreted end on into the road to stop just that.

Mercedes stuck out a hip, a dangerous hip despite the soft denim.

"Well 'Arold, aren't you going to ask?" Mentally Harold sighed, publicly he smiled.

"Will you ask me to get a firm hold on your delectable posterior, Mercedes, please?"

Mercedes burst into delighted laughter, her eyes flickering before she turned to the Hot Rods. "Now that's how you boys need to learn to treat a lady." The mutters about who might be a lady died when Mack glared, sweeping his eyes around to remind them where they were. Sharyn and most of the residents were looking puzzled, but Tessa wore a definite smile. There would be questions after this.

"As a reward." Mercedes paused to wind the gangsters up a bit. "No, but will you please put your hand firmly on my shorts. Right over the delectable bit, 'Arold." The temptress stepped up close and her fingers walked up his arms. "Then we can sit and negotiate." Harold took a firm grip on the denim and leaned forward. For a moment, Mercedes thought he was going to kiss her, but she didn't back off. Harold wondered just how she'd react if he did, then realised Mercedes had got to him again.

"There's more than one delectable bit, Mercedes, so do I get to choose?" Caddi had reverted to curious looks at the hands-on offer, but sod him and the rest. When Mercedes got up close like this, Harold couldn't help flirting. He wondered if the young woman gave off those pheromone things? At least the round of laughter distracted Harold a bit and this time a couple of his own people joined in. They were realising this had to be some sort of a private joke.

"Ooh, naughty 'Arold! Then again, if you keep trying and I like it, who knows?" Mercedes stuck her hand on Harold's to keep it in place as she turned, giving him the fun tour across her ass again but this time in public. She raised her free hand. "Do I have to ask?" Harold smiled and shook his head, so she put her hand in the back pocket of his jeans and squeezed. Harold's hand replied. Caddi and Mack, followed them into the embassy, along with the Orchard Close contingent. Harold headed for his armchair and sure enough, Mercedes sat on the arm.

He smiled up at her. "This is my chair, so does that mean I can make up new rules?"

"Maybe, in time, but right now be careful because these shorts aren't very long. Don't let your hand slide too far, 'Arold." Here we go, Harold thought. It might be a routine but the length of thigh across one of Harold's knees and her partially unbuttoned blouse made it effective. Mercedes smiled down at Harold, slowly undoing an extra button to make it easier for him to win the bra betting. Harold averted his eyes as Mercedes leaned forward a bit, smirking as she started their private game.

"If those stockings were longer I might be tempted. I'm curious how they manage to stay up all on their own." Harold gave the short length of stocking an obvious and appreciative look.

"They don't need help. They're called thigh highs because they come a long way up my thighs." Mercedes raised both legs, laying them right across his knees so Harold could see just how far.

"Lucky stockings." Harold moved his eyes away as her cleavage tried to intervene, looking around the room.

Bernie, Patty, Casper and Sharyn were in here, three of them fully armed as a statement of whose turf this was. Patty kept looking at Mercedes and smirking, while Casper and Bernie took their cue from Sharyn, who chose to treat the whole exchange with tolerant amusement. Caddi leant back, taking a swig of his beer before opening the bargaining. "I've brought charcoal, damaged machetes, knives and spears, and a broken knitting machine. I thought you could bring your smith to work out what the ironwork is worth." Caddi's smile at Patty faltered a little, when he noticed she had her crossbow cocked and a Liz special pointed at his groin. "The knitting machine might be useful for Patty. The Demon now, I hear?"

"Patty is already a knitting machine, and definitely a demon knitter." Harold didn't want gang names attached to anyone in Orchard Close. He didn't even like his own gangster name, Soldier Boy. Caddi wouldn't be giving the blacksmith a nickname, because he didn't know her name or even her sex. Liz lived in permanent fear of a gangster finding out, so she wouldn't look at the ironwork any place visitors could see her. A year after the last time one of Caddi's men had discovered who she was, and despite him dying before spreading the knowledge, Liz still kept the forge door barred to stop surprise visitors. "Hang on a minute." Harold used the phone to call Emmy, who promised to arrange for someone to inspect the ironwork and knitting machine.

When the phone went down, Caddi leaned forward expectantly. "Now why am I actually going to give you all my lovely loot?"

"Because someone forgot to mention just how screwed up some of the weapons are? Not only that but some of the last lot of radios were close to junk." Caddi waved a hand to acknowledge the truth of both allegations.

His eyes sharpened when Casper opened the bag and took out the repaired firearms. "That's nearly all of them, including the toy rifle."

"This two-two rifle was a mess, and needed serious repairs." Knowing how hard Caddi would bargain, Harold started straight away.

"I know. ET told me when he picked up the other radios. You showed him it had no firing pin?" Caddi smiled when Mercedes leant to look at the rifle.

Harold looked away to avoid winning the bra bet, but kept talking. "Yup, plus somebody had used it as a club, and possibly for cleaning toilets." Casper took out the bolt before passing that and the rifle to Caddy. "It took time to make the parts, but you get the usual guarantee that it shoots straight now." Caddi accepted that guarantee because if the weapon didn't work properly, Harold would sort it out as a freebie. He also accepted the charge for making the parts, because Harold didn't always admit he'd used spares.

Caddi grunted as he worked the bolt, inspecting the open breech. "The Spuds probably used it for growing spuds. All their guns are bunged up with crap." His face broke into a smile. "Which I can't complain about because it means they misfire or jam up. This rifle might have actually been used as a club, once it stopped working. What about that nine mil?" Casper passed the handgun over, after checking that both the weapon and clip were empty. Handing Caddi a loaded semi-automatic handgun was not on anyone's to-do list.

Harold gestured at the weapon. "That was jammed up solid. The clip, the action and even the barrel were full of crud. I also did some straightening and the mechanism had a couple of broken bits. Some idiot probably used a crowbar to try and clear the jam."

Caddi went over the weapon thoroughly. "Yeah. I couldn't even get the bloody clip out. Ah, that's better. Here." The warlord popped the clip in and out a couple of times, before holding the handgun out to Mercedes.

She ran through the operation quickly and smoothly. "A lovely job, 'Arold. Would you like to check over my weaponry?" Mercedes licked her lips while her muscles did a little tango under Harold's hand. "Maybe you could strip and oil it thoroughly, and check the action?"

Harold didn't have to try for sincerity. "If you bring everything down to my workshop, I promise I'll strip it down there and then. I'd do it right now, but then everyone would know my little secrets."

That raised a long, slow flicker behind her eyes. "Mmm, tempting. Secrets. You could show me yours, and I could show you mine. I'll just put this on there, shall I?" Mercedes leaned far enough forward to put the nine mil on the back of Harold's chair, but he managed to avoid burying his nose in her cleavage. Harold already felt sure any bra must be the size of two postage stamps, and held on by glue or magic.

Now he'd seen what he had to pay for, Caddi swung into negotiating the value of his loot. The knitting machine came first, or rather, whether Orchard Close wanted it. When Emmy arrived to let Patty go and find out, Caddi raised his eyebrows. "Hello, I'd heard you'd retired to run a market garden."

Emmy patted the sawn-off shotgun she must have borrowed from Seth, curling a lip at Caddi. "Pleasure before business. I don't get much chance to practice and it's ages since I shot someone up close and personal. Wouldn't want to miss a chance." Casper laughed and so did Mercedes, but although Caddi kept his smile, it seemed a little uncertain. While Patty went to look at the machine, the talk revolved around gardening for a couple of minutes. As usual Caddi complained about the quality of his veg, so Emmy promptly offered to sell him decent seed. Emmy and Harold were certain that Caddi's problem came down to how he treated the gardeners, not seeds, but why miss a chance of profit?

When Patty called Harold out of the room to talk, Mercedes pouted, standing slowly so that Harold's hand took its time sliding off. He paused after standing up. "I'll be back soon, so don't let anything get cold."

"Don't worry, I know just how to get warmed up again." Mercedes sat in Harold's chair and wriggled. "Mmm, still warm, that should do the job nicely."

Harold went through to the next room to talk to Patty, keeping his voice down because Liz had arrived. The discussion didn't take long, because the ironwork had been put in a garage to let Liz sneak in through the back to look. The best of the bent machetes were well worth having, maybe as good as GOFS work. The rest of the bladed weapons weren't as good, but she could straighten them if Caddi included charcoal in the deal. Liz could repair the knitting machine with a mix of rebuilding, fettling and artistic ironwork, but the result wouldn't be as wide as the original.

Patty asked for details, because there weren't any books with it so she'd have to work out how to use the thing. According to Liz, the size of the needles meant the machine would only take thin wool. Without a booklet they'd not be able to manage patterns or shaping, but someone unskilled could still crack out oodles of plain knits. After chewing it over, Harold and Patty reckoned that it would be good for scarves, and sewing strips of plain knitting together would make crude jumpers for the night guards. Patty thought they'd eventually work out how to shape the strips, enough to make woollens for the kids. That would be a big help because the children grew so quickly.

When they came back, Mercedes stood up and smiled. As soon as Harold sat, she parked herself on his chair arm, swinging a leg over his, so Harold placed his hand on her ass. Mercedes raised her eyebrows so he gave a little squeeze. "Cheeky, you didn't even ask." Harold tensed slightly but the muscles on Mercedes' ass said hi to his hand. "Warm enough?"

Harold shuffled in the chair, as if checking the seat. "Lovely."

She pouted, slowly stretching her other leg over Harold's before taking hold of Harold's wrist. With a mischievous smile, Mercedes took his hand on the fun trip, slowly, round to her opposite hip and partly onto her thigh, right up to the edge of the denim. "I didn't mean your seat."

"Oh, sorry. This is lovely and warm," Harold squeezed gently. "But I think I could get it hotter."

The flicker in her dead eyes suggested that Mercedes liked that idea, or maybe remembered the last time Harold had tried. "I'm sure you could, if we ever get the chance without all this boring business interfering."

"Speaking of which, if you pair can quit playing grab-ass long enough, we're supposed to be sorting out a price for that gear out there against my repairs." When Harold looked, Caddi didn't seem annoyed, so he still found Mercedes and her teasing funny. Harold could see why, because her thigh muscles started massaging his hand while he tried to negotiate.

Harold set into the spiel, stressing that plain knits with cheap wool weren't much use to the Orchard Close knitters. Caddi knew that and didn't care. The senior Hot Rod gang members, including Caddi, all wore thick Orchard Close knitwear. Patty poured on the cold water, sneering at both the quality and uses. From her little smile, Mercedes recognised the setup. Caddi probably did too. Eventually Patty admitted it could be useful for plain scarves and blankets for kids, before passing the decision to Harold as being well over her pay grade. Harold looked over at Caddi, who laughed. "You pair should be on the stage as a double act. I'm sure we can find some way of sorting out some cheap wool."

Mercedes chose right then to lean over and slide her hand into Harold's back jeans pocket. He avoided the bra-flash but she stayed a bit closer when she sat back up, and Harold felt the hem of her shorts under his fingertip.

He moved his hand back up her thigh. Mercedes pouted so Harold smiled and slid his hand down again, stopping just short of the hem. "Oops. Nearly touched somewhere really delectable."

Caddi smiled broadly because he'd caught on to the bra game. His smile widened, turning into speculation as Mercedes answered. "Then maybe it's time for you to try somewhere else, 'Arold. Now what would class as 'delectable'?" Since the captured hand had already tried her ass and her thigh, both normally considered off-limits, Harold didn't feel confident about making any suggestions. "I know!" Mercedes squeezed his hand gently for a moment while her thigh said goodbye.

"I'd rather live to remember afterwards?" Harold squeezed to return the goodbye.

"I think you'll remember. Now be very careful, 'Arold. Straying up or down could be painful." Too true, because Mercedes moved closer so she could slide Harold's hand right round her waist until it lay flat on her belly. "Nobody has ever told me if this is delectable. You must hold it firmly, and let me know later."

True because under her rules anyone who'd tried to touch her there, or most places, or even put an arm round her, had bled and sometimes died. Mercedes patted the back of Harold's hand while her tummy muscles said hello to his palm. Harold wondered if the woman had independent control of every individual muscle. Enough to be bloody distracting, Harold found out, because he kept wanting to return the gentle massage. Harold's own people were laughing as well now. They weren't aware of the lethal side but recognised a bit of a wind-up and some full-on teasing. Nobody realised just how far the teasing went under Harold's hand.

The negotiations took most of the afternoon because Caddi enjoyed bargaining. The haggling git probably enjoyed boot sales before the Crash, and this time he had a lot to haggle over. For once, Harold didn't care how long it took. He enjoyed hugging Mercedes, and the little games they played, even if it made negotiating harder. Eventually the other loot and gear came off the second pickup and into Orchard Close, this time mainly charcoal and beer making supplies. The negotiations finally wound down even if Mercedes didn't.

Orchard Close would be making a delivery of yeasts for both bread and beer in return for some of the goodies. The verdict from Harold's brewers and Pippa the baker, when they saw the results from the Mansion, were unanimous. The two yeasts had been mixed up or some other mould had got in there, and both were ruined. Between that, the firearms and the radios, Caddi came up short of goods in the end. He paid part of the shortfall in coupons there and then.

A handcart full of cheap, thin wool would come the other way to make up the balance, with a dig that Harold could use it in the knitting machine if he got it working. Caddi wasn't stupid and knew Harold wouldn't have traded for a totally ruined machine. The thin wool could be bought in the Marts so Caddi wasn't too worried about letting some go, not if it put fresh bread back on his breakfast table. He had different priorities on a winter morning to most of his subjects, and their warmth wasn't one of them.

Despite spending several hours with weapons pointed at him, Caddi seemed to have enjoyed himself. He'd bargained hard, but without his usual nasty edge or the foul language, and even made a couple of clean jokes. By the time he left, everything on the pickups had been traded. Caddi laughed and joked on the way to the gate, about how well Mercedes had distracted Harold. Harold hoped he'd not been stung too badly. Patty and Sharyn would no doubt berate him about it if he had.

From the way Caddi looked at Harold and Mercedes, the gang leader might be truly curious about what was going on. Until now Harold had wondered if Mercedes had been setting him up for a hit. Now all he had to worry about was if Mercedes wanted to kill him for her own reasons, or actually fancied him, or possibly both. At least Caddi didn't seem upset about whatever he'd come up with. The Hot Rod warlord wasn't the only curious one now. A good few Orchard Close residents saw Mercedes snuggling into Harold while they walked to the gate. She had to so Harold's hand could wrap right round her, and she could keep her hand in his jeans pocket.

As they reached the gate, Mercedes slid Harold's hand across and down onto her hip before swinging herself round to face Harold. This time his hand got the fun trip without an escort. Harold was sure on the bloody commando bet again, and the slow smile and arched eyebrows meant the realisation must have showed. Did Mercedes want him to know? "So which bit was the most delectable, 'Arold?"

"Oh no. To make a proper comparison I'd need a private session, just so that I wasn't distracted. I can definitely confirm that everything I've touched up to now has been smooth, firm, and truly delectable." Harold hoped that the long slow flickering in those dead eyes meant she realised when and what he was talking about. He sure as hell remembered!

Mercedes had remembered as well. "Maybe that could be arranged.

After all it's nearly dark, 'Arold. I thought we might get to stop overnight?"

Harold didn't have to fake regret, because he'd love to say yes. "I wish, but Caddi likes to have you tucked away safe in the Mansion at nights." Too damn true he did. Caddi wouldn't want his deal broken while the arse wasn't looking.

"Wouldn't I be safe here, 'Arold?" From the look, Harold thought he might not be.

It was out of his mouth before he'd thought about it. "Yes, but I might not be." Harold let the laughter from the rest die down a bit. "It's a pity I've only got a single bed, so there isn't much room." As soon as he said it, Harold wished he'd kept his big mouth shut. Caddi was always trying to find out Harold's sleeping arrangements and partners.

Her eyes lit up. "Oh, you'd be surprised how little room I might need with the right man, but I'll bear that in mind. Just in case I'm allowed a sleepover." Mercedes leant forward and up, and her lips firmly but briefly touched Harold's before she settled back with a smirk. "Just keep thinking about that, Soldier Boy."

She turned around, sauntering off while the rest laughed and followed her. Mercedes slid the coat back on after pointing at her shorts and giving an extra wiggle. Watch this, and think about that? Harold might be having some interesting dreams because as she kissed him, Mercedes stuck her tongue between his lips! It felt like an electric shock, too fast for Harold to react. Once again Mercedes had broken her rules in plain view, but without letting anyone else know.

Mercedes seemed to be slipping out of control, fraying the edges of her deal without actually outright breaking it. Harold wondered if he'd find her on his doorstep one morning, and hoped Mercedes brought Caddi's ears with her. A live Caddi wouldn't care about consequences; he'd bring every last Hot Rod and flatten Orchard Close regardless of collateral.

The crowd of spectators broke up, most of them laughing about the teasing. A good few were making comments about the shorts and stockings, and wondering how Mercedes got away with it around the gangsters. As expected, Sharyn wanted to know why Mercedes had been acting like that, but Harold refused to discuss it. To be honest, he didn't know.

Chapter 6:
Unexpected Visitors

Four days later, the first refugees from the war between Caddy and the Murphies arrived in Orchard Close. Doll called Harold down to the Embassy, the house used for meeting visitors, to meet the first pair. One of the women started talking as soon as they were seated. "There's a gang war over where we live, between the Murphies and the Hot Rods."

"We know. Who did your street belong to?" Harold had to be careful because if they'd run from Caddi, that broke the treaty.

"The Murphies. This morning the five Murphy men guarding our streets were dead in alleys or empty houses." The speaker shuddered before carrying on. "Including the nasty sod in charge. The ones I saw all had their ears cut off and were carved up." She glanced at the other woman. "That had to be the Hot Rods. We didn't want to wait for a vicious bastard like that to turn up so we came here. We've heard about the Hot Rods and women."

The other woman spoke up. "There's talk the Murphies are losing. We don't fancy what might happen next. The Murphies are arses but it had all settled down, if you know what I mean?" Harold nodded. Once the gangs were set up, some of them were content to take their cut and let the folk who lived in their patch get on with life.

The muttered "unless the bastards wanted more women" from the first woman meant settled down had a different meaning to some.

One thing puzzled Harold. The two women had trekked across the whole Hot Rod or GOFS territory to get here. "Why did you come here instead of a neighbouring gang?"

The first woman smiled confidently. "We heard a strong rumour yesterday, about a place over here next to the bypass. Someone said an orchard."

"Orchard Close, that's us." Doll sniggered, glancing towards the rear of the building. "We even planted a real orchard."

"This is the place then. Is it right it isn't run by a gang?" The woman looked from Doll to Harold, definitely confused because both were armed like gang members.

"We have gangsters, but not as you know them. Doll, take them for a drink in the canteen and give them the rules please. If they agree, get the girl club to collect them and explain everything." Harold paused as a thought struck him. "We'll need a bigger girl club if those sort of rumours are starting."

Two hours after the first pair of refugees arrived, a young woman turned up from the same street. Doll took her off to be introduced to the girl club.

As soon as he heard that a third refugee had arrived, Harold collected a work party outside Orchard Close, on the fields. "From what I was told this morning, we could have a sudden increase in refugees."

"Cripes, how big are you expecting Orchard Close to get, Harold? There's nearly a hundred and sixty of us according to the coven, and that's all we can take." Tilly, a gnome and Riot Squad member, hesitated before she continued. "Your Tessa and little Eddie took the last empty house, so the latest refugees will be sleeping in lounges and dining rooms."

Harold ignored the 'your Tessa' part. He pointed to the six big detached houses standing halfway across the cultivated strip, over three hundred metres from the walls. "I once thought of knocking them down to clear the field of fire across the fields, but we saved them for storage. Now I think we'll need them to live in."

Tilly turned to Harold, suddenly looking hopeful. "How many refugees are you expecting, because those houses have five or six bedrooms each. Maybe some of the residents can spread out a bit?"

"If people are going to live in those houses, what do we do with all the food and salvage already stored in there?" Fergie frowned, inspecting the big houses and then looking around. "I wouldn't fancy living outside the walls."

"We could start up another girl club, then the blokes will be keen enough to live there? That might also suck in a few raiders, crossbow target practice." Tilly grinned at the hopeful expressions on a couple of the trainee Demons. "Or put the single men out here, a boy club so we know where to find them?"

Harold shook his head in mock despair. "Calm down you lot. If we clear any ruins within seven hundred yards of them, out on the other side of the gardens, that'll stop scroats getting near. The bricks can be barrowed back to build walls." Several people groaned, because barrowing bricks to build walls seemed to be a continual job. "I'll sort out some sort of alternate storage."

"Aren't the walls big enough?" Louie squinted across the fields. "That's a hell of a distance if we're knocking down ruins and carting the bricks in. Over half a mile. Three quarters?"

"I meant new walls, around the houses. At the moment they're not much over three hundred metres from the ruins. Casper can build a new wall, out from Orchard Close to each side and right round them." Harold turned to Tilly and Bethany, both gardening gnomes. "Then they're inside the defences, and the bit between without houses becomes a protected garden for Emmy's baby plants. What do you reckon, Sweet Gnome?"

"That's bribery to get the gnomes on your side." Bethany adjusted her hat. "But since you called me sweet, I'll forgive you."

"I don't mind." Henry, one of the single men, smiled and glanced at the women. "As long as we can have a dance as a reward."

"At the end of the month. It will be a big dance if we're welcoming a lot of new people." Harold would chase Caddi's spies away and close the gates to visitors, as usual, to keep Caddi guessing on numbers. "Save a little bit of energy for that, but not much. The new refugees will be running from a gang war. They'll sleep anywhere to start with, but I want to get them into permanent accommodation as soon as possible."

"Fair enough. I remember how that feels." Henry spat on his hands, picking up the handles of a barrow. "Let's be at it." Two score men and women followed, heading for the ruins beyond the houses. Harold took Casper, Rob and Finn to inspect the actual houses, and work out what needed doing. It wouldn't be an overnight job.

All the windows had been covered in ply to stop pilfering, but now those on the perimeter would need bricking up the same as the ones around Orchard Close. Finding alternate storage for everything inside the houses stumped them for a while, because Casper cried off trying to build load-bearing walls. He wasn't confident about actual bricklaying with mortar, as opposed to long stacks of interlocked bricks to make low, thick walls. Rob came up with a solution, sectional garages and sheds. Anything wood had probably collapsed or rotted, but there'd be plenty of concrete ones and maybe a few plastic sheds out in the ruins.

Finn would need a new, heavy duty supply cable to bring electricity from Orchard Close, buried deep so nobody hit it with a fork. The electrician expected a lot of minor problems from dampness as he connected each one up. Unfortunately, that would take him away from the windmill project.

After some discussion on how far Finn, Rob and Charlie had come with the project, Harold decided they could leave it for a while. Not completely, he wanted a small demonstration as soon as possible. That would prove the theory, and encourage the scavengers before Harold sent them back out for more wire and bits for dynamos. Meanwhile, the scavengers would provide extra labour for clearing ruins, to give a clear field of fire from the new accommodation.

Rob, the plumber, had an easier job. There'd be no argument about composting toilets because the sewers under these houses had already been sealed to store water for the gardeners. He agreed to put in a bidet by each toilet, to cut down on the gross factor. That wouldn't take long, nor would fixing the small leaks that always appeared when houses were left empty for a couple of winters.

With water and electricity, the houses would be habitable. It would take longer to build a decent wall but Patty had the answer. She'd move her Demons into the first one fit to live in, which would clear some accommodation in Orchard Close proper. In her opinion, if some scroat tried to kidnap the women it would be excellent weapons practice. Or as Casper put it, "May all and any gods take pity on the fool that breaks in."

* * *

The very next day the gate guard phoned for Harold. "This one is your call," Emmy told him. "A young woman with a little girl, but she might bring trouble."

Harold had her brought into the Embassy to make it official. At first glance the small Asian woman didn't look like trouble, nor did her four-year-old daughter, and just for a moment he thought it might be an April Fool's setup. A quick exchange told him her name, Ruhika, that she preferred Ru, and didn't want her daughter, Gulab, to hear her story. The bloodstained kitchen knife Emmy put on the coffee table might be the reason, and banished any thoughts of this being a joke. In stark contrast, the bags of clothes, the coupons, the sheath knife on a belt and the aluminium baseball bat all looked pristine.

As soon as Emmy took Gulab to find a babysitter, Ru started talking.

"It was one of the Murphies, he said he was on guard and couldn't get to the brothel. I'm not a gang woman. I said no so he threatened to hurt Gulab." Ru looked decidedly apprehensive at the next bit. "I told him yes but in the kitchen where Gulab wouldn't see. Then while he was dropping his pants..." Ru stopped and looked at the kitchen knife.

"You stuck that knife in the bastard. Fair enough. It won't happen here because we don't allow abuse or even foul language. In fact, if anyone threatens you, run and call for help or stick a knife in him yourself. I'd prefer him alive so we can kill the scroat publicly, it's a better deterrent for the other visitors." Harold stifled a smile at his next thought. "If Patty gets there first she'll stick a crossbow bolt in him, but not to kill him immediately."

The young woman stared, trying to see if Harold meant that. "Are you a real gangster? Someone said there weren't any here." Ru eyed up Harold's weapons. She'd also seen the gate guards, heavily armed young men and women.

"Not a real one, but the others call me Soldier Boy."

Ru's eyes widened. "The Murphies talked about you! They didn't want to upset you because you can shoot... Um. A gnat?"

"Possibly." Harold smiled, making a quick decision. The Murphies were busy fighting Caddi, too busy to chase this woman. In any case, Harold had no treaty with them. "You can stay if you keep your trap shut about the knifing. I'm not supposed to take anyone running from a crime, even if we don't think what you did is wrong. Nobody from the Murphies will look for you in Orchard Close, in case someone shoots their gnats."

That raised a small smile. "I promise. I don't think anybody saw what happened. I set fire to the house when I left, so they might not even realise we aren't all dead."

Harold knew no gangster had seen her or Ru would be dead. She'd stabbed a gangster, stripped his weapons and coupons, packed her belongings and then set fire to the house? Harold wondered how long it would be before Ru joined Patty's squad. The aluminium baseball bat she brought went into the armoury, but Ru kept the sheath knife as a Murphy deterrent. No one came asking about refugees; the Murphies were too busy trying to survive.

* * *

To help keep the new refugees safe, Harold took Patty away from training her squad to see Liz. On the way to the forge, Harold introduced the idea of a slimmer machete. Harold stressed the long sharp point for better stabbing, but Patty didn't seem convinced. Twice during the short walk Harold had to swear this wasn't an April Fool's setup. There'd been an outbreak of pranks this morning, and not from the kids.

Once Liz let them in, she handed over the new machete. Patty hefted it a couple of times, unimpressed, so Harold took it off her and ran through a set of exercises meant for a sword. Patty took it back and ran through a set of machete exercises, added a couple of stabbing thrusts, and a huge grin spread over her face. "Oh no, not a new style machete. This is a super deluxe scroat-sticker. And from what I just saw, you know how to use it properly." She practiced a couple more slashes and a thrust. "It feels odd, the balance is off or maybe just different."

"But I can do something about the balance, unless you think learning how to handle the difference is the best way?" Liz watched intently while Harold sat on the workbench, smiling at Patty acting like a kid with a new toy. The rifle or the squad seemed to have lit a fire in her, given her a surge of confidence.

"If you don't mind altering it?" Patty swished and stabbed. "Could you make it a bit lighter, so I can wiggle it around like Harold just did? Maybe that's the answer, it will feel right if I use it like Harold. I'll still want enough weight for a slash or chop?" She frowned, inspecting the blade. "How does this work? If you cut too much off it can't go back on."

"If you want me to show you the moves, let me know. Otherwise I'll leave you two together, because Liz assures me that her test version is designed to be redesigned." Harold bowed to Liz.

Liz nodded, preening a little. "Because I'm the best. That one isn't tempered, Patty, so I can do what you want with it. Despite the boring lack of artwork, I made it just for you to ridicule."

Patty swished the machete again. "I can do that. This will be just the thing to make the scroats remember their manners around my girls. My own personal version of April Fool's, at any time of year." Harold left the two of them taking turns at whacking and stabbing a piece of wood.

*　*　*

Her new scroat-sticker didn't distract Patty from preparing the new home for her Demons. She chivvied any spare pair of hands into clearing rubble or collecting bricks for Casper, even including brick-carting as a strengthening exercise for her trainees. Over the next eight days, the pair of walls crept out from Orchard Close towards the six big houses. More and more residents, even if they'd already done their stint, found themselves press-ganged as more refugees turned up. At least half the current crop were Asian, which brought an entirely unexpected change.

When Harold walked into the canteen he didn't expect to be met with, "What's in this curry?" The GOFS wasn't complaining, more like smiling and smacking his lips.

Harold went through to the kitchen and leant over to sniff at the pot. "Is there something different in this curry, Elizabeth?"

"That'll be the spices from our new refugees. We've been testing them on visitors before we risk giving the residents Delhi belly. Today's came from Ru, along with some tips on how to use them." Elizabeth proffered a spoonful.

From the smell, Harold wasn't risking that. He mixed it with a bit of rice but still gasped. "That's a real tonsil toaster, different from the usual. Can we get any more?"

"I'll keep an eye open. I'm still looking for rat poison to spice up any Hot Rod curry, but I promise to keep them separate." From the look on her face Harold wasn't sure if Elizabeth meant that, but he laughed as if she'd cracked a joke. She still hadn't forgiven the Hot Rods for her lad dying, but wasn't usually homicidal.

Harold asked about Ru, to find out where to get more spices. He'd have won one private bet because she'd already joined Patty's squad. "That didn't take long."

The small woman turned, carefully keeping the crossbow aimed at the ground. "Oh. Is it all right? They said it was?"

"Don't worry, I just sort of expected to find you here. As long as you'll actually stick an arrow in some scroat if necessary, I'm a believer in everyone having a crossbow." Going by the number of trainees practicing, Harold needed more crossbows.

"Really? Oh good. I don't want the next banchod to get close enough for a knife." The other Asian-looking trainees all nodded at that. Harold didn't ask, especially since he was pretty sure he'd never repeat whatever it was accurately. Instead he asked about spices, and those were from West Bengal, because her parents came from there. Unfortunately, Ru had only brought what she snatched up in a hurry.

When he arrived home, Harold wondered if he should have asked for a translation. "Uncle Harold, Wills and Rory have a new word that I'm not allowed to say or I have to wash my mouth out with soap. Not spam, real soap." Daisy waited, poised, but Harold wasn't asking so she reverted to drawing. This time her ship had crashed at night and needed Uncle Harold to draw the Red Cross Bat. She did consider the Red Cross Orca or Squid for the cat-pirates in the water, so the school must be teaching about sea life again.

The new words, only a few, came from little Gulab. The teachers taught her English, or rather they improved what she had, but the youngster occasionally reverted to the mixture spoken in her street. June, the ex-trophy-wife-turned-teacher, hadn't known what the foreign words meant, but the context of some led to her asking. An embarrassed Ru explained, whereupon several went onto the soapy mouth list.

* * *

The numbers of crossbow trainees he spotted in the next few days sent Harold looking for Patty. "Patty, can you spare a moment from beating your squad into shape?"

"We're in shape. Look!" Fergie posed with her wooden machete and stick, but Harold didn't comment on her shorts. Several of the young women were wearing shorts or shorter skirts now and then since Mercedes visited. "She's just beating on us for no reason. Help, help."

"As you can see, they can manage without me for a while." Patty passed her wooden machete to a trainee. "You can beat on each other while I'm gone." She started down the road with Harold, her smile growing as they moved out of earshot. "More rifle practice?"

"Sorry, no. How many have you recruited now?"

Patty frowned, thinking about it. "Thirty-six, but there's more want to have a go. Some are men but most are women. I haven't put them all in the squad yet. They have to reach a certain standard first, with crossbows and machete sparring."

"I want to split them, to give Doll a squad, then we can move yours into the new housing once it's habitable." Harold explained about how primitive the conditions still were, but Patty wasn't bothered. "Liz thinks Doll is ready, what do you reckon?"

"She's chewing her nails down to her knuckles because she's bored, Harold. That's why she keeps taking a stint at the gate." Patty glanced back towards where the mainly female trainees were still beating on each other. "We'll get more blokes volunteering for guard duty."

"You seem to have plenty of fans."

"Not as many as a definitely younger, much livelier blonde." That idea didn't seem to bother Patty. "I'll take the women who aren't looking for a bloke, because they won't mind sharing a house in the Annex. Possibly two houses if more volunteer."

"Your own girl club? The Annex?"

"Those six big houses is a bit cumbersome for a name so yes, the Annex." Patty looked over at the six houses. "I don't mind moving out there because I'll be surrounded by fields, so if a deer turns up, pow."

"Luck with that." They both laughed because there'd never been a second deer. "Since you've already decided how to split them, you can come with me while I make it official with Doll." Harold stopped for a moment, frowning as he realised. "Now I'll need even more crossbows. There'll be another squad on guard, and they'll need weapons, so there won't be many left over for practice."

"Let's hope the Geeks need more knitting." Patty smirked and rubbed thumb and forefinger together. "I charge them and the Hot Rods extra."

Both Liz and Patty were right about Doll being fed up and ready for a challenge. As soon as Doll realised that Harold wasn't joking, she lit up and more or less exploded in sheer excitement. Harold left her in a deep discussion with Patty about who to transfer, and how to share out the weapons yet leave some for practice. He wondered what Orchard Close had to sell that would buy crossbows. He had some coupons saved from gun repairs, but wanted to keep them for a true emergency.

*   *   *

Doll took over Patty's section of the wall around Orchard Close, which allowed Patty's squad to spend all their spare time furnishing and fortifying their new home. The eighteen single women split into three shifts to ensure the new housing wasn't left unguarded, which also meant they could work on their new home while on duty.

The houses were definitely going to be needed, because as April progressed, the refugee numbers escalated. When the gate guard called him,

Harold headed for the Embassy, curious about why he'd been called to these refugees. These days, the guards and Coven usually processed new-comers. The new arrivals came alone or in pairs, so he hoped this trio were an exception and not a new trend. Few houses in Orchard Close had any spare room left, not even a couch, and the new houses still weren't fit to live in.

Harold, resplendent in his Soldier Boy weaponry, waited in the Embas-sy until Patty brought in the young women. She pointed at Harold. "That's him, Soldier Boy. Now remember what I said, just tell the truth." She put two aluminium baseball bats, three sheath knives with the belts and a good quality machete on the floor next to Harold. "They came with these."

Harold didn't need to ask anything. "We've run away from the Mur-phies. Will you give us sanctuary?" The one who spoke seemed a little more confident than her two companions. "We brought those to buy our way into here, into Orchard Close."

"You can have sanctuary without paying. Where did you get the weap-ons?" Harold wondered because even the confident woman looked nervous and unsure, definitely not a fighter.

"Some of the Murphy men were laid in the street this morning with their ears missing, and these weapons were laid next to them." She glanced at the other two women. "The ears thing means the Hot Rods are coming, so anyone who doesn't fancy living under those lunatics should get out if possible. It's all rumours but everyone says we should bring a buy-in, weap-ons if possible. There's supposed to be women here who kill gangsters."

Harold chuckled and pointed at Patty. "You can believe that part. This is Patty. Later you can meet her disciples, who all want to kill gangsters. Take them away for a beer please, Patty. Explain about scroats and caning, then issue them with these knives." He knew Patty would get any useful information out of them over a pint, more than they'd tell the gang boss. In any case, Harold needed a few minutes to think. Presumably Mercedes had killed those men because she collected ears, but according to the Hot Rods, Mercedes brought any decent weapons back with her. Harold won-dered if Caddi had sent other attackers in to cut off ears, just to spread alarm and despondency.

He'd barely put the weapons into the armoury when Patty came back up the street. "You need the three witches, Harold." She meant a meeting with some of the Coven, and probably Casper and other squad leaders.

"Do we need Emmy?" Harold preferred not to drag Emmy away from

Tammy and haranguing the gardeners, her gnomes, because both seemed to make her happy.

"No, I'll tell her later." Patty looked decidedly mischievous. "I'd say get Alfie but Hazel would kill me. She's finally got him cornered. Ah, forget I said that." Harold had thought Alfie was now chasing Veronica, but as usual he hadn't a clue. Hazel still alternated between calling him Uncle Harold and berating him for frightening boys away.

"Why, I don't say anything about who Hazel sees, not now she's grown up and moved into the girl club." Harold paused as Patty shook her head. "I don't!"

"Maybe not, but you definitely get that Uncle Harold look if you see her larking about with one of the lads." An embarrassed Harold promised he wouldn't do it again, hoping he could figure out what look Patty meant. Patty didn't seem completely convinced. "Hmm. If you start again I'll tell Liz and your new wench." Patty's eyes lit up. "Both of your wenches."

"Don't. Tessa is a friend." Now Harold wished they'd stuck to talking about Hazel. Even worrying about hordes of new refugees would be a relief.

"But all those new women have come in, and you picked her name as a possible wench." Patty put on a bit more speed, almost trotting. "Come on, let's round up some folk because we might have to build bigger and faster." They rounded up Tessa, Liz, Casper and June, and descended on Sharyn.

"Sorry sis. Coven plus meeting, or so Patty tells me." Harold bowed to give Patty the floor.

"The three latest arrivals found bodies on the street this morning." Patty recapped for everyone but Harold. "A beer and being allowed to carry a knife loosened their mouths. We might have a problem." She nodded towards Harold. "His other wench is sending presents, but not choccies and flowers. She's sending clubs and machetes."

Sharyn looked from Patty to Harold, puzzled. "That does seem more her style, but how is Mercedes sending them?"

"Not tied up with a ribbon. She's spreading rumours, and from today's example might be getting careless about stripping bodies. The Murphy streets are alive with rumours about this place, Orchard Close. They stress that lover-boy here is mucho scary to Hot Rods and Murphies, but a pussy-cat to his own people." Patty looked Harold up and down and shook her head. "The Murphies reckon Soldier Boy is bad news, which seems to mean the rest has become gospel. If anyone, man, woman or child, gets out before the Hot Rods arrive, they can find safety here. There's even directions. Go over the Barbie border and head into the sunrise to the bypass. Keep hidden in the ruins until they reach the fields then come straight across them, out in the open."

"Which takes them through GOFS territory but avoids Caddi's men. That's bloody specific. They're still risking the Barbies and GOFS but that wouldn't be too bad, going by what we heard when we sorted out the refugees from the General." Harold switched to the other bit that puzzled him. "What about the buy-in part?"

"The rumours tell them to bring weapons or whatever tools they've saved, and that anyone with a skill can earn plenty of coupons." Patty patted her machete. "Allegedly there's women here who kill gangsters with guns and crossbows. A few rumours are a bit over the top, like the one about every woman carrying a gun."

"Rumours tend to grow. That one probably started because we all carry knives." Real alarm showed on Liz's face as she thought it through. "Cripes, Harold, start building. You'll get snowed under if Caddi wins, and a lot of them will have trades or be women." Her face cleared and she looked round with a big smile. "On the bright side, they'll be armed women."

"I thought there was nothing between you and this Mercedes." Casper's face also broke into a big smile. "There again, she is sending you other women. Maybe it's so you'll leave her alone?"

Harold smiled right back. "You shouldn't be so happy. We need those walls built and windows properly bricked sharpish, and you're our bricklayer."

"Cripes, Harold, all I've done is build loose brick wall." Casper shook his head, looking definitely worried. "About a thousand miles of it by now I suppose, all round Orchard Close, and if I'd had cement they'd be a real wall. If I'll be doing a lot, I should have a proper trowel instead of a spatula." The rest broke up laughing. Casper used a metal spatula for spreading mortar on bricks, on the rare occasions he used any, because there wasn't a trowel in Orchard Close.

"I'll buy you one from the Geeks when we buy the cement. For now there's another thousand miles to build connecting us to those houses." Harold paused, pretending to count on his fingers. "Maybe only a couple of hundred miles."

"Hey, I didn't measure them. It seemed like a thousand miles."

Sharyn and Liz lurked when the rest left. "Give, little brother. Is there more to this Mercedes thing than you let on?"

"No, Sharyn, I swear. She's the furthest thing from my mind, except when she shows up and then I can't help it. She must give off hormones or pheromones." Harold looked from one to the other. "I swear."

Sharyn rolled her eyes. "It'll be hormones, his hormones."

Liz nodded, then smirked. "Maybe his pheromones are what's affecting her?"

"Cripes. Double cripes."

* * *

Harold didn't think about Mercedes if nobody mentioned her, but people kept teasing him so he thought too much for his peace of mind.

At least when Caddi turned up to trade a week later he only brought Charger. Harold actually felt relieved, even if he wondered why Caddi had decided to trade here again. Last year the Hot Rod boss had insisted Harold came to the Mansion for any business. Perhaps Caddi had worked out that this way he could jump the queue for weapons and radio repairs.

There were more guns to clean and repair, some of Caddi's own that had jammed or just fouled up, and one where the brass had split inside. There were also more captured firearms, so maybe Mercedes still took some trophies home. "Are you going Wild West, Caddi?" Harold looked suitably serious. "It won't work, you know, it'll never shoot round corners." Harold picked up the weapon, a rifle with a bowed barrel.

"Very funny I'm sure. You should go on TV." Caddi's scowl held no humour at all. "The Murphy who had that is very, very lucky he's dead. He'd jammed it in a grate and started bending the bloody thing even as my men closed in." Caddi held out a hand so Harold handed the rifle over. "I'd have roasted the, er, person over a slow fire." Caddi glanced at Patty's crossbow as he avoided a fine for obscenity. He worked the underlever. "The damn thing still works, and look at the engraving. It's a real Winchester, the proper cowboy thing. Can you straighten it?"

"Not a chance. Rifle barrels are tubes so they distort too easily, and even a tiny bit will jam the bullet part-way down. You really, really won't want that, especially if straightening it weakened the barrel." Harold looked the weapon over. "I can cut the barrel down to where it's still circular, before any bend? If I clean it up and check the mechanism that'll make a big clumsy pistol?"

"Not worth paying for because there's only five empties. We haven't got any more brass to fit. Even if we had, there's more shots in a revolver." Caddi sighed and reluctantly held the weapon out again. "What about you? You're always saying you want spares."

"It's no good as spares, because nobody else has an underlever." Harold assessed the weapon again, especially the smooth curve of the barrel. "I'll take it and the empty brass in part payment for the other work, but you don't get much for it." Harold worked the action, and it didn't seem to be damaged at all. "This will be a clumsy pistol, with only five shots, but if the bastards are closing in then five shots might be enough. Especially five big rifle bullets like these."

"Okay, but I'm not giving you the bloody thing."

Eventually, with the rest of the dealing over, Harold sort of asked about Mercedes. "You'd have made a better deal with your distraction along."

Caddi laughed at him. "Mercedes? If it's any consolation, I get distracted watching you two. Christ knows why but I think the, er young lady actually has the hots for you. Nobody even got to hold her hand and then pow, she can't get your hand on her ass fast enough." He chuckled, shaking his head. "I didn't tell her I'd be coming. She's supposed to be out there, putting the fear of God into the Murphies, not lusting after you."

"Won't she be mad at you?" It did cross Harold's mind that if Mercedes got mad enough to top Caddi, she'd solve her problem.

"Probably, but she daren't do anything about it. If she tries, she gets staked out in the yard on a mattress for..." Caddi glanced at Patty. "Mack and Cooper would punish her, same as you would if someone attacked Soldier Boy?" Patty narrowed her eyes but accepted the point with a sharp nod. Caddi turned back to Harold. "I'll bring her next time, if it won't cause any strife with your woman, because I can see the difference in prices."

"A visit from Mercedes won't upset any of my friends, will it Patty?"

"Oh no, we had a lovely little chat while I checked her over, in private." Patty smiled sweetly as Caddi jerked and stared. "I reckon she'd have preferred Harold to search her. Sorry, I mean 'Arold."

Caddi relaxed again. "If he ever gets to do that and lives, he'll have women turning up to have their picture taken with him like that blonde of yours." A hint of a sneer showed as he eyed Patty. "It's a pity about her being so hot and a blonde, or you'd have all the fans, what with being on the TV as well."

"You are so wrong about who has the hard-core fans. No man volunteered to risk death for the chance to sit and drink beer with Doll." Harold held Caddi's startled look. "Patty said yes and he put himself up as a target, a live decoy. I didn't miss so he lived and got his drink, and he even bought the beer." Caddi looked from Patty to Harold, both smirking, and then at Alfie who tried hard not to laugh.

"Come on, give me the punch line."

"There isn't one. Ask the GOFS. Cy's even got a picture and he insisted on getting Patty's crossbow included. He's got a picture with Doll in her hat and boots as well, because of the time they spent together at Beth's. He only has to get one with Emmy and her rifle for the set." Harold wouldn't put it past Cy to get one, if only for his help in getting Emmy's rifle.

"You could have had one with Mercedes, or a video, if you weren't so shy." Caddi smirked, but it faltered because Patty just laughed.

So did Harold. "Why would I need that, Caddi? I've got a 3D full technicolour memory."

The gang boss gave up on trying to tweak either of them. Instead, Caddi chatted about this and that, including capturing another pair of streets with a lot of Asians. That part Harold knew about, but reading between the lines, Mercedes seemed to be equally valuable as a scout or a killer. Harold could see why. He worried about someone getting a female spy into Orchard Close because a woman would be accepted much more easily.

*   *   *

The gang boss eventually left, with beer because the brewer he'd found wasn't as good as Nigel and Berry. Not surprising, the father and daughter had owned and run a micro-brewery before the Crash. Patty gave Harold a hand to carry the weapons to his workshop. He found out why once they arrived. "Are you really going to cut that gun down, Harold?"

"Probably. I can't see a kink but I doubt we could straighten it. On top of that there's only five rounds, or will be when I reload the brass."

Patty unwrapped the rifle, holding it up as if shooting which looked comical with the bend. "Are you going to teach me to shoot like Emmy? Long range with a bigger rifle?"

"Yes, I told you I'd teach you to shoot. You'll end up practicing with both mine and Emmy's, just in case."

"I thought you might just mean the little one. If I can shoot properly it'll be a waste if there's only rifles for you, Emmy, and Alfie. Wouldn't it be more useful to have an extra big rifle? Then I could help out and switch to a two-two when the five shots were done." Harold stared as Patty blushed a little, giggling nervously. "I've never been a gun freak but I've gone all girly and gimmee over this one. Look at it, it's gorgeous." She stroked the engraving.

A little smile tugged at Harold's mouth. "Won't your two-two get jealous?"

"Stop it! I'm serious."

"So am I, sort of. You learn on the little one first, if only because I don't want to reload those five brass cases too many times. If we're dead lucky there'll be more here somewhere." Harold waved at the jars and tubs holding empty brass found in the ruins. "Help me look."

Eventually they admitted defeat, but while they looked, Harold considered Patty's request. The extra five shots before any attacker closed in would help, and Patty could switch to a two-two for close-up. He wasn't sure about accuracy, but the weapon had a fitting for a scope so it must shoot a reasonable distance. After all, this wasn't deer hunting, so Harold didn't mind if the target crawled away and died later.

"I've thought it through, and we'll try. Liz will beat on you over the wasted charcoal if this doesn't work, but those five rounds might matter." Harold watched the huge smile spread over Patty's face. "You'll be spending long hours working on this very carefully, and might still end up with a clumsy pistol?" Patty's smile didn't falter so Harold gave her the last downside. "I don't think it'll ever shoot like the other big rifles."

"I don't care, Harold. I'll risk it if you will?" Patty stroked the rifle again. "Close-up I can get off five rounds fast enough to scare the bejesus out of a bunch of scroats. Caddi will choke."

"Oh no. Caddi will go crackers, so you'll have to hide it." Harold laughed at her disappointed look. "You do that with firearms anyway. Come on, let's work on Liz."

As Liz pointed out, if the bore was already flattened there wasn't any point in straightening the barrel. After a bit of fettling she produced an iron ball the same diameter as a bullet. It rolled right through. Now Patty was on a mission, Liz was intrigued, and the following discussion definitely included diagrams. The straightening would include both soot and sweat, and very careful heating and pressure. Harold left Patty and Liz working out if they needed some type of rod, or softer tube with rod inside, to put inside to help keep the rifling intact. Both were wondering how little heat they needed to straighten the tube without any more damage. Liz had started talking about car jacks and customised clamps so the pair were definitely serious.

* * *

Liz and Patty spent ten days getting the barrel true again, without wrecking the metal by overheating or leaving a kink. Liz claimed to have stress-relieved the result and swore it would stay put. Harold had intended trusting to luck on the accuracy as it would be used at shortish ranges, but Patty more or less begged him to make it truly accurate. Liz and Patty had repeatedly rotated the barrel while looking through it, to judge their progress with the straightening. They were adamant the actual bore now ran true.

Harold went out four times to get the sights right, a bloody pain because he had to keep reloading the brass. Patty came every time, and the last time, the trainee riflewoman tried the Winchester out. Probably due to the repeated nagging by Harold, Patty managed to keep the kick under control, actually dancing a little jig after hitting the target. While testing the other repaired firearms, Patty practiced again. After that Harold started taking her out into the ruins in daytime just for extra training, and Patty quickly became lethal with either the two-two or the Winchester up to a hundred yards. That made her the fourth and, potentially, the third best shot in Orchard Close, because Alfie's eyes spoiled his shooting over three hundred yards. Meanwhile Patty kept the rifle hidden; if anyone saw it they would talk and eventually Caddi would find out.

More refugees arrived but fewer came alone, and now most brought tools or weapons. Many of the men were older, bringing their wives and teenage daughters or young children. Several newcomers claimed some amateur skills, some of which would complement what Orchard Close already had. Others brought brand new crafts. One of the oldest, fifty-one year old Kharon, carried a rucksack full of tools and parts for repairing clockwork from watches to grandfather clocks. He found himself inundated with work, because every battery watch had died long ago. The scavengers didn't need asking, they scooped up every broken watch or clock they could find.

Work on preparing the new housing moved into overdrive, because most of the new arrivals were sleeping on settees or floors. Rob and his apprentices broke off from finding leaks to fit one bidet per house, so that the first composting toilets could be installed. Eager refugee labour dug the trench for a thick power cable to the houses, which Finn connected to a custom junction box. In a massive three-day purge, willing hands dismantled and transported sectional garages from deep in the ruins. More hours of dedicated labour relocated the stored goods and food into the garages. Even while the protective walls were still being built around the Annex, the first of Patty's Demons moved into the first habitable house.

*　*　*

Meanwhile, Rob, Finn and Charlie continued their work on another project, and announced a proper test. The trial run needed darkness so as dusk fell two days before Easter, all the lights in Orchard Close were turned off. Along all the streets almost every resident came outside and waited hopefully. Finn and Charlie ran back and forth with their apprentices, water gurgled, and more and more windmills squeaked and rattled. Eventually the creaking and squeaking of bearings smoothed out, almost dying away as they sped up. Charlie, Finn and Rob presented Harold with a box trailing several wires. "You do the honours. Just pull the handle from there to there, contact."

"This looks a lot like those things in the films about demolition. Are you sure Bernie didn't help with the wiring?" A ripple of laughter ran round the people nearby, because Bernie made the pipe bombs. "Shouldn't we have a celebrity Beauty Queen?"

"I voted for one in a swimsuit." Fergie looked Harold up and down. "The girl club and Coven voted for beefcake, but had to settle for you." The laughter rippled again.

"In that case, we have to hear a countdown. Four!"

"Three!" That included everyone nearby. "Two!" Harold took hold. "One!" Harold wasn't sure how many voices said that, but they were drowned by the cheer as he pulled the switch. A score of Christmas lights came on here and there nearby, then moments later more further away. Even more lit up soon afterwards until small clusters glowed all over Orchard Close, bright in the gathering dark. They were strung across streets, around windows, on trees and walls, and even around some chimneys. A hush fell over Orchard Close as the coloured lights transformed their home into some sort of fairy grotto.

"Wow!" For once Liz sounded awed, hesitant. "That's beautiful, sort of magical." Phones flashed as some tried for a picture. Harold could hear people talking in hushed tones, and some quiet laughter.

Despite the ethereal effect, what excited Harold was much more prosaic. The little clusters didn't produce a huge amount of light, but these lights didn't rely on the government electricity! "These little wires did that?" Harold peered suspiciously at what came out of the box.

"No chance. There's apprentices all over the place tripping switches, but the first few lights told them when." Finn pointed to a cluster that barely glowed. "Some are flickering, some are a bit dim and a few didn't come on, but we can do it Harold." He looked around, assessing the result. "Or at least we can if there's enough rain and wind."

"There isn't much wind tonight, and no rain?"

"But just as Charlie said, it doesn't take much wind if the windmill is balanced right." Rob pointed up towards the rooftops. "We cheated over the rain. There's tanks of water in some attics, to provide a flow down the drainpipes and simulate rain for the test. We can collect old header tanks and store more water up high in case there isn't enough when we want it. Just in case the government cut our water as well."

Looking up and down the street Harold could see people, some of them families with children, wandering about just looking up at the lights and windmills. Some were also listening to the gurgling in downpipes, explaining to others. Here and there couples were dancing, slow dancing without music, or staring up at the lights with their arms around each other. "You three done good, Finn. I honestly don't think they'll be cutting us off tomorrow, but by the time they do?" Harold spread his hands to take in the scattering of bulbs. "We're all believers now, so you'll get your scavengers and helpers. For now, I'm going indoors to get warm."

Harold walked home deep in thought. This would be a hell of an operation and might still be going on next year, not something to share on this night of this success. Already, voices were calling for the monthly dance to feature a lights and lighting theme. Two nights later, many of the dancers wore fairy lights, only glowing because they were powered by rechargeable batteries.

* * *

The next visitors were definitely not fairy-like. Three days after the dance Casper rang from the gate to report three heavily tattooed Barbies in a car. That seemed strange because Barbie visitors usually sneaked through GOFS territory on foot. Casper told him the one in a blonde wig wasn't Chandra, but she wanted to talk to Soldier Boy—officially. Harold phoned to ask Patty if she could come and be his bodyguard, and arrange for another guard, a man. He also phoned Sharyn to ask her to join him, in case the Barbie wanted to trade.

Harold waited at the end of his road for Patty and Sharyn before walking to meet the Barbies outside the Embassy. One glance showed him that these Barbies were one of the elite and two serious fighters. When Casper explained the delay, he'd needed an extra two people to carry the weaponry off, the Barbie laughs confirmed they were on a friendly visit. The delay had given Patty time to dress as a real bodyguard, with a sheath knife and her sabre in a machete sheath. She stood to one side, just behind Harold, with her crossbow loaded and no doubt at least two pistols under her thick jacket.

The senior Barbie wore a long blonde wig caught up in two bunches by red bows. Her clothes were new, but the flowered blouse with short puffed sleeves clashed with her extensive tattoos. The very professional tattoos of hearts and knives, snakes and skulls and a wolf's head looked to be new. Some of her faded, amateur tattoos would have broken the foul language rules if anyone had read them aloud.

"Hi there. I'm Cherry Pie." Harold blinked, startled, and the Barbie laughed at him. "How much do you know about us?"

"Barbie Girls. Female. Blonde wigs. Nutters. Have a shopping mall and a really firm way with shoplifters. Handle with care." Harold smiled to make at least part of that a joke.

Cherry Pie laughed again, pointing at Harold. "Soldier Boy. SAS. Has a tank. Can shoot the tits off a mosquito. Good beer and stew. Castrates rapists. Do not annoy." She looked around. "I'm here to clear up any misunderstandings, because you might have something we want." Cherry Pie looked Patty up and down. "Maybe more than one thing."

Harold glanced at Patty. She grinned, so he put up his hand for the high-five. "You win." Harold looked back at the Barbie. "Patty said you'd offer her a job."

"I didn't. Not yet but if, Patty?" Patty nodded. "If Patty wants a change of scenery, she'll be welcome."

"If you're going to poach staff, we'd better get comfortable." Harold gestured to the other two Barbies. "Do they know the rules?"

"Oh yes. No effing and blinding, no groping anyone without asking, and if they start a fight someone might finish it with a crossbow. It would be boring if it wasn't a complete novelty." The other two headed towards the canteen for a beer, and to look at some fresh talent, according to one. Harold led Cherry Pie inside the Embassy.

He invited her to sit while Sharyn asked if the Barbie wanted a drink. "Beer please. It's the best around here. Who's the brewer?" Harold laughed and the Barbie laughed back. The female gangsters were always after names but everyone avoided giving them, just in case the nutters came back to kidnap them.

"Do I call you Cherry or Pie?"

"Cheeky. Soldier or Boy?"

"Harold."

"F... Blimey, that's informal. Aren't you afraid someone will take the piss?" Harold mimed aiming a rifle. "Ha, yes, do not annoy." The Barbie sat down where indicated, turning to grin at Patty who sat a little behind and to one side. "Well since we're informal you can call me Cherry, even if I mislaid mine quite a long time ago." She waved at Patty. "You can call me what you like, and any time."

Patty smiled back, shaking her head. "I lost my cherry a long time back as well, but not in a way you'd be interested in. Ask Chandra."

"She warned me, but she reckons some of yours are a bit friendlier after a couple of drinks." Casper had followed them in but now Tessa arrived. Cherry looked from Tessa to Sharyn to Patty. "How many women have you got, Harold?"

"One."

"None."

"Two."

"Depends how you count."

Harold had answered none, so he quickly sidetracked them all. "Business first. Then gossip, dirt, winding people up, all the good stuff." He wanted to know why a different Barbie had come to trade. Cherry had the blonde wig and the relaxed, confident attitude all the top Barbies showed, but Orchard Close usually did business with Chandra. The Asian-looking Barbie, who wore a scanty version of a silk dress, usually combined business with visiting Louise, her girlfriend. "You are unexpected and definitely different to the usual visitors, apart from Chandra."

"Ah well, it's all to do with names. Cherry Pie, for instance." Cherry looked from Tessa to Sharyn. "Did either of you ever have Barbie Dolls?

Tessa's smile looked nostalgic. "Yes, the one with a horse and one with a few frocks."

Cherry twisted to look at Patty. "I suppose you had Action Man?"

"Cindy dolls."

"Ouch. Bitch."

"Backatcha."

Cherry laughed, turning back. "I like her. If she ever wants a change of scenery, please let me know." She glanced around at the others. "If any of these ladies had real taste in dolls, they'd know that the different Barbies had different names. If we climb up the ranks far enough, we get a new name. A Barbie name."

"So Malibu, Christie, Ken and Chandra are names of Barbie dolls?" Harold checked but his friends looked as surprised as he was. "There was a Barbie called Cherry Pie?"

"There's a long list, believe me." Cherry stared as Jeremy, armed with a shotgun, came in and sat in the corner. "Whoa. Am I that dangerous?"

"No, that's because Harold should have one other bloke in the room." Casper smiled at Cherry's quizzical look. "I wanted a Barbie, the one with the pink car."

Cherry looked round the room and everyone nodded. She eyed up Casper's muscles. "I heard about the big gay bloke, but didn't realise just how big you are. The Pink Panthers would love you."

Casper's curled lip was impressive. "Not me. I like to wear my frillies inside my jeans, and I've got past my thing about pink."

"Fair enough. We've got a couple like you and they don't fancy moving to the Pinkies either." Cherry turned back to Harold. "The names mean I'm far enough up the ranks to talk seriously. I'm here because we want to have a real chat to your radio man." All the banter stopped. Harold had mentioned more than once he'd talk if the Barbies stopped trying to steal Trev, but never expected it to happen.

Eventually, as Cherry continued, he had to believe she meant it. The Barbies wanted someone to decide if the transmitter could be fixed, and had been asking around all the neighbouring gangs. Even if the Barbies couldn't identify Trev, they'd worked out the Orchard Close radio man would be their best bet. An offer of twenty biros and a dozen writing pads, just for a first opinion, underlined how keen the Barbies were. Both were rare and expensive, and almost extinct outside of a Mart. The school would want them for teaching kids to write, so Harold agreed Cherry could call in her expert to explain properly.

Cherry made a radio call and a few minutes later the Barbie radio expert, called Skipper, walked down the road from the traffic island and presented herself at the main gates. She wore a red striped jumper and leg warmers, and carried a transistor radio, but unusually for a Barbie, didn't carry any weapons.

After Trev put on a balaclava and Skipper allegedly put on her special knickers, the pair were put in a room with chaperones. While they talked, Harold came to a tentative agreement with Cherry Pie. If Orchard Close made a bit of electrical kit that the Barbies could use to fix the transmitter, the Barbies would part with musical instruments, sheet music, and maybe some CDs from the shops in Beth's. Regardless of the transmitter repairs, Cherry wanted to trade for the live music the GOFS had been playing on the border. She agreed to trade sheet music for Jilli's recordings, because it had been years since anyone heard a new singer.

Trev, still in his balaclava, sounded relieved to get away from Skipper alive. Barbies were his own personal bogey-women, so even when he came into the meeting he sat as far from Cherry Pie as possible. According to what Trev had just been told, the transmitter must be a complete mess. He'd need pictures on a phone before giving any sort of opinion. Cherry agreed she'd get as many as possible, but then she tried to get pictures of Patty in return. According to the Barbie, if Patty wore all her weapons but less clothes she'd attract more Barbie customers for Orchard Close. Trev looked ready to pass out at the thought of more Barbie visitors.

"Off you go, mystery radio man." Harold made it a joke but he had no intention of letting the Barbies find out Trev's name. They'd be tempted to spirit him away in the night.

As Trev left, Cherry leant back in her chair and looked around the room with real anticipation. "Now that Skipper's had her jollies, it's time I got some fun out of it. Who gets to give me the down and dirty on how a Soldier Boy counts women?"

Sharyn volunteered to enlighten her. Cherry looked suitably impressed when she found that one of the women really was Mercedes. The Barbies knew of Mercedes and her rules through the GOFS, and one had seen the public part of her visit but only at a distance. Only that one Barbie had ever seen the Killer Queen, because the Hot Rods and Barbies never usually met. Cherry Pie repeated what Mack had told Harold; anywhere outside

Orchard Close the Barbies killed Hot Rods on sight. The Hot Rod soldiers had also told the GOFS about Soldier Boy getting eyes on, and some sort of hands-on, but it was all rumour.

Now Cherry sat looking from Tessa to Harold with a very quizzical smile, because Sharyn included Tessa on the list of women. Harold sat with a gang boss smirk, as expected, and hoped he didn't blush. "So, are you his woman or not?"

"Depends on if Mercedes is here." Tessa beat Harold to an answer, and shut him up completely. If he argued, he'd have to explain buying her. Worse, if he tried to stop the whole conversation, Tessa, Patty and Sharyn would ignore him because they found it funny.

"Very tolerant of you, and probably a good idea." Cherry frowned, looking from Harold to Tessa. "Let me get this straight. Mercedes is a stone-cold killer, everyone agrees on that, and no bloke gets to touch. But you"—she pointed at Harold—"have not only seen her stark bloody naked, according to the Hot Rods themselves, but she lets you grope her in public?"

"No comment." It took some doing but Cherry Pie finally accepted she wasn't getting a blow by blow account. It helped when Patty and Tessa finally realised that Harold really had dug his heels in, and stopped teasing. Harold didn't mind his friends teasing, but Cherry Pie and the rest of the Barbies would embroider anything he said and spread it far and wide. He didn't want Mercedes thinking he'd been bragging, or giving whatever 'details' the Barbies invented.

Cherry had already spoken to one eyewitness account of the visit, the Barbie. "Okay, I get it, a gentleman. Even so, what our lass saw was a gold plated invitation at the very least. When does she move in?" Cherry looked around, suddenly wary. "Is she already here?"

"Mercedes is killing Murphies, but after that, who knows?" Harold shrugged, managing to look indifferent but only because Mercedes wasn't anyplace nearby.

"Bloody hell, Caddi will go crackers. It couldn't happen to a nicer bloke." Cherry put her hands up as if aiming a rifle. "Keep in practice."

Harold did his gang boss bit. "Yeah, no problem. Anyway, it might never happen."

Cherry Pie smirked and turned to Patty. "If he plays hard to get, knit her a dress like that one of Chandra's. There's girls in Beth's saving coupons for one, because when Chandra wandered down the main drag wearing it the place came to a dead stop. Can you knit a cheaper version? Just thin wool because that clings in all the right places."

"Maybe. Do you mean just plain knit, because the lace stitch will be expensive regardless of the pattern." Patty glanced at Harold, but he indicated she should keep going. Bodyguard or not, he didn't want to turn down business. After a quick discussion, Patty had orders for one cream and two black dresses, short, tight and hot as hell, once someone brought the sizes.

Cherry came back to the radio deal, or to the number of deals that might go through GOFS territory. The GOFS tolerated a few crates of beer or a bit of knitting, but they'd want a cut of any increased trade. Since Cherry wanted blank CDs as well, if Harold could prise any out of the Geek Freeks, she eventually agreed to pay a fee if necessary. As the visit wound down, one thing still nagged at Harold. "You said you were here because this is serious, but Chandra usually deals with serious business. I've met other Barbies as well, ones with wigs, so are you telling me they aren't important?"

"It doesn't get more serious than Malibu, Christie and Ken. The problem is they all met you elsewhere, so they couldn't assess this place properly. The soldiers that come for a beer like this place, so they aren't exactly reliable as judges. I never even met Doll, so I'm a clean pair of eyes. Maybe a little bit biased, because of those rabbits you sold us." Cherry swept her hand round to include everyone in the room. "I'm supposed to get a read on your top people, while the other two assess your place, your people and the setup. Chandra has rose coloured glasses, because she's got a severe attack of lust." Her wry smile came back to Harold. "Now I'm impressed by the Mercedes thing and your bodyguard, so I'm not quite neutral either. Even so I'll recommend doing real business, long-term."

They chatted about types of business while Cherry finished her beer, then claimed she had to go before Patty seduced her into staying. Harold phoned the canteen to let her soldiers know, so they could finish their beers. As he said goodbye Harold saw Skipper, and learned that the original Skipper doll also wore a tight, red striped jumper and leg warmers. She complained loudly about not getting a chance to show the radio man her special knickers, which fitted perfectly with the usual Barbie style. The four climbed into their SUV, driving off with rock music blasting out.

The car stopped by the ruined houses close to Caddi's watchers, and Harold realised why Cherry hadn't been worried about Skipper waiting outside the walls. When four heavily armed Barbies came out of a garage, riding two quads, Harold wondered briefly if the Hot Rods were still alive. Once the music and motors faded in the distance, one of Caddi's men cautiously crept out to check they'd really gone.

Tessa came to the gate, standing with Harold while the car left, and walked back up the road with him chattering about the radio. As the news spread, a good few people in Orchard Close seemed excited about getting Barbie Radio fixed. The Barbie transmitter could punch through the government interference, so their manic mixture of slander, gossip and heavy rock had made a welcome change from the BBC. As rumours grew, Trev even had to confirm that the damage didn't sound like a government hit squad.

The radio interference that isolated the city made everyone a bit paranoid, as did relying on the BBC for any news. The Barbies might not be the best of neighbours, but their transmitter had let everyone know about the local gossip, and any wars.

Chapter 7:

May

Precinct Nineteen / Dudley Zoo:

Miles away to the west of Orchard Close, someone waited to welcome his neighbours. The enclaves were two miles apart, but the Zookeepers had promised to show Precinct Nineteen a very secure direct route. The man in a tattered police uniform, watching a canal tunnel entrance, wasn't totally convinced. He changed his mind as sunlight gleamed on metal in the entrance, quickly speaking into his radio. "Six-one-three here. Contact. Send fifteen because he was right." The man paused then fumbled a phone out of his pocket, raising it to take a short video clip. "You really should be here to see this." The prow of a canal barge had appeared from inside the tunnel, followed slowly by the rest of its forty-foot length. David, 613, stared at the sandbags across the front of the superstructure, blocking any windows there. The portholes along the side had steel shutters with slits. As he watched, weapons poked out of them.

A loudspeaker blared. "Ahoy there."

A startled David ducked, putting his phone away before standing again, slowly. He kept his stubby automatic rifle pointing down at the ground, because now he could see the sandbags didn't cover the front windows, not quite. Familiar looking tubes poked out here and there, two of them centred on him. David raised his empty hand in greeting, speaking calmly despite his silly grin. "Ahoy there. Did you come all the way underground?"

A hatch on the top of the boat clanged, and David registered that the whole thing must be made of steel. A man showed his head, cautiously. "Ahoy yourself. My name is Teddy. This is one of the longest canal tunnels in England, dead handy if you've got a boat. I'm supposed to meet someone called 'fifteen'." The boat had cleared the tunnel now, revealing a second one being towed behind.

"He's on the way, unless you keep going and meet him?" David stuck out a thumb. "Can I hitch a lift if you are?"

"We'll wait, then if it all goes wrong the third boat can tow us back out of trouble." The man smiled, but it had a bit of an edge to it. "You probably wouldn't enjoy following us in the dark for two miles." The boats stopped with the towed barge just clear of the tunnel, but the taut rope behind it told of another still out of sight.

David nodded agreement. "We'd all be blind with the muzzle flashes, and shooting back at them. We'd probably end up falling off that footpath."

Teddy showed him a tube with a small metal bottle attached. "What muzzle flash? We'd use hypodermic darts. Worse, for you, that footpath doesn't go all the way."

"Ouch. Do you want to come ashore?" David gestured around them. "My squad have the area well covered so it's safe." He stopped, listening carefully, then an incredulous grin spread across his face. "Is that a pig?"

"Sort of a piglet, but not as you know it. We've brought young tapirs, African boar piglets, two types of antelope and two types of deer. There are zebra foals and buffalo calves as well. That's why we didn't come sooner, we had to wait until they were weaned." Teddy looked down and sniffed. "We'll be pleased to off-load and clean up."

David stared, completely gobsmacked by the list. Sarge had said the Keepers at Dudley Zoo might swap live animals for weapons, and expert advice on using them, but all these? "How can you spare so many?"

"We have to let the animals breed to keep the milk coming, but usually kill most of the young because we haven't enough grazing. You have plenty of land and can help us defend a bigger area, so we'll both eat better."

David managed to croak, "Milk?" He shook his head, speechless. He'd risked his life, time after time, to get the thin crap the Marts called milk. Now this bloke had just delivered the African equivalent of a herd of cows.

"Hello Six-One-Three. One-five is here." The radio brought David back to himself. He snapped back into his role.

"Send One-Five in. I'm by the tunnel entrance." A flicker of humour touched his face. "With the Ark, Six-One-Three out." As he waited for the sergeant to arrive, the ex-police constable decided to volunteer if these people wanted guards and training. A real zoo would be a sight to see these days, even if he didn't fancy a two-mile boat trip in the dark. David thought about what these people must have gone through to keep the animals alive since the Crash. Sarge had said they were bloody paranoid about even letting him close enough to talk, and no wonder.

* * *

Sutton Park:

The eight gangs who had taken Sutton Park were definitely paranoid, but not about their close neighbours. Controlling the Park had turned out to be more of a job than expected, because just patrolling the area left the gangs over-extended. They all needed fighters in the Park to protect their interests and watch the residents, but that left them with less people to protect their home turf.

"This is bloody stupid." Angel, the bleached blonde bossing the Valkyries, kicked the body on the ground in front of her. "We've got all that lovely meat and fish, but we can't protect it."

A smaller woman with mousy hair hesitated, then went for it. "We're protecting the park and the meat and fish well enough. It's the isolated streets, the ones out in the ruins that are hard to defend. Most of this area is ruins, so we could just abandon it?" She looked a little embarrassed. "I heard the Skins are pulling the people out of anywhere vulnerable, and setting them up on the edge of the park."

"Been getting some Skin, have you? Be careful, you'll end up wearing big boots and polishing your head." Angel had replied more or less automatically, but now she thought about it. "How far did your new boyfriend tell you Shiner's lot have pulled back, and how do you know he told you the truth?"

The woman hesitated again, a slight blush on her face. "Not exactly boyfriend, but the Skins treat women all right. After a couple of beers his jokes were funny, then I had a couple more and you know how it is." A wicked little smile grew on her face. "He had a few as well, enough to loosen his mouth and a few inhibitions. He got downright gobby once I loosened a few things as well. I can't promise it's all true, but the Skins have definitely pulled back."

"I'll ask Hangaku. She's tight with Shiner ever since we carved up the Studs together. If it wasn't for Shiner's missus, Chelle, I'd wonder if they'd been loosening things." Angel considered it properly for a few moments. "No, it'll never happen even if Hangaku's standards fall that far. Chelle would take a shotgun to her and cut Shiner's nuts off." The bleached blonde looked at the surrounding houses, many with broken windows and doors, and the frightened people gathering outside them. "The bastards cleaned these people out, so they may as well move now. Tell them to get their gear together and I'll call up some transport."

As Angel made her radio calls, she wondered who else might be having the same problems. Her headquarters had a big wall all round it, and always had plenty of well-armed fighters in residence. That left the oiks, the ordinary people, scattered among the ruins in their small clumps of useable housing. Angel might not be angelic but she took protection money from those people, so the least she could do was to stop some passing arse from killing and robbing them. Once the move had been organised, she went to see Hangaku.

Hangaku confirmed that the Yakuza, the Skins and the Hard School were all having trouble with raiders. Something had to be done, and startling as that might be, maybe Shiner had the right idea. Not just about moving people out of harm's way, Shiner had some ideas on how to deal with the cause of the problem.

*   *   *

Eleven days later, an SUV carrying two men and two women, all heavily armed, drove away from two inhabited streets in a wasteland of empty ruins. A few of the residents waved, then everyone in sight either went indoors or back to gardening. Hidden in the surrounding ruins, a scruffy, heavily armed man turned to his companions. "I told you. The Yakuzas only send patrols round these little places. It'll be at least four hours before they come back, and it might be tomorrow."

"So how long do we wait?" This man patted his shotgun. "There's enough of us to kill the patrol as well, then we'll have plenty of time and we'll get their weapons. I fancy one of those swords."

"No chance. Killing a few civvies isn't that serious but their boss, Hangaku, doesn't like anyone killing Yakuza fighters. She'd hunt us down, and everyone heard what happened to the last one she caught alive." Uneasy muttering from the rest of the men confirmed they'd all heard about that. "We go in now, but no shooting this time because that patrol might hear. I was watching and this lot don't have weapons, just tools like hammers and axes and probably kitchen knives." He pointed three fingers at three of the men, then pointed to the left. "Find a good spot in the ruins and make sure nobody escapes that way. I'll call you in once we've sprung the surprise." After sending two more trios to surround the houses, the remaining seven stood up and checked their weapons.

"What if they've got guns?"

"I got this information the same place I did for the last two raids, so it'll be right. The plebs aren't allowed guns, and none of them can fight or they'd join the Yakuza." The leader looked down at the man's shotgun. "Only crossbows, guns are too noisy. Unload that shotgun because I know you, you like using that bloody thing way too much. We'll walk out there nice and steady, stick an arrow in anyone who runs, and round everyone up without raising an alarm. We'll have time to rob them blind, pick up a couple of fresh women, and be long gone before the patrol gets back."

"I want a woman of my own, just once." Despite grumbling, the gangster unloaded his shotgun and slung it across his back. He wound his crossbow as he joined the other six striding out of cover.

*   *   *

The leader waited until a few of the gardeners noticed him approaching, standing up and glancing nervously towards their houses. "Don't do anything stupid and nobody gets hurt. We want food and any coupons, then we'll be gone. If you run we'll shoot." Ahead of the seven men, some of the gardeners turned towards the houses. The leader of the bandits aimed his crossbow. "Call your people out of the houses. If we have to go in and get them, someone will get hurt." The armed men watched carefully but the first sullen-looking residents, men and women, came outside without any argument. "Well done, now I want you all in the middle of the street, out in the open." The leader raised his voice, shouting to the men he'd sent to surround the housing. "Move in, everybody. Check the houses as you come."

For a few minutes it all went to plan. The unarmed men and women were obviously reluctant, but a few more appeared and they were all drifting in the right direction. The crack of a shot jerked everyone's heads around! Or not everyone's, the bandits realised much, much too late. At the sound, every apparently cowed and helpless victim dived for cover. "Who was that?"

Nobody answered at first but more shots rang out, followed by a shout from one of the men sent to surround the houses. "Fucking Yakuza!"

"That's us." The seven men turned and all of them dived for the ground, because they'd all recognised the young Oriental woman framed in a doorway. The extravagant Oriental dragon on her dress might have been enough, but the long, curved blade confirmed they'd run smack into Hangaku, queen of the Yakuza. When the seven men hit the ground, only three were still capable of bringing up a weapon.

Even as Hangaku spoke, the hapless victims who'd dived for shelter mere seconds earlier came up with pistols and crossbows and opened fire. Rolling away from the riddled bodies of his comrades, one bandit pulled his shotgun round to load it. He'd tried with the crossbow, but thought he'd missed. He broke the weapon, fumbling for the shells, but a shadow fell across him. "Too late, asshole." The bandit looked up in time to see the young man's arm and sword, but not in time to scream before the blade ripped his throat out.

"There's two running, back here." As the voice finished, a loud crack echoed. "There's one running, but he's in the ruins now."

"Hunt him down. We wouldn't want anyone learning any lessons." Hangaku strode out into the road and toed a body. "You could have saved me one."

"That's your own fault, ma'am. It worked too well." A young man cleaned his sword before picking up a shotgun. "This needs cleaning, but it must work or he'd not have been loading it."

"A bonus." Hangaku sheathed her sword with a sigh of resignation. "I can't take all the credit. Half a dozen of us worked it out, and believe it or not, Shiner came up with the actual idea." Ripples of laughter rang out as the Yakuza stripped bodies, and cut a couple of throats to make sure.

"Are we going to set up again someplace else?" The bonus shotgun had definitely encouraged one fighter.

"No point. We've just killed our problem so now we'll abandon all the vulnerable housing. If the other raids persist, the other gangs will to do the same, set a trap. I'll call in our watchers and the other two traps." The Yakuza boss looked around at her fighters, a slow smile starting. "Angel's fighters are all women, so they'll need some blokes to make it look right. Does anyone want to play happy families with a Valkyrie?" From the big smiles there'd be no shortage.

"The Skins' fighters are all blokes, so they'll want volunteers as well." The young woman posed with her hand on her hip. "I wasn't planning on playing the housewife just yet, but maybe I could practice?"

* * *

Conan:

While Sutton Park sorted out their raider problems, and Precinct Nineteen learned how to milk a zebra, others still had conquest in mind. In the northwest of the city a bloodthirsty paranoid psychopath led his gang from strength to strength. Conan and his Barbarians had taken another two very small, weak, enclaves, to give him eight in all. The ninth conquest would be harder, because he couldn't find a way through the enclave gates.

Conan needed a way through the gates, because the Lambs of God had cleared a wide area around their enclave. Any attacker would have to run half a mile, straight into a hail of bullets and arrows. Conan loved the thrill of bloody, hand-to-hand combat, but this time his nutters would be cut to pieces before they could get over the walls.

Bribery and threats hadn't worked either. The Barbarians had approached the Lambs of God while they were shopping, but the men and women had laughed at the gangsters. The Lambs were confident in the strength of their walls, and knew the Barbarians daren't target them while shopping because of the Mart guards. None of the Lambs of God seemed susceptible to the usual incentives, offers of wealth or women, and Conan had run out of ideas.

Now a frustrated Conan stood in a derelict office block, using binoculars to watch the Lambs working in their fields. He cursed, turning away and passing the binoculars to his lookout. "Keep watching. I want to know about every single one of those fucks that comes outside the walls, how near they get to the ruins, and how long they stay out there. I want hostages."

"I've been watching for a fortnight now, Boss, and none of them come into the ruins. The only people to leave the farmed area were in a convoy going to the Mart." The man kept it respectful, because Conan had been in a foul mood all day. One of the others had warned him, the boss was pissed off because he'd hit his bitch too hard and she might die this time.

Conan stormed back down to his vehicle and roared off back to base. He tried to come up with a plan, because he had to keep taking enclaves to provide the fighters with loot and women. Once his advance stalled, some would leave or some twat would try to take over. Right now he couldn't think straight, which was all the Bitch's fault, her and her smart mouth. He couldn't just kill her because he'd bragged that he'd break her, but the Bitch just wouldn't give in. Conan strode through the small enclave, the last one he'd conquered before running into the Lambs, with his head going in circles. Lambs of bloody God? Well Conan's Barbarians were the lions, and they were hungry. He thought through what the lookout had told him. If he shot up the Mart run, it wouldn't get him inside the walls; he needed someone inside for that.

Suddenly galvanised, Conan went to find the Barbarian he'd put in charge here. "Garth, find anyone with brains and meet up in my place. We're going to work out how to get at those nuns."

Within ten minutes a dozen men had gathered. They soon realised that Conan had already made up his mind what to do, and their job was to find a way to get away with it. Coming out of the meeting, one of them summed it up for the rest. "What the fuck happened to him? Has that bitch sent him soft in the head or what? This is stupid. If we attack a Mart the whole city shuts down."

"If you don't keep your gob shut you'll be strung up in the square, begging him to let you die. If he wants us to attack the Lambs in the Mart then that's what we do." Garth looked from one to another, right around the group. "Unless any of you reckon you can take over?" One by one the men dropped their eyes, cowed. "In that case help me figure out a way to attack the Lambs while they are shopping, one that doesn't end up with the Mart guards using their machine guns on us." He looked towards where they'd left Conan. "The doc tells me the bitch made it, so we've got some time. Conan will be busy either beating the shit out of her or fucking her."

"Fucking stupid, that is. Why mess up a good-looking woman?" The speaker glanced nervously towards Conan's house.

"Because she won't give up. She keeps fighting back and he can't handle it." Garth shrugged, turning away. "Which keeps him occupied, so let's get thinking."

* * *

The General:
Much nearer to Orchard Close, only a few miles to Harold's northwest, Patton had been doing exactly what Conan wanted so much. He'd been leading his Bloods in a mad charge to capture yet another small enclave. Patton preferred this sort of conquest, serious carnage without any attempt at traps or trickery. The man running this place had been a nasty little tyrant, and stupid enough to think he could tell the General no when offered the chance to surrender. Not that the General, Patton or the Bloods cared

how the bloke had run the place, but for once their victims might find the new landlords an improvement. Patton finished wiping his machete on a torn shirt and tossed the bloody rag away. "That was fun, and the Bloods have been having a ball. Even so, after three like this we need a bit of a break for everyone to heal up. Are we going after the SIMS or that Orchard Close next?"

"Neither. There's a couple more like these, where we won't take enough serious casualties to slow your maniacs up. You'd best get back in there so they don't burn the place down." The General smiled to take any sting out of that, it was the plain truth. "Once they've sobered up, come and see me and we'll decide on what order to take them."

Rhys sidled up, notebook at the ready. "I've got details on a couple, possibly three." He watched with distaste as Patton waved to a couple of bloodied fighters. "Ones where a bit of finesse might help." The General sighed, he hoped Rhys never seriously annoyed Patton or he'd need a new spymaster.

*   *   *

Professors:

Only a few miles north of Patton and the Bloods, four cars stopped at a checkpoint. The occupants were definitely annoyed but also apprehensive when they saw the firepower aimed their way. "Prof paid up front."

"The boss has put up the tolls." The surrounding gangsters laughed, but their weapons never wavered. "It's four times as much, or you can pay with weapons." He eyed up a female despite her weaponry. "We'll take livestock, even armed livestock?"

The radio crackled. "Back off. We'll sort out something else. We'll write off the coupons for now." The occupants of the cars kept their weapons ready, with fingers on the triggers and safeties off. The trip home wasn't far, but long enough for some serious worrying. Two other gangs had set the price of a safe passage to the Mart ruinously high. Prof kept saying their enclave mustn't take part in the local gang wars, but more than one teenager thought slapping one of the neighbours down might back the rest off.

*   *   *

Reivers:

All across the UK, the TV showed that neither the government nor the Reivers were backing off at all. The latest news item included pictures of a supply convoy for a Mart, fifteen articulated lorries scattered along a stretch of highway, all burning furiously. An armoured Land Rover lay on its side in a ditch, torn open by an explosion. Between the vehicles lay scattered bodies in uniform and still, bearded figures wearing plaid or ragged jackets.

"The inhabitants of Inverness will be short of food after the latest outrage by the bandits operating out of the Grampians. Some of the foolish inhabitants of the city, the criminals and rebels and malcontents, have been spreading rumours that these savages are here to help them. They try to claim a link to historical figures such as Robert the Bruce, but would he have burned the very food needed to feed women and children? The Army managed to stop the criminals stealing the food, and killed this band so they will not repeat their terrible actions elsewhere."

The scene switched to the gunsights of warplanes as they swooped on a small band fleeing along a mountain path. Cannon fire tore through the figures and the rock of the path itself, sending both tumbling down the steep slopes. Uniformed men climbed a hillside and some fell. Others raised their weapons, firing at figures flitting among the rocks ahead. The scene moved forward to show the soldiers passing through the rocks, and dead rebels. A long view followed, of a dam and reservoir framed by snow-capped mountains.

"These brave soldiers are fighting tenaciously, disputing every inch of the mountains to keep the innocent citizens safe. The savages are threatening to destroy the Hydro-Electric generators which supply much of the power to the cities in England. Despite their losses, and the difficulty of maintaining air support among the mountains, these soldiers will not shirk their duty. Once again the rebels and traitors have been thwarted. Hopefully, the efforts of your government and the armed forces will continue to keep the electricity flowing, to bring you light and heat."

In Orchard Close, Harold kept his mouth shut about the differences between the uniforms and weapons in the mountains and those on the road, and how both were different to those on the bypass nearby. Not many differences, and most wouldn't notice, but Harold had lived in the Army uniforms up on the bypass and used their weapons.

* * *

Cabal:

Only five people watched the screen in the bunker, and none seemed happy about the alleged victories. Owen, the chairman, scowled at the spymaster, Maurice and pointed to the screen. "That rubbish is fine for the scum, but according to Ivy, the Marts in Inverness know the real situation. How?"

"They don't know the real situation. Those freed from the work camps are spreading rumours among the gangs. The Mart managers are listening to the gangsters, who are taunting the guards. It is true more convoys have been attacked, but those are real bodies." Maurice clicked to show close-ups of a couple. "The rebels can't afford losses because unlike our forces, there are no reinforcements." He sighed. "In reality, burning lorries is a plus for us since that means the Reivers didn't get the food."

"They don't actually need any more, do they, not after their invisible raiders popped up again?" Ivy lifted her lip, sneering at the spymaster. "They'll be well fed for a long time because four other convoys disappeared briefly. We only found them when patrols investigated the smoke, after The Bruce burned the empty vehicles." She turned to Joshua, the Army man. "I hope you can supply some decent armoured vehicles to escort convoys, because in all five cases the so-called bandits destroyed or captured what you've supplied to date. Why didn't the RAF catch them? Where's Faraz?"

"It's not down to him or the RAF because we are using the European aircraft in that area. We can't let the RAF see how many foreign soldiers or aircraft we have, or that they're targeting women and children. The air-craft are working deep into the Grampians, supporting the ground forces or attacking the home bases and families of these Reivers. We pulled them back when your convoys were attacked, which cost us dearly." Joshua took the TV controls to show about thirty uniformed bodies scattered across a hillside. A succession of clicks showed similar scenes elsewhere. All the uniformed bodies had been stripped of weaponry and equipment includ-ing boots, jackets and protective vests. "The counter-attacks and ambushes happened as soon the controllers pulled the air support, so the Reivers actually planned it. We can't use RAF personnel so the controllers haven't any experience, and were having trouble working with crews from different nations. That won't happen again."

"Ivy has a good point about the armour you supplied for the convoys, or rather the lack of it. My contractors are being slaughtered. The business about no replacements for the Reivers' losses are bullshit, because every time the Reivers free a work camp, some of the scum join them. The scum have been fighting each other for years, so they are already trained." Vanna, the Asian woman who controlled the armed civilian contractors, glared at Joshua. "We need real armoured fighting vehicles, the wheeled versions, not Land Rovers and other relatively soft-skinned vehicles. The tracked armour we used in York will rip up the roads so we can't use that."

Joshua held up his hands in surrender. "My apologies. I should have said they can't replace trained personnel, because the scum from the work camps won't be anything like as disciplined and effective as the original group. Most of the Reiver casualties are the new recruits, because they haven't learned how to fight as soldiers." He shuffled through some papers and pulled out a printed list before offering Vanna a few vehicles. The two of them argued fiercely over what mothballed vehicles would do the job, and how many Joshua could find crews for from the military prisons. None of the crews could return to tell the Army what they'd seen. He finally freed up enough armour to mollify Vanna, and agreed her contractors could provide most of the crew in each one.

"I hope this unrest won't spread south?" Owen looked around all those present, most of them nodding agreement.

"We have regular troops patrolling a line from Glasgow to Edinburgh, with RAF support, supposedly to stop these raiders coming south. They are actually there to police the imported troops." Joshua glanced at his figures. "This will stop any further clearances even in winter, because I can't spare the troops."

"That's not too bad just now. The farms are producing plenty of fruit and veg while the Falklands and Argentina are sending fuel and meat. The meat is mainly for the enclosures because the fishing fleet is feeding the Army and the useful citizens." Owen turned to Grace, the aristocrat supervising the work camps. "Once the harvests are in, you can send more parties out to scavenge the abandoned villages and suburbs outside the enclosures. That turned out to be very productive in the spring."

There wouldn't be much scavenging in Scotland this year. Most of those present had now skimmed the reports and were startled to find out six thousand inmates had been freed from work camps, and less than half had been recovered. At least most of the rest had gone back to their cities, rather than join the rebels in the mountains. Joshua's Army checkpoints and Vanna's Mart guards would be arresting people all over the country, on the slightest pretext, to make up the shortfall.

A relieved Owen moved his attention to Maurice. "What about your plans to eradicate the democratic enclaves?"

"Some are gone, and others will go soon. Some have been forced to band together and will take more careful handling. One item has come to my attention." Maurice brandished a thin file. "You insisted on rotating Army personnel, to stop attachments between them and nearby enclaves?"

"Yes. We don't want them getting too cosy. This way the Army personnel are all exposed to the worst areas to harden attitudes." Owen answered but the others nodded.

"Maybe it works another way. The hardened troops move next to one of the democratic, friendly enclaves, and lose their edge." Maurice started passing copies of a report around the table. "As you can see from the feedback, the Army as a whole might actually become more tolerant, not less. Overall we might be better off letting some soldiers stay and become friendly, then wipe them out along with the enclave."

Joshua barely glanced at the report before tossing it down. "I'm not happy about deliberately killing regular Army personnel like that."

"We'll all monitor the situation, and look at it again in a few months." Owen nodded to Maurice, ignoring the huff of displeasure from Joshua. "Please let us see the reports so we can assess the situation properly. After all, south of Edinburgh the situation is stable so we don't want to rock the boat until the Reivers are dealt with. Is that all?" Owen looked round the table before moving on to the next problem. Henry, the farm manager, had complained about the cancellation of all planned clearances. As usual he wanted more land for growing food. "Ivy, please liaise with Joshua to move the Army nearer to the enclosures. That will leave more land where the Army can't see Henry using mechanised farming equipment. Reorganising his farmers will keep Henry off our backs." The rest nodded agreement, happy to move on to more mundane matters.

*　　*　　*

As the meeting broke up, four of them paused briefly, letting Joshua get out of hearing. Maurice glanced after him. "Is that what you wanted, Vanna?"

"More real armour? Oh yes, the tracked tanks have uses but some of the wheeled versions will be a big help. Our own non-Army armoured force is building nicely." She smiled hopefully at Maurice. "What about our private snipers?"

"The first tests worked, and your nosy Army officer is no more. The test subject performed perfectly." Maurice hesitated, then admitted the problem. "We still need more traumatised people as raw material, because the wastage is very high. I'm having them buried in the woods, well spread out."

"Good idea. We don't want anyone to notice and ask awkward questions. I'm sure Grace can scour the work camps and find more inmates with breakdowns?" Owen waited until Grace nodded before moving on. "Did the anti-aircraft and anti-tank weapons arrive?"

"Yes. They came to work camps labelled with the wrong delivery address, and were put into storage pending return." Grace laughed briefly. "Maurice's off-radar delivery lorries picked them up. No trail, Owen."

Maurice picked it up. "They are now installed in the city centres, with Vanna's people, ready to antagonise the regular Army and RAF if necessary. We'll blow up a few tanks or planes if there's any hesitation when we finally send in the armed forces."

"Better yet, when we have enough paramilitaries and finally disband the Army, those weapons will be a big help if any of the armed forces mutiny." The four conspirators split into pairs and left.

Vanna glanced to make sure neither Owen nor Grace could hear. "I'm a little worried about the amount of ammunition in the enclosures, Maurice. After all, my paramilitaries will face it sooner or later."

"But we can cut the supply at the right time, since we know exactly where they shop. They'll shoot their weapons dry within a few hours. In the interim, the scum are thinning themselves so there'll be fewer for your people to face." Vanna nodded in agreement, but looked thoughtful as they hurried to catch the rest. She didn't think the scum would run out of ammunition as quickly as Maurice seemed to believe. She might not like them, but she recognised that they weren't all idiots.

* * *

Cyn Palace, London:

The six leaders of five gangs, Sin and Sinner, Kermit, Preacher, Ike, and Imam, weren't buying ammunition or propellant from Maurice's supplier, because they were isolated in London. Fortunately, the sealed city contained both the experts and materials to produce their own. These six had bought some of it to try a new method of deterring raids, and now they were ready to act. The combined reaction force had beaten off several raids without losing any food, even if each fight cost them fighters and ammunition. Now the Imam and Preacher had come up with a real long-term answer.

Today, the first part of the deterrent meant Sinner crouching in the rubble, keeping his head down so the raiding Gatts could pass by without spotting him. He could hear quiet voices and the sound of boots trying to sneak over broken bricks, but he couldn't see anyone. "Don't look. Stay hidden." Her words were barely breathed in his ear but Sinner turned to make a sharp retort, then stopped and smiled. The sheer mischief in Cyn's eyes held him, and she'd been right. He'd almost risked sticking his head up far enough to see.

Sinner nodded, then leant to kiss her. "You keep down as well. No need to join the attack." A vain hope, he knew. She'd led her people from the first time he'd seen her, three long years ago. Cyn had been frightened of her gun and sick at the sight of bodies when they first met. He hadn't been much better. Sinner looked across the rubble to where the librarian crouched. If it had hadn't been for her, he might have never met Cyn, and would probably be dead. He'd been watching the library from a block of flats, wondering who was in there, when a bunch of yobs had knocked on the door. A little fat bloke came out to negotiate and when the gangster shot him, everyone in the library froze. So did Sinner, though he couldn't do much anyway with only a cricket bat. Nita hadn't frozen for long, just a few heartbeats, then she'd emptied two pistols in a continuous roll that mostly missed. The shots that didn't miss killed the gang leader, dropped his second, and hit another three. The other four ran.

Sinner hadn't been called that, back then. He'd been sneaking around looking for someplace, anyplace, his small group might survive the chaos. When he saw Cyn coming out of the library, the pistol in her hand wobbling all over the place, his brain took a holiday and he'd charged out of hiding to help her. He'd not seen Nita until she followed Cyn outside and pointed a pistol at him. The smoke coming out of the barrel told him this one would shoot, so he'd started talking as fast as possible. A couple of Sinner's friends had come over to help finish off the wounded attackers, exchanged stories, and within days his small group had joined those in the library.

Right now, Nita, usually called the librarian these days, carried at least four pistols, a shotgun and a hatchet, and had that look in her eyes. Her religious fervour frightened Sinner, it frightened most sensible people, but that fervour came in handy in a fight. A light touch brought his mind back to the present. Cyn, known as Sin these days, mouthed, "They've gone." Sure enough, the noise of feet had faded away.

Sinner clicked his radio, twice. The rest of his Sinners knew what that meant and began to crawl out of deep cover, moving into firing positions. If everything went to plan, they'd be waiting when the Gatts ran for home.

*   *   *

The faint noises were now approaching Eli and Preacher, as the Gatt raiders crept through the rubble directly between them. Eli clicked three times, and four clicks answered. None of his gang, or Preacher's, moved. They'd set this up very carefully, which meant waiting for the right moment so they'd kill plenty of Gatts. Eli fitted a bolt into his crossbow. Arrows didn't ricochet like bullets so there'd be less chance of friendly fire casualties. A single click sounded on the radio. Eli waited for a count of five, but no more clicks came.

"Allahu Akbar! Allahu Akbar!" One voice called the first time, but even Eli joined in the second time. He wasn't religious but that cry would scare the shit out of the Gatts, the gang creeping up to steal food. "Allahu Akbar!" Eli came up on his knees and aimed his crossbow.

In the street, over forty fighters froze for vital moments, staring horrified at the horde pouring out of the houses ahead of them. Every coloured fighter in the other four gangs had joined Imam's men, to encourage the jihad impression because most people still thought of Moslems as non-whites. Even as Eli fired, half the fighters ahead of him broke and ran. Crossbow shafts sleeted in from both sides and ahead, and most of the remaining Gatts staggered or went down. A few fired, but by the time they'd decided which way to shoot, the Imam's shock troops had hit.

Eli charged forward, dodging a wild swing from a machete and striking for the bloke's arm. Before his opponent's machete hit the ground, someone else had brained the bloke. "Keep going, keep going. Allahu Akbar!" Kermit came bounding past, blood flying from his blade, and set off after the Gatts who'd run away.

"Don't let them get away. Strike now, in the Lord's name!" Across the street Preacher and a dozen men cornered three Gatts who'd run the wrong way. Eli turned to join the chase, kicking at a wounded man on the floor.

"Come on!" A long, curved sword, the real deal, skewered the wounded man. For an old geezer the Imam could shift, even if the younger fighters were leaving him behind. "Finish them now, before they recover." Eli did as he was told, encouraged by the roar of gunfire up ahead.

*   *   *

The gunfire came from the Sinners, a volley that hit the fleeing Gatts at point blank range, just when they thought they'd escaped. Sinner thanked God, either Preacher's or Imam's, because none of his gang had opened fire early and given the victims a chance to break away to the sides. He might have waited too long to be absolutely certain, but an elbow had smacked into his ribs at exactly the right time. "Fire!" Pistols and shotguns swept at least half the runners away, and wounded or stunned the rest. "Cease fire, cease fire, use your blades." Sinner leapt to his feet, cringing as he half-expected Nita to keep shooting. His relief didn't last long as he came face to face with a wild-eyed Gatt wielding a big old sword. Sinner blocked the first three swings, almost losing his machete, then stumbled and fell. The Gatt lifted his sword to finish Sinner and froze, a crossbow bolt sticking out of his chest.

As the bloke crumpled, his sword clattering on the rubble, he revealed a smiling Sin. "Sorry, I daren't shoot before. I might have hit you." She reached down and helped Sinner up, then handed him the big sword. "Here, try this for size."

"Hey you two, fighting before loving." Eli stopped, trying to catch his breath. "Bloody hell, I'm knackered." He looked around at the bodies, and the wounded Gatts who were rapidly becoming bodies. "Did we get them all?"

"Most of them. We let two get away just like you wanted." The young man scowled in the direction the Gatts had run. "We didn't have to. We could have sent the bodies."

"You know why they're alive. By the time they've finished shitting their britches and telling everyone Imam has started a jihad, every surviving Gatt will be praying the nutters head someplace else." All the humour left Sin's voice. "We all saw the real thing when that lot round Paddington decided to set up a new Islamic State. A lot of people died wiping them out, and nobody wants to find themselves in the way of that sort of thing again."

"Then you should all give thanks to Allah, that he sent you true believers." The little smile on Imam's face acknowledged a good few of those present weren't on speaking terms with any god, let alone his. "The Sinners you loaned me seemed to enjoy their religious experience."

Sinner laughed at him. "You might even convert a couple if we do this too often." As Preacher arrived, the six gang bosses walked slowly back towards the old school used as a barracks. The idea had worked, so now they had to decide which other local gangs needed the same treatment. Once they'd all learned some manners, maybe they'd be more willing to negotiate a permanent peace. Then the idiots could buy the food they kept trying to steal.

Chapter 8:
Demon Spawn

Despite all the action elsewhere in their own city and country, Orchard Close had more prosaic problems. The beer sales took a hit at the beginning of May, when the Hot Rods' production started back up. Since Caddi hadn't given them any warning, that left the brewers with gallons of surplus beer.

Despite his reluctance, Harold arranged to visit the Geek Freeks to try and sell in bulk. He rarely visited outside the scheduled trading trip once a month, because Harold didn't like the Geeks much. They were liars, cheats, and probably treated their women worse than Caddi did. The gang boss, Branson, had stiffed Harold over his share of the loot when they'd combined to stop the General, and Harold hadn't finished evening up yet.

Harold parked up and walked towards the Geek trading post, an old Burger King that had been left mostly intact. It sat in the middle of the cleared area around the Geek compound, where neither side could spring a surprise. As he crossed the open ground Harold braced for some winding up, because he'd be dealing with Marconi today. The Geek radio and electrics man still hadn't forgiven the Orchard Close women for his caning.

The bodyguards settled at tables either side of the Burger King, while Harold sat at a central table opposite Marconi. Sure enough, the Geek started prodding. "I don't suppose you're here to trade for women, Soldier Boy." The Geek manager inspected Patty, who had come as one of Harold's bodyguards. "You seem to have enough already. I'd heard you even took one from Caddi, or that nasty bitch of his was chasing you?"

Harold just shrugged. He wasn't discussing women with this little scroat, or any Geek. "Patty is as nasty as you'll want to meet, so warn any of your lot who get near her or her trainees." Harold gave the nastiest smile he could muster. "Then while they're bleeding out they can't complain it came as a surprise."

"Christ!" Marconi looked at Patty a bit more carefully, noting the amount of sharp metal she carried. She sneered at him. "I'll mention it. Darwin spent a night at the Mansion with that bitch of Caddi's and he's got a scar to prove it, a long one down his arm. He swears she cut him for no reason, and gave him the choice of his arm or an eye. She reckoned she felt his filthy eyes looking at her and that counted as touching. Where's your scar?"

"You already know I haven't got one." Harold smirked now because that would wind Marconi up, a bit of payback.

"Darwin won't come to trade with you. He says if you crow about it, he'll go apeshit because it's still a bit sore." Marconi laughed at Harold's baffled look. "The memory, not the scar. A couple of the girls had a bad time until he got it out of his system. We had to recycle one of them." Harold wanted to hit the little shit. Recycled in Geek-speak meant hurt or disfigured badly enough to be rejected as a sex slave.

"Well that would be a bloody shame, since I've got beer and some very different spices to trade. The spices make the Mart dog chews fit to eat." Harold wanted to move the subject on, and genuinely wanted to sell the beer at least. "Try this." The plastic tub held a bit of cold curry, a real Ru special. Orchard Close had plenty of Indian spices now. Some of the later refugees had more time to pack, so they'd brought the contents of their pantries.

The Geek tried just a little, cautiously, then took a bigger mouthful. "Whoo. Nice. How much have you got, and what do you want?"

"There's plenty of beer as well, our home brew. I know your blokes prefer it." Harold smiled at the sour expression looking back at him.

"Yeah. I've told Hawkins we should trade with you to buy in bulk. Then our men would spend their coupons here instead of your bloody pub." Marconi glanced at Patty before continuing. "Some of them fancy those women of yours as well, enough to be polite. The wilder ones visit to score a Barbie, since I'm told those crazy bitches go to Orchard Close for beer as well?"

Barbie visits weren't a secret, so Harold nodded. "A few do. After all, the road to the bypass is neutral and everyone has a treaty right to use it. Sharp left and our front gate is right there, and it's a canteen, not a pub. Do you want bulk beer then, because I've brought a lot? If not we'll set up a pub here and flog it to your men."

"What do you actually want?" Marconi looked out at the pickup. "You didn't bring that for fun." Marconi always tweaked Harold about his habit of walking rather than using diesel.

"Quite a lot, but I've brought a few bits apart from beer." Harold swung into proper trading. He'd brought skinny jumpers in Mart colours, but with a stripe of something brighter. Patty, Liz, and three of the latest refugees had worked out how to shape simple garments, and put in simple stripes, using the knitting machine. When he asked about the music CDs, Harold hit the jackpot. The Geeks wanted more live music, and were willing to part with a karaoke setup with music. It came with a booklet giving all the lyrics, but no tracks with a voice. After some back and forth he bought it, and thirty blank CDs, in return for one copy of Jilli singing every tune on the machine. The Geeks would rip it, but only sell copies to their neighbours the other direction. If Harold heard a copy being played by any nearby gangs he'd never sell the Geeks another new song.

The preliminaries over, Harold finally got to the real reason for his visit. "I'm after cement and sand again, and I haven't any soft loo rolls to trade this time. I need a couple of trowels for the bricky as well."

"So soon? Are your lot breeding like those bloody rabbits?" Marconi grinned, but it faded. "Ours have died again."

Harold tried not to show how happy that made him. "Ours haven't, so I guess my cement will be cheaper than I expected. We'll sell you three more, and instructions? Stick to them and your bunnies will prosper."

"Maybe. Probably." Marconi threw up his hands. "What the fuck, sell us five but this time the troops can look after them instead of the women. I'll castrate the arse that lets them die this time." He calmed down again. "So what are you building? More hutches?"

"We've had more refugees come in so we're using the houses in the fields, the storehouses. We'll be bricking up the windows and doors." Harold's scowl had a message in it, for Geeks in general. "So nobody bothers the women. There's a whole squad of guards sleeping in there, in case someone tries."

"The guards will be alert then, but if there's women in there they might not be watching the fields." Marconi thought that was funny, but the small smile on Patty's lips wasn't for the same reason. The Demon now had twenty-one single female trainees living in those houses, with their weapons. A few were wondering just what it would take to persuade a gang to raid, so they could try out their practice. "So how much cement? A lot I hope, because I've got this."

Marconi produced a nine mil that presumably needed attention, handing it over for inspection. Initially Harold assumed a Geek gun, because they cared for their firearms and this one looked clean. Closer inspection showed only the outside had been cleaned. "Captured?" Marconi didn't answer so Harold smirked. "It's been neglected until the action jammed, then some idiot tried to prise it open. The clip might have jammed before then, or after some burke used it as a hammer. Your lot look after their firearms better than this, and one of them tried to fix it." Marconi's eyes narrowed but Harold kept smirking as he continued. "Since he failed, you know it's going to cost double."

"Yeah, yeah, right." Marconi sighed, looking out at the pickup. "That'll carry a ton, right?" Harold nodded. "Which means we still get your beer and spices, but I might have to buy the jumpers. No, I definitely will because we want the rabbits. Our blokes can buy the jumpers themselves." Marconi leant back, smiling again. "The gun is a capture because Welly sucked our neighbours into the right place. We hit them with all four onagers loaded with pipe bombs. We killed seventeen and sent a lot scampering off to find a bandage. We captured more guns but they're still working, even if they're gunked up. I reckon they'll all need your attention in the end."

"Sooner is actually cheaper. There's less wrong with them." Actually they'd be bloody expensive whenever Harold fixed them. Despite ripping the Geeks off over the rabbits, twice after this deal, Harold reckoned Hawkins still owed him over the loot from the General.

"Maybe, once this one is fixed, or depending on the prices we agree for the cement, jumpers and spices." Marconi looked towards Patty again, at her weapon this time. "We can always sell you some more crossbows, better ones than hers. I'll get the two roughest pistols out here if Hawkins agrees." They settled down to work out just what a ton of cement and sand came to in knitting, repairs, beer, rabbits and spices. The guns came for repair so Harold bought crossbows to make up the balance. At least this time he felt as if he'd won on the dealing.

Despite the warning, Marconi and his guards kept eyeing up Patty as she helped Harold and the other guards load the gear into the pickup. Patty noticed, so it might have been a good thing none of them actually insulted or tried to touch her. Harold heaved a sigh of relief when the vehicle finally pulled away from the meeting. As usual, a trip to the Geeks had left him feeling as if he needed a good scrub.

* * *

Patty had sneered at the crossbows as she helped to carry them to the pickup, but chuckled once away from the Geeks. "My girls, and Doll's squad, will split these if that's all right Harold. We can get in more practice with the extras."

"Check with the other squads first, but that should be okay. Did you enjoy your first proper bodyguard visit to the Geeks?" Harold grinned, already sure of the answer.

"Not really. I didn't get to kill one." Patty didn't smile at all.

On the drive back Patty didn't say much for most of the trip. A half mile before coming in sight of Orchard Close, before the road came clear of the ruins, she asked if Harold would walk the rest of the way with her. "I need a bit more practice, Harold."

"Okay." She meant with the two-two rifle in the pickup cab, but the others would assume crossbow practice. Harold tucked the faulty hand-guns in the glove compartment, picked up his rifle and waved the driver and guard onwards. "Get that cement and the tools to Casper, will you, please, and make sure the guns are put in the guardhouse for now. We'll be in after you hear a couple of shots. While Patty is playing, I'm going to check the sights on this rifle." Harold headed into the ruins.

They found a spot, which wasn't hard in daylight, but Patty didn't load straight away. "Did you mean that, Harold? Back there."

"Which bit?"

"About Geeks bleeding out."

"If the stupid bastards touch you after a warning like that, feel free." Harold curled his lip and almost spat in sheer disgust. "The species would be better without Einstein for starters."

"It's just that the Geeks give me the creeps. The slimy bastards always seem to be deciding if they can get away with anything. You know, with women." Patty smiled, but only a little. "Except Wellington, and possibly Galileo and Tell. I don't think of Wellington as a real Geek, but the rest make my crossbow finger twitchy." She still seemed wary, unsure of Harold's reaction. "I just didn't want to cause trouble for you, if one of them gave me half a chance and I took it."

"Do you want me to post a set of rules? Something like those Mercedes uses, but point out the Demons have adopted them?" Patty still seemed unsure, so Harold confessed. "I don't like the Geeks either, and I definitely get an itchy trigger finger near some of them. They might even be worse than the Hot Rods." He pointed at the rifle. "Practice your long range, because if you ever get Darwin or Einstein in your sights you have my permission."

"Yeah, after what Marconi said I've moved Darwin up my list." Patty's smile didn't have any humour this time. "I'll only shoot them if we can prove you're somewhere else, unless I've got the Winchester handy because nobody knows you've got that." She looked around at the ruins and pointed. "That gable end with the buddleia growing up the end. The patch of pale brick is what, a hundred and fifty yards?"

Harold found the spot and checked with his monocular. "A hundred and forty but you'd be near enough at that. You're getting better."

"I practice at judging distance. The target might not be very big if he's hiding and I don't want to miss." Patty sounded utterly serious now. She settled in while Harold raised his monocular to watch the wall.

Four shots later Patty whooped when Harold confirmed four hits, all well inside the chest area. Harold tried not to laugh. "I've got a scope for that rifle. You can have it now."

"You rotten sod! I've sweated blood to hit with the peep sights and you've got a scope?"

"Which means hitting with a scope will be a doddle. If it gets fast and furious the scope is useless. Toss it aside because the view's too small. It'll concentrate you on one man and you'll kill him, but meanwhile his three mates have scattered and you didn't see where." They walked the rest of the way in deep discussion over the difference between picking off a single man, and a battle with a lot of moving people. She'd learned how to hit her target, but Patty needed her horizons broadening to make her hits much more effective.

Patty's shooting would definitely make Orchard Close safer. Now Harold needed a way to do the same with the Mart runs.

*   *   *

The Mart shopping trips were getting bigger despite the food coming in from the fields. All the extra people needed extra corned beef to supply fat in their diet, on top of the usual coffee, chocolate, underwear and contraception. That meant carrying more coupons, and unfortunately the shoppers were vulnerable after leaving the bypass and before entering the Mart. Muscles and fists weren't enough if someone with a machete picked on them before the shoppers had time and privacy to unpack their iron bars.

When he bemoaned that fact during some private sabre practice, Patty had a possible solution. One of the earliest refugees from the Murphies, Wamil, had started teaching a few women a type of unarmed combat.

Harold went to visit Wamil at home, just to have a look at a few of her lessons without any trainees present. When the tall, quiet, twenty-seven-year-old Indian woman agreed to run through her full training routine, Harold had a hell of a shock. She bounced around the room kicking, chopping and punching like some sort of Bruce Lee clone, though her sari made the strikes seem more graceful than lethal.

"What the hell is that? Sorry, but it's a bit more than self-defence." Harold chuckled, trying to cover his reaction. "Have you ever actually hit anyone like that?"

Now Wamil looked shocked. "Only my brother. He taught this to others as a combat skill, but we only sparred for exercise so we pulled the strikes. I've never hit anyone properly, because that could cause serious injury." She looked a little embarrassed. "This is not supposed to be for women and I only learned it to keep fit. I don't teach my classes the dangerous moves."

This time Harold's chuckle came much more naturally. "It'll definitely get everyone fit, the way you bounced around here. Dangerous moves? Exactly what is that lot supposed to do, except scare me to death?"

"It won't hurt anyone as an exercise." Wamil seemed defensive about that, so Harold asked about the keep fit exercises. Once she'd relaxed he came back to the dangerous moves. Wamil demonstrated a few in slow motion against a decidedly wary Harold, so he could see where the strikes would land. Harold felt relieved he'd met Wamil on friendly terms. Her so-called "exercises" would deliver a nasty combination of groin, eye and throat strikes with elbows, knees, feet, thumbs and knuckles.

"What about defence? Does it include any way of breaking free if someone grabs you?" Harold cautiously took her wrist in his hand. "Be gentle with me please."

Wamil barely took hold of Harold, showing where she would apply pressure rather than actually using any force. Harold recognised some moves, such as the thumb between his knuckles, and assumed the rest would work as well. Wamil moved on to a nifty selection of throws and blocks and some painful looking ways to grip or twist to release a weapon or cause agony. "Is that what you wanted to know?" Now Wamil seemed very worried for some reason.

Harold nodded enthusiastically. "Oh yes." The result looked ideal for hand to hand combat, especially smaller fighters facing heavier, stronger opponents. It wasn't judo, which he'd seen, but some of the throws had that flavour while the strikes might be nearer karate. "I like it. Nasty, and most of it doesn't rely on brute strength. Could you start proper classes for any of the women who want to learn, please? Patty's Demons will be interested."

"A keep fit class?"

"No, teach them how to actually use the moves, to hurt someone. You'll get a few men as well, once someone like Ru dumps them on the floor." The tiny Murphy ex-tenant had turned out to be a real firebrand. Harold felt sure Ru would be at the front of the queue for lessons, just in case the banchod got past her crossbow, machete and knife.

"I can teach enough to get the woman out of trouble, if the man won't accept no?" Wamil still seemed cautious.

"I was thinking more of crippling the scroat. I would like you to teach them as much as you can, the nastier the better." Wamil still looked confused. "Can you make the women truly dangerous? Show them how to hit the person properly, full contact, not just exercise?"

"Yes, but." Wamil dithered, and then took a breath. "These disciplines are meant to hurt, or even kill if used properly, so what if one of your men gets hurt?"

Harold laughed, shaking his head. After three years of the Murphies, some of the new refugees couldn't believe the Orchard Close fighters had no privileges. "It serves them right for stepping out of line. Is that what's bothering you? One of the guards pushing it with a woman and getting slapped down?"

"Yes, because. Well. They're the fighters, and fighters usually expect women to put up with…. It's just, they seem better here, but I wasn't sure." Wamil sounded flustered, and looked embarrassed.

"At least half the fighters are women anyway. Clear and simple version. If I grab a girl without permission and she breaks my arm, that's my fault. Now can you make the women dangerous?" Harold looked her straight in the eye, because Wamil needed to believe this. She seemed relieved but still a little embarrassed about the dangerous part, which didn't make sense to Harold. "How come you learned the dangerous moves if you didn't want to use them?"

Wamil's embarrassment became a nostalgic little smile. "My brother shouldn't have taught me, but he couldn't say no when his baby sister insisted. I only wanted to keep fit, but he wouldn't corrupt the teaching so I had to learn properly or not at all. Women aren't allowed to learn this fighting, but I think he was a little bit proud of me even if it had to be a secret." Her smile morphed into downright wicked. "He will have a shock if he meets some of your women. I can make them very dangerous, if I can find the time. I daren't teach Ru before, even if she is my friend. She would have hurt someone, or killed them." Her face fell. "I'm not sure I can actually hit someone myself, not full strength."

"Don't worry, because others like Ru can and will. Take all the time you need, because you don't have any other work now. This is an official job even if nobody else knows exactly what you are doing, apart from keep fit classes." Harold looked around the room, thinking about how Wamil had been leaping about. "I'll sort out a schedule for the keep fit classes, in the dance rooms. We should keep the advanced keep fit exercises separate. I'd like them to come as a surprise sometime." Wamil nodded enthusiastically and with real anticipation. "I'll want some tuition myself, because in a brawl I usually revert to knuckles, knees and head-butts. A bit of finesse might come in handy."

Wamil looked startled. "But I thought the Murphies are frightened of you?"

"Because I can shoot them a long way away, or beat them with a stick or machete. None of them have seen me fight without weapons." Harold sobered, trying to convince her. "So I'd be obliged if you keep very quiet about my practice." Wamil nodded, speechless. As he left, Harold smiled quietly at the thought that, unarmed, the quiet woman in a sari might possibly be the most dangerous person in Orchard Close.

*　*　*

For now, Wamil's lessons would take second place to Emmy's needs because it was planting time. The gnomes moved into top gear, dragging anyone who looked to be skiving out into the fields. The new recruits were torn because some were both garden gnomes and fighters, and there just weren't enough hours in the day to practice both. As the weather improved, some residents were finding time for football again. That took off properly when Fergie announced the weather had warmed up enough for the first swimsuit match of the year. The new refugees were stunned, then some became enthusiastic.

Harold had to agree the players could have a second pitch near the walls, providing the teams cleared extra land for planting. Despite the gnomes, enough people found enough spare time to make a start. This time they weren't waiting for the grass to grow, overgrown lawns deep in the ruins were dug up and brought back as turf. A few of the gang visitors were intrigued by occasional remarks, then fascinated when they asked for details. Nobody mentioned swimsuits, but the first enquiries came in about ordinary football matches, visitors versus Orchard Close. So far nobody felt that confident, even after a few Barbies and GOFS were allowed to watch. Harold didn't know how the players found the energy to play football after a day gardening and practicing with weapons.

*   *   *

Some residents had found a way to combine fighting and gardening. "Hup two three four, hup two three four." Harold looked up from weeding as seven women and three men marched past with Doll calling out the time.

"Hey, no fair. You should be gardening." Harold stood up, frowning despite Doll's sunny smile. "Is this the firing practice you wanted, because you never mentioned skiving to do it? Emmy will skin me."

"Your skin is safe. We are cutting down the undergrowth under the baby trees for rabbit food, and machete practice, and so the scroats can't hide there. Later on we are gathering leafy stuff from the ruins, more garden gnome work. We'll stop for the shooting practice before bringing back more yummy rabbit food." Doll brandished one of the sacks for the greenery. "Tomorrow we'll go out to get bricks for the wall around the Demons, and practice some more."

Harold looked them over, and all wore a pistol but none carried a crossbow. "Are your cowgirls going in for pistols, because I'm short on propellant?"

Doll nodded enthusiastically. "There aren't enough crossbows, so we let the Demons have most of them. A few have crossbows but we all want to learn how to use a pistol. We only fire three shots each but practice as often as you'll let us. That will save ammo in the long run, because we'll be accurate if there's a fight." She indicated her recruits, still marching off towards the line of saplings. "Come with us, because I'd like you to make sure I'm doing it right."

"As long as you protect me from Emmy."

"Deal, wimp." They both hurried to catch up with the group. Because he'd come along, they kept going through the saplings to practice immediately.

The group all knew where to go, stopping in front of a whitewashed house. Everyone began to adjust their belts. Fergie tied her holster to her leg, western gunslinger style, and when he looked around Harold saw the rest were now all slung low. "Accuracy, not speed, Doll. Just because they're cowgirls isn't an excuse."

"Not cowgirls because some are boys. They'll find a name sooner or later." When Harold turned, Doll had also tied her holster down. She dipped her hand and her gun came up fast, aimed away from the people. "We practice speed for if there's an emergency close-up, but don't waste ammo when we do." She smirked, because she knew what Patty kept under her jacket. "A fatal surprise, just like Patty keeps saying."

"Fair enough. Where are the targets?"

Doll pointed. "Drawn on the whitewash."

Harold looked at the figures drawn on the house, then the line of trainees. "That's about eighty yards. I thought everyone practiced at fifty with pistols?"

"But if we can hit one man reliably at eighty, it's got to be worth the practice." Doll looked a little unhappy. "That crowd would have broken thirty paces sooner back at the Mart fight. Patty said you taught everyone to hit a group a lot further away, and used that on the General. This is one step further?"

Since Doll had nearly died in the Mart fight, Harold could see her point. "Fair enough, and they are your squad. I've never learned to shoot pistols, not properly. I just went on what a couple of soldiers told us in London, and a few leaflets found in shooting ranges. How is it going?"

"There's five of us who can hit a man nearly every time at eighty yards. We could do with more practice?" Doll flashed a brilliant smile. "I'd say pretty please, but I reckon you're immune just now."

"Not immune, but my resistance is high." Harold hesitated, but Doll's request made good sense. "Just the five best. They can have another three shots a day. Will that be enough?"

"Can we save them up and shoot twenty off at once? That works better because we can correct and try again a few times."

"I'm convinced." Harold looked at the group. "Or I will be if you prove your point." Ten minutes later Harold agreed the point had been proved, which made sense in retrospect because rifle shooters improved by practicing. On the way back, he wrestled with a problem. He couldn't afford the propellant for everyone to practice like that.

*　*　*

The practice seemed more urgent with the Hot Rods involved in a war. When Caddi made another move into the Murphy streets, the warlord sent a hostage and asked Harold to visit the Mansion. Harold assumed the recent visits to Orchard Close were at an end for whatever reason, so he braced himself for the usual hassle. Caddi met him at the gate, his first surprise since usually the gang boss waited in his house. "Are you running short of diesel, Caddi?"

"I've got enough put by if the electricity suffers a mishap. The sort of problem your man can't fix." Harold thought he knew what sparked Caddi's half-smile, but waited until he'd been searched and most of his weapons were locked up. Sure enough, once they were out of earshot of any Hot Rods, Caddi admitted he'd realised why the residents deserted Glasgow. He had a couple of diesel generators tucked away, but wanted to buy the expertise to copy the Orchard Close system once it had been perfected.

"But we can't actually deal for that until it's perfected, so why are we wandering away from your house?" Harold looked around but couldn't see any obvious reason for Caddi's detour.

"I've got something needs looking at, a very special prize. The usual weapons for repair and some loot to trade are in the house." Caddi unlocked a garage, and stood aside to let Harold see a heap of electrics. "What do you reckon?"

"Pass. I don't even know what it is."

"That is supposed to make up a transmitter, when it's put together. The Murphy who surrendered reckoned this lot came out of a radio station." The pair of them stood looking for a few moments. "There's not many obvious controls or dials, and it's been sat in a shed for several years."

Harold believed that because dust, dead leaves, spider's webs and general filth caked every bit he could see. The biggest problem seemed to be... "Why is it in so many bits?"

"Back then, someone set the radio station on fire. The blokes who ripped this out were in a hurry but didn't know which bits they needed."

Caddi shrugged. "I've got no idea what's there, and nobody else has. Do you reckon it will work?"

"I've no idea. It looks like one of those 3D puzzles without a picture to help me put it together. My radio man might know?" Harold walked around the heap but still couldn't make sense of it. "There's got to be pieces missing, and who knows if any of the rest still works?"

"Yeah, well I need your man to have a look at it because Hot Rod Radio sounds good to me. That'll stick it to those fucking dykes as well. I'll pay for your bloke to work out what it needs?"

"I'll want Cooper as the hostage." Caddi opened his mouth to object but Harold kept going. "You might trade one of the others to get my radio man. You would for our brewer or the GOFS smith, and they know it."

Caddi relaxed, laughing. "They're right. Cooper it is, but that means there'll be no overnight." The warlord shrugged, still with a smile. "He'll never behave himself that long, then when your women try to cane him he'll go fucking crackers and get killed."

"Short visits, as many as needed?" Caddi nodded. "No guarantees." Harold didn't want Caddi getting his hopes up because the supposed transmitter looked more like scrap. "I'll take a couple of phone pictures back so he can think about it."

"Fair enough." Caddi waited as Harold took several shots from different angles. "Now let's get comfortable and sort out the guns."

* * *

When they finally made it to Caddi's house, the maid showed Harold into the lounge. "You may as well come in here now, since you made yourself at home last time." Caddi grinned and Harold smiled back because he had... sort of.

"Hey there Mack. Don't nod off in that comfy chair." Mack had a seat, instead of standing as he usually did when the trading took place in Caddi's study.

Mack smiled amiably, completely unfazed. "Not unless Mercedes is 'ere to keep an eye on yer, 'Arry. I 'ad a night off last time."

Harold sat in the same armchair as last time, asking the maid for coffee with two sugars. He looked over the collection of weapons on the coffee table and pointed. "Those must be your guns and will probably be fixable. The others are a mixed bag. I hope your blokes know enough not to use crowbars on jammed weapons?" Harold didn't care much if they did, but he was jacking up the price at the moment. "Some idiot Geek did and actually made it worse, so I doubled the price of course."

Caddi burst out laughing. "I'll bet that made them happy. My men know I'll use a cane or crossbow on them if they cause any extra damage." He gestured towards the captured weapons. "So what about them?"

After looking them over, Harold nodded slowly. "I'll have to let you know about the rifle but the rest look to be the usual neglect, unless there's split brass jammed inside?"

"In that one. How come that happens?" Caddi waited while Harold looked steadily back at him. "Yeah, all right, but I'll bet none of your rounds blow up in the gun, do they?"

"Nope." Harold wasn't offering to anneal or resize Hot Rod brass, he'd rather it split as often as possible. "Have you got original ammo for testing?" Harold would swap out Caddi's good rounds and test with his own reloads.

"Yes. I've also got this." Caddi lost his scowl, turning to reach down behind his chair.

Harold did a double-take. The weapon looked about five feet long, definitely a firearm but it must have weighed a ton. With relief, he recognised the swan-neck device right where the bolt should be. "That's a flintlock musket, what they used to call a Brown Bess."

Caddi chortled. "I knew you could fix it."

"I didn't say that." Harold looked the weapon over. It had been hard used but nothing appeared to be broken. "What's up with it?"

"If I knew that I wouldn't need you, would I?" Caddi ran his eyes over the weapon, not at all happy. "It won't work, and none of our people have any idea why. The bloke was stuffing things down the barrel when he was shot so maybe he blocked it." Caddi reached down and round and brought out a leather pouch, which he threw to Harold. "Here, this was with it." Caddi rooted around again. "He was using on the barrel."

That was probably the ramrod, Harold thought. He was keeping a carefully blank face. Until he had the musket in Orchard Close and in bits, Harold had no bloody idea what it would want. There were a couple of things he remembered, from films and historical novels. "It'll be short ranged and a bitch to aim." He looked pointedly at the ramrod. "Bloody slow to reload as well. Do you really want to spend coupons on it?"

"Too true. I reckon Mack could handle it." Mack grinned genially, and Harold thought the big man probably could. "The bloke who was hit with the bullet had a fucking great hole right through him, and did a back flip after he was dead. Something like that might come in handy now and then."

Harold opened the pouch. Rough looking powder, a scoop, bits of cloth, some bits of stone that might be flints, and… Harold held up one of the musket balls and grinned. "So would you if this hit you, Caddi." The ammunition looked to be well over half an inch diameter and might be getting on for twenty millimetres. He threw the ball to Caddi, who rolled it back and forth on the chair arm, smiling.

The maid brought the coffee, but Caddi didn't ask if Harold wanted a blow job or something similar. That puzzled Harold, and it must have showed because Caddi laughed. "You never say yes, Harry, and even if you did it would be a terrible waste. I reckon Mercedes would take a knife to any woman who looks twice at you. Then she might kill you as well, which would spoil the fun."

Harold smiled, relieved that something had finally stopped the hassle. "You mean it would stop her getting you better prices."

"True, but she's busy tonight so you can use both hands to eat." Caddi eyed Harold and thought about that. "My mistake, but I'll make sure she's here next time. You'll have to sleep in that cold hard bed over in the other house tonight." The bed would be soft enough, but definitely colder without Mercedes. Harold dragged his mind back from memory lane to concentrate on haggling.

The prices for the work took some serious negotiation, with the usual question marks left until the weapons were stripped. The musket stayed a big question mark until Harold had inspected it properly. Caddi loved to bargain but Harold thought he'd done all right this time. Along with beer making supplies, charcoal and coupons, more thin wool would head to Orchard Close. The women using the knitting machine had nearly run out. Someone the other side of the Geeks actually liked the thin jumpers so the Geeks wanted a score, a bit longer and plain black without the stripe.

Harold insisted on plenty of charcoal, the type without chemicals, because he accepted a selection of bent machetes and broken crossbows as part payment. The new recruits needed both. Liz would sort out the blades while Harold, Liz and anyone else with any idea would repair the crossbows. At worst Harold would pay the Geeks to sort them. Patty's Demons in particular would be pleased.

*   *   *

The evening meal tasted delicious, so Caddi must still have the chef. Oddly, despite being relieved about Mercedes not helping Caddi in the negotiations, Harold missed her. A pretty young woman in a very short, tight white dress sat down next to Harold. Caddi smiled happily and pointed at her. "Not up to your usual standard, but just in case you feel playful. This one will let you have your hand back no matter where you put it."

"I'm all fixed up these days, ta." Harold let the lass eat in peace. She didn't join any of the conversation around the table. Only Cooper and Dodge ate with them tonight, with their women, neither of whom spoke much.

Back in the lounge, Caddi went to take coupons from the safe to pay Harold for half the repairs upfront. After turning back, the warlord's face broke into a wide smile. As Caddi looked over Harold's shoulder a very familiar voice said, "Why didn't someone tell me 'Arold was here?"

"We didn't expect you back tonight, Mercedes. I had to find him another dinner guest." Caddi looked a happy boy, because the evening's entertainment had arrived.

Harold sighed inwardly as a miniskirt moved past at eye level, a real bloody mini with the hint of stocking tops already showing. "I didn't know until I came down. I had to go back upstairs to take off some clothes." More stocking top showed as Mercedes seated herself on the arm of Harold's chair and installed her legs across his thighs. "Have you been unfaithful, 'Arold?" She pulled Harold's hand round her with a, "Hardly worth all that asking business these days" and put it on the skirt over her thigh.

"Never unfaithful in word or deed, Mercedes. How could I be, with all those lovely memories of you?" The answering long, slow flicker in her eyes surprised Harold. He'd expected to have to try harder.

"It's a good thing I've undressed for company, or your company anyway. You might want something to keep you remembering." Mercedes glanced down at her legs so Harold made a point of giving them a long look.

"Oh yes. Those are definitely memorable." Harold wanted to ask if Mercedes wore stockings normally, or just when she wanted to torment him. For some reason a bit of stocking top looked sexier than just legs, or it did on Mercedes. Thinking about that and what Patty said about Mercedes and underwear, together with the comment about undressing for company, screwed Harold's concentration for a moment. Mercedes gave Harold a big smile before very obviously undoing a button on her blouse. She smelled lovely and Harold asked without thinking. "What's that lovely smell, scent or soap?"

"Why 'Arold, don't your other women wash?"

"Yes, but they don't smell like that." They didn't, unless Harold's reaction came down to those damn pheromones.

"Well since you like it, you should have a proper smell. Here." Mercedes leant in so he could smell her properly, which involved her blouse gaping invitingly and Harold sliding his eyes away. Mercedes smiled and her eyes did as well, a little, as she put her neck so close that Harold almost kissed it.

"Mmm, so lovely and so tempting." Harold blew out gently so Mercedes would feel it on her neck. She'd done it again; he'd started flirting without a second thought.

"You could have helped to soap me, if someone had told me you were here." Mercedes swivelled slightly so that Harold's hand had a little trip down her thigh. He avoided the hem, just, and her thigh muscles rippled hello. "You rotten lot could have told me about 'Arold." Mercedes actually sounded annoyed. "I had trouble reaching my back properly. 'Arold could have washed it."

Harold knew that part was bullshit because Mercedes couldn't take anyone into the en-suite, but it was a hell of a thought. "I would love to hand wash anything you need me to, Mercedes. Even if there's no shower or water."

"Naughty 'Arold, but don't give up. If you keep asking, who knows?" Her thigh muscles told him they liked the idea. Harold didn't need more distraction; he needed his full attention on where the captured hand touched. Mercedes swivelled her hips a little when she talked to the others, enough so his hand stroked up and down her very short skirt. Touching her stocking meant bleeding, so Mercedes had raised their game to a new level.

That didn't stop Harold from playing. "In that case, I'll keep asking."

Mercedes looked him over, very obviously. "Well, 'Arold. Since you didn't get to wash my back, will you be staying over? Just in case something else needs washing in the night?"

"My loofa is yours to command."

Harold tuned out the comments about his loofah, because he'd got the response he wanted. Mercedes looked down with that slow flicker in her eyes and smiled, a real smile. "Mmm. Tempting. But if your loofah strayed,

I might cut it off."

"Only if it strayed someplace you didn't want it. Unfortunately, my business is finished." Harold sighed, and found that he meant it. "If I'd only known, then I would have made the haggling last." Actually he'd be staying overnight, but daren't ask for another night in her bed. He wasn't sure if he could survive a second time.

Mercedes sighed as well, leaning in until Harold had to turn so his nose wasn't in her cleavage. "Maybe it's just as well I'm not allowed to take you to bed again. My won't-power might not survive another night." Apparently, judging by all the laughter, second nights in her bed weren't allowed.

"Once will have to do then, luckily it was unforgettable." Harold sighed dramatically, making sure the expelled breath went downwards without letting the spectators realise he'd just blown straight down Mercedes' cleavage. He considered the eye flicker and a small, private smile his reward.

"And tempting. If you'd stayed another night, I might have been tempted to stray." She sighed again, and her lips were close enough to... Harold stopped that thought sharpish, just in time to keep his fingers off the stocking tops as her legs swivelled.

Caddi interrupted, his face and voice showing his curiosity and some anticipation. "Well since you couldn't stop over in his gaff, maybe we could make an exception? Would you like Mercedes to take you to bed for the night, Harry?" Harold saw the surprise in the young woman's eyes, and then another tiny smile that nobody else could see.

"Of course I would. Frustrating as hell but a man's gotta take what he can, when it's offered." Harold kept his eyes, and his smile, aimed firmly at Mercedes. "After all, if I keep asking, Mercedes might take pity."

"Take your ears."

"Take your nuts."

Cooper and Chevy reacted but both Harold and Mercedes were waiting for Caddi, and everyone shut up smartly when the answer came. "Well then, if Mercedes asks you can say yes." Dead silence followed, while Mercedes made a great play of pursing her lips and looking Harold over.

"It has been a busy night, so perhaps I need a bit of fun and some relaxation?" Harold saw it then, a warmth in her eyes, deep inside but more than the flicker. "You look to be up for fun, 'Arold. Will you spend the night in my bed?" She paused. "With me?" Mercedes licked her lips. "Please?" The please wasn't actually necessary after the invitation in her voice.

"Yes Mercedes. How could I resist when you ask like that? I will do what I can to make sure you enjoy it." Her small, real smile morphed into the wider public version.

"Oh, I'm sure it will be memorable. Nobody ever wanted to come back for more! A few had so much fun they had to be carried out in the morning." Mercedes swivelled her hips a little to slide Harold's hand and her muscles did that little tango.

Harold winked at her. "If that's going to happen to me, please tell me first. You know why." He squeezed her thigh.

The Hot Rods guffawed as Cooper gave the answer, "So you can make it worthwhile." Harold had to ask again, because Mercedes had gone well past any rules he'd heard of. After all, Caddi had certain rules as well.

"Caddi, are you trying to kill me, or are you trying to recruit me?" Everyone went quiet, and even Mercedes looked curious.

"I must admit that I'd love to recruit you, but Mercedes doesn't screw anyone to order. In fact, she doesn't screw anyone." Caddi gave a short laugh. "I'm beginning to get curious myself, so no matter what happens, Harry, I've no argument with you. It's between you and Mercedes."

"So are you trying to kill me or recruit me, Mercedes?" Harold wanted to find out, even if he didn't expect Mercedes to tell him. She'd already screwed him, in his head.

"Yes." That young face and her old eyes looked at Harold. The tip of her tongue came out, for a moment. "To help you decide which option you need a hint. Would you like to put your other hand somewhere delectable, 'Arold?"

"I would love to, Mercedes, providing I manage to survive to remember it."

"Please put your hand somewhere delectable, Harold. Somewhere you'll remember until you die." So she still might kill him. The room had gone dead quiet again. One hand already rested on a very short length of skirt over her thigh, both too high and too low for Harold to relax. Where the hell should he put the other? If he refused, Harold lost their game. Not that he even seriously considered refusing.

Harold left his stick propped against his chair and raised his hand as if about to give an oath, before giving Mercedes a very slow inspection, toe to top. At the end of the delightful trip, Harold held her eyes. "So much delectable, and only one small hand. Where do I start?" The flicker was even stronger this time. Harold tuned out the chorus of suggestions because they were playing a private game, oddly enough.

"It's not where you start, 'Arold." Harold felt her hand take his wrist and pull it forward and wondered for a moment if he was going to confirm some betting by touch. Down went their hands, and for one wonderful moment her eyes twinkled.

Mercedes would be bloody gorgeous, must have been gorgeous, before something had killed that twinkle. That promise of laughter in her eyes finished the package and made it irresistible. Harold felt something smooth and warm, and a hem under his forefinger and the edge of his palm. Without thought his fingers followed the curve around. Then he registered just what he had hold of and... Harold glanced down.

She'd put his hand on her nearest leg with one finger on her skirt and the other three fingertips round her thigh but not between her legs. Cooper and Dodge immediately urged Harold to stick his hand up the short skirt. Caddi's attention fastened on Harold's hand, then switched to Mercedes with a real question in his eyes. A startled Harold did his best to keep his face straight as Mercedes leant in, giving him another chance to look down her front. As she did, the minx slid her nearest leg forward a couple of inches, so her stocking top came out from under the miniskirt. Harold had a strip of bare skin under one finger! As Harold slid his eyes away to decline the flash, he realised nobody else would know because his finger covered the bare strip. Mercedes laughed. "Now where do you expect to finish?"

Dead or with you biting the bedding wasn't a good public answer. "Just here is perfect. Higher and I lose that lovely smooth leg, lower and I move away from all the other truly delectable bits." Harold put just enough pressure on his second finger so Mercedes felt it on that strip of skin, and gripped the other thigh a little harder. He realised what he was doing and took a deep mental breath. Mercedes had got him to do something she'd have to kill him for, if anyone realised!

Mercedes looked triumphant. Caddi looked from her to Harold, curious what had amused her so much, so Harold spoke up quickly to divert him. "Where have you been tonight? It's dangerous for a young woman out in the dark." The gist of the various comments settled on it being dangerous for who found the woman, and certainly distracted Caddi.

"I've been wandering about, to see who is still stupid enough to follow a short skirt and an unbuttoned blouse into a dark place." Mercedes gave 'Arold a questioning look at that.

"It would probably depend on who is in the skirt and blouse, but right now I can see the attraction." Harold gave Mercedes a visual once over again, in case anyone missed the point. They didn't and the rest of them agreed, laughing. Despite her reputation, Harold thought Mercedes could still lure most of the Hot Rods somewhere private. They might be wary, but hell, Mercedes had got both Harold's hands occupied and hers free right now. Not both, because one slipped into his back pocket and squeezed his ass. Mercedes had to move in closer for that, which made it harder to avoid her cleavage.

At least Caddi stopped being so curious about her agenda with Harold, and wanted to know how her scouting had gone. Mercedes genuinely had just come back to the Mansion. She had killed two lone fighters, but neither were one of the remaining Murphy leaders. Those were getting very wary, and weren't venturing out without lots of bodyguards. Mercedes had also collected some useful information on sentries, weapons and strongpoints, which Charger entered on a map. Nobody noticed a young woman, and this one occasionally attracted a customer into an alley and took their ears. No wonder Caddi kept advancing.

The others in the room were watching Mercedes repeatedly move her cleavage about, trying to win the bra bet themselves now she'd undone that extra button. Their distraction helped Harold, as it wasn't so obvious he was having a lot of trouble with concentration. Not strictly true, Harold's concentration worked fine, but had to stay on his hands with side trips into his boxers. Harold tried harder to pay attention to the conversation when he suddenly realised that not everyone had been distracted. Caddi sat watching Harold try to avoid looking for Mercedes' bra, and his lieutenants try to see if she wore one, with a little smile.

The talk became more general, about the better beer now they'd found another brewer. As a bonus Caddi had captured the Murphies' brewery and the equipment, and installed the lot in one of the Mansion houses. Harold winced a bit when Caddi gloated over the brewer being a family man, so there'd be no screwing around with the yeast this time. "Did you want some chickens, Harry?" That came out of nowhere.

They all laughed as Harold stared. "I would love chickens, but not at any price you'll accept."

"Not proper chickens, not yet," Caddi clarified. "But they are real chicks that will grow into chickens. The Murphies were so busy fighting they didn't realise their hens had been laying in the bushes, and sitting on the eggs. I've captured the lot. I'm keeping the adults because they are producing eggs. Or the hens are, and some cockerels will make a lovely roast dinner." Harold realised that the bastard had done it. He'd got the breakfast everyone had considered extinct, bacon and eggs! "I've just realised that selling you a few chicks will pay for my musket."

"I'll want a lot of chicks for that, especially if they might not give eggs in the end." The negotiations about buying some chicks would have gone better if Harold could have concentrated on haggling. He broke every rule about touching her bare leg while not letting anyone know, while Mercedes kept moving her thigh muscles under his hand and trying to give him an eyeful. His concentration went walkabout when Harold wondered if he'd get the full view at bedtime. He privately thanked all and any gods the gun prices were sorted out.

When Caddi finally announced time for bed, Mercedes held each of Harold's hands in place for a last slow massage from her muscles while she slid that strip of flesh back under her skirt. She finished by standing up slowly so Harold stroked her as his hands came free. This time Mercedes didn't say anything about the view while following her, just pointed to her ass and gave it a little wiggle. Watch this. Caddi intercepted Harold at the bottom of the stairs.

"Just to make it clear, Harry. If you screw her brains out, you walk free, no problems. You even win the commando betting since you won't be doing it through her knickers." Caddi laughed, possibly a genuine one. "You don't even have to confirm."

"Fat chance. She's screwing with my head, but not the rest."

"No. For the first time she might, I only say might, be considering it so don't say no." Caddi wore a little smile that for once Harold thought might be sincere.

"Cripes, what makes you think I would say no if she means it? She'd kill me! Hah, fat chance I could actually say no. The bloody Pope wouldn't say no after the treatment I've been getting. Cripes Caddi, I'll be walking funny for days as it is!" Harold shook his head. "You heard her, she does this to blokes all the time."

Caddi laughed, thank all and any gods. "Oh yes, she could kill most of this lot the same way." The warlord patted Harold on the back. "Off you go and remember, have fun, or at least make it worthwhile." Caddi chuckled as he left, probably hoping he'd finally get his chance at Mercedes. After all, according to the Deal, if Mercedes let anyone into her pants, she had to screw Caddi for as long as he wanted.

*   *   *

A fulsome greeting awaited Harold when he arrived in her bedroom. "What took you so long, 'Arold? Don't you want to sleep in my bed?" Harold laughed, because both of them knew that was a silly question. Mercedes opened the drawer full of temptation. "Decisions, decisions. What should I wear for a second time? I've never had to pick a second outfit for the same man." Mercedes gave Harold a good look at a dozen skimpy versions of nightwear he would have loved to see her in, so why lie?

"I would love to see you in any of those, Mercedes. I would love seeing you coming out of them even more." Mercedes' smiled, full and delighted, and her eyes warmed but Harold kept going. "But I'm worried that you might not sleep comfortably, not with those little lacy bits and ruffles on your fair skin. Perhaps you should wear the same as last time? You seemed to be comfy in that."

That earned Harold a happy laugh before Mercedes headed into the en-suite. A few moments later she called out. "Will you pass my shirt, 'Arold? I came over all hot and bothered and forgot it." Harold picked up the big shirt and cracked the door open. "Over here 'Arold, you can stick your head in."

Harold half-expected another quick flash, but not tonight.

Her skirt and blouse landed at Harold's feet but he didn't see them, because Mercedes stood there posing in just her boots and stockings. This time Harold didn't get the full benefit, because his whole attention fastened on her face. Her mouth and her glorious, sparkling eyes were laughing, really laughing, probably at his expression. When Mercedes suddenly said, "Careful," Harold realised he'd started to put his foot inside the door. A blinding smile and an imperious hand beckoned, so Harold threw the shirt. He stayed right there, smiling back until finally Mercedes pouted regretfully. "Naughty, 'Arold, you can't expect me to get into my nightie with you watching." Harold picked up the skirt and blouse, closing the door before putting them on the chair.

This time Mercedes wanted 'Arold to get into the bed in his shirt and boxers. Once he had, she pursed her lips thoughtfully. "I've changed my mind." Harold didn't care because they were only playing to the sound and vision. "I want you to take off your tee. Not your boxers 'Arold, or I might forget myself entirely." Mercedes pursed her lips again as Harold sat up. "No, I think you should take it off under the covers. Slowly, 'Arold, so that

I can imagine your shirt sliding over everything." Harold obliged. "Mmm, that's lovely. Just thinking of all that sweaty muscle moving about is getting me all hot and bothered." From her eyes and smile Harold thought that might be true.

"It's a good job I've taken it off, because I'm a bit hot and bothered myself." Harold took the chance to send his boxers south save to some wriggling about later. They weren't going to be needed, not after the bathroom greeting.

Mercedes looked around at the cameras, wherever they were, waving the knife. Harold turned his back while the light show and music went on and Mercedes flipped back her side of the covers. "I hope this big muscly beast isn't as tempted as I am." Mercedes slid the knife, and herself, under the quilt. "That would leave a terrible mess on the bedsheets." Her hand passed Harold the knife.

Mercedes pulled up the covers and snuggled up. Harold didn't have a chance to go to sleep this time, because a hot tongue started drawing patterns on his neck. Moments later he felt her slow, careful wriggle as the buttons came undone, so Harold helped to slide her shirt clear. "Mmm, a gentleman," breathed gently into his neck so Harold kept going, tucking all the shirt out of the way behind Mercedes. He knew he'd got it all because Mercedes plastered herself against his back.

Mercedes moved up as he pushed the shirt clear so Harold reached the Holy Grail of the Hot Rods. He gave the smooth curve a firm squeeze, and then several slow, appreciative strokes. "Mmm, nice," preceded a slow writhe that massaged most of his back. Soft breath tickled his neck as Mercedes sighed contentedly. "I've been dreaming about this." She lifted her knee over Harold's leg before sliding her hand onto his six-pack and heading south.

Her soft chuckle when Mercedes found the boxers gone tickled Harold's neck. He concentrated on not making any noise, while sliding his hand over her hip and down. "Oh God, yes." Despite being thoroughly distracted, Harold worried about the amount of shuddering and writhing that followed. Mercedes eventually calmed down a bit, gently kissing his neck and stroking his belly so Harold returned the stroking. He would have loved to return to the kissing.

It wasn't long before her tongue started up again and she breathed, "More, please?" A lot more wriggling and shuddering and muffled noises later Harold felt Mercedes' breath panting against his neck. "Mmm, lovely.

Thank you, kind sir." Harold retrieved his hand while Mercedes cuddled in to get every possible inch in contact. Her hand rested on Harold's six pack again as they slept.

Harold's early morning call included an extra surprise towards the end of the action behind him. He stifled his exclamation at a sharp pain on top of his shoulder. After her breathing had settled down Mercedes kissed it better. "Don't worry, 'Arold, nobody saw your shoulder last night. They'll blame your woman." Her snigger felt wonderful as it worked downwards. Mercedes kissed Harold's shoulder again. "This is cheaper than biting through pillows." She'd bitten him!

While Harold worried about hiding that from the cameras, Mercedes kissed his shoulder again. "Look at it another way, 'Arold. What I actually wanted to do was roll you over and straddle you, then ride you into screaming ecstasy." A long sigh rippled down Harold's back and he stifled a murmur of appreciation. "But then we would have to kill everyone in the Mansion to get clear." Harold appreciated her giggle even more than the sigh. "We'd probably be too tired to manage that, which would be a terrible shame."

Mercedes snuggled in close again while Harold continued stroking whatever he could reach behind him. Her hand, much gentler now, wandered slowly over the muscles of Harold's chest and belly. "Mmm, that's nice." Harold could take a hint and kept stroking. While they were still calming down again, gently and very enjoyably, the door rattled. Harold tensed but a muttered "No!" from Mercedes kept him under the covers.

The cursing outside stopped and someone called out. "There's a problem. I've been sent to tell you about it."

Mercedes turned away from Harold. From the volume of her reply she must have put her head out of the covers, and wasn't happy. "So what is it? Just bear in mind that you're disturbing my fun. If it's sod 1 somebody is losing body parts." It went dead quiet outside. Harold felt the covers being pulled back up and over, and Mercedes snuggled up again.

"I'll find out in the morning," her soft voice breathed. "Meanwhile, will you repeat that stroking? Please? Just to get relaxed again." The giggle at the end wasn't necessary to encourage Harold. Eventually he heard the young woman's breathing calm down, and Harold drifted off with her warm body up against him and soft breath on his shoulder.

* * *

The usual cheerful rousing rattle and call roused them. Mercedes quickly did her shirt buttons up while Harold passed her the knife, then under cover of Mercedes getting out of bed Harold retrieved his boxers. As he sat up Mercedes gasped. "Your shoulder!" Her hands went onto her hips. "You came here from some other woman's bed! Have you been unfaithful to me 'Arold, when I've saved myself?" Mercedes should have been on the stage.

Harold had forgotten about hiding the bite, but now he realised Mercedes hadn't expected to anyway. "I promise, I swear, my mind was only thinking of you when that happened. How could it not be? I mean, a night with you is so utterly unforgettable." Harold got a snort in reply.

"You can take your boxers home this time, because I can't keep bloody trophies. The knicker sniffers grabbed the last pair. They were hung up where all the perverts could see them." Mercedes glared at the sound and vision, then suddenly beamed. "There again, it might be a good thing if you take them home. If your other woman has to wash your sweaty undies it might tire her out a bit. Quieten her down enough that she keeps her bloody teeth to herself." She was blaming Tessa! Mercedes looked Harold up and down. "Mmm, you do look tasty, so perhaps you'd better nip off and get dressed. I'd be tempted to even up but she might be rabid."

Mercedes was on fire this morning, keeping up a constant stream of comments while he used the shower room. Harold realised that she would be in straight afterwards, which gave him a wonderful opportunity. When he came out clean and dressed, Harold felt relieved. When she went inside Mercedes would see the short lipstick message on loo paper, about Caddi losing patience and encouraging Harold to break the Deal.

Mercedes came out of the bathroom in jeans and tee and a different pair of boots, treating Harold to a little pose in the doorway. A lovely twinkle showed in her eyes, just for a moment. "So you can check just how delectable everything is." Harold, very obviously checked her toe to top, while wondering if Mercedes kept a knife in each pair of boots or moved the same weapon about.

"I could be tempted into checking properly, if we find someplace private." Harold meant it and it showed, as did the warmth in her eyes when Mercedes smiled back.

A young woman arrived for the bedding, and letting her into the bedroom meant showing Harold a big new bolt on the inside of the door. Mercedes must have bolted it while he was in the bathroom last night. "That's new." In fact, it was unique as far as Harold knew. The Mansion bedrooms where Harold usually slept had neither bolt nor lock.

Mercedes gestured to a large square of slightly cleaner carpet, a new piece just inside the door. "Some idiot thought I fancied him, and came marching in as instructed." Mercedes glanced back towards the bed. "I woke up and threw the knife in pure reaction. The cheeky little shit bled out before telling me who gave him the message. I had to replace the piece of carpet." Harold looked at the distance to the other end of the bed, and made a mental note about Mercedes not needing a crossbow under twenty feet.

"What gave him that idea, about you fancying him?" Harold would have asked about a lock, but the screw holes where one had been removed were obvious.

"I'm supposed to have sent for the stupid bastard because I'm frustrated, or that's what he told the guards. They were right outside the door, waiting to see what happened. The incompetent bastards were probably disappointed that I had my nightshirt on." Mercedes sniffed and glared at the sound and vision. "Since the guards were no bloody good, I found another way of getting some peace and quiet. I'll see you later, at breakfast." Harold headed downstairs, while Mercedes escorted the maid and her bedding off out of sight.

All the Hot Rod lieutenants but Roller, still in Orchard Close as the hostage, were waiting at the table. Mercedes arrived, relaxed and putting on a lovely show, tweaking and teasing, but throughout the whole performance everyone had the question on their lips. Eventually Caddi sighed, looking straight at Harold. "You're not going to say, are you? Even when we saw her skirt and blouse land at your feet?" The gang boss gestured to the sideboard where the bundle of coupons now had a twin. "The betting went crazy after last time. You might even be able to afford Mercedes with that lot, so I've got to ask. Harry, can you confirm the commando and bra bets for last night?"

The totally honest answer wasn't what everyone wanted to hear. "I can only confirm that Mercedes wasn't naked in the bathroom when I looked in."

Most of them looked a bit disappointed and a couple muttered "towels," but Dodge smiled and said "boots" loud and clear. The room went silent again as all eyes turned to Harold, then Mercedes.

"So she was wearing just boots and stockings, or maybe just the stockings. That's not naked but it means the bet's still on. Come on Soldier Boy, look at the coupons, man!" ET was almost begging now.

"I've said my piece." Harold looked at Caddi and grinned. "Anyway, some women are priceless." He waited a couple of moments. "Especially if you might get it for nothing if you ask right, and you might lose your nuts if you ask wrong."

Caddi laughed, shaking his head. "If anyone is getting into her pants with permission, I reckon it's you. That's if she's wearing any. Come and stay over any time because this is getting interesting." Caddi wore another real smile, which widened when Mercedes didn't interrupt.

Harold knew only the camera had stopped him last night, when he helped Mercedes open her shirt. He'd lost count of how many times he almost turned over during the rest of the night. Now Harold just wanted to get Mercedes someplace private, face to face, even if it wasn't for sex. "Maybe when you've finished the war, Caddi. You don't want Mercedes distracted just now." Harold wondered if Mercedes might not want his ears if she killed enough Murphies. He'd already accepted that if Mercedes said yes he'd risk it anyway!

"Good point, if Mercedes is getting frustrated it'll encourage her to kill the rest of the Murphies sharpish." ET grinned at them all. "There won't be enough left to shoot at us." The round of agreement ended when Mercedes moved the conversation on. She wanted to know who'd rattled her door last night, but nobody would answer. They all shut up when the bacon, eggs and fried bread arrived, because everyone had their mouths full.

Eventually the bacon and eggs became grease smear and happy taste buds. "Since you haven't bought any women this time, Harry, you can go straight home." Caddi gave a knowing smile. "If your other woman is that keen, you'll need to rest up today." Mercedes scowled on cue.

Dodge chipped in. "If she's still biting like that, the last one has plenty of mileage left. Makes you wonder what's made her so lively."

Mercedes concentrated her scowl on him. "But 'Arold hasn't had a really lively woman. Not yet." She licked her lips, slowly with a wicked smile. "But when he does you'll know, because you won't need the microphone to hear us." Everyone stared at her after that, even Harold, without a single comment or joke. Mercedes had just made it absolutely clear what she intended, without any tease at all. Nobody even tried to tweak her or Harold while they all finished their coffee, because she'd answered most questions. Most of the Hot Rods seemed stunned but Caddi looked hopeful, while Cooper darted occasional jealous looks at Harold.

Harold couldn't leave without a Mercedes goodbye of course, and this time a small collection of people sort of hung about near the vehicles. Word about last time had spread. Mercedes got a good grip on his ass in return for Harold's grip on hers, but didn't risk the tongue trick with the quick peck. Not with four lieutenants a matter of feet away, though her lip contact was firm. "Back to your other woman 'Arold, and what can I do to keep you thinking of me?"

"I told you there's only one woman in my mind, Mercedes. Unfortunately, not in my bed. Yet?" Harold smiled right into her eyes and his reward came. That thaw, momentary but definitely warmer and longer than a flicker.

"Ambitious, I like that in a man." Mercedes trailed her hands down Harold's chest to his belt. "Among other things. Now, there must be something? Ah." Mercedes lifted Harold's hand away from her waist and twisted away from the hand on her ass, then patted her jeans. "Remember this? Now I said that last time and you seem to have strayed, so." Mercedes took a step backwards and smoothly fitted her ass into Harold's crotch. She bent a bit and rubbed it up and down once, firmly and slowly.

"There." The open-mouthed spectators got a real Killer Queen smile. "Bet he watches this all the way out of sight, and remembers it a lot longer." Mercedes patted her ass again and set off, giving her hips a good bump and grind. Harold watched it out of sight as instructed. So did the other men, letting out a round of sighs when she turned the corner.

"Bloody hell man, what did you do to her?" Cooper looked downright jealous even if he'd never even asked.

"Nothing, yet, but I'm going to have some very interesting dreams once my mind is out of my boxers." But they wouldn't be about that ass, or not in jeans anyway.

"You and the rest. Reckon she really fancies you?" Dodge thought he had the answer already.

"Dunno. If she does, that might be even more frightening. After all, imagine waking up in bed every morning with Mercedes beside you." Harold's little smile remembered how she'd woken him up.

"Too true."

"You should be so lucky."

"I wish."

"Yeah me too. But if she wakes up in a bad mood? PMT? Chipped nail varnish?" They all laughed at Harold, even Mack.

Dodge shook his head. "Good point. Now if we've all finished drooling over Soldier Boy's other woman?" Another flurry of good-natured obscenities sent Harold off home with his escort.

*   *   *

On the way home Harold puzzled over the reaction of Caddi's lieutenants, until he realised they didn't know the Deal. Maybe Caddi didn't want his men to know he wasn't holding off totally by choice? He also mulled over the news about the war. Caddi had won, taken his original objectives, but wasn't settling for half as originally planned. If he could take their headquarters, a big old stone house with a high wall right round the grounds, the Hot Rods would almost cut the Murphy's territory in half. After that, if Caddi took one more small estate with three streets, he could turn and crush one half or the other. At the moment, Mercedes spent much of her time probing the headquarters area for a weakness.

The gate guard on Orchard Close went onto alert when the vehicles turned up the road towards the entrance. A convoy with two pickups and an estate car full of guards led by a Hot Rod, Dodge, might be a threat even with Harold's pickup following. Harold parked next to Roller's motor, not a Rolls Royce but the grille and the winged lady from one were fastened to the BMW. Harold would compliment the Orchard Close guards when he had chance. Their response to the alert looked smoother and much quicker than usual, so all the practice must be working.

Harold hopped out, asking for barrows to bring in the trade goods and the damaged machetes and crossbows. He sent the first barrow-load of charcoal off to the forge, for Liz to check in case Caddi had sent the cheaper crap. Liz would stay out of sight, but she'd send a message if Caddi had pulled a fast one. Dodge loaded a barrow with the firearms, carefully covered, and Harold sent them to his workshop. Within minutes Tessa arrived, to let Harold know the blacksmith had accepted the charcoal. Harold cursed silently as he saw Dodge's eyes light up.

"Hey, Tessa, you'd better be careful how you mark this man of yours. His other woman uses a knife you know, so teeth might not be enough next time." Dodge sniggered, glancing to include the other Hot Rods in the joke. "You must be livelier now than you were with us." Tessa blushed as the men laughed.

Harold stopped it right there and then. "Oy, enough." Dodge suddenly realised that Soldier Boy's rules on his turf might not include someone teasing his woman. The senior Hot Rod and all the men with him stopped laughing, concentrating on unloading.

Dodge glanced from Harold to Tessa. "Ah, sorry. Big mouth. No offence?"

Tessa smiled at Dodge, a patently false one Caddi would have been proud of. "No offence taken as it's true. I'm a lot happier and what was it, livelier, now nobody is considering selling me." No offence taken but Tessa put some bite in the last bit.

"All business, nothing to do with me." Dodge turned to Harold. "I'll tell herself you arrived safely. You wouldn't want her to worry. Come on you lot, get going!" Roller looked puzzled as Dodge hustled him to his car to get moving. As the last bits came off, the Hot Rod vehicles immediately turned round and the men scrambled aboard. They were gone while the Orchard Close residents were still getting the collection organised. Dodge wanted to get out sharpish, before someone actually took offence. Patty's look would be encouragement all on its own.

The Hot Rods were barely moving before Tessa started. "Marking, teeth, other women," a pause, "livelier?" She still had a bit of her blush and definitely wanted answers.

"Big mouth? No brain?" Harold tried, "Later?" because the other words weren't stopping Tessa's look.

That got a smile. "Oh, yes, I think so." Tessa relaxed a little.

The small gang of helpers dragged everything inside the gates and split up to deliver it. Harold took the broken radios straight to Trev, to show him the pictures on the phone.

*   *   *

Thandia, the mastiff, reluctantly moved aside to let Harold into Trev's workshop, a modified garage. Elise unpacked the two-way radios, then very carefully and methodically started stripping and cleaning them. Trev looked at the pictures of the alleged transmitter, and gave his first reaction. "This is a shocking mess, Harold. I can't tell much from these."

"Caddi will send a hostage and pay for you to go and look." Harold smiled reassuringly. "He'll send Cooper so you're safe, and pay top rate."

"Can I take Elise, to clean bits up and help sort through it all?" Behind Trev, Elise froze.

"Nope. If Elise went to Beth's, would you go as well?" Harold thought he'd made a mistake and given Trev a heart attack, because he went sheet white and staggered.

"Barbies? No, not Barbies." That came out as a squeak as Trev recovered slightly.

"I reckon that's how Elise feels about the Hot Rods. Leave her a list of work and I'm sure she'll keep busy." Behind Trev, Elise started work again. "You won't be gone long anyway, because there'll be no overnight. Caddi doesn't think Cooper would last that long without incurring a fine. He'd object and swear again, then refuse the caning." Harold laughed out loud. "Then Patty would skewer him."

"Oh. I suppose she would." The colour started coming back to Trev's face. "At least there won't be anyone like that Skipper at Caddi's." He lowered his voice. "She kept on about me checking her special knickers."

"She's a Barbie so it's expected. I'll call Caddi's watchers on the radio and we'll sort out your visit." Harold bid Trev and Elise goodbye and went to see Liz.

*   *   *

Liz looked like a younger, feminine scrooge, hunched over the charcoal and bent machetes and rubbing her hands. "Do you need these as machetes, Harold?"

"Not necessarily. Sort of yes and no because they're for Patty's Demons and Doll's squad. I'd rather wait until the slimline machetes are perfected."

"Sabres, according to Patty. The back is nearly straight, but the widening and curve towards the end of the sharp edge makes them look sabre-ish. The extra metal weights them nicely for chopping. Patty is happy with the latest version so the sooner the Demons and Cowgirls have them the better." Patty looked over at the charcoal again and smirked. "If I keep getting enough charcoal I'll get this tempering business right. Providing you don't want too many sabres, and stop taking broken weapons in trade?"

"Be fair, bent not broken and I take them because then Caddi has to give me charcoal as well. Let me know when you get to the crossbows and I'll give you a hand." Harold turned to go. "If I've got time. I've got more guns as well."

"You need an apprentice. Now scat because you don't want to be anywhere near when I get sweaty and sooty." Liz gave a wicked little chuckle as she reached for her music player. "You've already got at least two women." Harold heard the iron plate slide into place, locking the door behind him. Liz's paranoia about being snuck up on hadn't abated. On the way to his workshop to put the firearms away, Harold thought about the amount of work he had, and how much Elise helped Trev just by cleaning the gear.

Maybe Liz was right. An apprentice would help with cleaning if nothing else, especially now with the state the captured Murphy's weapons arrived in. From the state of the latest ones from the Geeks, there'd be more badly gunked weapons from them eventually. With the worst crud removed, Harold could concentrate on the actual repairs. Cleaning was a lovely peaceful part of the job, but too many other things needed his attention these days. Unfortunately, the apprentice had to be someone he'd trust completely, someone who could defend themselves, and also inconspicuous. That would take some real thought.

* * *

The following morning, before he left to start work, Tessa brought Eddie round to play with Daisy and Wills while she spent a few hours working in the canteen. The "it's later" from Tessa meant she hadn't forgotten Dodge's comments, and brought an anticipatory smile from Sharyn. Once the three children were busy playing in Daisy's bedroom, Harold had an audience of two. No matter how Harold put the situation with Mercedes, they wouldn't accept the game as a wind-up, not if she bit him. He had to mention the bite to explain Dodge's comments, and then explain why Mercedes had blamed Tessa. Actually, biting him did seem a bit extreme even to Harold, but Mercedes epitomised extreme. "But only on the back of my shoulder."

"Was she wearing clothes when she bit you?" Sharyn wore a little smile as she pressed the inquisition.

"Yes." Sharyn raised one eyebrow. She didn't look convinced even if it was the truth. Harold wasn't going to prove it by telling Sharyn that Mercedes still had her shirt on, underneath her and on one arm.

"But you had your shirt off, so was it at bedtime?" Tessa picked that up much too fast. "So was she wearing a little frilly nightie?"

"No." Harold wanted to bite his tongue because he should have lied.

"No nightie? Did you get another flash?" Tessa grinned. "Another full frontal? All the Hot Rods swear you got one last time."

"I'm not saying any more." This would be much easier for Harold without Sharyn because he'd lie. His sister could read him like a book. Worse, the Hot Rods would tell everyone he'd been in bed with Mercedes again, and saw her naked in the bathroom. The gangsters all assumed that, even if he'd refused to confirm it, and not getting proof wouldn't slow them up one bit.

Tessa could mind read as well. "How did she do that without showing the Hot Rods?"

"Do what? Just let me be, right?"

Sharyn laughed. "You're my little brother. Tormenting you is a required skill. So when did she bite you?"

"Last night, now that's it." If it had been just Sharyn, Harold might have felt better about this. Then he realised, no he wouldn't, she was his bloody sister!

"In the bedroom? Nearly naked?" Tessa looked intrigued. "Nearly naked in bed? It must have been under the covers, so they didn't see her bite you." Tessa continued with a lot more speculation in her voice. "Were you? Nearly naked I mean." Harold tried to work out how to get them to accept no comment, because it wasn't working.

Too late, Sharyn answered for him. "That shifty look and silence means yes to all of it. So Mercedes bit you from behind, almost naked, in bed, and you definitely had your shirt off and probably don't sleep in your jeans." Sharyn smiled at whatever she saw on Harold's face. "Another yes. Did you help her off with her clothes?"

"That's enough. Stop putting words in my mouth. "

"So yes again. If a woman strips off in bed, rubs herself all over a bloke and bites him on the shoulder in the middle of her jollies, it's not a wind-up." Sharyn grinned at Harold as she said it, which meant Harold blushed again. She was his bloody sister and worse, put like that she was right. "Mercedes is an 'other woman' at the very least. Unless you've gotten a lot more casual about how you treat women, little brother?"

"Low blow, Sis. Look, it wasn't like that, not how you said." Harold knew he sounded defensive but he didn't usually kiss and tell. He hadn't actually kissed Mercedes yet, but he doubted anyone would believe that either. The Hot Rods would confirm the rest, and that he only wore boxers in the bed, so he was only putting things off. They'd be falling over themselves to be the first to tell everyone what Mercedes said about the bite.

Tessa moved forward. "There's one way to find out."

Harold looked at Tessa, puzzled, then shouted, "No!" He twisted away.

"Oh yes. Come on, little brother. Get that tee off. After all, it'll be almost gone if Mercedes wasn't serious." Sharyn and Tessa were both trying to look now but Harold fended them off.

"I've got weapons to fix. I might even sleep there for a few nights until you stop this nonsense." Harold could feel a magnificent blush warming his face, probably why neither of the two women were the slightest bit impressed by any denials.

"Is that where you'll be taking Mercedes, if you can prise her loose of Caddi? What was it, to strip her down and test the action? Cripes, little brother, if she's enjoying the foreplay this much she might not kill you afterwards." Harold had already come to that conclusion. "The whole place will be livelier if she moves in."

"Moves in?" Harold floundered, his brain trying to wrap itself around those two words.

Tessa patted Harold on the shoulder. "Well there's that spare bedroom now I've moved out. Perhaps I should bite you as well, so you can see the difference and how serious she is? After all, I'm getting the blame for this one." Harold jumped back again but Tessa made no move to follow up. Both women were holding onto the backs of chairs now because they were laughing too much to stand. Harold stood in the doorway with his mind spinning, but not at Tessa and Sharyn's teasing. He didn't know how he'd handle it if Mercedes really had the hots for him, as in not being satisfied with once. He already thought she'd break the Deal with Caddi and run for the hills, but what if she wanted to stay here with him?

* * *

Once the pair of them got their breath back Tessa made a cuppa all round, while Sharyn started talking about accommodation. That came as a big relief for Harold, at least to start with. The population explosion had reached breaking point because a man, woman and a youngster arrived last night and had to sleep on the dance house floor. Now another young woman had turned up this morning. The last three big houses weren't ready yet so something needed doing to ease the pressure. "So I'm moving back in here." Tessa smiled cheerfully.

Harold had just got his head back together but now he stared open-mouthed. "What!"

"Two Army mothers, we're already friends, the kids get on and this is a big house." Sharyn waved her hands around the obviously spacious lounge. "Plenty of room in here for another two. I'll stick an extra bed in Wills' room so Eddie doesn't have to double up. Two couples will cram into that two-bedroomed house of Tessa's, problem solved."

Harold wasn't getting into another hopeless argument. "I'll doss down in the workshop."

"No you won't!" Both of them glared at Harold as Sharyn continued. "You're Soldier Boy and this is the boss's house so you live here. If you don't you'll lose credibility, and the other gangs will start making moves. Cripes, the residents of Orchard Close expect it!"

That gobsmacked Harold. "Haven't you pair been paying attention? If Tessa moves in here then the gangs will be certain I bought her for, well, that I bought her."

Tessa lost it a bit while Sharyn smiled and let her rant. "You stupid thick prat! They already think I was bought! They already think you're banging me! So do most of bloody Orchard Close! Now they'll all be told I bit you with your shirt off! What do you expect them to think? Living here won't change a bloody thing except two couples get a house. So what's the problem?" Tessa calmed down a bit and got her breath back. Harold kept quiet so she didn't start again but no such luck. "Harold, why did you buy me?"

Harold tried to wriggle round answering. "I didn't buy you. I paid off a debt."

"She was a prisoner. You paid over the coupons or games to the right value. Caddi handed her over. That sounds like buying her to me, so what do you think the rest of the world think? I only believe you because I'm your sister, and know what a soft shit you are. The rest think you're a hard as nails gangster or SAS sniper gone rogue." Harold stared at Sharyn, speechless. He'd thought his sister would back him on this one!

Tessa sniggered, an improvement from Harold's point of view. "Being bought hasn't turned out too badly, and apparently it's made me livelier."

Harold had to smile a little bit at that. "Maybe. But it's still not a crime to help a friend."

That earned him a long look and a slow nod from Tessa. "That's good enough for me, and since I'm a friend there's no problem with me moving in. Is there?" Harold gave up and shrugged.

"After all," Sharyn added, "if you're friends, it means Tessa can see you in just your boxers now and again without blushing."

"I already did, several times when he dossed down at Stones' after a night out." Tessa smirked and stuck out a hip. "He's seen me in just a towel, coming out the bathroom." The pair of them were enjoying the teasing too much so Harold tried to distract them with practicalities, but to no avail. There were two bedrooms with en-suites upstairs, and the kids could use the other two rooms and the bathroom. Harold refused to use the bathroom up there if Tessa would be streaking about, but they just laughed at him.

"It won't be me causing raised blood pressure if your other woman stops over. Mercedes streaking down the road to use the shower in the workshop should liven things up." Tessa curled up, almost weeping with mirth while Sharyn nearly choked laughing, probably at Harold's expression. Harold's hormones liked the idea of Mercedes staying overnight too damn much for him to argue, so he headed for the gun room. This time the gun cleaning didn't calm or distract him, the thought wouldn't go away.

Chapter 9:
Old Weapons, New Weapons

It wasn't just Harold who couldn't get Mercedes off his mind. When he went home to get a bite to eat at lunchtime, Sharyn and Tessa carried on teasing. Their continual digs about Mercedes and showers might have been why Harold came up with a way to divert them, possibly in pure desperation. "The workshop bedroom and shower might be in use, if I get an apprentice." It worked much better than expected, because both women immediately became serious and wanted to know who he'd chosen. "Nobody" led to the pair running through a list of who in the inner circle knew enough about guns, but wouldn't be missed elsewhere.

Sharyn stopped coming up with names because she hadn't got one vital bit of information. "So just what would the apprentice do?"

"Only stripping down and cleaning the weapons to start with, because that's the bit that takes time." Both nodded, and Tessa asked more detailed questions about how difficult that would be. Both women had been around soldiers, and sometimes guns, for long enough to lose any awe or fear. Harold soon realised Tessa had handled Stones' collection of souvenirs, and she confessed to posing for pictures with a few of them.

Tessa's eyes narrowed. "Didn't you see any? He had them in his wallet."

Harold told the truth. "Stones only showed me one in a mini skirt and bikini top, and the ones with Eddie."

"If you ever decide to advertise, add a gun and that would work." Sharyn laughed, but then looked more serious. "Send a few to the Barbies and they'll be over here buying Tessa drinks."

"Some of Patty's Demons already sent a few, to encourage more visitors so they can sell them a beer." Tessa looked speculative. "Not porn, they reckon the pictures are no worse than some of the old adverts on TV. Bikinis and crossbows, that sort of thing."

"My apprentice won't be posing. He has to be a secret, and I really do mean that, otherwise someone like the Barbies would kidnap him." Harold nodded as realisation dawned on their faces. "Most of my work is very simple. Once the apprentice has been doing the job for a bit, that'll be obvious. Worse, the apprentice will know about the Mad Max versions. One slip and the nutters out there will think that means I'm a gunsmith."

After a short description of the Mad Max weapons, clumsy single shot firearms built using parts of wrecked guns and short lengths of ruined rifle barrels, a short silence fell. Sharyn suddenly pointed at Harold and sighed. "You, soft lad, are already a gunsmith as far as this city is concerned. If you can build a gun that works, they won't care how crude it is."

"Not a gunsmith, because they are crap weapons mostly made out of bits of others." Harold fixed Sharon with a serious look, trying to get through to her. "Even if that's what you think, you have to understand one thing. If either of you ever say that word out loud, anywhere, then the gangs will bury Orchard Close in bodies looking for me."

"Using the name doesn't change reality." Tessa might be right, but Harold still thought Mad Max was a long way from gunsmith. She paused, then continued slowly. "Out there, a crappy gun is valuable, so I understand that a man who can produce one from broken bits and scrap is priceless. Will your apprentice learn how to do that? Make one from scratch?"

"From parts rather than scratch but yes, I suppose so. If the apprentice is smart enough to be useful, eventually it will be obvious I'm making up weapons from parts I buy as scrap. They'll also realise I'm stitching the other gangs over the time taken to repair guns, and charging them for making bits when I only fit salvaged spares. It's to make everyone think the repairs are really difficult, so nobody tries it themselves." Harold shook his head in frustration. "That's why I've got a problem finding someone I can trust, totally and absolutely. One word and all hell breaks loose."

"How much will you teach them?" Tessa's eyes narrowed in speculation. "Will the apprentice learn to shoot, to test the weapons?"

"Yes, because the sights might need setting." And whoever it is might need to defend themselves if word gets out, Harold silently added.

Both Sharyn and Harold stared as Tessa burst out laughing, until she stopped long enough to speak. "Sorted, I'm the apprentice. If the other woman has a knife I'm going one better."

"But." Harold tried to think of a but. The other woman thing had thrown him.

Sharyn weighed in with a very good point in favour of Tessa. "What's your deepest, darkest secret? The one that all the gangs would pay seriously to know?" She pretended to type, so she meant Harold being an Army clerk instead of an SAS sniper. He hadn't started the SAS story, but that and his marksmanship certainly backed off the gangsters.

"What's the next deepest darkest secret?" Tessa tapped Harold's stick. Stones had a similar one.

"You know. You both do, both of them."

"And we haven't told anyone, so who can you trust with another big secret?" Harold didn't have an answer for Sharyn.

While he tried to find one, Tessa nailed it down. "Better yet, nobody will realise I'm your apprentice, so there's no danger I'll be snatched for information."

"Why not?" Harold blushed, bright scarlet. That was the wrong question because...

"Because nobody will wonder why you spend hours locked away privately with your wench, somewhere away from your sister and the kids. They all know there's a bedroom off the gun room so they'll be watching for bite marks, not gun oil stains. I can even confirm I'm stripping in there." Tessa laughed with true delight. "Your face is a picture."

"But you're not my wench or anything, so what if you find a bloke you fancy?"

"What if you find a woman you want, apart from Mercedes?" Tessa looked uncomfortable for a moment. "I don't want someone just now, and if I pretend to be your wench nobody will bother me."

"Or you, little brother. You've complained enough times about the new refugees leaving you alone." Sharyn wasn't joking at all as she continued. "I reckon there's a serious contender now."

"Yes there is, if I ever end up on my own with Mercedes." Harold relaxed because he'd admitted it now, right out loud. "Now let it be because that's freaking me out."

"So that's all settled. I move back into the room upstairs, everyone assumes I'm your wench, and you can have an apprentice." Tessa high-fived Sharyn. "Now you can concentrate on finding a way to get Mercedes on her own."

They were both having too much fun now so Harold gave up, at least partly because everyone else would come to exactly that conclusion. "In that case you should have some respect."

"What, like the other woman? I should bite you on the other side." Harold smiled as Tessa moved forward, clicking her teeth in a mock bite. "Does that smile mean yes?"

"No!" Harold had to laugh. At least in here there wasn't a gang of maniacs listening and hoping for blood. A bit of more sensible discussion settled the details. The move helped both women with child-minding and now Harold found out Tessa served the visitors to help keep them in line. She'd quickly realised that the gangsters stepped carefully round her in case Soldier Boy took offence. Better yet, she'd not been able to wear nice clothes for three years, but now she could dress up a bit and nobody dare comment.

Harold found that part funny. "We should let Wamil serve a couple of times. An elbow in the Adam's apple would teach respect just as well." Tessa wanted to know why so Harold explained, admitting Wamil would flatten him hand to hand. Both Sharyn and Tessa decided his new apprentice should have lessons, just in case someone realised what she actually did in the workshop.

Harold went off to work on the guns, because he needed to sort out the quick and simple repairs. Caddi would push for them. The stripping and cleaning and oiling worked its magic on Harold's peace of mind. A few hours of that and he'd got his head round it all. Harold could live with Tessa in the house, because she actually did know more about him than anyone here except Sharyn.

That evening, when Harold did his rounds, he met two new recruits. The young woman ran because her dad died, caught in crossfire, which left her and her younger brother alone. A woman living further up the street told her about Orchard Close, and advised her to run before the Hot Rods took over. Another woman told her the safest way to cross the border to the Barbies. Word must be spreading fast, and the new houses might not be enough.

* * *

A few days later Tessa turned up eager for her first gun lesson. Harold still found the work restful despite teaching someone new, up until Tessa left. "You'd better look happier than that when you leave." With an impish smile, Tessa added, "Otherwise everyone will think I'm not up to the job. Not lively enough." Harold spluttered a bit, but before he could answer the smiling young woman continued. "You're lucky. You just have to look happy. I have to look happy, lively, and as if I've just had a mouthful of steak as well." Tessa left still laughing at Harold's expression, which more or less gave the right impression.

Harold thought about what Tessa said when he left, and found he was smiling as instructed. It was time to give up and go with the flow. Letting a good looking woman hang on his arm now and then wasn't the hardest thing in the world. Better still, Harold liked Tessa and they could tease each other without her expecting to go any further. Now he'd better fix some weapons, and have a proper look at that musket.

*   *   *

Two days later Harold had something much more serious to consider. He'd taken the old musket apart and fixing the problem turned out to be simplicity itself. After removing the load, which hadn't been rammed, and after some fruitless inspection of the parts, he realised the flint had fallen off or been taken out. A quick inspection of the pouch and the bits of rock were flints, and fitted. Harold phoned to ask Veronica to look through the library for books about muskets, then inspected the dismantled weapon again. He bundled up the bits without the barrel or stock and went to see Liz.

"Open up or I'll huff and puff."

Harold heard the bar clank out of the way as Liz opened the door. "You'll have no puff left after spending all that time with your new wench."

"Don't start. That's for show so don't give her grief."

When Harold hopped up to sit on the bench, Liz started grinning. "One of those visits. Is she acting up already?"

Harold shook his head, and explained his non-love life. He spread out the bits of musket. "Can you make these? They look nearer to artwork than ironmongery, so you should enjoy it."

After looking them over very carefully, the smith smiled happily. "No problem, and they won't even cost much charcoal. So give, what are they for?"

"Repairing a musket. A bloody great honest-to-god baby cannon." Harold explained muskets and Caddi. "The Murphies have more, allegedly. Well, definitely, because the sound and fury are distinctive, according to Dodge. There'll be more to repair because Caddi is winning."

That bombshell warranted another close inspection, and a discussion about the workings of a flintlock. The mechanism basically consisted of a bit of twangy steel, a hammer and an anvil, with a simple catch and a trigger to release it. "There's all sorts of thin steel plate still out there to make these, but it'll probably be rusty." Liz frowned. "There's springs in all sorts, or just springy steel I can adapt, and the trigger is the same as a crude crossbow. How hard does this thing need to smack down?"

"Enough to make a spark." Harold rolled his eyes. "You can explain the scavenge list to Patty. She'll be unhappy because the damn things are too big for her to handle."

"Bernie deals with most of the scavenging these days. Patty won't care about muskets because she's got her secret poser baby to play with, though she'd be happier if you could find more ammo." After thinking about the scavenge list, Liz sobered, because the state of the nearby housing meant most thin metal plate would be badly corroded. Her first suggestion, nipping over the border to raid someone else's ruins, ones that hadn't been shelled, wasn't practical. The other gangs only scavenged for their own personal luxuries, but they'd object to anyone else searching their property.

"I heard the GOFS have let their tenants extend their scavenging, so they don't have to buy any more kettles and furniture from us. I'll bet the Barbies have as well, after the heap we sold them. Maybe they'll flog us some thin metal, if we can find a reason for wanting it?" Liz looked over the bits again. "Steel tube might be a problem. How likely is it that a barrel will be damaged?"

"Likely, but they'll straighten. They aren't rifled or even a tight fit. Can you make a couple of sets up so I can give Caddi these back?" Harold left after promising to get even more charcoal.

*　*　*

Harold headed straight for his lesson with Wamil. He arrived early, expecting to have to wait until her pupil had finished leaping about the front room. Instead, Harold found Wamil alone and she seemed flustered. "I can come back later?"

"No need, I have been practicing on my own but I can finish some other time."

Harold followed her into the front room, cleared for the less public practice. His attention immediately fastened on two strange objects shaped like fancy knife blades, laid on the small table under the window. "What are they?"

Wamil hesitated a moment before answering. "They are practice weapons, knives. My brother taught others to fight with many different blades but I only learned these, the Katari. Not with real knives, just with these."

"Those are fighting knives?" Harold eyed them. "I can see that those are blades if sharpened, but the two bars make a very wide and clumsy hilt."

Wamil smiled, picking up the two practice weapons. "Not held like this." Harold inspected them closer now, because Wamil slipped her hands between the bars and gripped the crosspiece. Now she held them as if ready to punch, with the blades jutting out in front of her knuckles.

"Punch daggers? I'd have thought they'd be shorter, broader?" Wamil moved, slashing and punching thin air, and Harold reassessed bloody quickly. "So they slash?"

"This one, the slimmer one with curves, is for punching through armour and should be sharpened to slash as well. The broader one can hack and stab, and take a solid blow from even a sword. I learned them because this discipline sharpens reflexes." Wamil turned one to show a notch. "If the opportunity occurs, this can catch an unwary blade and twist it out of an opponent's hand. Then?" Wamil punched air with the blade and Harold winced.

"Even a smallish person could get a lot of power behind a punch like that. You've never used them, fought with them?" Wamil shook her head. "What happened to your brother's weapons?"

"He is in the west of the city, across the motorway. I came here with my husband-to-be, but he died when the Murphies came. He defied them and they shot him down like a dog." For a moment, Harold thought the usually calm woman would spit. "The gangsters are not warriors, true fighters. I hope my brother met them with all his weapons, with bow and sword, and taught them some respect."

"So do I." Harold hoped that when her brother saw the guns the gangsters carried, he'd hidden his bows and blades rather than challenge them. He spent a few minutes inspecting the blades, to give Wamil a chance to calm down again. "Could you show those to Liz, and explain what you just said? No, hang on, will you spar with me?"

Wamil looked worried, backing away a little. "You can't use these, or not properly. I might hurt you."

"I want you to fight against a machete. I'll pad it of course, and those, and I'd rather you didn't cripple or kill me." Harold grinned, winning a small smile from Wamil. "But strike hard enough so I'll know you got me." Five very energetic and sweaty minutes later Harold nursed his bruises, as did Wamil, and both wore big smiles.

"The last time I did that, sparred properly, I fought my brother. He won of course." Wamil's smile faltered. "Did I strike too hard?"

Harold stopped rubbing his ribs. "Hard enough so a sharp blade, or even that one without the padding, would have done the job properly. Are you all right?"

"The padding on the machete is thick enough. My brother would strike me as hard as that, and blame me for being slow. He said it served me right for pestering him until he taught me." An imp of mischief showed in her eyes. "You didn't hit me very often."

"Too true I didn't, and I took a blow every time I actually got through. Next time I'll have a second weapon as well. May I?" Harold held out his hand for one of the weapons. He hefted it to judge the weight then tried it out, punching and slashing. "That feels strange after a sword, er, machete. I think you should train people who have never fought with machetes, once there are more weapons." Harold held her eyes. "Will you, please?"

Wamil still seemed fired up by the sparring and nodded without hesitation. "How will you find more Katari?"

"Hopefully you will talk to Liz and show her these. She'll shout cripes at me and demand charcoal, but you'll end up with a few more practice versions. Then she'll make the real thing." Harold assessed the weapons again. "She'll be annoyed, because this will be yet another job that eats up her charcoal."

As expected, Liz shouted cripes and stupid soldier and wimp because she'd barely finished making her first sabres, then settled down to talk properly. The smith had two old trailer springs, discovered when the heap of bricks that used to be a house wall were cleared to create more gardens. According to Liz the springs were still tempered, and she wanted to make some real weaponry with them. First on her list were a couple of the sabre type weapons for the Demons. They could practice while she made more from damaged machetes.

Nobody paid much attention to practice, mainly because the Demons were always training with both machetes and crossbows. Patty had already passed on some of her stabbing lessons from Harold, but the skills didn't transfer properly. The pointed machetes the other Demons had were still clumsy weapons. Patty's brand new custom-built blade only emphasised that, and the select few of the Demons who saw it wanted one, now please.

Harold wanted to get as much charcoal as he could, because Liz swore she had almost perfected her tempering. Once she did, there were sabres and now Wamil's blades to make, both lethal surprises with just a bit of luck.

*　*　*

Meanwhile, Trev continued with his visits to the Mansion, much keener after the first two passed without incident. After the fifth, he finally announced his verdict on Caddi's radio ambitions. A large part of the partial transmitter might be repaired, if the Geeks had enough parts in their electrical warehouse. The repairable part still wouldn't actually transmit, but with a few new parts it might fix Barbie Radio. That depended on whoever did it having a bucket full of fuses, connectors and... about then Harold lost track. The last part got Harold's full attention. The radio man had come to one definite conclusion, someone had deliberately blown up Barbie Radio. A crucial part of the transmitter had been more or less obliterated, so Trev couldn't fix Barbie radio without the parts from Caddi.

The next time he saw Caddi, Harold told him the first part, that Hot Rod Radio would never work. He suggested Caddi did a deal with the Barbies, which was how Harold found out why Caddi never dealt with the feisty women. "I can't. They won't deal with me even if I tried, and I won't try." Caddi's face showed real anger but not at Harold. "Not after what they did to Porsche."

"I heard they got Porsche, but no details." After what the Barbies had done to the raiders, Harold didn't want details.

"They sent me pictures of what they did, then what the Pink Panther fucking perverts did to him." Caddi glared, his fists white-knuckled. "That went way past revenge, the bitches."

"Revenge for what?" Harold had thought the treatment would be gross, but wondered why the Barbies had gone that far with a local gang captive. As far as he knew, Porsche hadn't been raiding them.

"While we were first settling boundaries, we caught a couple of the women before they were the Barbies. When they reckoned their gang were all women I thought I'd teach them a lesson, take the piss. We fitted them with thick dog collars and kept them on chains, with a mattress so the blokes could show them what women were really for." Caddi stopped and shook his head. "I misjudged the crazy bitches. They took all the beatings and fucking without even fighting back. One of the blokes must have been careless, or thought they were tamed. They killed him with his own blade and cut the collars. One made it out alive and got home to the Barbies. I thought they'd left it at that but suddenly, out of the blue, the bitches sucked Porsche into a trap. He had three others with him but the bodies were carved up, not shot, so the Barbies paid in blood to get Porsche alive."

Caddi stayed silent for a long time until Harold prompted him. "I heard about the ones who attacked Beth's, what the Barbies did to them."

"Porsche would have preferred that. They gave us five phones, one at a time. Each one full of pictures and video clips of what they did, with all the Barbies and their civvies watching because he was in one of the big shop windows. Porsche lasted nearly a fortnight. The bitches took turns to work on him. In between they gave the fucking Pink Panthers free use, didn't even rent him." Caddi punched the chair arm, hard. "Bitches! Fucking a woman is natural whether she's willing or not, but chaining a man down to be fucked is wrong!" Harold thought he might have just found out why Caddi had a real hate on for gay blokes.

The Barbies probably didn't see much difference between raping a woman or a man. Harold didn't. He wouldn't react quite the same as the Barbies, but he'd sure as hell kill the scroat.

Caddi took a big breath, letting some of the tension go. "Our territories don't actually meet, or didn't until I invaded the Murphies, but I tore down a wide strip of houses along our nearest border. They did the same, and we both keep sentries there. If I sent out a white flag, they'd kill whoever carried it."

Harold could understand the Barbies' attitude, but there was another way to fix the transmitter. "Will you sell them that heap of electrics through me?" After the outburst, he thought Caddi would rather burn it out of spite. For once the urbane pose had gone, and Caddi wasn't hiding how he felt.

Caddi kept quiet for a long time, fighting an internal battle. "I have to, if it'll get that fucking radio working. My men will go fucking ape if they find out I could have fixed it and didn't." Even so, it took a couple of attempts before Caddi forced himself to make the offer. "So what are you offering for the electrics? After all, you trade with the bitches and they actually visit your place."

"Fixing that heap of wires will cost me, then I'll be paying the GOFS to send something that valuable through their territory." Worse still, Harold couldn't be sure Trev's fix would work and Caddi wouldn't give a refund.

"You can get through the GOFS once without them stopping you. Those bitches do it all the time." Caddi settled down to trade. Despite Caddi's objections, Harold insisted on taking into account a cut for the GOFS. He could avoid paying once, but had no intention of screwing up a good relationship even if Caddi would no doubt like that. At least he knew that this time Caddi had to trade, because his men expected it, though Caddi held out for more than he'd paid out for Trev's work. After all, as Caddi pointed out, Trev's cleaning and testing now benefitted Orchard Close so he shouldn't be paying for it.

*　　*　　*

Harold sent messages to both the GOFS and Geeks asking for a trading meeting. He sent a hint with the GOFS message, to make sure whoever attended could make decisions about through trade and selling housing. Selling territory would be as much a favour as it would be business so Harold asked Roy, still standing sentry on the border with the General, how the GOFS seemed to feel about Orchard Close. If they were getting annoyed about the number of Barbies coming through, the trading wouldn't go well. Roy confirmed that they still treated him well, even if the four Orchard Close men weren't actually doing much. All the news and rumours agreed the General's men were busy the other side of his territory, and had conquered several gangs over there.

While he waited for replies, Harold spent time on the gardens, gun repairs, helping Patty to master her new sabre, and sparring with Wamil both with and without weapons. Harold sparred with a blade and a stick, and Wamil agreed that the combination made him harder to kill. With a smile, she also admitted he 'killed' her closer to evens when using a stick as well. After watching Wamil with her knives, Patty and Doll found three fit and limber volunteers to learn. That became easier once Liz produced three sets of practice weapons, just un-tempered steel so she didn't use much charcoal. Harold looked forward to seeing a Katari with a real blade.

Harold had just finished unarmed combat practice with Wamil when Hazel caught him in the street. "Harold, Harold." He smiled because that meant she'd got over her latest embarrassment, over him seeing her kissing Alfie.

"Yes Hazel."

"There's a woman trying to run over the fields, Bess says she looks in a bad way." Harold's smile died and he ran to Bess's guardhouse, number six, as fast as possible.

"Here, have a look." Harold took the binoculars from Bess. The young woman, dressed in rags, seemed to have trouble running, stumbling and limping even after she'd cleared the rubble. As some of the gardeners moved to help her, she fell down. The first people reached her, and then one of them fell.

A radio crackled. "Crossbow or bow from the ruins! Who's on duty with the rifle?"

"Billy. I've already called for him." Bess took her finger off the radio button. "That's a bit far for him, Harold. Unless you are taking it?" As she spoke, Billy came in carrying a two-two rifle.

Harold ignored the proffered weapon. "That's well over half a mile from here, too far for that rifle. Run out to the Annex, Billy. You'll still be over three hundred yards away and probably won't touch the crossbow-man, but try. If you get near it'll make him duck. Remember, use the firing slots and shoot and duck just in case." Out in the fields everyone near the woman had dropped flat.

The radio buzzed. "Harold? I'm on the way." Emmy didn't mention rifles on the air.

"Go to the Annex and wait. Don't do anything yet."

The phone rang, Casper from the gatehouse. "Harold? There's three GOFS, two Barbies and a Hot Rod inside the walls at the moment. And the two Hot Rod spies up the road of course."

"Put the visitors inside Orchard Close into the overnight house and explain. If they crack one curtain to peek, promise I'll shoot them all. I don't want them seeing who shoots and what weapon they use." Harold tried, but couldn't think of an answer to the Hot Rod spies. "I don't know what to do about Caddi's watchers, except hope they don't use radios. Broadcast that, they'll be listening and might keep their gobs shut." Harold hoped so. Whoever was out there would be listening, so any radio reports the Hot Rods sent home would go to them as well. "Send a runner to ask Demon to get dressed for trouble and go to the Annex." Casper agreed and rang off.

Harold spent a few minutes getting his own rifle and thinking about what had happened, and it didn't add up. The men with crossbows were suicidal against a good rifle, unless they had backup, and what did they hope to achieve by killing gardeners? Patty called by on her way to the Annex, with a big wrapped bundle as well as her two-two so she'd understood the message. Harold explained quietly without anyone else hearing. "You might need both your rifles, but only use the two-two for now because this stinks. There's more to it. Whoever is out there has to have backup so remember, shoot and move." Patty didn't waste time, setting off at a run.

Harold used the phone again to call the gate, asking Alfie to bring the 303. That took a few minutes because Alfie's leg still wasn't up to running. As Harold waited, a two-two started shooting from the Annex. Just as Alfie arrived a second small rifle started up, then after a couple more shots a deeper note joined in.

Harold handed his radio to Alfie as he arrived with the 303. "That wasn't Emmy's rifle. Ask who fired what, and if the person with the two-two is all right."

Moments later Bethany's voice answered. "Someone is out there and he shot clean through a loophole! He missed, er, the person on our rifle is all right." A two-two cracked again to punctuate that and moments later the other two-two fired. "Billy is trying for the crossbows, while the other one is now trying to hit the rifle but it's a long way away. Too far for a two-two I'm told." Patty must be hinting through Bethany that she wanted to open up with the Winchester.

Alfie passed Harold's instructions on by radio, because Patty's bullets would be getting close and he didn't want the whoever to know it wasn't Soldier Boy shooting. "Get a bad girl on the phone in the Annex. Until then keep trying with the two-two." Harold swapped weapons with Alfie, before sending him out to the Annex with the Blaser and instructions.

He called the Annex on the single telephone connection, and Bethany answered. "What's happening?"

The strain showed in Bethany's voice. "We think there's only four, all with crossbows, hiding in the edge of the rubble. They'll be lucky to hit anyone in the Annex since that's over three hundred yards away, but they've got eight of our gardeners and the woman pinned down. Patty wants permission to shoot the bastards."

"Tell Patty not yet but she can try to kill the rifleman, even if it's a long shot for a two-two. She's to duck and move after every shot and I'll speak to her in a minute. Tell Billy to keep taking shots at the crossbows with the two-two to keep their heads down, but duck after every shot."

"All right Harold. Emmy is here now."

"Hello Harold. I can't see him, the sniper, even from an upstairs window. He's chosen a good place, about six hundred yards out, in the rubble among the houses we're still demolishing. I can't nail him from the smoke because there isn't much, and anyway he keeps moving. I could kill the crossbowmen? They're hiding just beyond the saplings, where they can reach some of the gardeners and that refugee, but they're in plain view from upstairs." It all came out in a rush, because Emmy wanted to nail someone, anyone.

"Calm down, Emmy. Don't shoot at all unless you have a clear shot at the rifleman. They'll know about our big rifles but I'd rather keep them guessing where they are. Billy and Alfie shoot well enough to get close and keep the crossbows pinned with the two-twos. Give me a minute." Harold thought quickly, then went through the situation with Emmy.

The fleeing woman had to be a decoy, but maybe not a willing accomplice. She'd crawled into one of the buried baths used to store water, but had a crossbow bolt in her back or leg. The gardeners were all laid flat and crawling to get behind barrows, carts, greenery, or into a garden pond or bath. At least three were carrying pistols but weren't close enough to hit anything. Two had crossbows and were duelling with the attackers.

"Emmy, Alfie is bringing the Blaser. Do you want to use that or your sniper rifle?"

"I've used it before, and I'd rather have the four extra quick shots using the clip if I get a chance. Who uses my rifle if I use the Blaser?"

"Patty can. She's not used to it, but she's only got five shots for her baby and it isn't as accurate with only a peep sight." Harold thought about it. "Can you get Patty on the phone? Take a couple of shots with the two-two while I talk to her? Be careful, someone out there is a good shot. When she gets back, go upstairs and lay for the scroat. I'm going to stalk him if he's stupid enough to wait. Try not to shoot me by mistake, but be ready if anyone with a rifle breaks cover."

"Good hunting, Harold."

When Patty came on the phone, she cursed fluently without breaking the rules. "He's got a better rifle than me, Harold. Why can't I use my baby? Can I use that rifle you took off the General's sniper?"

"Yes to some of that because he's here to kill me, Patty. We need to set him up."

Patty didn't sound convinced. "He was shooting at me a minute ago."

"But nobody knows where I am, so he shot at a shooter. How near do you reckon you got with the two-two?"

After a pause, Patty replied in a quieter, thoughtful voice. "I winged one of those with the crossbows. I'm not sure how much damage it does at that range, but I used a special."

"Then it will have penetrated and done some damage. As far as the gangs or even most people in here know, how many people can shoot like that with a small rifle?" Patty didn't answer. "Billy will be getting close, but not as close as you did, and everyone knows about me and my two-two. When did the rifleman open fire?"

Despite his own conclusions, Harold still hoped he might be wrong, but Patty's reply scotched that. "After I shot the bloke with the crossbow. In fact, if I hadn't moved after the next shot like you keep telling me... Crap!"

"Billy had already taken a few shots without reply. This bloke waited to fire until after you hit a partially hidden man with a two-two at three hundred yards." Harold sighed, because until he'd put it like that he hadn't been sure.

Patty sighed as well, in exasperation. "I can't see him so how are you going to kill him?"

"I can't from here. He'll have different spots sorted out and will move from one to another, or I would. If we send out a lot of people to flush the bastard, he'll kill a few and then be gone. I need to get out there and flank his position without him realising I've left."

Once Patty worked it out, Harold could hear the anticipation in her voice. "So if I keep shooting at him, and getting near? He'll think it's you, until it's too late. With the sniper's rifle and scope, I might even hit the sneaky little git."

"Good idea. Use the sniper rifle, slowly and as accurately as possible. Save the Winchester for five rounds rapid, covering fire or if the group run. Aim where he shoots from, but if the crossbow users try to move out, kill one to pin them so he'll wait. Shoot and move bloody fast because otherwise he'll get you." Harold paused, then realised he hadn't told Patty everything. "Emmy won't shoot unless she gets a clear chance at the rifleman."

Sheer exasperation coloured Patty's answer. "How do I shoot at him if I'm ducking? I need to see the smoke."

"Good point." Harold thought about it but Patty had already got there. "If I roll sideways and get my eye to a crack on the bricks, will the smoke hang long enough to be spotted?" There were periodic slits, just slightly larger gaps between bricks but lined up through the wall to see without being seen. A few widened towards the rear for a rifle barrel.

"Then find another place to shoot from and try to hit the spot. Keep him convinced that I'm accurate but shooting at the smoke, so he's still got a chance of getting me." Harold immediately thought of one problem. "Ask Bethany or someone else to spot for you through a crack in the wall, well away from you, in case you take too long. Make sure nobody looks over the wall. Fire nice and steady. If his info is good, he'll think you are tempting him for the other rifle, which you are."

"Then if she gets a chance, Emmy can empty the damn Blaser into him. Sorted." The next part came out with definite venom in it. "Now kill him. At least two of the gardeners have crossbow bolts in them, and without that rifleman I could kill the swine that did it."

"I'm gone." Harold put the phone down and called the gatehouse. "Casper?"

"Hang on." Moments later Casper came on the phone.

"Casper, wait by the main gates with shotguns, crossbows and twenty fighters. If this goes wrong, charge the bastard. Use shotguns for covering fire. Shoot, dash and drop. Rinse and repeat until you get close." Harold hesitated before explaining why it would be urgent, in case Casper objected to him taking the chance. "I'll be out there and I'll need you to drive him away, stop him finishing me off if I've been hit."

"You're going out there, right where he wants you? Why the hell would…" Casper paused, thinking it over. "Because it's the only way, and only you can do the sneaky bit. Okay, we'll do dash and drop but I'll bring the tank round so we can get closer faster. Don't worry, if you're only wounded we'll get you and might kill a few as they run."

"Cheers." Harold put down the phone, checking over the 303 and the three full clips before heading to the end of Orchard Close. He left through the terraced houses, crawling quickly but carefully along the tarmac between two rows of potatoes. If the attackers had infrared, he hoped they'd be concentrating on the shooters. Behind him he could hear the two-twos pinning the crossbows, and the steady exchange as Patty and the sniper fired towards each other's smoke. Hopefully she'd keep her moves random, and the muzzle far enough back he wouldn't spot her before she fired. If Patty moved as soon as she fired, he'd never correct fast enough for a hit. Harold fervently hoped not, because he'd asked her to risk it.

The continuing exchange between Patty and the rifleman confirmed that he wasn't trained as a sniper, or any sort of military shooter. The attempt to kill Harold had failed, so the man should pull back and wait for another opportunity. Harold had plenty of time to think, because he had another half mile to go and some of it would be on his belly.

As he reached the ruins to the north, a short scream sounded on the heels of the sniper's shot. Harold clicked his radio, just once, and two clicks came back. Despite more cries of pain, whatever had happened hadn't altered the plan. Whoever had been hit wasn't Patty or Emmy. Patty impressed Harold, still keeping to her instructions instead of killing a crossbowman as payback. Emmy had done just as well, because the temptation to shoot at least one must be almost unbearable. Harold rose to his feet and began to run, crouched over with the 303 held across his body and a round up the spout.

*   *   *

Seven or eight minutes later the shooting still continued. The rate had slowed, as both shooters tried to tempt the other to take a better look. Harold looked cautiously around the next row of houses and saw movement. He eased back a bit, sighed, and went down on his belly again. He had to keep well clear to get past whoever this was without being seen, at least far enough to kill the sniper. Patty fired, but a long silence followed. She'd got him! Then another thought hit Harold and a chill went down his back. If Patty thought so and stuck up her head to have a look? The silence continued until Harold began to wonder.

After what seemed an age Patty fired again, and the reply came almost immediately. Now Harold worried if Patty had been careless, thinking the man might be wounded or dead? Her next shot came as a relief, or he hoped that Patty fired it. The two rifles continued their duel, with the two-twos firing now and then as well, while Harold wondered again who this man was. Probably someone who'd been a club shooter or a deer hunter, sticking with a plan that had worked on other occasions? He couldn't be a local or someone would have talked about him.

Harold saw movement straight after he heard the next shot. Got him! A few moments later he saw someone moving, but the man held a crossbow as he headed towards Orchard Close. Harold mentally drew in a slow crawl around the intervening partially demolished housing towards the shooting, avoiding the direction the man went. Within minutes Harold could see the legs and ass of a man who must be a flank guard. He was tempted to shoot the bloke through the legs, to panic the attackers and flush the sniper, but decided against it. If the sniper held his nerve he might still get away. Harold crept on.

* * *

Harold finally caught a glimpse of his target. The sniper changed position after another shot, but unfortunately Harold could only see a leg once he settled. That would cripple and pin the rifleman, but there were others out here as well. If they were trying to kill Harold, the wounded shooter might get his chance. The man fired again as Harold closed so he peeked quickly to see where the bloke went. Perfect. He'd hidden just over a hundred yards away. Next time he moved, Harold would be ready.

Even as he slid the big old rifle forward Harold heard a shout from his right! Damn, he'd been too eager and forgotten to check his flanks. Harold turned his head to see a man stood on the rubble, pointing. "Here! With a bloody rifle!" The man started to raise his crossbow, less than twenty yards away, then ducked a little as Patty took a shot. It must have been aimed at the sniper, because the man straightened and raised the crossbow again.

Harold glanced around for cover but there wasn't any so he tried to beat the man to the shot. Rolling up and almost into a sitting position, Harold twisted to bring the long barrel round but he'd be too late. As he moved the Winchester sounded, firing as fast as Patty could crank the lever. The crossbow man flinched even as he fired, looking towards Orchard Close instead of his target. Harold jerked as an impact on his chest and sharp pain told him he'd been hit, but the crossbow man dropped his weapon and staggered sideways before falling out of sight. A glance down showed a crossbow bolt jutting at an angle from Harold's jacket, but it hadn't gone deep enough to put him down immediately. Harold twisted, still sat up, looking for his original target.

The sniper had been caught between two rifles, undecided, but now he tried to do the same as Harold had and get off his shot first. The depression in the bricks that concealed the sniper worked against him now, he had to sit up to turn whereas Harold only had to swivel his hips. Harold already had the 303 to his shoulder, but took a snapshot rather than waiting and giving the man any chance. The butt kicked hard and Harold worked the bolt. His first shot clipped the target, knocking the man back while his arm and rifle swung up to one side. Harold took time to aim the second shot properly, putting the big bullet into the sniper's chest. The man flopped back and his rifle clattered down into the rubble.

Two men came up out of cover with crossbows, and then a third, all looking back at Harold. The nearest, the flank guard only forty yards away, flew backwards into the rubble when Harold shot him. Another man staggered, dropping his crossbow as Patty clipped him with the Winchester, which gave Harold all the time in the world to nail him. The third man sprawled forwards, towards Harold, as Emmy joined the party.

Two men further away sprang from the ruins, running as fast as they could, trying to dodge about while negotiating the rubble. Another stood, hesitated and went down on his face. Patty had switched back to the sniper rifle. One of the runners staggered and went to his knees as Emmy fired again. Emmy's victim's knees barely landed before Patty's bullet knocked him right down. Harold settled his sights onto the last one and waited patiently as Emmy took another shot but missed him. Sure enough, he eventually ran straight for a few steps, long enough for Harold's bullet to throw him forward onto his face. He tried to drag himself back to his feet but flipped over and sideways as both Patty and Emmy fired.

Harold put another clip in the rifle, waiting. Both Patty and Emmy started firing steadily, presumably at the men with crossbows among the saplings. There were noises from three places around him, men in pain, but nobody obviously moving. A man with a crossbow burst through between two half-walls, running as if the Barbies were on his heels. Harold took a moment to make sure of the shot.

The radio burst into life. "Harold? We're on the way."

"I'm okay Casper. I think they're all hit unless there's one hiding wherever the cars are. Don't use firearms unless you have to because I'm in the line of fire. Shooters Two, Three, Four and Five keep off the radio but good work. If anything moves make sure it isn't me." Harold grinned, he'd almost used Patty's name. "Shooter Three, hide the evidence. Patty, report in please."

Two almost simultaneous shots sounded before Patty answered. "One of the wounded moved so shooters two and three made sure." Harold could hear the laughter in her voice, but that was a pity because now he'd calmed down, Harold wanted survivors.

He called Casper. "Try for a live one Casper, but take no chances."

"On it. We're nearly there. Stretchers going for our people." Casper grunted in the middle of speaking and Harold could hear the lorry engine revving. The heavy vehicle would be a rough ride over rubble.

* * *

Harold carefully undid his jacket, hissing with pain when the point came clear with the cloth. The protection in his jacket, a layer of bits of flat metal fastened to a padded lining, had been enough to slow the bolt. He had no idea how big a hole the head had made, but it wasn't fatal. Harold bit off a yelp as he slid a dressing inside his shirt. He smoothed the tape into place, and found he could breathe without too much pain.

Noises nearby, from where the crossbowman had spotted him, prompted Harold to head that way. When he peered over the bricks, very cautiously, he found five cars but nobody standing. The crossbowman lay spread-eagled but moving feebly. With the amount of blood pulsing from the big exit wound just above his waist, the bloke wouldn't last much longer. Harold quickly removed the pistol, knife and machete from the man's belt, tossing them to one side. Another sound brought him up and round, rifle pointing at one of the cars. He approached cautiously then lowered the weapon. The woman in the car, almost naked, badly bruised and firmly tied up, stared back from above her gag. "It's all right, you're safe." Her eyes didn't believe him.

He checked over the lip of the hollow, but Casper's people were in among the bodies so there'd be no surprises. Harold put down his rifle and pulled a knife, slicing quickly through the strips of material binding her arms. "Here, cut yourself free." He left her to it, picking up his rifle to keep an eye on the places the other attackers had fallen.

"Bastard!" Harold turned. The fallen man wasn't quite dead yet because he thrashed weakly and tried to scream, probably because of the woman stabbing Harold's knife repeatedly into his groin. She had both hands fisted round the hilt, lifting them above her head for each blow, so his jeans weren't stopping the blade. The woman noticed Harold watching but drove the knife down twice more, into his throat. Her glare at Harold had a real challenge in it.

"Patty or Emmy might not have cut his throat after." Harold saw the shock as that hit her. "Why don't you calm down and introduce yourself. I'm Harold, also known as Soldier Boy." He tried to make his smile reassuring, but must have failed. She dropped the knife and stood up, apprehension on her face.

"I'm not with them."

Harold had another go at looking and sounding friendly. "I guessed that, but you'll be safe now. Do you know who they were? Which gang?"

"No. He was going to kill you. With the big rifle. For coupons." She pointed in the general direction of the sniper's position.

"He's dead. Any idea who sent them?"

She shook her head. "It was a big payday they said. Where's Julie? They told her if she reached the walls she'd be safe." She sobbed and kicked the body, then hopped a bit so the kick must have hurt her bare toes. "When she'd left he told me the others would stamp on her feet first, to slow her up, then shoot her anyway if she got that far."

"Far as I know she's okay. If she kept her head down she's hiding somewhere out there, safe and sound." Harold pointed at the body. "Put his boots on if you want to kick anything. What's your name?"

"Amelia." She knelt and pulled at the man's boots.

"Where from?"

"The Geeks."

"The Geeks set this up?" In that case Harold would declare open season on Geeks, and turn Patty and Emmy loose.

"No. We were taking the rubbish outside the wire, for burning, and our two guards were killed with crossbows. We were grabbed and had to run for ages." She shuddered at the memory and tugged her rags around to cover up a bit more. "They kept us going with knives until they got to the cars. We had to lie in the back on the floor while they drove away. Then last night they had some fun."

Amelia put on the boots and stood to kick the body, several times. "That's better. The fun was to make us keen so we'd run when told to." Faint but bitter humour showed briefly. "They weren't any worse than the usual bloody Geek fun, if the wrong ones picked us. It's usually only one at a time, but sometimes a bunch of the sick bastards want to play pass the p..., parcel."

She sighed, suddenly sitting down fast enough for it to be almost a collapse. "It's over, isn't it? If you're Soldier Boy that must be Orchard Close. We made it." She burst into tears as Casper came over the lip of the hollow.

Harold looked up at Casper and shrugged. "Not guilty. I think she's happy. Did you find any survivors?"

"No. They'd all bled out by the time we got to them. Those big bullets really tear them up. Bloody hell, Harold, when did, er, Shooter Three learn to do that?"

"A natural, then quite a lot of careful practice whenever we could. Secret practice that should stay a secret." Harold tried to be serious but couldn't help the snigger. "You've seen Shooter Three with a crossbow."

A big smile spread over Casper's face. "Oh yes." He looked at the body and the bloody groin and throat and glanced towards Harold with a silent question.

Harold shrugged and indicated the woman. "Payback."

"Fair enough. He's lucky he was dead then."

"Not quite, but that did the job. This is Amelia. I'm heading home to get patched up, and to congratulate the Coven on the protection in this jacket. Can you get the rest to strip the bodies and throw them together? Either bury them in bricks so they aren't an eyesore, or burn them, but get pictures first. This is an attempt to get me, personally, and I'd like to return the favour." Harold suddenly felt very tired, exhausted, as the tension bled away.

Casper nodded towards Harold's open jacket and bloody shirt. "Can you drive? We brought the pickup as well, it won't knock you about as much as the tank."

"I can drive, thanks. It hit me at an angle." Harold pointed at the discarded weapons. "That crossbow doesn't have a crank, so the plates inside my jacket were enough to slow the bolt." He hefted the rifle. "Come on Amelia. Let's get you somewhere you can have a shower and put on some nice new clothes. We'll have a party to welcome you later."

Harold wasn't sure why, but Amelia looked shocked and apprehensive at that. She turned as Casper threw his coat. "Here." She pulled the big coat round herself and eyed up the corpse, but her payback had ruined his jeans and shirt. "Don't poke about in the pockets. I keep all sorts in there and some is sharp." Casper's reassuring smile worked better than Harold's.

Amelia gave him a cautious smile in return, hesitating by the knife she'd dropped so Harold pointed. "I'll want that one back. Take his belt and keep his knife if you want to." She nodded enthusiastically, buckling on the belt and checking the knife while Harold repossessed his and cleaned it. When he set off she limped alongside to the pickup, and climbed in without hesitation.

* * *

Amelia went into the girl club for a shower, new clothing and a gentle interrogation by the women. Within ten minutes Liz came to find Harold, waiting to have his wound looked at. "The only new clothes she's seen for two years are the knitted jumpers. Those thin ones." Harold frowned, he'd have expected the Geeks to make them wear something sexier. "The Geeks like their women wearing a thin stretchy jumper and nothing else. Those longer ones make a tight mini-dress when one of the captive women is washed down for some special fun, for a Geeky sex party."

"Okay, enough. I get the picture and I actually offered her all those, without the Geeky parts. Please explain that a shower, new clothes and a party don't mean the same here. The knitting machine is broken as far as the Geeks are concerned. Oh shit." Harold looked for something to punch.

"What?"

Harold glared at Liz. "Under the treaty, I'm supposed to send them back to the Geeks."

"No." Liz crossed her arms with a truly stubborn look. "There'll be a rebellion. The Demons would rather go and kill the Geeks, all of them."

Harold turned as Tessa, Sharyn and Emmy arrived to check on the wounded. "So would I, but that breaks two other treaties so how do we make two women disappear? The bodies are a big hint about what happened, and our visitors will know." He glanced down the street. "Are the visitors still safely locked up?"

"Yes, they never saw a thing. By now they're probably having an orgy." Emmy's smile disappeared as she remembered the other spectators. "What about Caddi's watchers?"

Liz produced a huge grin. "Doll went to have a word. Something about big mouths and deep graves." She shrugged when Harold stared at her. "She meant offering them a deep grave as an option, not handing them a shovel. I think?"

Emmy ignored her, thinking hard. "That means nobody saw the lasses properly. We'll need two refugees who aren't those two."

"What?" Harold looked around, baffled again.

"Two of those running from the Murphies will do. They were captured on the way here and used by the sniper to tempt us out so they could shoot at you." Emmy smiled happily, but Harold couldn't see why.

"But why would new refugees agree to say that? And keep it a secret?"

"Because they are either running from, or have been, in the same situation? Don't worry Harold, we'll find the right ones to supply names and a street they came from, a Murphy street. You won't recognise Amelia or Julie again, unless they introduce themselves." Emmy seemed confident so Harold let it go.

Patricia, the nurse, looked up from her current patient. "Unless you see Julie before Lenny gets the crossbow bolt out of her ass. She reckons it's lucky the bolt hit a bit with some meat on. The medication she's just had might be helping her mood."

Emmy patted Harold on the back. "Get your sympathy bandage, then go and do Soldier things. We've got it covered. Just remember, you rescued two ex-Murphy girls."

"Okay. Murphy girls. Go and do Soldier things." Harold turned to Patricia to find out who else had been hurt. The answer killed any humour because four of the gardeners out in the fields had been hit by crossbow bolts. Worse, the sniper had shot another two gardeners, no doubt trying to force Patty into a mistake. He'd gone for making them scream rather than kills, but one at least would never walk properly again. Two crossbow victims would never heal, because they'd bled out before Lenny the medic got to them.

* * *

A quick inspection showed that Harold wouldn't be one of the urgent cases, because the steel plates had slowed and deflected the bolt just enough. It had hit a rib, not hard enough to break through, but solidly enough to stop it glancing off and reaching his lung. Patricia bound the dressing properly and told him to come back later. Harold found Patty waiting outside the hospital, literally twitching with excitement. He pointed towards the gate. "Come on, let's see what Doll has done to Caddi's sentries. That way you can tell me about it on the way."

Sure enough, as soon as they were clear of the gate Patty started. "That bloke shot right through my firing slit twice, and was too close most times!" She looked a bit wide-eyed. "Sorry it took four shots. The first bloke who stood up. I had to shoot quickly."

"Good. I got too eager and made a mistake. If you'd waited he'd have taken time to aim properly, but you distracted him so the bolt hit me off-centre. How did you know?" Because Patty hadn't waited very long.

Luckily.

"I didn't but he stood up, shouting and pointing. I took a shot but too fast and I missed. I ducked, but the sniper didn't reply so I used the Winchester to shoot as fast as possible. Then I heard that cannon of yours and figured you'd nailed the sniper, so I shot at the next one to stand up." Patty shook her head. "It wasn't real, not like a proper fight with machetes. More like targets that fell down."

"Thank you for making them fall down. I'd give you full credit but I reckon you work better as a secret, Shooter Three. Nobody will think Shooter Three is the Demon, because she's only little and knits. Even if she uses a big needle in her crossbow, she can't possible handle a big butch rifle." They both had a snigger about that.

Patty's voice sobered. "Will Alfie be upset about you calling me Shooter Three?"

"No, because Alfie already knows three hundred yards is about his limit, which is why he doesn't have one of the better rifles." Harold would talk to Alfie, just to be sure it hadn't ruffled any feathers.

Doll met Harold outside one of the damaged houses up by the traffic island, looking apprehensive. "You didn't want radio messages."

"Do I need a shovel or just new undies for them?"

Doll sighed in relief at Harold's humour, then smiled. "Possibly underwear. Five of my squad are guarding their radios and explaining alternatives. Those do include deep graves and also accidental house collapses, or possibly tripping and skewering themselves on a variety of sharp stuff."

The two Hot Rods looked relieved to see Harold. One started to look indignant, probably going to complain, but Patty caught his eye and tapped her crossbow. Harold nodded towards her. "The options are still open if you act up. We didn't need you telling the world what we were doing, not until we'd sorted the problem."

"Caddi will say this is the neutral road." The man flinched from the look on Doll's face, so she hadn't been as diplomatic as Harold usually was. "Just sayin', right?"

Harold smiled before answering, and knew how nasty it looked. He explained that radio messages weren't neutral. Doll butted in to point out she could have shot them or buried the pair in a lonely grave, and blamed the attackers. Both of them became much more amenable, asking for details just so they didn't get shit from Caddi, and seemed grateful when Patty inspected their weapons but gave them back. On the way back down the road, Patty and Doll reckoned the pair would tell Caddi about the rifle, but not mention they'd been captured.

When the group reached the gates, still teasing Doll about her methods of getting boyfriends, the visitors were waiting with questions. One of the Barbies waved her radio so they'd been listening. "Shooter Four? Five?"

"Shooter Six maybe, now we've got another rifle? One free beer as compensation for missing the fun?" Harold waved a hand in the right direction. "We're a bit busy clearing up right now, but you'll get the gory details from someone later." The visitors headed for canteen, happy with the freebie, while Harold went to check on the wounded again.

He met a surprisingly cheerful Julie, laid on her front until her crossbow bolt could be removed. She had her ankles on a pillow to take any pressure off her badly bruised feet and two broken toes. Two of the other wounded weren't conscious. After one look at Lenny's worried face, Harold left his own wound for later. A glimpse of Gayle the dentist in a medical mask meant someone needed serious anaesthetics. The conscious ones seemed cheerful if pale, so they'd probably had the same medication as Julie.

When Harold returned an hour later, Patricia cleaned his wound properly for Lenny to have a quick look. Patricia had learned a lot about battle injuries, but still preferred an expert opinion. According to the paramedic, Harold had ended up sliced rather than skewered. The gash would be sore, as would the bruised or cracked rib, but Harold would take that over a punctured lung any day. According to the medic, everyone still alive should make it. Patricia put on a fresh dressing and supplied details. In addition to the four gardeners and Julie, Amelia would be spending some time in the hospital. The nurse wanted to make sure the rough treatment hadn't left any lasting damage. Going by the way she'd dealt with the wounded kidnapper, Harold thought Amelia would be fine.

*   *   *

The Hot Rod spies must have confessed, or Caddi had wondered why they'd not transmitted the action live. Either way the Hot Rod boss knew because just before dusk, Casper called Harold down to the gate to meet Charger. The Hot Rod seemed apprehensive, but came inside without asking for a hostage exchange or bringing in a bodyguard. Harold wondered if Caddi had sent Charger because he tended to get on better with the residents. The slightly older Hot Rods' mechanic didn't seem as violent as the rest, and had always treated women with more respect.

Charger looked apprehensive because Caddi wanted him to get an explanation. The Hot Rod probably toned down the actual demand, but even so telling him to piss off would only cause trouble. Caddi would be offended, and the nutter might even kill someone, ambush them, out of sheer nastiness. So instead, Harold explained there wasn't a problem if the watchers didn't report every movement over the radio, to any scroat out there who might be listening. As he pointed out, they could come and sit in the canteen to spy in comfort.

Charger looked relieved, leaving straight away without a beer. The radio messages from the spies dropped off after that so either Caddi accepted the point, or his watchers had now realised just how vulnerable they were.

The next person to talk to Harold about the attack went all around the subject to make his point, because he couldn't speak openly. The sergeant on the bypass tried to let Harold know he'd seen the rifles, illegal weapons, without actually admitting it. Going by what the TV showed, the NCO should have called in either artillery or an air strike, and reinforcements so he could invade the enclave and capture any rifles.

Harold arranged for extra chips and beer to go up to the soldiers from now on. They were a thank you for the warning, and because despite his standing orders, Sarge hadn't even fired a warning shot. A serious discussion led to all the rifle and shotgun users agreeing they would try and shoot from inside houses in the future. Meanwhile, the joiners looked into ways of making a simple frame, a cover for the firing steps if necessary. To help with that, the Coven asked the sewing circle to go through the salvaged curtains and bedding. With luck the women could make a screen to hang on the frame, so even drones wouldn't be able to see what weapons were being used.

*   *   *

Two days later, Mercedes turned up with two Hot Rod escorts. There were a good few glowers, from people who thought that the Hot Rods were somehow responsible for the attack. Doll must have been very quick with the search, because Mercedes marched up the road while Charger and a bodyguard were still being inspected. No joking or teasing this time, Mercedes didn't even take off her coat. "How many were hurt? How many are women?"

Harold could see the anger in her eyes and a little something eased inside him. If Caddi had been involved, Mercedes didn't know. "Seven hurt, two died and three are serious enough to be in hospital for a while. Three were women, a gardener and the two decoys. Only one of the men will be left with a serious long-term handicap. We killed all the scroats."

Mercedes looked around. "Where are they, your injured?" She steadied up a little, and looked a little bit embarrassed. "I'm sorry. Can I visit the sick please, 'Arold?" A real Mercedes smile broke out. "I haven't got a little white nurse dress and white stockings, but the girls won't mind that, will they?"

"No, but the blokes will be heartbroken." Patty smirked, looking at Harold. "Unless you've come to kiss them better? One of the wounded is near enough to start now. One who didn't put himself on that list."

"Not all of them. My lips belong to 'Arold and I would love to kiss him, then kiss him better, if I could get him alone?" The little warm spot in her eyes appeared and went, and her voice softened. "Two dead, no more?" At the curious looks, Mercedes shrugged very slightly. "A big pyre or so I heard."

"One big and two smaller. We didn't want the scroats to stink. They were all dead before we burned them, which is a pity." The sheer venom in Patty's snarl caught Mercedes' attention.

"Why, what did they do?"

"Had a party to make sure the decoy women would run." Patty suddenly looked wary as fury blossomed in Mercedes' eyes.

"The bastards are never satisfied. Are you sure you got them all?" Her hand twitched towards where her belt knife would sit. "None of the wounded got away?"

"Not a chance. Those big bullets don't take prisoners." Casper stood blocking the road as it became obvious that, instead of heading for the Embassy or the canteen, Mercedes wanted the hospital. The hospital, originally the house Patricia lived in, stood outside the usual allowed areas.

Mercedes hesitated at Casper's folded arms and the 'Keep Out' sign. "Please, 'Arold?" Her eyes twinkled and she posed just a little. "I'd strip for an extra search, but this isn't exactly private."

Harold didn't have the heart to argue. "I'll have to stay close?"

He'd hardly finished speaking before Mercedes put an arm round him. "You'd better get a grip then." Harold put an arm round her waist and headed for the hospital. "Do you know who did it?"

"Not yet. They aren't local, so I reckon someone hired them in." Harold hesitated, then told her. "The coupons were from scores of different people and the weapons were a mix."

"I'll ask around, and if I find out who I'll let you know." Several people exchanged glances because that wasn't expected. "In fact, if I find them I'll send their ears. I am sick of the way women are treated these days. Stolen and passed around like bloody trophies. The bastards are worse than animals." Nobody nearby would argue with any part of that. There were no other Hot Rods in the group now as her escort were only just leaving the gate, and anyway, gangsters weren't allowed near the hospital.

Harold looked around those near enough to hear, and leaned over towards Casper. "Make sure nobody passes that gem to anyone else, especially Hot Rods, will you?" Casper looked around and nodded in understanding. Caddi definitely fitted the group Mercedes described, and wouldn't like a public statement like that.

Mercedes calmed down by the time the group arrived at the hospital, morphing into a cheerful, sympathetic young woman. She asked Patricia about everyone and spoke to every invalid. Each one of the wounded received sympathy and jokes, to their bafflement and then delight. Mercedes apologised that she hadn't brought flowers or grapes, and left them smiling. Harold saw her eyes while she spoke to them, and it wasn't an act. Whoever had been buried behind those dead eyes had started to break free.

As they left the hospital Mercedes saw Charger, waiting nervously at the 'Keep Out' sign, and turned back into her Hot Rod persona. Waiting wasn't optional, because Casper had gone back there with three others and a bad attitude. Mercedes raised her voice. "Too late Charger, 'Arold has already given me a full medical inspection. I stripped him down to check his wounds, and kissed them all better." She laughed at the look on the Hot Rod's face. "I couldn't get him anywhere private enough, or we'd still be in there and you'd hear at least one of us screaming."

Charger looked relieved. "Sorry, but you know, Caddi told us."

"Oh yes, I'm not to be trusted alone with Soldier Boy." Her hand in his hip pocket squeezed Harold's ass. "Am I safe alone with you, 'Arold?"

"Absolutely not, Mercedes. I hope that makes you keener, not worried?" Harold returned the favour, since Mercedes had wanted to know what his hand felt like in her back pocket.

"Ooh yes." Mercedes sighed and snuggled in a little. "I suppose I'd better get back, or himself will have a cardiac. What a waste, I never even had any delectables stroked." She carried on chattering down to the gate, then insisted that 'Arold stroked her jeans over her ass with both hands, just to keep her going. A bemused Harold watched her walk down to the cars with a finger pointed at what he should watch.

Chapter 10:
June/July

Dudley Zoo / Precinct Nineteen:
Precinct Nineteen and the Dudley Zoo residents had reached a balance. The extra acreage Precinct Nineteen controlled meant that more of the young zoo animals matured for meat, and the Zookeepers could support more of the mothers just for milking. The children drank real, full cream milk while the fresh meat reduced reliance on the Marts. The residents still needed some essentials, but now they could leave a couple of months between shopping trips. Less trips meant taking less risks and expending less ammunition, especially as the additional numbers meant a stronger convoy. The protein and the milk, and their secure positions, even led to a steady influx of refugees. Not gangsters, ordinary people who saw a chance to buy a decent life for their families by trading their old skills. With the extra labour, more land could be farmed, and many of the old warehouses were cleared to provide pasture.

Some of the neighbouring gangs began to bury their old hatred of the police to trade for milk and meat. That didn't suit the Cabal, so local agents were sent new instructions.

* * *

Sutton Park:
After a brief period of unrest, while families relocated from the ruins to the edge of the park, the gangs settled down. The forcibly removed civvies realised that they were safer, and if they worked in the nearby park their kids could get real meat and milk. The extra labour dug over more of the park for crops, the part not used for rearing stock or preserving wildlife.

The eight gangs began to realise just how knowledgeable their new tenants were. Better still, the park wardens knew the area intimately, and were perfectly happy to show the fighters the best places to put guard posts and lookouts. In return, the gangs agreed to leave the less edible wildlife alone rather than use it as target practice. It wasn't much yet, but the barriers between conquered and conquerors began to weaken. The boundaries between the gangs were definitely crumbling, especially after mixed forces lived together for up to a week. They acted as families while setting the traps, and some of the liaisons continued after the operation ended.

The gradual coming together wasn't entirely unplanned. A very few people, definitely not the type to work for the Cabal, were intent on welding all the gangs and residents into one integrated community. They hoped that if the result acted relatively civilised, that would be enough to stop the Army attacking them. These select few had a couple of alternatives, just in case the Army attacked anyway, but were keeping them secret for now. They were determined that this enclave at least would survive.

* * *

Conan:

Conan wasn't worried about snipers, or any other sort of attack, but the knock at his door made him wary. The rest usually left him alone when he was in this sort of a mood, but this knock sounded brisk and confident. Conan even knew the reasons for his mood. Between the Lambs of God and that fucking Bitch, it seemed as if the whole world had conspired to defy him. He'd had to storm another enclave, suck up some losses, just to get the edge off. The men were muttering, and sooner or later one of them would take a shot at being boss. "Come in."

"Hi boss. I've got a proposition." The heavily armed man wasn't a typical Barbarian, clean-shaven and relatively neat and tidy. He'd been here a while, and had made a couple of suggestions that worked out.

Conan searched his memory for the man's name. "Sylvester? What do you want in here when I'm supposed to be planning? Unless you've come up with a way to get into that compound and have a Lamb of God barbecue."

"Oddly enough, I might have. You won't like it because you'll have to make a deal with the God-botherers, but it should do the trick." Sylvester smiled confidently in spite of Conan's scowl. "The thing is, I've got an in with the Mart guards and know which assholes can be bribed." He smiled at the incredulous look on Conan's face. "Yeah, you don't trust them. Nor me, but I know a couple from way back, and I know where we buried the bodies."

"Bribe them to do what, exactly? Hang on." Conan opened the door and called to a passing Barbarian. "You, stand outside this door. It's closed for business. You let anyone in I'll cut off your nuts." The man didn't flinch, that wasn't an unusual threat from Conan. He took out his machete and stood a bit clear of the door when Conan went back in, so the mad bastard didn't think he was trying to listen in. With luck, whatever it was would cheer the crazy fuck up a bit.

*   *   *

The General:

While the Bloods picked up small enclaves and extra fighters, the General looked closer at both the SIMS and Orchard Close. Both had exactly the sort of fighters he needed, the steady sort who'd stand and trade bullets and arrows all day without breaking or launching a mad charge. There were steadier types in among his fighters, the sort that tended to keep clear of the Bloods when they weren't actually fighting. He needed more of them, under their own commander so he could use them and the Bloods separately. Patton wouldn't like the idea, he'd either think he was being replaced or resent splitting the command. Either way, he'd kill the other bloke and probably try for everyone else because that was Patton's way. The General looked again at the sheaf of notes from Rhys. The mass of information had its uses, even if he'd need a bloody civil service to keep track if it kept growing at this rate. He sent a runner for Rhys.

When the spymaster arrived, he thought he knew what his boss wanted. "Caddi is still in the middle of his war. If we go now, we go alone and those dykes will fight, and so will the GOFS."

"I've complained about all this shit a time or two, how you make a file even if I'm not interested in an enclave." The General waved a sheaf of papers. "I apologise. I've been looking at the rejects, the ones that are too tough just now because we'd lose as many as we gained. I want to take out Napoleon." He laughed as Rhys sucked air between his teeth, the exact noise a mechanic made before telling the punter the repair would cost a fortune. "I don't want to conquer. You'll love this. I want you to make him an offer he'd be bloody crazy to turn down. He gets to keep his men, and his rank. After all, Napoleon is a good solid general's name."

"Like the MiB? You want another commander, this time one with troops that are personally loyal?" Rhys shook his head firmly. "Bad idea. He'll start looking for promotion. Worse, him and Patton might face off, the Bloods against the rest."

"No, he'll surrender, not buy in, because if he doesn't we'll make an example of the families of his soldiers. This file says the officers and steadiest men are loyal because their families get privileges." The General ran a finger down the figures. "We'll split out his nutters for Patton, and do the same with our other men. Then we'll put our solid men in with his, so they won't all be loyal to him. Make Patton his boss, that'll give him a problem if he wants promotion." He tapped the stubby automatic by his chair, a present from the MiB, and chuckled. "The office ponces only had guns, so letting them join as allies wasn't a problem. I doubt they could find anyone to follow them, let alone the Bloods."

"Shit yes. I don't think I could find anyone else to take Patton's job, or leastways not one who isn't as bloody crazy as the Bloods are. His second in command usually lasts two or three months before one of his own men tops him." Rhys bent over the papers. "The Bloods will be pissed if they miss a fight. We'll have to have them there, wound up ready to go, or someone like Napoleon won't roll over."

"Which will keep Patton busy, slapping them down." The General sat back with a big smile. "Well? You can do all that devious shit you like, blackmail and threats, treachery with a smile, all wrapped up as a box of goodies."

"It's probably doable, with care, because he's got to know we can take him if we pay the blood price. I can't let him realise you need him, not if he's got to surrender." Rhys took the papers from the General and began to read. "It's a nice prize anyway, even if you end up topping Napoleon after he's surrendered."

"No rush, there's still plenty of little stuff to keep the Bloods occupied once they've healed up. I don't want to rush this, because we're moving into the big league now." The General leant forward across the small table and lowered his voice. "I daren't have another fuckup like the one at Christmas, or getting knocked back when we tried that night attack across the water. Patton for one might fancy his chances on his own. Even if he just took off with the Bloods, we'd be screwed."

"He wouldn't. ..." Rhys reconsidered. "He might, because of how many of his men we lost. That loyalty goes both ways. Okay, slow and steady it is until we've got enough men, and the right ones, to take Soldier Boy."

* * *

Professors:

Midway between the SIMS and Sutton Park, just south of the motor-way, the Professors and their students had beaten off a sudden rash of small attacks. Just as bad, none of the gangs would let the students through to the Mart. When a van sporting the colours of Benny's Boys approached the border, flying a white flag, Prof expected another extortion attempt. Benny's Boys had barricaded any roads between the Professors and the nearest Mart, and kept asking for women or territory to allow any vehicles through.

"It's Benny himself, with only two bodyguards." The border guard sounded shocked, because the gang boss usually sent a lieutenant and a score of fighters to any meeting. "Hang on, he's shouting." Moments later the guard came back on the radio, sounding even more shocked and puzzled. "He wants to meet Prof, one on one, and he'll disarm and come inside if we give up a hostage."

By now, the student manning the radio in the main accommodation had called for the Prof, and the senior fighters. One of those, a college rugby player called Chad, turned to the old man in a suit and a teacher's robe. "I'll go as hostage, Prof. This has to be important." He turned to two of the other fighters. "You stay close to Prof all the time. If anything looks off, don't hesitate. Kill the swine."

"As a last resort, Chad. We don't want to lose the team captain." Prof turned to the radio. "Tell Benny we agree, but he will be searched. Chad is on the way as a hostage."

* * *

Five minutes later, because Prof authorised the use of precious diesel to send a vehicle, a very inquisitive gang boss walked in through the front doors of what used to be a shop. Despite the heaps of produce on the shelves, the sandbags and determined, heavily armed guards would deter any casual shoppers. Prof met him just inside, holding out a hand. "Hello Benny. We haven't met but I'm Prof, the senior lecturer."

"A posh way of saying gang boss. Can you agree things and make them stick?" Benny shook hands, nodding towards the well-armed young man and woman stood to one side. "When I was that age, I didn't like old fogeys slinging orders about."

"Prof doesn't sling orders about." The young woman looked the gang boss up and down. "We pay attention because Prof is smarter than most of us put together. He whupped your gang, and all the rest that tried it on."

Benny visibly relaxed, just a little. "Good. I was told it wasn't him, but nobody here is disputing what you said. That's what I want to talk about, things I've been told. In comfort?"

"My study is this way. These two youngsters will stay with us." The Prof's smile had a bit of steel in it. "They don't totally trust you."

"That's the usual way we do it. We don't usually have a meetings with you, boss to boss, so you won't know." Benny smiled properly and bowed slightly. "After you."

*   *   *

Once everyone had found a seat and had a drink, Benny didn't waste any time. "You've had more attacks lately. A lot of gangs broke their agreements." He looked around at the bookshelves. "Do you know why?"

"Food, and our young people, and because some people just like violence." Prof nodded towards his bodyguards. "Our young people are more experienced now, so none of the attacks succeeded."

"And because someone in here has set up a very good system of defence." Benny hunched forward, intent now, and began to explain why there'd been so many attacks. Word had spread through the nearby gangs that the old duffers in here relied on their books. The catapults, the fire bombs that couldn't be put out, the medicines, treatments for wounds, the amount of food grown, every benefit came out of the books. According to the rumours, capturing those books would give any gang all that knowledge. Winning would be easy. There wasn't any real organisation, because the kids didn't rate the old duffers.

Benny had fallen for it as well, until he caught one of his men releasing a pigeon with a message tube on its leg. The message had been in code, and the man had killed himself, but he'd had another four pigeons. Since the same man had been the one who had been telling Benny about the rumours, the gang boss had reassessed. He'd never been convinced by the rumours claiming that the enclave was run by old duffers and kids muddling along, Benny had lost too many men for that to be true. Now he'd just confirmed that Prof was the real boss, and wanted the truth about the books.

Prof explained, the books had a lot of knowledge, but he had genuine University tutors and students to make the most of what they learned. The midwife, for instance, had actually been a Biology tutor. It took a while, because Prof didn't trust Benny's sudden change of heart, but eventually he had to take the approach at face value. Finding out he'd been suckered had really pissed off the gangster, now he wanted to stick it to whoever had set Benny's Boys up. Unfortunately, despite wanting to make as many deals as possible, Benny had to refuse one request.

"I've got a confession. I can't give you access to the Marts. We closed the roads to stop you finding out, because we don't want others knowing we have to pay for Mart runs ourselves." Benny scowled, but not at anyone in the room. "The Lycans have blocked all the roads except one, with bloody great heaps of rubble. The only way through has big steel-faced gates and a shit-load of fighters. We pay up if we want to go shopping. It's cheaper than paying two other gangs or fighting through two other territories."

"That's a pity, because that's the main thing we want. We have to pay at least two gangs, and the prices are getting higher every time." Prof sat for a moment, deep in thought, missing the nasty grin on Benny's face.

"But you could open the gate with those catapult things. Then we'll tell the shits, either let us through or we'll bust them again." Benny must have seen the rejection on Prof's face because he pushed on quickly. "We'll give you free access across our territory. You'll still pay the Lycans, but not too much or it's cheaper to knock the gates down again."

That was a huge incentive, but Prof wasn't sold yet. "No fighters. I'm not using up our young people like that."

"Okay, as long as you break the gates and set fire to the wall either side." Benny sounded downright gleeful. "Don't worry about fighters. My boys have been taking shit every time they pay up, so they'll enjoy sticking it to the fuckers for a change."

"Language."

Benny looked at Prof, startled, realised, and glanced at the teenage guards. "Er, sorry? I never even thought about it." A terse nod from a young woman acknowledged the apology. "Right, back to gate breaking?" This time Prof nodded, and Benny began to describe exactly what they'd be facing.

Prof still wasn't completely sold, he wanted time to think about the idea. He didn't want to ally with gangsters, but Benny had offered a very tempting prize. Benny left without an agreement, but with a promise that he'd get an answer within days.

*   *   *

A week later, Benny stood with Prof on a rooftop. Behind them, in a large car park, were two huge, angular metal constructions. Both were surrounded by Prof's fighters, but only a quarter were armed with the usual gangster machete and pistol. The solid block of black, armoured Kendo fighters intimidated most who came near them, but some of the gangsters made jokes about the light troops dressed in gaily painted body suits. Not directly to their faces, the locals had all found out the hard way how bloody quick those kids moved, and how accurate they were with their javelins and pre-Crash bows.

Benny had a huge grin on his face as he watched his men swarm through the shattered gates and spread out beyond, hacking down any surviving guards. To either side of the opening the walls had big lumps gouged out of them, with fierce fires still burning on the bare brick. "I don't know what shit you put in those things, but I'm glad I'm not trying to put the fuck... damn things out." He pointed beyond the fighting, now almost over. "A car full of fighters just arrived but we've already taken the wall. They'll report back to their boss, then we'll get a parley." He tried to act nonchalant. "My blokes actually did the fighting, so we get most of the loot, right?"

"Not a chance. Our trebuchets probably killed more men than your guns and machetes. I'll settle for fifty-fifty, including ammunition, as agreed. It would be a pity if we got into an argument just now." The Prof didn't even turn his head to argue.

Benny reassessed, again. He kept being fooled by the old geezer's appearance. Now he glanced back at the car park where the throwers were ready to fire, loaded with the bright red containers that set bricks alight. A few volleys of those and the Prof could probably help himself, because half of Benny's men were out there around those gates, sitting ducks. "Done. Fifty-fifty." He shook his head, bemused, looking out at the fires and bodies. Who would have guessed what a nasty murderous bastard hid behind that frail-looking, gown-wearing exterior?

*   *   *

Reivers:

Far to the north, in Scotland, the group of ragged men and women with beautifully maintained weapons weren't bemused, they were between grief and rage. The Reivers knew they were facing killers, but hadn't realised just how cold-blooded they were. "We've been careful, Bruce. I've no idea how they tracked us to the cave." The speaker, his clothing stained with blood and soot, looked exhausted. "We've got to the back but everyone in the cave is dead, and some died badly. We had the bairns and women well away from the entrance but it didn't help. It looks like a hurricane went through there, a burning one."

"Thermobaric bombs. They were used against caves in Afghanistan." Bruce looked up at the clear sky. "The weather isn't helping us at all." He thought hard, turning to the group with him. "Any ideas?"

A woman with a long scar down her cheek and a haunted look in her eyes glanced up as well. "They've got an eye in the sky, a long way up? Probably at night because that's when we move about. If the cameras record all the hot spots moving about, and put them through analysis or even run them fast, a pattern may show up. I read that in a book once, about a future war but it might work in real life. It might just be enough to show which are sheep and which are us." She shook her head sadly. "We'll have to do something, Bruce. We can't lose more bairns."

"That might also explain why a couple of raids went wrong. Our people must have been spotted moving into position overnight. I'd thought it was because we'd only half-trained all those volunteers and they'd made a mistake." Bruce frowned, working at the problem. "We can't stop drones. We'll have tae give ground, slowly, and make sure any raids move randomly. Individuals can spread over a large area, or maybe get among small flocks of sheep. They can backtrack and take an extra day or two tae get into position."

The exhausted rescuer shook his head. "That won't stop attacks on the refuges and stores. We can't keep everyone underground all summer." Most of the group shook their heads at that.

"It'll cost us a lot of ammunition and sugar for rockets, but we can stop any low runs tae lob bombs into the caves." Angus looked leaner, more tired, but also more savage and intent. "We can slow up air attacks on our front line troops as well, if we take down a few aircraft and helicopters. They will assume we've protected any non-combatants the same. We will if we've got enough sugar."

Bruce scowled. "That willnae stop a bomb launched from high up, a standoff weapon."

Another man spoke up. "No, but thermobaric relies on the explosion happening in the right place. If the fuel cloud or missile is ignited too soon, too far from the target, it won't have the same effect. We'll have to capture a military vehicle, or maybe just a fishing boat that has some sort of radar. Just passive, but enough to see a plane coming and launch something to set the bomb off early." He looked around them all. "I've no idea how we'd actually do that."

Angus's eyes narrowed. "I've a thought or two, and we've some smart lads and lassies out there."

Bruce hunkered down, bringing out a map covered in scrawled lines and symbols. "We should send yon foreign troops a message as well, to persuade them to leave our families be. For now, we keep everyone indoors for a month, except if there's heavy cloud and preferably rain." He glanced up at the clear blue sky. "Never thought I'd hope for a wet summer."

*   *   *

The Cabal:

The Cabal were jubilant. Two nests of rebels cleaned out, a dozen raids had been mauled, and more new troops from the continent were settling in. The refugee pilots had already punished the Reivers, because the rebels had no answer attacks from the air. The sheep and deer made identification difficult, but the analysis of overnight videos had finally borne fruit. It had taken time because there were too many miles of mountains to cover them all, and most of the drones had to be deployed near the borders in defence.

Despite more raids for food and even more liberated volunteers, the Reivers were giving ground. Scores of Reiver volunteers were being killed during attacks, which didn't always save the convoys and guard posts. Joshua thought there had to be a trade-off point. The more volunteers the rebels freed from work camps, the more food they needed so the more chances to kill some. He hoped the new troops would be enough to find the break point, to stop the rebels feeding all their new troops.

Maurice kept training snipers, and trying to extinguish relatively democratic enclaves. A few of the latter were tenacious, actually growing stronger so he encouraged the worst gangs to grow larger. Here and there, even the nutters began to wonder where the convenient information came from, but as long as they kept winning most didn't look too closely.

* * *

Cyn Palace, London:

The jihad idea had worked another two times, then once more but dressed up as a Christian crusade. By the time the surrounding gangs realised there wasn't a real religious uprising, the four strongest had all lost a lot of fighters. One by one the local gang leaders were invited to the library and given a choice. Peace and trade, a truce, or they could raid again. If any of them raided, the counter-attack would wipe the gang out. Facing five combined gangs, none of whom had lost many fighters, none of the neighbours chose war.

Some gangs went further than trading. The Gatts, originally based in Gatwick Airport but driven out by a stronger gang, were between the cleaver and the block. Squeezed from three sides and with most of their leaders dead, the remainder came to Cyn Palace with their own proposal. They would disband, giving up their territory in exchange for membership of whichever gang their members preferred.

A trickle of new arrivals arrived from further away, lured by stories of fields and security, but they caused their own problems. "We haven't enough room." Eli ignored the looks from Sinner, Sin, Imam and Preacher, concentrating on Kermit because he looked the most worried. "The ones who are arriving now aren't fighters. They'll eat all our food, and we'll spend our time protecting them and repairing housing."

"He's right." Kermit turned to the others. "Taking the Gatts in was a mistake, because hardly any of them stayed in their own territory. Now we've got to protect more ground and it barely feeds the fighters."

"Because the Gatts were useless at farming." Preacher pointed in the direction of the school playing fields, now full of crops. "We are using our methods on their cleared areas to get a better return."

"It still won't feed them, or barely, and they'll still need protecting." Eli glared at the little smile Sin wore. "Go on, spit it out. What do you know that I don't?"

"Nothing." Sin spread out a map. "But you keep on about refugees. Sod that, we want recruits. Tell them there's a price for living here." She swept her hand over the area given up by the Gatts. "We've put guards in there anyway, so we may as well farm it properly. The price for their safe home is that every refugee has to clear a section of ruins. They can dig up the foundations or roads, turn the whole area into a field so we can plant on it."

"Bloody hell Sin, that's a hell of a job." Kermit leant over the map. "I suppose they could start where it's already overgrown gardens, or garages that have fallen down. Even so, eventually there'll be too many coming."

"No, because there are other enclaves out there who will attract some of them." Imam moved to look at the map. "We should insist that a certain number of the refugees—" He turned to Sin with a smile. "Sorry, recruits, join the fighters. Then if we run out of room we'll have enough troops to take a bit more."

Sin did her best to smile innocently. "Maybe here?"

Preacher leant closer, suddenly intent, then chuckled. "That would take us almost to Gatwick Airport. Have you got designs on all that open land?"

Eli squeezed past Imam and Kermit to look, suddenly a lot more interested. "Nobody claims the airport, just bits around the edges because it's too big to defend. Still, a strip along this edge, properly farmed?" He looked around them all with a wry smile. "All right, you got me. We'll do what Sin said, but the new arrivals had better give up some fighters." He looked at the rest again, alarmed now. "Who gets the extras?"

As the group settled into working on the details, Imam and Preacher exchanged knowing looks. If the new arrivals fought in the current mixed groups from the start, they'd never truly belong to any one gang.

Chapter 11:
Expanding Opportunities

While the Reivers plotted their response and other gangs dealt with their problems or made their own plans for the future, Orchard Close settled down after the sniper attack. As the weather warmed up, more residents joined the football teams. The GOFS and Barbies pushed hard for a chance to play, and now a few residents were interested in letting them. Harold said he'd think about it, privately wondering if that might soften up the GOFS before he met their leaders.

Meanwhile, he had other problems clamouring for his attention. Harold still wasn't sure how he could arrange repairing Barbie Radio, even if Trev could work out how to. He'd suggested bringing the whole thing to Orchard Close, but it was too big. Now the blondes were pushing. While Harold considered ways and means, Trev made two more trips to the Mansion because Caddi wanted the multimedia system in his study fixed. Harold needed parts for that, as well as Barbie Radio, and hoped to get a better deal for bulk.

Before getting too embroiled in radios, Harold had to make his copy musket. Caddi seemed to think the primitive firearms were some sort of super weapon, and kept harping on about getting the original back for Big Mack. Harold thought Caddi's miserly soul would cringe at the amount of powder it ate. It had shocked Harold when he'd unloaded the thing, because it used one of those scoops full for one shot.

Liz copied all the metal parts, allegedly just for spares, which Harold made up into mechanisms. Stephan carved four stocks and forearms, also for spares in case one came in split. The result looked good enough but Harold wanted barrels because, looking at the sets of spare parts, he didn't want to be restricted to what he could scavenge from ruined weapons. He also wanted to buy all the useable tube in one purchase, but didn't have enough machetes to trade until Liz produced the improved versions. Going back several times for a few more lengths of tube would make the Geeks curious.

When Mack brought Trev back from his third multimedia inspection, Harold had to admit he'd repaired the musket. Mack took the weapon with him, chortling and telling Cooper what he would be blowing holes in. Trev confirmed that the multimedia could be fixed, but thought it might take a couple more trips. He'd certainly got over his worries about Caddi kidnapping him.

A reply came back from the GOFS, confirming they would trade for a few houses and access for the Barbies to trade in Orchard Close. Not a firm proposal, the GOFS wanted to talk face to face about exactly which houses and how much access. Harold's curiosity piqued when instead of him taking his pickup to the meeting, a GOFS SUV escort turned up to collect him. Harold had decided to take Patty as his bodyguard, armed with everything short of a rifle, because with the Barbies the other side, the GOFS would know women were dangerous. The driver told Patty it was more of a pleasure than he'd expected, but claimed to have no idea why he'd been sent.

Harold had expected the usual meet near the border. When the SUV kept going deeper into GOFS territory, both Harold and Patty wondered why but the driver played dumb. The reason became clear as the car crossed an area of cleared rubble, heading for an imposing building. Harold only had Rob's and Finn's descriptions from when they'd fixed plumbing and electrics a couple of years ago, but realised the old school ahead had to be the Castle, the GOFS HQ. Now he started to worry, because if they'd be going in there the GOFS would want to disarm and search Patty. That wouldn't go well. The GOFS usually met their neighbours nearer their borders, where all the bodyguards stayed armed.

Harold could see why the GOFS called it the Castle, the thick stone walls and ornamentation along the edge of the roof were meant to look like battlements. The place was old school, literally, even down to the gargoyles and a coat of arms carved into the stone over the entrance. The arched windows were blocked but they'd been filled in neatly with stone, leaving crossed firing slots. A heavy, metal clad gate, and the cleared area around the building, completed the castle impression.

Harold walked in through the big gates to find his first surprise, no search. The second was when the GOFS leader, Gofannon, met them personally. He looked Patty up and down. "So what are you, Soldier Girl?" He took another, slower look and whistled. "Blimey. What does your boyfriend say to that lot? Unless?" He eyed Harold.

"I'm Patty, and I'm dressed for visiting. I thought that if Harold can't deal with whatever, it will be serious." Patty smiled happily. "You'll have to ask the boss how many girlfriends he has at the moment. It varies. My boyfriends usually say please, very politely."

Harold tried to keep his surprise from showing, because that definitely wasn't Patty-like, but Gofannon burst out laughing. "I've been told about Patty the Demon. The Barbies will love you."

"They do, and they've got pictures. So where do I have to put this lot? I hope whoever is searching has some manners." Patty smiled again. "And that she's warmed her hands." Harold tensed because that wasn't a hint, Patty wasn't letting a bloke search her.

"Ha. I reckon we could find a volunteer but there's no search. If we allow you to get this far it's because you aren't stupid enough to try anything. You're only here because we want to have a proper chat with your boss, away from prying eyes." Gofannon looked back at Harold. "Patty can keep her gear if she promises to behave, and so can you, but we want to talk to you alone if possible."

Harold turned to Patty. "Seems fair enough. Have a beer or whatever and relax." She looked a little worried about splitting up so he grinned. "If you hear shooting and think it's gone adrift, you know what to do."

Patty smiled because a bodyguard's job was a sort of joke between them. "Yup. I kill them all and rescue you." The half dozen men and two women nearby joined in the laughter. Patty's instructions were to get out if possible, and come back with help if feasible. In reality, both of them would die if a fight started in a place like this, as everyone here knew. The concession just meant that the GOFS weren't as paranoid about visitors as either the Hot Rods or the Geeks. From what Gofannon had said, the paranoia had to be appeased before they let anyone through the gate.

Patty turned to find three men and two women waiting, all happy to take her to a beer and curious about her gear. Patty was armed very thoroughly but didn't dress like the Barbies, which made her unique in GOFS territory. Harold noticed these women all carried knives, but none had machetes. They were relaxed around the men, and it went both ways. Gofannon noticed Harold's inspection.

"We don't make a big fuss about it, but we don't abuse our women.

The Barbies sorted that out and it's sort of relaxing anyway, now it's settled in. How we live in here isn't public knowledge but we reckon you won't rock our boat." The GOFS boss hesitated a moment. "To be honest, it wasn't voluntary to start with." He fell silent, but Harold thought his escort seemed to be working out what to say so he kept quiet.

They walked halfway across the tarmac quadrangle, still marked out for netball going by the posts at each end, before Gofannon spoke again. "Your plumber saw the first arrangement, the room where we kept the women, so I should explain. We started off like a lot of gangs. We collected up some women and put them in that dormitory, the one he saw. They were sort of volunteers, but only because this was the best of a bad set of options, and leaving wasn't an option once they moved in. There were real volunteers among them, because there always are." From his expression Gofannon still wasn't happy about the next part. "We'd been here about six months when one of our blokes came in, stripped naked and shaved bald all over. His arms were tied behind his back to make sure he arrived that way. He brought a message from the Barbies."

"Cripes. Saying what?"

"The Barbies had captured a score of our men, fighters. When we asked why they'd surrendered, the bloke said they'd been surrounded. The Barbies must have used every fighter they'd got to show how hopeless it was. The men were told they'd be sent home unharmed after being ransomed, providing they surrendered." The GOFS leader glanced at Harold with a wry smile. "I would have probably chosen that over dying."

"A ransom?" Harold hadn't heard of the Barbies ransoming anyone.

"A very simple swap. Every woman being held against their will in exchange for all our blokes including their weapons. Otherwise our blokes would be taken to Beth's and used in the same way as the women." Gofannon gave a little laugh. "It was actually fair. Like for like. So we made the swap and then we"—he waved a hand ahead—"had a meeting."

"That must have been some meeting." Harold kept his face straight and his tone carefully neutral.

"Oh yes, but there weren't many options. If we locked up more women, the Barbies would snatch more blokes. Then we'd swap. We'd be supplying the Barbies with women who hated us, and the Barbies would give them weapons. Strangely enough, once we actually talked about it, most of us were a little uneasy about the dormitory. We'd sort of drifted into it, and the women were sort of resigned to it. Only a couple of our council really objected to turning them loose, and were out-voted. Now all the women in here are genuine volunteers, and that's worked out better all round." Gofannon stopped, and gave Harold a long look before he continued. "We keep the arrangement private, because otherwise some arses among the neighbours would take the piss. The stroppier Geeks or Hot Rods would push, until we killed one of them out of sheer bloody annoyance. Then it would get bloody." The GOFS boss voice sounded reluctant, probably because he was admitting a weakness to another gang. "Early on we weren't strong enough to stand against a serious attack, and even now we need to concentrate on the General."

"We have a similar problem, we daren't confront the likes of Caddi head-on." Harold remembered Rob reporting the room full of beds. "So you shut the dormitory down?" He wasn't sure he quite believed Gofannon, because Caddi always got 'volunteers' when he wanted them.

"No, but the girls in there are genuine whores. The lads pay up and get serviced. A few of the men, and all the top blokes, have personal volunteers of course. You know how some women always want to screw the boss?" Gofannon looked at Harold with a half-smile, fishing for information.

"Yeah. They always did, or some of the old geezers would have never got near some of the women in the scandal sheets." Harold could see how that would work here, out of sight. There were a few in Orchard Close who wanted to get into the boss's pants, just because he was the boss, and Harold knew at least two women were selling sex. "Have the Barbies grabbed any more blokes?"

"Yes, once, because some of the troops didn't believe the new rules. We swapped for our men and explained properly, and painfully. A couple died, including one of our council, which finally convinced the rest." Gofannon showed absolutely no humour in that statement. "The rest of us have found out this way has benefits." The usually serious Gofannon grinned properly this time. "Wait until you meet the Head Girl."

"How come I'm getting to hear this?" Harold's couldn't work out why the GOFS dirty linen had been displayed for a rival gang boss.

"We have to talk seriously which means you have to meet our council, the top blokes with daft names, face to face. Quite a few want to meet you anyway and we don't all gather together anywhere else, it's too tempting a target. Once inside the Castle, how we run things is pretty obvious so I may as well explain." Gofannon glanced at Harold. "You only got in here because of what our blokes tell me about Orchard Close. With your rules and the way some of your women act, you're hardly likely to rock the boat or take the piss about us." He glanced back the way they'd come. "I can't see your bodyguard spilling the beans to Caddi, and she proves a point. You don't allow abuse, you're consistent in how you treat women, and you really don't care whose men you beat or kill to keep those rules." Gofannon opened a heavily carved wooden door. "When we get in here I'll explain why the talk is serious."

*   *   *

They entered a large room, obviously the library Wayland had spoken of. As he'd said, most of the books had gone, while the shelving showed the marks of blade and fire so the place had been trashed at some time. A long table down the centre of the clear space claimed Harold's attention. The table had seven men seated round it, including several Harold had never seen before. The introductions broadened Harold's knowledge of old gods, ending in, "And Cyclops, because he's only got one eye."

The man in question took off a diver's facemask, to show two eyes behind his spectacles. "I'm bloody careful with me specs cos we can't find an optician."

"Nor us. Maybe they're with Ronald McDonald." The rest laughed with Harold as Gofannon indicated a vacant chair.

Gofannon sat at the head of the table but Harold sat near him, not at the far end, so the GOFS weren't playing gang games today. The gang boss opened up the real meeting. "We are concerned about you and Caddi."

"Why?" Harold didn't understand. He became even more baffled when Gofannon mentioned Mercedes. Eventually he got it. The GOFS had heard rumours about Harold and Mercedes, and then that Mercedes might be moving to Orchard Close. That led to some of them wondering if Caddi had made a private treaty with Harold, and handed Mercedes over as the sweetener. Harold stopped laughing long enough to reassure them, he would join the Barbies before teaming up with Caddi. Mercedes might decide to move on at some time, but if Caddi ever tried to hand her over to anyone as part of a deal she'd probably cut his arm off.

Explaining all the rumours and what had actually happened took a while, even after Harold cut out anything private. At least the GOFS seemed to understand Harold's reticence, and didn't push for more. When it came to the betting, Vulcan commented that the commando coupons would have bought the housing Harold wanted. Vulcan confessed to being treated to a night with Mercedes, but she hadn't marked him like she had Darwin. He reckoned she wore a tent, and declared a no-go area down the middle of the bed. When Harold ignored the implied question about what she'd worn, or if there'd been a no-go area, everyone smirked.

The GOFS warchief confessed to keeping his jeans on, staying wide awake all night, and realising about two a.m. that losing some street cred might have been smarter. Klaus, one of the GOFS soldiers, wanted to meet Harold to check he didn't stand nine feet tall and fart thunderbolts. He'd had his hand nailed to a door post with a knife while Mercedes explained her rules. Klaus didn't blame her, but he wanted to get the Hot Rod who'd suggested patting her ass in a quiet place sometime.

Finally, Gofannon leant forward a little. "There's one last little worry. You do a lot of work with Caddi, sometimes more than for us and the Geeks combined. How much does his business mean to you?"

"I do more work because he offers it, but it's pure business. He's a nasty little bastard and I'd shoot him tomorrow if I thought I could do it without a war." Harold looked around the table and shrugged. "Cripes, when we made that alliance with the Barbies, we all more or less agreed to trim his ears sooner or later. It came up again when the refugees arrived from the General."

"But then this Mercedes thing started so we wondered." All the men at the table leant in, so this had to be the important part. "Caddi is greedy. What bothered us was the thought of suddenly finding your gang and his both coming at us. Our only line of retreat pushes us into the Barbies." Everyone grimaced.

Harold didn't see why. "At least that flank is secure."

"Against Caddi or the General, but the Barbies aren't exactly welcoming neighbours. Now, if Orchard Close is still independent, Soldier Boy can ensure Caddi doesn't spring a surprise." Gofannon gave a big satisfied smile. "Better yet, you won't warn him, so if he tries he'll get more than a bloody nose."

"How? He's probably got as many fighters as both of us combined." Despite that, Harold would live up to the treaty and help the GOFS if necessary. He didn't fancy being surrounded by Hot Rods and Geeks.

"Later. Once we've worked out what you want, we'll tell you how you pay." The rest chuckled about that while Gofannon reached down and brought out a hand drawn map. He handed it over, after pointing to a shaded area of housing that he wanted to sell. The narrow two mile strip joined Orchard Close to the Barbies, along the edge of the flooded area that held back the General. Harold didn't fancy it, because he'd be guarding that frontier, but the GOFS insisted they'd keep their men there as well. Surprisingly, the GOFS accepted the Barbies coming down the new access for a beer and trade. Now Harold started to worry about how much it would cost him.

When he tried to nail down a price, Gofannon included a wider bit, where the border bent round the water's edge to meet the Geeks. Harold gave up even pretending to negotiate. "I can't pay for all that." A pity because despite having no electricity or water, and the broken windows, the houses were mostly weatherproof. They'd be perfect for Orchard Close-style scavenging.

All the GOFS started laughing. "Yes you can." Wayland managed to straighten his face. "Do you need any swords?" He started grinning again.

Harold looked at the map and back at Wayland. "Don't you think I'm far enough in debt?"

"We're not sure." Vulcan stroked his short coppery beard, looking towards Gofannon who nodded. "We haven't said what we want yet. You still might have credit, so do you need swords?"

"Your Patty could do with one, to finish the set." Gofannon explained Patty's armament to the rest, and that she'd come as Harold's bodyguard.

Harold shrugged and didn't answer directly. "I'll have a look at the swords, but we haven't got a lot of gear to trade for extras." He wondered if it might be worth buying just one, because having an example of Wayland's tempering might help Liz with her experiments. Casper or Alfie could swing a GOFS sword, no problem, as could Henry or Logan.

"We'll sort out a trade." The GOFS still looked confident, but Harold still couldn't figure out why. He went to look at the swords but they were too expensive to buy, even if Liz could make two thin ones out of one larger weapon.

*   *   *

The GOFS left Harold and Patty to eat in private, presumably so both they and the GOFS could talk among themselves. Patty had also seen some of the houses being offered, and agreed with Harold that rabbit burgers and a bit of knitting wouldn't be enough. She had news of her own. "It might be because I'm a woman, but a couple of the GOFS women un-wound enough to swap dirt. We had a really good natter. These women are all volunteers, the bed mates as well as the workers."

Harold explained what Gofannon told him. "I wondered just how vol-untary he meant."

"Totally as far as I can see. The bakers and that type of worker don't provide sex unless they fancy someone, and could move back out to one of the estates if they wanted to. Some have regular boyfriends, proper ones, among the GOFS soldiers or other workers in here." Patty looked impressed, so the women had been convincing. "There is a brothel but it sounds like a larger, more official version of the one in Orchard Close, women who choose that life. There are a few who volunteer for the dormitory as a way of making a few extra coupons, or to pay a debt, then leave again."

"Gofannon reckons the top men have volunteers."

"They do, but nobody seems frightened they might be chosen with-out an option. Vulcan dropped by to check what he'd heard about my weaponry and a couple of women flirted with him, just fun stuff. He's a real smoothy, old style. When he'd gone we swapped more dirt and lies and Gofannon's woman is called the Head Girl. She organises the brothel, wears a gymslip, and is well past just voluntary. She carries a hockey stick to back off any others looking at her man. The other GOFS women seem to think their deal is better than most women get these days. They get treated better than Hot Rod women, but aren't expected to fight like a Barbie or an Orchard Close woman." She suddenly burst out laughing. "They all think I'm here in case you feel randy."

Harold laughed as well. "Cripes, I'd cut myself to bits."

"But if we were staying longer, and you needed a shower?" Patty laughed again, at Harold's blush this time. After the meal, she threatened to walk out looking a bit dishevelled, still adjusting her clothing. Maybe strutting around in all that weaponry had woken up the knitting Demon's wicked side!

*   *   *

The GOFS took Harold back to the forge, and right through to the big reveal. "That's a bloody cannon!" Harold inspected what looked like a Na-poleonic era cannon, the real thing, from the thickness of the metal mak-ing up the barrel. A rusted mess attached to the side of the blunt end must have been a firing mechanism. Once he'd finished laughing at Harold's reaction, Wayland displayed three rams and sponges on sticks and wanted to know if Harold could fix it. The GOFS weren't put off by the amount of powder a cannon would use, they had a stack of small barrels! A mixture of musket and cannon powder, according to the labels, which led to Vulcan uncovering four rusty muskets and what had to be a blunderbuss.

He picked up the blunderbuss. "Either this or the cannon will turn any mob of charging assholes into mincemeat, so we can afford to use a lot of powder. We heard you can fix muskets?" Vulcan had a challenging look about him.

"Yes, but I've only fixed one so far. It was in a lot better nick than those, or that cannon." Harold wondered if Caddi knew just how much information the GOFS were getting from someone in the Hot Rods. "They're not accurate, and bitches to aim because they kick. Caddi wanted his for Mack."

"But a body does a backflip, which makes them scary." Wayland smiled as wide as Mack had. "Or they will be once you fix them."

Harold looked at the collection and shook his head. If the GOFS had these from the start, they'd have been asking about repairs long before now. "Where the hell did you get this lot?"

"From the Murphies. One of their men decided to jump ship, and bought his way in here with the location of an armoury." Gofannon smirked and the other GOFS laughed at the next part. "When we nipped over there the Murphies never even noticed. We think they were distracted by your new girlfriend."

"We nearly told the bloke his deal was off, because all the weapons are useless." Wayland gestured to a crushed 9mm hand gun. "That's the only modern weapon we found. We brought them anyway, mostly because Vulcan fancied owning a cannon even if it's scrap. We reckoned the powder would make bombs. When we got back, one of our guys reckoned the Hot Rods were getting a musket fixed. That has to be you?"

"Yes, and I can probably fix some of those. If I do it'll cost you." Harold would charge the GOFS serious numbers of coupons regardless of what work the cannon needed. It might need a lot going by the amount of rust and crud.

"No, if you fix all of them and the cannon you'll have those houses. You sort out our problem, including the Barbies wandering all over the place, and we sort out yours. I can easily cast a few cannon balls, or maybe a shitload of smaller lead balls so the cannon is a giant shotgun." Wayland chuckled in anticipation. "The next time the General tries to get across the water, or if Caddi gets ambitious? Splat. I reckon an iron cannon ball will stop even an armoured truck."

Harold agreed, the plate on his tank wouldn't stand a chance against an iron ball the same diameter as that cannon barrel. He headed back into the library in a daze. He soon snapped out of it when the real trading started, because most of it depended on how many of those weapons he could fix. Harold ended up with his streets, mainly because the GOFS were so keen to have the cannon. If he could fix all the weapons, Harold would also get two barrels of musket powder. He'd build new weapons round the old barrels for that deal. Gofannon threw in the nine mil for spares to sweeten the deal, when Harold insisted he didn't need blades just now. By then Harold was in a daze again, because the GOFS kept toasting with rotgut.

*   *   *

The GOFS took Harold to his new border with the Barbies, so Soldier Boy could tell the guards. The Barbie checked with Ogou to confirm their cars could come through without asking the GOFS, then switched to offering Patty a job. As Harold left, the Barbie commented that Soldier Boy must be getting careless. As a gang boss with only one guard he might be kidnapped, even if the bodyguard was the most dangerous sex.

When the chauffeur took them home by way of their new housing, Harold and Patty quietly discussed the state of the buildings they could see. Harold had remembered right, the housing would be a gold mine for Orchard Close. When they arrived back home and the chauffeur left, Patty revealed what else she'd been thinking about. The Barbie on the frontier had made a good point. With this war on and extra people arriving, and now extra territory, Harold needed two bodyguards to prove that Soldier Boy was a proper gang boss.

Harold started to argue because he hated all that posing crap, but Patty just suggested getting more opinions. She meant Tessa and Sharyn, but Harold wanted Liz, Casper and Emmy at least. Alfie and Doll came as well, and Harold thought they'd all agree he didn't need all the gang boss rubbish. He got a shock when everyone agreed with Patty. He needed bodyguards when he went outside the walls.

At the beginning, the gangs had been scared off by the sniper or nasty

SAS reputation. Now Orchard Close had grown from a couple of dozen people to a full enclave or gang, so one guard wasn't enough for the boss. Especially since, as Patty pointed out, the GOFS thought she'd been there as a joke. Harold surrendered on the bodyguards, but insisted on one being a woman because half the wall guards were female. He wanted to hammer home that the women were real fighters, to keep the likes of Caddi cautious.

Some worried about women guards causing trouble, because gangsters wouldn't rate them. Patty's wicked smile when she listed a few possible bodyguards persuaded any doubters. As the Demon pointed out, all the gangs would get the message after the first stupid scroat bled out. She wanted the job permanently, but her squad would be keeping her occupied.

As part of the new image, Tessa tried to get Harold into a better motor. He refused, because the battered old vans and pickup worked fine. More to the point, the diesel would run out soon, so he may as well drive a useful vehicle. An SUV wouldn't be as much use as the pickup for scavenging or trading. Once they'd settled that, a grinning Harold told them exactly what deal he'd got. Most of them were gobsmacked about the amount and quality of the housing. Tessa looked stunned at the idea of working on a genuine cannon.

The following discussion included a lot of laughing and toasts in small beer, or fruit juice for Harold because he'd had too much GOFS rotgut. Once Tessa recovered from the idea of working on a genuine cannon, she wanted to know if they'd all see it fire a test shot. From the enthusiasm, everyone else here and probably most of Orchard Close would want to watch. After assuring everyone he could fix all the muskets as well, so they'd get both the housing and powder, the rest left. Harold agreed with Tessa and Sharyn, the squad leaders and Liz had to be let into the secret, but not until the first new musket worked.

An hour later, a GOFS SUV pulled up by Caddi's watchers and they were invited inside and taken away. Within five minutes a convoy rolled down the road towing the cannon behind them. The weapon needed careful man-handling through the steel girders set in the road to stop cars, then willing hands rolled it up the road and parked it at the side of Harold's house. The GOFS were serious about surprising Caddi, they pitched in to move a stack of salvaged timber so their artillery couldn't be seen by visitors. The muskets and blunderbuss, and enough powder to test them all, came in as anonymous bundles and went straight to Harold's lair. Ten minutes after the convoy left, Caddi's spies were dropped off in their usual place. Harold doubted Caddi would send any complaints to Gofannon.

* * *

Fifteen minutes after the GOFS left, the bullhorn started up on the bypass. Harold sighed, checked that he had taken off any possible weapon, and walked to the edge of the zone. He twirled as instructed, and since he had no jacket the bullhorn invited him up to the guard post.

"Hello Sarge."

"Hello Soldier Boy, or should it be General with your own artillery." No hint of humour showed in Sarge's face or tone.

"It doesn't work." Sarge's face didn't alter. "It's not a rifle?"

That brought a faint lip twitch. "It's not exactly a pistol either. What's its range?"

"About three feet, as far as a cannon ball will roll if it falls out the end because it doesn't work." Harold glanced back towards the cannon. "That is a very heavy blowgun, in a really fancy shape. Get your binoculars on the firing mechanism."

"A touch-hole? You'll drill that clear in ten seconds."

"The hole isn't in the top so I doubt that would help, and there's some rusted junk over whatever hole there is. I reckon it used to be flintlock or caplock." Harold laughed at the unconvinced look on the sergeant's face. "If I fired that at one of your armoured vehicles, even if the driver stayed still long enough for me to hit it, the ball would only scratch the paintwork. Then he'd run over the cannon, and me."

"Don't point it this way. I'm serious, because the barrel length means some sergeants wouldn't worry about technicalities." The sergeant frowned, lifting his binoculars to take a closer look. "Why do you want it?"

"I don't. It came in trade. We'll clean it up and flog it to some idiot gangster to put outside his front gate. He'll think he's Napoleon."

Sarge lowered his binoculars, pinning Harold with his glare. "Fair enough, but if anything resembling a firing mechanism appears on that thing, the RAF will drop by. Do we understand each other?"

"Perfectly. If you don't mind, I'd like to clean the crap off, including the crud on the side. I want to polish the barrel inside and out so it looks shiny and pretty. And expensive?" Harold hid a sigh of relief when Sarge nodded. At least he could make the cannon look like he'd spent a lot of time on it, though now he'd have to work out a firing mechanism that could be fitted after the GOFS collected it. As he walked back down Harold mulled over ways to do so, coming up with a couple of possibilities.

Before he started on the cannon, Harold should finish building a musket. He'd just been given four more examples to help him, five if the blunderbuss mechanism worked the same way. They were badly rusted examples, but Liz could replace everything except the barrels and those would clean up. Before he could finish his experiment and build one from scratch, Harold needed tube for barrels. That meant tempting the Geeks. Hopefully Liz had repaired the damaged machetes from Caddi, or could give him a timetable.

* * *

Harold tried the forge door, but Liz still kept it barred. "I'll huff and puff?"

Liz opened up with a huge grin. "Not with your extra woman to de-puff you. The heavily armed one you take with you in case you feel lonely?" Harold laughed because Liz knew better. "Your turn first. What do you want?"

Harold hopped up to sit on the bench. "I need those damaged machetes modified as soon as possible. Not specifically, but I need the machetes the Demons have now. I can sell them once you finish their new sabres."

Liz smirked, not what Harold expected. "Is that all? Do you know Ant? Anthony, actually, but for some reason he prefers Ant."

"Came in from the Murphies a while back, end of April or beginning of May?"

"That's the boy. It took him a month or two to realise how we work here, then he came to see me. Not for my body, but because of my skills." Liz preened, then reached down and picked up an object about three feet long. "He had a couple of very interesting ideas, and one ended up as this." She handed it over.

Harold took hold of the rubber grip on the end of the shaft and swung it experimentally, then started to smile and looked round. "Can I bash something?"

Liz pointed at a chunk of splintered timber against one wall. "There."

Harold looked the weapon over before he swung. The club head looked like a giant iron egg with ridges, while the shaft had been wrapped in wire to make it harder for a machete to damage it. Harold swung and the thump and splintering as it struck impressed him. "The balance is perfect. What is it supposed to be apart from scary?"

"That is a mace such as ye olde knights used for battering men covered in steel, so it should go straight through those shields the scroats use." Patty picked up a second and swung it. "I swing hammers for a living, so of course the thing is balanced. How much is it worth?"

"More to the point, what does it cost?"

"A shaft the same diameter as a sledgehammer shaft, or maybe a lump hammer for a lighter version. I have to shape the hammer head and weld the ribs on, then I harden the lot. I can only use hammer heads because I can't cast metal to get different sized holes, not yet." Liz looked a bit more uncertain. "Can we sell them for enough coupons to be worthwhile, or for more hammer heads and shafts? I might be able to adapt a big axe head?"

Harold grinned and opened his arms, then folded them. "I'd hug you, but you're in the forge and all sweaty and sooty and you wouldn't stop there."

"Then I'd shoot myself for letting a wimp ravage my fair body. I'll settle for that big grin." Liz's grin had to be bigger. "Now I'm not sure I dare show you the rest." She picked up an iron bar, then tapped a knife blade against it so it rang. "Remember this?"

"Yes."

Liz picked up another knife and did the same, and the clear sound rang out again. Harold wasn't paying attention to the sound. "What on earth is that? Did you leave a randy sword and an amorous knife in here overnight?" He looked harder. "Maybe in a threesome with an axe?"

Patty twirled with the weapon, dancing half a dozen steps to silent music. Harold smiled, because when Liz did that she'd usually just had her sooty fix. The smith was completely blown away by that bit of steel. "Ant mentioned short stabbing swords for close work, but I went a bit further. This, philistine, is a perfect fusion of heavy metal blacksmithing and artwork. I call it a Rambo, because nobody will want royalties so I can." When she handed it over, Harold could see where the name came from.

"Did you ever see a real version?" Harold had seen pictures and various survival knives, but this looked more like Rambo's big rough cousin.

"No, those were illegal. This is designed for a woman to use as a short sword or an axe, or just to slice up her steak." A wicked smile lit up Liz's face. "Ooh, will your other woman want one?"

Harold inspected the Rambo. The knife blade, sixteen or seventeen inches long, widened to three inches before tapering again over the last quarter. Liz had sharpened one edge, and the reverse curve back from the point. He thought Mercedes would love one. "Probably."

When Harold ran a thumb over the big, rounded, chequered boss on the handle, Liz chuckled. "I might not fight but I've seen you maniacs practice, and how you use the boss on that stick. If you're using that knife and bring your fist down to hammer on some scroat's head?" Harold carefully put the knife down on the bench, then without warning he lunged forward, picked Liz off her feet in a bear hug and swung her round. He plonked her back on her feet and sat on the bench again, laughing out loud at her expression. Liz recovered enough to speak. "Risky. If I didn't have standards and iron self-control? You like it?"

"How many can you make?"

Her face fell and she glanced over to one corner, and a long piece of plate. "Not many because I've only got one trailer spring left. It's them or sabres and Wamil knives, those Katari things. I can make sabres out of the better quality machetes, but my tempering using anything else is still a bit hit and miss." She cheered up as she pointed at the knife. "That's one of my better efforts. I made it from a bit of leaf spring that had lost its temper in a fire."

"But I'll get you oodles of charcoal when I trade maces and Rambos, so you can perfect your tempering this time." Harold left Liz singing loudly, hammering away to something by Hells Fayre that his eardrums refused to recognise as words or music. Once he could hear normal speech, Harold went to the canteen to find a Geek, to pass on another message about trading. More Geeks had started visiting again through the summer, the numbers cautiously increasing when people stopped blaming them for Hawkins stitching Harold over loot. Their welcome had cooled again, after Orchard Close learned that some Geeks held parties that included gang rape, so it took a couple of days for Harold to find a messenger.

* * *

The reply the next day, suggesting as soon as possible, didn't mention the two-car escort waiting for Harold at the Geek border. That came as a surprise, because the Geeks didn't usually bother to escort him through their territory. The puzzle grew when Harold arrived at the meeting place, the wrecked Burger King. The Geek negotiator usually walked the two hundred yards from their compound, but today Marconi came in a big shiny SUV. Harold parked up in the usual place and walked the last hundred yards with his two bodyguards. He stopped short when two more guards got out of the SUV, giving Marconi four. "Too many, Marconi." Casper raised his shotgun, not quite aiming it, while Ru centred her crossbow on one bodyguard.

The Geek manager hesitated, then two men climbed back into the vehicle and drove about halfway back to the compound. Harold couldn't see why the Geeks were so on edge, so he carried on to the Burger King. Once inside, he sat in the centre opposite Marconi, as usual, while Casper sat at one side with Ru leaning against the table. Marconi's guards sat the opposite side of the leaf-strewn dining area, definitely on edge. They only unwound their crossbows after Casper took the shells out of his shotgun. "What's the problem?"

Marconi hesitated, then scowled before answering. "Remember when those two women ran towards you, a couple of weeks back?"

"Don't start. Two of your women were allegedly stolen by a bunch of scroats. Just afterwards a rifleman tried to kill me, using a woman as a decoy. They'd got a second woman for another try, both of them caught running from the Murphies. A couple of your men met both the lasses, after we killed the sniper and his happy band." Harold curled his lip and sneered. "Maybe you should have killed whoever stole your women? Stole them because one of your men mentioned how the guards died. The women didn't run to us or anyone else."

Now Marconi looked embarrassed. "Yeah, all right. It's just that you've got a lot of new women over there and we've misplaced some." Marconi glanced at Ru, then away when she glared.

Harold scowled, he'd been expecting some sort of comment about all the new refugees. "They're all from the Murphies."

"So you say. While we were searching for those two in this direction, someone cut a hole through the wire at the other side of the compound. We lost half our women. We've checked on their families and friends, and they didn't break out and go home. The pair taken from this side were a diversion while the rest of the gang stole the rest." Marconi both looked and sounded totally pissed off. "The bitches in the bedding store never even shouted to warn us."

Harold thought the 'bitches' probably decided it was at least evens their new owners would treat them better. "The men who came to Orchard Close had been paid to kill me, not steal women. The gang who raided you will have kept the first pair as well. Maybe you should treat your women better, then they might not want to be stolen."

Marconi shook his head sadly. "We'll treat the ones who are left better anyway, because most of them are pregnant. The first two pregnancies had to be deliberate because we give them the pills. We were going to abort the bitches, but Hawkins reckons we need the kids. Otherwise, we'll just die out eventually. We stopped the pills, and brought in extra women so a few getting pregnant wouldn't matter."

Harold usually ended up wanting to punch the Geek negotiator on these visits, but this time he wanted to use one of Wamil's daggers to do it. Deliberately breeding from unwilling women had to be a new low even in the city. "Are you trying to wind me up and start a fight, or do you want to trade?"

The Geek looked at Harold's bodyguards and sneered. "A fight? Those two? Or are they along so it doesn't matter which way you swing if you feel randy?" Marconi must be too pissed off to think straight, because Casper could probably break either of the two Geek bodyguards in half.

At least Marconi's jeering gave Harold his opening. "If Casper swings, be sure to duck. It won't be a handbag. Show him, Casper." Casper unhooked his mace from his belt so everyone could see it properly, and the two Geek bodyguards promptly put their hands on their machetes.

"What the hell is that?" Marconi looked suitably impressed.

"It's a mace. We thought you might like to trade for one, but if you keep winding me up I'll take it elsewhere. Do you have a shield we can wreck, or should Casper show what he's here for? Then you'll have to send for another guard, and he'll have to wipe that down." Harold kept his voice light while the Geek eyed up the weapon. Both the Geek guards now looked decidedly nervous.

Marconi held up his hands. "Point taken, all right? By shield do you mean an old traffic sign, that sort of thing?"

"Perfect. You might not want the bloke to be holding it?" Harold held his grin, not hard because one of the guards flinched. "It doesn't matter to me, but he'd probably be pissed off about the broken arm."

"Yeah, right." Marconi turned and muttered to a bodyguard, who beckoned a watcher from the cars. Meanwhile the Geek switched targets to Ru. "You may as well sit down, since it won't make much difference to your height. Unless you're here to lie down when necessary?"

"Careful, you are forgetting what you were told when Patty came. Ru has a similarly sharp way with anyone who gets too personal." The look Ru gave Marconi came close to removing skin anyway.

This time Marconi seemed to dismiss the warning, or felt he needed to show off. "Yeah right. She can't even manage a full size machete. How the hell can she be a real bodyguard?" The Geek bodyguards laughed, because Ru stood barely over five feet tall. Harold knew just how long and hard Ru practiced; she could probably kill or cripple either of the much bigger men without needing a weapon.

"Ru? Show the bigmouth what you use to make a point?" Marconi had his mouth open to object to bigmouth when Ru sneered, and slid her Rambo out of the sheath.

Two low whistles sounded from behind Marconi as his guards saw the blade. "Where did that come from?"

Harold ignored the question. "That's a Rambo. Ru is very good with it, so anyone sticking a hand up her skirt should remember that Ru studies at the Mercedes school of rules and forfeits." Ru wore jeans under her reinforced skirt so they wouldn't touch her leg, but Harold felt sure that wouldn't save the Geek.

"Christ, the Barbies will want to meet her." Despite his answer, Marconi seemed more interested in the big knife than the woman and Liz had got it right. The weapons were going to sell really well.

"They have, and made her an offer, and they want her as a fighter not a girlfriend. Now if you've finished taking the piss out of my bodyguards, do you want to deal?" Harold concentrated on keeping his smile and his tone light, because he knew Ru's tolerance levels weren't high. If the arses kept pushing and one actually stuck out his hand, he'd bleed long before getting near her skirt.

Marconi nodded, his eyes still on the knife. "Yeah, too true. Bloody hell, your women should carry warning signs."

Harold glanced, and Ru had settled for smirking now they'd taken her seriously. "You mean the armour and weapons aren't a message? You know the women from Orchard Close don't let blokes maul them about."

"Okay, okay. Can I look at that, the Rambo? How much?" Marconi had already been hooked by the look of the Rambo, because he hadn't even tested it yet.

"After Casper gets his mace back, because in a moment you'll want to look at that." A fighter arrived with his shield, a metal 'No Entry' sign with a strap on the back. "If you prop it against the counter or something solid?" At a gesture the man propped his shield on the counter, braced against the till.

"That's about the height it would be held at." Marconi looked at Casper. "Go on then, swing your handbag." The four Geeks grinned and then cursed. Casper had taken a step, let the mace swing with his movement and driven the head clean through the thin metal. He yanked the weapon back out of the crushed till and smiled at the Geeks.

"Anybody want a handbag?"

"How much? No, hang on, give me that knife first." Harold looked back steadily until Marconi got the message. "Please." He smiled properly at Ru. "Pretty please to you. Ru, was it?"

"Ruhika. Boss?" Harold understood the look Ru gave him. She didn't fancy giving a Geek her weapon, even if she still had her smirk.

"No, he can look at Casper's. After all, Casper's still got his mace if someone gets creative." Harold didn't think they would, but pure avarice had flashed over Marconi's face for a moment.

"And I've still got my crossbow." Ru wasn't actually arguing but Harold suddenly realised that Ru's crossbow only needed the bolt. She hadn't let the tension off, though a casual glance confirmed that the Geeks had. Harold ignored her little mistake and turned to Casper.

"Let him see the Rambo, please, Casper. I don't think anyone's got designs on your underwear." That diverted the Geeks as they all denied any interest in what Casper had under his jeans. The fighter retrieved his shield from the floor, scowling as he put his fist through the hole.

"Don't worry. I'll get you one of those clubs instead." The man perked up, whistling happily as he left. Marconi sighed, shaking his head as both the bodyguards asked if they could have one as well, or a Rambo knife. "Bunch of bloody prima donnas. So how much will it cost me to buy some of each? How much is a Rambo, and how much is a club?"

"I told you, that's a mace. We can only get a few so it's resale and I need a profit."

Marconi smiled but his eyes narrowed. "Who made them?"

Harold shook his head. "Not the GOFS, so deal with me or don't deal."

"Smartarse. Through the Hot Rods then?" After a moment's silence Marconi accepted he wouldn't be getting any more information. "So what do you want?"

"Big hammers and lump hammers, spare shafts for them, axes and cement. We're finishing that extension to Orchard Close because we've had a lot of new arrivals." Harold let the increase in his gang numbers register. "We'll also need electrical bits. Quite a lot for a radio, but our man is also trying to fix a multimedia system."

"That set-up of Caddi's?" Marconi hesitated, thinking hard. "From what I can remember, we're getting a bit low on spares for radios."

"I don't mean a hand-held. We've got part of a real transmitter." Harold paused for effect. "We might be able to fix Barbie Radio with it if you've got the rest."

Smiles broke out on all three Geek faces. "I bloody well hope so. They might be mad bitches, but radio is boring without them banging out that lively shit. If they could have managed to stray into decent music now and then it would be even better." Marconi straightened up suddenly. "Hey, what about more CDs, like those you made for us with the karaoke machine and your singer? How much more of that live stuff have you got? Folk, blues, that sort of thing. Shit, anything but heavy rock would be good for a change."

Harold thought about that. He couldn't be sure of getting any instruments or CDs from the Barbies unless he fixed the radio, but any new songs by Jilli would sell somewhere. "We need words and tunes, but I told you we've only got a guitar. Send anything you've still got, on a player or phone, and you'll get a free copy of it sung by her."

"Anything?" Marconi made a half-gesture to his pocket, pausing as Ru put a hand on her Rambo. "Just my phone, right?" Ru nodded so he took it out. "There's a few on this I'd like to hear her sing."

"If she gets the lyrics and the tunes, our nightingale seems to sing anything. If you give me a copy of those, you get them sung and we will sell the other copies elsewhere." Harold sneered because he'd heard what some of the Geeks liked. "Nothing obscene, unless you want cripes instead of anything we don't like?"

Marconi laughed in genuine humour and so did his guards. "I might go for that, even if a Sodom Awl album would be more cripes than original words. If you include a video clip of her singing, we'd pay extra?" Marconi held up both hands at Harold's glare. "Just singing, right, nothing gross. If you get new stuff, songs we haven't got, we'll be interested in those."

"We might have a lot of new music soon. If we can fix Barbie Radio they'll give us some instruments and sheet music, and maybe some CDs they don't use." Harold saw Marconi's eyes narrow in calculation. "Don't try and crank up the prices for the spares. I'm not paying out a fortune when we still don't know if we can fix the bloody thing, or get in and out of Beth's alive."

"We want Barbie Radio fixed so I'll go easy on the prices, providing we have an agreement first. If the repair doesn't do the job, we get a good deal on buying whatever kit you've managed to get working. I've been trying to boost our CB into something that will punch further through the fuzz. For the songs we've got a dozen original CDs we can give you copies of, though most of them are a bit scratched. I'll get anyone here who knows words to anything else to record them. The tunes and singing might be a bit rough?" Einstein looked keen, and so did his bodyguards, very keen if he'd offered to copy personal CDs. "Though you don't sell copies of the original CDs. Deal?"

"As long as you don't copy Jilli's CDs and sell them to anyone we trade with."

"Deal. We'll only sell to the gangs the other side of us. We trade a bit when we aren't shooting at each other. We'll pay you in blanks?" They settled down to thrash out what everything cost, relative to each other. Part way through, Harold casually asked if they'd got anything he could use as bars for windows. He rode out the comments about bar being good ammo for the ballista, and Harold having to cage the new women. Once that died down, Harold suggested steel tube, which would work just as well for upstairs windows.

Marconi thought about it, long enough for Harold to start wondering if they'd still got any, but after a radio call the Geek gave Harold a list and asked what sizes he wanted. Harold asked for a price for the lot, because he really could use any surplus for upstairs windows. Another radio call arranged for the Geeks to drag the rack of tube out here for inspection. Marconi got back to the profitable deal, the electrics, and agreed Trev could go round the shelves in the old shop to find the right parts.

Harold sent Jeremy in to guard Trev, because he'd had a few years to get used to the Geek version of gross. The newer men all seemed a bit too keen on finding an excuse to practice their new combat skills. Just to stop any messing about, Harold insisted Marconi stayed in the meeting place until Trev came back. If Hawkins tried to snatch the radio man, Harold would take the Geek version. He spent part of the wait explaining the extent of the housing Orchard Close had just bought from the GOFS.

Harold nearly had a fit when Trev showed him the bags of gear he'd brought back with him. Eventually most of the spares were kept, on the proviso that a big bag of connectors, fuses and mystery electrics were on sale or return. If Trev used them, Barbie radio had better work. Even then Liz needed to get busy on more maces, or the Barbies would be paying for their radio in soft loo rolls so that Harold could pay the Geeks.

Marconi wasn't as keen on coupons, knitting or curry, not now he'd seen the new weapons. "We'll want maces and Rambos in payment, and rabbits. We wouldn't mind one of those big rifles you've got. Four now we heard? We could deal for Shooter Three as well." Marconi smiled, and this time he meant it. "I'll get Hawkins out here to make him a bloody good offer, and give you most of this gear in compensation?"

"Not a chance. Have any more of those captured firearms jammed yet?" Harold grinned at Marconi's disgusted scowl. The pistols needing attention came in the SUV that towed out a rack of steel tube in half a dozen diameters. Harold inspected the tube for rust but despite not having a use for it, the Geeks had kept the rack out of the weather. After some more haggling, Harold 'allowed' Marconi to pay the balance, and buy the curry and knitting, with crossbows. The final bill for the purchases depended on what Trev used, and the work needed on the firearms.

The Geeks stood around laughing as Harold's party loaded up the steel tube and the cement to get it home. The lengths of steel tube were unwieldy, and unfortunately the total weight of that, the hammers and cement pushed the pickup and van close to their limits. The loads had to be rearranged several times to balance the load. Eventually one of the guards suggested using the trailers in Orchard Close's new territory.

"All right, I'll bite. What trailers?" Even if they were broken, Harold might be interested.

"Follow the railway line." The guard laughed again at Harold's puzzled look. "At the end of the cutting where the line comes out of the water onto your new territory, there's three derailed flatbed wagons. I reckon one of those would be long enough for the tube, and probably the van and pickup. Then you can push the lot home." Harold joined the laughter because yes, a railway wagon would do the job.

"I'll keep an eye open for a railway engine." Harold talked with Casper on the way home, and agreed the guard had a point. Orchard Close needed a working trailer or two, for moving whatever the scavengers found in the new housing. He also talked to Ru, to find out why she'd smirked when

Marconi started tweaking her. Apparently, Patty had told the Demons that the Geeks and Hot Rods would be gross on their own turf. Instead of getting annoyed, the women should imagine the scroat running up and down as a target for crossbow practice. From the smiles, that idea worked for everyone else in the pickup.

When the steel tube came into Orchard Close, Liz looked at it, at Harold, and back at the tube with a big "Oh" on her lips. Harold had to get his musket built and come clean with his blacksmith.

*   *   *

After working on four more muskets and the blunderbuss, Harold decided his would be an improved version. He finished the paying job first. The repaired weapons went back to the GOFS as flintlocks, even if two had been caplocks when they arrived. Flintlocks didn't work as reliably and not at all if they got wet, handy if the GOFS ever aimed them at Orchard Close. Harold sent extra flints as spares, made from smashed cobblestones, which made the GOFS very happy. The caplocks had been a big help, because now Harold could design an improved version.

Vulcan almost salivated over using the blunderbuss on a bunch of unsuspecting prats with machetes and attitude. All the GOFS with him loved the size of the musket ammunition, and thought the big, heavy weapons would double up well as melee weapons. Harold expected some back for repair after they'd been used as clubs. A steady stream of GOFS came to check how the cannon repairs were progressing. They progressed very quickly, because the weapon only needed a good clean and a firing mechanism.

Once the rusted bits were cut off and the hole cleaned, Harold and his apprentice inspected the result and went to see Liz. While she produced some artwork, several volunteers in Orchard Close polished the inside and outside of the cannon until it shone. Harold left it a week before calling for the GOFS to come and collect it.

This time, Caddi's spies were joking with the GOFS when they left, because they knew it would be temporary. Caddi would go crackers trying to find out what happened. While a cheering crowd of GOFS and residents manhandled the cannon through the gates, Vulcan wanted a serious talk. "Why can't our lads join the football matches?"

Harold stared, perplexed, because he hadn't thought Vulcan or any other top GOFS even knew about them. "I'm a bit wary. We play in the evenings, after most visitors have gone home."

"Our lads stop over sometimes and haven't given any trouble for ages, have they?" Harold had to agree. The GOFS were cheeky, and flirted, but kept it clean. "One reason is that I told them they can't expect an invite if they don't behave. The women won't trust them. They'll play in male-only teams to start with?"

"We haven't got one." Harold couldn't help his little smile because Orchard Close had a single-sex team, all women. "Don't you play football at your place?"

"Yes, but your people play without weapons, swearing or fights, and everyone sticks to the rules without threatening to kill the ref. It's a novelty, and the players are definitely more attractive. Allegedly." Vulcan sighed, dramatically, then chuckled. "I'm asking because they're bending my ear, so any chance? If you let a couple have a go it'll shut the rest up and make them even better behaved, hoping for a chance. Cy reckons the Barbies want to play as well?"

"They do, and if I let a few of your lads have a go, they'll insist." Harold couldn't help a snigger. "The Barbies want to join the swimsuit league."

"Er, cripes, nobody mentioned that. I might even come to see myself." Vulcan laughed and slapped Harold on the arm. "Cheer up. Imagine watching our blokes or the Barbies trying not to swear when they've been fouled."

"I'll ask our players if they mind, and they'll decide who gets the chance." Harold glanced towards the cannon, now hooked up to an SUV on the access road. "Now do you want your toy or not?"

"Oh yes. We'll send you a video clip of the first shot at a live target." Vulcan headed for his car with a definite spring in his step.

When Harold stopped the convoy just inside his border, Vulcan came to see why. "It's not actually fixed yet." Harold showed him the shiny clean hole. "You can't fire it using that hole, but I daren't put a firing mechanism on it where the Army could see. The sergeant threatened us with artillery and napalm if it looked operational. I told him the idea was to make it look pretty so someone would buy it and put it outside their front door. We've stopped to sort out a test firing." He pointed at a nearby garage that still had a door and roof. "I'm going to shove it in there straight after, and hide in case a helicopter appears."

Vulcan looked up at the sky, alarmed. "F... Cripes. So how do we get to fire it?" He looked crestfallen and the other GOFS were as bad. Harold got the impression Vulcan would be looking for an excuse, any excuse, to use the cannon in real combat.

"When our welder fastens on our smith's contraption, you'll see." Harold had stopped near a house with electricity. Liz and a welder lurked inside the garage, but now she came out and got busy. While she worked, Harold explained how it would work. "You'll need a blank two-two cartridge." He held one up. "This goes into the hole, there, which swivels into the box like a pistol cylinder. Pull this bar to cock it, pull the toggle there and boom. No safety, so be careful. You'll want to use this length of string or the recoil will bruise your shoulder." Vulcan laughed and the other GOFS followed suit. Harold caught Liz's little smile as she finished the welding. She knew the mechanism was just a single-shot two-two in a box, without the trigger, butt or barrel.

Ten minutes later Harold rammed a small charge down the barrel while the GOFS braced the tail against a kerb. Vulcan stood well to one side, and pulled the string. The GOFS whooped and cheered at the thunderous noise and cloud of smoke. So did Doll, Patty, Casper, Alfie, Tessa, Sharyn, Fergie and a score of others from Orchard Close, who'd followed just to see a real cannon fire. A good few of the spectators took video clips on phones to show to others. The GOFS put their shoulders to the cannon and ran it up the driveway into the decrepit garage as the spectators scattered. After half an hour peering at empty skies they all agreed the Army didn't care what happened, providing it happened far enough away. Finding out exactly how far away could be a matter of life or death.

* * *

From Harold's point of view, the range of a cannon or how far away from the Army they would object to banned weapons weren't a matter of life or death. Pistol and rifle ammunition might be. The neighbours always seemed to have plenty of propellant but Harold never had enough. He already knew, from what happened in every serious attack, from the original rioters through to the defence of the Mart, a big fight would burn up every round in Orchard Close in no time. He just hoped the likes of Caddi never realised he could spin out a fight until Harold simply ran out of bullets. Worse, Harold found himself in a catch-22. If he allowed the fighters to use up propellant in practice, he had less ammo for a fight but they'd be more accurate.

Meanwhile, Emmy's garden gnomes were working flat out and commandeering everyone possible. Every other project, including improvements to the walls connecting the Annex to Orchard Close, had to be almost abandoned. The weather had been kind this year so Emmy had been able to stick to Curtis's timetables, and expected a real surplus. Even the drier weather through July didn't matter, except that bucketing out the water stored in the old sewers became a major chore.

At least reloading the brass, and cleaning weapons, became less of a chore for Harold as Tessa quickly learned to be useful. The extra help meant Harold had more time to train the fighters with blades, and even get out into the fields and relax. Tessa still teased Harold now and then about what they were allegedly up to in the workshop, and Sharyn helped her. Harold found that relaxing, something normal when he went home on an evening, while Sharyn enjoyed Tessa's company and having a babysitter sometimes.

Within weeks, even repairing the guns became less of a chore. Harold knew it wasn't rocket science, but the speed of Tessa's progress still surprised him. Tessa finally admitted that she pushed because she wanted to repair a few herself, then she could actually shoot one to test it. She'd handled various firearms, even watching Stones stripping them down, so unlike most civvies Tessa felt comfortable with guns. Once she had a refresher about safety and safeties, Tessa could soon load or dry fire all the various weapons. Harold gave in and promised she could try a two-two rifle the next time he tested a repair. Tessa acted like a kid with a birthday coming up.

The squad leaders casually brought up rifle shooting among their new squads. They reported that among the best with a crossbow, at least another eight fancied a rifle. Harold wasn't surprised to find Ru was on the list; the small, feisty Asian woman wanted anything that would kill a banchod before he came into knife range. Doll begged off for now, because she wanted to concentrate on improving her pistol shooting and fighting with blades. Most of the potential shooters were women, to let the larger fighters concentrate on training with melee weapons such as maces. Many of the smaller fighters who were accurate with crossbows bemoaned the fact they weren't as big as Emmy, so the best they could hope for was a chance at a two-two 'toy' rifle. Bethany and a couple of others knew about Patty, but kept their mouths shut and hoped that moved them up the list.

All the fighters were complaining about there not being more long range guns. According to many of the women they would be more accurate than any gangster, because they hadn't all that testosterone messing with their brains. The sight of the two new mainly-female squads sparked a rush of even more volunteers, and this time a good few of them were men. Some refugees weren't looking for sanctuary to hide now; the women in particular had decided that if this was home, they would help to defend it.

Chapter 12:
Spring for Liz

The Barbie Girls took advantage of the new free passage to drive over and have a beer more often, which led to more GOFS visiting. Harold finally bowed to the pressure, and the football players allowed a few GOFS and Barbies to join in. The first football matches with gangsters among the players were hilarious, with Barbies stuffing fingers in their mouths to stop from swearing. After seeing Lenny administering first aid, nearly all the Barbies claimed they'd got severe sprains that needed massage. Patricia administering ice packs didn't help, because the GOFS and some of the Barbies immediately wanted her to deal with their mystery sprains. Nobody took offence because the laughing faces made it clear they were joking. After a few matches without incident, almost all those looking for treatment were genuinely injured.

The Barbies tried to recruit Ru, and most of Patty's or Doll's squads whenever they saw one in her fighting kit. Others wanted Alfie or his squad to search them twice, but none of the guards accepted the offers of a sleepover at Beth's. All the Orchard Close fighters began to wear what definitely became light armour, as the outbreak of enthusiasm among the residents moved on to protective clothing. As details of Harold's near escape spread, many of the fighters made their own version of the plated jacket that deflected the crossbow bolt. The other squads began to copy the Demons, sewing lengths of thin plate down their skirts. Experiments showed that the plates stopped slashes from a machete, so even male guards started to wear reinforced skirts over their jeans. The women fighters adopted that, wearing jeans under their armoured skirts, with a few sewing or strapping protection to their shins.

So far, Wamil remained a secret or the Barbies would definitely be after her, which became a private joke among the Demons. They thought it would be a good idea to let the Barbies know, so they would try to kidnap Wamil. Harold could make good money, ransoming the kidnap squads back once the quiet woman had beaten them senseless.

*　*　*

The next bewigged Barbie came in openly, not to kidnap anyone. Instead of getting a phone call, Harold found out when Casper knocked on the door of the gun workshop. "There's another of those kooky Barbies with a wig at the gate, wanting you to search her personally." He grinned at Tessa and Harold. "I told her that Alfie had to search her first, in case she had anything sharp in there."

"How kooky? Is it one we've seen?"

"This is a new one. She's called Ski, but at least she's not carrying any. Oh, and she wants us to tie her up first, and offered her own handcuffs." All three of them were laughing now.

"Well I'm off to change into something tighter and not as comfortable." Tessa headed for the door. Harold didn't even argue, he'd lost that one too many times.

Once she'd gone out of sight, Casper murmured, "She fancies you, you know." He sniggered at Harold's look.

"Fairy off. She's just pleased to be here instead of in Caddi's place." Harold kept going because Casper didn't believe him. "I've known Tessa for years and she's a friend, enough of a friend that we've been drunk together without getting amorous. So what does Alfie reckon to this one?"

"He's in trouble this time, because she's younger than most of the others and very wriggly." Casper's shoulders shook as he tried to keep in his laugh. "She's a pretty young lass under the manic crap, so Hazel won't think it's funny if she finds out."

"That's mean."

That sobered Casper up. "No. She asked for a woman to search her, and not so she'd be safe. I don't always know if they do that to get a bloke, or actually want a woman to do it, but this one was easy. Either way, if I give the job to some of the lads they'll be too interested in searching her to look for any weaponry. Alfie will blush but he'll do it right." Harold had been packing his gear away while they spoke but Casper nodded to the tools. "You'll need that lot later. She's carrying a well wrapped something that will probably be a shotgun or rifle. That and there are eight guards in two cars as escort. I came to let you know rather than phone in case you don't want the news to spread."

"Cripes, we've never had any firearms from the Barbies before. I sometimes wondered if the GOFS had passed some through without saying, but thought maybe they didn't trust each other enough." Harold finished packing and clearing up. "Let's go and see what brought this on."

Ski wore a bright blue scarf round her blonde wig, big skiing goggles on her forehead, and ski pants. She looked to be late teens, had no visible tattoos, and complained vociferously about not being tied up as she came into the Embassy. By that time Tessa had perched on the arm of Harold's chair, wearing tight jeans and a tee. She smiled sweetly at Harold because she knew how much it wound him up.

Alfie came along, definitely looking flushed. He offered a long wrapped object. "It's a rifle, Harold, and, er, Ski says it's broken." He turned to go, obviously relieved to get away.

"You'd better stay, since I'm supposed to have a bodyguard in here." Harold couldn't resist, and Alfie often did that job anyway.

"Ooh, so if I try to attack you, Alfie will leap on me? Who knows what you'd end up with your hand on this time?" Ski had a pretty smile but Alfie blushed harder; searching must have been lively.

"That'll do. We're not on show any more." Harold smiled as he spoke, because the Barbies were funny when they weren't annoyed.

"Yeah, sorry. It's just that, well, it's a novelty to find a bloke who has to be tricked into grabbing, er, well. Oops, nearly forgot where I am." Ski sniggered, then made a definite effort to be serious. "It really is a novelty though." She looked round very obviously, and pulled a face. "That's mean. Where are the Demons? I was told there would be at least one. I've seen the pictures and hoped to get Tilly." That told Harold which Demon had spiced up the pictures, or one of them.

"You caught us by surprise, while they're all busy. Beer, cider, tea or coffee?" Tessa went into her hostess routine, which usually settled visitors down. It worked now, not least because she wasn't a servant, serf or peasant. Soldier Boy's wench getting the drinks acted as an ego stroke for the type that cared.

"Beer please. It's good stuff regardless of what berries you use. You should open a pub." They all laughed at the old jokes, both about the name of the beer and a pub. So far no gangsters had realised that Berry Beer was originally named after the brewer's daughter. There weren't any labels now, but the name had stuck. "Seriously, some of us have been talking and you could set up a pub in here, in Orchard Close. The other idiots we've heard about tried to set up on their own, without enough protection. If you put in proper bar skittles, music and a dartboard, we'd be setting up shifts at Beth's for those wanting to come over here. I want ten percent for the idea of course." Ski reached out for her beer and took a long drink. "Aah, lovely."

"Not ten percent. If we set it up, you get one free beer when you visit." Harold shook his head but began to seriously consider the idea. Put like that, the idea sounded feasible, because the canteen already served beer. Rig up the right atmosphere and sheer nostalgia would attract the surrounding gangsters in droves. "No using a crossbow on the dartboard."

Ski giggled and raised her arms to mime using a crossbow. "You could arrange crossbow darts in the back yard?"

Fergie arrived in full kit, as a bodyguard, because Harold always had one of each sex now. "Casper said you needed someone who won't blush if they have to handle a Barbie."

"Bloody hell. Er, sorry. You weren't in the pictures." Ski started to give Fergie a slow once-over and stopped. "I keep forgetting where I am. Are you a Demon?"

"Yes, there's quite a few of us now. I didn't pose for the pictures because I don't usually have to advertise. You must be Ski. I had a Ski Barbie, a million years ago." Fergie sighed nostalgically and everyone sobered for a moment until Harold moved on to business.

"Bet you didn't come for a beer, or to give me ideas about new ways to part you from your coupons." Harold looked very obviously at the wrapped package. "Did you want to sell that?"

"Not sell. One of the girls found a friendly Geek, a very talkative Geek wanting to show off his new weapon. A big, sharp knife? He called it a Rambo and apparently that's what it looked like." Ski looked pointedly at Fergie's belt so Harold nodded to the young woman.

"Show Ski a Rambo please, Fergie." The knife came out to be duly admired.

"We might trade for those." Ski hesitated, eyeing the knife again. "No, we definitely will trade for those, but not until I get back and someone okays the prices. That's if you can get more?"

Harold didn't mind a new customer for Liz's wares. "We can, but only a limited number."

"That's a pity. Anyway, back to the Geek. Flashing the Rambo got him up Steph's skirt and under her shirt, but not into her pants. He showed her his other weapon, a sparkly clean nine mil. She commented on its lovely condition and the prat even let her try the action. Sort of an exchange for trying out hers?" Ski smiled as she carefully phrased it to keep within the Orchard Close language rules.

"We get it." They all did, because the Barbies tried swapping sex for information on anything, from the number of reloads the guards carried to the name of the radio repairer or the brewer.

"When Steph told him we preferred revolvers, because they didn't jam up, he reckoned a local friendly Soldier Boy sorted out little problems like that. Apparently the guns come back looking like new and shooting straight?" Now Ski looked straight at Harold, with a sort of challenge in her eyes.

"True. Not good as new, but clean and working if possible. I can repair most firearms if they aren't too badly damaged. That includes clearing jams, sticking clips and split brass, fixing broken mechanisms or making new firing pins, that sort of work." Harold shrugged and pointed at the rifle. "I'm surprised that's the first one from you. I get work from the GOFS, Geeks and Hot Rods, but to be honest I thought some of it might be from you or others beyond, passed through at a profit but without telling me."

Ski scowled, not at all happy. "No, your neighbours have been very quiet about it. How come you've been so shy?"

"I don't want somebody thinking it would be a good idea to kidnap their own repairer. They might decide it's worth putting together enough people to take Orchard Close." Harold didn't have to fake his glum face or sigh. "There are some real idiots out there."

"Well it's out now, and someone at Beth's did mention kidnapping. A lot of others pointed out that nobody with a working brain cell will try to kidnap Soldier Boy. That brain cell should point out that every weapon in Orchard Close must be in good nick, so the place would be very expensive to take. Especially with at least four big rifles and real shooters." Ski's brow wrinkled a bit. "If it's been a secret, how come the Pink Panthers know? Perhaps the Geeks have been loose-lipped, or one of them has got a boyfriend."

"The Pink Panthers know?" Harold couldn't hide the shock on his face, so much for secrecy.

"That rifle is from the Pinkies. We'll get a commission if it's fixed, and if it is and the price is right there'll be business from us as well. Above my pay grade but I'd bet coupons Ken is using the Pinkies as a test." Ski smiled at Tessa and gestured at the parcel. "If Tessa would unwrap it, nobody will get nervous." All the Barbies were meticulous over calling both Tessa and Sharyn by name. The other gangs often called them 'your wench' or 'Soldier Boy's sister' even if they kept it carefully polite.

Tessa unwrapped the weapon, a single shot rifle, and after checking the safety she tried to pull back the bolt. It went part way and stopped. "Is there one up the spout?" Tessa kept the rifle pointed at the ceiling, and her finger away from the trigger, while she jiggled the bolt some more.

"We don't know. The Pinkies sent three rounds for testing which is supposed to be the system?" Harold nodded and Ski handed them over. "You look very comfortable with that, Tessa. Can you shoot?"

"My bloke was a soldier, and so was Sharyn's, so we've been around weapons." Tessa didn't answer the shooting question but Ski answered it mentally, as yes.

Her eyes lit up. "Are you Shooter Three, or Five?"

Tessa stared at her in surprise. "Me?"

"Er. Well. Since someone heard the radio talk to Shooter Two, Three, Four and Five, everyone has been wondering which of your blokes they are. Two were on little rifles, but our lass heard two bigger rifles and then that old Army one. Near the end two new rifles fired four or five times, quickly so they've both got clips. One of the first two was the sniper, and now you've got his rifle as well. We know about Emmy and Alfie, and since we are women we aren't just looking at the men or big women like Emmy." She looked at Fergie for a moment, assessing her size. "We know it isn't Patty or she'd have been shooting in the battle on the TV, and Doll didn't go to the Geeks as a shooter either. It's the range that interests Ken. One shooter pinned that sniper at over six hundred yards, and the other two killed men at the same range. From the sound, the Army rifle was a lot further away so it got round behind the sniper. Ken says that part had to be Soldier Boy SAS shit." Ski looked at Tessa again, then turned to Harold. "A couple of our people looked over the ground, after all the fuss died down. From the blood, they sort of figured out where everyone must have been. It wasn't exactly a secret."

"Not guilty. Though since we've got someone handy who can teach shooting?" Tessa smiled happily and swept her hand round to take in all of Orchard Close. "Who knows, we might have a Shooter Six or Seven? Seventeen?"

"Not then, or they would have been joining in because you've got more little rifles. You got that bloke's rifle, so maybe eight altogether, or nine now?" Everyone just smiled until Ski sighed and continued. "Never mind. Back to that rifle there, can Soldier B… Can Harold fix it?" Ski had trouble with the informal bit.

"Possibly. If not you get it back and I'll show you why, or maybe make a deal for the rifle as spares." Harold held out a hand and Tessa passed over the weapon. "Unless something very odd has been done to it, apart from some prat using a hammer to try force the bolt, I can probably have it ready in a week. Do you know how many other gangs have found out about the repairing?" Harold hoped nobody else had been quite as enterprising as the Barbies when it came to estimating shooters, and that they'd keep quiet. He daren't ask them to be discreet, in case they took it as confirmation.

"No idea, but the news is spreading. We've heard about the new ones, those muskets. Apparently you've made some broken ones work?" Ski waited until Harold nodded. "We can suggest that the Pinkies keep it quiet and just take commission, but you might be too late. It's your own fault. We can trade with the Geeks now and believe me, they are very happy to give up all sorts of goodies for what we can offer. Malibu won't let us trade the soft loo rolls, but they are very loose-mouthed if they get another sort of roll… er." Everyone ignored the hesitation since it wasn't actually outside the rules, and Ski was trying.

"Yeah, and as a bonus you can rob me blind by looting my nice new houses." Harold wasn't too worried by that because the GOFS had already taken what the Barbies wanted, booze and potential weapons. He only commented to keep them from being too blatant.

"Oh no. We've had to spank a couple of our lot for getting carried away. The hard word is out from the very top. Barbies are to leave your houses alone, because if anyone f… Er." She paused, then started again. "If anyone messes up the free passage they'll be in deep, well, a lot of trouble?" Ski shook her head in mock despair. "I've spent three years talking like that, and it's hard to stop."

"You'll survive." Tessa sounded sympathetic. "I found it a bit strange to start with."

"Oh, I don't mind. It's just difficult, remembering. Maybe I should spend more time here, in the canteen, learning how to say cripes?" Ski looked over at Fergie and smiled brightly. "Maybe I can buy you a drink? We can practice cripes while talking about all your weapons and shiny armour, or maybe my handcuffs?"

"If you're buying." Fergie smiled back, just as brightly. "And I'm off duty." Some of those present did a double-take, but Harold had known about Fergie's preferences since the private training sessions.

Ski looked a very happy Barbie Girl. "I'm buying so let me know when you're free."

"You could discuss that later? In the canteen, maybe?" Harold wanted to stop the flirting and get back to business, especially now it had suddenly gone beyond flirting.

"Sorry boss." Fergie straightened her face and back.

"No problem. But not on duty." Now all Harold needed was a subject change.

"How come you've still got loo rolls after four years?" Alfie must have been thinking about them, and now everyone else realised that even with a shop full, the Barbies should have used them up.

"Ken thought about it, right at the beginning. The original Barbies, before I arrived, went out and looted every shop and house they could get to in the neighbouring territories. Loo rolls, sanitary pads, Tampax, moisturising creams, cotton buds. The other gangs weren't interested in all the woman stuff, and they wanted booze and fags rather than loo rolls. We've still got quite a lot, all rationed of course." She looked around hopefully. "Do you need any? In return for Rambos?"

"No, we've sort of fixed ourselves up." Tessa smirked. She had been intrigued, and then definitely converted to bidets.

"Yeah, some of the girls said you've got a water jet thing that, well, you use a sponge? They reckoned it works, strange but quite gentle." From the look, Ski wasn't too sure. "I'm sort of looking forward to it. There's not a lot of novelty about these days."

"It's a bidet. We've got a plumber so while your lot were nicking loo rolls, this lot were searching houses and ripping out bidets. We've got a lot of soft, natural sponges as well." Tessa sighed dramatically as she sat back on the arm of Harold's chair. "All these years with Mall loo paper, and bidets were just down the road." She sighed again, even more dramatically. "If Harold had only said, I'd have moved in years ago."

"It's a good job the idea didn't spread. The Geeks have parted with tons of cement and some gas bottles for our sort of luxury item. We've even been able to reinforce the approaches. We'd run out of cutting gas a bit back, but now there's chunks of steel set into the roads on the approaches." Ski made a seated half-bow to Harold. "Cherry liked your road defences, but we've adapted them to leave a way through for our cars." The conversation drifted into who might trade what for luxuries, until Ski headed off to the canteen to try some Orchard Close stew and buy another beer.

Ski stayed overnight and did spend time, and coupons, buying Fergie beers and talking to everyone she could. Her bodyguards spent coupons in the canteen, flirted with everyone, male or female, and played loud music in the visitor's house. The Barbies left the next morning with big smiles and carrying crates of beer. Ski took back a mace for Ken, and a Rambo, and promised to be back in a week for the rifle. As the convoy roared off down the road, the car stereos blaring out Motorhead's Eat the Rich, Caddi's watchers crept back out of hiding.

* * *

While Harold found new ways to prise coupons out of the neighbours, the normal day-to-day work around Orchard Close produced its own rewards. Emmy's garden gnomes worked their magic, the seasons turned, and more salad type goodies appeared on the tables. One tea time Daisy triumphantly produced her own, personally grown tomatoes. "One for Mummy, one for Uncle Harold, and one for Wench Tessa."

"What?" All three adults stared. "What did you call Tessa?" Sharyn cast a helpless glance at Harold and a definitely pink Tessa. "She's Aunty Tessa."

"But everyone knows she is Uncle Harold's wench. Georgina said that Joey told her and he heard it." Daisy hesitated, thinking hard. "Somewhere but everybody calls her that."

"But you called Holly Aunty."

"Oh, is Tessa a gartered wench? We know that's different. Why is it different? Have you got a garter, Tessa?" Daisy looked at Tessa, and two more pairs of bright inquisitive eyes joined hers so Wills and Eddie wanted to know as well.

Harold recovered first. "That's a mummy question for later. You call her either Tessa or Aunty Tessa, all right?"

Daisy nodded and Harold relaxed, much too soon. "All right. Is Mercedes your wench as well? Nobody else has two."

"No, Mercedes is not my wench, and where did you hear that?" Harold knew the question had to be a mistake as soon as he opened his mouth. He could feel his cheeks heating up.

"But Milly said you kissed her by the gate because her mum said. Sukie said her mum is wearing shorts because if you can play grab-ass in the street…" Daisy stopped and put both hands over her mouth, eyes wide.

"Yes young lady. Definitely soapy-mouth." Sharyn's blush matched Harold's and Tessa's, and the meal finished hurriedly in embarrassed silence. Except for Daisy, who tried to spin hers out because of the upcoming retribution.

Once the children had gone with Sharyn to get washed, Harold tried. "Look, I'm sorry."

"I volunteered. I didn't think it through but of course people talk at home, and little pitchers have big ears." Tessa shrugged, saw Harold's expression and giggled. "At least I'm not the one playing grab-ass."

"I didn't!" Harold hesitated, because he usually ended up with his hands on Mercedes' shorts, skirt or jeans. "I suppose I did, but on the main street where the kids don't go."

"From what Sukie said, the shorts and probably a bit of grab-ass could be spreading. Doll and Fergie have already strolled down Main Street in shorts, and quite a few of Doll's squad wear them, even some of the blokes." Tessa smiled happily at the next bit. "The scroats who saw Doll kept their mouths firmly shut. She had a pistol and a machete, and one hell of a kick-ass attitude."

"I'm worried because if the dress code relaxes, it'll encourage the likes of the Hot Rods." Actually Harold wanted to beat his head on a wall, because he'd spent three years teaching the local scroats some manners.

"Not necessarily." Sharyn must have heard that, as she came downstairs. "Remember what Holly said? It took a lot of training before the scroats accepted short skirts without getting out of hand, but it was worth the effort. The training slipped when you had your timeout, but you've straightened them out since. Some women like to wear shorts or short skirts, and if they are truly safe here, they're safe to do that."

Harold frowned because yes, the scroats had accepted Holly's skirt. "Keep the garden canes handy."

Sharyn glanced at Tessa. "Maybe your wench should carry one, as a hint." Harold opened his mouth to object, but Tessa's face told him he'd be wasting his breath.

"We agreed I'd pretend to be your wench, so I'll keep pretending until the real one arrives. We'll know her because you'll start playing grab-ass." Harold left to check something, anything, with laughter still ringing in his ears. It didn't help that he knew if Mercedes turned up, he probably would end up with his hand on her ass.

*   *   *

Working on weapons kept Harold from dwelling too much on grab-ass, and a week later resulted in a working musket, a brand new one. He inspected the weapon, and the other two he'd almost completed, and knew it was time for the big reveal.

Harold invited the squad leaders, Casper, Alfie, Patty, Doll, Matthew and Bess, for a meal. He added Liz and Emmy, Sharyn suggested inviting Stephan the joiner, and Patty wanted Ru there because she'd soon be second in command of the Demons. When the group sat around the fully extended dining table, instead of an informal meeting in the lounge, the usual visitors started looking curious. "I invited you all here for a meal, the same food you'd get from the canteen but as a social occasion. The kids have gone off to Suzie's for the night, supposedly so Tessa and Sharyn can enjoy the meal in peace. The real reason is so we can have a long meeting, without making anyone curious." Harold looked around the intrigued faces. "As you know, Liz has expanded her repertoire to Rambos and maces. We must decide which are needed most, what they will cost, and how much of what to trade. We will be getting enquiries about both weapons, and can probably sell all we can make, so over to you Liz?"

"I can re-temper old spring steel now, but I can't make blades from any old scrap. If you find any broken or burned trailers in the rubble, rip off the springs and bring them in. It's not thick enough for blades like the GOFS swords, but it'll make Rambos." Harold could see the distinct effort Liz made to bite off "and Wamil's knives and sabres" when she realised everyone here might not know.

Alfie picked up that small springs meant only small weapons. "So the bigger the better?"

"Yes, because they are thicker. That heavy duty trailer you found had some lovely, long, thicker plates under it." Liz sighed. "It's a pity we can't find any big trucks, or old cars."

"What about caravans? Can you use those springs?" Matthew had found a burned out touring caravan when scavenging, and brought the springs back to Orchard Close.

Patty answered for them all. "Yes, because they're just trailers with little houses on."

"If bigger is better." Alfie looked around with a smile starting. "Does that work for caravans?"

"Ooh yes. One of those big mobile homes would have…." Liz's eyes opened wide, and half those present realised they knew where there were big mobile homes. Only the burned out remains of them, but springs weren't combustible. Alfie now wore a huge grin.

"The ones the assholes burned." Harold didn't need to say which assholes to some people here.

"The night I got my hairstyle?" Emmy put up a hand to stroke the crewcut side of her head.

"Anyone else lost? Because I haven't suddenly seen the light, or anything else." Tessa looked from one to the other and Patty, Ru, Stephan, Bess and Doll looked back, baffled.

"Before your time, before Bess or Patty, a dozen scroats came in here before the walls were built." Casper nodded towards Harold. "Harold shot the leader because he pointed a big pistol at us, then I shot the one with a shotgun after he tried for Emmy." Emmy tapped the small scars on her cheek and forehead.

Harold answered the question in five pairs of eyes. "Then I told them they could keep their clothes if they left nice and quiet. The residents chipped in to say how they'd prefer to kill a few, so the scroats dropped their weapons and scarpered."

Liz grinned at Tessa. "You know that big tarmac park the other side of the neutral road?"

"The one dug up in strips for potatoes? Yes."

"There were over a dozen big mobile homes on there when the roads were sealed. We were stripping them for gas fired stuff in case the electricity died. There were beds, carpets, fitted units, a miniature house inside each one. The assholes set fire to them and boy, do they burn." Liz looked unhappy now, and fell silent. At the time she'd cried about all the good gear that went up in flames.

Harold finished up for her. "We dragged all the wreckage to the far end so we could see anyone sneaking across the tarmac. When the Army used a bulldozer to clean up bodies after the big breakout attempt, they shoved the whole lot a bit further. The RAF turned the bodies into a pyre that included the wreckage. Nobody wanted to go near that mess for a long time." Harold didn't mention human bones and charred meat or the stink. "We've chucked other rubbish on there since."

"Rubbish that is burying big flat springs!" Liz finished triumphantly. "They've been there forever and I'd forgotten about the caravans." She hit herself on the forehead with the heel of her hand. "Cripes!" Liz spun and glared at Alfie. "There'd better be the right sort of springs in there!"

Alfie cowered in mock terror. "I can't remember. I've only looked to see if any of the metal sheeting might be thick enough to use for shields. It's all caravan walls, thin aluminium I could sneeze through where it didn't already melt."

* * *

That ended the discussion because Liz had to go and look, right now. The inhabitants of Orchard Close were treated to the sight of the whole group being chivvied down the access road, and across the potato field to the rubbish heap. One good look at the tangle of metal, melted plastic and charred wood and Liz gave a big whoop. By the time she had danced through the entire group, hooking arms to whirl each person, everyone there got the message.

Harold managed to shut her up until they got back and indoors, where the residents, Caddi's watchers, the world and his dog couldn't hear. Once allowed to celebrate, Liz wouldn't stop crowing about how she could make Rambos for all the guards, and Harold could sell oodles. She wanted all the springs dragged out and across the road, now! Alfie agreed to get a work gang organised and start shifting the springs in the morning. If he used the pickup and vans to block the view, and scavenged all the aluminium as well, Caddi's watchers wouldn't have a clue.

Liz wouldn't make sense for a while, so Sharyn, Tessa, Matthew and Casper went to get the food from the canteen. It took until the end of the meal for the smith to calm down enough to discuss how many Rambos and maces the defenders needed. Even then, Liz's excitement kept the group amused until everyone had helped to clear the table. The talk revolved around the springs and what they would make, of course, but also about trying to get materials for more maces. Searching the burned-out ruins of small garages and sheds went up the list of priorities, as the metal hammer heads would still be intact. They all had a good laugh about how Bernie would react to another scavenger hunt over the same ground. Stephen suggested adding banisters to the list, the better ones were made of straight-grained hardwoods so he could split and shape them into shafts.

"No brandy and cigars, just tea or small beer." Harold raised his small beer. "But now you find out why you are really here. We are building our own very crude muskets, which is why I invited you, Stephan. I'll need more stocks and forestocks, because the three spares you made are already in test weapons."

"I'll go through our woodpile for any suitable bits of timber." Stephan frowned gently, thinking about it. "Forestocks would be another use for banisters. I would have been curious if you'd suddenly wanted... How many are you making?"

Harold confessed he didn't know, too many to pretend he needed the stocks for repairs. "But keep quiet about it, because this is the sort of secret every gang in the city will kill us for." Sharyn wasn't known for being alarmist and Harold saw her words hit home. Even Liz sobered up.

"So why risk it?" From their expressions several others thought Stephan had a point.

"We are growing and need more protection, especially because a large part of our population is women." Harold looked pointedly around the current group.

"And most of those are young women." Stephan, in his late twenties and single, smiled. "Not that I'm objecting, just making the point."

Sharyn didn't smile back at him. "Exactly, we are creating a pool of women under thirty as well as having so many tradespeople. Sooner or later someone will look at this place, and at how many troops Soldier Boy has, and decide the losses are worth what they'd get."

"The more attackers we can shoot before it gets to hand to hand, the better. A volley of muskets at close range will also demoralise any attackers, shock them. The more the merrier." The faces around the table understood what Harold meant. The Hot Rods were frightened of the Murphies' muskets, even if they were slow and inaccurate.

Tessa put in her sixpennorth. "I've lived in the zoo and they won't rate the armed women when they count fighters." She curled a lip, remembering. "They don't rate women at all, or not for fighting, unless they are Barbies."

"Caddi." For a moment Harold thought Casper would spit. "He'd love to get the women."

"So would the Geeks." Emmy's hand twitched towards her belt knife. She still thought Einstein had set up the assassination attempt that had cost Pippa her hand. "Either would want the tradespeople as well. Both are always bitching that ours are better."

Harold sobered his voice and face. "How many secrets do you want to have to keep, Stephan?"

"What? Oh." Stephan thought about it. "I'll be curious, but if I don't know I can't say the wrong thing. How much do I need to know?"

"That's all for now, thanks. We'll want more hilts of course, for the Rambos and any repairs." Harold glanced across at Liz. "Some of the hilts will be a bit different. We're trying to make the machetes and Rambos easier to handle for the smaller men and women."

"That's not a problem. In that case I'll go now, and thank you. For the option." Stephan left, sober-faced and deep in thought.

"Do I need to leave?"

"No Ru. What do you keep pestering me about?"

"Something better than a crossbow. We get them? The new muskets?" Ru's happy smile was infectious, especially when Harold didn't say no.

"You'll get one if you can handle it. I'll show you now." Harold went into his bedroom for a few moments and came out with a test version. All the speculation stopped as he put a half-dozen musket balls and the musket on the table.

"It'll be good for one shot, but then they're slow." Patty had been out at night with Harold, testing repairs. "Muskets take forever to reload."

"No good for Bess then. Or maybe a good idea, it will conserve ammo." Matthew ducked away as Bess took a half-hearted swipe at him. Despite her protest, everyone knew Bess usually emptied her pistol as fast as possible.

"That's a big bullet, but the barrel is shorter than the usual muskets. Is it lighter?" Ru's eyes were alight because this would definitely nail the banchod beyond knife range.

"How hard does it kick?" Casper wouldn't be bothered by the recoil, but he had to be wondering how many others could use the weapons.

"Give me a second! First of all, you are right, Ru. The barrel is a bit shorter and also lighter because it's steel tube. The bore isn't as big either. It's still thirteen millimetres but hopefully the kick will be less, which answers you, Casper." Harold smiled at Patty, waiting for her reaction because Tessa already had a big grin. "Watch this." He flicked the simple catch and the weapon broke open like a shotgun. "Poke the load in there." He clicked it shut and pulled back the big hammer. "Stick a cap in there and boom. It will slow Bess, but not too much."

"Oh man, I want one." Alfie stared at the weapon. "The assholes will think they've survived the volley and rush in before we can reload. That's what the Hot Rods reckon they do against the Murphies. But a few seconds later, ours will go boom again."

"Not yet. This needs testing and then taking apart and inspecting, and maybe altering and testing some more." Harold handed the musket to Tessa. "They'll be stored in pieces as spares so nobody realises they are complete weapons. My apprentice will now demonstrate." Tessa rapidly reduced the musket to four pieces and three bolts. "Those will be in different boxes until we need them."

"It'll still take time to put in a wad, the ball, a wad, and powder. We'll have to be careful with the powder." Patty had only loaded a musket twice but already hated the lengthy procedure. "We won't be able to ram it all in tight. Will that matter?"

"I don't know about the ramming, and hoped someone could help with that. Perhaps with a cartridge?" Harold looked hopefully at Liz. "They'd be faster if everything went in at once, like a shotgun?"

"I don't know. I've got brass from Yale locks, door handles and ornaments." Liz shook her head in frustration. "I'll never get enough made. It's the time, because I have to make the stupid things individually. How would you make that hammer set off a cartridge anyway?"

"Would it burn through cloth? The cap thing on the side I mean." Ru looked towards Patty. "I was just thinking the powder could go in a bag so it wouldn't spill or need ramming. We could make a little hole in the bag before loading. If the spark will burn through a bag it'll speed the job up, and this way we don't need brass."

"I saw film of the Americans doing that on a Civil War re-enactment thing. They shoved one long sausage down the barrel and rammed it home." Doll's brow furrowed in concentration. "It was in a cannon, so the lot went in from the front including the cannon ball, but surely it would work the other way?"

"I reckon, and that solves one problem." A big one that Harold hadn't found a solution for. "I worried about the ball sometimes just shoving the first wad out of the way and rolling off down the barrel, followed by the powder. If it's all inside a baggie there's no problem."

"Is there a way of testing some different types of cloth, to find out what works? Until we sort that out we can cut a hole in the bag as we load. Can you spare one of those for me"—Patty glanced at Ru and Doll—"us, to experiment?"

"What's the range?" Casper eyed the bits and the length of the barrel. "The Hot Rods reckon the Murphies wait until it's point-blank, but it's about fifty yards down to the neutral road. Could we hit anything at that distance?"

"If you do it'll tear a big nasty hole in a man at that sort of range, according to Mack. Muskets aren't what you'd call accurate, but with practice the musketeers should be able to hit a crowd at fifty yards." Harold could see the disappointment on some faces. "It isn't exactly a superweapon. A crossbow has more range and is probably more accurate."

"But it's brutal, noisy and scary, and close-up will blow a hole clean through who it hits. With luck it'll kill the one behind as well. The Hot Rods worry about those few Murphy muskets a lot more than they do about all the crossbows. If we can reload faster than crossbows that's good enough for me, since we'll be using them on crowds." Matthew looked from the weapon to Harold. "How much practice can we get?"

"Not enough, even if I increase the number of tests at night. Whoever has a musket can have at least one shot to experience the fire and the fury, and the kick. After that, they can practice loading and aiming until their fingers are raw." Harold laughed at the long faces. "Hey, if we have enough of them the scroats will die of sheer fright."

Bess didn't seem keen, then her face brightened as she picked up one of the musket balls. "If we aim below the waist and it kicks harder than expected, then at worst it blows their heads off. If it doesn't kick that badly, I can't see anyone getting up with one of these somewhere between his nuts and his neck."

Tessa rolled one across her fingers and smirked. "I'll let you know how hard it kicks."

"Hell, yes. Apprentice? So all that time you pair are spending in Harold's hidey hole, supposedly getting some privacy away from his sister?" Doll broke up laughing while Harold felt a blush starting.

"Ask no questions, sister. I never said why we were in there." Tessa still wore a big smirk.

So did Doll, now. "No, but everyone has come up with an answer. A few were wondering if there would be room for all those guns, you two and Mercedes."

Everyone had started laughing now, except Harold. "We were fixing guns."

Tessa looked him up and down. "Stripping, lubricating, testing the action. I swear I never realised it could be so much fun until Mercedes mentioned it."

"Don't you start as well!"

"Well you'd better let me have some real action then." Tessa lost her smile and teasing tone. "When do I get to shoot something?"

"When we finish here?" Harold sighed in relief as the idea of getting to actually shoot a gun took Tessa's mind off winding him up. "If anyone has any bright ideas about the kick, about a way to let more people try it, please let me know."

"I would like to try a musket, to see how bad it is." Ru looked a bit worried. "It looks very heavy to hold steady. If the kick is a lot harder than a crossbow, that could be a problem."

"Me too. How heavy is it?" Bess gestured at Matthew. "Neither of us is a weight-lifter, especially since Matthew's arm never quite healed right."

"Since you aren't having to ram a new load in, the barrel could be rested on something. Veronica found some books that showed a long stick to support the barrel, but that has to be awkward to set up. We'll probably be shooting from the walls but the barrel will slither about if it's resting on bare brick. A sandbag would be better, if we had any sacks." Even as Harold finished speaking, Patty and Sharyn looked at each other and grinned. Sharyn quickly explained that most of the damaged curtains, bedding and clothes from demolished ruins were washed and saved for cleaning rags. Making sand or earth-bags to provide extra protection on the walls wouldn't even make the sewing circle curious.

Eventually, the discussion moved back to the caravan springs. Liz could only make a limited number of saleable weapons, because the defenders needed the rest. The maces looked brutal and would have psychological impact, while the Rambos could be used by smaller fighters instead of a machete. They all agreed that a man with a baseball bat wouldn't want to face a mace, even a woman with one. Casper brought the mood down, pointing out that the GOFS would produce maces and Rambos as well. Then everyone would have them and Orchard Close would lose the deterrent factor. He looked downright despondent because the GOFS might even be upset at losing some heavy metal business.

"Cripes, I was only trying to help!" Liz looked alarmed and a bit guilty.

"But they will help, Liz. Initially, the new blades will put anyone off attacking, and by time they've made their own?" Harold tapped the pieces of musket on the table.

"You bloodthirsty lot will have more muskets than any of them can dream of." Liz had her smile back.

Harold admitted to another ace; it was time he came clean with this group. "Not just muskets. Over time I've also made some Mad Maxes, to give us extra weapons shooting modern ammo."

"The different sizes of tube! I knew it! What will they look like?" Liz started bouncing up and down in her seat again. "Have you made one?"

"That tube won't handle modern ammo." Harold put a big, clumsy single shot pistol on the table, opened it and unloaded a long, fat rifle bullet. The breech consisted of a hinged block of iron with a shaped groove in it. "The barrel came from less than half a rifle barrel. This is a single shot 50 calibre, slow to reload and clumsy, but brutally effective if it hits. That odd stock is so you can brace it to help with the recoil, and even then only someone with really strong wrists should risk it. I've made two of these and eight other patched-together weapons. Remember, this is a very big secret."

"That's a pity. Knowing about this lot might help back them off." Casper picked up the Mad Max pistol, tested the weight, and tried aiming it. "A bullet like that will go through a car."

"The ones with hardened centres will, but keep quiet about that as well. These are only spare parts cobbled together, but if anyone knew I made them they'd come after me. That or they'd try to capture people to force me to work for them." Everyone realised there were at least two people like that in the room. Sharyn and Tessa knew Harold well enough to realise there were more he'd buckle under to save.

Ru kept her smile until she tried to aim the pistol. "Oh well, I suppose someone like Logan will get this. On the bright side, ten unexpected modern bullets and however many big nasty muskets should stop the first scroat to try and kidnap anyone. Before that, with a bit of luck, Harold and Shooters Two to Four will use those big rifles to kill whoever is in charge. Five if Roy is at home. Do you need a Shooter Six?" Everyone looked at her but nobody answered, because some people here didn't know the identity of Shooter Three. "What? I'm just saying. With four big rifles and all those little ones?"

"It's no bigger a secret than the others we've spoken of tonight." Harold watched Patty as he spoke and she nodded very slightly. He waved a hand towards Patty. "Ru, Liz, Doll, meet Shooter Three."

"I knew it, and you kept saying no!" Doll leant back from the table, her eyes wide in shock.

"We guessed because we saw her head out to the annex with a long something, bigger than a two-two, and we were there when Harold spoke to the Annex." Matthew looked apologetic as several shot him accusing looks. "We heard all the guessing but Harold never said who it was, so we kept quiet." Bess nodded in agreement.

Ru wasn't that surprised, but her eyes narrowed in accusation. "You told me the kick on a big rifle would be too much for a small woman?"

"I thought so, but it wasn't once I knew what to do. Harold inflicted some serious nagging, and I bruised my shoulder at first even with the little one." Patty preened, buffing her nails on her lapel. "Then he fixed me up with a big rifle, a secret one." Her face sobered as she continued. "The actual rifle has to stay a secret because it's a real poser job, one that will upset Caddi." She explained the Winchester.

"I could learn to shoot a little one." A whole new world had suddenly opened out for Ru. "Just in case you find another bigger rifle, or Patty is in the bath or something?"

"After me, sister. I've been working on him longer." Tessa preened a little.

"Ooh, do I have to do the stripping and lubricating thing first?" That was the first truly risqué thing Harold ever had heard Ru say, and it stopped everyone for a moment. Her hand went to her mouth. "Sorry." Ru recovered and smiled. "You've all corrupted me. That and, well, a real rifle?"

"Don't worry, Patty hasn't done any of that." Harold carried on quickly as he saw Patty's mouth open, "And it isn't necessary. I've got all the apprentices I can deal with right now." Harold looked slowly round the group, trying to calm them down. "We will be testing, very carefully, to see who has a good eye, and the muskets and crossbows will help with that."

"What about you, Casper?" Bess looked from Casper to the musket. He seemed a good fit for one.

"Only close-up at a crowd, and if we've got plenty of them, because I'm useless at shooting. That's why I have a shotgun if there's real trouble." Casper pointed at his face. "It's my eyes."

Ru had been thinking and now she looked at Patty, but hesitated before finally speaking. "If your rifle is a secret, then there's five altogether. Do you need another shooter?"

"How many shooters for rifles do you need, Harold?" Bess and Ru leaned forward a bit, hopefully. Bess licked her lips, quickly. "If there's at least one spare big one."

"Four Mad Maxes are rifles, then we have five big ones including mine, and four of the little ones, the two-twos. Those need an accurate shooter at any sort of range. Patty keeps one because her rifle has limited ammo." Harold smiled ruefully. "Luckily she usually hits what she aims at. We also need people accurate with pistols, preferably different people."

Patty realised she might have an answer to her limited ammo. "Are the Mad Max rifles single shots? I could use one until I need the five quicker shots."

"Two are only shotguns with a copper sleeve and fire pistol bullets. You saw one of those. The other two are single shot with salvaged rifle barrels, but none of them are as accurate as a real rifle." Patty looked disappointed but the others were still keen.

"What about the other Mad Max weapons, the pistols?" Doll hefted the one on the table. "Are they lighter than this?"

"The two like that fire rifle ammo which makes them pistols with a massive kick. The other four pistols are single shot as well, but smaller calibre. In addition, there are the weapons we've accumulated. We have seventy-eight semi-automatic pistols, half a dozen revolvers, four single shots like Finn's and twenty-one shotguns." Harold let the exclamations die down. "A lot of them came from the Mart fight, but we've fought off small groups and fined a few scroats. I've sold some well-worn or small calibre weapons now and then, and some weren't fit for anything but spares."

"That's an arsenal." Ru spoke quietly, almost whispering.

"Not quite, but probably as many as any other gang but Caddi. The Geeks may have more after what they'll have scored when the General bounced, maybe not because a lot of those went into the water. Some of the others would be useless after being in that fire." Harold picked up the big rifle round and tossed it up and down. "We'll need every weapon if there's an attack. The problem is the ammo and spare clips, not the weapons. We used up nearly every round at the Mart. If we had more propellant I could make up more ammo, but we still wouldn't have spare clips. Unfortunately, we need a lot of other things as much as propellant, so if I concentrate on that the other gangs will realise I've got more guns than expected. They'll put the prices up for starters. We also need charcoal for Liz, as much as possible. At least the GOFS gave us powder for the muskets, enough until we build more weapons." Harold stopped, watching them all try to work out the pros and cons.

"So we'll scare the shit out of any attacker with the first volley, but then it drops off." Patty thought hard, then sat back and shrugged. "To hell with it Harold, get the propellant. Buy a lot before anyone has a chance to jack up the prices. They won't know how many guns it's for, will they?"

"She's right." Casper nodded, still eyeing up the big pistol. "Better that the gangs know we have plenty of ammo than having empty guns. We could always have people behind the shooters, refilling empty clips?"

"Better put two behind Bess." This time she hit Matthew properly, but he just smiled.

"I'll still need charcoal for making the Rambos, maces and..." Liz looked around the table trying to work out who knew what. "Harold?"

Harold shrugged, because all this group should know. "Some of you know we've been testing thin machetes, cutlasses, sabres or giant pointy needles. It's time you all knew the sabres have been perfected, but not for sale. You also need to know about Wamil's little secret as well." He explained Wamil's surprise. Patty put her sabre on the table for inspection.

"Can we keep the sabres in the old machete style sheaths so it isn't obvious? I keep the iron bar in there as well so it's hidden." Patty weighed up Ru's Rambo, and her own bar and sabre combination. "I'll keep with these, not a Rambo. Or as well as, if we have enough? How about a smaller, ladylike mace as well?" The rest relaxed after all the doom and gloom stuff, laughing and making jokes about how Patty could hide all the extras.

The following discussion went around charcoal versus propellant, leaving Harold with the minor problem of prising either out of someone. Hopefully any new customers for gun repairs wouldn't know about the local charges, and might even give up clips for pistols. The meeting broke up with Harold reminding everyone that this was all top secret. Even as the rest left, Tessa put the musket back together for the test tonight.

* * *

Tessa managed to keep quiet while Harold found a suitable place in the ruins. The three test shots sounded more like a cannon than most firearms, unless the listener had heard the real thing. Similar loud bangs had happened other nights when Harold tested musket repairs, so there shouldn't be any additional curiosity from Caddi's watchers. With work coming from three directions, even Caddi's men never knew whose guns Harold tested.

The muskets all fired without any problem. Harold inspected the target doors with big white circles on them, and two of the crude iron sights with the white dot on the back were pretty good. Only one needed serious adjustment, because muskets would miss a barn anyway beyond fifty paces. Tessa's excitement left her twitching after she hit one corner of the big white square of wood with the two-two rifle.

Tessa chattered rapidly but as quietly as possible all the way back, only shutting up when she turned on her glows to approach the guardhouse. Once inside the workroom, they put the muskets and rifle on the bench and Harold turned to Tessa. She punched the air and exclaimed "Yes!" Suddenly Harold had his arms full of Tessa and she had a full lip lock. Unfortunately, Harold was also excited, or maybe he'd fancied Tessa, sort of, for years. For whatever reason Harold kissed her back. They held it for long moments, too long for either to pretend they hadn't, before the pair suddenly sprang apart. The light in here, bright so Harold could see the weapons, showed the shock on her face as a scarlet Tessa whirled and ran out of the door!

Damn! Harold sat down, stunned. He'd gone on and on about not buying Tessa for his woman, then he'd gone and grabbed her. Then again Harold hadn't actually grabbed her. No, but he'd had a good firm hold of Tessa and had kissed her a lot harder and longer than friendly. What shook Harold was that Tessa had kissed back—or actually, she'd kissed him first. Did Tessa feel obligated? She kept saying everyone thought that's what Harold brought her for, so why had she done that? Damn!

Harold worked the whole episode around and around his head, until he came to one definite conclusion. If it wasn't for Mercedes playing silly sods with his head and hormones, Harold probably wouldn't be as worried. After all he'd had a couple of mad moments with Liz and Patty, and the world didn't end. But this had happened while he was getting into another woman's pants, or would be if Mercedes wore any! Even worse, if he tried to give up on Mercedes it wouldn't work. The bloody woman would smile, stick out her hip and he'd start flirting and playing grab-ass. Cripes didn't even come close.

*   *   *

Harold wasn't sure how long his brain had been buzzing round when a knock on the door roused him. "Come in." He braced himself but Sharyn

came in, smiling happily. Harold felt about six years old as Sharyn extract-
ed Harold's version of events, and then laughed at him! "It's not funny. I've
only just persuaded Tessa she wasn't bought to, well, for exactly what just
happened."

"I'm laughing at you both. You are a pair of silly sods." Sharyn shook
her head in mock despair. "I knew she'd started to get interested in you,
soft lad. I half expected to wake up one morning and find that one of you
had been sleepwalking."

"That's news to me. Anyway I don't two-time." Harold paused, then
sighed. "I'm not actually one-timing."

"Only because you can't get Mercedes on her own. You do know that
Tessa likes dangerous men, don't you?"

Harold had a full scarlet blush now. Sharyn could always do this to
him. "Well, not put like that." She made Tessa sound like an adrenaline
junky of some sort.

"Well she does, and Tessa knows now I've made her sit down and think
about it. That's probably why she ended up with Stones, but she lost him
when everything went to hell. You came back, but in the Mart you still
seemed like soft lad. Then you did the white knight bit. Tessa found out
that soft lad has a Soldier Boy wild side, one that has all the local bad boys
crapping themselves. She's been reassessing you ever since, even if she's
never admitted it even to herself. I knew because her teasing ramped up,
but you treat her like a china doll and you've got this thing going with
Mercedes." Sharyn laughed at Harold's expression, or maybe the blush.
"Tessa is back there complaining about your timing. If this had happened
a year ago she'd still be in here, finding out just how interested you were!"

"Cripes, Sharyn. There's things a bloke doesn't need to know, especially
from his sister!"

Big sister smiled and patted Harold on the shoulder. "You need to
know that Tessa isn't mad at you, in fact she feels like a proper prat. She
made a big thing about being bought supposedly for sex, and you've been
falling over yourself to prove you didn't. Despite that, and you already being taken, sort of, Tessa says her hormones took over." Sharyn tried to stifle
a giggle, but failed. "She got a bit wound-up about shooting a real rifle, and
then you were stood there all handy-like."

Harold shrugged and stood up. "I'll move my stuff down here. Ow!
No need for that!"

"I'll clip the other ear if you come up with any more stupid suggestions.

Tessa can accept she made a pass at a bloke at the wrong time, but if you move out she'll feel responsible. At the moment, the lass is wondering how to set the clock back about an hour." Sharyn giggled again, without any attempt at stopping it. "She reckons it might be worth a rerun once the dust settles."

A baffled Harold stared at his sister. "What? When the dust settles? Oh. Mercedes?"

"Oh, Mercedes? Yes, Mercedes. Either you will or won't get into her pants or the other way around. Then depending on the result, Tessa might decide she wants to try again sometime." Sharyn's look had a lot of mischief in it now. "Since she reckons you were definitely interested?"

Harold hesitated but he couldn't honestly deny it. "She's not exactly repulsive, you know, and yes, I already worked out I might not have fought too hard. You know, without the buying and Mercedes."

"Well then, can you work with a woman without grabbing her if she gets near?" Sharyn looked a breath away from laughing again.

"Of course I bloody well can!"

"Don't be so indignant. Some gang bosses can't, you know." Harold recognised that tone; Sharyn had switched to having fun. "So that's settled, as long as you can accept bad timing and nobody's fault. Tessa will be over here in a bit to get on with her job." Harold nodded and hoped Sharyn had finished. "Tessa isn't interested in a repeat just yet, maybe never. Can you deal with that?"

Enough was enough. "Stop it!"

"Cripes, Tessa is as screwed up as you are. Talk about pouring out hearts." Sharyn ruffled Harold's hair, making him feel about thirteen. "This one was free but another consultation will cost both of you, big time." She left, still laughing, leaving Harold to wait as instructed.

He'd started wondering if Tessa had backed out, but eventually a slightly flushed, definitely cautious apprentice gun repairer came through the door. She looked at the floor and the table, embarrassed, and sort of hesitated for a few moments, debating. "Did Sharyn explain?"

"Yes, sort of. Look, I'm sorry." Harold knew he sounded embarrassed as well.

"Cripes, I bloody well hope not! I thought you were enjoying it!" They both went a shade pinker and looked away.

"Stop it!" Silence fell again until Harold couldn't stand any more. "I've always liked you, but hadn't thought of you like that, you know?"

"I know. Bitch, weapons, wars, bitch. Just my bad timing. I got a bit excited. Nobody let me shoot before!" Tessa giggled, then stifled it and glanced up. "Can we leave it for now?"

"Not if we keep talking about it." Harold sighed, looking around the room instead of at Tessa. "I'll try to carry on as usual if you do the same, because I don't know what else to do."

"Deal. Now tell me, did it damage any of the muskets?"

"It wasn't that passionate!" Harold held up his hands in apology once they both stopped laughing. "Sorry. I don't know because I haven't checked them since the test. I've been sat here thinking of something else. We'd best split them down and have a look, but keep the bits of each one as a set."

"Why, I thought they were interchangeable?" Tessa's manner became brisker now they'd found a nice neutral subject.

"Maybe, but until we are sure about that, and how accurate they are, we won't take chances." Tessa nodded, then picked up a musket and used a marker to put one dot on each of the components before starting to strip the weapon. Harold and Tessa spent an hour discussing just weapons, while cleaning and checking the three muskets and working on other firearms. Talking through the problems and solutions calmed them, and the pair gradually relaxed again. They packed the marked sets of components in separate boxes after dismantling the weapons. That wouldn't fool anyone who truly suspected, but at a glance the parts would look like any other box of spares. After that, the pair finally finished listing all the Orchard Close weapons by ammunition type, and worked out how much of what calibre Orchard Close needed.

Eventually, both were yawning because it was well past midnight. The pair had managed to move past the kissing, right up to when they finished packing up. Tessa gave Harold a little smile. "Hmm, this is difficult. I'm supposed to forget earlier, but go out there looking as if we did." She put her head to one side and looked at Harold with definite curiosity. "The bitch has never kissed you properly, has she?"

"Mercedes? Cripes, no! Just a quick peck, but not properly because that would really cause the shit to fly. Caddi would probably consider a proper snog breaking the Deal."

"Why did you buy me, Harold?" Tessa wore a little smile because she'd already had two answers, too nice and a friend. Those were before the clinch.

Harold sighed because there was no point in going around it now. "I like you, too much to let the animals have you."

A big smile broke on Tessa's face. "With that, I think I can make sure they all know why we've been in here half the night." She opened the door. "If I need a booster, I'll remember that even if Mercedes gets into your pants, I got first dibs on the lip lock!" Tessa left Harold shaking his head and smiling. That was the teasing Tessa he'd always liked, which didn't help just now. Harold still wore the smile when he left the workshop, so anyone wandering about this late would be convinced.

* * *

Harold needed a bit of space the following day, away from Tessa who still looked a bit embarrassed at breakfast. He went out with the scavengers who were working over the new houses, and used the opportunity to look around the area. His bodyguards followed but gave him some space since Harold was obviously wrestling with something. After a quick check on what the scavengers were finding, Harold called by to talk to Roy and his men. The four experienced fighters were still bitter about having to retreat from the General, twice, but confessed to being bored while waiting for him to attack. They promised to stick to it anyway, because if the General came it would probably be across this water. Instead of going back to the scavengers, Harold decided to explore a bit. He followed the edge of the water towards the Geek border.

Working along the edge of the floodwater, exchanging greetings with the GOFS watchers now and then, Harold found a single railway track. It came out of the water and curved off between the houses, reminding Harold of what the Geeks had said about trailers. He followed the rails in the general direction of their border. Sure enough, the track curved that way and disappeared under the floodwaters that filled the railway cutting along the Geek border. Three huge flatbed rail wagons sat close to the edge of the water, all at odd angles, completely derailed. Another stood nearby, still on the tracks.

Harold couldn't see any rust on the beds so he thought they might be thick ply, which would be useful. He went closer to check, and saw the Geeks had been right about the size and weight of the trailers. One pair of wheels had come loose, rolled across the nearby road, and embedded itself in a car. The casual look at the end of the wagon without wheels turned into a stare, before a big smile broke over Harold's face.

After spending another couple of hours helping the scavengers, Harold went back to Orchard Close with the first van load of plunder. As he arrived, the pickup came bouncing out of the old caravan park, up the access road and around the side of Orchard Close. Out of sight of Caddi's watchers, the caravan springs were heaved over the wall and carried away to Liz's lair. Her extended lair now, as the adjacent garage had been cleared for the smith's new stock.

Bethany met Harold to let him know Caddi's watchers had tried to get a better look. "I told them that we had some target practice scheduled, and they were on the range." She pointed across the rows of potatoes to the four man-shaped targets at the other end, all painted with Hot Rod logos. Harold just laughed, then thought about it and sent a message asking Ru, Patty, and Emmy to bring the dead sniper's rifle to the gates.

Instead of standing about waiting for them he followed the latest load of springs to Liz, finding her rubbing her hands together like a miser inspecting his gold stocks. Harold didn't need to ask if they were suitable, her smile lit up the garage. Harold asked her to come and check on the scavengers tomorrow, keeping it as casual as he could.

Liz barely glanced away from her springs, just commenting that it would stop people collecting things she couldn't use yet. Harold suffered another recital of how she should be able to melt the scrap steel and cast anything, because the Celts could. He butted in eventually to ask her to come early, so he could get back to muskets. At least that diverted Liz, while Harold explained about him checking, testing and checking until even Tessa had got bored with them. Once clear of the smith, Harold went off to sort out the Caddi spy deterrent, and test one potential shooter.

*   *   *

Harold took Patty, Ru and Emmy up into the bedroom of one of the guardhouses next to the gates, out of sight of the Army but with a clear view over the potatoes. The four man-sized targets were clearly visible at two hundred metres, a good distance for amateurs. Patty tried the sniper's rifle and, with the scope to help, showed off a bit with head shots. Harold offered her the rifle, instead of her Winchester, because it had plenty of ammo. As he'd expected, Patty dithered but settled for keeping her Winchester. All that lovely engraving made it a doubly unique weapon, if she could ever flaunt it. Emmy tried the new rifle next, also hitting her target in the "eyes" with both rounds, but pointed out "her" 308 rifle seemed just as good. By now Ru had realised where this must be heading, and started to twitch.

"Your turn now, Ru." Harold pointed towards Patty. "The squad leaders have been assessing everyone during crossbow practice, and Patty put your name top of the list for a rifle. You'll train with a little one to start with, then end up with this or Patty's baby if you do as well as expected."

Patty nodded at a stunned Ru. "I had to train with a little one first. I promise, it makes a big difference. Kneel down there, use the bedside table as a rest." Harold stepped back as Ru knelt, letting Emmy and Patty explain the kick and help Ru get the butt tight into her shoulder. The first shot hit at mouth height, well above where she aimed but almost central. Aiming and shooting a heavy crossbow had been good preparation.

Four shots later Harold stopped them, he'd seen enough. "Remember, Ru, nobody knows who the shooters are. Practice with the little one, especially loading. Patty will teach you, then I'll check on you once you've got the basics. Collect the rifle and ammo from my house in an hour or so, and take them home. One of this pair will call by to drop off a cleaning kit, and teach you how to use it." He watched them leave, chattering and laughing as the usually intense Ru turned downright giggly. Rifles had an odd effect on some people.

Harold stuck a bullet through the fourth target's head, and one through its groin for Caddi's watchers to report on. That should stop anyone connecting the three women with the shooting.

*   *   *

The following morning Liz kept strictly off the subject of caravan springs around other people, but had a little skip in her step. On the way, sat in the cab with Harold, Casper and Ru, she relaxed and chattered about all the lovely weapons she intended making. Liz quietened again while instructing the scavengers on the type of metal plate and small springs she wanted. She also took the opportunity to stress how much any hammer, axe and pick heads would be appreciated, even if they'd been in a fire.

Once she'd finished her talk, Harold asked Liz to come and look at some possible salvage with him and headed towards the railway wagons. He swung wide to approach them without giving her a clear view until the last minute. When the group came round the corner he waved a hand at the derailed vehicles. "See anything you could use?"

"What? The rail wagons?" Liz looked them over. "Those wheels and the ironwork underneath would make all sorts if I could melt them down, but that's not going to happen. Those posts are iron or steel so we could cut them loose for road blocks, but it will cost in gas. What are the beds made of? Is it plate or plywood?"

"What's stopping the wheels from banging on the wagon chassis?"

"Suspension of…" The other three knew when Liz realised what sort of suspension, because she took off running towards the nearest one. By the time they reached her, Liz stood tapping the leaf springs with a knife.

"Ooh, listen to that music. It's all still tempered. I can make all the Rambos you want from this!" Liz stopped a moment as a beautiful smile spread across her face. "I can make a sword that will turn the GOFS green." She whirled, suddenly looking worried. "We have to get these back to Orchard Close, quickly. If someone else sees them they'll be gone!"

"They've been here four years, Liz. The GOFS scavengers have already seen them, but that can't have included their smith." Harold pointed at the wagon with one end up in the air. "I didn't realise either when I first saw the wagons, because the springs are just a tall stack of flat plates without a curve like the others I've seen. If the end of that one hadn't been up in the air without wheels I might have missed it. The only reason I came here was curiosity over some comments from the Geeks, so they've seen them as well and nobody realised."

Casper quickly filled Liz in on the teasing but Liz didn't really listen. The smith kept moving from wagon to wagon, tapping and scraping at the springs. There were fifteen plates on each corner, and sixteen sets of them once they'd stripped all four wagons, enough tempered steel to make an armoury. "Yes, yes, but if you realised, Harold, someone else might. Then there'll be a convoy of pickup trucks in the night and they'll all be gone! We'll have to take the weight off them to get the springs loose. How will we get them over the wall?"

"Calm down Liz." All three of them were chuckling because Liz had been smiling happily and bouncing around for almost two days. That made a welcome contrast to her mood the last year or so, ever since the Hot Rod had threatened to tell Caddi she was the smith. Even killing the scroat hadn't taken the hunted look from her eyes. This Liz seemed a lot nearer to the one who used to have a few too many beers and bemoan the lack of big sweaty men pounding iron. When that thought occurred, Harold couldn't resist a chance to tweak her. "Will you want an apprentice, to help with all the heavy metal pounding this lot will need?"

"An apprentice?" A sparkle grew in Liz's eyes. "Mmm, someone big. All muscles and built like a—smith? I could audition. Get them to take off their shirts and pound metal for a while?" She giggled, then stood up straight and visibly calmed herself. "Before any of that, we have to get these safely into Orchard Close. Preferably without anyone realising what we've got. After all"—she waved an arm to encompass the whole city—"there may be more out there."

"This is where a lorry would be handy." Everyone laughed at Casper because a lorry would cause a gang war. Every warlord would want it. The lack of any big lorries was another of those niggles about the Crash that puzzled Harold whenever he thought about it.

"We will need the pickup, both vans and several runs. The springs can be covered up with some scavenged gear, or well wrapped up in case anyone gets a glimpse." Harold pointed back, towards the scavengers in the new housing. "If we throw some of what they're collecting over the top, nobody will have any idea." Not for the first time, Harold felt tempted to disappear Caddi's watchers, because the precautions were mainly because of them.

"We can break them down to move them." Casper tapped the big band holding the plates together. "Cut through this with a torch and, bingo, a lot of smaller plates."

"Don't you dare! Nobody gets any heat near my lovely tempered spring steel. I'll chisel them off in my lair. Mmm, that might be an apprentice job." Casper started laughing because Liz tried to get between him and the springs, as if he was going to produce a set of burning gear on the spot. "I can make you a trailer to carry them if you find me a plain axle with decent wheels, but it'll bounce all over unless you find some coil springs I can fit?"

Harold wasn't being diverted. "First these springs, then making weapons. Once you've got time, any sort of trailer will be handy."

"These wagons will take some lifting." Casper brought them back to the wagon stripping problem. Car jacks, the bigger the better, went onto the scavenge list, or would once Liz had stopped drooling over her prize.

"All finished with drooling for now, but I'm making no promises about what happens when this lot is back in my lair." Liz looked at the rail wagon reared up almost on end. "We could pull that one over onto its back with the pickup, then the other wheels might fall off as well."

"We really should get back before someone gets curious." Casper looked pointedly at Liz and Ru and chuckled. "Otherwise, with Harold's reputation there'll be all sorts of rumours. Two women and me?"

After another lecture from Patty, the scavengers extended their lists. Bernie had been on the scavenger gangs from the very beginning, and warned the new recruits they'd end up taking everything but wallpaper and floorboards. He wasn't far wrong. To help equip the new refugees from Caddi's war, the list now included any electrical equipment, even if it didn't work. Finn, Charlie or Trev, or their apprentices, were stripping it all down for components.

Even damp bedding, plastic or glass containers without tops, broken kids' toys and brass ornaments were taken. Useable curtains, carpets and furnishings were moved to weatherproof rooms, to be collected later. The old housing near Orchard Close had been damaged by shellfire just after the Crash, then scavenged in stages to meet different emergencies. These houses had broken windows but mostly intact roofs, and had barely been searched by Orchard Close standards. They were a treasure trove!

* * *

Some of the salvage went straight to the big houses in the Annex, to furnish them. Once Casper finished the two long connecting walls to Orchard Close, at least another forty people would move in to join the twenty-five Demons and a dozen other hardy souls. The rest of the work could be finished around the residents. Even when the Annex houses were all occupied, Casper and his assistants would keep raising and thickening the walls until they matched Orchard Close itself. Casper had more help when another rash of refugees turned up, and one claimed to be an apprentice bricky.

This time Susan and June, two of the Coven, smelled real trouble brewing when they vetted the incoming. Among the latest nine were six attractive young women in a group. All six were dressed in the gangster idea of women's clothing, short and tight, and all looked pale and still in shock. The girls turned up with coupons, three belts with knives, two baseball bats and a machete, not that unusual now Mercedes had become careless with weaponry. What put the Coven on alert were a small calibre single-barrelled shotgun with a dozen rounds, and a crossbow with a full quiver.

June quickly gave Harold the story. The six had been collected from their homes by the street fighters of the Murphies and put in a house with a guard. All of them were in a terrible state over what had happened next. They were told that they'd got a new job, because that bastard Caddi had taken the brothel and the usual whores. The place became the gangster brothel, even if the whore part didn't apply because the girls weren't voluntary, or paid.

They'd had five bad days and nights. On the sixth day, a woman dressed for sex arrived just as it was getting dark, and knifed the guard on the front door. She'd dragged the body inside, told the girls to keep quiet and asked where any other Murphies were. After knifing the gangster who'd gone upstairs with one of the girls, she slit the throat of the guard at the back door. The girls gave vague descriptions, but they came down to a scary woman with long red hair and a big, bloody knife. None looked too closely, because she kept cutting bits off the bodies even while telling them to take the weapons and coupons from the dead. The instructions on how to get to Orchard Close and safety were precise.

Harold met the girls briefly to assure them this really was Orchard Close, he really was Soldier Boy, and he'd shoot any scroat who came after them. Their liberation happened as they'd said, because from their state of mind the girls weren't up to killing their captors themselves. After what had happened to them the previous five days, Harold didn't think the girls would have even thought of robbing the bodies without instructions. He told them to never, ever, mention the woman, or they'd be putting her in danger, then left the girl club to supply clothes and sympathy, and get them settled in.

Susan, Rob's missus, carried out a bit more quiet investigation. Several of the young women refugees over the last month had been told about Orchard Close by a single young woman. Mercedes must be using wigs as the reported hair varied in length and colour, but in all cases the mystery woman sounded about the right size. Susan agreed that the identity of the woman must be kept a secret. Those in the know didn't mention Mercedes' name to the girls, or anyone else.

Sooner or later Caddi would find out and kill Mercedes, or she would get him first. The warlord would do it for letting the weapons go, even if the women weren't considered important. Harold stopped further questioning about the woman in case people came to conclusions, but other refugees mentioned getting instructions from her. Others were told by a neighbour who'd heard about Orchard Close from someone else. Mercedes was, as Harold had said, getting reckless.

*   *   *

A message from Caddi asking Harold to visit worried him, but when Harold asked about Mercedes, ET just laughed. The Hot Rods hardly saw her at the Mansion, but rumour said she'd gone on a rampage. All the Hot Rods thought that once the war ended Harold had best brace himself. According to ET, Caddi wouldn't let Mercedes come for Soldier Boy until he'd won, so she'd decided to finish the Murphies on her own.

That sounded like Caddi using the public displays to help spread rumours, and probably encourage his troops. Still, if Mercedes would be out somewhere killing Murphies, that wasn't why Caddi wanted Harold. A casual request for Harold to bring a mace, and one of those new knives, actually reassured Harold. Caddi must have heard about the new goodies. Even so, Harold still felt himself tense up as he started the drive to the Hot Rod stronghold.

Chapter 13:
Novelty Heavy Metal

When Harold arrived, Mack waved the pickup through the gates and inside the Mansion, the first time that had ever happened. Caddi waited to greet them, only the second time he'd done that, which racked up Harold's anxiety. "Lovely to see you Harry. I thought you might be too busy with all those new people." That told Harold one reason for the visit. Caddi considered the Murphy civvies his property, even if he hadn't captured their streets yet, and hated the idea of any escaping.

He smiled quietly, because Caddi couldn't argue with the answer. "They're all from the Murphies, Caddi, and I've got no treaty with them so they aren't runners." Harold offered his weapons to Mack, who only took the pistol and mace and didn't put either in a locker.

"True, but so many of them are young women. Mercedes will be getting very jealous, even if it might be her fault. Considering how many young men she's killing, there can't be enough Spuds left to keep the women warm at night. Maybe that's why they're leaving?" Caddi sounded relaxed, but that didn't fool Harold. The warlord could switch moods in a heartbeat. Caddi waved a hand, directing Harold between two houses then walking beside him. "Such careful young women, coming over all that rubble instead of up the neutral road."

Harold kept his smile, with an effort because they'd moved out of sight of anyone else. He couldn't work out why Caddi needed privacy. "Yes, I've put people on the border to tell them where the boundary runs. They all seem to prefer to play safe, so we've cut them a path through the brambles out past the fields."

"Why Harry, don't they trust my lads to respect the neutral zone?" That was a joke, Caddi's watchers were installed in houses that were technically Harold's. "Whoever you've got spreading the instructions is very good, because Mercedes hasn't found them. The runners all disappear into Barbie territory where we can't follow."

"They aren't runners, just people who have had a bad time lately. Refugees tend to play safe and after all, misunderstandings over an exact border are fairly common." Harold relaxed again, a little. He could play these games all day and Caddi's tone said it was just that, a game. Harold certainly wasn't telling the nasty sod he hadn't sent anyone to spread rumours. "I understand you have some new refugees of your own, young women."

That brought a genuine laugh from Caddi. "True, so true. We captured the Murphy whorehouse so all their whores are refugees. Not that you'll be seeing any of them, they've got a new employer." All the humour left Caddi's face and both he and Mack put hands on their weapons. "Now I've caught you playing away Harry. I know there's no agreement who you repair weapons for, but I'd rather you stopped helping the Spuds."

The tone of voice warned Harold as much as the way Caddi and Mack braced ready for trouble. Caddi had wanted privacy in case this turned violent. "Quite seriously, Caddi, I have never knowingly repaired a weapon for the Murphies. There's been a few from the Barbies, and the Geeks and Barbies passed a few through, but that's it. The rest are the usual." Harold put his hand on his knife and gripped his stick as Caddi started taking a pistol from his belt.

"Calm down Harry, I just want to show you. Tell me you didn't fix this, because the Murphies know fuck all about how to treat guns." Caddi handed Harold the pistol so he relaxed, but not much.

Harold took the weapon, unloaded of course, checked the action and inspected the clip. "Not guilty, but someone who knows his weapons did this. He's used different oil to me, but decent stuff. Unless the Murphies have attracted someone new, unlikely given their situation, they've found a repairer in a neighbouring gang. There have to be others in the city."

Caddi scowled at that, and the gun, but accepted the answer. "I'll pass the news to Mercedes. This time I'll want the bloke still attached to his ears, and preferably still breathing." Volatile as ever, the warlord grinned. "That'll be cheaper than dealing with you." He took the weapon back and put it in his belt. "Have you scored a blacksmith, Harry?"

"What? Why?" That baffled Harold again, because Caddi had obviously expected to catch him out a second time. No wonder the suspicious git had got Harold on his own.

"I went to visit the neighbours, the GOFS." Caddi had his half-smile so Harold braced for the punch line. "I wanted to buy one of these maces I'd heard about. Imagine my surprise when they didn't recognise what I described." He glanced at the mace Mack carried, the one Harold had brought with him.

Harold's little smile didn't look at all innocent. He wasn't worried now so he didn't mind playing Caddi's games. "Fancy that, how strange."

Caddi laughed at him. "So then I went to ask the Freeks." He glanced at Mack, who smiled back. "Guess what, they'd got some, and some local, friendly Soldier Boy had sold them. Better still, they were bragging about their Rambo knives. They'd won some in exchange for cement and steel bars and radio components." Caddi looked pointedly at Harold's belt. "The size of that sheath looks about right, Harry."

"That's because it's for a Rambo." Harold wasn't too worried now because Rambos weren't a secret, even if the smith assumption still seemed odd.

"I called on the GOFS on the way home, and asked about knives." Harold smiled at the enquiring glance so Caddi continued. "They had some very nice knives and I bought a few, but nothing like those Rambos. That meant someone is being very bashful and keeping quiet about making them, and how many suspects did it leave?"

Harold laughed and shrugged. "One, Caddi. It isn't a crime."

"No, but it is intriguing. Could I have a look at that knife you're carrying please, Harry?" It wasn't exactly a request.

"Of course, but I'll want it back. If I lose it I'll get nagged." Harold took a good firm grip on his stick as Caddi took the Rambo from him. "Careful, it's sharp." Mack snorted from the other side.

"I know, I saw one." Caddi waved the knife about, presumably testing the balance. Satisfied, he led Harold to a stack of salvaged timber and chopped a couple of lumps out of it. At least that brought them back into view of the other Hot Rods. Caddi inspected the edge, making a beckoning motion at his house. "It stays sharp as well." A woman came out carrying what turned out to be a pig's leg.

Caddi put the leg on the timber and this time put his muscle into the swing, then again to shear through the bone. "No sign of a nick and it's still sharp. This is very good work. So I'll ask again Harry, have you found a blacksmith?" At a gesture the young woman picked up the two pieces of pork and headed back into the Mansion.

"No, Caddi."

"Are you sure, because Mercedes can't find the blacksmith the Murphies had, and believe me, she's looking." Caddi wasn't happy, and still unwilling to let go of his theory. "That's another one I want breathing."

Harold hoped he'd run far and fast. A blacksmith could get a job any-where. "What's he look like?"

"A bloody blacksmith. Six-two and a brick shithouse. Used to shoe horses and suchlike. Now where the fuck is he because I want him!" Caddi sounded bloody annoyed and that wasn't a request either.

"Running like a rabbit if he knows Mercedes is looking. Nobody like that has come in." Harold looked the mad bastard right in the eyes. "As your blokes have told you." He may as well ask. "I thought you'd got a blacksmith?"

"Yeah but this one's the real deal. The Murphies have got some damn good machetes and knives and he makes them so I wanted him. Shit!" A thought struck Caddi. "So you've already got a proper blacksmith?"

"No, Caddi. What I've got is good steel that is easy to make into blades. We found some in the ruins but when it's gone I'm screwed again. In the meantime we're too skint to keep them all to ourselves." That was a safe statement. All the gangs thought Orchard Close sold everything they could, just to get by.

"No machetes made of this stuff?" Caddi indicated the Rambo.

"Just those knives. We call them Rambos and there aren't a lot of them." Caddi hadn't asked about sabres so that wasn't even much of a lie.

Caddi frowned. "Plus those rifles of course. Fucking great holes at long distance sort of make knives redundant. I got your little message to the lads, the target practice."

"Just getting the sights right on the new one." Harold had hoped they'd pass it on. "I wouldn't want to miss and waste a round."

Caddi scowled, then switched subjects yet again. "What about the clubs?" He pointed at the mace Mack carried. "Are they for sale because Mack would love one? It would take the lock out of a door sweet as you like and if he hits anyone, squish." Caddi had that half-smile back. "Is that more special steel?"

"My metals bloke says it isn't steel, just shaped iron. Nothing magic. You know us, nearly everything we can make is for sale."

"But bloody expensive. My bloke tried making one out of a hammer head and Mack tested it on some bricks. It doesn't handle right, the head had dents in it and the ridge things came off. The Freeks reckon yours are hard enough to smash a shield without being damaged, so your bloke does something different." Caddi held up a hand. "Yeah, and you aren't telling.

Can Mack test that one?"

"What's up Mack? Isn't he buying you any toys these days, or did you break them all?"

Mack grinned and brandished the mace. "Not toys like this, 'Arry. It feels dead right and don't look breakable. Can I bash something to find out?"

"Yes, as long as it's not me? You pay for any breakages." Mack grinned and smacked the woodpile a couple of times. After inspecting the result, he headed for a heap of cleaned bricks, quickly reducing some of them to rubble.

The big man came back wearing a huge grin. "Can I 'ave this one Caddi?"

Caddi took the mace, inspecting the head before swishing it back and forth. "There's no dents or damage and the ridges are still all there. How much if I supply the shafts and some hammer heads?"

Harold finally relaxed because if Caddi wanted to deal, he'd got no more complaints. "Depends on the size of the heads, and what else you've got, and have you got the wire to wrap the handles?"

"Bloody hell, I may as well make them myself! I'd wait until Mercedes got back to help with the negotiating, but Mack might cry if he doesn't get one now." Caddi had a real smile now, heading for the house where they settled down to haggle. Harold made a deal for hammer heads, charcoal, shafts and wire. He came home without either the mace or the Rambo and with orders for more. Harold spent the trip home worrying about Mercedes, as well as the interest Caddi showed in the new refugees and products in Orchard Close. The warlord's closing words hadn't helped.

Caddi had actually told Harold about his deal, sort of. "If Mercedes turns up and chucks her knickers on your bedroom floor, then screws you brainless, that's fair enough. But we've got a deal. After the one night, Mercedes comes back or she's doing a runner. That would break the treaty Harry, and that would be bad." Caddi actually believed Mercedes would turn up at Orchard Close. Harold knew he wouldn't even consider turning her away, and he might not insist she left after one night, or ten.

That took care of keeping Harold's mind occupied on the way home. If Mercedes came to Orchard Close and didn't want to go back to the Hot Rods, Harold knew he couldn't make himself insist. Even if he could physically chuck Mercedes out, Harold wouldn't, because he knew what Caddi wanted the young woman back for. Caddi's comments about the betting didn't help. The assholes were betting on whether Mercedes would top the other woman out of hand, or if Tessa would just get the hell out of the way. A few were betting on Harold keeping both, but only because the odds were astronomic. Nobody bet on Tessa backing off Mercedes.

Harold should have a bit of time to think, weeks or maybe months, because the Murphies had found a way to slow Caddi up. According to the warlord they had abandoned battle lines or concentrations and were relying on hit and run. The Murphy gang members now hid in the rubble, or among the streets they knew and their own subjects. The abrupt change of tactics had already cost Caddi men and time, and had stalled the attack. Without any strongpoints or troop concentrations to hit, the Hot Rods couldn't find a way to break the resistance.

The lack of fixed lines allowed Mercedes to add to her ear collection, but she couldn't get to the bosses. The Murphies were bleeding to death but now they were bleeding Caddi as well, shooting his men from ambush before fading back into the population or the ruins. Caddi suspected somebody new was directing the fighters. The warlord had pushed Mercedes to find the new general, or a weakness that would finish the Murphies and make him irrelevant.

*　*　*

While the Hot Rods fought and died, the Orchard Close pickup and vans burned diesel, running back and forth as the railway springs were retrieved. The sets of springs were very heavy, heavy enough that the workers had to take half the back wall down to get them over. Liz kept hopping around like a demented frog during the work. She still refused to allow anyone to burn through the band holding the spring plates together, or the pins holding them onto the wagons. The rusted pins had to be beaten out with big hammers so no heat came anywhere near her new steel.

The men might not have realised, but Liz gleefully used the opportunity to audition for trainee blacksmiths. The five candidates were willing enough, because the smith wasn't the only female eyeing up the well-muscled men stripping off their shirts. Despite a few adventures getting the wagons jacked up and chocked, the last springs were eventually deposited in Liz's store. Scavengers descended on the wagons, levering up and removing the plywood floors. They also unbolted various bits of ironwork, which disguised what else had been taken.

Liz promised oodles of blades, and selling some of them would buy the extra propellant Orchard Close badly needed. Just in time, because the increasing numbers of refugees made Orchard Close more and more tempting. If Caddi teamed up with the Geek Freeks, the inhabitants would need every weapon and every bullet. The squads trained hard, especially the ones with improved weaponry. Meanwhile, Harold pushed on with building muskets, but carefully with a lot of testing.

* * *

Some of the Murphy refugees came in broad daylight now, usually along the path through the brambles to the fields around Orchard Close. Harold had to put a score of fighters along the GOFS border to direct them, in case Caddi got creative. After interrogating captive Murphy civvies, the warlord now knew the route, but he couldn't intercept anyone and Harold knew why. Once inside Barbie territory, at the first landmark, the refugees found a different set of instructions. The new path twisted through derelict Barbie and GOFS territory, even including cellars with water if they needed to hide out overnight. The Barbies and GOFS must know about the refugees, but made no attempt to stop them. Harold wondered if they'd caught a few but were keeping quiet.

More of the refugees came with weapons, hidden if possible because sometimes they brought firearms. The best of the visible weapons, Murphy-made machetes and good quality crossbows, would be giving Caddi indigestion. The rest varied from pre-Crash high quality steel to new and often amateur attempts.

Four days after Harold's meeting with Caddi, the hammers, axes and shafts started to arrive. The refugees had heard rumours about them being particularly valuable, well worth bringing despite being heavy and unwieldy to carry cross-country. Mercedes must have heard about maces. Refugees now brought any tools they still had, ranging from hand mincers to electric drills, a router, and a professional spray painting kit. Some, like wood chisels or the Stanley stainless steel hatchets, must have been kept well hidden from the Murphy fighters.

It became obvious who Mercedes concentrated on, as only a third of refugees were male and the largest proportion of the females were teenagers. A few had already been abused by Murphies, while others were under pressure to join the brothel. The rest were running before Caddi captured their streets. Rumours about how badly the Hot Rods would treat them, and Orchard Close being safer, probably didn't need much help from Mercedes. At least all those fit young women could go straight out to help Emmy in the fields, allowing the fighters more time to practice.

Two dirty but working nine mil pistols arrived with ammunition. Those were carefully concealed and carried in by two separate teenage girls, on different days, and both came with machetes and belt knives. Better still, both came with spare clips, six in all. These women hadn't been abused, because the gangster pressuring each of them died before he could get physical. The rest of their news brought a little smile to those in the know. The number of Murphies who had died nastily, either in their 'brothel' or after grabbing or threatening a woman, must be having an effect. The gangsters had stopped trying to replace their brothel, concentrating on fighting for survival.

*   *   *

Nearly two weeks after Caddi bought the mace, Alfie called Harold to the Embassy. He arrived to find a limping man, a woman, a young lad and a girl who looked to be in her early teens. Alfie waited with his shotgun. "These are Fredrick, Kathleen and their kids. I've not searched them properly, because of what he said. I thought you might want this to be a secret." Alfie nodded to the man. "Show him."

Both the man and the woman looked at the kids. "Maybe the kids shouldn't hear? We'd rather stay here together, if you can find someone from our area to watch them. Please?" Kathleen took Fredrick's hand as he nodded agreement. "We know some of our neighbours headed your way."

"Sit down, everyone." Harold used the phone before he joined them. "Sharyn? Can you come to the Embassy to meet some visitors, please? Not gangsters. I'll need a refugee to look after a couple of kids. Someone from?" Fredrick supplied their names and the street. "Find one the children will recognise, please." Harold gestured to armchairs.

"I'd rather stand for now." Fredrick looked apprehensive but Alfie nodded, so Harold shrugged and sat.

Alfie picked up two big bags, a workman's leather type and a rucksack, and placed them next to Harold's chair. "One is carpenter tools. You'll want to look in the rucksack when the kids have gone."

Harold waited patiently, trying to ignore Alfie's mischievous little smile. Emmy arrived with Sharyn, no doubt to cover the secrecy part. "Sharyn didn't want to bring someone covered in armour and sharp steel." Since she'd brought Tammy in her carrycot, Emmy definitely looked more reassuring than a fighter despite her pistol and machete. She beckoned to the young woman following her. "A neighbour of theirs. She's one of my new gardening gnomes."

Harold didn't need telling, all the refugees obviously recognised each other. He sent the trainee gnome off to the canteen with the kids, asking her to get them drinks and something to eat. "Fredrick has brought presents." Emmy and Sharyn's curious looks moved to Fredrick and then the bags. Once Harold opened the rucksack, he wanted answers as well. There were two pistols in there, both looking clean and well maintained. "I assume you haven't been keeping these in the attic."

Fredrick gave a nervous laugh. "Not likely. They came from the new men. I didn't do anything, honest." He firmed up. "I was told those would buy a place and keep my family safe."

"Definitely. I'm very interested in whoever had them." Harold knew his smile would look happy, because of his next thought. "I'm half sure I know how you got them." He could already imagine the comments about the presents his girlfriend sent. "Wait a few minutes, drink your coffee, and get your thoughts in order." Harold checked the bag properly, becoming even more curious. There were four spare clips for each of the pistols, all loaded, two good quality machetes, knives, and two almost full boxes of rounds for a rifle. One box were originals while the others looked to have been reloaded with care, not the usual gangster slapdash. The telescopic sights had to be for the same rifle.

As the women sat, that left only Fredrick still standing. The man opened his coat and undid his jeans in spite of the females present, revealing a familiar shape. He had a rifle down his trouser leg! Harold watched it come all the way out and yes, this would be a secret. "Where do I put it?" The man looked apprehensive, holding the weapon as if it might bite.

"I'll take it, Fredrick." Harold took the rifle, checked it over, and found the weapon in lovely condition.

"That'll cause some competition." Emmy had something very similar, at home. "It is, um, one, isn't it?" She bit off sniper rifle.

"Yes, it's a 7x64 hunting rifle, because this scope and ammo must fit and it's written on the boxes. Now shush and let Fredrick sit down and talk." Emmy gave Harold a sour look but shut up.

Fredrick sat and took a deep breath. "I'll just start at the beginning, right?" Harold nodded. "The Murphies are losing their war. It's getting close to our house, but we can't leave. I mean we couldn't. Didn't dare." He took another deep breath and Kathleen leant over to murmur something. It seemed to firm him up. "The Murphies brought two strangers to our house. One man slept in the front bedroom upstairs, while the other man stood outside the door to guard him. The guard slept when the first man went out. Four Murphies picked him up each day. The Murphies brought food for him but Kathleen had to cook it. They said we had to act normal, not tell anyone about him, or they'd do things to the kids. If he got a stomach ache, well, it would be bad." He shuddered, that still bothered him.

"We're safe now." Kathleen glanced at Harold and shut up.

"Yes you are, Kathleen. If you'd rather miss this, Emmy will take you to sort out accommodation?" Harold had come dressed up as Soldier Boy so the meeting might not be reassuring for her. She shook her head so Harold turned back to Fredrick. "Was there anything special about the man? Something different?" Harold wanted to know if the man had been hired in, and if he maintained his own weapons. "Did he fix guns?"

"I don't know. He went shooting, from what the escorts said. He hadn't any gang markings on his clothes, not even a Murphy shamrock. We never heard a name." Fredrick shrugged helplessly. "We tried to keep away. I took their food up so Kathleen never went near them. Some nights the Murphies brought women round, you know?"

Harold nodded. "But then?"

"The night before last, a woman knocked on the door. She said she'd come as a bed warmer for the men, but she didn't have any escort. Some of the women are willing so I let her in." Fredrick looked nervous while Sharyn and Emmy both had tiny smiles. "She had a long coat on but I could see her face, a pretty young thing with long blonde hair. She took off the coat and, well, she was dressed for, you know? She said to make sure the kids didn't hear anything which seemed odd, but kind." Fredrick stopped.

"Tell him." Kathleen glanced at Harold when Fredrick stayed quiet. "She gave us a lovely smile and went upstairs. We heard voices then the bedroom door. After a bit the door opened again. We heard the guard say something. She answered but it was drowned out by a thud and clatter." Kathleen stopped and both her and her husband looked pale.

Harold didn't need telling. "She'd killed them."

"She came downstairs with blood all over her blouse and skirt, and her legs and arms and boots." Fredrick swallowed hard, something between horror and disbelief on his face. "She still looked happy, in spite of the blood and that big knife. I thought she would kill us next. Instead she told us the Murphies would blame me, and told us where to run and how to hide everything. She promised the Murphies would be too busy to chase us." He glanced at Kathleen. "She told Kathleen to rouse the kids quietly and pack our gear. To take tools rather than kettles, because you'd fix us up?" Harold nodded, he'd make sure they got a full set.

Sharyn butted in, smiling reassuringly because Harold looked a bit forbidding dressed like that. "You'll get everything you need. Bedding, furniture, the full trip, even if the actual rooms might be a bit cramped."

When Kathleen smiled and nodded, Fredrick sighed in relief and continued. "She took me upstairs to get all those weapons. I had to search the bodies, take their coupons and their belts, ammunition, everything. She told me how to hide the rifle. There are spies near here?" Harold nodded again. Fredrick shuddered again before continuing. "The men were lying in pools of blood. While I collected everything, she started cutting the bodies up, cutting bits off. She followed me downstairs and gave us instructions on finding this place, and a route out that avoided the front lines. Then she wiped the blood off her face and boots, put her coat back on to cover up all the rest, smiled again and left. So did we." He flopped back in his seat. "We stayed in a cellar last night, right where she said it would be, and came in today."

"We are safe now, aren't we? She said we would be, and Rosalyn when she's older?" Kathleen looked hopefully from one to the other.

"Too true." Sharyn nodded towards Harold. "I'm his sister. I'll get you settled in personally, and he'll deal with the protection bit. All you have to do is forget it happened."

"It's all over now. You can't forget the woman and the weapons, but never mention them to anyone." Harold tapped the rifle. "This is a secret and so is how you got it." Fredrick nodded jerkily, followed by his wife. "Good. Take your tools with you. Stephan will welcome you like a long-lost brother, because he's snowed under with carpentry work. If you help him that'll cover your contributions, and leave you extra coupons for the kids." Both Fredrick and Kathleen looked relieved.

"We'd rather the kids didn't know about the woman and all that." Kathleen waited for agreement, then the pair followed Sharyn to collect their children and find a meal and bed. They'd probably be sleeping on someone's settee tonight, until more scavenged beds were dried out. Fredrick's first job would be helping Stephan build bunk beds, so Patty's twenty-five Demons could squeeze into one six-bedroomed house. Every one of the six houses in the Annex was needed, because right now some of the single flats in Cherry Tree House held a family of three or four.

Harold saw a gleam in Emmy's eye as Fredrick and Kathleen left, and braced himself for some teasing about girlfriends and presents. Later he told the rest of his top advisors about the 7x64 hunting rifle, explaining what Caddi told him about the gun repairs. He'd already mentioned the change in Murphy tactics. Now they all agreed that Mercedes had killed the new Murphy sniper, and possibly the alternative gun repairer. Harold rode out more humorous abuse about his girlfriend's idea of gifts, begging off discussing what he intended giving her in return. He'd love to give her a Rambo, decorated with a big bow, but that might take some explaining.

Nobody had much time to dwell on Mercedes because the refugees kept coming. The weekly queue at the armoured bus to collect coupons became a little longer every fortnight, as the newcomers went in to register their new address and thumbprint the receipt. Everyone had to collect their coupons personally or they didn't get any, so Caddi's watchers tried to count how many filed out of Orchard Close. As the numbers crept up above two hundred, that brought other changes.

Harold now walked around with a pistol, Rambo knife and a machete as well as his Soldier Boy stick. His own people insisted, to back down any challenges and reassure the newcomers. He also had to have two almost permanent bodyguards. One or sometimes both were female, because many female trainees took up Wamil training and some became very dangerous. Ru became a vicious infighter and a very good shot, at least partly due to her fierce dedication to training. Her close escape from the rapist drove her. She lost her wary edge around Orchard Close men, but Ru still sharpened up near any visiting gangster. Once the diminutive fighter started thinking, rather than reacting to scroats, Patty made her the official Deputy Demon. A few of the Asian Demons started calling her Myrtyua or Aneka Myrtyua but Ru didn't answer to it. Eventually someone told Harold it meant many deaths, or something similar, a reference to the wide variety of weapons Ru practiced with.

Because of the status boost, Harold had to stop going to the Mart. Someone might take the chance to attack a 'real' gang boss who came unarmed along the bypass. Emmy pointed out that Caddi, the General, or someone like them might start a war by taking out the gang boss. That was how Caddi opened his campaign against the Murphies. All an attacker would need was a decent rifleman in the abandoned houses, three hundred yards from the bypass across the exclusion zone. Harold knew Emmy, Patty, Roy, and probably Ru or Alfie could do the job, and conceded.

Casper usually supervised visits to the Mart now because of his size, and took big men including all Liz's potential metal beating apprentices. Other men went as well, including some without unarmed combat training because the volume of shopping had doubled. The shoppers started going the other way along the bypass, to SainsMorr Mart, on the week they didn't visit TesdaMart. The soldiers didn't mind because most gangsters went shopping any time they wanted, armed to the teeth. The Orchard Close shoppers were still searched, so they had to rely on the unarmed combat specialists until they could unscrew their iron bars. So far, apart from a few minor skirmishes, they'd got away with it.

* * *

When Harold suddenly received notifications about the issue of new computer games, delivered by a man in a small car, it meant the shoppers could avoid those days. The man never actually spoke to Harold, or came inside Orchard Close, just dropped off a leaflet and drove away. The Coven suggested Harold had now got a big enough gang to make it onto some list. In late August, Soldier Boy made it onto another list. One morning, four very clean, smart SUVs with dark windows pulled up at the bottom of the road to the gates. A Hot Rod followed in a smaller car. He beckoned to the watchers, driving off with them down the road towards the Mansion. By now Harold had arrived at the gate.

A short, slim man, dressed in new or almost new jeans and a plaid shirt, climbed out of one vehicle and walked up the access road. He stood in front of the gates and turned slowly on the spot with his arms out, the universal declaration that he was unarmed. He had no knife, which made him more unarmed than the gangsters ever were. "I would like to speak to Soldier Boy."

"Speaking. You are?" Harold wondered because that wasn't a gangster or even a local voice. He had clear diction and the man's accent sounded good enough for the BBC, even old style BBC.

The man gave a small smile. "I am usually known as Dealer." His smile interested Harold, a slightly mocking smile that invited him to share the joke about all the bullshit names. Harold didn't think the same smile would go down well with Caddi, which meant the man knew something about Soldier Boy being different. "Probably because I make a lot of deals."

"What sort of deals?"

"That would be better discussed in private." Dealer raised a hand. Eight men climbed out of the cars, quickly followed by the four drivers. All of them had Army buzz-cuts and wore suits and shades. Harold would bet all twelve were armed under those jackets. "I spend a lot of coupons on protection. Advertising to everyone might mean I needed many more men. Could we speak privately, please?"

"We don't deal in flesh or drugs. If it isn't either, come on in and we'll talk. Privately." Dealer didn't even hesitate. Once through the gate he held his arms out again but Harold shook his head. "You're not carrying any more than the nutters do. If you are and you use it, you'll be committing suicide." Harold indicated the people walking about nearby. Nearly everyone, man or woman, wore a knife while many had a machete, a pistol, or carried a crossbow. The guards, of course, carried them all.

Dealer took a slow look round but didn't look particularly worried. "Definitely different, especially the mixture of sexes. Are you expecting trouble?"

"No. All my people carry weapons if they wish and are trained if they ask." Harold led the way into the Embassy, offering a beer from the crate. He only used one room now, the rest of the house had been furnished for refugees. Casper had thickened the dividing wall, making the room smaller but more or less sound-proofing it for private conversations.

"No big house?"

"No marching a stranger through Orchard Close, where he might see too much before I know just who he is. I can sort out coffee or tea if you prefer it?" Harold felt twitchy. He would have pegged the man as official, government, except the government didn't come into the city. That had to be a deliberate act, along with the FBI act by the bodyguards.

The man raised the bottle. "This will be fine, thank you. I am known locally as Dealer, and I do make deals. You have just appeared on my list of people who might be interested. Do you require percussion caps, primers, propellant or powder for reloading ammunition?" Dealer produced that little smile again, probably at the look on Harold's face. "I also have a limited number of empty brass cases, and I can source clips for some weapons.

Possibly some very good ammunition for the right price."

Harold sat there gobsmacked. Orchard Close propellant came from other gangs as part of Harold's gun fixing trade. The gangs sometimes offered reloads, but they tended to skimp on the filling and use damaged brass so Harold preferred to load his own. He'd spent hours wondering why the gangs always had plenty, and now it turned out to be a bloke called Dealer. "The other gangs keep you a deep dark secret."

"So will you, or I won't come back. I talk through the possibilities with the gang boss and nobody else. One on one without any guards. We make the actual deal out there, and you can bring a trusted man for that." Dealer smiled again and this one had real humour. "Armed to the teeth if you wish, because my man will be."

"What do you want in trade?" It wouldn't be beer, or soup in jars.

"If you've got a Rembrandt or a Rodin tucked away, I can make you a really good offer?" Harold laughed at him. "No? Oh well, I live in hope. There are still people who will buy them. Gems of course but only good ones. Bulk gold in ingots but I will test it first. Gold jewellery, ornaments or other paintings. A Banksy would be wonderful but I doubt a single one survived."

Harold laughed again. "Wrong place, Dealer. We have plastic containers with sealing lids, glass jars with tops, good soup, real rabbit burgers, the best homemade beer and some novel ironware."

"Definitely novelty ironware. I like the maces and definitely want to discuss the knives, or are they short swords? Someone told me they are called Rambos and I would love to see one properly. I might buy a small amount of beer, judging by this." Dealer paused, just for a beat. "Do you sell the guns you make?"

"Naughty. Someone has been indulging in the Barbies' most infamous product. I fix guns but I can't build them." Harold laughed again and hoped it sounded natural. So much for secrecy.

"Odd that. Nobody can any more. How good are your repairs?" Dealer still wore a little smile, the one that invited Harold to share a joke.

Harold duplicated the little smile. "You know, because you've asked."

"I've got some idea, and I might do a deal over repairs in the future. I've just added black powder for muskets to my product line, and understand you might be interested?" That had to be a probe. Muskets were very new and publicly Harold hadn't got any yet.

"Not unless I get into a war, because I traded for enough to keep us going. I am interested in propellant for reloads and maybe some brass, if I can find anything you want." Harold wanted to know the propellant prices, if only for trading with the gangs. Black powder as well, because if he made a lot of muskets that would be important.

"I've heard that you are responsible for the number of muskets in use around here." Dealer raised a hand as Harold opened his mouth to object. "Not building them, repairing them, because up to now nobody in this part of the city had tried. They are slow to reload, short ranged, and nobody understood their shock value so most people considered them useless. There aren't a huge number in use, just a few here and there, but now the gangs on the receiving end are searching for them. Then there are maces, as I've just seen, and Rambos. You appear to have some history buffs among your people."

"I do, and they have been very helpful."

"Lucky man, or is it luck? I have already been told you have more than your share of resourceful people." Dealer still wore that little smile. "Some of your neighbours get a little annoyed when the subject comes up."

"It's not luck. They could have their own experts." Harold waved towards the rest of Orchard Close. "It's called freedom. People get very excited and surprisingly productive when they get a taste." Harold had started getting a bit fed up of the joke now.

Dealer definitely looked intrigued at that. "I can imagine. If you won't relieve your people of their ornaments, or your girlfriend of her jewellery, I will make you an offer for Rambos and maces. What are they made of?"

"My friends don't have jewellery or valuable ornaments, or they would probably volunteer them. They would probably give me the shirts off their backs to make this place safer. My metals person uses very good steel in the knives, and very solid iron in the maces." Harold gave Dealer a little smile and some payback. "As someone has already told you."

"True, but better than that they are also distinctive and nasty looking. I travel all over the city. A long way from here both of those items will make me a substantial profit. An even bigger profit if the quality is as good as I am told. Not as much as firearms repairs, those will buy you more than any steel weapon." Dealer rubbed his forefinger and thumb together. "Then there are always coupons of course."

"I'm not sure how we manage a deal on firearms, because usually the price depends on what I need to do? As for the Rambos, our supply of steel is limited but we can spare a few." Harold had started wondering how a bloke with powder and propellant could drive around the city openly dealing with the gangs.

"If you repair a personal weapon, that will get us started. I'll collect the weapon and pay next time. Please don't be tempted since all my people are similarly armed." This time Dealer's smile had some steel in it.

"That makes absolutely no sense."

"It's an automatic weapon. Not Army because they are very fussy about that, and not an AK for the same reason." Dealer still had a smile but seemed more watchful now, looking for the flash of avarice no doubt.

Harold thought that honesty would be the best policy. "I don't want one. I'll fix yours if I can, but we are too close to the Army for any automatic weapon to go off. I won't even test fire it except on single shot." Harold glanced up towards the bypass and remembered the not too subtle hints Sarge had dropped. "My personal bet is that there's artillery on call for little incidents like that, or possibly a helicopter with napalm."

Dealer's smile widened a little. "Good guess. Well in that case I might have some very lucrative business for you. Quite a few nutcases out there have a favourite toy that doesn't actually work. It's difficult to find a repairer who won't try to steal automatics."

Harold stared, because that caught him out. "That doesn't sound like a safe idea. You are giving nutters automatic weapons?"

Dealer laughed, without a hint of that sly undercurrent. "It's the best way to get them killed, preferably after selling them a lot of expensive ammunition. The worst of them won't be able to resist running around blazing away. They think a man with an AK is bullet proof." Dealer sobered, looking at Harold without any smile at all. "But they aren't, are they?"

Harold smirked, fairly sure Dealer already knew Soldier Boy's reputation. "No. Nobody is bulletproof. My neighbours understand that, which keeps me and mine safe."

"Nor is your tank or your battle trailer, I understand, even if they come closer than many." This time Dealer had just a little question in his voice and look.

"An Army bullet would go straight through the plate. Someone made a better version that might have stopped even them, using old target plates from a range." Harold let his own little smile come, a totally genuine one. "They didn't do much to stop the Eurofighter that came calling."

"I heard. Just to stop any unpleasantness, I should tell you that your tank may not be bulletproof but my cars are. The real deal, pre-Crash, just in case someone is ambitious. I tell them all so there's no excuse if they scratch the paintwork." Dealer had answered Harold's unasked question, sort of.

"Cripes! How come none of them have swamped you for the cars alone?" Harold couldn't get his head round it. A real armoured vehicle should be irresistible.

"Automatic weapons in bulletproof cars is a deadly combination, because nobody has any real anti-tank weapons any more. We've had a couple of gangs try. They bounced, messily, and one now has trouble finding ammunition. The other one didn't have enough men left to survive their neighbours." Dealer straightened, becoming much more formal and business-like. "It's been fun, but now I should get back to earning a crust. I don't get to visit a new gang leader very often these days, and even then they have usually just inherited from the deceased. This is my first new territory in almost two years."

"How does the actual trading work?"

"You bring what you'll trade to one of those houses down the road, out of sight of the nosy. We agree on how much of what you want, and work out how you'll pay. Just you and one very trusted lieutenant who can keep quiet." Dealer chuckled as he stood up. "You have knocked down everything nearby so the meeting will be fairly obvious, but not what it's about."

"The ruined house on its own, about a hundred metres away on the other side of the road, will do nicely. We left that one deliberately, for trading, before we started the open door policy. It'll take me a little while to see what we can raise. Half an hour?" Harold had no idea how much Orchard Close could spare, but real brass for the Winchester would be very handy. So would some extra propellant, it had to be cheaper this way. While he was dreaming, maybe some clips? "Would you all like a beer while you wait? A free one."

"My men would appreciate that, thank you. Half an hour." Harold escorted Dealer to the gate and watched him walk back to the cars. After warning the guards not to point anything obvious at the cars, Harold phoned Liz and Casper for starters. A guard went to find a couple of Demons who were off duty. They were to dress sensibly, not for fighting, and take beer and a dozen mugs to the cars.

* * *

Harold phoned to ask Patty if she'd come fully dressed to go shopping with prejudice, but wouldn't explain. A frantic discussion followed with Casper, Doll, Sharyn, Tessa and Liz, because Harold had no intention of keeping this from his inner circle. Runners scattered to collect maces, Rambos and a score of Liz specialty crossbow bolts, because Dealer had said distinctive and dangerous. Liz could make more artwork, and as many Rambos as Harold wanted just now.

The knives for Wamil were suggested, but Harold didn't know if this bloke had loose lips about where the stock came from. Another time he might offer one of each. Sixteen Rambos and two dozen maces, most of the current stock, went into a wheelbarrow. Liz added two big bronze ornaments she'd been going to melt down. A woman and a dragon, and both were lovely, which was why they hadn't gone into the melting pot yet.

Harold didn't see half the scavenged goods these days, but Liz would pass word to the groups to find her more ornaments if these traded. The scavengers would look for hidden jewellery in future so that Liz could turn the gold into ingots. The blacksmith hoped Harold could buy brass cases, because she still didn't fancy making them. Sharyn brought a selection of the jewellery the Coven held, either to sell to residents or to trade for food if the coupons weren't enough. Since she kept the stocks, not even the Coven would know if Harold bought ammo with some of it. Tessa put a battery CD player on the barrow, with a CD of Jilli singing a dozen songs.

Patty turned up armed to the teeth, including her baby in its custom tasselled sheath. If she couldn't flaunt the weapon, Patty wanted to flaunt the disguise. She asked how she could go shopping dressed like this, unless it was to Beth's? Everyone there laughed at her until Tessa explained. Harold stuffed one of the Mad Max 50s in the back of Patty's belt, under her jacket alongside the pistol already there. "For shoplifters, because I reckon the smartarse will bring a bodyguard in Kevlar."

Harold put a pump action shotgun in the barrow for himself, covering it so the Army didn't get agitated, while Patty carried a crossbow. She slung her Winchester sheath down her side where it might be a quiver. Harold put a .45 revolver and a nine mil pistol in his belt. Dealer said to come armed so both wore machetes, Rambos and carried a mace. After all, Harold could always throw those into the trade if necessary. Patty swapped out her sabre for a good quality machete, so she could sell it.

Harold had no idea where Dealer came from, or if he'd be back, so he wanted to get as much ammo or propellant as possible while he had the chance. The bloke's stockpile might be enough to tempt some gangs to combine and run right over any defenders, regardless of the armoured cars and automatics. That would leave Harold paying gang prices again.

*   *   *

Dealer waited while Patty went in to check the room, then came out to wave Harold forward. Dealer's guard followed them in, producing a little machine pistol like those the police used to have. So did Dealer. They both wore loose waterproof jackets over their clothes to conceal the automatics from the Army. Harold picked up the shotgun, letting it almost aim at Dealer's knees. Patty dropped her crossbow and swung her sheath round, putting her hand in the end. The Winchester barrel pointed at the guard's groin.

Harold looked pointedly at the two automatic weapons. "Maybe we are both heavy on weapons for a friendly discussion. Those little sods are much too handy for my peace of mind, and even I can't miss with this and it's not birdshot. Patty can't miss with that either, not at this range, so how about we sort of calm down?"

Despite the weaponry, Dealer seemed more interested in Patty. "What is that, exactly?"

"Winchester 30-30 underlever. Not automatic, but the next best thing." Harold smiled just a little as the guard tensed. "Even Kevlar might not save you at this range, not with her ammunition."

"Maybe not. We wouldn't want to find out, so perhaps you are right. We could lower the heavier firearms?" Dealer gestured at the guard, who hesitated before hanging his arm and the machine gun straight down. Patty's weapon never wavered. Dealer looked her over, and smiled. "I tend to go over the top at first, just to warn the ambitious types. Since your bodyguard looks more civilised than most, maybe we could ease off a little more?"

"One in each corner of the room?" Harold glanced at the distances. "Far enough away so we all get a warning if someone gets uncivilised."

Dealer looked round the room. "I think so. Except that one, because now I just have to know if it is what I think. Especially in a sheath like that." Dealer nodded at Patty. "Hello. I am both surprised and delighted to see you. You are a vast improvement on most bodyguards."

"So I've been told. People keep offering me a job." Patty eased the sling off her shoulder without the muzzle wandering much. "Boss?" Patty must be in full bodyguard mode if she'd started calling Harold boss.

Harold looked at Dealer first. "Providing the weapon stays a secret?"

For once, Dealer didn't smile at all. "Consider this room a confessional. In my business, I can't afford to have loose lips."

Turning to Patty, Harold nodded. "Pull the sheath off carefully to let the nice man see it, but only once the rest of us get rid of the heavy artillery." Which is what they did. As the bodyguard put his automatic in the corner, Patty placed the Winchester on the cloth Harold had taken from the barrow. She took hold of the end of the sheath, removing it without getting near the trigger.

"Very nice. There aren't many underlevers about and with all the fancy engraving, that's a custom job. The barrel work has been damaged, but not too much so would you like to trade it?" Dealer hadn't mentioned buying or selling firearms before, or not after the probe about making them, but now he sounded dead serious.

Harold laughed when Patty stiffened. "She'd kill me. I'd like some brass for it, if I can afford it. It was damaged and only came with a few rounds."

"The barrel? Slow, careful work, straightening one of those. Does it work?" Now Patty laughed and Dealer smiled. "Of course it does or it wouldn't be here. I'm surprised your bodyguard wants to keep a weapon like that a secret."

"I told the owner it was scrap and took it for spares, because I didn't think the barrel would straighten. He'd be a bit annoyed if he found out." Which was a bit of an understatement. Caddi would burst a blood vessel.

"I can understand why. Do you need brass for anything else?"

"Yes please, a few fifty calibre rifle, and do you have any 410 shotgun cases? Then I'd like some propellant for modern weapons." Harold pointed to the contents of the barrow. "If I can afford it."

"You've got a fifty-cal rifle? I thought there were only two and the one this side of the city ended up smashed. Badly. If you repaired that, you're a gunsmith." Dealer had suddenly become watchful and very serious.

"No, it's a Mad Max." Dealer kept that look so Harold explained. "A weapon made from bits. In this case part of a fifty calibre rifle barrel but the actual firing mechanism is something else. Nothing any manufacturer would put a name to."

"A rifle?"

"No." Harold sighed because from his face, Dealer wasn't letting it go. "I don't want any sudden moves, all right?" Dealer and his guard nodded so Harold reached for the Mad Max in the small of Patty's back. The guard suddenly had a very modern pistol in his hand, pointed at the floor. "Don't get excited because this is single shot. I'm going to unload it without pointing at anyone. Right?" Harold spoke to Patty as well because she had a hand inside her jacket, no doubt on one of her nine mil pistols.

"That's a long pistol barrel." Dealer snorted in amusement. "God knows what the rest is." He glanced over at the guard. "When the breech opens, lose the Glock." The bodyguard looked unhappy but resigned.

"That's something well under half a badly damaged rifle barrel. Something big mangled the actual mechanism. The rest is two blocks of iron hinged together, with a chamber between them filed to take a rifle round because it came with five empties. The trigger mechanism and hammer came from a ruined revolver, and the grip is custom carved by our carpenter to help with the recoil. It can be braced on a shoulder or maybe a hip." Dealer nodded so Harold let the block hinge sideways, taking out the long, fat round. "There, no magazine so it's safe." As the bodyguard put the Glock away, Patty brought her empty hand out of her jacket.

Dealer relaxed a little. "The damage came from a sledgehammer, apparently. I told the owner to use the rest as a club. Why is the bullet red?"

"It's hardened and then painted with nail varnish. For Kevlar."

Once again, the guard tensed slightly. "That's Teflon. Teflon coated bullets work on Kevlar." The bodyguard thought hard. "I've never heard of using nail varnish. Does it work?"

Harold grinned because he'd asked Patty the same question when she'd suggested it. "I've no idea but with luck we'll never need to know."

"You can make metal jacketed rounds?" Dealer also looked closer at the long red round.

"No. Hardened steel core centre in a lead bullet." Harold tapped the metal plates covering his jacket. "People are armouring up."

"Right, I'm convinced. Not a gunsmith but good enough for what I want. Can a man bring in the weapon for repair?" Dealer noticed Patty's hand twitch towards her belt. "His hands will be empty, and he'll hand the bag to your bodyguard for her to take a look."

"Okay, but just for your information there are rifles aimed this way. If you two come out without us then you will die. It would be silly to pull such a complicated stunt for a few coupons and these weapons, but some people are well past silly." Harold didn't think that Dealer worked like that, but these were not trusting times.

"Ah. Ditto. We may have to exit hand in hand." Dealer looked from the guard to Patty. "I'll swap dancing partners?" The bodyguard smiled and so did Patty, but neither answered.

Once the bag came in, Patty opened it to show another of the little automatics. When Harold inspected it, as asked, the guard didn't even put a hand near his pistol. Somehow the tension seemed to have eased. Harold wasn't sure when he'd passed a test, but both he and Patty obviously had. "If I fix this I'll be looking for empty clips in payment. If you've got them? Maybe loaded clips?"

Harold almost held his breath but Dealer didn't hesitate. "No problem if you tell me what weapons need clips. I can supply reloads or original ammunition, though the prices will be different of course." Harold gave the makes and models for empty clips, deciding on new, empty brass to make up any shortfall. Original rounds and even reloads were expensive. While they talked, the guard started asking Patty about the Winchester, how it handled and how many rounds it held. Whether the rounds had hardened centres might have been more than casual interest.

Soon Dealer and Harold were busy haggling over powder and brass and heavy metal. According to Dealer, all the maces and Rambos were headed well away to the other side of the city, so as not to spoil Harold's local trade. Dealer would sell two or three of each to gang leaders, who would pay top price for them as poser but effective bodyguard weapons. The name of the Rambos made a good selling point. The maces and Rambos carried by Harold and Patty went into the barrow to be traded. Dealer pointed out that if Harold had anyone who could manage some engraving, a bit of fancy work on the Rambos would improve the prices.

Dealer paused and frowned at one item. "Crossbow bolts?" Harold pulled one from the bundle to show the point. "Good Lord, what is that?"

"That is a special, and each one is unique. A lot of gangsters around here worry about finding one in their leg." Patty smirked as the guard leant in a little and grimaced at all the little sharp spikes and hooks. "We don't have to hide crossbows."

Dealer looked fascinated and definitely curious. "I would have thought in their leg would be the least of their worries."

"No, because this is what happens when a metal worker has artistic leanings, and a vicious streak." Harold saw Patty's smile grow as he continued. "They are designed so that removing the bolt costs the victim the limb."

Dealer inspected the point again. "I can see that. How well do they work against that jacket for instance? Doesn't the, ah, artwork affect penetration?"

Harold smiled sunnily because Patty had tested a few for just that reason. "Not much at a hundred yards. The extras tend to shear off if they hit something hard enough but the point keeps going. Those using the crossbows pride themselves on accuracy, so if some scroat plates their body the shooters aim at any unprotected bits. There are a lot of big blood vessels in limbs, and as a bonus, intense pain is incapacitating."

The bodyguard actually flinched slightly. Dealer gave Harold a long look. "That is a particularly nasty mind-set."

Harold held his eye. "Not if you've just escaped one pack of animals, and another lot try to get you. Many of the best with a crossbow are women. They will not hesitate."

The chuckle came as a surprise. "That solves a puzzle. Sanctuary is real, even if it turns out to be called Orchard Close. There are vague rumours about you in the strangest places." Dealer's face showed just a little annoyance. "I hadn't connected the dots, even after seeing the armoured vehicles and realising you were the ones on TV. I'm usually a bit quicker than that. How good is your armoured vehicle against something that isn't an Army bullet?"

"Crap against anything but plain lead pistol ammo. Luckily a lot of people only use that, and skimp on propellant." Harold opened another of the bags on the barrow. "We've collected a couple of other things to trade as well. Are these ornaments the sort of thing you want?"

* * *

The trading took a while. Harold tried to push the prices up, but had no idea if he'd been stiffed. Both bronze ornaments were accepted, as were several brand new pairs of impractically high-heeled shoes. Harold had no idea who'd volunteered them. Dealer produced a loupe to look at the jewellery, rejecting over half the gems. He offered to take the settings, or any other scrap gold, providing he could test it first. He liked the CD of Jilli singing, promising to use it to tempt other customers.

Gradually the gear in the barrow moved over to Dealer's side, to be replaced with items Orchard Close needed. Unsurprisingly, Harold found that the other gangs had always stiffed him over propellant, though it still wasn't cheap. Percussion caps and primers weren't cheap either when he asked. Harold didn't need any, but not asking a price would have been strange. He parted with a few coupons, but few enough that he thought he'd done all right. Next time, Dealer assured Harold, there might be a few gang firearms to fix. Dealer would bring them, and make a decision when Harold produced the repair.

Harold's purchases went into the barrow with the bagged broken weapon and his shotgun, all covered with the cloth. Nobody held hands as they left, even if Patty offered with a smile, but Harold and Dealer came out of the door like Siamese twins so nobody ended up shot. Harold and Patty headed straight for the gun room to hide the automatic. Two of Dealer's men went into the house to remove the trade goods, then the four cars left.

Harold had a long talk with his trusted lieutenants. The notifications about games at the Mart and Dealer's visit arrived at almost the same time, so they must get the same information. The trigger had to be the numbers of residents, which meant a bloody great leak from the government somewhere. Either that or Dealer was official, which nobody wanted to even consider. None of them wanted to find out the government kept feeding ammunition into the conflicts.

Harold had tried, but he couldn't get any hints about the other gangs. The impromptu meeting agreed that being discreet had to be part of Dealer's stock in trade, underlined by nobody ever telling Harold where their propellant came from. That came as a relief because Harold didn't want word spreading about Soldier Boy making crude firearms. He definitely didn't want Caddi to come looking for the Winchester. In retrospect, they agreed that Dealer probably already had other weapons repairers in the city, but wanted options. With a smirk, Emmy pointed out he'd probably just lost one local repairer, compliments of Harold's girlfriend.

* * *

Harold didn't have much time to reflect on Dealer's visit. The Barbies were pushing hard to get their transmitter repaired, but had promised not to attempt a kidnap. Three times, groups of women came to look at the partial transmitter and talk to Trev, always with Skipper and her special radio knickers. Real bargaining began because the bewigged blondes were absolutely serious. If Barbie Radio went back on the air, Harold could empty the music shop of instruments and sheet music.

Despite Harold pushing hard, the Barbies didn't want to part with any music CDs. They might need that bargaining power later. "What will interest you, maybe prise something loose?"

"As the actress said to the choirgirl?" Cherry let her eyes drift over Ru and Patty and back. "You won't pay." She suddenly grinned, hopefully. "Unless you've got a spare musket?"

"What makes you think I've got any?"

"Common sense? A GOFS with loose morals said you'd taken musket powder in part payment for some repairs." The Barbie looked decidedly smug. "The border guards, ours and theirs, sometimes find it more fun to guard from the same bed."

Harold had two muskets now, the original type. Both had been given in part payment for other repairs, for spares because they were useless, but he'd fixed them. "So what might a musket get me? They're slow to reload and a long way from accurate."

"But scary. A big weapon like that, all that sound and fury, will certainly get you places the actress didn't expect." Cherry's smile grew more calculating. "With two, you might be allowed to get downright adventurous."

Harold laughed, he had to because the Barbies were funny in this mood. "We'd want to run riot in the music shop."

"You want to get at the whole choir?" Her eyebrows shot up in fake astonishment. "Greedy." Cherry's smile faded, becoming more serious. "For two muskets in full working order, we could let you have a rummage through some sections. We'd keep our favourites."

"As the choirgirls said to the actress? Deal. Let us know what genres and we'll put together a shopping list. If you let us have extras we'll let you have live versions in return, sung by Jilli?" Choirs and actresses didn't come into the following discussion on genres, and what a live version of a recording might be worth.

At least discussing that backed Cherry and the rest of the Barbies off a bit. The Barbies were already convinced the repair, whatever it was, would work and even insisted on making solid plans for transporting the gear to Beth's. With a grin, Cherry Pie promised they'd send enough fighters to stop any thieving bastard being tempted. Harold asked who'd protect it from Barbies, and insisted on having some of his own fighters along. Again and again Harold emphasised the repair might not work, but the Barbies didn't seem to hear that part.

Harold told the GOFS exactly what the convoy would be carrying, so nobody got creative. The gear would be useless to anyone else and worse, if anyone interfered the Barbies might start a full blooded war. The musical instruments on the return trip weren't valuable either, except to Jilli. Gofannon asked about the possible new music, especially Country and Western, and bought more copies of Jilli singing songs donated by the Geeks. He also wanted compilations of the Spice Girls, Adele, Rihanna, Scuffin Lether, Mutha's Ruin and the Beatles for the GOFS women. The Head Girl kept complaining about the lack of decent music, and according to the GOFS leader he'd never sleep safe again if he stopped the radio being fixed.

*   *   *

In the meantime, another opportunity came up because all refugees were asked a list of questions when they arrived. Among the expected questions about troops and weapons were a few about which roads were clear, and were the railway lines blocked by wagons? Hopefully the refugees never realised the wagons were what mattered. One day the questioners hit the jackpot.

Now Harold was in a quandary. He wanted the steel, badly, but it would be a big risk. Worse, if he didn't raid for the spring steel, Caddi might realise what it was when he captured the location. For the first time in years, Harold took a small group on a midnight trip across gang territories, but to look rather than to loot. Over half of the long line of abandoned rail wagons had flat springs, the sort that made Liz dance. After long discussions with his friends, Harold decided he had to run his first real raid, an armed incursion because he absolutely could not sneak those damn great things away.

The raid had to succeed, or Caddi would hear about it and wonder what Harold wanted off the wagons. Once he'd worked out the answer, Caddi would be able to upgrade the Hot Rods' weaponry, something none of his neighbours wanted. Luckily, even if Harold didn't even know the Cabal existed, for once their agents were helping. Their local man didn't think that improving the Hot Rods' weaponry even further would help his bosses.

Chapter 14:
August/September

Precinct Nineteen / Dudley Zoo

The ex-police and the Zookeepers would have loved to have some spring steel, or any idea of where to find some. More decent blades might help them deal with their current problems without expending more ammunition. Sarge summed it up. "The automatics in particular are running short, and they're all that keeps the gangs from launching a full-scale attack."

"It's the small raids, trying to nick a calf or a pig, that are the problem." David, Six-One-Three, held up four clips for his automatic. "We'd break a real attack with these. The trouble is we keep having to use a short burst now and then against small groups. Sooner or later we'll run low. Then if word gets out?"

Teddy, without his tiger-skin cape for an informal meeting, looked thoughtfully at the small number of clips each of the ex-policemen carried. "I thought you reloaded them, with the powder from the captured ammunition?"

"We do, some of it, but the gangsters don't put enough in theirs so we need three of theirs to load two of our rounds." Sarge held up a brass case with an obvious crack down one side. "Not only that, but the brass itself is deteriorating. If we use just one like this, by mistake, it'll jam the gun. Then the automatic is useless until after the attack. If the damage is bad enough we might lose the weapon, permanently."

The Zookeepers looked horrified, none of them knew much about firearms even after their crash course in shooting one. Eventually, a voice spoke up, an unusually tentative Inga. "So if they attack now you'll slaughter them, but we'll still get further raids. Maybe you'll have to stop using automatics, accept a casualty now and then to hold on what's left as a final deterrent."

"We'd get whittled away, one fighter at a time. There's too many nutters out there who fancy a barbecue." Sarge, or One-Five, turned suddenly towards Teddy. "What if we stop firing, and some of your people complain, and we shout we've run out? Then no automatics against the next raids?" He looked around at the doubtful faces. "It would take a little time, but we have enough ammunition to rely on captured firearms for a while. We'll reload it, and weed out the worst brass, but it should be enough to fight off several raids." It took a while to persuade everyone, because there would definitely be more casualties. It would also mean some of the ex-police taking shifts in the darkness, sitting out any raid while they waited for a real attack.

*   *   *

David, Six-One-Three, wasn't keen on the result of the discussion. The next time a bunch of yobs raided, the Zookeepers shouted for backup and he called back he had no ammo left. They beat off the raid, but he felt sure it cost several more wounded than it should. Some of the following raids pushed hard, encouraged by the machine guns staying silent, which had cost one death as well as too many wounded. Some of the Zookeepers grumbled, but Teddy couldn't explain in case of leaks. To try and compensate, to make sure the gangsters didn't cause too many casualties, Precinct Nineteen supplied the zoo with extra pistols and a squad of ten men under Eight-One-Four, Simeon. While the men above kept fighting off raids, below their feet two squads with automatics waited for their chance.

The policemen understood they'd lose men, but most considered it a fair trade for the steady supply of milk for the kids and the fresh protein for everyone. There were other compensations for defending the zoo, chief among them the social life. A good number of the ex-policemen were single men in the twenties, whereas the zoo staff had been mostly women. The gentle teasing and flirting over the occasional barbecue lifted spirits despite continual raids.

*   *   *

Sutton Park:

The score of people meeting in the burned out hotel near Sutton Park, armed and unarmed, weren't either flirting or barbecuing. The gang leaders had stopped treating the park residents as conquered assets, but this was the first time any had been invited to a war council. Not quite war, but rumour and the occasional refugee had warned the gang leaders. A big gang were expanding, rapidly, in their direction. Luckily the aggressor wasn't a neighbour, not yet, so Sutton Park had time to prepare. Shiner, the youth dressed as a skinhead, banged a baseball bat on the table to stop the talking. "The bloody prophet isn't heading this way. He might never come near us, someone out to the east might chop him and his disciples up."

"The Last Prophet, and his gang are called the Children of Cain. Nobody out that way is big enough to stop him. We are, but it means leaving here, launching an attack." The older man looked slowly around the room. "I don't fancy that, because we'd be leaving this place nearly helpless. Some ambitious bastard to the north or west could cause real damage, killing people and stealing animals, especially if we got badly cut up. That could happen even if we won."

"Fair enough Headmaster, but if we wait until he's big enough, we'll be in the shite." Hangaku, mistress of the Yakuza, tapped the hilt of her sword. "The time to chop him is now. I'm sure Angel agrees." She nodded towards a bleached blonde.

"I'd like to but we can't, Hangaku." The blonde shook her head despite the scowl from the Asian woman. "The best idea is to get ready for him. We'll have a better chance to stop the bastard if we make plans now. We can map out approaches, maybe dig a few ditches where they'll fill with water and steer an attacker into some real pain."

"It only has to be enough to slow him up, then whichever gang is attacked can whistle up some help. Good thinking." The man wearing a gold painted safety helmet nodded enthusiastically. "Once we combine we'll carve the bastard up."

"Better yet, Odin, we can streamline the command. Screaming for help, and then trying to organise six more gangs when their fighters turn up, will be a nightmare." The Headmaster swept his arm around the room. "We are working closer and closer together, and two of the smaller gangs have already amalgamated with Shiner and Hangaku. If we pool our resources, create an army that fights together, we can bloody anyone's nose. We'll have to do it sooner or later. The Army will come to clear the rest of us out of here, but not until we've done killing each other. By then we want to be trained as one unit, with a shitload of ammo."

"Not combined, the gang members won't go for it." Hangaku looked thoughtfully at Shiner, the skinhead. "Attitudes are definitely softening, but individuals, not whole gangs." Her own people already mixed easily with Angel's Valkyries, and now many of them had friends among Shiner's Skins as well as the Park residents. The recent combined operations had accelerated the process, but not quite far enough to combine.

Shiner nodded slowly. "We can make plans, and meanwhile start making up mixed guard groups of the most tolerant. The pairs who were playing happy families to set up ambushes for starters, most of them still keep in touch." He looked around the rest. "We can flog a bit more meat and fish to buy extra ammo, and make sure everyone knows where it is. A central stockpile?"

"But even combined, we'll have no chance against the Army. None of us have that level of expertise." Odin shook his head despondently. "Nor that level of weaponry. A few rifles won't even slow the tanks and squaddies up."

Behind the leaders, one of the park keepers, Asif, glanced at another of the original inhabitants. Jer shook his head, very slightly, so the two turned back to listen. The gang leaders had listened to the hints and were taking the first steps to solving the problem themselves, so they didn't need to know they already had an ace. These gangs weren't too bad as gangsters went, but they had to learn to fight together. A few of the park keepers would drop more hints here and there to help them organise that. Fighting off the Last Prophet would toughen the combined gang, and prepare them for the main event.

* * *

Conan:

Conan didn't know about rail wagon springs or the Cabal, even if one of their agents had paved the way for today's operation. Parked up outside the local Mart, he looked over his assembled men and scowled. "Right, you know what to do. Remember, don't touch the Mart guards even if they arrest one of us." Conan didn't mean us, because he stayed in the vehicle when most of the rest headed into the Mart. He might like violence, but Conan didn't want to be in a Mart if the guards opened up. His men were armed, but none of them wore gang signs so if it all went wrong the Barbarians wouldn't be blamed. He settled in to wait, wishing he could get in among the action.

When a bus sheathed in metal plates pulled up outside the Mart gates, Conan whistled softly to alert his men. The big white crosses painted on the outside identified his target, the Lambs of God. The nuns and other shoppers on the bus had barely gone inside the store when a Mart guard came over and insisted the driver moved it further away from the gates. Conan smiled happily, because that meant Garth and Sylvester's bloody crazy plan must be actually working.

Inside the Mart, Garth and a small group waited, poised for action. For the tenth time, Garth checked the cameras in the women's toilets, but they'd all been smashed. For the seventh time, he reminded the men they had to stay in the stalls and keep quiet until all the targets were inside. For the twelfth time, he hoped that bloke of Conan's had fixed the Mart guards. For the ninth time, he hoped the woman they'd brought would keep any other silly bitch coming in here and springing the trap.

Five minutes later the doors opened and a group of confused nuns came in, talking quietly and wondering why a Mart guard had ordered them to come here. "Now!" The stalls burst open and armed men poured out. Two made for the doors to block any exit while Garth raised his voice. "Any of you that resists ends up in the brothel. Surrender and keep quiet and we won't touch you." Within seconds the noise died down, and an older nun approached Garth.

"What do you want? We have no coupons, so you may as well let us go." She glanced towards the door, uncertain. "The guards will be here soon."

"That guard has gone off to collect his pay. The vicar has your coupons but that's not what we want, we want hostages." Garth turned to his men. "Did any of them fight back?" A nun staggered forward, pushed from behind, and a voice told Garth she'd struggled. "Not fighting so not the brothel, yet. Strip her down and give her a taste of what that means." As the other women surged forward, voices raised, Garth held up a hand. "We can do the same to the rest of you."

As a gag muffled the nun's screams, Garth opened the door to the shopping area, briefly. "Come inside vicar, your girls want a word." He shrugged as the priest hesitated. "If you leave them we'll cart them all off home to amuse the lads." The priest headed into the toilets so Garth pointed to the exit, and the Barbarian woman went to let the others know the trap had worked.

*   *   *

Ten minutes later most of the nuns came out of the toilets, two of them supporting the sobbing victim. None of them were allowed to cover her up, because she was a lesson. Another five of their number were still inside the toilets, but still in their underwear and those four hadn't been beaten or groped. The Barbarians just wanted their clothes for now.

Outside the Mart, a lone nun and the priest approached the bus, talking urgently to the guards. The twelve heavily armed men left their crossbows behind, heading into the store with the priest. As soon as they'd gone inside Conan sauntered over with a dozen of his men and pointed to the nun who'd come from the Mart. "What did you tell your fighters?" Conan knew what the pair should have said, but he wanted to check.

She looked at the floor, ignoring the accusing looks from the two nuns left on the bus. "One of the novices has been attacked. They are to bring all our shoppers out of the Mart and escort them to the bus."

Conan turned to the women left to watch the bus. "If you keep quiet when they come out, all the nuns keep what's left of their clothes on, right?" The two pale faces looked confused but the other nun quickly explained what had happened to one of them. "If you show any sign we're in here, the five still locked inside the Mart toilets will be the star attraction in our brothel. We'll do the same with any survivors here when the shooting stops." Another two short nods answered him.

The sister plucked up courage to ask the important question. "How do we know we can trust you?"

"You can be absolutely certain what happens to your five friends if you don't behave." Conan didn't glare or threaten, he needed these fools to believe they could save the women. He kept pushing, because Sylvester had stressed that he shouldn't give anyone a chance to stop and think. "There'll be plenty of loot and sod all fighting, so the men won't mind missing out on women. Not only that, but I've heard that your nuns are nurses and doctors."

"Nurses, not real doctors even if some of them are very experienced." The sister sounded a little more confident now.

"I can get plenty of women, but I can't find willing medics. My men won't touch anyone if you agree to doctor our wounded. Now just sit there and wait." Conan climbed aboard the bus and picked up one of the loaded crossbows the guards had left behind. Several of his men followed, collecting extra crossbows and crouching behind the loopholes in the windows.

* * *

Conan didn't have to wait long. A group of mixed shoppers and guards, with the nuns crowded together in the middle, came out of the gates and headed for the bus. Conan let them get over halfway, well out in the open, then moved forward into the doorway of the bus. His men came around either side of the bus and others followed the shoppers out of the Mart. "Stay right there. If you don't fight, nobody gets hurt." As expected, some of the fighters had to try. Two were cut down from behind when six men in nun's habits produced machetes. Another six were killed by crossbows before they got anywhere near the bus. "I warned you. I've explained to the sister here, and we've made a deal to keep you all alive." Conan pointed towards his own bus. "Five nuns will be going home in that."

"But you said they'd all be safe!" For a moment the priest hesitated on the edge of rebellion. The Mart was only metres away, and maybe some of the shoppers would help nuns.

"They'll be safe, and so will all the civvies and their shopping, but only as long as you all do as I say. One hint of treachery and I'll pass those five round the whole gang." Conan's big smile had absolutely no mercy in it now. "There's over three hundred fighters now, scattered around the en-claves." He turned to let his eyes sweep across the entire group. "If you start giving me trouble now, I may as well start shooting and take the surviving women straight home. My men can strip them off and have some fun on the way."

Some of the shoppers might have argued at least, but Conan's men shoved the naked nun forward. "This one objected, but we were in a hur-ry so she's only been beaten. We'll do a lot worse to the next one." More Barbarians came out of the Mart gates and drew machetes, cutting off any escape, and the last resistance collapsed. The priest ordered the remaining four Lambs' guards to drop their weapons, and the Barbarians moved in to split up their captives. Ten minutes later only eight naked bodies showed where the Lambs of God had met Conan's wolf pack. Conan had his key to the enclave door, and it hadn't cost him a single round of ammunition.

* * *

The General:
The General knew about spring steel from rail wagons, and had a few

suspicions about where some of his information came from. He had no intention of telling anyone else about it either, especially Caddi. The General had called the current meeting, being held six miles to the northwest of Orchard Close, because he'd heard about Harold's gun repairs. The General scowled at his spymaster. "Are you certain the bastard isn't building weapons? If he is we go now and suck up the losses."

Rhys shook his head, emphatically. "No, just repairs but up to now it's only been for close neighbours. I've got a sort of source in the GOFS, or someone I know has. I already told you Soldier Boy cleans and unjams weapons, but now I've got a better idea of his level of expertise. The Pinkies have had two repairs turned down, one's a gunsmith could have rebuilt. I sent them, as a test. Cadillac isn't so sure, but he's a real paranoid and also has a thing about this Soldier Boy. I reckon Caddi is scared of him." Rhys smiled slightly at the sceptical look from the General. "I can't find out why, but he must be to let the bastard rub all over a Hot Rod woman."

The General's frown broke into a grin. "I'll let him rub over a dozen women if it gets us close to him."

"So far even Cadillac can't get into this woman's pants, and doesn't push it. She's a stone killer and a full gang member, but she's got the hots for this Soldier Boy." Rhys thought for a moment. "That might give us a chance, if it causes a war. Mind you, Cadillac is already busy with the war he's got. If he wins and joins us in the attack, the Hot Rods will be big enough to insist on a full share." The spy glanced at the uniformed men. "You'll want to get rid of her anyway, before turning on Caddi. She's his assassin, which is why she isn't in his bed."

"Good point. I'll share Orchard Close and maybe these GOFS with Caddi, but by then I want you to find a way to kill her. I'd rather someone else soaked up that GOFS cannon fire, so don't tell Cadillac about it. Then when I've gobbled up Welly and the Geeks, and got the Pinkies and Barbies onside, we'll see whose is biggest." The General turned from the map on the wall to one on the table. "But first we want those rockets. Are you sure of your man?"

"I'm sure I've found the right man, and the right approach, but we haven't agreed on the payment. Are you sure we can get the Pinkies and the Barbies?" Rhys shrugged at the hard look. "The Pinkies are still not frightened enough to roll over, and the Barbies are downright bloody scary. It might be easier to scare the GOFS off and take on the Barbies."

"We won't scare the GOFS now, with good reason. That fucking cannon will probably fire as far as our rockets can, unless we lob the things into the air. That'll get us another visit from the RAF. Worse, anything short of a shell hitting the bloody thing will bounce off. Once I've got these new rockets, I'll invite the Barbies to a parley and show them their options. I've got to hold up until the harvest is in but by then we should be ready. It'll be handier if we let the SIMS sweat at collecting their food first. Patton?"

"Yes sir."

"We'll take another enclave in the interim, Napoleon's." The General pushed the map and a thin file across to the leader of the Bloods, a file he'd been careful not to mention until now. He hadn't wanted to give Patton any chance to brood on the possible change to the command structure. "According to Rhys, there's one man in charge and he might be approachable. If he isn't it may be bloody, because their fighters are good and well disciplined. If we get in position to shoot the leader and top officers, even if there's a fight the rest might surrender. If not we'll use automatics to punch a hole. Once the Bloods are through their line, discipline won't help them. You've got three weeks with Rhys to check the defences haven't altered, and for you to train your people. They'll need that to learn where everything is, so the fucking lunatics don't burn something useful."

"No problem, and three weeks will be more than enough. You'd better use all the automatics, or the Blood's injuries won't be healed in time to attack these SIMs. Remember, I need two to three months to get the worst hit fighters back in action." Patton glanced at the map. "Is it worth risking for one more medium sized enclave?"

The General didn't take a deep breath first, but definitely tensed up as he finally told Patton exactly why he wanted these fighters in particular. "Yes, because I want more disciplined fighters before going after Soldier Boy. Your nutters work well, but at the moment our steadier fighters are mixed with them. I'd like two forces, nutters who charge whoever is shooting and the types who'll stand under fire." The General tapped the file. "Even if we kill the leaders, these troops have been well trained. We'll find an NCO among them and give him women, or whatever the hell else floats his boat."

Just as the General had hoped, Patton looked and sounded worried but talked rather than reaching for his weapons. "Two commands? I thought I led your Army?"

"You do and you will. You'll just have to rely more on your deputy to kick the Bloods into action for you. Promotion, Patton." The General slapped the bigger man on the shoulder. "Cheer up, you'll get twice the women and loot this way." Patton didn't cheer up. He watched the General leave and wondered if the arse had decided to get rid of a potential rival. Patton didn't want the top job, but that might not save him if the General wanted to clean house. He needed a couple of men to lurk, handy-like. Then if some arse tried to top him? The trouble was, most of the Bloods weren't the sneaky type.

As he left the house, the General beckoned to three men wearing motorbike leathers. "I want you to go around all our enclaves. Tell everyone I want to know as soon as our workers have their crops in." As the messengers left, he turned to Rhys. "Do you trust Patton?"

"Yes. He doesn't want your job. He prefers the actual fighting, not the planning, but be careful about promoting others or he might feel threatened. Patton doesn't run the Bloods by being a deep thinker, so he'll act first and worry later." The spy glanced back at the house with Patton inside. "Maybe you need someone with a knife at his elbow, just in case?"

"Don't worry about that, I'll deal with it. Just concentrate on finding a way into that SIMs place without getting half the Bloods slaughtered." The General followed the spy's look. "We'll need Patton and the Bloods to scare the shit out Napoleon, then the queers, and to keep those dykes in order."

"I'm trying, but it's slow work. I doubt we'll be able to hit the SIMs much this side of Christmas. We need the extra disciplined men, but the delays after every fight to let everyone heal have slowed the whole job up." Rhys perked up a bit. "That'll be just in time to give the Bloods a whole new set of Christmas stocking fillers, and we might still get at Soldier Boy's women for Valentine's." They parted, both laughing.

*   *   *

Professors:

Despite learning about the mystery spy among Benny's Boys, Prof hadn't been able to find anyone in his own enclave who kept messenger pigeons. All the pigeons were clipped so they were incapable of flight, as were the few ducks they'd caught, so none of them flew off before going into the pot. Not enough birds to supply all the protein, but at least buying corned beef had become easier after making that new deal. Unfortunately, after a short period when Prof's cars could visit the Mart for a reasonable bribe, Benny brought bad news.

The Lycans, as the gang called themselves, hadn't repaired the gates Prof had smashed but they'd recovered from the shock. Benny had a woman in the other gang, a spy, one who worked around their headquarters, cleaning up. She'd heard some complaining lately, and suggestions on ways to fix the problem. The Lycans' neighbours had been taking the piss about how they'd been stuffed by a bunch of old men and schoolkids. It hadn't turned into anything yet, but Benny wouldn't get much warning when it did. He tried for getting a trebuchet permanently installed to cover the broken gates, but Prof didn't trust Benny or his Boys enough for that.

Instead, he started making plans. According to Benny, the gang were talking about payback, something more than just closing the road. Some of the Lycans wanted to stop a shopping run to ask for a hugely inflated price. Not too bad, but according to Benny it wouldn't be optional, the cars wouldn't be allowed to back away. They'd take the weapons and cars, and the more militant Lycans wanted to take a couple of the girls, to make a point.

Prof asked the engineering department to construct trebuchets that were easy to dismantle for transporting, and adapt as many of the existing ones as possible. He'd finally reached the end of his patience, even if he wouldn't tell the students yet. If the Lycans wanted to push his students into a fight, they could have one, but they definitely wouldn't enjoy the result.

* * *

Reivers:

In the Scottish mountains, there were no Cabal agents and no rail wagon steel. Machetes weren't much good most of the time, because the foreign troops now had varying degrees of air cover. One particular unit of Italian troops had perfected working with their top cover, a Greek Chinook transport helicopter with machine guns firing from openings on each flank. Not a true warplane, but more reliable than hoping the controllers would send support when asked. The Chinook hovered above and behind the soldiers to give covering fire, following them as they advanced.

The chopper came with a liaison officer who, in the Italian commander's opinion, fell a long way short of the usual standards of the British Armed Forces. "Follow them, close-up, you've got them running. Don't let them get away!" The Greek pilot rolled his eyes to his comrades as the liaison screamed into his radio. The soldiers below had chased groups of these so-called bandits before. Any time now there'd be an attempt to set up an ambush, or the Scots would settle into a new defensive position.

The stink of spent ammunition filled the helicopter where the three flank machine guns had been laying down covering fire. They were silent for now as the pilot moved slowly sideways, keeping well back from the soldiers and jinking now and then. The Germans had lost a helicopter to snipers. "That's it, they're trapped. Flank them, push men up the slopes either side. Then when they break you've got them." The pilot could hear the officer down below answering through the radio, trying to explain why he shouldn't and couldn't.

The rebels, now digging in across a small valley, would probably love a flanking attack. Either the steep slopes either side would be mined, or there'd be more men waiting there. The ragged fighters had broken contact, fleeing in apparent panic until they'd suddenly stopped right here. Even as a pilot he could recognise a pre-planned fall-back position. A death trap if the Italians had a larger force, but sending soldiers up both flanks would leave the pinning force too small. These Scots would counterattack at any opportunity, and they loved hand to hand. The pilot rotated the big helicopter to use the machine guns along the other flank, to give the first three a chance to cool.

*   *   *

Ahead of the Italian soldiers, up in the valley, a man in ragged plaid crooned quietly to himself. "Come on, ye bastards, just a wee bit further. Come intae ma bluidy great nasty parlour." He raised his voice a little. "The men or yon Chinook, Angus?"

"The Chinook. That's why we picked this unit. They've got a system, a guid one, but this time it's perfect for us. Are the men too far forward or too far back?" The speaker didn't raise his eye from his rifle, tracking his first target.

"Too close, they could charge with nae warning when yon bird goes doon."

"No, they're good troops so they'll wait for the officer. That means they'll freeze for a second or two, and a few might even forget to keep in cover and stick a head up to look." Everyone could hear the hunger in his voice. "Remember, lads, just how we've been training ye. None of yon mad charges from the Mel Gibson film. Aimed shots, pick your target and drop him." His voice took on a cadence, calming the half-trained ex-gangsters and farm workers while reminding them what to do. "Rabbie, don't hurry, make sure of the Chinook. If the Italians charge, these lads are used to hand to hand." Angus thought he'd prepared properly, but now he worried the Italian bastards would smell the trap and ask for real air support. An Apache or a jet would cost the Reivers a lot of fighters. Around him occasional shots spat out, the shooters hugging cover afterwards as the machine guns in the helicopter responded.

*   *   *

As the valley sides began to get steeper, and he began to lose a man here and there, the Italian officer asked for real air support. He needed something carrying rockets or bombs, even an Apache's nose cannon would do, just to break up the prepared defence ahead of him. "Air support? You've got a bloody helicopter and fifty trained soldiers against about thirty rabble. They're trapped so there's no real danger, no need to call the jets off a real target." The liaison didn't give the real reason, he'd been told to economise on the more expensive munitions.

Many of the foreign troops had been low on missiles and bombs when they arrived, and the British Armed Forces needed what they'd got. There were plenty of bullets, which was why the Chinook had so many machine guns. The liaison officer had been told to drive the foreign troops hard, regardless of casualties, to push the rebels north. "If you can't do the job, we may as well send you back across the Channel." That should do it. None of the foreigners wanted to take their wives and kids back into that mess.

The officer gave up, moving his men forward slowly and carefully. The fighters ahead weren't rabble, and probably had more than thirty men, but he had enough soldiers to take them. Real air support would have cut down on his casualties, something they'd had too many of when they'd first met these Scots and the enemy sucked off the air cover. The officer contacted the helicopter, warning the gunners the ground pounders would be going all the way in. A bullet whined off a rock, much too close, and he ducked further behind cover. The machine guns behind him fired short, efficient bursts in reply, and then the ground trembled and he heard a strange sound. As he turned the officer began to scream, "Terra, terra!" quickly changing it to, "Get down, land." The pilot might not understand, but the officer knew exactly what those pillars of fire were.

The pilot saw the ground in front of him erupt and the streaks of fire climbing upwards, and immediately realised most of them would miss. He poured on the power and tried to throw the big, cumbersome machine up and sideways. He daren't land, the chances were he'd never get off the ground again because bullets were already punching through the Chinook. The enemy had brought heavy rifles and snipers. The Chinook began to twist in mid-air, the pilot began to hope because nothing had hit him yet, and then he found out the rockets weren't meant to.

In a ripple that started below the aircraft and worked up past it, spreading tens of metres all around, scores of explosions enveloped the helicopter. Not too dangerous in themselves, each burst sent shrapnel sleeting through the air in every direction and enough found a target. The windshield starred, gunners cried out in pain, the rear rotors stuttered, and the helicopter slid downwards and backwards. The pilot fought the failing rear motor, then screamed as a rocket went off near the window behind and to the side, open for a machine gunner. Crude shrapnel tore through the gunner and the cockpit, silencing the liaison and the radio, while the pilot collapsed forward. The Chinook slid further backwards before twisting and dropping, the surviving gunners barely having time to realise before it struck and crumpled. Pure shock brought too many of the Italian soldiers to their feet, or up on their knees, staring back at the unfolding disaster.

"No! Scendere! Anatra!" The Italian officer shouted at his men to get down, take cover, but all the Reivers opened fire. Within moments over a dozen soldiers were down, and several more had been hit. "Fall back in sections. Dig in round the helicopter, it's got machine guns." The officer peeked out round his boulder to check the enemy weren't charging, then flipped over backwards. Angus had been waiting, knowing the officer would have to check.

Despite losing their officer, the Italians began an ordered withdrawal, taking turns to lay down covering fire. Their ranks faltered as the Reiver snipers retargeted from the helicopter, and began shooting anyone giving orders. The soldiers were soon without NCOs but they were professionals, so they kept leapfrogging back towards the wreck with its radio and machine guns. Angus took occasional shots, content to let them go for now. Fifty yards later the survivors found out why. The trap had cost a fortune in sugar, first for the rockets and then for the mines, but the result was worth it. As the operator behind Angus held down the second switch, a long strip of ground erupted. The bombs weren't efficient, being buried deep to avoid detection. Most of the shrapnel went upwards, but just for a few moments the soldiers in among the explosions broke. As even those on the edges of the mines scrambled to get away, the Reivers finally had their clear targets. Bullets scythed through the shocked Italians, and man after man toppled before the survivors threw themselves into cover.

Angus had no intention of letting the enemy recover. "Charge! Don't let them get to the chopper!" The Reivers, mostly recruits used to the bloody hand to hand in the cities, bounded forward screaming war cries while loosing off the rest of their clips. Machetes glittered in the sun, these men and women had never even trained with a bayonet. None worried about casualties, not after gang wars, soaking up what a few Italian soldiers threw at them before being targeted by snipers. A few soldiers ran towards the cover of the wreck to make a stand, but none survived long enough. Angus's snipers killed any soldier who didn't stay behind cover, and then the wild-eyed, ragged mob struck.

Angus wasn't using a machete, nor was he intent on killing. He made his way through the frantic melee, using his bayonet and rifle butt only if necessary, heading for the helicopter. So far, it hadn't burned, but it only needed one smart Italian or Greek to realise what a prize it was. He snapped a shot at a man with a grenade, hoping he hadn't pulled the pin yet. Closer to the wreck Angus saw a thin trickle of smoke, and movement inside. He fired at the movement, a quick burst, and headed for the smoke. The ex-soldier mashed the smouldering mess of wires with his boot, grinding it into the turf, then turned at a cheer. The Reivers were celebrating and had started looting the bodies, taunting each other about how well they'd done.

"Leave those. Just make sure they're dead. Get the machine guns and ammunition clear of this wreck. Quickly, I can smell smoke." The young men and women stopped looting and rushed to get the heavy weaponry. Angus thumbed his radio. "The shop is open." He headed for the cockpit, hoping the liaison officer's radio and codes had survived.

Five minutes later the dull thud of fuel igniting announced the end of the looting. The last three running away from the already burning Chinook were smouldering or actually beginning to burn, but they didn't drop their prizes. Willing hands slapped out the flames or poured water on their clothes. By now the group of unarmed men and women who had been hiding nearby were loading quads, horses and ponies with the pick of the weaponry and ammunition. "Time to go!" A man on a quad held up a radio and pointed east. "An Apache has just been pulled off an attack and it's coming this way. We've got two minutes, tops, to be off this hillside." He gunned the engine, bouncing up the slope with four machine guns and boxes of ammo strapped to the vehicle. Behind him the remaining Reivers snatched what they could and ran.

Most of the Reivers were over the crest by the time the attack helicopter came up the valley and circled the tall plume of smoke. The pilot saw the fleeing attackers, but he had his orders. Four helicopters had been shot down in the last hour, all along the front, so he wasn't to chase anyone. He stayed high, watching a scattering of targets spreading out and then disappearing into the gulleys and valleys seaming the hillsides. None of the targets were big enough to warrant using a missile, the largest being electric quad bikes. An hour later two lorries full of soldiers, with two jets circling high above, came for the bodies and any weapons the Reivers had missed.

*   *   *

A week later, despite their recent success in downing helicopters, the nervous groups surrounding two small radar sets deep in the Highlands weren't entirely sure Angus's latest idea would work. The fifty partly-trained volunteers at the head of each of two valleys, laid flat in shallow trenches and almost covered in turf, weren't all that confident either and they were uncomfortable as well. Nearly a month had passed since the attacks that had scoured the Reiver caves, killing men, women and children. Hopefully the government would think the Reivers were getting a little bit careless while moving about at night. With luck, they'd also think the Reivers could only target helicopters, so they'd have no hesitation over sending a jet. The bait had been dangled for four days now, but nothing had happened and confidence was waning.

"One, three-ten, four, one." In one of the valleys every man or woman on that wavelength tensed, then tried to relax or scrambled to get set. The turf erupted as figures carrying automatic weapons ran frantically across the end of the valley. The string of figures told them how many aircraft, one, the bearing, not quite the best approach which was why the gunners were running, four hundred feet high above the ground so low-level, and one minute away. Around the radar, the group picked up their weapons. Their particular response wouldn't work against low level so they'd throw a few bullets and hope to hit the missile.

Almost a minute later a small rocket, a firework, rose from the top of the pass above the valley to show where the plane would appear. The running figures laid on their backs and pointed their weapons upwards while a voice began to chant "five, four, three, two, one, f...." The scream of jet engines, and the cacophony as fifty automatics and machine guns fired until their clips and belts were empty, drowned the last word. The Bruce had taken serious weaponry from the front line to give this his best shot.

The French pilot knew he'd been picked up, but by a general, low-powered sweep rather than targeting radar so his threat detectors stayed silent. He'd seen the firework, but didn't think the rockets used against helicopters would be quick enough to catch him. In any case, he'd been given strict instructions. The English controllers had told the last pilot who'd broken off an attack run, if it happened again he was of no further use. His family would be sent to live in Inverness.

The pilot gritted his teeth as he cleared the ridge, eyes firmly on his sights as he locked the missile on the cave mouth and launched. His plane bucked and he fought to turn it, wondering what had happened because there'd been no explosions. Even as his missile streaked home and the cave mouth gushed flame, bullets punched holes or starred his windscreen. He looked for the attacking aircraft, but didn't live long enough to realise why his instruments weren't picking anything up. Pain tore through his leg, something in the fly-by-wire system failed, and the sleek war machine became a flying brick doing what flying bricks did best. As it struck the valley floor and bounced, pieces flying in all directions, dumbstruck men and women rose to their feet to stare.

"It worked." The man watched as the tumbling wreck exploded into a fireball. "It worked!" A cheer swept across the hillside and the fifty men and women began to run down the hill. "Check all the wreckage. We want every bullet, anything useful you can find."

The group around the radar at the other end of the valley raised their heads, looking at the flames still gushing from the cave. "I'm a believer. I've heard stories, that the Vietnamese did that to stop American planes, but never believed it. It still doesn't seem right, firing straight up without aiming. You'd think the bullets would be too spread out, that not enough would hit." The man pointed at the pilot's pyre. "That takes some arguing with."

"Angus said it probably wouldn't work, that it might just frighten them off. We might have got lucky and nailed the plane, but that still isn't good enough. If that had been a real refuge, they'd all be dead." Maeve tore her eyes from the cave, looking back towards the plume of smoke up the valley. "That's too high a price to pay for one plane."

A man placed a hand on her shoulder. "You heard what Angus said. We can't stop them, we just want to force them to launch from a distance." He patted the radar set, taken from a fishing boat. "Then this will take care of it." He ignored the muttered "we hope" from behind him, and hoped Maeve hadn't heard.

Regardless of what happened in the valleys, the enemy pilots were about to have a few rough days. Now the method had worked once, Angus and Bruce would set up something similar near the front lines. The first few should be easy, especially if this pilot hadn't warned the others, because the government forces had reverted to low-level runs with jets. Losing a few warplanes on top of eight helicopters should stop the close air support coming in quite as close.

* * *

Three days later, it wasn't a radio call that alerted the defenders waiting near another cave. "Got one. Up high, and a plane not a drone. It's not messing about, coming in on a straight attack run." Around the speaker anxious hands gripped small boxes and fingers hesitated over buttons. Two people took out their cigarette lighters and held them above the ends of a dozen fuses. For long minutes the radar operator hunched over his screen, completely engrossed, searching for that one small new return, the bomb. At the other end of this valley the gunners in their shallow trenches stayed under the turf. If this attack failed, the jet might still try a low-level run.

"He's launched!" Around the cave entrance levers were pulled and buttons pressed. Inside the entrance to the cave a strange, wobbly shape began to grow. An old hot-air balloon, sealed as well as they could, was being inflated as fast as possible using nitrogen. With luck, it would snuff some of the fire. Other, smaller balloons headed upwards, some trailing smoke, some trailing wires and others hauling small wire cages. Another hot-air balloon, filled with hydrogen, wobbled into the air quicker than the others because men had started inflating it at the first warning.

The radar operator counted down towards the estimated impact time. As the numbers dropped, air rifles popped some of the smaller balloons, filling the air above the cave entrance with smoke that included iron and any other metallic filings they could find. Nobody could be sure what would spoil the bomb's targeting, but some of the mixture might. Likewise, the wires below some balloons, and between some, might have no effect even if the bomb hit them, but maybe they would. Frantic searching had come up with optimal figures for when a thermobaric bomb should discharge its load, and releasing or igniting the cloud early should reduce the impact. At least the plane hadn't dropped one of those pallet things from directly overhead.

The numbers chanted by the radar operator dropped further as more small balloons rose, while the hydrogen-filled version wobbled on a tether, waiting. A billowing, fireproof mass almost filled the cave entrance, but nobody expected it to take much of a blast. Instead, nets full of rocks fell from the hillside above the cave. Their cables, looped around pulleys, yanked up the door laid flat under the dirt outside the entrance. The collection of welded bar and beams, plated with whatever the constructors could carry this far, covered the opening. It wouldn't stop a missile, or make a proper seal, but it might reduce the amount of fuel that got inside. As numbers fell lower, men and women raised automatic weapons. The guns were desperately needed at the front, but first these bombs had to be stopped.

The radar operator passed zero, supposedly the moment the bomb would release the fuel cloud. Lighters were applied to fuses, then moments later the next, then the next. Flights of ordinary fireworks rose into the air and burst into globes of coloured sparks. Every gunner opened fire into the air above and to the front of the cave, hopefully firing through the fuel cloud. Hundreds of supersonic fireflies hurled upward, because every weapon had been loaded with tracers. They might ignite the fuel early, they might damage the bomb, they might not have any effect. More fireworks exploded, spitting waves of coloured sparks across the sky and hopefully the expanding fuel cloud.

The cages below some smaller balloons were burning fiercely now, phosphorus hot, again hoping to ignite the payload or interfere with aiming. An explosion and a ball of flame wasn't failure. The hydrogen balloon created a crude thermobaric bomb all by itself. Hopefully it would serve two purposes, a back-blast to divert the real bomb or the fuel cloud, and it might burn off some of the fuel cloud. Smaller balloons and some of the smoke and rockets disappeared in the blast, but they'd already done their work or failed.

Nobody would ever be sure if anything affected the attack, or if the bomb operated perfectly. Even in the worst case, the wires and smoke in the sky, and the other balloon inside the entrance, might have helped dissipate the explosion. Flame bloomed and the area around the cave disappeared in a fireball. The ground slapped everyone, hard, some people falling over or being blown down.

As the smoke lifted and began to drift, all eyes turned to the cave and the scorched surroundings, all except the radar operator. "Drone! Just above the hills, watching."

"Can we get it?"

"Nobody near enough, but next time we'll know." The radar operator kept watch on the plane flying out of range, while the rest watched the flames around the cave die down. As soon as possible the cables were released and the remnants of the door fell away, letting two men in fire-fighting equipment inside. Nobody needed the report, the men came out waving their arms above their heads and one did his best to dance in the clumsy suit. The wall, built out of sight inside, had held. There'd been nobody in this cave, but the wall and as much as possible of the defence would be duplicated at the real targets.

One woman in particular wore a savage smile as she reported over a radio transmitter. This transmitter reached right across the Highlands, telling all the other caves to duplicate the system. They couldn't, not entirely, but the bloody government listeners wouldn't know that. She glanced over towards the drone and added that the decoy system had worked, they'd fooled the bastards into attacking empty rock. She didn't mention the ship radars. If the Reivers could nail a few drones, the bastards would find it harder to pinpoint a real target.

*   *   *

Cabal:

Safe from both Reivers and the gangs in the cities, the Cabal were getting all the messages and weren't at all pleased. Owen, the chairman, rapped his gavel to stop the chatter. "I understand how unhappy you all are, and I share your frustration. Joshua, Faraz, why is this rabble in Scotland still causing so much trouble? I thought you had them on the run."

"Don't blame me." Faraz scowled. "The RAF is excluded from the area so the refugee air power can kill women and children without causing any ripples. I am working through four sets of liaison officers, English, French,

German and Spanish, and that's not always helping because some of the aircraft and troops are Italian and Greek. They are all asking how the hell this rabble could have anti-aircraft weaponry." He gestured to the wall screen and used the control to click through several pictures of wreckage. "Eight helicopters and three jets were shot down within days, and another helicopter and two jets are missing but might have been mechanical faults. Two of the helicopters were Apaches, and we were short of those to start with."

"They haven't got real SAMs, surface to air missiles." Joshua, the man in Army uniform, grimaced. "Despite that, someone has come up with an effective strategy against low level attacks." He changed the picture to a tube with crude fins resting against two rails, pointing skywards. "The sugar rocket, a straight copy of the ones used by Hamas against Israel for two generations at least." The next picture looked more like a firework display. "We aren't sure how many they threw up in a volley, but after all the food convoys they've captured, the Reivers have plenty of sugar and bleach."

"How on earth did they hit a plane?" Several heads nodded to agree with Ivy, because that didn't seem possible.

"They didn't." Joshua explained how even one bit of shrapnel in the wrong place would be fatal for a modern, fly-by-wire aircraft. He explained about the wall of bullets, and how they worked just like a wall of exploding rockets. The questions kept coming, even when Joshua showed how the Reivers had sucked the planes onto the right attack runs. None of those present were happy with the solution, launching from further away rather than low-level runs. Even the helicopters would stay higher and fly faster. Joshua and Faraz had already issued warnings about careful scouting before following retreating Reivers.

Faraz had to confess the RAF didn't have many stand-off weapons, and couldn't get replacements. The stockpiles would be needed for London, or when the Cabal finally reconquered Europe. Some of the survivors in Europe might have genuine SAMs. The clearly unhappy RAF man glanced at Owen. "You won't even let us use RAF stocks of dumb bombs, or relatively dumb rockets. That leaves us with what the Europeans brought, which wasn't much. We've started manufacturing the sort of rockets used in the Second World War, barely any better than the Reiver version."

"We used too many at the beginning, against mobs and ships, and we haven't the facilities or personnel to replace the fancier weaponry, not yet. Any chance of buying some elsewhere?" Owen turned to Boris. "From our colleagues in America or Russia?"

"Most of the armed forces there are either fighting internal uprisings or confined to defending areas around their bases or barracks. They aren't exactly under control, just enough to stop them interfering." Boris looked apologetic. "We daren't give them a hint this was planned, especially the international scope of the operation. Selling off their munitions would make the wrong people curious. The Cabal in South America are still pushing north, and will need everything they have to deal with Central America."

"You should use your planes to keep the Reivers from the eastern coast, from the convoys and farms. The soldiers can deal with them in the mountains." Vanna used the controls to show an armoured vehicle, a personnel carrier, slewed across a road. Smoke still seeped from a hole in the side, the open doors and the turret hatch. "Somehow they appear to have armour piercing weapons as well?"

"Yes and no. I warned you these are soldiers, or at least their leaders are. That might have been a shaped charge, but not from a missile so they'd have to get close enough to place it. Your contractors on the lorries have machine guns to stop them, so destroying that vehicle had to have cost the attackers." Joshua glanced at Faraz in wry acceptance of what they both knew. "The deaths bought the Reivers the machine guns and ammunition from the lorries. At least they couldn't dismantle the heavy weapons from the armoured vehicle but they took the ammunition. All the weaponry captured with the convoys is the reason the fighters in the mountains can throw up a wall of bullets against aircraft, or our troops."

"So what is the answer? I've got plenty of lorries, but Vanna's people are going to become very reluctant to drive them." Gerard, the youngest there, put up a map of Scotland on the screen. "We can still push the low-level attacks, tell these foreign pilots to try harder, to risk the rockets and bullets? We have their families."

"The imported troops and pilots are fighting to buy safety for themselves and their families, not for a cause. The Reivers aren't scum or rabble any more, they have a cause and many have no families left." Joshua looked around the table, his face grave. "If we threaten the families of our foreign troops too often, or worse still actually harm any, they may as well join the Reivers. Boris"—he nodded towards the diplomat—"is recruiting more military groups from Europe, specifically groups with armour, and those will deal with the Reivers. A sweep is underway to drive them north of Loch Ness. That valley runs coast to coast and can be held by light armour and machine guns if they dig in."

"But in the meantime, you can still target the Reivers' families and stores. That should slow them up." Vanna didn't care how many kids burned if it would take even one of these nutcases away from attacking convoys.

Faraz hesitated, then operated the control to show why that wouldn't work either. "We launched a low-level attack against the first refuge. The next time we used a standoff weapon." The TV showed the take from the drone watching the defensive measures, then played the radio message telling the rest to adopt the same system. "From that we know we attacked two dummy targets, lost a jet, and failed to destroy the second. Even the experts aren't sure if that firework display affected the weapon."

"Let us pen them in for this winter, for a start, and look into the cave problem." Joshua might be asking permission, but his tone of voice wasn't accepting any arguments.

"When will that that happen, the line of steel thing?" Ivy sighed, and the rest could see her fatigue. "I'm fending off the retail consortiums but I need answers. They've lost a senior manager as well as staff, and some workers daren't leave the Marts to go home at night in case the Reivers strike."

"It'll be done by the time the heavy snow arrives. That line will also keep the Reivers from most of the east coast farmland. They'll be able to reach the part north of Inverness, but we'll have armour in place to prevent free access to the city. There'll be no more recruits from Aberdeen or the work camps south of that, so we'll gradually wear them down." Joshua's smile had a savage edge. "They can spend another winter under the snow, but further north, and this time the aircraft will keep harassing them. That's providing there's enough avgas?"

Owen beamed, tapping the control to put up a spreadsheet full of figures. The rest turned to them with some relief. Their allies in South America now had enough fuel for military operations and were driving north into Central America. The news that the Argentinian and Brazilian-led forces were capturing intact military vehicles that had run dry brought smiles all round. As Joshua pointed out, that should happen in Europe when the time came to cross the Channel.

More good news came on the food front. The UK had almost become self-sufficient, and would be once the city populations were processed and the land around them could be used for grazing. At the moment most food imports were coffee, tea, and chocolate, or meat for the cities. When asked,

Maurice admitted the enclosures were still reluctant to kill each other fast enough, despite his encouragement. He'd resorted to setting loose small flocks of goats, in the hope that some gangs would fight each other over fresh milk.

To Maurice's complete surprise, the goats sparked a fierce row between Vanna and Joshua, about who could be trusted to insert the animals, professional soldiers or contractors who wouldn't get weepy-eyed and rescue children as well. The row soon concentrated on the real problem. Vanna wanted heavier armour for convoys, while Joshua didn't trust contactors with that sort of weaponry. Eventually, the rest told Joshua he may as well turn the armour loose, because it wouldn't be used except for clearing another city. He compromised, agreeing to one battle tank per main convoy, on a transporter, but he still wasn't happy about contractors helping to man them.

"For God's sake, make sure those Reivers don't capture one. They'd not get far into the mountains before an air strike took it out, but they'll take the shells to use the explosives." Joshua stopped, paling a little as something crossed his mind. "Actually, they are bitter enough to launch some sort of kamikaze with a tank, and neither your contractors nor the Army guard posts want to face that, Vanna." Vanna winced at the thought, and promised to make sure it didn't happen.

"What about elsewhere, Maurice? Are you working on destabilising the gangs and keeping the pot boiling?" Owen smiled hopefully, the discussion needed lightening up. "Will we be seeing our pinups again soon?"

Maurice's smile wasn't at all pretty. "You might see them as a tragedy if either of two plans works out. At least one of them might give us the blonde, somewhat traumatised but that will work well for our purposes. We believe the Army have warned her not to get arrested or go to a Mart." Maurice put up a picture of Doll walking through Orchard Close wearing her Stetson, boots and shorts and carrying a crossbow, a machete and a tied down pistol. "Once we get hold of her, these pictures will be priceless propaganda. They'll make a sharp contrast against the state she'll be in by then."

"The Army have warned her? What happened to your vaunted Army discipline?" Vanna sneered at Joshua. "You keep pointing out my contractors are a bit loose around the edges."

This time the perennial squabble about the relative merits of soldiers and contractors led to a practical plan. The soldiers near the civilised enclaves would be left in place longer, to let the ones elsewhere harden their attitudes. After six months, the results would be assessed.

Nobody would have any reluctance about shooting some of the opposition. "There are a good few gangs the Army will shoot without any qualms. Some are becoming very useful tools to destroy the rest." Maurice changed the picture to show a still of a huge bearded man wielding a crude battle-axe. A battered, scarred auburn-haired woman on a leash knelt beside him. "I'm still growing some gangs to deal with others. This one, for instance, is coming along particularly well…."

*   *   *

As the meeting broke up, Vanna and Maurice once again paused to speak with Owen. Vanna reported that more launchers had been delivered to work camps, then diverted to her people deep in the cities. Maurice would be working on diverting more anti-tank and anti-aircraft missiles from the stocks brought over by the foreign troops. When the Army and RAF were sent in, they'd be shown pictures of what the Reivers were doing. The first missile taking out a tank or plane should banish any reluctance to fire. Maurice promised suicide bombers and snipers, and assured Owen the enclaves would be out of ammunition by the second day.

"Run out of ammunition? They seem to have plenty now, with that new, smoky powder?" Owen glanced from one to the other. "You were going to find out how that happened. Just how much do they have?"

Maurice waved a negligent hand. "I'm making progress. There's not enough ammunition in the cities for a real battle. Seriously, don't worry Owen."

Vanna quickly diverted the chairman. "I'm more interested in the snipers. Are they perfected, Maurice?" She gave Owen a sour look. "I've got a target or two for anonymous snipers, and I'll bet Ivy has a couple of Mart managers on her list."

Maurice pursed his lips, thinking how to answer honestly. "Not perfectedb Vanna. There are a lot of failures and we don't always find out until final testing. Enough are working out to create a small but potent ace in the hole. Now we'd better leave."

As Vanna and Maurice hurried to catch the rest, Vanna spoke quietly. "Owen is getting curious."

"If he pushes harder, I'll tell him how the gangs get ammunition. Owen is a realist, and knows I need a contact network." Maurice sniggered then glanced enquiringly at Vanna. "We can always cut him in on the profits?"

"We can always task a sniper?" Maurice didn't reply and a faint smile touched Vanna's lips.

*   *   *

Cyn Palace:

On the new borders, close to the edge of the old Gatts territory, a guard nudged his companions awake. "Got someone, but it's weird. There's only one for starters. He's not a loony or a runner looking for sanctuary, because he's sneaking."

"What, a scout? Is he after us?" The second youth took the infrared scope and aimed it where his friend pointed. "He's got a bloody great pack." He chuckled suddenly. "Looks like one of those Army things, a Bergen. Maybe he's on a training march and got lost?"

"If so he lost his helmet and rifle as well. Nip over that way a bit and let him get nearly between us." The lookout debated, but he didn't want to use the radio to call the boss. Everyone listened to the bloody things and the neighbours might snatch this bloke. Then they'd get whatever was in that pack. He settled down, aiming his crossbow in the right direction and checking now and again with the infrared. He needed the scope, because this bloke kept to the deepest shadows even when it meant a detour. Definitely sneaky. "Okay mate, far enough. Don't do anything stupid because you're in a crossfire."

The figure sank down a little, so only his head showed. "I didn't think you'd got night sights. Most assholes with them start moving about when they first see me so I can avoid them." The low chuckle came as a complete surprise. "Not a crossfire, which means you haven't got coms to your friend. He hasn't got a clean shot."

"I have, so up on your feet with your hands up." The lookout glanced quickly to the side where the third guard had her crossbow tucked into her shoulder, then put the scope to his eye again.

"That crossbow hasn't got night sights, and you can't shoot accurately with a handheld scope. I've come in peace but if it has to be the other way?" The voice sounded a little uncertain this time. "I might be too late anyway." His head disappeared and came up in a different place. "Tell your friend to stop trying to get a shot, or I'll leave. I just want to know if Marcie survived."

Two of the lookouts exchanged glances, and shrugs. "I don't know a Marcie. Which gang?" He wondered if she'd belonged to the Gatts. "Some of the Gatts joined us."

"I don't know. There weren't any gangs when I left. Who are you?" The voice sounded uncertain again, then suddenly sharpened. "If you keep trying to flank me I'll fucking shoot you. Which part of talk don't you understand!"

The lookout clicked his radio. "Keep still. He can see you, so he's got some sort of night vision." Louder he called to the hidden man. "Okay, I've told him to stay still. We're the Muppets because Kermit is the boss, but there's four other gangs who share this bit. There's another gang someplace behind you. What's this Marcie look like?"

"Real pretty. You'd remember." The sigh could be heard clearly. "What about Cullen, or Nita, or Cynthia? We left them in an old library near here, but the streets have been wrecked since I left so everything looks different."

The woman with the crossbow leant over to whisper in the lookout's ear. "The Librarian's called Nita, I think, but I don't know many other Sinners. This Cynthia could be Sin?"

The lookout passed that on, and the man's head came further out of cover, then ducked again. "Cynthia is here? Harry called her Cyn, and we called the library Cyn Palace. Did Nita have her baby okay?" He stopped talking and the lookout lost sight of the man.

"The Sinners call the library Sin Palace sometimes, but we thought it was a joke about the gang name. The librarian has a kid, a two year old… Shit, when did you leave?" Dead silence answered, until the lookout began to wonder if the bloke had sneaked off.

He reappeared, a good five yards from where he should have been. "Send one person forward, unarmed, as a hostage so I can get out of no-man's land. Then send for Cynthia, Nita or one of the originals from the library. Be quick, your neighbour's sentry is out cold but they'll hear the radio message." The mystery man's good humour came back briefly. "Tell Cynthia that Davie has brought a refill for the steel box."

"Why would we give you a hostage?" But even as he spoke, beside the lookout the woman had put down her crossbow and started removing her weapons belt.

"Maybe us women talk to each other more than you blokes, but I've heard the Sinners have a steel box they use for ammo. They reckon their first guns came in it." She started to wriggle forward. "We want him be-hind our lines sharpish." The lookout started talking, quickly. Within min-utes he got a good look at the bloke, or what bits weren't under a shapeless camouflage overall. The Army crewcut, the dinky night vision on a head-band and something about the look on his drawn, tired face stopped the lookout from insisting on a search. The semi-automatic pistol in his hand might have helped with that.

The three guards debated briefly, but there wasn't much point in using the radio and rousing everyone. In less than an hour they'd be relieved, and could escort this bloke straight to the library. Their new companion seemed content to wait once he knew they couldn't tell him about this Marcie, settling down with his back to a wall and the pistol ready. The Army canteen he pulled out from inside the overalls and the hilt of the knife on his belt were ringing big bells in the lookout's head now. That knife was an Army bayonet.

*　　*　　*

The relief arrived on time, but they were Imam's blokes and didn't know Marcie either. The three Muppets tried to talk to their companion on the way back, but he seemed more and more reluctant to answer. That altered when the library and church came into sight. "That's it!" He took a quick step, then hesitated. Davie wasn't quite a captive, but there were now a dozen armed people following him. One had run ahead to warn the Sin-ners. While Davie hesitated, the door of the library flew open and a woman hurled out and down the street towards them.

"Davie! You came!"

The man dropped his pistol and opened his arms wide. "Marcie!" About ten years seemed to fall from his tired, lined face in the brief time before the two connected. From the impact, it would be a while before either would be talking, but from the expression on the face of the second woman coming out of the library she knew Davie as well. That came as a big shock to most of those present. They'd never seen the Librarian smile, let alone a big happy one like that! The couple were still saying hello when Sin arrived, even if neither of them was speaking.

Sin had a big smile as well, and the three guards caught the end of what she was telling Sinner. "Davie is a daft sod, a bit of an innocent. When he couldn't marry Marcie he didn't want to leave, but Harry told him not to risk it. It was still a bit touch and go, and we kept expecting him to turn up, but then the Army sealed London." She came to a halt, waiting a few moments but Davie and Marcie didn't notice. The second loud stage cough finally got their attention.

"It's Davie. He came back for me!" The lookouts still couldn't remember the young woman, but Davie had been right about pretty. She'd never been to any of the parties, but maybe this bloke was the reason.

"I can see that, Marcie. Now how about we go into the library so Davie can sit down." Sin's eyes swept the small crowd. "We don't want to open his present here, do we?" With that Marcie began tugging her man towards the library, not hard because he wasn't struggling.

*   *   *

Despite some casual questioning, the lookouts never did find out exactly who the bloke was, or what he'd brought. The gear and the way he'd acted might mean Army, but the next time anyone saw him, Davie didn't look very soldier-ish. He had the crewcut, but worked in the fields rather than as a guard or fighter. Those who worked with him reckoned Davie was a bit young to be Army during the Crash, and seemed a bit simple. Maybe the young man was just besotted, because he talked about Marcie most of the time.

Sin and Sinner, and any of the originals anyone asked, just said Davie was an old friend of Marcie's. A few found out Marcie worked in the library, but nobody dare ask the Librarian unwelcome questions. Interest waned when the mystery man slipped into the gang without a ripple. In private, Sin, Sinner, and a few close friends including the Librarian, had a small celebration when Davie gave Marcie her present. Marcie passed it on to Sin, because she'd already got the only present she cared about. The few in the know agreed the contents of the Bergen would be very useful when their backs were against a wall, but until then it should stay secret.

Chapter 15:
Shopping with Barbie

In Orchard Close, Harold already had more secrets than he felt comfortable with. He'd been working on turning one secret into an opportunity, planning a raid, when Trev threw a huge spanner in the works. The radio man had finally bodged together a fix for Barbie Radio. A probable fix, not a certainty, because there were too many unknowns. The explosion, even if the Barbies denied any such thing, could have thrown crap deeper into the transmitter's entrails, and there were almost certainly blown fuses.

Trev offered to write instructions, the best he could manage, but nobody else in Orchard Close knew enough about radios to improvise. Harold considered asking Marconi, the Geek radio man, but the Barbies would kill him regardless of any agreement. The be-wigged maniacs had most of the Geeks on their 'Most Wanted' list. Harold couldn't just tell the Barbies he couldn't fix their radio. Despite all the attempts to inject some realism, the Barbies were convinced Trev could do the job. They wouldn't believe anything else, and would try to kidnap Trev or possibly launch a raid. Harold didn't fancy pissing the Barbies off that badly, and the other gangs wouldn't be happy if the blondes went on a rampage.

Plenty of people were wondering what the Barbies would pay to get the transmitter fixed, but Sharyn came up with the real question. She asked what the Barbies would put up with. Harold came up with a possible answer, but if it didn't work the radio delivery would be on a one-way trip. He sent messages out around Orchard Close for volunteers, fighters willing to come with him on what might end up being a suicide mission. Any candidates were to meet him in the back garden of the dance house, fully armed, in two hours.

Harold took Trev and Elise in through the front door, fifteen minutes early. One glance out of the back window told him all he needed. He turned to Trev. "What you've told me is that the only way to fix Barbie radio is for you to go there."

Trev paled, glancing at the door as if weighing up the chances of escaping. "I didn't say that. I told you, I can't go there. Please?"

"You said nobody else can do it, which means you have to. Would you go if you were safe?" Harold raised his voice. "Bring them in, Patty." When the back door opened, fighters poured in until the dance room, and the extension at the back, were full. Even then voices could be heard outside, complaining they were being left out. Harold turned back to Trev. "Everyone here is willing to die to protect you."

"Bullshit, er, no they aren't."

"Too true we are." Patty scowled at Trev. "We didn't know that you were the job, but Harold asked for volunteers willing to die to help him get a job done." She swept her hand round to include the rest. "There's more coming." Suddenly she grinned as realisation hit. "You want us to go shopping in Beth's don't you?"

Before Harold could answer the cheering started. He'd thought that might cool the volunteers off a bit, but most of the idiots loved the idea. "It will be very, very dangerous but if everyone sticks to the script, the Barbies should stand for it." Harold turned back to Trev. "Do you truly think the Barbies can get to you with this lot as bodyguards? Or put it another way, will they take the losses to get through me and them, because I'll be there."

Trev looked over the fighters, dressed in their plated jackets and skirts and festooned with sharp stuff and firearms. "I daren't, Harold." That came out as a whisper. "I'll tell someone what to do."

"I'll go, if Trev gives me instructions." Everyone stared at Elise because she never spoke up. The lass flinched at shadows, but now she'd volunteered to walk into the tigress's den. She stroked her big mastiff. "If Thandia can come? I owe you, Harold, and everyone here." Her white face and trembling hands said Elise didn't fancy it one bit, but her voice showed real determination.

Fergie pushed forward and eyed Trev. "Are you going to let her go instead of you?" Her lip curled in disgust. "Maybe you aren't worth dying for." The young woman turned to Elise with a big smile. "She is."

Logan rested a hand very gently on Elise's shoulder. "Don't worry luv, I'll be right there with this." He showed her his mace.

"Trev?" Harold held the man's eye. "Your call, because otherwise Elise is our best bet. We can't afford to toss out all the work we've already paid for. Nor can we afford the losses if I tell the Barbies no, or Elise can't do it. They'll come for you, mob-handed." Harold held his eyes until Trev's dropped.

"I'll do it." Harold barely heard him, but Trev's voice strengthened on the second attempt. "I'll go. If you and this lot will come with me. You've got a proper plan?"

"Of course he's got a plan. Cripes, he's Soldier Boy, remember?" Bethany grinned and tapped her gnome hat. "But after this I want my real gang name, Sweet Demon. All official, right?"

"That's if you come. There's half a garden full of lunatics out there and I've got to leave a couple of people on guard." Harold tried to look stern, but he couldn't hide his grin nor the tear stinging the corner of his eye. Patty had told him the new recruits would do whatever he asked, but this definitely went over and above gratitude and they weren't all newcomers. "Now use that sweet smile to get them organised so we can get on with the planning. I'll want permanent guards on the kit, starting right now before I tell the Barbies it's ready." He glanced at Trev. "And a couple to watch over Trev until we go." Bethany grinned triumphantly at the "sweet" before herding fighters outside.

A dozen hands patted Trev on the back as they left; four fighters promising to put up a tent in his garden to watch the back door. Half an hour later, Harold had everyone's names, and had sent most home or back on duty. He settled down with a small group to plan properly. Harold thought they could get Trev into Beth's and out again, alive, but only if the Barbies didn't fancy paying what it would cost to keep him. The rest set into helping him work out how to make the price so high even a Barbie wouldn't consider it.

Once Harold told the Barbies the parts were ready they'd want to collect the kit immediately, so Harold held off a few days. Barry and Bernie needed at least two more days with Kharon the clockmaker to get their contribution prepared, with several others chipping in to help design the ultimate deterrent. Harold spent those days refining his ideas, thinning out the volunteers, or pacifying those he would leave behind. When he told a Barbie the repair was on, the woman downed her beer in one and ran to her car. Within the hour a message came back, the Barbie escort would arrive the following morning.

* * *

Five days after Harold asked for volunteers, the Orchard Close escort formed up. Their shotguns and some other weapons were concealed, but the escort were festooned with pistols, machetes, Rambos, maces, and crossbows. Definitely an escort, not a mob, thanks to the latest creation of the Coven. Since learning about the possible visit to Beth's, they'd had teams of women sewing overlapping steel washers onto padded jerkins. The result, real armoured vests, gave much better protection than the usual mishmash of flat plates sewn to jackets. Better still the thirty-five identical versions looked like a uniform. In a melee it would be easy to tell who belonged to Solder Boy's Army.

Ru and Alfie came as Soldier Boy's personal bodyguards. The Barbies liked them and both volunteered. Alfie would definitely do anything necessary to keep Hazel safe, and she'd insisted on coming to prove she didn't get the cushy jobs from Harold. Patty came as Harold's second in command, because both the Barbies and Orchard Close fighters respected her. Doll agreed she liked the Barbies too much after her stay there, and might not look determined enough for the deterrent to work. Her five best gunslingers came, with holsters tied down. All five swore that if it went to hell, they could draw and shoot faster than anyone else could raise a weapon. A hail of seventy-five bullets should disrupt even Barbies enough to give the rest a chance.

Casper, Emmy, Matthew and Doll assured Harold they could hold Orchard Close. The new muskets, and all the Mad Maxes, were loaded and hidden in the guardhouses. In addition, all the rifles but Patty's baby and a two-two for Harold would stay behind, because any fighting at Beth's would be short range. The rifles should hold off a daylight attack on Orchard Close if someone like Caddi tried to take advantage, and Harold should be back by dark.

The Barbie escort came down the road with "Born to be Wild" blasting out from their CD players. As soon as the first vehicle came in sight, the Orchard Close escort marched down the access road, standing in ranks to greet them. Harold shook his head at the natural blonde leading the Barbies. "Are those your party clothes?" He'd seen her at the refugee negotiation, but now she wore a one-piece studded leather swimsuit over her clothes.

"I'm Beetch Barbie, so what else should I wear? A hard Beetch so just what you need for a serious job." She looked over Harold's fighters, stood in two ranks. "Soldiers on parade! I should inspect them like they used to on TV." Which she promptly did, strolling up the ranks commenting on imaginary flecks of dust. On the way down behind them she threatened to slap a few bottoms, allegedly improve their posture. "You'll do. Would any of you like to sign up?" Beetch looked up at the nearest man, Logan. "Especially you. You can inspect me first?"

Harold thought her mood might have something to do with the heap of electrics sat in the back of Harold's pickup. "Sorry, they've all got a job, baby-sitting our radio man."

Trev sat in the back of the crew cab of Harold's pickup, wearing a balaclava, with one of Patty's blacksmith candidates each side as protection. Beetch waved at him, but her smile died as she inspected the load. "What's that?"

"That big lump attached to the top of the electrics is five gallons of oil and paraffin, with a bomb strapped to it." Harold held up a little plastic box with a button on, an old garage remote. "If anyone tries to nick the gear or our man, you lose the lot in a big bonfire. I considered taking the tank but that might just be a bigger temptation to your lot."

Beetch looked and thought, while a lot of the Barbie hilarity died away. "Fair enough. After all, some arses round here just can't be trusted." She turned, her smile breaking out again. "Come on girls, let's get the guests to the party!" The Barbies cheered, turning their cars around but leaving a gap in the middle for the Orchard Close vehicles. The Orchard Close escorts cheered as well as they broke ranks and loaded up. Most went in the pickup and vans, except for one in each Barbie vehicle to keep everyone honest.

The convoy set off, the Barbie Girls playing "Titanium Plated Bitch" at full volume with the windows open and generally showing off. On the way past, each carload shouted insults and promises at the houses where Caddi's watchers lurked. The Barbies were creative, but the Hot Rods didn't fancy a trip to the Mall. The pair might have felt better if they'd known Harold included their safety in the negotiations. He didn't want the Barbies starting a war on his doorstep.

The Barbies produced another exuberant and obscene display going past the GOFS sentries, but the GOFS expected it. The convoy wasn't on their road anyway. Roy and his men waved as they went through, and the GOFS sentry nearest the Barbie border even blew kisses. When the convoy drove over the border the Barbie sentries cheered them through. Even the civvies, the inhabitants of a clump of houses halfway to the Mall, seemed happy to see the convoy. Men, women and children came out of the houses to wave as the vehicles came through, smiling and cheering, which wasn't what Harold expected. He sure as hell hoped the transmitter worked, or the downer could be fatal.

* * *

The final approach to Beth's wound through a maze of low walls, girders and concrete blocks, covered by crossbows and several firearms. More Barbie guards stood on the roof of the concrete and glass structure, each side of a huge sign reading Queen Elizabeth II Shopping Centre. Someone had spray-painted BETH's in big letters beneath it, on the glass front of the entrance atrium. When the convoy finally drew up outside the main doors, Beetch called for people to come and collect the gear. Harold lined up his people either side of the pickup and revealed the rest of his conditions. "We all come in with the radio man. Armed."

"No way! No stranger goes into Beth's. We'll let him in to fix the radio, but nobody else." Beetch looked a little wild-eyed just at the thought.

"Nope. You all know I don't let any of my experts go alone. If he goes in there without us I've lost him, and that doesn't happen. We'll still be outnumbered but you won't attack us." Harold put as much confidence into the statement as possible.

"We won't?" Beetch had a real edge in her voice, while several Barbies put hands on weapons. Those already aiming weapons tensed. Harold glanced at his own people. Doll's gunslingers weren't the only ones with their hands near their pistols, ready.

Harold held up his hand, the one holding the little remote. "Don't do anything stupid until we show you why." Beetch nodded, a short, jerky, tense movement. "Okay, troops, show them the deterrent." Half of Harold's escort pulled out plastic bottles with lumps taped to the sides, holding them up. "Guns." Fifteen shotguns including the sawn-off appeared from under long jackets or the vehicles, along with extra handguns. Harold waved the box with a button. "If I press this, the transmitter is a bonfire. Then they'll shoot out your front doors and chuck those fire bombs into the shops and into your marijuana." Harold could see a huge patch growing under the glass roof of the entrance hall.

"You're bloody crazy. We can't allow you in Beth's with that lot!" Beetch tensed but kept glancing at the electrics and Harold's button. Harold thought that might be the only thing stopping a bloodbath, which was what he'd counted on.

"I'm not suicidal. You know that, and my people want to go home as well. We don't want to die so we won't start anything. This is just our insurance." Harold looked round at the poised Barbies. "If it kicks off we'll do what I said, because we're all dead anyway."

Harold could have kissed every man and woman behind who muttered "too true" or "believe it" and similar comments loud enough to be heard. The crazy sods sounded as if they meant it as well! "Burn, Barbie, burn" followed by another voice saying "Barbie-cue" had to be Harold's personal favourites.

"We could kill you now, you're right out in the open." Beetch glanced up to the weapons on the roof.

"Probably, but it wouldn't be easy and your transmitter would be gone forever. Anyone who survived the initial attack would blow straight through those doors, and burn as much as we could." Harold grinned and let it be as manic and crazy as he knew how. "By the time we're dead, you'll bloody well wish you'd talked." The mutters behind agreed while bombs, firearms and melee weapons were lifted, ready. "Now is it still a deal?"

Beetch glared at him, then at the escort behind him. "You mad bastard! Why didn't you say? Why not tell me this up front?"

Harold laughed, and it wasn't forced. "What, so you could snipe at me and ambush us on the way in, bury us in machetes?"

Beetch snorted, but some of the edge went off her stance and she raised her voice. "We wait for the bosses." The other Barbies also lost their edge, or a bit of it, as Beetch continued but quietly. "I might be a named Barbie, but I'm not senior enough to let armed anybody in Beth's. Only Barbies or prisoners go in there."

Harold pointed at the cab containing Trev. "He's neither, and he was supposed to go in and come back out." Trev had been well fortified with cider, but still looked as if he would faint every time a Barbie looked at him. The bombs were the final thing that had persuaded the radio man.

Beetch thought about that for a few moments. "Fair point, and no, I didn't think that through. We'll still wait here for the bosses because"—she suddenly grinned—"maybe he wasn't supposed to come back out." She glanced over at one of the Barbies. "Get them, all three. Tell them what he said, and that I said it's worth considering." The Barbie went off at a run, into Beth's. Beetch turned back to Harold. "Five minutes, tops, because they'll be in there waiting for that." She gestured to the mound of electrics and shook her head. "Can your lot sort of lower the bombs, please? Shit, only Soldier Boy would bring hand grenades and a fucking suicide squad."

"Whatever it takes." Harold didn't relax, not yet.

During the next three minutes, several civvies and Barbies came to look out through the glass doors. None came out because Beetch sent someone to stop them. "So there are no fatal misunderstandings." A small crowd appeared, walking rapidly towards the doors with three out front. "You got all three, Soldier Boy. Those are Christie, Ken and Malibu."

"I know. We've met, remember, but they looked happier last time." Beetch made a choking noise, not a happy one. She went to the doors, and after a short consultation the three followed her towards the convoy. Christie, Ken and Malibu looked the whole scene over, while Harold repeated the reasoning for letting his army into Beth's.

Malibu, the real blonde wearing a twinset and pearls under her machete and pistol, seemed to be in charge. "You were such a sociable type when we met before. I thought your reputation might be exaggerated, but now I find out you really are a brass balled crazy bastard." Harold looked round at the Barbies in their wigs and extravagant clothing and borrowed a trick from Caddi. He raised an eyebrow. Ken chuckled but Malibu just nodded. "It takes one to know one." She looked up at the electrical gear on the pickup, assessing both the gear and bomb. The Orchard Close troops got an equally thorough inspection. "You had better behave, and that thing had better work."

"I can be nice if you can. Remember, we don't actually want to die." Harold shrugged, trying for nonchalant. "I keep telling you I can't guarantee the thing will work, but we are definitely motivated."

Malibu finally smiled, just a little, nodded and turned to Ken, the big one dressed like a bloke. Christie, a tall slim black woman with a small blonde wig perched on top of a big afro, joined them. After a few tense moments of muttering, Malibu turned to those watching and raised her voice. "Get your lippy on girls, the Army's in town!" She continued in a lower voice as the cheering spread. "We talked on the way to meet you. This is definitely a one off because of the radio." She paused, looking over the Orchard Close group again. "Soldier Boy gets to bring his army into Beth's, fully armed. You come in, fix the radio, and get out. Any adventures and it goes Apocalypse Now. No casual shopping. Deal?"

"We fix the radio, collect our payment and leave. Anyone sneezes hard at us and it's burn, Barbie, burn, Barbie-cue time." Harold just couldn't resist that bit. "Deal." Everyone smiled as all three top Barbies shook hands with Harold, then with Patty, Alfie and Ru, which meant the Barbies recognised them as the elite. Harold wasn't sure that Ru considered it an honour, but Patty loved every minute. Alfie kept blushing as various Barbies called out, reminding him they'd been searched and asking if they could return the favour. Hazel looked ready to kill them all but managed to keep quiet.

In reality, the electrics on the pipe bomb taped against the container of paraffin and oil might not detonate anything. The string hanging from the side definitely would set off a very short clockwork timer, and ignite the bomb. In case nobody could get to it, two people would chuck their petrol bomb on the pickup to set it off. They'd promised to do so out of spite, because if it did kick off they were all going to die.

The small pipe bombs taped to the bottles of oil and paraffin were Barry's burning version. Kharon's clockwork fuses should release between four and six seconds from string being pulled, detonating a percussion cap and the fire bomb. Every person on this trip had volunteered three times during selection, knowing the odds. Harold had weeded out those who were a bit too keen on payback against anyone, then any showing hesitation. Except Trev, who was terrified but resigned, fortified with cider, and reassured by the sheer number of armed friends along.

Now, the force spread out either side of the transmitter. The big double entrance doors were unbarred and opened, and a small group of unarmed civvies came out. "The servants will strip down enough so you don't get nervous." Beetch called to the men and women and they shed jackets and jumpers, and in a couple of cases, shirts. The servants carefully picked up the timbers under the transmitter parts, sliding the impromptu litter off the pickup and heading inside.

"You are the first armed outsiders into Beth's since we arrived." Ken didn't look happy, but then suddenly smiled. "Caddi will have a fucking heart attack, because Barbie Radio will tell everyone you came for an orgy." She actually laughed, though it sounded a bit manic. "It might turn into one, once the radio works. I'm going ahead to make sure everyone behaves." She left, shouting at a couple of Barbies to take their hands off their effing weapons.

The immediate escort of Barbies shed their weapons apart from small blades, also to avoid accidents, Beetch explained. Harold would bet a horde of heavily armed women lurked just out of sight, probably with Ken in charge by now. Curious faces peeked out from all sides, while equally curious Orchard Close guards looked back as they finally made it inside. The first shop each side had no glass in the window, but a sheet of steel set at an angle sealed the bottom half of the opening. At least the women standing behind it were showing their empty hands, not aiming crossbows. The crossfire from there should rip any attackers apart as they came through the doors. Unless, Harold thought with a private smile, they brought hand grenades.

Conditions in the rest of Beth's weren't anything like as bad as Harold expected. A wide strip of the floor had been torn up, but only to grow marijuana. A few of the shop windows lining the sides of the wide hall were smashed, and some displays ransacked, but most looked intact and many still contained goods. The store dummies were arranged as an orgy, and graffiti decorated everywhere, but otherwise the place didn't look that much different from before the Crash.

The civvies looking out of the shops, or from beyond the broad staircase ahead, seemed healthy, decently dressed and not at all cowed. Given the reputation the Barbies had, their servants shouldn't be smiling and excited. The two men and a woman on leads, and one tied to a post who'd definitely been whipped or caned, were almost a relief.

The servants carrying the transmitter were reminded to be careful by several of the spectators, servants as well as Barbies. The Barbies referred their civvies in here as servants. They spoke to them quite reasonably, definitely better than Caddi's lot spoke to the serfs in the Mansion. The servants treated the misshapen lump and clumps of wires with tenderness and caution, which didn't make for quick progress.

It seemed to take forever to get across the wide foyer. The whole procession kept to one side, well clear of the wide strip of luxuriant growth running directly under the glassed strip in the roof. The Barbies grew what many considered to be the best marijuana in the city, a major source of revenue for the nutters which was why Harold threatened to burn it. He'd need a lot more fire bombs to get it all. The plants continued back beyond the stairs, directly under the glass roof, as far as Harold could see. The Orchard Close guards tensed when savage barking broke out. "Maggie, leave! Down." The young Dobermann, looking very much like her sire Fury rather than Lucky her Labrador ma, obeyed and laid down. She still watched the armed intruders intently, and the Barbie guard next to her kept a firm hold on the leash.

"Even if you sold her, we can hardly tell her you're a friend." Beetch looked Logan up and down. "Unless you let your boys come shopping on a regular basis?" Harold watched, but the dog seemed to be under better control than her sire ever was. Casper would have tried to make friends.

"Casper would have wanted to hug her. He might visit just to see her." Harold paused when the name registered. "Maggie? I thought you'd call her Mz Fang or Ball-biter."

"Margaret Thatcher. Hardest bitch to ever run this country." Beetch smirked and chomped her teeth together with a click. "Ball-biter would work because she goes for the nuts." The Barbie looked up ahead of them. "I'll go up the stairs first to clear the riffraff." She quickly cleared the people waiting at the top and the procession started up. As they did some of the tension seemed to ease, with a couple of Barbies calling out to some of the Orchard Close guards. None of them answered, staying with the job, but Beetch called back. "Not now. If you want to get friendly, wait until the radio is fixed." A few cheered or laughed at that.

After a short trip along the balcony, the servants set the gear down inside the radio room and left. As the Orchard Close escort settled in, after checking the room for surprises, quiet comments were exchanged at the state of the transmitter. Harold already knew the pictures looked like bomb damage. Now he could see the whole setup, the thought a small bomb had been shoved inside the front of one panel.

Trev started stripping out the ruined section, sending everything down to the transport outside. With luck, some of it could be salvaged to use or sell elsewhere. People clustered at the bottom of the stairs and within minutes Ski and Beetch came up to see Harold. "Will it work?"

"Give us a chance! I keep telling you, maybe. Trev has already told me there's big nasty surprises the pictures didn't show." Harold glanced back at Trev, who hadn't said any such thing but the Barbies needed slowing up. "Just keep clear of him. We nearly had to carry him in."

"What's the matter with him?" Ski seemed genuinely curious.

"We don't know what's the matter with a lot of our refugees, men and women, and we don't pry. He arrived in a bad way, and hasn't said why." Harold glanced back again but Trev seemed engrossed. "Let him be because he's got to concentrate. He's trying to find out if the bomb threw any crap deeper inside, and messed up more of it."

"It wasn't..." Beetch relaxed and shrugged. "It won't happen again." She left with Ski, speaking to several people outside, servants and Barbies. The small crowd in the foyer started up a low-key party, with a bit of dancing and some animated talk and laughter. The maniacs appeared to be on holiday, or just missing because the crowd out there were a mixture of relatively unarmed fighters and servants. Harold was looking carefully, ignoring his first impressions, but these people were definitely too happy for gangster slaves.

Not that Harold relaxed. He knew the real maniacs had to be just round a corner someplace, gripping serious weaponry. The ones below were the ordinary soldiers, mixed with people who kept the toilet unblocked and the food grown or cooked. All of them were obviously fond of what was a genuine radio station. Barbie Radio appeared to be a proper studio with mikes on booms and turntables as well as disc players. They'd ripped off the complete article and someone had installed it properly, unless it had always been here. The way everything neatly fitted in meant Harold thought that a real possibility.

The components Orchard Close brought started going into the hole, or partially anyway because the repair would never fit. Harold doubted the Barbies would care how it looked. Trev sweated, and said cripes a lot, but kept saying not to worry. Meanwhile, the escort ate their own food in shifts, drinking their own boiled water to avoid drugging. Patty came back from talking to the Barbies at the top of the stairs. "They're not worried, but that doesn't look to be coming along very fast." She nodded towards where a couple of his escort were holding wires or bits of electrics for Trev. "It gets dark early this time of year. What happens if Trev hasn't finished? I don't fancy trying to load up and keep this lot off us at night, not once that's working."

"Good point. Ask your girlfriends out there to send for one of the top three." Patty flashed a grin and went to do so.

Malibu turned up so Harold beckoned her forward. She looked in at the mare's nest of wires, and Trev busy testing and fitting together. "Fucking hell, that's a mess."

"It was a worse mess until he started repairing it?"

"Possibly." Malibu squinted. "Something certainly seems to be going in."

"Then how about we start on the payment?" Harold looked up and down the shopping Mall. "Lovely though Beth's is, we don't expect a sleepover."

"If that thing works, I could guarantee you'd all enjoy it. What do you have in mind?" Malibu kept watching Trev, but Harold didn't think she understood any better than him.

"How about one of my people goes down and supervises emptying your music shop, then raids your CDs and DVDs?" Malibu didn't look keen, but Harold kept going. "If Barbie radio doesn't work, the loaded vehicles won't move."

"Maybe." Malibu took a long hard look at the lump still attached to the electrics. "What about that bomb? How come it's still stuck on there?"

"If your transmitter works, the bomb will make sure we get clear with our payment. Once we are back at the border I'll remove the battery and disable my remote. We'll wait there with your escort until you confirm the bomb has come off." Malibu still hesitated, so Harold tried a diversion. "Who would you like down there to supervise?" He grinned, sticking his chest out, and Malibu enjoyed the joke.

"Would Soldier Boy like to go down there among all those lovely girls? They'll make you really welcome and would love you to supervise them, all of them." Harold would never have believed the word supervise could sound so downright filthy.

He feigned disappointment, not very well from Malibu's expression. "I daren't. These women would pine or be jealous. They'd nag me about it for months afterwards."

Malibu's eyes roamed over the Orchard Close party and her lips curved in a big smile. "How about Patty, so we can show the Demon all the benefits of Barbie membership? Just the sight of that fancy sheath is loosening knicker elastic."

"By all means go for it. Maybe she'll persuade a couple of yours to follow her home instead?" Harold pointed at the decorated sheath on Patty's rifle. "She might let someone look under her tassels if she's asked right." He raised his voice. "Patty?"

Once Harold explained, Patty nodded happily. "No problem. A teacher once told me it's a good thing to broaden my horizons." She tapped her rifle and blades. "I'm sorry but I insist on staying dressed." Malibu agreed so Patty followed her out the door, then looked back. "If I don't come back, a Demon expects a decent pyre. Something hot, downright incendiary and definitely memorable." Several of the escort waved their bombs in the air, but the Barbies loved it. Those near enough to hear burst out laughing, passing her comments on to the rest.

* * *

Once Patty left, Harold once again tried to reassess the Barbies because reality wasn't gelling with the rumours. Some of the people downstairs could have fitted into Orchard Close without a ripple. It kept him occupied, and calmed his nerves, as time slipped away without the electrics producing even a burst of static. The Barbie troops were nutters, but so were Caddi and the Hot Rods. Barbie humour had a real bloody edge, but being surrounded by gangs who thought women were natural prey might cause that. Any captured Barbie could expect a long slow death, probably chained up as a sex toy.

A tiny worm of unease stirred in Harold because outside, when they'd been shaking bombs, some of his people were definitely as manic as any Barbie. Was he training up an Orchard Close version of the local nutters? Yet in here that savage edge seemed dulled at least, so maybe the Orchard Close fighters would calm down once they were homem A woman introducing herself as Vinnie underlined the relaxation, by bringing Splash up to say hello. Now a full grown Staffy, Splash wouldn't come near until Vinnie said Harold was a friend, but then went wriggly and waggy-tailed. A few casual questions confirmed that the dogs spent their nights on guard.

A succession of Barbies came to spend time guarding the Orchard Close guards, chatting with both men and women. Harold watched, wondering if the GOFS and Barbies had rubbed off on each other a bit. Perhaps the fabled sex slaves and slave labour didn't exist? The Barbies weren't enlightened, but neither were they tyrants. Harold visited Caddi's headquarters on a regular basis, but only met the other gangs at agreed trading posts. Maybe Caddi and the Hot Rods were worse than most of the other gangs? Not the Geeks, Harold had plenty of evidence showing how nasty the Geek Freeks were. What he saw here matched with the way Finn told him the Barbies treated their tenants, those outside Beth's. Those were treated much better than the Geek or Hot Rod serfs.

A continual stream of top Barbies talked to Harold, Alfie and Ru, making it clear that the Barbies were interested in more trade. Chandra, wearing her silk curtains of course, seemed keenest. "We didn't just come for the beer you know." She very obviously ogled a few of the nearest women. "Or your women and polite men, as lovely as they are. Malibu kept sending different fighters to have a beer and a look and ask questions. She wanted to know how your women are treated when nobody is looking, and if we can trust you. Those football matches were unexpected and are very popular. We've threatened some really bloody retribution if anyone fucks them up." Chandra looked into the radio room, at all the armed Orchard Close fighters. "We had to find out what made you tick, especially before we let you near Beth's. Near, not inside. None of us expected you to get this far, as the choirgirls said to the actress."

"I might have been a bit pushy, but I never expected to see that." Harold gestured to the relaxed and definitely not tortured Barbie servants dancing below. "As the actress said to the choirgirls."

"Is that what happened with Mercedes?" Chandra grinned, her eyes alive with mischief. "Come on, give us the latest dirt."

"It was a bit like that, I suppose, and I definitely didn't expect what I saw." They bantered for a bit about choirgirls and actresses, and how far they might go or what they might see.

"We've had questions asked about your gun repairs. Where did you learn?" Chandra slipped that in, then smiled sort of innocently at Harold's look. "Seriously."

"In the Army, and I'm probably not the best out there. The Trainspotters had someone and I'll bet the General has a gun repairer. Some might even be the real deal, from pre-Crash." Harold chuckled because where he'd learned was obvious. "What I learnt is enough for running repairs, because HM likes the Army's weapons to work."

Chandra found that funny, but soon got back to business. "We definitely agree with HM about weapons. Some of us agree with your wench, the home one, about those bidets. We had a look in the shops, and we've got a few with all the fittings but they're still boxed up. Can your plumber fix them up, and maybe a couple of the fancy baths with bubbles and suchlike?"

"Are you serious, after this?" Harold looked at all the weapons on display. "You'd be tempted to keep him, so are you inviting this lot back inside again?"

"Above my pay grade but maybe, if you don't leave a mess on the floor?" Chandra seemed serious, but Harold wasn't so sure. "We'll expect you to keep quiet about this place, what we're like at home. Some arses would think we were getting soft. We'd have to make another example, decorate a couple of lamp posts."

"Is that what happened last time, the raid?" Harold had often wondered why the idiots had attacked a gang headquarters.

"Just idiots, we reckon, because until now nobody but Barbies ever saw inside Beth's and left alive. Malibu must trust you, at least that far, so maybe your plumber would be safe. Fergie and Louise could come as escorts?" Despite her laugh, Chandra wasn't joking about the last part.

They talked about plumbing and this and that until Harold dropped in his own innocuous question. "So how many Murphy refugees have you intercepted?" He did his best to look innocent as Chandra gave him a long look.

"Not quite intercepted, but we've got people hidden in the right place to inspect them. If the runners look mad as hell and ready for a fight, we make them an offer. Most people look frightened, running for sanctuary, so we let them go." A tiny question appeared in Chandra's eyes. "You could have told us your girlfriend had found a way under our border."

"I don't know how they get out, not exactly, just that there's a place they all aim for. I don't even know it's Mercedes, not officially. Why don't you make them all that offer?"

"We don't want the unwilling ones, just those ready to fight. We'd like some of their weapons, but if word got back I'm sure the refugees would suddenly find another route. This way, if Caddi or the Murphies follow one of them, we get their weaponry. We've only had two fighters come through, following a lass who was too frightened to be careful. They didn't go back to report." Chandra's amiable manner took on a serious edge. "If Caddi takes over the rest of the Murphy estates, we can use the same bit of sewer to go right under his border guards."

"Someone might be lurking at the other end." Harold didn't want the Barbies and Mercedes coming to blows.

"I reckon she's more likely to leave a map showing where Caddi sleeps. If she wanted to give us any grief, she'd have saved that route to help her boss." Chandra thought for a moment, then smiled in anticipation. "Let her know we've got an ambush this end. She might send him through there once the war is over." They discussed what might happen when the war finished, until eventually Chandra left. When Harold checked, Trev seemed to have connected a lot of wires in the interim.

It wasn't dusk but time dragged on so Harold told a few to doze. They'd be sharper later. Trev took another break, coming to talk to Harold but keeping his voice down. "I'm ready for the first test, but it won't start transmitting. There might be a few lights but that's all."

"Okay. I'll keep the Barbies out of sight of the kit and won't tell them.

They'll only get wound up." A quick word with the guards and they made sure no Barbies wandered nearer for a while.

Trev ran the first test. The speakers inside Beth's crackled! A stampede of women came up the stairs to ask what had happened, led by Beetch. "Is it fixed?" A crowd behind her hung on every word, ignoring the weapons the startled guards were aiming.

Harold held up his hands, palms out, trying to calm them down. "Steady on. It's just a test to see if the power is going where it should. We didn't expect any noise because it's not transmitting." Harold pointed at one of the speakers that made a noise. "How come that fired up?"

"It's our tannoy. We make announcements on there or sometimes play different music to what we transmit. Does that help?" Harold passed the message. Trev nodded, keeping clear of the door and turning back to the transmitter straight away. Down on the ground floor of the shopping centre the party picked up a bit. Beetch spoke to the succession of senior Barbies who'd come to investigate. Despite that, they looked happier because something had started working.

Harold considered prodding Trev along, but that would probably make the radio man more nervous. Lights came on inside Beth's before Trev came to see him again. "This time the tannoy should work. Warn them and try to keep them clear. Please?" The stampede had wound him up all over again.

The second test produced a burst of music through the speakers, and a bloody great cheer went up. The tannoy worked at least, which livened up the dancing in the foyer. Four obviously elite Barbies, Cherry Pie, Ski, Beetch, and one wearing jodhpurs and holding a whip, stayed permanently at the top of the stairs. At least they kept the rest from trying to look in the radio room. "The decks are working now, it's just the actual transmitting part. Whoever set that bomb knew where to put it to cause the most damage." Harold passed the first part of Trev's comment to Beetch. Someone down below produced a big boom box and set it up on a table.

Ru came across to Harold, speaking quietly so Trev didn't hear. "Ski says that thing is tuned to Barbie Radio, and the volume is on eleven." Despite the dancing and laughter below, the revellers all kept glancing at the radio and up at the radio room. Someone even lowered the volume of the CD player. The tension began to rise again, expectation rather than aggression.

Trev kept testing, twisting and joining, and the rat's nest turned into a thick braid of connected wiring. He tested controls again. More lights came on, but Trev confessed he didn't actually know how to operate the kit. Harold passed that on. Within minutes Skipper turned up in her red striped top and leg warmers, a denim skirt, and carrying her old transistor radio. "Stop playing about with those controls." She rubbed against Trev. "You can adjust anything of mine you like? Maybe stay over so you can tune it all?" Everyone but Trev laughed.

Harold rescued him. "Are you here to help him, or give him a heart attack?"

"I came to help because I usually operate Barbie Radio. I know what to press to get it to work." Skipper started poking buttons and turning dials. "Your radio bloke can turn on anything else he likes, as long as it's me?" She couldn't get a reply, even his name, so Skipper settled for telling Trev which lights should have come on and what they meant. When Trev traced wires and did some more twisting and taping inside the front panels, Skipper got on her hands and knees to see better. "Don't look up my skirt, because I put these knickers on for the radio man. He can look, or put his hand up to check?"

Trev refused to check, or even answer, so she went back to playing with controls. More lights came on and dials lit up until finally Skipper put a CD in, then tapped a microphone. Nothing happened but after consulting, Trev rewired a small section. This time Skipper sent a message to turn off the CD player downstairs. Silence fell. The next tap sounded loud and clear down below, from the radio! Skipper picked up the mic and announced triumphantly that "Barbie Radio lives!" Her words boomed out at eleven and the real party started. Harold even knew where the armed to the teeth maniacs were lurking, because he could hear them cheering.

Beetch opened her arms to include everyone. "Stay the night! Join the party!" Right now, Harold thought the invitation might be genuine. The Barbies in sight were totally relaxed and happy, only interested in dancing and celebrating. Just as well because they were already mixing with the Orchard Close guards, wanting them to join in. The weapons weren't even slowing them up. Harold wondered, just for a moment, but the invasion seemed totally friendly and not the prelude to a massacre. The only assaults were lip to lip, and those victims weren't actually fighting back.

"Sorry, I'm on a curfew." Harold quickly organised the guards with Trev in the middle, heading downstairs while the good mood lasted.

The dancing crowd reluctantly parted, just far enough to let them through before closing up behind. The Orchard Close group all had a lot of invitations on the way out, but declined. Not all of them were against the idea, Harold heard several promise "next time." His own people were a bit too relaxed and happy if they were considering coming back!

Except Trev, who might be surrounded by guards but had a companion and wasn't relaxed at all. He kept cowering away as Skipper made increasing desperate pleas for him to check her knickers, tweak her nipples, anything please to remember him by. Harold received his own set of offers, a couple of them from female servants which somehow seemed more startling. He accepted one offer, a large Union Flag to drape over his shoulders, which raised a huge cheer.

Harold heaved a sigh of relief when the doors opened, and took a deep breath of fresh air. Patty, stood by Harold's pickup in the full glare of the light from the glass doors, also looked relieved and definitely ready to roll. "They kept telling me you'd stopped to party, and asking me back inside. I thought I might have to go home alone." Several Barbies promptly offered to keep her company; the party had spilled outside to the sentries. Harold chivvied the rest of his people along, because he wanted to be over the border before the euphoria wore off. He still had the button and the muskets until the convoy reached the border, and hoped the bomb stayed enough of a deterrent. Full volume Barbie Radio, with vocal accompaniment, blasted from the transport as the escort poured out of the doors to take Harold home.

A small army of additional Barbie troops trotted alongside the vehicles, but fell behind as the vehicles accelerated. When the convoy passed their housing, the civvies were actually dancing under the street lights, waving and cheering. Barbie Radio blasted out from their houses, loud and clear. "We Will Rock You" hammered out of the radios as the convoy reached the border, loud enough for the GOFS to know that Barbie Radio lived. On this clear, still evening maybe even the General, Geeks and Hot Rods would catch it.

Harold took out the batteries and crunched the remote underfoot. "Pull out the battery and remove the bomb without pulling the string. Then pull the string and chuck it where it won't do any damage when it goes bang. It might not anyway without the batteries." Harold kept his voice and face dead serious despite Beetch's huge grin. "In which case shoot it until it does, because you don't want to take it apart." He didn't want the Barbies getting an example of Kharon's clockwork fuse.

Beach Beetch calmed down enough to send a Barbie to pass that on through the field telephone, and wait for confirmation. "What about the liquid?"

"Five gallons of oil and paraffin, harmless without the boom. If you put the mixture in a big tub the two might separate and then they're a bonus."

Harold and his party refused offers to join in the dancing for the few minutes until the Barbie came back. She spoke to Beetch who gave a whoop. "All clear, the bomb is off!"

Harold handed over the two muskets. "Careful. They're loaded, because we weren't sure if you'd be getting the gun or the ball." Harold grinned as he said it because by now he knew what the result would be. Sure enough, the Barbies fell about laughing, that was their kind of joke. Beetch promptly let one musket off straight up, which knocked her onto her ass.

People on both sides put a hand on a weapon or cocked what they were carrying, then relaxed. Beetch looked round and started laughing. "Here, you try." She threw the other musket to one of the border sentries before using the empty one to help herself up. A few seconds later, smoke and flame erupted skywards again. It looked spectacular now darkness had almost fallen, so the GOFS would know the Barbies had muskets. They were a negligible increase in firepower, but the big noisy weapons were becoming a status symbol of sorts.

Harold handed over the small bag of musket balls, half a dozen flints and a glass jar full of powder. "This is the right powder. It's a bit rougher than the type you put in reloads, but that will work as well. The balls are just lead."

"Yeah, yeah, yeah. We've all been looking at books and a couple of old videos to see how they work." Beetch threw the empty musket and the ammo to another border guard. "Get those back to Beth's. Just one of you, the rest can party when you're relieved."

She turned back to Harold with a wide smile. "I'm in charge of your escort, all the way home. You should ride with me to give directions. With a bit of luck I'll find out if your balls are lead or brass, and you can check if I'm a genuine blond?" Harold managed to keep his smile, though he hadn't been planning on that. It would be an interesting trip but he couldn't refuse, not without losing his fearless SAS bastard reputation.

Beetch wasn't just being chatty, she seemed downright manic even for a Barbie. She put the inside light on, just so Harold could read the big tag now fastened to the zip down the front of her swimsuit. It read 'Pull to

Initiate Orgy' in big letters. Then Harold had to look at her ass to see that the zip came through and nearly up to her waist, "in case I meet a beach doggie." Harold could pull the tag if he wanted to check if she was naturally blonde, or the back zip if he didn't care either way. The act carried on, unrelenting.

The driver and gunner joined in, with increasing precise offers of what they could do for Soldier Boy, individually or together. When Harold kept declining they switched to offering to party while he watched, then maybe he'd be tempted. He found out later that the others in the Barbie vehicles had been subjected to a similar set of probably genuine offers.

*　*　*

At least the harassment kept the Orchard Close escort alert, which almost caused a massacre. The Barbies didn't mess about with coming across the rubble to Orchard Close, they came up the road with their lights blazing. The road to the bypass was neutral regardless of how Caddi felt about it, and anyway they were the Barbie Girls so noisy and blatant were required behaviour.

The fourteen or fifteen armed men clustered around the vehicles blocking the access road to Orchard Close nearly died. Harold heard weapons being cocked all around him and yelled. "Stop, wait! Turn the bloody radios off!" The radios were turned down, not off, but relative silence fell, a silence punctuated by comments about cheeky Hot Rod bastards and dead meat.

Meanwhile, the men froze in the glare, pinned against their vehicles. "Shoot them in the legs, girls, so we can take them home to the party." Beetch sounded totally serious.

"Don't shoot yet, they aren't any sort of a threat." Harold laughed to pretend he felt relaxed, but he knew how much the Barbies disliked Hot Rods. "They're fifty yards from Orchard Close and bright shiny targets. Crossfire." Harold laughed again as loud as he could. "I trained the people aiming at them."

The comments started to brighten, with the suggestions moving on to taking the Hot Rods intact and keeping them after the party. The edge came off Beetch and the gunner in with Harold, and he breathed a bit easier. One of the men stepped forward with a hand up to shade his eyes, calling out. Harold recognised Dodge and shouted again for some quiet.

Eventually he could hear what the Hot Rod shouted. "Where you been, Harry? Caddi wants to know."

"At a party with my new girlfriends." That raised a big cheer from the Barbies, and various offers to party in different ways. Dodge realised who Harold had in all these motors.

"Barbies! You brought them back? Are you f… bloody crazy?"

"Manners, Dodge. Ladies present." That just increased the offers. This time Harold wasn't sure all the voices were Barbies.

"Ah, sorry Harold." Dodge must be sorry because he actually said Harold instead of Harry. The Hot Rod had finally realised he was asking Soldier Boy a possibly unwelcome question, while pinned neatly between a horde of Barbies and whatever pointed his way from Orchard Close. "It's just that Caddi wondered, and then we saw lights coming."

"So why does that affect me? I'm on my patch, Dodge. Cooper tried this once, but had the sense to stand the other side of your border." Soldier Boy had to keep up his public image. Privately Harold would have laughed and told the man, but right now he had to be a gang boss.

"It's just, ah shit, someone killed a couple of the lads and took their motors. Nothing special but Caddi knew you'd left with some of your lot, armed to the teeth. With you teaming up with the Barbies, you know? Ah, shit, forget it." The last part tailed off. Dodge didn't want to be here, or asking that question.

"Caddi sent you to ask me if I've raided the Hot Rods and nicked his motors? Doesn't Caddi like you, Dodge?" Some gang bosses would have sent Dodge's head back, or maybe the man but without his balls. Several of the Barbies had already suggested something similar, for all the Hot Rods.

"Not right now, because the blokes and the motors were mine. Look, can we have the lights off and talk please?" Harold had never heard Dodge trying to sound reasonable before. The usually bullish Hot Rod had finally realised what a bloody dangerous place he'd ended up in. Nobody present liked Hot Rods and his own people were blocked in, lit up, night blind, and daren't use rifles or shotguns or the Army would shoot them.

"Go inside the gates, Dodge. Your men leave their weapons in the motors and are searched at the gates. These nice ladies are staying the night so their weapons get locked in their vehicles as well. The troops can all have a free beer in the canteen to start the party." Harold managed to keep his voice level as a hand gave him a friendly fondle, and a low voice pointed out he wouldn't be sorry. The Barbie convoy waited, shouting promises about the party while the Hot Rods filed through the gates and were searched. Meanwhile Beetch passed a message, warning her women to leave everything but knives in the motors.

When the Barbies moved up for searches, most of them asked if Harold, Alfie or Patty could search them personally, please. It felt like dealing with a score of manic Mercedes wannabes, which kept Harold smiling. The offers continued as the mob spilled in through the gates, until Tessa walked through the scrum and put her arm round Harold. A momentary hush followed as the Barbies noted the short tight skirt and top, the smile, and the proprietary arm.

"Welcome home Harold. Everything's been kept warm for you. There's beer or stew in the canteen for the others." Tessa gave Harold a firm kiss, what a gang boss would expect from his woman, while Harold tried to ignore the emphasis on everything. The Barbies made comments about what had been kept warm, until Beetch reminded them where they were. The comments moderated to slanderous innuendo.

Tessa had definitely backed the Barbies off, so Harold put an arm around his official wench and walked up the street to home. On the way he nodded thanks to Casper, Doll and Emmy, who'd lined up thirty heavily armed fighters just inside the gates. The fighters who had been to Beth's calmed down, forming ranks again which neatly cut the Barbies and Hot Rods off from their motors and weapons. Up ahead the Hot Rod troops were heading into the canteen for their beer, watched by Matthew, Bess, and a dozen of their squad. Within minutes Harold reached his home, and as soon as the door closed Tessa and Sharyn started laughing at him.

"Emmy phoned from the gate to say someone should rescue you." Sharyn offered a cup of coffee.

"I put these on and came to the rescue." Tessa posed in her tight clothes. "I suppose I'd better put real clothes on now so you don't get ideas." She licked her lips, then smirked. "I'd say sorry about the kiss but you wouldn't believe me." Harold opened his mouth to answer, then decided no comment might be safer which made them both laugh even more.

Regardless of what Tessa thought, Harold knew he couldn't stay in here. "There's Hot Rods and Barbies loose out there. I ought to keep an eye on the idiots."

"Don't worry about it. Doll has the job of chaperoning whoever's in charge of the Barbies because they all know her. Casper is bigger than Dodge, and will threaten him with a gay search if there's any crap. The Hot

Rod and Barbie troops will end up either arguing or pairing off with each other. They're not heavily armed so it won't come to much." Sharyn smiled and patted the big chair.

"We'll need extra guards in the canteen with that lot." Harold wanted to go and help. He definitely didn't think he should be sat at home with his feet up.

"They won't start a gang fight, because Emmy is keeping those guards by the gate armed and on alert tonight. Doll reckons putting the two gangs in two of the Annex houses will keep them from causing trouble in the main compound tonight, especially with the Demons next door. Someone is already moving residents out to make room, just overnight. All our fighters were ready for trouble anyway, in case Dodge felt ambitious before you arrived back. Casper already made the Hot Rods wait out there for over an hour. We wouldn't let them leave, in case Dodge went to ambush you coming back in just the pickup and vans." Tessa smiled and posed. "Now do you want me to sit on the chair arm so we can play that game? The where does the hand go one? Or are you going to tell us all about the trip?"

"I'll phone the canteen first."

"In that case I'll get comfy." Tessa headed off upstairs to get changed, while Harold made his call. Emmy answered the phone and told Harold it was all covered, and he was to keep out of it. This would teach the Barbies and Hot Rods they weren't important enough for Soldier Boy's personal attention. Harold laughed and sat down with his coffee to tell Sharyn and Tessa that, and about the trip. Sharyn answered a knock on the door within minutes and came back with a message from Casper.

Harold stayed in his chair because Tessa insisted. She'd dressed to make a deliberate impression out there. The "everything warm" and the kiss should keep anyone from bothering Harold tonight, until everything cooled down again. Even the residents would get the message, because Daisy, Eddie and Wills were sleeping with Susan and Rob tonight. The two women laughed at Harold again when he objected.

Casper's message confirmed the muskets and Mad Maxes were still a secret, while a phone call from Matthew told Harold to relax, the night shifts were sorted. A little later Patty called to promise that her Demons would be up early, to take over guard duty. According to her, Harold should have a late breakfast and make the Barbies and Hot Rods wait around a bit. There weren't any more interruptions. Soldier Boy had very efficient officers in his army, Sharyn and Tessa reckoned. Harold had to laugh because yes, his friends had got it all under control.

Harold, his official wench and his sister relaxed while discussing Dodge's visit. They agreed either the GOFS had taken an opportunity to sting Caddi, or the Murphies were biting back. They also agreed that Caddi had deliberately sent Dodge, a bullish type, to test Orchard Close. He'd known Harold left with a lot of fighters, because the spies must have reported. The response would make Caddi think long and hard before taking any liberties.

They discussed the Barbies knowing about the escape route, but letting most refugees come through. Keeping those who looked like potential fighters seemed a Barbie sort of thing, but letting the others keep their weapons wasn't. Harold spent some time explaining how some of what they thought they knew about the Barbies didn't seem to be quite right. Sharyn wondered if some of it was extra people joining and calming the original nutters down a bit. After all, the original founders of Orchard Close were completely outnumbered by later arrivals. They all agreed enough nutters remained to make the Barbies bloody dangerous.

Despite Harold's misgivings, none of the nutters, Hot Rods or Barbies, started any trouble inside Orchard Close. Harold slept better than he'd expected with nearly forty non-residents inside the walls.

* * *

Harold had a late breakfast as instructed, with Dodge and Beetch as well as Casper, Doll, Ru and Alfie. He'd wanted all the squad leaders, but Patty, Emmy and Matthew told him they were busy so they'd see him later. Sharyn had barely put the bubble and squeak on the table when Beetch started. She triumphantly announced that Logan, one of the Orchard Close escort, had pretended to tug at the big tag. Beetch told Logan he had to pull it now, at least down to her waist. Logan reckoned he didn't mind inspecting her blouse and pulled the tag. Beetch smirked until Dodge had to ask. "What happened?"

"There's nothing under the swimsuit. The arms and top of the blouse are sewn to it." She preened, pushing out her chest and the tag. "He seemed interested, if a bit flustered, so I asked if he wanted to check my roots. He only had to pull the tag a bit harder."

Dodge waited, but not for long. "Well?"

"Oh no. Anyone wanting to know has to check for themselves." Beetch refused to confirm anything else.

"There were a lot of roots being checked last night. I found a sleep-walker. She wanted to check out how hot my…." The Hot Rod glanced at Harold and left the rest unsaid. He seemed quieter this morning, nothing like his usual abrasive self.

Beetch glanced at Doll. "You should get a swimsuit, the blokes seem more interested in checking out blondes."

"No need, my Stetson and boots seem to attract enough attention and anyway, we don't want to confuse them." Doll inspected Beetch. "You'd be a natural for the swimsuit football league in that get-up, but you'd have to get rid of the sewn-on bits."

"You've got a whole team of Beach Beetches? I thought it was a windup when Chandra and Ski were on about them." Beetch glanced down at her leather and studs. "I'll have to look out for another swimsuit, in case I get an invite. I suppose you'd insist on one without studs or zips, a non-Beetch version?"

The others made jokes about what constituted acceptable dress for swimwear football, while Dodge wanted more information. He was teased about having to design Hot Rod swimwear if he ever had the chance to play. Harold looked round them all and thought about how he dressed and acted in public. They were all at it, living the whacko identities they'd chosen. Doll wore her Stetson and boots, while the others from Orchard Close all wore their newest clothes and poser weapons like Rambos. Ru had a lot of extra blades, as usual, while Casper brought his mace and giant machete. Alfie had arrived with his spear, the one with 'boyfriend' inscribed on the blade.

Tessa sat close to Soldier Boy, wearing a tight blouse, feeding him bits of toast and pouring his coffee. Soldier Boy had an arm round his wench, because Tessa put it there with a murmured "and no wandering." She seemed to be enjoying herself. Casper, Ru, Doll and Alfie were a bit startled by this version of Tessa, and the two visitors were definitely amused. Harold recognised the teasing, flirting Tessa he'd known before the Crash. The breakfast felt a bit like those he'd had at the Mansion, without the foul language because Dodge and Beetch kept to the rules.

Sharyn found a neutral subject, by promising eggs for breakfast next time if the chickens had started laying. Nobody could sex chicks these days so Caddi had included some cockerels, which meant there would be more chicks in time. Beetch immediately wanted to trade, either for eggs or, hopefully, chicks. Dodge wanted to deep fry the bloody cockerels that lived behind the Mansion, because of the crowing every morning. He warned them everyone here would feel the same eventually, and even eggs wouldn't compensate.

When Beetch teased him a little about losing two motors, Dodge admitted, with a shrug, that the Hot Rods had pushed a bit too far too fast. Caddi had sent Mercedes to kill a few Murphies to put off any attempt to take advantage. Dodge's eyes brightened and he explained to Beetch about Mercedes being Harold's woman.

Beetch already knew, but had to ask Tessa the obvious. "So what does that make you?"

"The wench that bites," from Tessa surprised Harold. She followed up with, "And the lively one, I'm told." Dodge promptly told her Mercedes had promised competition, but Tessa just smirked and pointed out those were words, not action. Harold sat gobsmacked and kept his mouth shut while Dodge updated Beetch on the latest scandal.

As a gang boss who had women competing, Harold had to look smug about it all. It wasn't too hard, because thinking of the real circumstances kept Harold amused. Meanwhile, talking about a possible catfight between his supposed women led Beetch and Dodge onto how many fighters Orchard Close seemed to have. They were both impressed by the numbers on duty last night. Dodge reluctantly admitted that even the women looked like real fighters, though he daren't tell Caddi that. Beetch kept trying to work out how Orchard Close could afford such a high proportion of fighters to workers. Harold and his friends weren't giving them the answer, all the fighters were also workers. The meal closed with some fairly innocuous banter about naughty boys and girls who'd wandered into the wrong house in the night.

While the commanders ate, all the gear came off the pickup and vans or out of the Barbie van. Jilli danced round them, squealing in delight as each instrument came in sight. She sang them 'Mull of Kintyre' and then 'Who Do You Think You Are' by the Spice Girls as the Barbies left. Harold promised there would be CDs but no, he didn't think Jilli would be coming to play live on Barbie Radio. Not yet, because after all, he'd just survived one shopping trip and needed to get his breath back.

Dodge looked interested in that because nobody had seen inside Beth's for years, and escaped to tell the tale. Harold confessed it was interesting and just survivable. After the very lively sleepwalking reported by the Orchard Close guards, Dodge would no doubt get the Barbie version. Despite the tension between the top Barbies and Caddi, the rank and file were young people with flexible morals meeting strangers of the opposite sex. It was a match made somewhere a long way from heaven.

Barbie Radio blaring out as the women headed home gave Dodge the basic story anyway, especially with the boasts about the Army dropping in for an orgy. Harold noticed a lot of Orchard Close houses switched to the rock channel once they knew it worked again. Harold kept Dodge for a half hour in case the Barbies had set up an ambush, then let the Hot Rods go.

*　*　*

In the weeks following the shopping trip, an increasing number of Barbies turned up for the canteen and the football matches. Even after the novelty of driving down the new route wore off, the Barbies kept coming, many of them walking to save on diesel. The extra Barbies attracted more GOFS, until the weekly football games became twice-weekly games. The Coven even parted with coupons to buy new footballs from the Mart and settled teams developed, with a definite rivalry between them. The GOFS and Barbies eventually created their own teams, or sometimes a combined one, and some joined one of the three in Orchard Close. A few of the more polite Hot Rods and Geeks were finally allowed to watch football, but not the swimsuit games.

Despite the squaddies being keen, Sarge wouldn't allow them to play football. Instead, the soldiers lined the bypass where they could see part of the pitch, and cheered whoever had the ball. As the weather cooled and the nights drew in earlier, the swimsuit league put on clothes.

While Orchard Close played football, Dodge and Mercedes spent three weeks hunting Murphies, payback for the motors. A sudden Hot Rod advance, one that almost cut the Murphy territory in half, probably explained the real reason Mercedes had been on a rampage. Rumours claimed that Caddi walked into the Murphy HQ virtually unopposed. The more extreme rumours claimed Mercedes had killed everyone before the Hot Rods arrived. Wounded Hot Rods, visiting Orchard Close for a beer, scotched that. Some had been injured storming the building, but they confirmed the Murphies' gates had been unbarred and the guards were dead.

The fall of the Murphy stronghold led to a surge in refugee numbers arriving in Orchard Close. The newcomers filled every other available house, even sleeping in the lounges and dining rooms. In many houses, the kitchens and bathrooms were the only rooms without people living and sleeping in them. Harold offered the dining room in his house but the Coven were adamant. The big house had to be available for Soldier Boy to hold confidential meetings with his top people, including the Coven if necessary. Harold also offered to give up the room in the Embassy to provide a bedroom, and take future visitors to his house. He rejected one idea, meeting them in the half-ruined house outside the walls, because the gang bosses would be insulted. Again his top people objected. They didn't want the likes of Caddi off the main street, in case one of them realised which building housed the forge, or the brewery, or maybe the gun repair room.

Harold asked again about building new accommodation, but Casper repeated he couldn't build proper walls, not safe enough to live in. His bricky apprentices, two of them now, refused to even consider it if Casper wouldn't. The amateur builders returned to improving walls. Since all the housing was full, some of the residents began to look for alternatives. Here and there, scattered among the ruins, some of the houses outside Orchard Close had relatively intact roofing. If water and electricity could be connected up, and the windows replaced or filled in, some serious renovation would make them habitable.

The nearest group of relatively intact houses sat on the edge of the demolition zone, nearly half a mile away near the traffic island. They'd been damaged by rioters and shrapnel, then exposed to the elements for three years, but had never burned. Harold had used them for the first meeting with the other gangs, and Caddi's watchers used them because despite broken windows and some missing tiles they were relatively weatherproof. Even so, Harold wasn't keen, because living there would leave the occupants isolated from the main enclave.

Giving the residents a clear field of fire would be a huge job all by itself. The ruins for six or seven hundred metres beyond would need clearing, almost to the border a mile away, as well as the same distance each side. The huge area could then be farmed but would need defending, so the residents would need their own wall to form a small separate enclave. Demolition would provide plenty of bricks, but connecting the houses the half mile to Orchard Close just wasn't practical.

Harold talked it over with Tessa and Sharyn before having a look at the practicalities with Casper, Rob, and Finn, his bricky, plumber and electrician. Doll, Patty and Liz took Stephan the carpenter for a stroll out there to assess the job, and how secure they could make it. Alfie and Hazel told Caddi's watchers to move back, because these houses were needed. Ru, Matti, Jeremy, Matthew and Emmy all took fighters out there to train, and discuss the possibilities. Finn reported that electricity could be run in from a junction box if he salvaged enough heavy cable from elsewhere, while Rob located water in an intact main under a road, close enough to run half a dozen connecting pipes. Word spread across Orchard Close and more groups walked over to assess the houses.

A surge of new confidence ran through Orchard Close, even the old hands. In their eyes, they had stood off both the Barbie Girls and the Hot Rods in one day and night. The new refugees were especially impressed by the large number of gangsters meekly giving up weapons, staying overnight, and leaving without trouble. Meanwhile, having GOFS and supposedly lunatic Barbies making friends, playing football and keeping to the rules lessened some of the paranoia. The growing confidence included the future. Orchard Close wasn't just a place to hide and hope, it was a place to live, and grow, and bring the kids up.

Harold tried to put some realism into their dreams, without demoralising anyone, and found the realism already there. Orchard Close wasn't up to a war, but if they stood together the residents could back the scroats off. For most, especially the new arrivals, that was more than enough and in some cases almost euphoric. Harold expected the old hands to calm everyone down, but now there were too many newcomers. Worse, the likes of Patty, Casper and Doll seemed to be just as enthusiastic.

A dozen plans for fixing the houses were offered to Harold. A sanity check threw out the wildest and the teams inspected the best of the houses again, with real intent. Within days the project had a name, the Farm. The people living there would be the non-specialists, the ones who dug the fields rather than tradespeople. Casper found another amateur bricky among the newbies to help him build the outer walls quicker, when the time came. For now, he had all three apprentices practicing by thickening and raising the two long walls to the Annex. In the evenings, after work, demolition gangs started to clear the area surrounding the potential housing. Caddi's watchers had to move even further away as the work gangs tore down their new location.

* * *

In Orchard Close, their new confidence spread to the brewers. "We want to open a pub." Harold had stopped when the pair stepped in front of him but hadn't a chance to ask why.

He looked from Berry to Seth and back, and the idiots meant it. "We already sell beer in the canteen. There are a thousand rumours about pubs and they all end the same way, everyone dead."

"But they don't have Demons, Boyfriends, Elves, Lovers and Gunslingers as the bar staff or security." Berry beamed.

"Boyfriends, Lovers and Elves?" Harold knew who the Gunslingers had to be, Doll's squad. "I thought they'd all decided on the Riot Squad?"

"Yes, the guards, all of them, are the Riot Squad but calling Patty's squad the Demons sparked off the rest." Berry giggled, then tried to straighten her face. "Hazel said that Alfie is her boyfriend and the men with him would all make terrific boyfriends. She even had Sorcha engrave 'Boyfriend' on a spear head, with love hearts, and persuaded Alfie to accept it. I don't follow the logic, especially when Hazel joined the squad to make sure there's no poaching. Worse, a few other women joined, probably because of the blokes."

"Elves and Lovers?" Harold had strong suspicions about the Elves, but he may as well get confirmation.

Berry pointed down the street. "Matthew and Bess are gartered, and so are most of the guards based in number six. Some aren't but those two attract mainly couples so Lovers it is. Casper's squad reckon that if he's the Orchard Fairy, they must be his Elves. Blame Emmy and the garden Gnomes for starting it."

Harold opened his mouth to point out that the motley collection of men and women in Casper's squad, mainly men, weren't at all Elf-like, and gave up. "As long as they don't all start wearing stupid hats."

"No, they all want helmets. The Demons want Viking horns on theirs. Doll's squad want cowboy hats, steel ones of course, and you know some already tie their holsters down." Berry nudged Seth. "They wanted him to be Doc Holliday because of the sawn-off. Now it can live behind the pub bar with a couple of maces, the last of the pistol bows, and a crossbow with a Liz special."

"Expecting trouble, are you?" Both of them laughed at Harold. "Where will this pub go? We're short of housing."

"Those living in number seven, where Old Harry lived when we first arrived, have agreed to the downstairs being the pub. They're all singles in there, and will put bunks in the bedrooms. There's a huge conservatory on the back so it'll have room for a lot of customers. The scavengers have collected four dartboards and lots of sets of darts, Stephan repaired a set of bar skittles, and we'll scrounge or buy packs of cards for the snug. We'll organise a karaoke night, with that machine the GOFS sold you, and a quiz night, all that sort of thing." Berry looked anxious now. "It'll bring in loads of coupons, honest." She sighed, gazing soulfully into the distance. "I always wanted a pub of my own, one day."

"Stop trying for sympathy. I'll want four people behind the bar, and two fully armed members of someone's squad on duty. You can't sell hard liquor." Harold thought hard, remembering the discussion with Ski. "Set up a couple of crossbow targets outside, and some boules or something like horseshoe throwing. You'll want a punch-bag for anyone wanting to show off, or let off steam. What are the rules?"

"All the Orchard Close ones of course. In addition, if the staff decide someone's drunk, they get no more. If any customers get out of hand, they're barred for any period we decide, up to life. That has to include bad language or trying to grab the staff, on top of the fine or caning. If they fight among themselves and use blades, or damage furniture, barred for any period up to life." Seth shrugged dismissively, apparently not worried about the customers fighting. "With the two guards there, attacking the staff will be fatal. Especially with number six just along the road on the opposite side. It always has a guard shift on duty."

"The threat of being barred will work better than caning." Berry handed Harold a list. "Here, we'll be serving fruit juice, small beer and the other watered booze as well as real beer and cider. There'll be burgers and soup, chips, and snacks of some sort once we get Pippa to work her culinary magic. She might even manage real crisps."

Harold looked down the list. "They only drink from plastic. No glass, especially not bottles. I suppose you've got a name?"

"No. We thought everyone can choose, all put a name up and the most popular one gets it. Well?" Berry had grabbed Seth in some sort of bear-hug, anxiously waiting. From her half-smile, she knew what the answer would be.

"Go for it. My vote is for The Pub, because there's only one left." Harold didn't think Berry heard past the first three words as she whooped and picked Seth off his feet to whirl him round. As her lips connected, Harold got out of there.

A week of intense discussion later Harold supervised a vote. The Pub came in well ahead of The Highlander, also popular because there could be only one. Stephan, Fredrick and a couple of amateur woodcarvers took a circular table top and carved both sides with a representation of the Orchard Close tree logo. They decorated it with four dartboards instead of fruit, carved The Pub around the top edge, and hung it outside the door. Two weeks after Berry suggested it, in early October, The Pub opened. Twenty-four gangsters cheered as Tessa cut the ribbon, then surged inside.

* * *

While Berry and Seth kept the locals amused, Harold considered the shrinking heap of spring steel in Liz's lair. He took a deep mental breath, and showed Wamil a secret. Wamil tried it and agreed that any fighter could use a similar sword, one much lighter than a GOFS version. Harold's sword had a twenty-six-inch long steel blade less than an inch wide, curving in to a sharp point at the end. The blade had been sharpened a third of the way up both sides and left thick enough and flexible enough through the middle to take a solid blow. A fighting rapier, not a fencing epee.

They sparred a little with padded weapons. Wamil agreed the slim steel could be downright lethal, especially as Harold fought with a metal bar in the other hand. They sparred again, really going for it this time. Eventually, Wamil admitted Harold would have killed her about evens, the best he'd done so far. Harold enjoyed real sparring instead of solo exercises, because as they fought, his old lessons came back so Wamil had to work harder and harder to keep at evens.

On the way home, Harold called by the forge to make Liz shout cripes and beat on him. When Liz let him in, he hopped up on the bench. She grinned. "One of those visits? With your stick as well, so all official. Am I in trouble?"

Harold just gave a bland smile. "How good is your new steel? Does it make truly flexible, strong blades?"

"Oh yes. What do you want? A big berserker double headed axe?" She stopped as Harold took hold of his stick with both hands as if using it as an axe, then squeezed and twisted. Liz's eyes narrowed at the click, then widened as the stick parted at the band of decoration. Harold pulled and the gleaming steel weapon slid free, leaving him with a twenty-eight-inch tube in the other hand. "Ooh, you sneaky, nasty soldier you! Cripes, you've had that all along?" She put out a hand. "Gimmee."

Harold held out the sword so she could take the hilt. He waited for Liz to swing it a couple of times before asking. "Can you make me one or three?"

"Probably a lot. It'll take less metal than a machete or even a sabre, even if it's thicker in the middle. That railway spring steel is already thick enough." Liz swished the sword again. "Cripes Harold, who knows about this?" She swung and stabbed at thin air. "Not the gangs because I've heard the scroats saying you only carry a stick."

"I only use it in an emergency. Berry saw it once but not properly. Sharyn knows, and Tessa because her fella had it made. Then Wamil, and you." Harold smiled quietly at the memory. "Plus a bunch of SAS blokes, but none of them are about at the moment. Two of them have something similar."

"I should beat on you, because this means I can't make as many sabres and Rambos. But look at it, it's gorgeous, real art. What's the writing on the blade? I know you told me the bit around the inkpot on the boss says 'The Pen is Mightier than the Sword' in Latin, but what does this bit mean?" Liz made a couple of attempts at it.

"I had to learn to pronounce it when I had lessons. The top bit is 'Stilus gladio fortior,' which means 'The Pen is mightier than the Sword.' The blade says 'Si tamen habes in gladio,' which translates as 'But if you also have a Sword?" Harold watched while Liz tried to work out why. "It's an in joke from when I won the medal. The SAS lads reckoned I lacked finesse with the pointy stuff."

The blacksmith had picked up on something else he'd said. "Lessons? You can use it properly? Do that jumping in and out with a facemask?" Liz pretended to jump forward and back, stabbing as if with an epee.

"Yes I can use it properly, but not the facemask stuff. This is a fighting sword or sword-stick, more like Walter Raleigh I think." Harold held out his hand and she handed the sword back. He ran through a couple of exercises, dancing and prancing as Sharyn called them. "Slashing, stabbing, parrying, clubbing with the boss, a smack in the teeth with the stick and maybe a knee in the nuts. The unsharpened bit shrugs off a machete and will break an arm. Now, can you make them?"

"Cripes yes, and these are almost artwork. That lass with the engraving kit could put some fancy on the blades, like she does the Rambos." Liz stopped grinning and sighed. "You're no fun at all. I've got to keep it secret, haven't I?"

Harold laughed at her crestfallen expression. "Just think of all the crowing you can do eventually, about these, the Katari, the sabres and the muskets." He looked round very obviously. "Where's your apprentice?"

Liz tried to look sad then really frowned, looking at the rapier. "The applicants are all with the other Boyfriends or Elves, learning how to beat scroats as well as heavy metal. I suppose I'd better keep the secrets from whoever for now. I can work on these while the successful applicant plays at soldiers, then when he comes back all hot and sweaty?" She looked upwards with a blissful expression. "Now you've done it. Go on, soldier off and leave me to my sooty dreams."

"I'll either drop this off now and then for you to look at, or Tessa will bring it." Harold rolled his eyes. "Nobody will wonder why she's carrying my stick."

"Keeping it warm? That wench is loving it, stuffing it to the Hot Rods after living under them for three years." Liz switched from having fun to curiosity. "If it wasn't for Mercedes, she might be serious?"

"Smith off. I've known Tessa for years, and she saw my acne." Harold slid the sword back into his stick with a snick. "There, just a thick wooden walking stick with a brass boss." Liz frowned, inspecting the exterior so Harold explained. "I have to file marks off the steel now and then, but it came with a little pot of paint to touch up the scratches so it still looks like wood."

"There's even proper woodgrain etched into the steel. Sneaky and artistic, I like it." Liz reached for her music player. "Now scamper off if you value your hearing." Harold scampered.

*   *   *

As the October nights closed in earlier and earlier, work slowed on the new houses. Getting them ready for habitation proved to be too much before winter. When frost crusted the early morning fields, even the keenest enthusiasts reluctantly admitted defeat until spring. Work gangs carried on with demolishing the surrounding ruins, they could do that all winter. The bricks from demolition went into a huge stack the other side of the buildings, where they couldn't give an attacker cover.

Meanwhile, the visiting gangsters asked for an extra target in the pub yard, for knives. Shortly afterwards talk began about real competitions for knife throwing, crossbows, horseshoes, darts and even bar billiards, with titles and maybe prizes. Lively rivalries soon started between the visitors but the Orchard Close fighters daren't take part. Nobody in Orchard Close could throw a knife properly. When asked, everyone claimed that Harold wouldn't let them show off with either knives or crossbows. It wouldn't be fair to the visitors. A few residents watched the visitors, carefully, and began to get the hang of throwing. Despite the teasing, Harold didn't ask Mercedes to drop by and give lessons.

The Riot Squad practiced hard with their other weapons, where the visitors couldn't see, until Ant found them another use for their spare time.

* * *

Ant, the history buff, seemed worried but determined when he intercepted Harold on his evening walk around the walls. "I know I'm not a fighter, but I think Orchard Close should adopt a system for fighting as a group instead of one on one." Ant seemed wary, probably because Harold looked suspicious. He'd had some completely screwball ideas brought to him, including armoured knights on motorbikes.

"We are developing different ways to fight. What sort of system do you think would work better than this?" Harold gestured to the walls with the firing steps.

Ant looked along the walls and hesitated, then blurted it out. "But what about if they get inside, or if you have to go out there to attack someone?"

Harold spoke gently, realising that Ant was worried about him dismissing the idea or maybe the tone of his first reply. "I've worried about it myself, which is why the wall is so thick and high. The Riot Squad are all practicing for a breakthrough, but it will be bad. I'd rather not go out there to attack anyone, to be honest, because we would be outnumbered." Harold studied the history buff. "You came up with the maces, didn't you?"

"Yes. I thought that a baseball bat isn't designed as a melee weapon, so we needed something that was."

Harold nodded. "They are a lot better. Liz said you suggested short swords, which led to the Rambos. Now you've come up with a way to deal with a break-in. What weapons does it need and how much training would it take?"

"We have the weapons, or most of them." Ant held up both hands, palms out in mock surrender. "I'll confess here and now I studied the Romans, so I might be playing favourites. That's why I suggested short swords, though Liz went way beyond anything I had in mind. I noticed that with those metal strips on the skirts over their jeans, the armoured vests and the Rambos, the fighters are nearly there, nearly legionnaires. When I went with a scavenging party to take that plywood off the railway wagons, the last bit fell in place." Ant paused, obviously trying to find a way to explain. "The gangs tend to use the biggest men they can find, but we use anyone willing to have a go and many are smaller, especially women. The Romans were small. The Germanic tribes and Celts were generally taller and probably physically stronger, but got beaten badly. Hundreds were killed by the legions, for negligible losses." He looked at Harold hopefully.

"Good enough to get me interested. What are you doing this evening, after eight?" Harold smiled at the startled look. "We'll get no peace until Daisy is in bed, and I'd like you to come round to my place and discuss this with a few other people."

"Tonight?" Ant looked and sounded worried. "I can come but I've not got all the books to back it up. I could find them in a couple of days?"

"I'd rather you came tonight. Then if the theory is sound, we'll get you some help searching through the library. You'll need it. We've found loads of books in the new housing but they aren't all dried out yet, let alone sorted and shelved." Harold patted him gently on the back. "Better yet, we can work out who are the best fighters to test your ideas, and look for alternatives."

"I'll bring what I've got. Eight o'clock." Ant left, head down deep in thought, while Harold finished his rounds.

*   *   *

By the time Ant left, just before midnight, he had converts. Not to a straight Roman legion arrayed in the open for battle, because they'd be shot to pieces. According to Ant, Celts and Old Germans fought like gangsters, picking a target and trying to kill him one on one. The Romans would lock shields, refuse individual combat, and kill the attackers at a rate of five or ten to one.

Some research the following day confirmed that part. Harold felt relieved because he'd harboured a small suspicion that Ant pushed Romans a bit too hard. The talk resurrected a few previous suggestions about how to fight the gangs. Most were impractical such as the Greek Phalanx with super-long spears and the English Longbow arrow storm, both of those took years of dedicated training. There were others, including a Saxon-style shield wall with spears, maces and axes that were practical but favoured larger men. The defenders on the wall worked a lot like that, because the height gave them an advantage.

Even as ideas were rejected, some aspects were kept. For instance, lancers on pushbikes weren't practical but the scavengers now sent in as many bicycles as possible, even broken ones. A few had been kept for messengers, but a resident mentioned a dystopian book they'd read. Cycles were the fastest personal transport in the world that didn't need an engine. The larger numbers were to provide emergency mobility for a strike force, even after the diesel finally ran out.

Gradually a variety of possible fighting styles developed, each suitable for one aspect of the defence or a certain temperament. The five squad leaders began assessing their fighters, swapping squad members to get people with the right skills together. Most of the time that meant people with the right preferences, their training wasn't finished. In some cases, such as the legion shield wall, it hadn't even been designed.

All of the five smaller units making up the Riot Squad would patrol their section of wall, and defend it against a surprise attack. If Orchard Close had any warning, the off-duty fighters would join them and any specialists would split off. Patty's Demons would be sort-of Romans, with Rambos and hopefully plywood shields for plugging breakthroughs by groups. Instead of chucking spears they'd use a volley of crossbows before contact. The first experiments proved one of Ant's suggestions, plywood could be bent and made a very tough shield.

Doll's gunslingers were the best pistol shots, so they trained as assault troops. They'd use pistols, accurately at up to eighty yards, targeting scattered breakthroughs or launching attacks on enemy commanders if the opportunity came up. For close combat their members preferred sabres with iron bars or shields, one on one after shooting at the enemy as they closed. Casper's, Alfie's and Bess and Matthew's squads would provide the main defence on the walls, using shields and a mixture of machetes, spears and maces. They would fall back to hold the guardhouses if necessary, shooting into any breakthrough from the flanks. All the squads had some crossbows, and the brick walls would give them protection as the attackers closed. With the shotguns and rifles as well, and luck, they'd break an attack short of contact. The overall emphasis stayed on holding the walls, but the squad leaders watched for anyone especially good at shooting, or blade work, for specialist training.

Chapter 16:

October

Dudley Zoo/Precinct Nineteen

Teddy and Sarge, the leaders of the Zookeepers and Precinct Nineteen, hadn't any real specialists except the ex-police snipers and the Zookeepers using dart guns. Despite a series of raids, the zoo hadn't been either infiltrated or caught by surprise, but the defenders hoped someone launched an all-out attack sooner rather than later. Each raid put more of their men out of action, even if just temporarily, but using automatics even once would ruin the whole plan. The emergency squad hoped they'd realise when the main attack came, hopefully before it ran right over the rest of the zoo.

Tonight neither Sergeant Koos nor David, Six-One-Three, could see more than occasional shadows across the tunnel entrance, too many shadows this time. They could also hear triumphant shouts from the gangsters, and panicked radio messages as the defenders of Dudley Zoo retreated. The woodland echoed with gunfire, and the occasional bellow from Takato's elephant gun. Crouching in the canal boat in the pitch dark, too far back to be seen from the entrance, the twenty men could only listen and hope.

"Christ, no, we're done for! There must be two full gangs out there, too many men to stop. They're real fighters, not yobs. Fall back, fall back. Hold the castle. Let them have a few animals and hope they go away!" Simeon, Eight-One-Four, had panicked, or so it seemed. The message only contained one important bit of information, two gangs had combined using experienced fighters and enough men to take the place. This was what the defenders had been hoping for, while the rest of the radio message should suck the attackers right in!

In the tunnel, Sergeant Koos, One-Five, waited long moments as a few more shadows flitted past the entrance, then he tapped Six-One-Three on the shoulder. The ex-constable tapped the next man, and so on down the boat. The men picked up long wooden poles, padded at the ends, braced them against the tunnel walls and heaved. Very slowly at first, then quicker, the barge floated towards the opening. Just before it came clear the men put down the poles and quickly filed inside, heading for their positions and weapons. The last man held down the transmit and said, "One-Five here, full auto."

"What the?" The gangster died, eyes wide in astonishment as the long steel shape slid silently into view and a rifle fired. Others turned as more of the rifles poking from the sand-bagged loopholes spat death from behind them. In the woods, towards the zoo itself, automatics opened up in short, deadly bursts. Screams and curses echoed through the trees as the attackers realised what they were facing, and tried to get away. They were too late because more automatics were waiting, aboard the barge now floating right across their quickest, easiest line of retreat.

The gangsters might have made a better showing, but the automatic weapons came as a terrible shock. The mob charging forward to swamp the defenders disintegrated, many of them panicking as the flickering lines of tracer turned their front ranks into bloody heaps. Some of the survivors scattered into the woodland, throwing aside weapons and any chance of escape as the traps in the undergrowth, or pursuing Zookeepers, maimed or killed them. The rest, surrounded and facing professionals with superior firepower, tried to break out past the barge. Ten frantic minutes later, a man wearing a tiger-skin cloak limped up towards the canal. The steel barge, now sporting new scars and holes in the sandbags, had been joined by several floating bodies. Fifteen pushed open a hatch. "Hi there Teddy. Did one of them get you?"

"No, Teddy tripped in the woods. I told him, the commander is supposed to be calm and collected, not screaming and running about." The young woman put an arm around Teddy. "Did any of them get away?"

"A few, Imogen, but their neighbours will mop them up when they realise how badly those gangs were hit. Can we come ashore now?" Another two men had come out of hatches, throwing ropes to others in ragged police uniforms who were now coming out of the trees.

"Yes, and thank you. That should put off anyone but the Barbarians, and we are a long way away from them, thank God. We'll follow up just as we discussed, pushing out beyond the trees to make a proper killing zone with warning signs. The extra grazing land, and the browse, will mean we can let a few more animals mature." Teddy, the man with the tiger skin, grinned. "Not all of them, we will be barbecuing a young buffalo tonight to celebrate. I hope you are staying?"

A chorus of agreement came from the barge as the ex-policemen disembarked. This alliance had some very unexpected benefits.

* * *

A week later, Six-One-Three stood peering into the stretch of canal coming out of the tunnel. "Why are there so many?" The water below him teemed with fish.

Inga, a dark-skinned woman with exotic feathers threaded through her dreadlocks, joined him. "We put nets across two dead-end side tunnels, at those junctions you passed in the tunnel?" Constable Six-One-Three nodded, he'd seen side tunnels off the subterranean canal leading back to his own enclave. "We released all the fresh water fish in our aquariums into them, just after the Crash. We've had to more or less ignore them since then, because the other gangs could reach this entrance." She patted his stubby automatic. "Or they could until you turned up. The gangs were all wary of the darts and Takato, but your automatics scare the nasty sods shitless."

"Fair return for milk. We've had men killed trying to get that skimmed rubbish from the Marts. It still seems surreal, milking zebras and buffalo, but the kids will be healthier."

"And the children know it. They recite the names of those who have fallen to defend them, or on Mart runs to keep them fed, every morning at school assembly. There's a plaque on the wall so they remember everyone." Inga put a hand on his shoulder. "Most of the latest names are your men. We are all grateful."

Six-One-Three looked embarrassed, turning back to the strip of water to find a way to change the subject. "Won't these fish escape now you've set them free?"

Inga could take a hint that big. "No, we've put the net across the canal under the bridge over there. They've all gathered because it's feeding time. We breed maggots in the dung, to supplement what they find." She smiled as the ex-policeman watched the fish, entranced by the spectacle. There were fish from all over the world, many of them brightly coloured, all mixed together in a mad painter's piscine palette. "Would you like to help me feed them, Six-One....., surely you don't have to use your number all the time? Don't you know me well enough to drop the military stuff?'"

"It's not military, we shortened our police numbers." He glanced at her, smiling. "You already know my name is David, so I suppose it is a bit silly. I know your name is Inga. Luckily, because crazy woman with feathers in her hair is a bit of a mouthful."

"If we're being informal, you could take me swimming?"

David's eyes widened. "Swimming? In there?" He stared down at the crowded fish, in water he'd seen bodies floating in not so long ago.

She rolled her eyes. "Not in with the fish." Inga gestured towards the tunnel. "There's another small side tunnel in there that's netted off. There's floats to sit on and oil lamps. We didn't fancy fishy friends or the gangsters joining us in the water." She stifled her smile. "We could take a rowboat. I'd have time after feeding this lot, if you help me out?"

"Brilliant. What do I do?"

"The maggots are in those tubs." As she followed him, Inga's smile became a little more calculating. David was a strapping young fella, a polite one who had given as good as he got when she'd flirted a little at the barbecues. Inga would have made a real move sooner, but she hadn't wanted him distracted from killing gangsters. Now, if she could get him in the side tunnel with that soft romantic lamplight, David would probably go along with the skinny dipping part. After all, there weren't any swimsuits and he wouldn't know the swimming parties were usually single sex. Better still, the water wasn't exactly warm, which is why there were sleeping bags to warm up in after drying off. Some were doubles.

* * *

Sutton Park:

Around Sutton Park, the gangs were still slowly learning to live in harmony, and a few members here and there had progressed to the double sleeping bag stage. Others definitely hadn't. There were fights between members of different gangs, but the equivalent of duelling rules had developed. Letting the challenged choose the weapons cut down on actual fights, because some of the gangs had real favourites. Nobody wanted to take on a Yakuza with a sword, nor one of Shiner's Skins with just a baseball bat and boots.

Despite many of them being reluctant, the gangs were forced closer together because the Last Prophet and his men were expanding. Refugees, people running before he got to them, trickled into the area around Sutton Park. Gradually a ring of small groups of almost habitable houses around the park itself were renovated. The new inhabitants either worked in Sutton Park, or began to clear the easiest of the ruins around them to extend the fields.

At first the gangs claimed anyone settling in their section, but the better housing wasn't evenly spaced, which meant some gangs ended up with the lion's share. That meant more rents, and more extra food, and other gangs objected. After some discussion, the tense type with hands on weapons, the refugees were all called the Newbies. They belonged to no gang, or all gangs, and their rents and the extra food they produced were divided up. During the negotiations the smallest of the gangs dissolved, most of them joining the Newbies, which gave them a core of fighters. The remaining five gang leaders, or their lieutenants, began to meet more and more to deal with their new, joint tenants. They also had to agree on joint commanders for the fighters recruited from the Newbies.

None of them realised just how often the original park keepers asked for meetings, or brought problems that needed a meeting. Neither did they notice how often a park keeper happened to have a solution. Not always the best one, but the one that led to the least chance of strife. Despite being the conquerors, the five gangs were being gradually trained into a strange arrangement that wasn't democratic, but would be a long way from totalitarian.

* * *

Conan:

Elsewhere in the city, other enclaves made their own plans for defence but sometimes they just weren't enough. As midnight approached in one insignificant enclave on the north-western edge of the city, close to an Army outpost, none of the residents were thinking of sleep. Armed strangers roamed their streets, while teams of the locals frantically threw water onto the buildings near to what had been their guardhouse. The burning house had been a barracks for most of the fighters, its windows boarded up apart from weapons slits. Other teams carried in bodies from around the enclave, throwing them onto the blaze to join the rest on one giant pyre. The residents flinched nervously at the screams from elsewhere in what had been their home. Now it belonged to the Barbarians.

The leader of the Barbarians, Conan, strode through his new possession. Reaching a small, undamaged house with a prominent cross on the door, he knocked, identifying himself before the man inside opened the door. "You were right, Sylvester. We poured paraffin and oil through the weapons slits and torched the barracks doorway before the first shot. Those boarded up windows trapped most of the fighters, and the rest never got chance to organise. Better still, the Army never had a chance to stick their noses in." He looked around but couldn't see anyone else. "Does anyone know the God-botherers let us in? We killed the ones they drugged."

"No, nobody alive anyway. They're in the back room, through there." Sylvester, a tall man in his thirties, gestured to a door. "Give them a pat on the back to encourage them and we can do it again, when you have to. Not too often, or someone will realise."

Conan headed for the door in the far wall, pulling it open without knocking. The priest and four nuns stopped praying, their heads jerking up in alarm. "It worked. You did your job so the other nuns are safe, as long as they keep nursing my men. They stay safe as long as you'll do it again when I tell you." His eyes narrowed. "Why isn't she out there?" Conan inspected the sixth worshipper, taking in the woman's age and figure. "Hobbled, or keeping one of my men warm and happy."

"Kelly asked to join us, to become a novice. She didn't know what we were doing, so she is a true believer. It wasn't to save herself from your men. Can we keep her, please? We did what you asked, gave you this enclave?" Despite the priest's attempt to sound resolute it came across much more like pleading. "We'd like to see the others please, to make sure...." He trailed off as Conan laughed.

"Make sure they still have underwear? I kept my word. As long as they nurse my men, and you do as you're told, none of them end up in a hobble. Saving your sisters from that should be enough to keep you in line, without letting you pick up strays." Conan whirled round, his fist rising as Sylvester touched his arm. "Fuck it, you should know better."

"Sorry." Sylvester jerked his head to get Conan out of the room. Once the door closed he spoke quickly and quietly. "Let them have the woman, as a reward. This is the first time we relied on them completely and they made a big difference. If we'd tried storming the walls the Army post might have interfered, because this enclave is close enough to have made friends. It would have only taken one soldier with a machine gun getting a rush of blood to turn our attack into a bloodbath. The bastard wouldn't have even needed to leave the Army guard post." Sylvester turned to look at the closed door. "They've got close to this girl. Let them save her, then promise her special treatment if they fuck up."

Conan thought about it, seriously, because Sylvester wasn't usually wrong about this sort of shit. He'd suggested using the nuns again, after the captured ones had got Conan's men through the gates and in among the Lambs of God. The Barbarian leader wasn't sure where the lean, fit man had come from, but he had contacts among the Mart guards and sources that gave him solid info. Letting Sylvester win this one might keep him sweet. Conan nodded and opened the door without answering. He'd let the God-botherers take the girl with them, then put her to work in the hospital. The four nuns and the priest would get a good look at what he'd done to the Bitch, then he'd promise to make their little friend a special project if anyone fucked up.

*　*　*

The General:

Meanwhile, a few miles northwest from Orchard Close, too far to cause any alarm, the General hoped his own spymaster had persuaded an opponent to open his own gates. The morning mist wasn't too bad, barely softening the rubble and certainly not hiding the General's army as they drew up in front of the small enclave. A long way in front, because a half mile of fields and flattened rubble surrounded a continuous brick wall, with several half-demolished houses jutting out. The houses had been turned into strongpoints, their crenelated tops higher than the walls, allowing the defenders to enfilade any attackers who made it that far. The General glanced back and up, until a man at a house window gave him the thumbs up. The snipers in the nearby houses were ready. The MiB automatics were among the third rank of the Bloods, ready to open up once they had a target.

The General raised his loudspeaker. "Parley?" He turned it off and waited. After a few moments he frowned at Rhys. "I thought you said they'd been primed to expect this?"

"Yes, they are. I hope Napoleon goes for it. They've got some good intel in there and know about the snipers and automatics, so it won't be easy if they fight. Maybe someone got cold feet, or maybe some of them are having to be convinced." Both Rhys and the General shut up as a half dozen pistol shots rang out, inside the enclave.

Even while they were wondering if that had been a power bid that failed or a regime change, a loudspeaker called, "Where?"

Rhys chuckled. "He already knows. In the middle of the clear ground."

The General nodded and answered. "You come outside the gate, with your top four men. We'll start walking and meet you in the middle of the fields." He wanted the other blokes in view first because he had pictures on his phone. If the gang boss came out despite knowing about the snipers, he wasn't planning anything cute.

A radio crackled. All it said was, "It's him" but the General started walking. The man who'd reported also had phone camera pictures of this gang's boss, and binoculars. Patton and Rhys joined the General, as did Branson and Scrooge from the MiB. The General didn't fancy this but his fighters, especially the Bloods, expected their boss to have some balls. As he came nearer, the General smiled, because this bloke also wore some sort of military uniform. He'd only brought three companions, but the fourth might have been the cause of the shooting. The man stopped and saluted, so the General returned it.

"I am known as Napoleon, but I think this might be Waterloo. Your terms, sir?"

"Total surrender. Your enclave becomes mine."

"What about my men, the fighters?" All four of the men were edgy, surrendering but still worried it might be a mistake, so the General smiled reassuringly.

"If they march out, surrender, they can join my army. In fact, they'll be welcome." At least two of the men weren't completely convinced, and neither was Napoleon.

"March out? Do they have to disarm?"

Patton laughed but the General shot him a look to shut the idiot up. "That is what a surrender means."

"Can they keep their blades, since this is a negotiated takeover rather than unconditional surrender? They'll stack their firearms but, well, we have a certain esprit de corps here. If you want to use them, that will work for you." Napoleon finally asked what really worried him, because despite the negotiations there were no guarantees. "Who will command them? They would fight best under their current commanders?"

This time the General laughed, he couldn't help it, because there'd be no need to negotiate to get exactly what he wanted. Napoleon had just offered to do the job, without any conditions. "We'll discuss how much command, and how many men but you definitely aren't in charge anymore. Even so, the MiB prove that I am happy to consider some sort of position for others. What about the rest of the people in there, the ones who don't fight?"

"The civvies will do what they're told. We are surrendering to avoid a sack, so that is a condition, because otherwise we might as well fight. You don't want that because some of the tradespeople are productive, in return for which we keep their children or spouses safe. If their families get caught in crossfire, you'll lose assets such as my firearms repair man." The man calling himself Napoleon hooked a thumb back towards the fortifications. "Not only that, but my fighters will not stand by and see your Bloods turned loose on their families."

The General relaxed. If the fighters and that repair man had families, he could control them. "If you'd like to sit down comfortably, we can thrash out the details over a drink?"

"One man will go back to let the troops know. They will remain on alert until I give them the order to stand down." The General agreed and escorted his new ally to where beer, wine and coffee waited. He smiled quietly, because Patton looked thoroughly pissed off. The big man would be busy for the next couple of days slapping the Bloods down, because Hannibal, Patton's current second, didn't have what it took to boss those lunatics. Not now, when they were wound up for a fight.

*   *   *

An hour later the General watched the fighters march out and neatly stack their firearms. "Perfect." Beside him Patton grunted unhappily but the General chuckled. "Cheer up Patton. You've got a little time before we go after the SIMS, but there'll be no waiting for anyone to heal so start briefing your men. We'll use the break to reorganise, to go through all the men we have. I want you to sort out all the nutters, the nastiest bastards, from everywhere and move them into the Bloods." The General grimaced, because Patton might not like the reason. "We'll need plenty of them to charge over that open ground at Orchard Close, because every bloody gun will be working. Attacking the SIMS first will get them settled in together."

Luckily the MiB diverted Patton. "All our guns will work better now we've got a real repairer, a rifle club man. Pity his eyesight is buggered or we'd have another good sniper, because Rhys tells me he's got certificates on his wall." Scrooge, the MiB, frowned. "Are you taking some of our men?"

"Only swapping. I'll replace your nutcases with some of the less excitable sort. They'll be easier for you to keep in line, and won't fuck or cripple your workforce when they get spaced or pissed." The General smiled slightly at the cautious look. "Don't worry. I know you are allies, not conquests."

"How long do I have to reorganise, sir?" Patton still didn't look very pleased. "There'll be pissing contests between the Bloods and the new men. I can stop them killing each other, but they'll shed blood and that'll take time to heal." He hesitated, then continued. "I won't have time to train up the other recruits if the Bloods need that much attention. Hannibal can't handle that level of shit."

"Spend a month letting them get to know each other, then make it official. Throw a big party for the Bloods and new men at Guy Fawkes, to settle them in together. Depending on how Rhys gets on, we'll take the SIMS any time from then to Christmas. We'll let Julius Caesar head up the other troops, the steadier ones." The General chuckled. "He didn't fancy Napoleon any more when I told him we'd be fighting Wellington. Julius has his gang well organised and surrendered them as an intact force, so he gets the rest of the steadier men to train up. Under your overall command of course, Patton, just like Hannibal." The General looked down a list. "We'll find the right man to stand at his elbow, in case he gets ambitious."

Rhys drew a thumb across his throat. "I know just the man."

"Good, now show me how we get past those SIMS rockets, without losing half the men we've just recruited. Better yet, show me how I get hold of one of their experts, someone who can make more rockets." The General held up a hand as Patton opened his mouth. "Yes, we can make sugar rockets and those mortar things, but then the RAF will call by. The MiB reckon these bloody SIMS things were accurate and kept low." The three men bent over the map. "I want to be tucked up in this SIMS place by Christmas. Then I can get the Pinkies onside and everyone healed up for a spring offensive."

* * *

The Professors:

The Prof, not too many miles north of the General but the other side of the SIMS, was preparing for what would be either another false alarm or a massacre. Hopefully, if it went that way, his students would be doing the massacring. Three cars drove slowly and cautiously through their neighbour's, Benny's, territory, heading towards the Mart. They probably wouldn't get all the way, because Benny's spy reckoned the Lycans would break their agreement and snap up the soft, juicy target. There'd been two false alarms, but this time infrared scopes showed the men lying in wait in the buildings either side of the only open road.

Prof glanced at Benny. "You were right. They took the payment but this time they're going to stop our cars anyway." He raised his binoculars. "Tell your men to keep back until we cease fire."

"Too bloody true." Benny turned to send a couple of extra messengers to hammer that home. Some of his idiots might forget and charge early. Ahead of the three cars, half a dozen men left a building to walk out and form a line across the road. Five aimed their weapons while the sixth called out as the cars stopped well short.

Prof listened in, through the radio in one car. "They want five times the coupons, or goods and weapons up to that value, and if the cars try to back up they'll open fire. Chad is arguing but there's two automatics pointing at him. Are your men ready, Benny?"

"Oh yes. The assholes over there have pulled this stunt before, asked my blokes for extra, but not that much. They know I haven't got the fire-power to deal with those bloody machine guns." Benny smirked, glancing at the nearest trebuchet before raising his radio. "Three, two, one, fire!"

Prof shouted down his radio. "Get out Chad, now, fast as you can!" Out on the road four of the six men were cut down by a hail of accurate bullets from Benny's best marksmen, reinforced by Prof's few decent shooters. The pair with the automatics were the priority and were hit several times, which meant two of the others only staggered. The survivors ran for the shelter of the buildings. "Trebuchets, fire!"

As the three cars reversed as fast as possible, back across the cleared strip between the gangs, six thin lines of smoke arced across the sky. Two dropped a little short but the sides of two buildings, the ones either side of the road with a clear view of the cars, erupted in flame. The weapons that had started firing from the windows stopped abruptly. Benny chortled and lifted his radio again. "Move up, but wait until the bombs stop." Armed men, with a few of Prof's students, began to move across the wide border strip between the gangs. They moved in short dashes, lying down in the rubble to get some cover, but few weapons were shooting at them.

"Four and five, up seventy. Three and six, up eighty. Fire when ready. One, adjust fifty left. Two, adjust forty right and up ten." The trebuchets already had the approximate ranges and bearings. Prof's message confirmed the switch in targets, and corrected the range after their last attempts. This time the six lines of smoke were staggered, but by the time the last one fell the buildings behind and to each side of the ambush point were catching fire. "Again."

Some of the ambushers guessed what came next, they ran out of their buildings and tried to get away along the road. A hail of gunfire swept them away but Benny swore and shouted into his radio. "Rifles only you fucking idiots! Save the pistol ammo." He shrugged apologetically towards the young women making up the nearest trebuchet crew. "Sorry." Nobody had said anything, but Prof's kids didn't like swearing.

Prof smiled quietly to himself, but kept his eyes on the target as another volley landed. With the escape route firmly ablaze, he lifted his radio again. "Well done. The trap is closed. Burn out the rats." Benny winced, because Prof looked like someone's slightly dotty granddad but there hadn't been an ounce of mercy in that. One after another the trebuchets retargeted, three to each rat trap. Flames burst on the houses full of ambushers. The rest of those inside realised what was about to happen, much too late to make a difference. The fighters in the cleared ground between the gangs surged forward into accurate crossbow range, and waited for their targets to run out into the open.

Five minutes later, eight vans and minibuses, all with some sort of armour, drove up and took position front and back of the Prof's three cars. Ahead of the convoy, Benny's triumphant Boys were stripping the bodies in the road and front gardens before throwing them into the flames. There'd be plenty of loot, because most of the would-be ambushers took their chances with the bullets and arrows rather than burn. Better still, those semi-automatics had laid in the road throughout the fight so they weren't touched. Benny had made a deal about them, one for him, one for Prof.

Benny pointed towards the vehicles. "They'll escort your cars to the Mart, then nip off to finish the rest of the Lycans. We'll take both those machine guns, but you get one once we're done." Fighters were climbing into the extra vehicles, waving weapons and cheering. "If your people wait at the Mart, a couple of vans will call back to let them know it's all over and escort them home." He heaved a sigh of relief. "Shopping will be a lot easier now, for both of us."

"You'll let any of the ordinary tenants who wants to leave come to join us?" Prof still wasn't totally sure Benny meant to keep the deal, but there were enough of Benny's fighters leaving in the vehicles to reassure him there wouldn't be an attempt to take the trebuchets.

"I've had a better idea. How about we share the new tenants and territory?" Benny's smile might have looked better on a wolf. "Proper allies. We could use the same method to take over a couple more places. I'll supply nasty sods with machetes, you bring the artillery and strategy and stuff. Then your farmers and plumbers move in to make the place more profitable."

"We'll talk after we've got the Christmas shopping safely home." Prof wanted a long talk to his faculty before he agreed to that. One part sounded very attractive; Benny's nutcases would be the ones to die in any fighting instead of Prof's students. He'd just have to be very careful that his new ally didn't get greedy.

*   *   *

Reivers:

Deep in the Scottish Highlands, the group of heavily armed, ragged figures were more interested in flour and tins of beans than possible Christmas celebrations. "Did we get enough for the winter before they sealed us in?"

A one-armed woman with a sheaf of papers looked up from them. "Yes Hamish. We've even managed a bit of a surplus, thanks to Angus and Bruce raiding right up to when the armour sealed the line." Both paused for a moment, because the raiders had pushed hard and too many hadn't come back. "The foreign bastards are pulling out of some of the lowlands now the crops are in. Even the fishing boats and work camps are moving south to Inverness. We can scavenge the abandoned villages, if we take care. Better yet, we've got your fishing boats and volunteer crews on the west coast, willing to try for extra protein when they can." The woman looked a little uncertain. "If they can."

One of the men, Hamish, tried to sound reassuring. "We'll only operate when we're sure the visibility is bad enough, with high seas to mess with naval radar."

"We sent people to snatch a few more boats before the rest leave, providing the weather is bad enough to let them get away. If they can't, they're to steal the radars and any gear they can carry." This gaunt, blue-eyed man glared up at the skies, at the unseen watchers. "Can we help your fishermen, Hamish, set up to protect them in some way?"

"No, Angus. All we can do at sea is run or hide among the small islands. The crews have had plenty of practice while keeping in touch with the outer islands, and they'll be careful." Hamish managed a chuckle. "Luckily there'll be plenty of bad weather to hide us, now winter has set in."

Maeve sighed, a long, sad, weary sound. "Winter will be a relief for the women and kids with family among the fighters. They'll get to see them, spend Christmas together."

"And Hogmanay. We saved a little something for that." Sudden grief swept over Angus's face. "For those who have no family now."

Maeve put her hand on his shoulder, totally genuine sympathy because she'd seen her family die in the snow with Angus's, torn apart by artillery. "Aye, we know. We'll be expecting you for Christmas dinner, Angus. You need a little bit of time to relax as well."

"Until spring." The grief faded, replaced by savage anticipation. "We can use the winter to get ready, to properly train our new recruits. Then we'll see how their precious line of steel stands up to some real pressure." The rest smiled as his sheer confidence lifted their spirits.

*   *   *

The Cabal:

Deep under the Lincolnshire countryside, others were definitely confident. They weren't actually laughing, but most of the people in the bunker looked happy about the harvest and the prospects for the following spring. Owen, the chairman, rapped his gavel. "Henry, I believe you finally have food production under control."

The bearded man smiled happily. "Definitely. A combination of good weather and getting the work gangs running smoothly has delivered. Now that is perfected, I'd like more land please."

"You gained thousands of acres when we emptied York. Surely that isn't all planted up?" Gerard, the youngest member, looked startled.

"No, because a large amount of that is moorland. We can grow sheep or even cattle there better than arable crops." Henry changed the picture on the wall screen to show a map. "Cornwall would be ideal if we clear Truro. The weather is better there, and the problems in Scotland wouldn't have so much impact if we had additional production elsewhere."

"Enough to abandon the far north of Scotland?" Joshua the Army man had leant forward, intent.

"Abandon it? I thought the foreign troops were pushing the Reivers back?" Owen scowled, his previously happy mood extinguished. "Or so the reports say, in among the complaints about losses and the Marts whinging about the difficulties in maintaining supplies up there."

"We are winning, but it's costing us. Some bright spark came up with an idea, but Ivy and Henry told me we couldn't stand the loss of production in the coastal strip." Joshua beckoned for the control, changing the map to the north of Scotland. He quickly outlined the pros and cons. The long, relatively narrow coastal strip was difficult to defend, so abandoning it would save on men, ammunition and intercepted convoys. Some objected because that would give the Reivers the ruined villages, and a milder place to spend the winter. Any worries about the logistics of moving the work camps vanished when Joshua suggested processing the inhabitants instead, to save food over winter.

Several objected to the Reivers getting free access to the northern parts of Inverness, a source of recruits, but Joshua had planned for that. Once the farmers and guards were all south of Inverness and the line of steel, the foreign armour could clear the city. The gangs wouldn't stand a chance against a full armoured assault with close air cover. "The population can be pushed out of the city northwards, which will screw up the Reivers' logistics for the winter. The brave liberators can't let all those families starve or freeze, can they?" A big smile spread over Joshua's face and he smacked a fist into his palm. "The Reivers can't break through our prepared lines. They will have to come out of the hills in the spring to farm the lowland, to feed everyone next year. Once they have women and children, dependents, in those villagers, an armoured thrust up the flat land will force them to fight in the open for once. They can't reinforce or resupply with no city or work farms in reach, so with luck we'll finally break them."

Smiles grew around the table, especially the one on the RAF man. "Out of the mountains the aircraft will get a clear run at them. We can send the foreign aircrews in to smash any organised resistance because collateral won't matter, and it'll be harder to target planes if the anti-air rockets can't hide." Faraz sat back in his chair, his voice showing his relief. "If they are broken in the spring, the Reivers won't be launching any surprise attacks in the summer."

"If we aren't guarding or feeding Inverness, that will free up Mart and camp guards. We can use the extra men to push forward with other plans."

Vanna smiled happily, checking her own notes. "They'll enjoy taking over sealing the cities down south instead of freezing their butts off. Then the soldiers in the cushy billets can earn their keep in London."

Owen interjected a note of caution. "First we have to give Henry more land to grow food on."

"That depends, Owen. If Inverness is cleared we don't have to feed the population, so we can manage." Ivy looked sold on that idea, nodding her head in agreement and the discussion descended into details. This clearance wouldn't be easy, because Maurice couldn't trick this population into a breakout. Inverness and Aberdeen were fully aware of what had really happened in Glasgow.

Elsewhere, Maurice admitted that a growing number had worked out why the population of Glasgow left, and were making plans in case of a power cut. Onscreen, an enclave called Orchard Close lit up, a section at a time, with tiny lights. "This uses wind and water. Since it's England, we are unlikely to have a drought or a long calm, so losing the piped water supply will just mean them boiling rainwater."

Ivy watched as the scene reran, taking in the progression as the small clusters of lights sprang up. "Has their electric been cut off?"

"No. This is one solution to us cutting the power like we did in Glasgow, a test run." Maurice switched to close-ups of Orchard Close in daylight, highlighting the ingenious combination of wind and water generators. He clicked again to show other enclaves, in different cities. The precautions varied from hoarding diesel for generators through to full sized waterwheels in rivers.

Boris, the diplomat, still looked worried, because the only successful clearance had relied on cutting off the electricity and water. When Vanna explained they'd use armour first, then her contractors to process the survivors, he still wasn't satisfied. He hunted through papers to find the original assessment, where Joshua had explained the effect on Army morale if they were sent to attack civilians. Boris suggested using foreign armour to clear Inverness, then London, but Joshua didn't want the Army knowing how much had been gathered together. The numbers wouldn't matter in Inverness because the regulars wouldn't see them, but the foreigners would be obvious in London.

"I thought we were leaving London to wither away?" Grace looked startled, then began hunting through her paperwork.

"London isn't withering." Maurice's usual smooth presentation faltered and he looked a little embarrassed. "I have little information, because I can't keep regular contact schedules or replace agents very easily. What information I have suggests that fewer and fewer are fighting among themselves." He passed out small notes. "Because, and I quote the meeting printed out here, we should save the ammunition for when the bastards come for us. There is a spreading realisation there, and in other enclosures, of what we plan for them."

After reassuring Joshua the gangs weren't organised well enough to organise a breakout, Maurice confessed the whole situation had become messier than he'd thought. He had been working to build some gangs until they were large enough to be a real problem in the future, just to wipe out the stronger democratic enclaves. Wiping them out had become more urgent, because several Army units were making real friends. Since the enclaves in question were both peaceful and relatively democratic, the Army, and the RAF, once word spread, might refuse to target them.

"Can you still handle that, removing those enclaves?"

"Yes Owen, but as an example?" Orchard Close showed on the screen again, but on a map with the General's and the Hot Rods' territory outlined. "Each of those larger gangs wants to take out that enclave. Both are trying to do it alone, yet negotiating to combine. Three others gangs are in an alliance to stop that, but at least one of them would happily double-cross the rest. It's a rat's nest, poisonous back-stabbing rats. I'll still get the result we want, providing I can keep the two bigger gangs from fighting each other until after the enclave is taken." He clicked again showing similar situations elsewhere, Sutton Park among them, not quite democratic but not oppressive. Even those would have to go, because the Army might consider them acceptable after seeing the worst examples.

"Don't worry, my people will deal with souring relations when the time comes. That or just run over them with a tank." Vanna tapped the table, looking towards Owen. "I vote for Joshua's plan in Scotland, if only so I don't have to go up there for any more morale boosting visits."

Ivy scowled but nodded and tapped the table as well. "I vote for it to shut up the Marts. If we are clearing Inverness I'll agree to losing the farm produce north of there." Henry nodded and tapped the table to signal his agreement.

"I like the idea of getting rid of those work camps. They are too vulnerable and the raids by Reivers are making them rebellious. All in favour?" Grace raised a hand and the rest followed.

"Start your planning, Joshua." Owen rapped his gavel on the table. "Now we'd better go through the boring details. Gerard, are the shipments from the Falklands and Argentina keeping to schedule...?"

*   *   *

As usual, the members of the Cabal straggled out of the meeting. Vanna spoke quietly to Maurice. "Are you selling ammunition to the problem enclaves?" A faint smile crossed her face. "Since you seem to have a lot of information on that one."

"We are selling, not me, and yes." Maurice glanced to make sure nobody could hear, then smirked. "That should thin out the attackers very nicely."

"Napalm would be better. What about the snipers?"

"We still have a high failure rate. Some can go in with your special units on attacks now, the ones who will just shoot anyone in their sights. We can give those a proper test in Inverness. The others, the real stone cold killers to take out a specific target, are taking a little bit longer." He hesitated, but decided to come clean with this ally. "A lot longer and there's a lot of wastage. A few are naturals, their trauma does most of the job for us, but the rest are very difficult to programme. We are running out of lonely woods near the training facilities, places to put the failures, because I don't want the numbers to be obvious."

"Use one of my special facilities. You can bury as many as you like there without anyone being nosy." Vanna chuckled but it was black humour, reflecting on how many had already been interred in those places. "Most of the facilities aren't being used now, so pick one near the training and let me know. I'll make sure my people ignore a few mystery visitors."

"Excellent. Thank you." Maurice moved ahead to talk to Joshua about Inverness.

*   *   *

Cyn Palace:
Some of the London enclaves were relaxed, even triumphant, completely unaware of the Cabal's plans for them. "We warned them what would happen if they raided." Kermit wore a sling but it didn't affect his huge smile. "Hitting the shites with a hundred fighters didn't leave many survi-

vors, and they didn't even get into the fields. Following them home caught them flat-footed. I doubt they could raise twenty fit fighters after that."

The big man known as Sinner smirked, gesturing to the Imam. "His lot screaming that foreign stuff scares them shitless. I reckon the Smurfs are finished now anyway. Maybe we should grab a bit of their area, since our men are already over the border, something easily defended?"

The small redhead with her arm round him sounded more cautious. "Only if the rest of their neighbours get some as well, then none of them will object. We don't want to lose more fighters defending our new land."

"And only if we agree the area we take is used by all of us, not just the nearest gang." Imam scowled at Sinner. "The foreign words were Holy words, calling on His help in fighting the invaders."

"I'm good with that, and I'll bet Preacher's lot were asking for the same help." Eli wasn't wounded, but he had fresh bloodstains on his armoured vest.

"A God by any name is a powerful ally. Better yet the rest of the neighbours are a bit more civilised than the Smurfs, so the whole area should calm down." Preacher aimed a small nod towards the Imam. "I agree, we should take over a piece of their land and some of their people, the workers, but all of us should share the benefits."

"At this rate, we'll end up one gang." Sinner looked from Preacher to the Imam and frowned. "Maybe not."

"God moves in mysterious ways. For now, let's have a look at the map and choose our new boundary." The men gathered round a table, heads bent over a map. The small auburn-haired woman, Sin, smiled quietly as she saw the Imam and Preacher murmuring quietly together. God seemed to be on the job already.

* * *

Inside the enclosed cities, the fighting between gangs died down as the weather worsened. Most gangsters didn't fancy slogging through rain to end up dead or wounded, fighting was bad enough in the sunshine. A few gang bosses thought that with the others sat in comfort, fat and happy, winter might be the perfect time to make a move.

Chapter 17:
Christmas Presents

Orchard Close might not be contemplating an attack on their neighbours, but their trainee fighters didn't relax. Even so, quite a few of the trainees abandoned their practice temporarily at the end of October when Mercedes accompanied Caddi on a visit to Orchard Close. As word spread, a small crowd formed to watch Mercedes walk up the road to meet Harold. Despite the chilly wind, her coat came off to reveal a short skirt, a crimson flared one. These boots ended just below her knee so she showed a lot more stocking this time. Mercedes didn't seem worried by the cold, undoing an extra button on her loose white blouse when she got close to Harold. "Whew, I've come over all hot and bothered at just the sight of you." Mercedes slid both arms up around Harold's neck and the gap gaped invitingly. Harold dragged his eyes up to hers just in time to miss the view, but saw the welcoming spark.

After a hello peck on his lips, Mercedes stepped back. She stuck out a hip, lifting an eyebrow in a question or challenge. "Mercedes, may I put my hand on your ass, and any other delectable places on offer? Please?"

"Hmm. Maybe." Mercedes made quite a play of deciding this time, until even Harold began to wonder. Then he started wondering if he'd have to say no, because of his own rules in Orchard Close. "Not yet." That raised a mutter from a couple of the Hot Rods. "But if you put your hand on the skirt over my ass, I can imagine what it will feel like straying underneath." Caddi stood nearby, laughing, but his eyes sharpened at that because even the public script was history. Once he'd placed his hand, Harold stuck his hip out and Mercedes put her hand in his back pocket. It crossed his mind he'd already started playing grab-ass.

Harold's hand had the fun trip when Mercedes turned, and again inside the house as they all sat down. Mercedes draped her stockinged legs over Harold's lap and started the 'where does the hand go' game. Once again, she skipped Harold having to ask. With Mercedes almost leant against his shoulder, Harold's arm went right around her waist onto the skirt over her upper thigh. Dangerous, because every time Mercedes moved Harold had to stop his fingers slipping round her thigh. The front of the loose blouse swung enticingly under his nose.

Mercedes seemed to be fired up today. Harold soon found out why, because Caddi wanted to both brag and complain. "The Spuds haven't produced a military genius after all. The bloody Trainspotters have been giving them fighters and advice." Caddi sounded indignant, funny really since he'd attacked the Murphies in the first place.

"Trainspotters? Did they have a treaty with the Spuds?" Harold thought they'd been a bit slow in that case.

"Not that I know of. Maybe they don't want me as a neighbour?" Harold reckoned none of Caddi's neighbours were keen on that idea. "It isn't open and official support, but the bastards sent a proper shooter, a sniper. I might have had to hire you, Soldier Boy, because judging by the number of killings, he might have been as good as you. He's not a problem now because Mercedes got to him. I'm a bit pissed off, because there were too many others about for her to get away with the rifle."

"That's a pity, an accurate rifle would be a welcome addition to any armoury." Harold looked straight at Mercedes when he said that, and saw that warm spot come and go in her eyes. A real warm spot now, not just a flicker. "A present like that would have deserved a very special reward." The tip of Mercedes' tongue touched her lips, while her thigh muscles asked for the reward.

"She went back for her reward later, his ears, when the Murphies chucked out his body." Gangs didn't care too much about bodies, unless they were stinking too close to where the fighters lived. "I'm hoping he wasn't the gun repairer, because I'd still like him."

"Just as well Mercedes dealt with the sniper because I'm busy just now, sorting out all the refugees. Maybe the repairer is back in Trainspotters territory. They might not risk him further forward." Harold smiled, glancing across at Sharyn. He had to when Mercedes smoothly slid her cleavage between Harold's eyes and Caddi. Harold would already bet coupons on braless, but so far he'd avoided confirmation.

"You might be right." Caddi was scowling when Harold could see him again. "I know how busy you are. Bloody hell, there'll be nobody left soon. They're bringing weapons as well which is annoying." As expected, the weapons had really wound Caddi up. If Orchard Close fighters weren't patrolling the border, Harold felt sure the Hot Rods would try to grab some refugees.

"You'll take the rest soon, so then they'll come under the treaty." Patty didn't sound happy saying that, but Caddi's snarl didn't look that happy either.

"Good, because the runners know how to avoid my men on the way here. I found out where they were heading for, Barbie territory. I sent one man to follow them. He didn't come back and the runners must have another route now. That means your people are right there, on the ground, but the way the war is going you might want to pull them out. I'll get a description sooner or later, and then you won't get them back." Caddi scowled at Patty, then turned it into a sneer. "Maybe you think one of your Demons would get away. If I catch one, you'll find out what happens when they meet a real fighter. I'll make an example of whoever it is." Patty's eyes flashed, but even as Harold opened his mouth to stop her answering, another voice cut in.

"I've decided." Everyone looked at Mercedes as she spoke. Harold saw the twinkle of mischief in her eyes, and his hand automatically tightened a little around the top of her thigh. "Your hand feels lovely just there, 'Arold, but I don't think you should put it up my skirt. You might get carried away." There were a few gasps and a choking noise from over towards Cooper. The gasps came from the two extra Orchard Close guards, here to remind Caddi's party of where they were.

"Then I might carry you away?" Harold wondered more about where this might be going.

Mercedes knew just where she was, and apparently where she was heading. She'd definitely diverted Caddi from who might be giving the refugees their information, or goading Patty. "Maybe, but not yet. Before I find somewhere delectable for that hand, I'd better make sure the other one is occupied. We wouldn't want it wandering about unsupervised."

"Not much" came from Cooper, while Harold's guards snorted in amusement or agreement. Patty, Sharyn and Casper took it in their stride, but Mercedes fell well outside most people's experience of visitors.

"I think your hand should go on my leg, but only on the stocking as yet." Harold watched her eyes because that sparkle meant Mercedes planned some mischief. She lifted his hand and placed it on the hem of her skirt but mostly on lovely smooth stocking, so Harold gave a little squeeze. Mercedes leant forward, her leg slid forward just a bit, and Harold had that strip of skin to play with again. "I only wear these stockings for you, 'Arold, so you can stroke my leg without losing a hand." The sparkle in her eyes became a challenge.

Harold obliged. He tightened his grip and slid his hand forward around her leg a little, then back. Mercedes sighed. "Mmm, lovely. Now then, where can I put the other hand?" A lovely smile blossomed. "Move your other hand up a bit please, 'Arold." That puzzled Harold. Her waist wasn't exactly pushing any boundaries, but some of the others in the room gasped. He would have looked down but her open blouse neatly blocked the view.

Harold's thumb went up over the skirt waistband but not onto a blouse, and he stopped. He nearly lost the bra bet because Harold almost looked down to see if Mercedes had opened her blouse. "Further 'Arold, so it's all on delectable, but not too far." Too true, if he went too far Harold would be confirming the bra bet by hand. Harold thought he would get to do that eventually, but for now he obediently slid his hand up over the top of her skirt onto skin.

"Your wish is my absolute pleasure."

"Ooh that's lovely, 'Arold, and now I'm wondering what your hand will feel like sliding around to the front. You tried that on top of my blouse, but now you can tell me if my skin is delectable." As his hand started moving, Mercedes gave a sigh that Harold could confirm felt bloody wonderful. "Let me pull my blouse down over that, so it doesn't wander about too much. Is your hand happy there, 'Arold?"

Mercedes leaned back at last so Harold glanced down. She'd hidden his hand under her untucked blouse, leaving it loose enough for... Harold stroked her belly button, just a little, and her tummy muscles played a little hello on his palm and fingers. "My hand is very happy, Mercedes, as is the other one. The problem is that your skin truly does feel delectable. Now I want to stroke the rest and compare."

Mercedes laughed, squeezing Harold's finger ends slightly between her legs before letting go. "Keep asking, and you might get a yes."

"I think you will, Harry." Caddi couldn't keep quiet any longer, but he'd lost interest in who told Murphy refugees anything. "Where's your other woman? She should be taking notes."

"She's busy. Tessa reckons that it's more fun for Harold if he concentrates on one of them at a time." Sharyn shrugged. "I'm his sister so I don't see the attraction."

Casper and Patty chipped in and moved the conversation on from Tessa, and kept it away from people directing refugees. Casper had a genuine question, and the perfect diversion. "So what are you going to do about the Trainspotters?"

"I can send that bloody redhead Franco a message, pointing out that they should keep their men and weapons at home. The sort of message that will persuade them their advice to the Murphies is a bad idea." Caddi gave a short, humourless laugh. "A message carved on someone's, er, equipment." He glared, daring someone to comment on him nearly breaking rules.

Cooper diverted them all. "Not on an ear, like some messages." The Hot Rods started laughing but the rest looked puzzled until Cooper explained. "Caddi brought Mercedes over here before she goes delivering messages." Mercedes laughed again and Harold enjoyed the result. Her stomach gave his hand a thorough massage, which Harold's hand returned under cover of the blouse and movement. If Harold slid his other hand forward a bit, Mercedes also used a laugh to cover squeezing his fingertips between her legs, briefly.

From her little smile, Harold felt sure Patty had spotted something, but neither Cooper nor Caddi could see from their angle. Nobody could see that Mercedes had taken her hand out of Harold's back pocket and slid it up under the back of his shirt. She was doing a bit of stroking of her own. Luckily Caddi wasn't negotiating just now, because Harold kept losing track. Mercedes had gone well past grab-ass this time.

Cooper laughed again before continuing which gave Harold's brain time to recover. "Roller reckoned bringing Mercedes over to Orchard Close was a waste of time. He said Soldier Boy is that keen he's already tripping over his tongue, or possibly something else. Then Roller stood like a bloody statue while Mercedes cut a little notch out of his ear." Cooper started laughing again, but got out the, "For now. If he keeps interfering with her fun she'll get the whole ear eventually."

Most of those present were laughing hard now, but Patty at least might be laughing at Harold's face. Harold thought Mercedes kept laughing because she enjoyed the stroking and squeezing as much as he did. Caddi finished off the message. "Because the trip isn't for Soldier Boy. We're here for her to have some fun and get her ration of 'Arold." Caddi shook his head. "She's coming for you, Harry."

"I'm not running." Harold looked at Mercedes when he said it.

Her eyes warmed, really warmed, and stayed that way. "You'll need a bigger bed, or a thicker carpet, or someone's ass is going to get terrible bruises." Mercedes spoke with total sincerity, and meant every word because her eyes said so. Her eyes were quite vocal when no Hot Rods could see them. Harold hoped she could read his eyes and see that he wasn't running.

Caddi broke the stunned silence after that statement. "Maybe you should visit the Mansion once Mercedes has delivered her messages. There's a big comfy bed there." The gang boss wore a big smile now. He expected to close his Deal, very soon.

"Thank you but not yet, Caddi." This time when Harold looked up he tried to put a warning in his eyes. "There's more fighting to come. I wouldn't want Mercedes to be distracted and make a mistake. If that happened I would never get to find out just how delightful all those other delectables feel." Harold wanted to remind Mercedes to be careful. The tango under one hand, the muscles flexing under the other and her fingernails on his back said Mercedes might be hearing 'delectables' and 'feel' instead.

If Harold spent another night in her bed he'd turn over. Harold expected to survive but then he'd be trying to kill Caddi and a hell of a lot of Hot Rods. Caddi wasn't getting Mercedes unless she wanted him to, and she didn't. Her comment in bed, about having to kill everyone in the Mansion afterwards, had been clear enough.

Harold didn't think this was love, or any deep and significant feelings. On his part, he'd been snared by the lure of something beautiful, wild and deadly that might, just might, let him pet her. He had absolutely no idea what had fired up Mercedes.

Unfortunately, the visit wasn't all pleasure. During the haggling over the gun repairs that Caddi wanted done quickly, Harold lost track several times. Mercedes enjoyed the laughing game, and between that and avoiding the attempts to flash her lack of bra at him Harold had to ask Caddi to repeat himself. "If you've pulled your brain out of her pants, would you like to buy my forge?"

"What, complete with the anvil and all those fancy pincers and whatever?" Harold would, or rather Liz would. The blacksmith had mentioned human sacrifice as a way to get a proper anvil and tools, as long she could sacrifice a Hot Rod or Geek. "What's happened to your blacksmith?"

"He's fine. We never found the Murphies' blacksmith but now we've got all his kit. It's a lovely setup, all in a big horse box, so my bloke is happy to let the old gear go. Once the trailer gets to The Mansion, do you want the spare stuff?"

"I'll ask my metals person."

"Blacksmith. You've got a bloody blacksmith, and the proof is I'll sell the forge gear for maces and Rambos. Maybe my bloke can make them with the new stuff, but that won't be fast enough."

Harold set into haggling but his mind kept wandering into Mercedes' pants, if she wore any. As he avoided another bra flash, Mercedes leant in and whispered in Harold's ear. "You'll win if you look. I never wear one when I come to see you." Her nails dug into his back, more brain cells went into meltdown and Harold couldn't bargain like this.

"I can't make a deal until my blacksmith sees what's on offer. No, before you ask, my blacksmith doesn't visit." If Liz or any decent blacksmith visited the Mansion, Caddi wouldn't let them come home. He'd admitted he would swap a lieutenant for someone who made decent blades and maces.

"What a pity I won't be there." Mercedes turned to give Harold a reproachful look and her other leg came over a bit to rub his fingers. The sparkle in her eyes said Mercedes knew damn well why Harold didn't want to bargain now. Harold could forgive her, and not just because she tripped all his switches. The presents the refugees brought from Mercedes more than repaid any losses she cost him in trading.

"Yes, that is a pity." Caddi could have meant either not bargaining now or not getting his hands on Harold's blacksmith. "Where do we meet because I'm not bringing the gear here without a trade being agreed? That costs diesel." Eventually they agreed on a place in Hot Rods territory, but near the border so Harold's people could walk.

"If the trade goes through, your vehicles deliver the gear here and collect the price." Harold wasn't trying to carry an anvil over a mile.

"All right, but I'll definitely need the vehicles back because some dipstick lost two." Caddi snarled that bit.

"I thought that was sorted." Dodge seemed to be off the hook when Harold last saw him.

"Two more were ambushed and burned, and these little mishaps are all a bit too close to those lunatic bitches. Some of the lunatic bitches seem a bit too much at home over here. Have you got another other woman, Harry? One with a blond wig?" Caddi had switched to another regular complaint, the Barbies.

"Cripes no. I've got all the woman I can handle, right here in my hands." That won a lovely smile and more muscle interaction from Mercedes, but Caddi wasn't satisfied.

"So how come they keep dedicating songs to you? If another of my men mentions you and The Trooper, I might just shoot him." Barbie Radio had decided that "The Trooper" by Iron Maiden made the perfect dedication track for Soldier Boy. There were other fighting songs as well, dedicated to Patty or Ru or the sexy bitches in Orchard Close. Much to Hazel's disgust "I Want a Man with Slow Hands" had been added to smooch hour, dedicated to Alfie. Skipper always dedicated "Out in the Fields" to all the boys and girls working those rolling acres, and asked if the radio man could visit. Repairing Barbie Radio had been popular, and apparently the Hot Rod rank and file listened.

"Yes, 'Arold, I wondered as well. In the last smooch hour I'm sure that woman dedicated 'Je t'aime' to Soldier Boy?" Mercedes smiled with her eyes as well so she was teasing, not annoyed.

Harold grinned. "Maybe because they know about us?"

"Mmm, I'll practice the lyrics, just in case." Harold averted his eyes as she leant in again and felt hot breath on his ear. "Je t'aime, je t'aime. How was that?"

Deep, throaty, and sexy, definitely sexy, Harold thought. "Mmm, if I handle a couple more delectable bits, maybe we can get more feeling into it?"

Mercedes slid her leg slowly off Harold's hand where she'd brought it over as she'd leant in. "Feeling? Oh, I'd love to get more feeling involved, 'Arold, feeling and delectables." Her fingernails ran up and down his spine a bit.

At least Caddi stopped complaining about Harold and Barbies, because everyone could see which woman Harold wanted. The conversation went back to arranging the meeting, and if Harold would have the firearms ready by then. Caddi put off the smithy gear trading until he could get his weapons back at the same time.

Mercedes walked back down to the gate with Harold's arm round her, on top of her blouse. Both of Harold's hands were placed on her ass for goodbye and Harold smiled a little at the comments Suzie would make. When he pulled just a little, Mercedes swayed forwards without hesitation. "What a pity you can't stay here for Halloween, Mercedes. We could find you a lovely costume for trick or treat."

Mercedes smiled and walked her hands up Harold's front and around his neck. "Which would you choose, 'Arold. Trick or treat?"

"I'd invite you inside for a treat. Then I'd ask you for a treat as well." Harold looked right into her eyes, warm brown eyes just now with barely a trace of the dead ones. "We could swap tricks as well?"

Delight blossomed on her face, then she pouted. "I'm sure I could find a trick you liked, 'Arold. Now what can I do so you aren't tempted by anyone else's tricks or treats?" Both Mercedes' arms tightened around Harold's neck and her lips stayed on Harold's for long seconds this time. A ripple of murmurs came from the Hot Rods, while Harold's firm grip wasn't just because of the kiss.

As her arms tightened round Harold's neck, Mercedes moved those last few inches and pressed herself against his front! The fag paper would have been smeared into oblivion, and Harold had to stifle an impulse to wrap his arms right round her. Mercedes had smashed another of her rules. She pulled away with a smile, one that reached her eyes. "Imagine that, but without clothes." With that she turned away, pointing to her ass and giving it a wiggle of course. As everyone laughed, the Killer Queen pulled on her coat, swaggering off down to the cars surrounded by Hot Rods.

When he'd wiped the daft grin off his face, Harold started worrying about Mercedes. Her eyes were still dead if they weren't looking into his. If whatever she'd buried inside broke free, Mercedes was capable of more or less anything. Seeing Caddi literally lick his lips as Mercedes broke the clinch didn't help Harold's peace of mind.

*   *   *

Harold didn't have time to imagine too much, because he had to talk to Liz before she worried too much about meeting Caddi. When he managed to visit her, a little later, it wasn't the meeting with Caddi that Liz had heard about. "I'll huff and I'll puff?" Harold heard the bar being removed, to reveal a laughing Liz.

"From what I've just been told, you'll have no puff left." Liz beckoned, with a flamboyant bow. "Come into my lair, wimp. Are you thinking straight after that parting shot? Imagine that, but without the clothes? I'll bet you have, imagined it I mean." She smirked and posed, but her sooty apron and the lump hammer in her hand spoiled the effect. "I'm going to steal it when I get the last two prospective apprentices hot and sweaty in here. The one who likes the idea will be the right man. After all, my apprentice will have the same duties as yours."

At least this talk with Liz, and Harold's blush, were private. Once Liz stopped teasing, they worked on how to keep Caddi from identifying the blacksmith. Liz confessed to still having the occasional bad dream about that Hot Rod she hadn't heard, about if he'd come into the forge instead of going after Celine. Harold knew she still worried, because Liz still kept the door barred.

Once they'd worked out a way to keep her safe, Liz asked for charcoal, as much as possible because her baby trees still weren't growing fast enough. When Harold complained, she produced a bowl with a leather chinstrap, a helmet, a shiny metal one. "I've managed to melt some metal, at last. This is an alloy and a lot softer than steel, but it should turn a blade."

The two of them hit it a few times with edged weapons and the helmet deflected a blade unless it hit solidly, full on. Even then it might mean a cut and concussion instead of a split skull. They tested the weight and fit, and the helmet would be uncomfortable even with a bit of padded cloth inside. Harold reminded her they'd got all the middles out of ruined cycle helmets, and crash helmet linings. A bit of a diagram, and Liz reckoned she could make them fit inside the next attempt. As he came away, Harold briefly wondered who he could raid for trees to make charcoal. He'd laid awake nights worrying about the lack of decent head protection, now that the few crash helmets and bike hats were all ruined.

Harold had barely finished letting a few select people know about helmets, then explaining why there weren't any yet, when Patty wanted him to watch the new practice. The first dozen Ant-inspired shields were ready, curved plywood faced with thin aluminium to stop splintering. The old cladding from the caravans finally had a use. The Demons lined up with locked shields, and a Rambo to slide between them and stab an opponent in the gut. The second rank poked broom handles forward between their heads, to simulate spears, but in a real situation they'd wait until after the crossbow volley. Patty chose shorter women for the front rank to let the taller fighters reach through easier, ones who swore they'd stab a real person if necessary. A substantial percentage of these volunteers had been abused or threatened by the gangs, and now they fancied some payback. Harold worried once again about turning them into Barbies, but their own logic defeated any protests.

According to the front row women, their attackers wouldn't see any threat in young women hiding behind shields. Once the bastards were close enough for the big knives, it would be too late. Several intended putting on makeup if they had time, to help suck the bastards in because they had a score to settle. Their treatment by the gangs had made some women into potential killers just as efficiently as HM forces did to their recruits, even if the mental scars were different. This training should turn potential into deadly. After a quiet discussion, Patty promised to keep an eye on just how bloodthirsty some were getting.

There'd be backup for the Demons, because Harold and his biting woman had spent a lot of time together. The increasing number of hybrid firearms were split up, with boxes of 'parts' being stowed in three places while half a dozen complete weapons were scattered around in various houses, for practice. The squad leaders and their deputy knew where the weapons were, and who could use them. By the time Orchard Close had a score of the new style muskets, twice that number of people were training as musketeers.

The new musketeers spent long hours becoming adept at loading a hybrid musket and dropping the crude sight on a target. Now they also learned to ride the kick to keep it there. Thanks to Stephan the carpenter, Liz, Rob the plumber and some experimentation, the training weapons had a kick without firing. The butt plate on three dummy muskets included a spring that smacked it back into the shooter's shoulder when the trainee pulled the trigger. The beam of a torch, strapped under the barrel, told the trainee if they'd kept the barrel down and pointing at the man shape painted on a wall.

* * *

All the training stopped for Halloween. At dusk, curtains were closed and any outside lights were turned off, then the wind and water generators started up. Orchard Close lit up with various sizes of coloured bulbs, turning the familiar streets into a magical fairy grotto. The first ones to benefit were the youngsters, but one of them wasn't even slightly enchanted. "But I'm older than most of them. I can shoot a crossbow so I'm a guard, one of the Riot Squad." Daisy glared at her firework fairy costume. "I need a proper costume now, like Fergie or Sukie's mum."

Tessa, Sharyn and Harold all winced before Sharyn answered. "You are seven, young lady, not seventeen. You don't have to wear that costume or go trick and treating, but in that case you don't get any sweets."

"But I don't need this costume. Sukie's mum is wearing shorts and she says she'll get something better than buns and sweets for her treat. I've got shorts?" Daisy stopped suddenly, turning her curious gaze on Tessa. "What sort of treat, Aunty Tessa? Millie's mum said you'd get special treats as well." This time both Harold and Tessa had blushes to go with the wince.

"Enough! If you won't wear that, off you go, upstairs. Georgina and Joey are both older than you, and they'll be trick or treating with us. I'll tell them you want them to have your share." Sharyn's hands had gone on her hips, while Wills-Womble and Eddie-Pirate were watching round-eyed from by the door.

"Joey is going?" Daisy's rebellion collapsed. "Georgina said she would trick or treat him, but if he's coming with us she's got no chance. He likes me, he said so." She ran upstairs with the dress. "Bet I get more sweets than Wills or Eddie."

"Won't. Bet I win." Eddie wasn't as resigned to Daisy as Wills had become.

Sharyn rolled her eyes. "I swear I'm going to gag Suzie. She keeps opening her big mouth where little ears can hear." Her face softened into a little smile. "If she's wearing shorts, I wonder which character she's dressing as?"

Harold manfully withstood the thinly veiled references about who might wear shorts or stockings, and what treats someone dressed that way might get. Thankfully, now Daisy had made up her mind she didn't waste time and soon hurtled down the stairs again, ready to go. Tessa and Sharyn didn't give her time to speak, hustling the three children down the road to meet the rest. Harold stayed home to dish out treats.

This year over a dozen young children went door to door, an old-fashioned trick or treat. Mums, sometimes dads, and even some of the young teens escorted them to collect little sweets or fruit and pastry treats. Despite ferocious smiling and eye-fluttering, Harold only allowed Daisy one treat when the gang knocked on his door. Joey looked ready to run, with Georgina on one side and Daisy on the other, glaring at each other.

Afterwards the young teens gathered at Betty's house where she'd laid on treats, burgers and fruit juice with one drink of small beer each. The numbers in the computer club had grown to where they sometimes spread out of her front room, but the eldest resident liked having youngsters in her house even if she teased them about their terrible musical tastes. She also insisted that Alfie should stay in her spare bedroom, rather than move into a flat now he'd reached eighteen. There were quite a few thought Hazel would like to get Alfie in his own flat, or anyplace Harold couldn't see. A few were wondering if Betty might be more broad-minded than she seemed to be when she laid down the law to the computer club. Hazel certainly spent a lot of time visiting.

Later that night, a large number of strangely dressed young men and women ran around Orchard Close banging on doors. Not exactly magical and fairy-like, despite the lighting and several victims looking decidedly spellbound. Only a few really went for shocking, and most of those had a target. As Liz delighted in telling Harold later, a couple wore their version of a Mercedes outfit and offered grab-ass to their chosen victim. Suzie wore very small shorts, real Daisy Dukes, and found thigh highs from someplace but only Billy got an invite to grab. The gossip mill seized on that with rumours of gartering. Between then and Guy Fawkes, plenty of other rumours over who tricked or treated who spread through Orchard Close.

Five days later, the soldiers on the bypass accepted that fizzing and sparkling colours and lights, on Guy Fawkes night, wouldn't be threatening. The men and women with chips and soup might have helped, or maybe it was the line of young women in costumes, waving from the bottom of the access road and inviting them to the bonfire dance. Sarge warned Harold his squad would be rotated out soon, so the women should be more careful. This sergeant took a copy of Curtis's picture to pass around a few other NCOs. He'd get word back if anyone saw the gardener, just to confirm he'd made it. Harold kept that from Emmy, in case it came to nothing.

Barry the ex-fireman had been experimenting with chemicals again, because this year he presented a wider variety of colourful fireworks. He still avoided any bangs or shooting flares, just in case a soldier had an itchy trigger finger. Harold chased Daisy, Eddie and Wills around the bonfire until they were tired, while the dogs chased everyone and stole treats. Eventually Tessa and Sharyn helped him carry the children home to bed. This year Harold went to the dance afterwards. He'd accepted that the new refugees in particular were reassured by seeing him there, dancing with whoever asked. In any case, from the jokes, he wasn't on the hunting list because he'd already got two. Someone chose shopping as the theme, to celebrate the visit to Beth's, so the mystery competition contestants dressed as shop dummies. Their attempts at lingerie kept the single blokes intrigued and hopeful, as usual.

Fergie allegedly wore a lace dress, made from not enough lace curtain. During her dance, she wanted to know how she'd squeeze between Harold's women to get more machete training. Harold laughed because he'd known her secret for a year. This time Fergie didn't dance as much because the lads were realising she'd prefer a Barbie, especially one with Ski goggles and a wig. Not everyone had connected the dots, because several young men tried to trade for Fergie's number to walk her home.

As usual, who walked who and how long they took fed the rumour mill. Harold didn't need a rumour mill to know Alfie would walk Hazel home. He'd started to wonder if the only thing stopping a gartering might be him, because the idiots still tried to hide their relationship. Harold was already sure Hazel slept at Betty's house more often than not. He didn't spread the bit of rumour fodder he collected on his way home, and swore Tessa to silence. Roy, the refugee fighter, sat hand in hand with Celine, watching the stars. It looked as if Celine's unorthodox rape therapy had finally paid off, and she'd found her older version of dangerous but safe.

They'd need every dangerous fighter to keep Orchard Close safe. As November progressed, Harold became more certain that Caddi or the Geeks would come for Orchard Close, or at least launch a raid. Too many visitors made comments about the number of fine young women now living there, even if the cold weather meant everyone wrapped up more. Harold had nightmares about both teaming up, because the GOFS couldn't uphold the treaty against that pair even if they tried. At least the Geeks wouldn't team up with the General, while Caddi's and the General's current wars stopped them from joining up.

* * *

Two days after Guy Fawkes, Dealer turned up again. This time Harold knew the way it worked and the two of them were soon in the Embassy. "The weapon?"

Harold produced it. "This isn't one of yours."

"What makes you think that?" Dealer's expression wasn't saying either way.

"It's a gang weapon, probably taken from a policeman back during the Crash. I reckon your blokes cleaned up the outside but inside it's filthy. Someone's used axle grease instead of oil, and they haven't ever stripped it properly." Harold worked the mechanism. "It was jammed solid. I see a lot of it, especially using home reloads with the new propellant and old brass."

"Maybe my men aren't very good at keeping weapons clean? I should chastise them." Dealer started smiling properly.

"If the rest are like this, I'll tell the lasses taking the beer to bring back the guns and the cars. I'll bet you don't use reloads in those weapons, do you?" Harold gave a smile that showed he already knew the answer.

"No. I took this in trade because it's allegedly bloody useless. I will be keeping it now, because these are much too good for some asshole to spray the neighbours with." Dealer worked the weapon, peering down the barrel and into the breech. "Lovely clean job. Where do you get your oil?"

"I collected a lot from clubs and shops at the beginning, after the rest stole the propellant and weapons. I also collected reloading equipment: presses, dies, powder measures, moulds, and resizers for brass."

"If you have spares, I could give you a really good deal on any or all of those. Most people didn't think that far ahead." Dealer glanced up. "You didn't buy caps or primers last time."

"I found a few here and there, and I tend not to waste ammunition." Dealer smiled in genuine amusement, so he already knew Harold's reputation of one shot, one hit. "A few people in here thought further than day one. We collected up a lot of wool, for instance. Good Arran hand knits are a specialty." Harold gestured at Dealer's jumper. "Bespoke, not mass produced like that. We could make you some bobble hats and scarves with Dealer on them? Or balaclavas?" He wanted to get away from how many primers he might have. It worked better than expected.

"Seriously? Not the hats and scarves, but hand knitted Arrans? Any other sort of knitting, or craft work?" To Harold's surprise, Dealer seemed genuinely interested.

"More or less any sort of knitting, I think. We have one or two who can wield a mean needle now, for embroidery or crocheting as well. Some are quite artistic. The latest Rambos have a bit of fancy engraving and you were right, I get a better price for them." Harold chuckled at his next thought. "My bodyguard is known as Demon, but that's because she's a Demon knitter."

"Oh dear, I'd better not tell David or he'll propose. My bodyguard. He was quite taken with her." Harold thought this amusement might also be genuine. "Tell David she'll knit him a jumper and he'll want her to run off into the sunset."

"Get his size. Then you can buy him one for Christmas and tell him who knitted it."

Dealer laughed at that idea, a definite crack in his cool. "I'm going to enjoy visiting here. I am truly interested in quality hand knits, silly as that may sound. Will they knit to order?"

"Bring patterns, and wool if it's a special. Some of the children have pictures knitted into theirs and apparently that is easy. I'll bring Patty, providing David can keep himself under control?"

"He'll behave on duty, but once he knows he might want to hold her hand on the way out. Bring whatever hand knits you can spare, and next time we'll talk orders. What else do you have?" Dealer paused, thinking through what they'd covered. "I'll take a reloading kit this time, if possible. What about those helmets the gate guards have? They're new."

"Only alloy, and there aren't many yet." Harold ran through his very short list. "We've got the fancier Rambos, and a few other knives you might like. Maces of course. This time I have some little gold ingots, because now the scavengers look for jewellery or ornaments. My people are keeping an eye open for a Turner or a Banksy in case there's one in an outside loo or shed." Dealer's smile acknowledged how likely real artwork would be. He took the automatic back with him in the bag it had arrived in. Harold sent beers to the guards, and half an hour later wheeled the barrow down with Patty as his bodyguard.

David seemed very interested when Dealer started talking knitting and Patty answered, instead of Harold. "You bring a pattern, or maybe a picture, and we'll get close." Patty sounded utterly confident.

Dealer inspected the four jumpers, five scarves and three pairs of gloves whose owners had agreed to accept a replacement if these sold, then passed them to David for an assessment. The bodyguard inspected them closely and murmured something, so he had to be genuinely knowledgeable about knitting. Dealer nodded and smiled. "We can deal for this quality, especially if you can manage the less mainstream types of knitting. We'll pay a premium for anything knitted by whoever did these." Patty smirked when he pointed at two of the jumpers, because she knitted one of them. "What about crocheting? Can you make toys or dolls?" Dealer had to have a customer in mind, but Harold's mind boggled at a gangster collecting woollen dolls.

"We'd need more colours, vivid ones." Patty set into serious trading, taking orders for a black minidress in thin wool and a man's Arran jumper. Harold radioed Emmy to bring a bag of croqueted toys and any embroidery she could get hold of, and leave it outside the door. Dealer took them all. Next time he would bring patterns and definite orders for embroidery, croquet and knitting, and the wool for them. Part of the payment would be in brightly coloured threads and wool.

While Patty negotiated, Harold started wondering who Dealer wanted to see in a black minidress. The knitted ones were thin, stretchy, and fitted like a second skin, and Harold had a momentary wobble at the thought of Mercedes in one. She'd started getting to him when she wasn't here. Those pheromones must be strong stuff!

It was almost a relief when the dealing moved back to weapons. The three helmets were taken in trade, as were the two that Harold and Patty were wearing. In Dealer's words, in a week or two gang bosses on the opposite side of the city would be prancing about wearing shiny new hats.

Once again, Dealer took the maces and Rambos, giving a little more for the knives with the engraving. They each had something different, including stylised wolves and an attempt at a dragon. Sorcha, the engraver, used several pages of tattoo outlines from one of the computers as guides and had already improved from her first attempts. Dealer thought the word Rambo probably added as much value as the fancy work. He made a good offer for the pair of Wamil style knives. With the gun repair and the knitting, Harold came away without parting with any coupons for purchases.

There were five weapons for repair: three poser type hand guns, a hunting rifle and an engraved pump action shotgun. Next visit, in three months' time, Dealer promised an AK for repair at a truly exotic price. Harold remembered Dealer's comments about finding repairers who wouldn't steal automatic weapons, he must have passed that test. The repairs came into Orchard Close covered up in the barrow, along with propellant and brass casings for weapons that Harold hadn't much ammo for. He also had six new clips for his pistols as part of the pay for fixing Dealer's firearm, and twenty .38 rifle rounds to use in the adapted shotgun. Harold had an agreement to deal for another two of the reloading kits next time, once Dealer had sounded out how much he could get for them. Orchard Close might be wanting coupons from Dealer at this rate, or maybe Dealer had some more exotic stock. When the Orchard Close leaders discussed the visit later, Alfie thought half a dozen hand grenades would be useful.

* * *

Grenades might be more of a dream than a possibility, but Caddi's forge would definitely be a big help in defending Orchard Close. Two days after Dealer's visit, on the ninth of November, Harold lined up his guards before setting out to deal for the blacksmithing equipment. "This is Caddi's gang we are meeting, and it's not on our turf so the language rules don't apply. Half of you are going to get a lot of comment, and it won't be nice."

Logan, a metal beating candidate, sneered. "We can fix that." He hefted his mace.

Harold fixed him with a glare. "No you can't, Logan. Not without starting a war. If you can't handle the women being harassed, step back now."

"We'll handle it ourselves anyway." Several women nodded to agree with Tilly, and put a hand on a weapon.

"No, Tilly. I told you when you volunteered." Harold sighed, this could end up a total disaster because the Riot Squad had insisted on half the guards being women. "The same applies to you. Ignore the language."

"We don't care about the language." Tilly looked around the other young women. "We're all refugees so we've all heard it before."

"Last time we had to ignore it, and hope the bastards let it go at that." Rihannon looked as if she'd swallowed something disgusting, but that might just be memories resurfacing.

"Or they didn't let it go, and we remember that all right." Tilly actually smiled a little at that but it looked more of a snarl. "This time if they go further, they'll bleed. Unless we're supposed to ignore everything?"

Harold kept his face and voice bland, in case he wound them up any further. "Mercedes rules. I'll tell them up front."

Everyone understood Mercedes rules, because the residents had cross-questioned the Hot Rods after her visits. "Good. We can start up a Mercedes style collection." Eight heads nodded to agree with Tilly.

"But not for bad language." Harold didn't mind a bit of confidence, but he didn't want the women pushing for an excuse.

"No." Tilly relaxed and tried for a real smile. "Sorry Harold. Memories, they got a bit intense for a minute but we won't let you down."

"Fair enough. You heard what Tilly said, Logan? The women will deal with it if someone gets too frisky." Logan and other men nodded, so Harold turned to smile at Liz. "Having second thoughts about coming?"

"Cripes no, I'm feeling a lot safer. I just need to copy that attitude and stand back sharpish if a fight starts." Liz looked round and then patted her own gear. "I can't actually use all this armour and sharp stuff."

Tilly grinned and patted her on the back. "Don't worry, sister, we've got you covered. You just keep making us more sharp stuff."

"Keep in mind that you're supposed to look as if you're guarding Abraham. He's the metals man, as far as the Hot Rods are concerned." Harold smiled at the only unarmed man.

Tilly looked him over. "He doesn't really look the part. No offence Abraham, but you're old, and sort of scrawny for a smith."

"In that case the Hot Rods won't try to kidnap me, and they can see why I need bodyguards." Abraham flexed a non-existent bicep and smiled happily. "Caddi will know Harold hasn't got a real smith, and I get to put one over on the asshole."

"If he tries for the real smith, I don't care about the rules. I'll brain him." Henry, another candidate for Liz's apprentice, carried a mace and definitely had the muscle for braining.

"Only if he recognises me." Liz smiled and poked his bicep. "If you get sweaty rescuing me you might get the traditional reward."

"Calm down Liz, it's too cold for sweaty. If you're all sure you can behave, we'll get off. It's over a mile to the meeting place but we won't be rushing. Tilly, put a couple out front as scouts and let's go." Harold had to smile once the group started off, because Tilly struck up with "hup, two three four" so they were marching. Soldier Boy's army didn't have any morale problems.

*   *   *

When Caddi's men saw the guards with Harold, there were a lot of comments about surplus women. The looks the women gave the gangsters weren't encouraging. "Are you trading some of these for the gear, Harry?" Caddi grinned because he knew Harold didn't sell people.

"No Caddi, and a word of warning to all your lads. These young ladies might not be in Orchard Close, but it's safer not to touch. They've heard of the Mercedes rulebook and decided to adopt it. Now they want to start an ear collection." Harold looked over Caddi's men. "Or nuts, I don't think they care."

The Hot Rod warlord's smile slipped a little. "You training up more girlfriends, Harry?

Harold's smile widened as several of the women sniggered. "I don't need any more, Caddi. These lasses are all volunteers for this trip because it's the best chance they'll get of trophies. Just a word of warning, that's all."

"This isn't Orchard Close, so my men can say whatever they like." Caddi had his little half-smile back.

"Words aren't a problem. Now are we here for your lot to lust after my bodyguards, or to do some serious business?" Harold looked pointedly at the two pickups full of gear.

"Definitely business." Caddi turned to his men. "I'm here to deal so you'd better do your job. If one of you gets adventurous and loses a hand, tough shit." The gang boss turned back to Harold's party and laughed. "That's a blacksmith?"

"No, I told you I haven't got one. We'll give him a minute to see what useless crap you've included and then we can deal." Harold waved Abraham forward and four guards went to help him, including Liz and what now appeared to be her personal minder, Henry. Harold and Caddi watched while the loads were pulled apart. Abraham inspected various bits and scratched his head, genuine puzzlement because Abraham felt more at home in the garden. Once he'd looked, all the guards moved round Harold and Abraham so that Caddi couldn't hear the discussion.

Only a short discussion, with Liz right behind Harold, murmuring as he pretended to talk to Abraham. "The gear we need is here, and it'll be a big help. There's some crap in there but I need to look closer. There's some moulds and sand boxes that might be ok. Please get the useable tools and anvil at least."

"Is that all?" The pickups carried a lot more than that.

"I'd rather have charcoal than the broken tools and worn chisels. Decent charcoal because with this gear it'll be a lot easier to make proper blades." Liz paused. "I'll have another look at that heap in the second pickup with the electrics mixed in. It's ringing bells in my head but I don't know why. We'll pull it apart properly while you get the bloody stupid demands out of the way." Harold laughed, because Caddi always started a negotiation by asking for something outrageous.

"Be quick." Harold raised his voice. "Well go and have another look then. I'm not giving up good weapons for anything you aren't sure of."

Abraham spoke louder as well. "Okay, but I'll have to pull the heap apart properly."

Harold looked over at Caddi, who could hear that part. "We can start while he does that."

"Good. I haven't got all day."

"Neither have I but I'm not buying your scrap. Some tools are better than we've got and we want the anvil, but I'm not buying worn chisels and broken tools. We'll need a lot of charcoal as well." Harold tried to sound disinterested, but Caddi knew he wanted the anvil at least.

"Have a word with your new blonde girlfriends. Together you can raid the Trainspotters and cut down their precious bloody trees. It will serve them right." The Hot Rods all laughed because the Trainspotters controlled one of the old parks, with plenty of mature trees if they'd not already cut them down. Caddi inspected Harold's guards, again. "The Barbies might help you for nothing more than a date with your soldiers. No wonder we can't find any decent women among the Murphies. You've nicked the lot."

"Refugees so they're volunteers Caddi. They seem to prefer Orchard Close to the Hot Rods." Harold kept an amiable smile, because after all he'd told the guards they were to ignore words.

"That's not neighbourly, Harry. You could share them out a bit."

"They go where they want. That's how Orchard Close is run, Caddi." Harold pointed at the women and laughed. "Make them an offer."

At least Caddi laughed at that. "I still reckon the Trainspotters are your best bet for charcoal."

"It's a long walk Caddi, so I'll need some in the deal." Harold had listened to Liz often enough to know she needed all the charcoal he could get.

"You won't need much. That blacksmith isn't going to be making a lot of gear unless he gets one of the girls to help him." The Hot Rods supplied the laughter chorus, while several of the girls flexed their biceps to help Abraham to decide.

"I'll bear it in mind." The dealing began over how much of what, and Harold soon realised Caddi meant to push him hard. Maybe the number of women guards had annoyed the Hot Rod, because he twice offered to take a couple of them as part of the price. Harold asked for another talk to his blacksmith.

Liz didn't waste any time, once Caddi couldn't hear what was said. "Give the arse what he wants. I promise you'll be stitching him. You must get all the gear, don't try to pick and choose." Liz sounded intent, and focussed.

"Some's never been used so why am I buying it? Is it even blacksmith kit?" Harold could see the dust and muck coating most of the gear in the second pickup. Some looked like electrical gear, so maybe Caddi intended selling off half a shed full of crap. Harold bent closer, allegedly to discuss the gear quietly with Abraham, while Liz murmured from behind.

"All of it, and I promise you'll get the better of the deal. My word on it Harold." Before Harold could ask Liz for more of an explanation a short yell and some swearing interrupted him.

One of the Hot Rods nursed one hand with the other, and scowled. "I barely touched it, boss."

"Touched what?" Caddi looked suspicious. Both sets of guards had hands on hilts, poised and ready, but only Tilly actually held a weapon.

"Not the weapon he asked to inspect." Tilly looked over at Harold. "He asked if he could look at the Rambo, boss, so I took it out to show him. Since you were selling some I thought it would help. When the scroat moved in to look he put his hand on my ass."

The Hot Rod looked and sounded indignant. "Only on that bloody armour plated skirt!"

"And you're not bleeding. Seems fair." Harold could see most of his guards fighting a smile at Tilly's answer.

"So what did she do, Cal, if you're not bleeding?" Now Caddi sounded curious.

"I don't know boss, but it feels like the bitch broke my hand." Caddi walked over and grabbed the hand in question. "Aargh. Fuck. That hurts!"

"It's not broken." Now Caddi seemed more interested in Tilly. "What did you do?"

"Put your hand on me and I'll show you?" She looked back steadily. "Harold told them the rules."

Caddi turned away and glared at Cal. "Yes he did, and I warned you I'm dealing, serious business. If you want to get crippled, do it on your own time." The gang boss moved back towards Harold. "Let's get this sorted before one of the prats loses his fucking ears."

"I'll take the lot because sorting out the crap will take forever, but I'm not paying top price for the scrap." Liz had always done well by Orchard Close so Harold took a flyer. Working on the basis that he should trust the expert, Harold gave away more than he should have for the gear. Definitely more than he wanted to, because Caddi pushed hard on the price. The warlord seemed determined to make a point, and at least part had to be Caddi being furious at Cal for trying it on and failing.

Despite the extra cost, Harold stuck out for more charcoal in the deal. After all, even Caddi knew that any ironwork ate charcoal. The warlord admitted that he hoped the new setup didn't use as much or he'd be raiding the bloody trees himself. He promised the charcoal would be at Orchard Close by the time the residents unloaded the forge gear, and drove off with his guards. His annoyance had gone, and now Caddi seemed very happy with himself.

Too happy, Harold thought, wondering if some of the bad mood had just been Caddi faking to drive up the prices. Harold had cranked up the prices of some of the repaired guns, to try and even up, but even so he'd been stung. Too many Rambos and maces and some helmets were heading for the Mansion, he'd have to take some from the armouries to make up the price. Liz could replace them, eventually, but that would cost time, metal and a hell of a lot of the new charcoal. Harold couldn't even discuss it with Liz, because the two Hot Rod pickups carrying the purchases kept pace with the Orchard Close squad.

*   *   *

Liz literally twitched, pacing up and down as the two pickup trucks unloaded. She hovered impatiently while Abraham supervised counting out the helmets and weapons, and handing them over to the Hot Rods. It took a while to move everything from the Hot Rod pickups, and then their payment through the gates in wheelbarrows, and by the time they'd finished, the charcoal had arrived. Abraham opened a bag, near Liz so she could nod to tell him it smelled right. She seemed distracted, a lot more interested in the heap of junk. Once the gates were shut and the Hot Rods drove away, Liz whirled to face Harold. "Come on, let's get it all into my lair." Liz kept her voice down, fighting the grin that kept trying to spread over her face.

Harold glanced around everyone present, and they looked baffled as well. "Whoa, Liz. You want all the crap in there as well?"

Liz almost hopped up and down, bursting with something she didn't want to say in public. "Get it all into my lair and get me Finn, so he can help me sort through it. You may as well make yourself useful as well." The men and women with wheelbarrows looked baffled, but they carted the lot into her lair and unloaded.

Liz closed the door behind them as the last one left, leaving only Harold, Finn and herself inside. Harold waited while Liz whispered and Finn poked and pulled and tested, until finally the electrician said he might need Trev and it would still take a couple of days. The corrosion under the bird and rat shit didn't look too bad, nothing he couldn't fix once Elise cleaned it all up.

By that time Harold was wondering what the hell he'd bought, so as soon as Finn left he pounced. "I paid a bloody fortune for that crap. Now tell me why."

The little twirl before Liz spoke was an answer all by itself. "What do you want? Maces, knives, helmets, shields, a full set of fitted armour?

"From that lot? What does it turn into? A magic cauldron? It's well disguised." Harold stared at the mess, but inspiration didn't strike.

"As good as a magic cauldron, but the proper name is an induction furnace." The blacksmith's expression said that Harold should be performing cartwheels, but it meant nothing. Liz pointed at the shape uncovered when she'd pulled the wires about for Finn.

"I'm no wiser. It doesn't look like a cauldron."

Her smile almost split Liz's face. "You know I have trouble getting the heat I need to melt metal?"

"Yes, it's why I bargained for extra charcoal." Harold glanced at the heap of expensive bags in one corner.

"That'll be handy for working the blades, tempering and generally fettling, but I won't need charcoal to melt metal now." The sheer glee in her voice confirmed Liz's absolute conviction.

Harold looked at the heap of bits and wires. He hoped he understood. "So this will?"

"That really is the blacksmith's equivalent of a magic cauldron. Like I said, an induction furnace, and it's complete with crucibles, moulds and sand boxes. That heap of crap will melt pretty much any metal the scavengers bring, using electricity instead of charcoal." Liz couldn't keep her eyes off the heap of gear, shuffling and twitching while she spoke.

Harold started to smile and killed it quickly. "Did you tell Finn what it is, or anybody else?"

"Sort of, so he knew what it should do." Liz looked alarmed when she saw Harold's face. "What's the problem?"

"How about Caddi deciding to attack us to get it back?" Harold saw it sink in and Liz sobered. "How come nobody else recognised it?"

"Look at that heap of crap. Even I didn't get it at first and I've told you enough times, I'm a blacksmith slut. My dream chat up line was 'would you like to test my induction furnace,' or 'do you want to inspect my fettling gear' from a big muscly bloke. Caddi's blacksmith is either an idiot, a total amateur or is being dangerously uncooperative." Liz waved her hand over the tangle of metal and wires. "With the anvil and tools, this is a miniature iron works. I'll bet some scroat lifted it complete because they recognised the anvil."

"Caddi's blacksmith is an amateur because Caddi said welds broke, and his man couldn't harden maces like you do." Harold's smile didn't match Liz's, but it was getting there.

"I can do better now, cast the mace heads to fit shovel shafts, broom shafts, whatever we've got. No welding or cutting so we won't need rods and gas. How do you fancy steel helmets?" Liz laughed and made a show of inspecting Harold.

"Slow up, we'll have to sit down and make a list. Cripes, Caddi will never believe Abraham is the blacksmith, not if a stream of heavy metal comes out of here." Harold stared at the heap of crud, having trouble believing it himself.

"At worst he'll think it was one of the bigger blokes in the guards, one like Logan or Henry. He won't know it's me." Harold realised where some of the euphoria came from. Liz had got away with it, so nobody would be trying to kidnap her.

"Can you tear yourself away for a bit, because I'm serious about the list?" Harold needed more heads working on this because Liz wasn't firing on all cylinders. "Have you got a big hammer man organised?" He grinned. "Logan?"

Liz's smile widened if that was possible. "Not Logan, though he was a candidate when I carried out the first auditions yesterday. That's when Henry asked why I didn't put on my ear muffs, those rabbit fur ones. He's my secret admirer! After that offer today to protect my fair body, I think I should at least get him in here for a proper test." Harold had to laugh at the huge dollop of smug in that.

"No wonder he seemed so keen." Harold shook his head, trying to sound serious. "Make sure you put the bar on the door down, so no innocent walks in and has the sight seared into their brain forever."

Harold got to Finn before he'd talked to Trev or anyone else, and the electrician swore he could do the job alone but it might take him a bit longer. A quick meeting of the squad leaders came up with a list of what they needed Liz to make first, with steel helmets up at the top of the list. By that time even Liz had stopped laughing, while Doll complained again about the number of secrets she had to remember. She'd started worrying about talking in her sleep. Sooner or later something would slip, and she'd been pushing the training of her squad in case that set off one of the local nutcases. Several other sober faces agreeing with her set Harold worrying, and pushing himself to get more muskets built and ammunition loaded.

*   *   *

Everyone's good humour took a knock when the soldiers on the bypass were rotated out. For some reason the Army brass had doubled the time any unit spent in the same place, which meant that Orchard Close had made a few real friends among their guards. When the new soldiers arrived, the sergeant called Harold up to explain that he wouldn't be taking any crap or doing anyone any favours. Harold had heard the same from every new sergeant, but this time it seemed to be said more by rote than with real conviction. The sergeant didn't look at the picture of Curtis, but said he'd seen it and hadn't seen the man.

Harold made sure all the residents understood, they had to be extra careful. Quite a few, especially Doll's squad, had started wearing pistols openly. Now Harold drummed into everyone they mustn't point the barrel anywhere close to the bypass, even by accident. Hiding rifles and muskets, and firing practice, became even more important while all the squad leaders nagged the guards about keeping shotguns covered. The squads all put in extra practice raising the covers over the firing steps, until it was a smooth, quick operation. Hopefully, someone firing a rifle under there wouldn't attract an Army bullet while responding to an attack from out in the fields.

Only the most tolerant men went on the first Mart trip after the soldiers arrived. The shoppers reported that the sergeant and soldiers used the wand and searched, but were polite about it. After ten days, Harold sent Abraham, who wasn't at all big or threatening, up with a bowl of chips. He gradually reduced the gap between chips to every three days and increased the number of shoppers, but wouldn't risk any women.

Meanwhile Harold upped the rifle and pistol practice a little, because he'd scored extra propellant to reload the rounds. As Ski warned them, now that the Barbies knew about it a flurry of gun work came in. Just as well, the repairs from the GOFS had dropped off because they didn't get in many fights. Chandra 'accidentally' let slip they'd had a few repairs done in the past by someone the Trainspotters knew. The Trainspotters didn't accept many weapons, and must add on a big commission going by the prices. That might be why the blondes obviously knew to clean their guns, and probably cleared simple jams. They'd never be as good a customer as the nearer gangs.

Some gun repairs came from beyond the Barbies. Harold charged those a bit more than the locals, and Chandra admitted to adding even more, so others probably considered him expensive as well. The Geeks and GOFS jumped on the bandwagon and passed through repairs once the secret came out, admitting they'd kept quiet so their weapons worked better than anyone else's. Only Caddi never sent any outside work. Harold suspected the warlord didn't want to strengthen any of his neighbours. It didn't work, the Baggies and Ferdinands sent work through the GOFS, exchanging the weapons and payments near the Mart.

Two rifles for repair were passed through the Pink Panthers and then the Barbies, and they came with a goat! A nanny, who would give milk! Someone must be desperate, or have a herd, because she was the incentive to get the weapons repaired. Harold thought it might be another test because neither weapon could be repaired, but he made one good weapon out of the two and kept the goat. She produced the first real milk they'd seen in years, and helped to keep the weeds down.

The Barbies were intrigued because both the rifles were scrap in their eyes. They hadn't expected Harold to get the job done, and intended on buying the goat from the original gang. Instead the Barbies now wanted fresh milk. Eventually, they accepted that one small goat didn't give much milk and switched to trying to contact the original owners, hoping to buy one.

The goat's milk went to the young children. Those born just before or since the Crash took calcium tablets and multivitamins, but probably still had a string of deficiencies. The supplements Harold had looted on his midnight sorties just after the Crash were running low, and nobody trusted the versions sold in the Marts.

With more through trade, more gangsters, especially GOFS and Barbies, visited Orchard Close. Some came from further away, a few adventurous strangers as well as occasional Trainspotters, Ferdinands, Baggies and even Pink Panthers. Only a few of each came, all drawn by the rumours of a genuine pub. Some of the regular gang visitors, especially the pub customers, were now being greeted by name. After one corpse, several canings, and three being barred for life, the pub rules were accepted by everyone.

True to her word, the scrap around Liz's workshop reappeared as maces, helmets, plates for armour or spear heads. New greaves appeared, shaped to fit around a leg or arm, and curved plates to fit over the top of boots. The helmets gained sides and a nose bar to stop sideways chops and clubs. Scrounging teams brought in any bits of metal they came across now, and there were tons out there in the ruins.

Now she wasn't stuck with using hammer heads, Liz created a smaller version of a mace, mounted on half a broom shaft so even the smaller fighters could use them one-handed. The next version had a round spiked head, a Morningstar, according to the medieval enthusiast who suggested it. Harold didn't fancy a love tap from either. After a visit from Ant, Liz cast a mace with a slim iron shaft, saving on shovel shafts and wire.

Over an evening meal with Tessa and Sharyn, Harold brought up the explosion of creativity and the sheer enthusiasm generated over every project. Tessa knew what brought it on, or thought she did. She had arrived in Orchard Close before the new rush of refugees from the Murphies. At that time the gate guards had swaggered a bit, but were careful not to upset any of the other gangs. They'd accepted that Orchard Close couldn't match the larger gangs surrounding them.

The new arrivals didn't know any such thing. They'd run to Orchard Close following rumours of a place where every woman carried a gun and the gangsters daren't touch them. Even without guns, free access to machetes and training on crossbows had confirmed their belief. Orchard Close was a safe home, and a high percentage were only too willing to help defend it. These men and women had spent years under a gangster's thumb, where any new idea or bit of extra output was stolen or banned. Now they could suggest or make anything they liked and the ADT, Asshole Deterrent Tax, actually worked. No rent, no protection money, no swaggering gangsters stealing anything they fancied, it hit them like strong drink or drugs. The newcomers were drunk on freedom. Tessa confessed she sometimes wanted to slap a visiting gangster, one with a bit of attitude, for no reason. Everyone nearby would set on the scroat if he objected.

Harold checked, and Orchard Close now had over two hundred and thirty residents. With the recent influx, about a third were now women under thirty, and only a few were married or gartered. That brought some changes, such as the canteen setting up three shifts for meals. Most residents weren't in family groups, and many didn't fancy taking their meals home to eat alone. The weekly shopping trip now needed over a score of men. It would have needed twice that if the Army hadn't relaxed the rules. With only Orchard Close using the bypass for shopping, they were allowed to use handcarts to bring their purchases home.

* * *

The increased numbers still didn't make Orchard Close as numerous, or as strong, as their neighbours, but kept their people safer than most. Living in one enclave meant that everyone lived with their protectors, and many non-fighters had important supporting roles if the worst happened. In other gangs, most 'civvies' lived in estates away from the headquarters fighters, more vulnerable to raids or roving nutters. Their high percentage of fighters also helped Orchard Close, but only because the defenders doubled up in trades or the fields. By collating all the little snippets overheard when the Hot Rods came for a beer, Harold's inner circle finally came up with a firm estimate of Caddi's strength. The result wasn't encouraging. Caddi's fighters outnumbered Orchard Close over two to one, none of whom had to work so they could train full-time.

Orchard Close couldn't defend all their walls at the same time, so if someone attacked, sections might have to be abandoned. The most vulnerable walls were the two three-hundred-metre-long sections, sixty metres apart, connecting the original Orchard Close to the Annex. Two trenches were dug, one across each end of the enclosed gardens, to isolate them from the housing. At over two metres deep, and nearly as wide, set three metres out from the compound wall at each end, the result stopped any possibility of a mass attack across them. The huge amount of spoil wasn't wasted, it went into the old road beds to grow crops. Every night the guards in each compound removed all but one plank across 'their' trench, in case someone sneaked into the gardens to get to the Annex or Orchard Close. Maybe the residents were paranoid, but precautions like that helped them live with it.

The shorter days meant the Riot Squad could now practice earlier in the evening without being clearly visible. To keep their secrets, the Demons practiced with lengths of wood instead of Rambos. Any visitor catching a glimpse of them would see fighters with clubs. The trainees learned to keep formation, holding off the 'rioters' wielding baseball bats with their shields and jabbing with their 'swords'. The Demons were totally serious about learning to kill gangsters, so most looked downright savage while training, but none had the Mercedes dead-eyed look. Once practice finished they would chat and joke a bit, which relieved Harold.

When more very badly damaged firearms arrived for repair, Harold smelled a big rat. People out there somewhere were trying to get a read on what could be done, perhaps Dealer himself. To throw them off, Harold didn't try quite as hard with the worst weapons, hoping it wasn't too late. He didn't like refusing work, because the more distant customers paid with clips as well as propellant. Harold already had enough brass for a small war, once he'd got more clips and loaded it all.

More gun work came from the locals, a good third in terrible condition because all the gangs were now scouring their ruins for muskets. That meant they also found rusted firearms, buried since the original riots, and some that weren't real guns. Harold had to explain that display weapons would explode even if he fixed their mechanisms and fitted firing pins. Tessa became adept at stripping, cleaning, and oiling, and could clear simple jamming in some modern weapons. Meanwhile, between them, they perfected the musket building process and spent long hours creating more. The pair eased off a little after a few comments about how much time Harold spent with his wench. After that Harold spent some time working alone in the gun room, while Tessa assembled components at home where nobody would realise.

The influx of coupons were gratefully snapped up by the Coven, to help deal with the new residents. Now Harold took tradable items, ornaments, food, and electrical and plumbing components as well as coupons in payment, as did other trades. When Dealer came back in February, he'd be offered anything Orchard Close didn't use, including some good quality watches Kharon had repaired. To explain why he suddenly had a sale for all this gear, Harold told everyone that Dealer travelled around trading high value items between enclaves. In response, the Orchard Close scavengers brought in paintings and ornaments, anything in good condition that looked expensive, and many residents donated personal jewellery. The Coven sorted through the jewellery, putting any hallmarked gold or expensive looking gems aside for trading. The rest could be bought by residents, if they wanted any. A few joked that Harold should buy gold rings, either to mark his women or so Mercedes could put one through his nose to lead him about.

* * *

As November passed, the dwindling number of Hot Rods visiting The Pub weren't making as many jokes. That might be because only the wounded were given any leave. Caddi's anger and frustration showed when he visited to deal for repairs. He didn't bring Mercedes because, as he sourly pointed out, her job was to kill the bloody Murphies, not give Soldier Boy his jollies. The Hot Rods' attack had stalled as the hours of daylight shortened. The Murphies' hit and run tactics, with the added advantage of knowing the streets in the dark, made Hot Rod advances or attempts at infiltration almost suicidal.

Despite Caddi's preferences, Mercedes turned up with Mack when the big man delivered more abused firearms and collected the repaired ones. Harold thought it was defiance, winding Caddi up for not bringing her on the last visit. The warlord would know because both ET and Mack were there, stunned almost silent by the display. Mercedes pushed Harold's hand under her blouse without bothering with the where should it go, and told him to get a firmer grip on her leg. Then she tutted and slid his hand round, still below her skirt hem, so she could trap Harold's fingers between her legs.

It wasn't defiance, not all of it, because Mercedes made it obvious how much she enjoyed visiting her 'Arold. Harold no longer wondered if she meant it, that warmth in her eyes persisted right through the visit. The young woman had a definite twinkle in her eyes as she left. Mercedes put her coat on but left it open for goodbye, and her hips did a little shimmy against Harold during the kiss, invisible to the rest. The kiss itself stayed in contact for much too long, tempting Harold to kiss her properly.

After that, Caddi insisted on Mercedes hunting Murphies in the longer dark nights. The visiting Hot Rod elite kept Harold up to date, because Caddi had finally made the Deal public. He'd had to explain why Mercedes rubbed all over Soldier Boy, yet Caddi hadn't dragged her into his bed. Mercedes promptly declared that the Deal wouldn't last much longer. None of the Hot Rods bothered asking if they could touch these days, and even lieutenants were treating her with extreme caution because Mercedes had a hair-trigger. Anyone getting near 'Arold's territory bled for it, even if the last two swore they never actually made contact. Cooper visited a couple of times, short visits as the hostage while Trev worked on Caddi's multimedia. The Hot Rod told several people that Mercedes had made it absolutely clear. She was feeling lonely in bed at night and wanted 'Arold in there as soon as possible.

It wasn't always an empty bed, because the Killer Queen took another victim up there. The stories about Mercedes and Harold must have made Scarface hopeful or careless. Mercedes needed a new mattress and bedding, and the Bulls needed a new lieutenant. Caddi cheered up a bit, and even more when the next one told to ask turned it down. Throstle from the Baggies lost face, but kept everything else. No matter how keen she was, Mercedes wouldn't be closing the Deal until spring, until Caddi thought the days were long enough to try a real push. Meanwhile the Hot Rods consolidated, while Mercedes kept the Murphies on edge.

The refugees coming into Orchard Close dropped off dramatically as the weather became colder and the fighting petered out. Anyone venturing out after dark was conspicuous now, especially with the lines stabilising. The trickle still coming seldom brought weapons, tending to be families who sometimes brought hoarded tools instead. Most of these families included teenagers expecting to be recruited without option, as winter amusement or fighters.

Harold concentrated on being ready for either Caddi or the General. The Riot Squad loved their new shields, made of the thick plywood from the railway wagons. The youngsters seemed too confident about them, so Harold explained that plywood wouldn't stop bullets. These youngsters already understood. They were depending on Soldier Boy winning the firearms exchange, so they could get in close enough for blades.

The smiling faces all had faith that Harold would do that, scary because few had been in a hand to hand fight. No matter how hard they trained, or how much they hated gangsters, Harold knew some would freeze, run, or go berserk once blood began to flow. It isn't easy to stick a blade into a human. Harold stressed that, especially the sheer effort required. The Riot Squad responded by working harder on their strength and stamina, stabbing or beating sacks full of earth.

Soldier Boy worked just as hard at making sure his other trainees won any firearms exchange. Musket trainees progressed to a single live shot, at night out in the ruins. The noise and smoke were a shock to everyone the first time, so they needed to get over the surprise. At least those shooting at people were less likely to freeze than those stabbing, but some would. Harold knew others would shoot high the first time, or shut their eyes and hope to hit. He put extra effort into a few of the very best musket or crossbow trainees. They moved onto two-two rifles, and eventually live shots. The best of those were married to weapons, a Mad Max rifle or a two-two. Harold wanted at least two for each rifle, because someone would be shooting back.

Meanwhile the gangsters visiting Orchard Close were intrigued by the happiness and apparent wealth of the ordinary workers, even the latest refugees. By wealth the gangsters meant electric kettles, TVs, good clothes and plenty of food. The gangsters thought the skills in Orchard Close generated the wealth, when most came from scavenging and efficient gardening. Some of the people in Orchard Close told the visitors, but it didn't seem to get through to the Hot Rods and Geeks. The occasional comment showed some GOFS and Barbies were listening, and were extending their own scavenging.

Harold worried even more, because the supposed wealth made the place an even bigger prize. Even as he did, the scavengers went out finding more allegedly valuable items, still laid in houses left empty for years. They now worked in groups of at least fifteen, with at least three trained guards carrying firearms.

*　　*　　*

A visit by Dealer on the fourth of December surprised Harold. He'd repaired the weapons, but didn't expect to be paid until February. While twelve beers went to the cars, Dealer came into the Embassy where Harold turned on a blow heater and pointed out he hadn't put together a shopping list. Dealer laughed, relaxing into his chair with his beer. "No, but other people have. I've had to come out of turn because your rather different offerings are popular. Especially now, or rather for Christmas."

"Red hats with white pompoms? We've a good selection of plastic mistletoe, but they'd lynch me if I traded any of that."

"I wish I could find real mistletoe. I'd make a killing." A little gleam of mischief showed in Dealer's eyes. "First, I want to place a private order."

"For Christmas? You'll be back?" Harold couldn't understand, because Dealer had told him the schedule would be every two months in summer, three in winter.

"I'd like twelve balaclavas, black ones." Dealer paused and his lip quirked in an almost-smile. "With Dealer knitted across them above the eyes, in white." Harold burst out laughing, but Dealer wasn't joking. "Can you have them ready in time?"

"In time to wrap them for under the tree? Probably, if you make another trip on Christmas Eve. That would be another big seller, Christmas wrapping paper, or cards." Harold looked Dealer up and down. "You should have a jumper with your name on, like this." He opened his coat to show the Arran jumper Patty had knitted as an advert, with SB in a plain panel on the front. "I'm not sure there's time before Santa calls."

Dealer inspected the jumper, definitely interested. "Possibly, at some other time because I can buy myself a present out of season. I've got enough orders already to keep your knitters happy until Christmas, probably too many. We'll have to work out who will be disappointed, so I hope you'll be bringing the same bodyguard?"

"Come to the pub for a pint with her, then you can talk through what you want in comfort. We'll sort out the prices later so nobody knows what you sell? Your men could come as well, because our customers include any visitors." Harold grinned because he felt bloody sure Dealer's men didn't fraternise.

For once Dealer lost his cool, staring open-mouthed. "You have a real pub? I thought the other gangs were winding me up."

"Yup, with a dartboard and bar skittles. There's crossbow and knife throwing targets in the back garden, and horseshoe throwing even if these shoes never saw a horse." Harold piled it on, because Dealer still looked gobsmacked. "Some of the GOFS and Barbies want to start a darts league, and both of them have football teams ready for the better weather. Come and have a beer with me."

Harold expected an immediate rejection, but Dealer actually thought about it. "I can't. If I'm not out of here in a certain time, those men out there will come and get me." He hesitated, looking almost embarrassed. "Could you take a picture with my phone, please? Me in front of the pub? What is it called?"

"The Pub. It's the only one." Harold sobered, because Dealer had lost all trace of his trademark mocking smile.

"Are you serious?"

"Yes, because it really is the only one in this city, as far as I know. Certainly the only one open to outside business."

Dealer shrugged, but even that seemed embarrassed. "It's silly but I'd like proof, to show it can be done. Especially to people who insist you all live like savages."

"Would you like a picture in front of the dartboard, with the staff, or outside? I'll get Patty and Doll to stand with you?" Harold glanced at the door. "Do you have time?"

"For a picture, yes, just outside and not with your charming bodyguard. I would have to answer searching questions at home if I took her to a pub." When Dealer straightened, becoming more his usual self, Harold realised that just for a moment he'd caught a glimpse of the real man. "Please remember my request is private and I'll pay privately, in coupons. Did you repair the weapons?"

Harold phoned Tessa to bring the repairs in a bag and put them in the hallway, then brought them through for Dealer to inspect. "I'd like clips and propellant please."

"More clips?"

"We've been in three big fights. The pistols go through a horrendous amount when it gets close enough for them, so I want five spare clips for each, at least." Harold told him the truth, because Dealer must know roughly how many fighters the other gangs had. "Judging by the numbers of men the General used last time, if he gets close we'll need them all."

"I can't comment on that, but understand your reasoning. I'm sure that sort of firepower would be a real comfort to anyone." Dealer worked the pump action shotgun. "I know of one very happy boy when he gets this back. We'll discuss exactly how happy, and which clips you want, once we get trading. Would you bring these down please, and anything else you have?" His Dealer smile came back. "Since I'm here I may as well make as much profit as I can."

"Of course. The Pub is two doors up, and I'll take the picture myself." Which Harold did, taking three and making sure he included the sign and the price list on the wall outside. Dealer thanked him and looked genuinely pleased before heading back to his cars. As soon as the gate shut behind him, Harold began phoning round to collect trading goods, and to ask Patty to dress up. Too late, she'd been told and had already given her baby an extra polish.

* * *

The dealing had an edge of humour to it this time. Not outright joking, because Dealer had his persona firmly in place, but even his bodyguard seemed a little less tense. The gangster who had sent the engraved shotgun would be a very happy boy, going by the price he'd offered to get his toy fixed. The rest paid well, even without whatever percentage Dealer charged on top.

Harold had to ask and Dealer confirmed that all poser weapons were worth a premium, and he'd had several of them waiting for the right repairer. To prove it, Dealer produced a genuine AK for repair. He offered a very generous price upfront, a price the owner would pay if it worked regardless of what the weapon needed. The repairs on two poser pistols would be priced depending on the work required.

The black dress must have been just what Dealer wanted, because he ordered three more in different sizes, plus one in green and a white one. He also wanted eight cable knit or Arran jumpers for men, and six of different types and styles for women. As promised, Dealer brought patterns or pictures and wool for the orders, along with plenty of brightly coloured wool and all the requested embroidery silks. He discussed the work with Patty, which items were priority if she couldn't get them all knitted and who wanted a top class job. Patty bargained hard over price versus quality of knitter, and seemed happy with the result. With luck, she reckoned they'd all be ready by Christmas, along with the selection of crocheted animals and dolls. She wasn't so sure about the embroidery. Dealer had several shirts and sweatshirts he wanted decorated, and a list of sew-on patches if they could be produced.

Once he saw the new melee weapons in the wheelbarrow, Dealer thought long and hard. "I'll take all three Morningstars. Whoever thought of that as a woman's weapon has a sick mind."

Patty smirked, picking one up and twirling it. "No, the scroats have sick minds. This is a woman's cure." David the guard nodded in agreement, as did Dealer. Dealer mentioned the improvement in the usual maces but Harold just put it down to buying an anvil and better kit. The steel helmets were snapped up; they were as shiny as the first ones but tougher.

"Have you any more of those punch daggers?" That little smile hovered. "One of my men recognised them. Did you know they have a name?"

"Instead of punch dagger?"

"Hah, yes. I'd believe that act, except they are apparently a very specific style. My man would like to meet whoever uses them." The smile appeared again, briefly. "He might even be tempted into the pub."

"Sorry, you aren't the only deep, dark secret." As Harold expected, Dealer's smile acknowledged the dig.

Harold didn't expect him to turn towards Patty. "Can you use Katari?"

She smiled back at him, more or less innocently. "Is that what they're called? I'm versatile, so I carry a selection to deal with surprises."

Dealer let it drop, switching to making deals with Harold for the non-wool goods. The watches were accepted, at decent prices, with Dealer asking about bringing others for repair. Harold wasn't sure exactly what parts Kharon had, or if he could repair Rolex or TAG Heuer, but promised the repairer would try. He promised to find out if Kharon would consider broken watches for spares, as part payment. While he negotiated, Patty and David chatted. The bodyguard finally asked if he could try the action and weight of Patty's Winchester. He'd never laid hands on a real underlever. Patty's reply surprised Harold. "Okay, but only if I can point this at you?" She pulled the Mad Max 50 out of her belt.

David gave it a long, hard look. "Deal." He looked a little unsure. "I can't find anyone who knows if nail varnish will help penetration. Most of them thought it would just leave gunge in the barrel."

Dealer stopped dealing to laugh at him. "Go on, tell her what they actually said."

The bodyguard looked embarrassed, then confessed. "Everyone told me if a long 50, especially a hardened round at short range, hits someone wearing a vest the nail varnish won't matter." He worked the action on the Winchester and Patty caught the round, handing it back when he asked. David inspected the flat steel end before reloading it. "A hardened 30-30 like this will probably go through anything but ceramics, and that long 50 might even get through them. We'll never find out, because my boss is too tight to buy ceramic plates for us."

"It wouldn't matter. If I have to shoot you I'll go for your head or your nuts." Patty's big smile might have been joking, but David visibly flinched.

He rallied, even managing a chuckle. "Head please, just in case I survive. I might get a sympathy kiss?"

"Possibly, if you survive a headshot from either of these." Patty held out a hand and David handed her weapon back with a big smile. He lost it sharpish when Dealer looked over.

It was a sort of flirting and left Harold intrigued. Patty seemed to be finally out of that shell she'd worn when she arrived in Orchard Close. The change had started when she'd killed her first scroat. Since then, as Patty improved her accuracy, proficiency, and head count, her confidence grew. When the male gangsters as well as Barbies started treating her as truly dangerous, Patty had loosened up even more. This sort of joking and teasing with a virtual stranger, a man, was a whole new step.

Harold took part of his payment in empty brass and propellant, because the cars didn't carry enough of the right sort of clips. The Christmas orders would be paid with whatever clips Dealer could source from the list Harold supplied, and the difference made up with coupons, propellant or brass. This time Harold invested in a few genuine full metal jacket long 50 and 30-30 rounds, allegedly in case David armoured his nuts or head.

The gold had to be taken to one of the cars for testing, but then Dealer took it as well as two of the paintings and three ornaments. The trader produced his loupe and looked at the gems, rejecting all but six, but he paid well for two of those. Harold had no idea what any of the luxury goods were worth these days but they were useless to him, certainly of less use than the protection they bought. Dealer confirmed that if someone wanted decent jewellery, he would sell as well as buy. He told them he'd try and source anything anyone asked for, modifying that to exclude anti-tank weapons or grenades after Patty asked for both. Towards the end, in a sort of casual way, Dealer asked if he could buy videos of the football games.

"Not the swimsuit league. We don't allow anyone to film those, and anyway they've covered up until spring." Harold tried not to smile at Dealer's expression and failed. David the guard looked at Patty and opened his mouth, but said nothing.

"No I don't. Though I dress a bit less formally when spectating." She smirked when Dealer glanced at her, startled.

"Who does play? Once again I've heard rumours, but some of your neighbours like to wind people up." Dealer had to mean the Barbies.

"A couple of Barbies and GOFS played in the last of the swimsuit matches. Next year there might be more." Harold remembered a comment earlier. "I might get you a video of an ordinary match. The teams include men and women fighters from different gangs, but there's no swearing or violence. No animals or savages."

That brought a sharp look from Dealer, and his guard, before Dealer's little smile came back. "You'd get busloads of visiting fans, but you might need a machine gun for crowd control." Dealer still looked intrigued by the idea but quickly switched subjects, getting back to trading.

Once again Dealer and Harold came out like Siamese twins, with Patty and David following. This time the bodyguard grinned and took her proffered hand. Harold kept his big mouth shut. The wheelbarrow went straight to the gun repair workshop, where Harold stressed that Tessa mustn't mention the AK to anyone. One slip and he couldn't be sure even the GOFS wouldn't get greedy. According to Tessa she'd rather have the poser Glock, decorated with angels swooping down instead of the more usual eagles.

Patty enlisted the Coven to organise every knitter, and abandoned her squad to knit full-time. Explaining why some outsiders' Christmas orders, including crocheted toys, were a higher priority than any in Orchard Close wasn't easy. Nobody outside the squad leaders could know about what Dealer sold, or why Harold wanted to meet the deadline. Patty promised she would team up with Sharyn, Tessa and Emmy, who all knew about Dealer, to find ways and means. Hopefully, even Caddi would take Christmas off and leave them to knit and sew in peace.

The extra visit sparked yet another discussion about Dealer. He must have sources outside the city, and be able to smuggle ammunition in and goods out, but who were his customers out there? The consensus settled on him being part of an organisation with a genuine manufacturing facility somewhere, churning out propellant and ammunition. His customers for traded goods must be in the other cities, unless one horrific suggestion was the real answer. Casper pointed out that if the government wanted to get all the valuables out of the cities before attacking them, Dealer seemed to be doing just that. After a stunned silence several others pointed out the government wouldn't want to arm gangsters, because the Army would have to fight them sooner or later. Casper agreed, to everyone's relief.

Chapter 18:
Early December

In the three years since the mayor died and the city exploded in violence, random attacks by roaming groups had almost stopped. The enclaves lived in relative peace unless another gang launched a raid or an invasion. Despite their varying lifestyles and outlook, Conan, Precinct Nineteen and Sutton Park all had the same opinion of fighting just before Christmas. They didn't. In their own particular ways, most of the enclaves settled down to have a few easy weeks, and enjoy themselves as much as possible in a ruined city under siege. A few were more dedicated.

*　*　*

The General:

The General wanted a very specific early present, and wasn't relying on Santa. Rhys had finally found the ways and means to attack the SIMS, or more particularly, to get what the General wanted afterwards. As the sun rose on the sixth of December, the forward SIMS observers reported an army approaching their positions. Nobody even bothered to ask who, because only one nearby gang had an army. The observers promptly legged it for their enclave, where a well-practiced routine swung into action. The SIMS had been expecting an attack, sooner rather than later.

Defenders moved to blockhouses set into the walls, while the non-combatants gathered at the muster points. Just in case the General had managed to get hit men inside, a squad guarded the entrance to an old concrete office block. Three floors above, men and women were still making additional rockets. Two floors above them, on the roof, teams loaded the rocket firing racks and swivelled them to test the bearings. From there they could launch the projectiles directly at any target around the entire perimeter, singly or in groups, once the defenders gave them locations.

Stevie, guarding the office block doors, received a message that the

General's troops were coming out of cover, starting their assault. As he lowered the radio, gunfire broke out inside the building! "Julie!" Stevie's girlfriend, Julie, worked at preparing the rockets so without another thought he charged inside and up the stairs. Behind him explosions boomed and shrapnel rattled against the concrete walls and splintered the doors. By the time Stevie reached Julie's workplace, the shooting and screaming had died away. He glanced around the room, at the three bodies and bloodstains. Two rocket makers, Julie and Maisie, were missing. A trail of blood spots, and an automatic weapon firing on the roof, sent Stevie running up the next flight.

The blood trail kept going and so did Stevie. Even as he pounded up the last flight to the roof, gasping for breath, he heard the roar as a full flight of rockets were launched. Another salvo went off as he charged the door to the roof, but bounced off because it had been barred. "Look out, he's got..." Something cut off Julie's voice. Stevie got the message and dived for the floor, just in time! An automatic tore a line of holes through the door.

"Stay back. If I hear you use a radio, I'll kill them."

Stevie tried to place the voice and couldn't. "You can't get away. The only other way off the roof is the fire escape, and you can't take captives down that." Stevie hoped the shooter wanted captives. "Let me hear whoever you've got. If they're dead I'm calling the cavalry."

"I'm alive, Stevie." He could hardly understand Julie through the sobbing. "Maisie is alive, but in a bad way. He's set them all off. He's killed us all." The roar as the last eight rockets volleyed confirmed the launches.

"What does he want? We've got more rockets so wasting those doesn't matter." There were more on the roof, and boxes of reloads on the fourth floor.

The voice still sounded totally confident. "No you haven't, or rather won't have. Those rockets went up in the air, off towards the nearest Army post, so the RAF will be on the way to blow the crap out of this place. You can let me go, or wait and die with your woman."

Stevie managed to place the voice, and couldn't understand it because the man had lived here since the Crash. "You don't want to die either, Keith, so why are you doing this?"

"Stand back and let me start down, because that bloody RAF plane will be on the way. There'll be a machine gun in Julie's back so don't stop me." Keith muttered to someone, then raised his voice. "I'll explain on the way. You might even decide to join me."

"Do it Stevie. He fired them all towards the bypass." Julie had stopped crying.

Stevie didn't hesitate, because they'd all seen TV pictures showing the RAF response to rockets fired at the Army. The nearest soldiers were five or six miles away but the rockets probably had enough range, and it wouldn't matter if the missiles had missed completely. The RAF would still be coming, and their radar would already have the location nailed down. "I'm going down to the next landing. Come down slow. If you point a gun at me I'll start shooting because there's nothing to lose. If you hurt Julie or Maisie I'll shoot anyway." Stevie took the first two steps.

"Be quick, and turn off that radio. I'll keep this automatic pointing at Julie so don't get creative. Now move, for Christ's sake." By the time Stevie moved down ten steps to the first turning, the top door opened to reveal Julie. Behind her Stevie could see Maisie, slung over Keith's shoulder. "Come on, hurry up!"

Stevie didn't hurry too much, he kept it slow enough for a limping Julie to keep up. As he did, Keith followed but stayed safely behind her. The traitor explained, he'd sold out because one way or another the General would take their enclave. This way the RAF would destroy the building and all the rockets, and without their artillery the SIMS wouldn't last long against the Bloods. The General would win easily and capture the workpeople, but he particularly wanted someone who could make rockets. If Keith provided a rocket maker he'd get a good position with the General, bossing the workers in another enclave.

Stevie found out he should have died with the rest at the door, when Keith's hidden bombs went off. With nobody to stop him Keith would have hidden nearby with the women, coming out after the conquest succeeded. They negotiated as they went down the four flights of steps because Keith wanted the women, the rocket makers, and Stevie refused. Unfortunately, as Keith pointed out, without them he may as well start shooting. The General would skin him alive if he found out Keith had let them go.

Maisie's condition settled it in the end. She'd taken a bullet and needed urgent attention, attention the General would give her because he needed her alive. According to Keith he had a recognition signal, so the attackers would spare him and any captives. If Stevie managed to kill him, the Bloods would kill Stevie and kill or gang rape both women as they rampaged through.

Keith stopped on the bottom step. "Time to decide." Stevie stood in the doorway and braced himself. A quick glance had shown him that his squad were all dead, caught in the bomb blast. "If you come with me willingly, the General will reward you and Julie will be safe." Both Julie and Stevie shook their heads. "Idiots. All right, you can have Julie, and maybe the two of you can get away. I keep Maisie and I'll get her safe." Keith's eyes flicked upwards. "Providing we get out of this bloody building, right?"

"Do it Stevie. We've lost the battle anyway. Let the bastard go because at least that way Maisie might survive." Julie glanced through the door, towards the gunfire. "We've got time to hide, then get to the rally point and warn them."

"Listen to her. Drop the radio or you'll warn everyone before I get safe. I won't shoot you now unless I have to, because a machine gun opening up in the middle of the enclave will bring fighters in a hurry. Then they'll stop me getting away and I'll die when the RAF arrive. Now bloody move!" Keith pushed Julie forward just a bit, and Stevie almost went for it but the traitor had that automatic aimed right at her back.

"Done." He'd already realised, too late, that he should have held the transmit down from the beginning. Stevie scooted the radio along the floor, before stepping backwards out the door. A quick glance showed that nobody had come to investigate, but explosions and gunfire along the walls explained why.

"Here, now bugger off." Julie staggered forward. Stevie finally had his shot but that automatic might still get both of them, especially Julie, and Maisie would definitely die. He put an arm round Julie, pulling her outside and sideways.

"Grab a gun. We'll get him as he comes out."

"Too late. That'll just kill Maisie because he's right, we can't save her. She still might bleed out before he gets her safe." Julie bent, awkwardly because of her injured leg, snatching up weapons and ammunition. "Come on, move or we'll be blown to bits anyway. We'll tell someone when the RAF have gone." She limped as fast as possible towards one of the buildings. "There's a cellar in here." Stevie gave up, snatching up more weapons and ammo before running after her. He found Julie inside, struggling with the trapdoor to the cellar. Her arm had never healed properly after the attack by the MiB, which is why she'd ended up as a rocket maker.

Even down in the cellar the pair heard the rockets or bombs hitting, again and again. After what seemed like a lifetime, possibly five minutes, the noise died away so Stevie heaved on the trapdoor. Daylight and the stench of smoke streamed in because the front of the house had gone, blown away. The missiles or bombs had torn chunks out of the concrete office block, leaving fires that still raged through what was left. The RAF hadn't been precise, most of the nearby buildings were in ruins or burning. The pair clambered out, heading for the nearest rally point.

As they arrived, the big doors opened and a van sheathed in steel plates started out. The driver leant out of the window. "Just in time. Bug-out. The RAF blew up the bloody rockets and the Bloods are over the walls." Neither Stevie nor Julie even tried to explain, not yet. There'd be plenty of time if they all lived. The driver did a double-take at the number of weapons the pair had snatched up. "You've got extra guns so I want you both in the last vehicle as rear guards." Stevie nodded, all the SIMS knew about bug-out. If any attacker breached the walls in numbers, the non-combatants and a core of fighters would punch out of the unengaged side. They'd make for the nearest halfway civilised enclave, in this case the Professor's, through the two gangs to the north.

"What about the fighters in the blockhouses?" There were vehicles placed so those could join the bug-out as rearguard.

"Hardly any of their vehicles will start, and it's the same in all five places. We've been stitched. The blockhouses are going to buy us as much time as possible." The couple nodded, heading for the last vehicle.

* * *

Across the cleared strip outside the walls of the SIMS enclave, the General smacked a fist into his palm. "The Bloods are among the buildings. Got them! Rhys, that Keith gave you their names and the radio channels. Call those blockhouses and give them the choice. Surrender everything and everyone now, and live." He smirked. "Or any who survive the rape and pillage will live, because the Bloods are over the wall and God himself can't stop them now."

Rhys spoke several times, to different people, then cursed quietly. "They said no, and not very politely. The stupid sods mean it."

"Shit! I wanted to get Julius's men through the enclave and after the runners, the bug-out. Our road block will only hold for a while." The General sighed in resignation. "All right, get Patton and Julius on the radio. We'll get enough Bloods under control to help the steady troops, and take the bloody blockhouses one at a time. Fucking heroes, I hate the stupid shits."

* * *

Three tries later the swearing in the General's HQ reached a crescendo. Twice his men had launched an attack, but supporting fire from the adjacent blockhouses broke the assault. There were even a few rockets, a nasty surprise because his info claimed the launchers were all in the block of flats. The third time, one of his men got a bomb through a loophole which silenced most of the fire from one strongpoint. The General threw everything against the next blockhouse in line. Without the flanking fire from the burning blockhouse, the Bloods finally swarmed over their target in numbers. Just briefly, until the ground around the fortification erupted in flame, smoke and flying scrap metal! The Bloods were fighting mad by then, so even that didn't break them. They swarmed over the blockhouse and this time they got inside.

"Thank fucking Christ for that! Now we can roll them up each way, one at a time. We'll watch out for those mines at the next one." The General grimaced, glancing at his radio. "Too late to get the runners now, they broke straight through the roadblock. I didn't expect them to keep rockets and an automatic back from defence, just for their bug-out." A savage grin split his face. "At least we got a rocket maker. Better yet, that Keith swears all the rest died so I'm the only one with them. Tell the medics if that woman dies, so do they."

"They know. She should be all right. They've stopped most of the bleeding and are pumping fluids and antibiotics into her." Rhys, the spymaster, ran a finger across his throat. "What about that Keith?"

"Put him as an intel liaison to Julius. A backstabbing two-faced fuck like that might be useful if Caesar decides he wants the crown." The General scowled as he raised his binoculars again. "If too many non-combatants got away there won't be enough left to amuse the Bloods. We'll have to keep going and eat up that little gang to the north, just to get the lunatics some reinforcements and playmates."

* * *

An hour later a SIMS fighter with a bloodstained rag around one arm looked at the five survivors in his strongpoint. "We're the last, I reckon.

They're throwing bombs to detonate the mines outside, and we're out of rockets and pipe bombs. They'll get to us next time, or the time after." He held up a control on a wire. "You know what this does, triggers our mines. Or you thought it did." He flicked off the back cover and moved a slider. "Now it's an Armageddon switch. There'll be nothing left to loot by the time they put the fires out. Do any of you want to be alive when the Bloods get inside?"

"Not a chance." Tears trickled down the woman's tired, smoke-stained face. "Put it on a chair in the middle. The first one who thinks the Bloods are getting too near, press that button."

A youth with a bandaged leg, sat by a loophole, frowned at that. "I'm surprised none of the others did that, blew up their blockhouse."

"A few might have, further around the wall, but they won't have pressed this or we'd be gone as well. The council have been preparing for the General for over a year now. We were supposed to trigger this if we had to retreat, scorched earth, but when we found out our bug-out vehicles had been sabotaged the blockhouse commanders all agreed. The General has someone inside and knows our defence plans, including the bug-out, so he'll have someone waiting to slow them up. That's why, when the rockets were bombed, we asked for volunteers to dig in and die, to give the others as big a lead as possible. Now this will finish the job, make sure they're too badly mauled to try and follow." He looked around the bunker, meeting each defender's eyes in turn. "We've done it, but there'll be no cavalry." He straightened to a sort of attention. "It's been an honour."

"You daft sod, give me a hug." A woman put her good arm around him. "Killing those nasty shits has been a lot of fun, but we knew the score." Her big smile belied the blood and grime on her tired face. "I've been a bit pissed off about them getting the crops and gear, but now I'll die imagining that bloody General tearing his sodding hair out. Stick that button thing in the middle." She moved back to a loophole, sniffing as her bravado faltered. "If I go down, don't leave it too late. I really don't fancy being a Bloods prisoner."

* * *

As the Bloods closed in on the few blockhouses that were still resisting, a dull thud sounded and the ground vibrated against the General's soles. All around the perimeter smoke gouted from the loopholes on most of the strongpoints, and fuel tanks in the nearby garages exploded. Further inside the enclave, smoke and flames rose from stores and workshops as a wave of destruction spread among the houses. Everything stopped as even the Bloods were stunned into silence. The General turned to his spymaster, Rhys, rage suffusing his face. "Perhaps Keith won't be useful after all. Not after I've skinned the incompetent fuck an inch at a time, and the Bloods have finished playing with him." His hand crumpled the reports used in planning the attack. "I hope your reports about Orchard Close don't miss any little details like this?"

Rhys nodded and got the hell out, at least until the General had shed someone else's blood. He'd keep clear of Patton and the Bloods as well, because the nutters had too many wounded to take another place right now. They'd get no rape or pillage from this victory, which would make them even more short-tempered and vicious than usual. Maybe he should have a chat to Julius, just in case either of them suddenly needed a friend.

*　　*　　*

Professors:

The General had Keith staked out, but hadn't finished skinning the traitor, when the Professors had surprise visitors. A long column of vehicles pulled up at their southern border, led by an armoured van bearing the gouges and smoke stains of serious combat. The visitors had technically invaded the smaller gang to the south, but nobody seemed to want to argue. Prof wondered why they'd stopped, because the border defences couldn't organise fast enough to keep this many out. He stood in the road with four of the Kendo fighters, and raised a hand in greeting.

The tired voice from the van sounded female. "Hello there. Are you the Professors?"

"Yes. Who are you?"

The van door opened and a smoke-smudged woman with a bandage around her upper arm came out. She propped a shotgun against the vehicle and pointed back towards the convoy. "We are what's left of the SIMS. We come in peace." A bitter laugh from inside brought a wan smile. "Actually we are begging for shelter. The General has taken our enclave."

Prof looked behind her at the long line of vehicles, several showing battle damage. "How did so many get away?" His eyes opened in alarm. "Is he following you?"

"Eventually, maybe, but there's two gangs in the way. The second gang got out of our way after we blasted through the first, but they'll both be lining their borders for the next rude visitors." The woman glanced back at the vehicles. "A lot of good people died to give us a start, and more died getting us this far. The survivors are mostly non-combatants, but a good few have trades and they brought tools and equipment. We've even brought a woman who makes rockets, a sort of guided missile. They'll stop any of your neighbours giving you grief."

That didn't make sense to Prof. "So how come the General won?"

"Betrayal. He got to someone inside and the RAF blew up our artillery." Her shoulders slumped. "Look, we know we'll not get decent housing, but we need someplace to sleep tonight. Then if you don't want us we'll push on, try to find someone to take us in."

"No need. If you are willing to work clearing land and fixing housing, you are welcome. I must insist you turn in your weapons before coming inside our perimeter." Around Prof and back behind him in cover, hands gripped weapons a little tighter.

The woman's bitter laugh was echoed from inside the vehicle. "We've blown through the General's blocking forces and everyone else that tried to stop us. You can have the weapons, but there's sod all ammo." She limped forward, holding out her hand. "I'm Michelle, and very, very pleased to meet you."

* * *

The Reivers:

North of Inverness, and in some places south, the Reivers had also finished a fighting withdrawal. In their case, they'd been harried by troops and aircraft, and where they'd ended up wasn't exactly a safe haven. Even so their leaders were satisfied with what they'd managed. The air attacks had definitely eased off, or were launched from a distance so they weren't as accurate, and there'd been no more attacks on the caves. The government forces had established a front line, but too late because convoy after convoy had been pillaged as the government troops and work camps moved south. Most of the supplies were carried across the mountains in backpacks, and were now north of Loch Ness. With the crops raised in small patches scattered through the Highlands, the Reivers thought they might have enough food for winter.

Just as well, because the battle tank in a food convoy had come as a deadly surprise. The sides of what looked like an articulated lorry fell away to reveal an armoured behemoth, but a couple of the raiding party escaped, temporarily. They'd got off a warning message, one that explained why two recent raiding parties had disappeared without trace. Raiding halted, then resumed, but only on smaller convoys or outposts. Gradually, as more of the government's new mercenaries arrived, only spotters had stayed south of Loch Ness. Now they'd had to leave as well.

To the south of the sixty-mile Fort William-Inverness line, right across Scotland, the European troops built strong-points and manned them with machine guns. Spotters were established along the coast at each end, to stop any flanking raids, while artillery and light armour moved into position to respond if the Reivers tried to break through. North of the line, the Reivers started planning for when the snow melted. Somehow they had to break that line, or there'd be no food the following winter. For now, sneaking in and out of Inverness allowed the Reivers to recruit, gather intel and mix with the residents for a little R&R.

*　*　*

The Cabal:

Owen stood to address the Cabal members, a big smile on his face. "Not so much a meeting this time, more an excuse to exchange congratulations. After all, this is the season of goodwill." He gestured towards the one-way window showing the operations room. Tinsel and trimmings, and even a small fibre-optic Christmas tree, were decorating the consoles and workstations. "Personally, I am going to stuff myself with turkey and trimmings, and put my feet up. When we raise a glass to celebrate the New Year, I think we can definitely count the old one as a success. We now have enough European armour and air power, to solve the clearance problem. Providing Maurice continues to eliminate democratic enclaves, I believe the end-game is in sight."

This time nobody held back for secret discussions. Vanna had a quiet word with Maurice, just to congratulate him on how well the new snipers were working out. He had good news for her. The yearly bonus from their information-collecting operation, already turned into bullion, was waiting for collection. Maurice also handed her a large soft parcel, a Christmas present, a bonus on the bonus. He'd no idea which enclave had provided it, but going by Vanna's usual tastes, he thought the knitted shawl might be just the thing.

* * *

Cyn Palace:

In London none of the neighbours around Cyn Palace wanted to fight, and one or two wanted to trade. A strange, almost peaceful December left everyone in exactly the right mood for Christmas. Presents were in short supply inside the cordon, but in Cyn Palace a small group congratulated each other. Everyone would eat well this winter and next year, and even better they'd now turned the old school gymnasium into a giant pigeon coop. Not exactly turkey, but everyone would have roast bird on the table at Christmas.

There'd be a small break afterwards, but then it would be time to dig over the fields and any extra cleared ground for spring sowing. The cleared area grew daily, as the new refugees sweated to earn their places. Trade routes were spreading, so this year there'd be cauliflower if the seeds were viable. A small group of traders had sold cheese and seeds, then traded two weird-looking cows that had allegedly come from London Zoo. Despite the hump, they both gave milk, a real novelty. The traders had wanted some of the captured weaponry, and the chance to copy several library books. It wasn't exactly heaven, but hell seemed much further away than it had a time or two this last four years.

Chapter 19:
Digging and Dancing

Orchard Close had a similarly peaceful December, even with a war next door and refugees still trickling in. Rumours of a savage battle involving the General didn't worry anyone too much, the dying had been a long way from their border and might slow the gang boss up. As Christmas grew nearer, the coloured lights went up and the night defences took on a festive air. The new refugees looked astounded, while those who had already seen them quickly claimed the rechargeable fairy lights to wear. Lights twinkled on six of the young firs in the plantation this year, once Finn ran power cables out to the trees. Half a dozen residents laid a temporary extension cable from the new electricity supply in the Farm, placing a string of coloured lights across the front of Caddi's watchers. Not only did that blind them at night, it lit the spies up very nicely so everyone else could see them.

Several residents asked about a Christmas tree this year, a real one, not plastic. Liz refused to let anyone steal a single twig of her prospective forest, but the residents didn't want them anyway. This year they wanted a proper sized tree, bushy and two metres tall at least, providing someone could work out where to find one. Every decent sized tree for miles around, except those in the alleged Trainspotters' park, had been used for arrows or charcoal.

One mid-December morning, Harold answered a knock on his door to find six very nervous teenagers standing there. "What have you lot been up to?"

"Nothing, yet, sort of. If we sneak under the bypass we are out of sight of the soldiers, right?" Nate obviously wasn't keen on being the spokesman, but one of the girls had pushed him forward.

"Possibly, though there's supposed to be cameras under there." Harold frowned. "Don't try it, you'll get shot."

"Not the third span along, not since Rihannon, er, well." Nate stopped, but the girl prodded again. "Not since Rihannon started meeting a soldier under there. The camera stopped working. Now some of us go under there to meet, in private. Not soldiers." The youth floundered to a stop, his blush threatening to set his face on fire. Harold had started off alarmed, but this sergeant must have relaxed a lot more than he'd realised. Now Harold tried to keep his smile hidden. Same-sex houses for the young singles and no spare rooms left little privacy for a love life. Harold was impressed that some of the girls were relaxing enough to be tempted, and more impressed they did so out in the decidedly frosty night.

"I'm lost. Why do you want to see me about your love life? And regardless of what Rihannon is up to, I still think you are crackers going under the bypass." Harold would be having a word with the guards that side. There weren't many because the wall almost met the exclusion zone, but those on duty must know about the couples.

"We can't cut the mesh or climb it because that sets off alarms, but we could dig under the fence. If we put a board and some dirt over the hole in the day, we could do it in three or four nights?" Nate might have been warming to his theme, but Harold had started getting worried.

"Why? I wouldn't recommend escaping. You'd be out there with just what you can carry, a target for every soldier, pilot and escaped scroat."

"Not escape, we could go out and get a tree! A real Christmas tree." Harold looked at the rest of the group. The two lads might have their brains in their pants, but the four young women were determined. If he said no they'd probably have a go anyway. Cripes, at least a quarter of Orchard Close would help them.

Harold looked as stern as possible. "Not tonight, and maybe not tomorrow. I'm going to talk to a few people. It's a lovely idea but not worth dying for so I am telling you now, don't start digging." Harold forced a scowl because he didn't seem to be getting through. "Keep your mouths shut, really shut, because if I hear one rumour I'll stop you." He couldn't keep looking serious for much longer so he sent them on their way. "But decide who is going if we come up with a plan."

Harold wasn't sure they heard anything but, "who is going" because the group bounced down the path with a lot of laughter and some intense hugging. He'd make sure the wall guards understood. Harold looked back at Tessa and Sharyn, listening at the door to the lounge, and watched their smiles blossom when he said, "Charcoal."

* * *

Before he made any real plans, Harold had to check if the idiots were telling the truth. Several shamefaced guards admitted to letting couples go out through the potato field at one end, and head across to the bypass. Harold told them to stop it for the next couple of nights, then went to find the charcoal expert. He smiled when the door to Liz's forge refused to open, and knocked. "I'll huff and I'll puff?"

After a few moments he heard the bar being lifted, and the door opened to reveal a grinning Liz but no apprentice. "You'll have no huff left after carting all the new ironmongery down to the armoury. Oodles of helmets and maces, and Henry's hammer is ideal for making Rambos." She waved Harold inside. "Luckily he's off practicing with those rough Riot Squad types, or I might not have answered the door at all."

Harold hopped up to sit on her bench, raising a smile. "I'm relieved you're still finding time to smith, what with new toys and a new toy-boy. How important is charcoal now, with that new furnace?" He already had some idea by the number of charcoal bags that were now empty.

"I need it to temper and fettle, to straighten or repair the rubbish you accept in trade, and for hardening. Is there a problem?" Liz glanced at what she had left. "I know it's expensive, but the trees aren't growing fast enough."

"You made your own charcoal when we cut down all those trees just after the Crash. The thing is, getting timber is possible but risky, but from what you say may be necessary. Nobody has any but Caddi, and he's pushed his prices right up or maybe he has to pay more."

Liz stared at him, startled. "Cripes, are you actually going to raid the Trainspotters? How will you get trees back here?"

"Some of the teenagers want a Christmas tree."

"So do I." Liz stopped and frowned. "Where from and does it have relatives?"

"Outside the wire and it presumably has lots of similar sized friends at least, unless the squirrels have eaten them all again." Harold grinned when Liz scowled about the squirrel propaganda, then sobered again. "Rihannon has found a soldier boyfriend, who has disconnected the cameras. The idiots have been meeting under the bypass."

Liz thought about it for a few moments, then hopped up to sit on the bench next to Harold. "Give. Do we need diagrams this time?" Harold gave, and they discussed but without a diagram. Harold asked another half dozen people he thought were sensible, and they all either fancied a

Christmas tree or agreed with getting more charcoal. Just as a test, during the next two nights, Harold sent several couples across the exclusion zone to the bypass. Sure enough, the soldiers ignored anyone disappearing under the third span away from their post. A red-faced Nate explained that anyone going under the bypass should check with Rihannon first, so they didn't bump into her soldier. The squaddie should report trespassers and she didn't want to put Lionel, Private Vaughn to the Army, in an embarrassing position. Except with herself, presumably.

Harold didn't want to be embarrassed either, so Liz went to see Rihannon and explain. The lass agreed to schedule her future meetings with Lionel for three or four in the morning, at least until Liz gave her the all clear.

* * *

Mid-afternoon on the fifteenth of December, Harold invited the small group of excited teenagers, four couples now, to meet him in the dance house. "Nate, and the rest of you, we've agreed you can try to get a Christmas tree." He waited a moment until they calmed down again. "There are conditions. Matti and Jeremy are allegedly sensible adults, but look young enough to be sneaking off for a cuddle, so they will come as well." Matti's giggle at that didn't help. "If they say stop, you stop. There are a few more rules, or rather sensible precautions. Are you willing to stick by them?"

"Yes," came from eight pairs of lips without any idea of what they'd agreed to.

"Only couples can go, so the soldiers don't wonder why. You will be very, very quiet and careful, and bring the soil back to scatter on the fields. Use the same tracks there and back so your numbers aren't obvious. We will send other couples to collect soil as you dig but everyone has to be Cinderella, all home by midnight. If you are there too long the Army might get curious." Harold pointed to a selection of garden forks, spades, and empty home-made sacks. "Put those under your coats, even though it's dark. Dig gently, no clanging on rocks. We have thick plywood, and timbers for crosspieces, so you can put plenty of earth and grass on top to disguise the hole. Make sure there are no tracks outside the fence if you succeed, in case someone wants another tree." Harold gestured Matti and Jeremy forward. "I'll leave you to it."

Half of Orchard Close seemed to have heard of the scheme by the time the ten of them had the hole dug, two days later. The digging took longer than strictly necessary because the group wanted to get a decent sized tree! Any squaddie who noticed and watched them disappear among the concrete supports, and other couples wandering out there and back, must have turned a blind eye. The dirt collecting couples used the same tracks as the diggers, so daylight didn't show too many footprints in the hard frost.

On tree night, Harold arranged a carol singing competition to mask any sounds, and divert attention. He judged the night to be dark enough just after eight. "Remember to saw very slowly, and stop to leave plenty of silent periods. Absolutely no chopping because sharp sounds travel too well at night. All of you have saws and knives?" The group showed them and re-buttoned their coats. "If you have time, cut branches off other trees, but don't bring them tonight. Let's get your tree first."

"What are the branches for? Um, sorry." Beverley pushed Nate forward again but Harold answered her.

"We want more wood, to make charcoal, but not until you get your tree." A trumpet blared down the street. "That's Jilli warming up. The carol singing will start in a moment, and should keep the soldiers distracted. Off you go and good luck." As they headed along Orchard Close to their exit, voices and loud music rang out. Jilli had found volunteers to bash on impromptu drums, and some of the refugees remembered playing a recorder at school. A few others had dabbled, and more or less kept a tune. The singers didn't seem to care, some of them couldn't keep a tune either.

The crowd that gathered were vocal, the singers enthusiastic, and Jilli stuck to trumpets, saxophones and the one electric guitar the Barbies had parted with. She kept the emphasis on volume, and tried to keep the rest more or less playing the same notes. By midnight the lumberjacks were back with a bushy fir tree nearly three metres tall, swearing they took it from inside a small wood where nobody would ever notice. They'd cut decent sized branches off several trees, and stacked them for retrieval later. The squaddies must have wondered about the cheer when the tree went up in the canteen, unless they thought there'd been a singing competition. The carols picked up again with a vengeance until one a.m., when all those taking part staggered home to bed.

*　*　*

The following day Harold plotted with various people. Any wood collectors had six nights to work in, because carols would only work as cover until Christmas. When asked, Jilli volunteered to blow her lungs out every night if needed. The teenager now had five volunteers who would play simple backing notes, to give her some respite and increase the volume. Doll suggested a dance, of course, but not the usual one. If the weather permitted, everyone would dance in the street to help distract the Army. The party would also go on a bit longer than usual, until one at least. That night, fourteen mixed couples went off into the dark at intervals, the first just after eight when the music and singing started.

A flashing torch under the bypass at ten o'clock told the Orchard Close guards that timber had been collected. A succession of couples left the dance to collect the loot. The raiders came back well after midnight with the last of a good haul of timber, all thick branches cleared of side shoots. The dance wound down, until a shout went up for Jilli to provide a slow smoochy number to finish properly. The amateurs fell silent while Jilli started to play an instrumental only version of White Christmas, on a saxophone.

Nobody even called for the hat. For the first time since the Crash, people simply asked whoever they wanted to dance. A good few sang along quietly, and others were wiping an eye. "My job, I believe." Tessa slipped her arms around Harold and pulled him out into the street. "Unless you want more other women." Harold noticed the hopefuls, pouting and then looking elsewhere for a partner.

He had to laugh, because Tessa had done the right thing. A few of the new refugees had already made a play for the gang boss. It was a good career move for women already abused by the gangs and whose options were now, in their own eyes, limited. Tessa and Liz explained to all the new girls, very quietly, that Orchard Close was different so their past didn't matter here. A few simply didn't believe that, while a couple really did want the status. The persistent ones believed Tessa, when she told them to back off Harold or she'd come for them with a gun. Hazel had issued similar warnings; as a squad leader, Alfie attracted similar interest.

As the crowd dispersed, Harold led a group to assess the stack of branches now stashed out of sight of the bypass. Liz crouched over the timber with a small torch, cranking to keep the light going. "Perfect. All good solid timber. Is there more?"

The lumberjacks and jills were there, bright-eyed and triumphant. Beverley pushed Nate forward, but Matti took pity and answered for him. "Plenty, Liz. We cut the branches from several trees, and made a start on the trunks. The ones we've started are all deep inside a small wood. Unless someone follows our track, they'll never be discovered. Jeremy and I took turns standing guard but we didn't see any sign of patrols.

"How much of a track?" Harold looked at the stack and the cutters, and continued before Matti could answer. "Could we send more people down it, more woodcutters?"

"As long as they go from the fence to the wood along the single track, it shouldn't show up any more than now. We used an existing trail that wandered a bit, like deer maybe would." Matti smiled hopefully. "More people might look like a few more deer?"

"How many more?" Liz asked but everyone else had started wondering.

Harold hesitated, because he didn't want to push his luck too much but Liz needed charcoal. "Twenty-four couples? There were at least that many went across the exclusion zone, if we count those collecting the wood from this side of the fence. They'll have to leave a few at a time, not like some incipient orgy."

"I'll find volunteers, or more probably beat some off." Matti hugged Jeremy and they left, murmuring to each other.

*   *   *

A ripple of suppressed excitement swept over Orchard Close the following day, followed by a lot of blade sharpening. Rambos and machetes were pressed into action because there weren't enough saws or breadknives. As the couples allegedly seeking some private time left the walls in small groups, Harold watched the Army post. The last couple disappeared under the bypass without any alarm being raised. That had to be a deliberate blind eye, because despite the cloudy sky, the soldiers would be able to see them with night sights. Two hours later, more couples crossed to start collecting the logs, some of them substantial chunks of timber. Later, collections included two-metre-plus sections of what must be tree trunks. Once again the dance ended with a slow number, 'Lady in Red' this time, and now more were plucking up the courage to ask others to dance.

The lumber cutters confirmed they had cut down whole trees this time, claiming there were plenty more that were thin enough to be carried away. Harold waited all the following day for a reaction from the Army, or for a patrol to inspect the footprints in the light snow. The couples were using tracks left by others to reduce the impact, but still left half a dozen clear trails. Matti swore that on the far side everyone still used one track and tried to walk in a file. By evening Harold had decided the risk had to be worth it. He authorised thirty pairs of cutters, but this time he took some precautions in case the Army objected.

When Jilli played 'I Only Have Eyes for You' as the last dance, some of the woodcutters had already been home to get changed. The rest took off their coats and joined in anyway. After three dances in three nights, the residents were well into the swing of it. Some were wearing real party clothes despite the cold. Hemlines were rising, and so was the temperature of some last dances even when it snowed, but nobody complained or slapped a face. Harold let it go, his sense of fair play insisted. He felt sure that if Mercedes turned up, his last dance wouldn't be chaste, and would probably stray into grab-ass.

The following morning Harold couldn't understand how the Army were missing all the movement, or rather why they kept ignoring it. He wondered the next night, and the next right up to when an Army searchlight illuminated six couples carrying timber. The porters were in the middle of the exclusion zone, obviously carrying lengths of raw timber. Before anyone opened fire, Harold cupped his hands and shouted. "Don't shoot! Don't shoot! Just kids bringing firewood."

A long silence followed, with the twelve frozen in place, before the bullhorn sounded. "Straight home and stay there. Oh-eight-hundred, Soldier Boy." The sergeant! He wasn't usually on duty at night.

"I'll be there." Harold turned to shout to the wood carriers. "Come on home, nice and steady." He smiled quietly to himself as they did, because none of them put down their timber. Meanwhile Harold spoke one word into the short-range radio. "Oopsy."

A single click answered, then moments later a double click. The single click came from Alfie and Hazel, allegedly snogging under the arches but actually watching for the Army. Harold would bet coupons there'd be some real snogging, since the couple were safely out of his sight. Right now Alfie or Hazel would be ducking under the fence, to warn all the other wood carriers and cutters. The way home had been compromised.

Once under the fence the rest of the returning woodcutters moved along the bypass, ten more fifty-metre spans away from the Army post. They didn't cross the exclusion zone until they could do so beyond the end of the fields, straight into the ruins. As Harold hoped, they were far enough away to avoid anyone watching from the Army post. Better yet, Doll, the person double-clicking, waited with an armed squad to escort them home. The returnees brought everything they'd cut up to the moment they were stopped, despite the long detour to arrive home via the Annex. After stacking the wood there, everyone came across into Orchard Close and joined the dance.

* * *

The following morning, Harold presented himself at the bottom of the access road at eight o'clock as requested, unarmed except for a very big bowl of hot chips. "Far enough. What have you got there?"

"Breakfast. Chips for the squaddies. The girls just cooked them so they're hot."

"Coat off, give us a twirl, then bring them up nice and slow." Harold did as told, then turned his back to be checked with a wand. The soldier took the chips back behind the sandbags.

"Turn round." Harold did and tried to see just how annoyed the sergeant might be. The NCO wasn't giving any hints, keeping his expression as neutral as his voice. He looked Harold up and down. "Soldier Boy.. Someone told me you were a cheeky bastard. You don't think you can bribe the Army with deep fried potato, do you?"

"No. I'm just being friendly. At least consider them a sign of our appreciation. After all, nobody ended up shot." Harold smiled and tried to keep it light.

"I don't shoot people for being idiots, not when they've been encouraged by certain stupid soldiers." A quick glance along the sandbags led to two soldiers and the corporal looking decidedly apprehensive. The sergeant took another step along his side of the sandbags so Harold kept pace. "But I am annoyed, more than a few chips can make up for. What the hell were those idiots doing, and why did you send them?"

Harold thought for a moment while Sarge ate his share of chips and took a couple more steps. He mentally shrugged and went for truth. "We've had a lot of youngsters come in over the last six months, running from a gang war. They wanted a proper Christmas, so they came to me with a scheme to get a Christmas tree. The ones who'd been here longer picked the idea up and ran with it. I said yes to keep some control. Then there was this hole, and all those trees, and charcoal is bloody expensive."

"I thought you were a big bad gang boss." Sarge had perfected sarcasm.

"You could have told them piss off?"

"I'd have been trampled. Half the young people down there wanted a go, and nearly all of the people down there are under thirty." Harold smiled quietly, because he'd never dare say this to a gangster. "Anyway, I'm not a proper gang boss. Much too soft and all that."

The hint of humour in his voice didn't reach Sarge's face. "Yeah, I heard that. So you sent them out into the exclusion zone to get wood for charcoal."

"No, they volunteered. I had to beat back the rest who wanted to go. Most of those people lived under another gang before coming here, or ran ahead of conquest. Our smith needs charcoal to make weapons and stop a repeat." Harold looked straight at the sergeant, trying to show he wasn't bullshitting. "I tried to keep it sensible, but once they proved one of the cameras doesn't work? I didn't suggest the party either."

"No, but the noise and all that dancing allegedly kept these eagle-eyed defenders distracted." Sarge relaxed and a little smile showed at last. "I knew about the camera but turned a blind eye. That Rihannon looks a nice lass, and she wasn't selling sex or trying to get the idiot into the ruins. These days soldiers don't usually get to meet women socially, not decent ones." When he raised his voice, Harold realised how far from the other soldiers Sarge had moved. "I didn't expect you to take liberties, and only found out when I came early for my nightly inspection." Sarge turned to glare at the corporal. "Some people who should have known better had selective blindness."

"No harm done? We won't risk it again." Harold doubted it was optional. "I bet the camera works now."

"No it doesn't, but our night sights do." The sergeant had lowered his voice again. "So do the other cameras, those watching the other spans your people used to escape. I can't fix that particular camera, or Private Vaughn will no doubt try to meet her in the ruins and not come back one night." He held up a hand to stop Harold speaking. "Not because the lass will arrange anything, but there might be others lurking."

"I appreciate that. I'll stop the rest." Harold knew it made him look weak, but he wanted Sarge to think twice before shooting if someone else got adventurous. "Or I'll try because I have my own problem, two really. My own eagle-eyed defenders turned a blind eye as well, but worse is why the couples were risking it. We are too crowded, but up to now most female refugees were too busy avoiding men for it to matter. Now some girls have realised they are suddenly safe enough to dance and date young men, but that means they sometimes need a little privacy."

"Not just here. We came from near an enclave with morals and laws, but some local asshole ran right over them." Sarge shook his head. "The women who got away ran to us, and I had to take them in. A better option than getting caught, but not one I will sleep easy about. They went to work camps, and I'd rather not send any more women there."

"Our women understand that they might be arrested and sent to camps. That's why mainly men come up here with the chips, and the women hang back." Even as he said it, Harold realised Rihannon at least must have broken that rule. "Doll heard about the medal so she won't be coming near you."

The sergeant ignored the reference to Doll. "The camps are bad, but my worry is about how many young women seem to think joining brothels is a better option." He glared at Harold. "Which I didn't say." He glanced at the soldiers again, safely out of earshot. "The mushrooms don't get the same rumours as sergeants. I've had the night to think this fiasco over, and I'll make you an offer. If the animals come for you, and your women run to us, I'll have to arrest them. I don't want to get posted and find someone like Rihannon in the local brothel. If you promise not to take liberties such as lumberjacking, I'll forget to report the hole. If it all goes to hell, tell your women to escape through there and set off cross-country. They can make a life in the Derbyshire Peaks or the Scottish borders, someplace well away from big cities."

Harold's mind whirled. Why did Sarge want the women running about out there? "What about the roaming gangs and Army kill squads?

"The kill squads aren't Army, so they should hide from everyone. Especially anyone in uniform because they aren't Army either. The roaming gangs are smugglers, and armed, and will snap up any stray women." A nasty smile crossed Sarge's face. "If your women take their weapons, the bastards might get a nasty surprise." He looked Harold straight in the eye. "Otherwise all that's out there are occasional sweeps to round up livestock. The RAF won't report women if they hide any rifles."

"Cripes, Sarge, I daren't tell everyone that. They'd never keep their mouths shut to some of the visitors." Harold stopped and thought for a moment. "Agreed. I'll let a few trusted people know what to do if we get hit by too many."

"That's a relief, because now I can give these lads a reason for not reporting their little lapse. I'll tell them the truth, it's an emergency way out for the women. They'll keep quiet because they saw what happened to the civvies at the last posting." Sarge nodded towards the soldiers. "They'll feel better knowing those lasses with the chips have a way out. Your youngsters did a good job of hiding the hole, in the unlikely event some officer wants to walk the wire." Sarge flicked his eyes upward. "At least it happened at night when there are rarely any drones about, and mostly under the bypass or in woodland."

Harold nodded thanks, very slightly, for the hint about drones in daylight. "Good enough for me Sarge, and thanks. To show our appreciation, what's your policy on beer? We know you like a few chips and a bit of soup now and then, but we also do a wicked home brew?"

"Absolutely forbidden." Sarge smiled conspiratorially. "As is accepting French fries or soup. If some officer came by and caught a whiff of beer there would be trouble. There again we don't actually see any officers on these cold nights. It's a long way from the nice warm NAAFI, and they have to walk because HM doesn't like to waste fuel." He suddenly looked curious. "Did they manage to get a whole tree through there?"

"Yes. A proper bushy one nearly three metres tall, and then a smaller one for the pub the next night. Your lads could see them, if they came to the dances or the pub? They'll be made welcome and there will be no mishaps." Harold gestured down to Orchard Close, where half a dozen would-be musicians were practicing to a CD in spite of the light snowfall. "I'll send the tank to chauffeur them?"

"Cheeky sod. They'd love that, as you well know. Not a chance." Sarge chuckled, turning and starting back towards his men. "I'd let them, but the silly sods wouldn't be able to resist opening their big mouths in the NAAFI. The fallout would be spectacular." He waved a hand in dismissal. "Now clear off before you corrupt them even more."

"Cheers Sarge, and Merry Christmas." The sergeant just rolled his eyes, but Harold heard Merry Christmas at least twice from the squaddies before the corporal snarled at them. Harold spread the news among the small group he trusted to keep quiet, despite Doll's protests about yet another secret. She swore she'd be too scared of talking in her sleep to keep a man overnight, not unless she shot him in the morning.

* * *

One of the secrets, Dealer, turned up early the day before Christmas Eve to collect the Christmas knitting. He also collected the repaired weapons including the AK, an early bonus for Harold. Dealer inspected the balaclavas, paying Harold in coupons when they had their initial private meeting. After paying he hesitated a long time, then sighed. "I believe that you are an honourable man. Swear to me that you will never, ever mention you got this information from me."

Harold stared but Dealer looked totally serious. There wasn't a hint of that smile. "I promise."

Dealer let out a long breath. "I am about to break a very big rule. Make your walls thicker. Never, ever tell even your most trusted advisor I said that. I mean it."

Harold stared. "Why?"

"No. I don't tell tales and walls have ears. Right, here's the list of clips I managed to get together. The marked ones are not exactly pristine so we'll negotiate later." Dealer had obviously given all he either wanted to or dared. He left soon after, waiting with David in the trading house where Harold daren't press him.

This time, Patty had definitely relaxed around David, or maybe she just felt good about Christmas or getting nearly all the knitting finished. She actually teased the bodyguard about what might have happened if he'd brought some real mistletoe. On the way back to the gates with the clips and other supplies, and yet another very good rifle and two poser pistols for repair, Harold teased her about that and the hand-holding. Patty actually thought about it for a few moments. "It must be these dances. Six in a row, and all those kids smooching and waving mistletoe. I sometimes wonder who leaves the shower door unlocked, because yours is spoken for." She glanced at Harold and smirked. "Twice."

"Stop it. You know better."

"I do, but I know one someone who would get a key. Are you going to hang up stockings, or did you ask Santa for a present already wearing them?" Patty nudged Harold. "Next time Mercedes comes, tell the bodyguard to piss off and drag her into the bedroom." She giggled and nudged him again. "Given a chance, I reckon she'll drag you instead."

Harold stopped pushing the barrow and stared. "Cripes, don't encourage me! Caddi would start a war." As he started moving again he grinned. "I really am tempted sometimes."

"So do it. Live while you've got the chance, because we can't count on tomorrow." Patty stopped short of the gates, straightened and stroked the sheath over her baby. "If all the shooters lay for the bastard, we could kill Caddi and the rest of those arses with the stupid names in a couple of volleys. The rest would run." She gave Harold a mischievous grin. "Give Mercedes a gun and she'd help."

"She probably would, but don't you ever tell anyone that. I'd love to do just what you suggested, but Caddi has over twice as many fighters as we do and they are hardened now. They've been fighting for months and they've all seen blood." Harold put his own barrow down because he had to settle this where nobody could hear them. "I'll not get people killed because I fancy a woman. We could even lose. Even your Demons might break, because most of our people have never been in a real fight. Not up close and bloody."

That sobered Patty, wiping the smile from her face. "You're right. You've just reminded me what it's like, especially the first time. It's the blood and the smell. Shooting is easy compared to that." She sighed and bent to pick up the barrow handles again. "If it comes to the choice between that and Caddi getting her, I've got your back."

"Thanks." Harold smiled and swerved a little to nudge her this time. "If David ever brings mistletoe, I'll get Dealer out of there and guard the door."

"In that room? No thanks, I like my home comforts. It might be a different story if he turns up howling at my window?" Patty chuckled, then changed the subject to explaining how she'd got most of Dealer's knitting done. The squad leaders had contributed their own coupons to encourage the knitters to change priorities. Harold told her to call by and he'd repay them, explaining he'd put the extra coupons from the poser weapons aside as an emergency fund. They finished the walk tweaking each other about nearly-love life, then shifted to more mundane subjects inside the gates.

Once he had a moment alone, stashing the firearms, Harold thought long and hard about Patty's offer. He knew, deep down, that Casper, Emmy and Alfie had his back no matter what he did, and now Patty. Just thinking of that scotched any temptation to brace Caddi over Mercedes, because those four would step in and maybe get killed.

Harold didn't think long because several of the young women interrupted him with a request, apparently prompted by Rihannon's success. The chips and beer were taken up to the Army night shift by eight young women, one of them Rihannon, with tinsel in their hair and decked in fairy lights. The group came back giggling and asked if they could take the next lot as well, please, because the soldiers were very polite and wanted to see them again. The one with two stripes tried the beer, and reckoned it was better than the stuff they had back in the barracks.

* * *

The following day, Christmas Eve, Casper's voice yanked Harold out of wondering why the walls should be thicker. The weakest were a metre thick, the interlocked bricks making them a solid obstacle even without mortar. "What?"

"I said your Christmas present has arrived early. She's being searched at the gate right now, but judging by what she usually wears it won't take long." Casper laughed at Harold's expression. "Doll is searching, and complaining because she's got to keep another secret."

Harold came out of his workshop and locked up. "What secret?"

"Mercedes warned Doll she can't tell anyone what's under the coat, or not." Casper laughed again. "Your face is a picture."

"Who came with her?" Harold held his breath, because if Mercedes had come alone....

"Charger and ET. They've come to collect those last two pistols for Caddi. I've told them to go to the pub but she's is waiting for her escort."

"You could have phoned?"

"And missed the look on your face? Not a chance." Casper clapped Harold on the back. "It's cold out so don't keep her waiting."

Sure enough Mercedes had already started up the street from the gates, wearing a long leather coat that only showed her high heeled boots. Behind her, Doll's raised voice sounded more mischievous than annoyed. "I've searched her, Harold. She's not dangerous in the usual sense, but I'm not sure you should get near her."

"That just makes him more interested, doesn't it 'Arold?" Mercedes looked up the road to where Charger and ET were just going into The Pub. "You'd better take me into the Embassy. If you take off my coat, you can get started on the delectables. I hope it's warm in there."

Harold spoke before his brain caught up. "Why don't you come up to my house? It's a lot warmer?"

Harold heard a sharp intake of breath from Casper behind him, but his eyes stayed on Mercedes. Her eyes blazed with sheer glee. "You want to take me home?"

"Any time."

Mercedes moved the two steps to hug him, properly, and as Harold returned it she kissed him, quickly but firmly. "Oh dear, and those two are in The Pub. What a pity. Still, I'm sure you won't take advantage." As Harold turned she put her arm round him and held him close. "I accept." She pouted as Casper turned to follow them, then glanced up with a little grin. "Will you help me take my coat off, 'Arold? It could be interesting, depending on what I've forgotten to wear this time."

"If it's in my house, maybe we'd better step into my bedroom to do that. Just so that nobody else is embarrassed." Harold smiled and so did Mercedes.

Mercedes didn't answer for a short while, but then. "Soon, 'Arold, but not quite yet. If Caddi had managed to finish off the Murphies, who knows? If you'd hung up two stockings, they might both have been filled on Christmas morning."

Harold tightened the arm around her. "Mmm. I wouldn't need anything else. I could have played with my present all day and never got bored."

Mercedes laughed, and then sobered. "Unfortunately, we had better ask ET and Charger to join us." She giggled and hugged hard for a moment. "So that Caddi doesn't get the right idea, and think you are breaking the rules." This wasn't for show. Mercedes spoke quietly and both Casper and Doll had dropped back too far to hear her. "I can't come down your chimney this Christmas, but will you be my Easter Bunny please, 'Arold?"

"Then or whenever you want, Mercedes." Harold sniggered, hugging her a little tighter as well. "My burrow is your burrow."

"Mmm, sounds cosy. Just thinking about it should keep me going until then." Mercedes raised her voice. "Will someone point out to the watchdogs they've been a bit careless." Quieter she continued, "Maybe because I told them we'd join them." Doll put her head round the door into The Pub, and moments later Charger and ET came out carrying their beer. "Just in time, boys, because if he'd got me home alone who knows what our Soldier Boy might have got up to?" Both of them grinned and both opened their mouths, then remembered where they were.

Doll eyed them up and put a hand on her pistol. "I'm sure we can delay them, Mercedes?"

"Not this time, thank you Doll." Doll didn't actually delay ET and Charger much, but she kept them well back to give Mercedes a bit of privacy. Just before they reached the garden gate, Mercedes suddenly stopped. "Will your other woman mind, 'Arold?" For possibly the first time, Mercedes sounded hesitant.

Harold didn't hesitate at all. "I haven't got another woman, Mercedes. I've known Tessa since I had acne, and her fella was a very good friend. She backs off the volunteers among the refugees."

"Volunteers?"

"They want to be the gang boss's woman. The position is reserved, and the successful candidate even branded me." Harold knew what he'd just offered, and right now didn't care. Maybe all the dancing and smooching had got to him as well. "Tessa will step aside as soon as she moves in."

"In that case the candidate had better give you a Christmas present." She glanced up at Harold with that lovely twinkle in her eyes. "I've brought two but you ought to open one all alone."

"You'd better open yours away from sound and vision." Harold had thought long and hard about what to give her. The big fluffy white toy rabbit didn't look much, but inside was a souvenir from the trip to Beth's. It contained one of the special bombs, one with a five-second clockwork fuse, but with Barry explosives and shrapnel replacing the oil and petrol. The note explained, telling Mercedes it was to give her a running start or for her to leave as a parting gift. Now he wondered what Mercedes had given him.

Harold assumed that someone phoned ahead, because neither the children nor Tessa were in evidence. While Sharyn sorted out drinks all round, Mercedes asked 'Arold to undo all the buttons on her coat. She insisted he started at the bottom and worked up, probably a good idea when she moved closer while he did so. If he'd started at the top, Harold thought his nose would have been hooked in her cleavage. Her cleavage became more obvious when she licked her lips, slowly, and undid the extra button. "Sit down, 'Arold, so that I can get comfortable."

Harold sat and Mercedes perched on the chair arm, tucked in so she leant against his shoulder. "This is the first part of your present, 'Arold, the public part. You'll want to be more careful than usual." Harold was sure of it. Mercedes wore a miniskirt with short boots, but no stockings, and she stretched her legs over Harold's to make it blatantly obvious. Harold admired the view, then looked up and almost kissed her. The happy, cheerful twinkle in her eyes had just a touch of wicked. Mercedes was ablaze, even if only Harold could see.

"That's a lovely present, Mercedes. What can I do to say thank you?"

"The next part is the present, and mine as well. You have been a naughty boy, 'Arold. You've had your hands all over my stockings and I found that I liked it. So much that I'm curious. Now I want to know what your hand feels like without the stocking. Will you please put your hand on my leg?" She paused and the mischief in her eyes was even more obvious. "Exactly where it was last time." Harold heard stifled noises from Charger and ET at least.

"I would love to, Mercedes. But can you restrain yourself, because it might feel even better than you expect?" Harold didn't want Mercedes to get too creative, or not in public anyway. Despite that, right now he was seriously considering Patty's suggestion.

"Oh, I'm hoping it feels better, much better, 'Arold. I suppose you'd better untuck my blouse first, so your other hand can get busy. At this rate, you'll end up ruining my reputation." Or underlining it, because Charger and ET were witnesses and would report to the Hot Rods.

Harold pulled her blouse loose, slowly and gently, working all around her waist. Mercedes moved a little to let him, giving Harold yet another chance to win the bra betting. Even if Mercedes had told him she never wore a bra while visiting, the game was on if only to amuse the others. Harold ran his hand right around her back, just above her skirt, and received a big smile. "Mmm, I might have to come and get you to help me undress again, 'Arold. You are so gentle." Mercedes licked her lips. "And thorough."

Her body moved closer so she leant on Harold's shoulder, and he had no trouble reaching right round to her stomach. Nor did Mercedes have any trouble putting her hand up the back of his shirt, and running her nails down his spine. Mercedes glanced down. "Remember that when you get hold of my leg, 'Arold. Gentle and thorough."

Harold couldn't look down just now without losing the bra game. He lowered his hand safely clear of Mercedes' skirt, which earned him a pout. As Harold began to slide his hand slowly up her leg, delight blossomed in her eyes. Mercedes wriggled a little bit. "Careful, 'Arold. It's a very short skirt."

Too bloody true it was. Harold wondered for a moment if Mercedes had lifted the hem as she had the first time with her blouse. If so Harold was about to break every last rule. Then he'd take her into the bedroom and tell the bodyguards to sod off, or kill Charger and ET so Caddi never found out. Harold wasn't sure if he felt relieved or disappointed when his thumb touched fabric. "Very." Mercedes laughed as Harold cleared his throat. The second try Harold had his voice back under control. "Very short. Just for a moment I wondered if you were tired of waiting."

"When you put your hand up there, 'Arold, it won't be with all these spectators." Mercedes looked over at the gobsmacked Hot Rods. "In fact, you might never get up my skirt. I might insist you take it off before you handle the delectables."

"As long as there's no audience, I will happily strip off every stitch on both of us. But I can't promise to keep control afterwards."

"I hope not!" Mercedes closed her other leg on Harold's finger ends and rubbed it up and down. "Oh, I really hope not because this is very nice." Harold agreed. There was conversation about this and that, but Harold didn't even pretend to be keeping up. Snuggled in close like this, every time Mercedes turned towards him and spoke Harold could feel her breath on his face, on his lips. Harold wanted to kiss Mercedes, properly, and her smile and eyes said Mercedes knew. Her eyes said she might like it as well.

The visit didn't last long because evening drew in too early right now. Harold wished it had been longer, and saw the regret in Mercedes' eyes when Charger said they had to leave. "You could stop over for the dance at least? After all, those two are here as chaperones?" Harold squeezed her leg and stroked her tummy. "I promise to save you the last dance. All of them?"

"Not a chance, Harry. We've got strict instructions about getting Mercedes home before dark." Charger sounded genuinely worried, probably because he couldn't physically insist. "She wasn't supposed to be coming at all, she jumped into the car at the last minute. Roller nearly strained something getting the message to us before we got through the gates. Sorry Harry, but Caddi would kill me." Charger actually sounded sincere, which surprised Harold.

"Fair enough." He smiled up at Mercedes as she stood and his hands slid off her. "I can wait." When he helped her on with her coat, she stepped back into him so his arms were right round her. Once again Harold almost told Charger to sod off and leave Mercedes here. Instead he gave her the Christmas present, smiling because his attempts at drawing rabbits on the paper suddenly had more meaning. "For your burrow."

At the gate, Mercedes passed her present from 'Arold to Charger to look after. Goodbye wasn't quite a real smooch even when her lips stayed connected much longer. Harold could feel the moment coming and almost started the real kiss, but he wanted Mercedes to decide. Mercedes crushed herself against him and wriggled more this time as Harold wrapped his arms right round her. When she stepped back he watched the light and warmth in her eyes die as the Killer Queen took over. This time her real smile stayed. "Keep the burrow warm, 'Arold." Mercedes left with a wave, and a finger pointed at her ass.

Harold stood watching her car leave to a background of speculation from those around the gate. They all seemed to think the deal with Caddi would be history the first time Mercedes got Harold on his own. What the hell happened after that had a lot of people wondering, and would probably keep Harold awake sometimes. As he waved goodbye, Harold felt a lot of peace and goodwill, just in time for Christmas. He found himself wishing he had a pair of stockings to hang up, just in case.

When he turned from the gate Harold had to laugh. Roy and his three men stood in a line, mouths open. "Er, cripes, Harold. I thought the GOFS were winding me up." Roy looked in the direction the Hot Rod car had taken. "If she does a runner, send for us." A smile flickered on his face. "I've got a score to settle with the Hot Rods." Harold saw the smile on Celine's face as she stood just behind Roy, but managed not to smile himself. Celine had definitely found her protector, especially when it came to Hot Rods.

"If I don't get the chance and it goes all wrong, give Caddi a long-range migraine will you? Gofannon will take you in afterwards." Harold knew the GOFS would, because their boss had already offered Roy a job any time he wanted it. Several people cheered and suggested giving Caddi his migraine for Christmas. Others suggested Einstein, then more names and the serious moment passed.

When darkness fell on Christmas Eve, more beer and fried potatoes went up to the bypass. The girls came back laughing and high-fiving. They'd taken plastic mistletoe and reckoned they knew where Harold got his rules about being polite to women, from HM. Harold asked around quietly. The idiots really had been kissing the squaddies, but over the top of the sandbag wall so not exactly a clinch. Harold thought it more likely the sergeant's rather than HM's rules kept the squaddies polite, but the lasses had earned some extra goodwill up there. Liz promised to drive home to the women that they should run at the slightest hint of a grab.

*   *   *

Christmas Day dawned white, bright, and actually cheerful. Harold opened his present from Mercedes in private, spending some time wishing the two bits of silky nightwear weren't empty. He recognised them, she'd tempted him with this set the first time they met. The note said, "In case I don't have time to pack," so Mercedes wasn't sure how abruptly she would be leaving the Mansion. Harold manfully endured the teasing questions while he opened his other presents.

Daisy had managed to knit everyone a scarf apiece, with tassels. She enjoyed opening her presents, with plenty of squealing when she found a real Barbie doll. A Ski Barbie, because Ski thought any niece of Soldier Boy should have an appropriate role model. She'd still charged Harold a substantial number of coupons for the toy. After breakfast, Daisy pestered everyone until allowed out to round up a snowman building team. She included Joey, Georgina and Sukie so the Halloween spat with Georgina must be over. Wills managed to stop her opening most of his presents, retiring to his room with a large metal digger that had an operable arm. Eddie joined him with most of a set of Lego bricks. The new housing had plenty of scavenger material.

Another surprise present arrived, six cushions delivered by a smiling group of the ex-Murphy refugees. They'd all been embroidered with an Orchard Close tree covered in smiley faced fruit. The festive run-up before Christmas persisted through Christmas Day. Tessa answered a knock at the door just after a dinner heavy on potatoes, sprouts and rabbit, but light on turkey. "For you, Harold." When he joined her, Tessa turned, held up the mistletoe and kissed him. The cheer from outside came as an even bigger surprise, and Tessa winked. "Since she isn't here."

The line of young women with plastic leaves and berries, and a big smile, meant Harold had to smile as well. He soon decided that Tessa's display might have been a good idea, because several of the kisses were alcoholic and decidedly enthusiastic. The line of women left, laughing and waving their mistletoe, to bang on Betty's door until a startled Alfie answered. Hazel, standing behind him, didn't see the joke because Alfie's kisses also included several fairly enthusiastic versions. Harold wondered how much Christmas cheer had been drunk.

During the afternoon, every house with a male had a visit from at least some of the 'Kissmas Fairies.' It didn't take long for a group of 'Kissmas Elves' to form, and start on visiting the single women. By late afternoon, the 'Kissmas Elves' and 'Fairies' were trying out each other's mistletoe. The plastic leaves and berries were very popular this year, with occasional ambushes continuing after dark as some 'victims' looked for payback. The impromptu band played all day, even when the only expert took a break. Some players were already improving, while several children from Jilli's school class joined in with recorders. Plenty of people were willing to sing, with volume replacing musical talent most of the time. Even Barbie Radio played some old Christmas standards, though 'Christmas Time' by The Darkness, 'Mistress for Christmas' and 'Christmas with the Devil' jarred with 'White Christmas,' 'Deck the Halls' and 'Jingle Bells.'

Daisy asked for crossbow practice so the kids took turns with her little crossbow, shooting sticks at their snowmen. Outside the front gate, the Girl Club and apprentices scraped up enough snow for a snow-girl, equipping her with a Riot Squad helmet and spear. More snow scavenging from back gardens led to a series of brief snowball fights, until the ammunition ran out. It wasn't planned, but everyone seemed to have decided it was time to have a real, old-style Christmas. The squaddies declined an invitation to come and dance so their goodwill gift went up after dark, when the drones wouldn't see the beer and soup. Even Caddi's watchers were sent hot soup, delivered by half a dozen armed men without mistletoe.

* * *

Between Christmas and New Year, Liz organised making the first batch of charcoal. Volunteers helped her build a sod kiln on the cleared ground, cutting and stacking the wood as instructed. Liz rubbed her hands over the result, wearing a permanent smirk as she helped to bag it up and set up the next burn. Caddi's watchers could see the charcoal making, but had no idea where the wood came from because they hadn't seen any arrive.

In the end, one of them just had to ask. By then everyone in Orchard Close knew what to say if any other gang asked about the wood or charcoal. "Harold is very grateful for the tip about timber from Caddi." Most of the residents had no idea what the message meant, but those in the know reckoned it would drive Caddi crackers. The warlord would spend hours trying to work out how Harold had raided the Trainspotters.

The girls repeated the mistletoe trip to the squaddies at New Year. That earned them a rousing three cheers from the bypass as they came back, so presumably Sarge wasn't there. The New Year party was a blast, especially the music because the constant practice meant the band were now much better. The drummers had been whittled down to two, both of whom could actually keep the beat on sets of drums made from metal cans, boxes and barrels.

More of the women relaxed, which showed in their party wear because this time there wasn't a theme. Despite dancing outside in the gently falling snow, it wasn't just the usual suspects showing a bit more leg or skin. A couple of slapped faces led to apologies, and the women relaxed a bit more. The two knitted mini-dresses were given an airing and had the desired effect, the wearers had a full dance card. Most of the young men were being very cautious. They liked this idea, girls in proper frocks who would dance if they were asked, and didn't want to mess up. Here and there during the woodcutter dances and smaller versions after Christmas, the ancient art of chatting-up had been rediscovered.

When the BBC chimes announced midnight, every man had several New Year kisses, because there were more women than men. Several of the girls complained about the blokes all claiming more than one, and wanted equality. Harold neatly dodged the ensuing melee. He worried a bit that the newcomers were pushing boundaries too fast, but Sharyn reassured him. The Coven and Girl Club were keeping an eye open, even as some of them joined in. There would be no regrets over a hangover.

* * *

Harold's real New Year celebration arrived during New Year's Day, in the afternoon. When the phone call from Alfie told him Mercedes had arrived completely alone, Harold thought she'd made her break for it. Instead Mercedes waited outside the gate for Harold to come and talk. "Caddi wouldn't let anyone escort me, because I'm not allowed to visit. It's to keep me keen. Cheeky bastard." Mercedes grinned at him, totally unrepentant. "So I came on my own. What do you think, am I in any danger of being kidnapped?"

"Not exactly. I'll throw you over my shoulder and carry you inside if you like? Why don't you ask me to ask you if you'd like that?" Just for a moment, as the laughter danced in Mercedes' eyes at Harold using her own tease, he thought she'd go for it. The eventual shake of her head came slowly, and reluctantly. He stood aside and swept an arm to usher Mercedes through the gate. "Would you like to walk inside? I promise to carry out the searching personally. In private. In my burrow?" Searching wouldn't take much because she'd left her coat in the car.

"That would be lovely. But if I let you do that then I wouldn't want you to stop, 'Arold. If I didn't stop you, you wouldn't stop. Would you 'Arold?" Mercedes wasn't hiding the sparkle in her eyes today, especially when she read the answer in Harold's face. There were no Hot Rods here and her laughing eyes and the real, full, Mercedes smile were out in the open. "I can't come inside, but will you please search my ass?" Mercedes pouted. "On top of my jeans but remember, that's all that's in the way."

She'd done it again. When Harold's eyes went to her blouse, Mercedes laughed. "Nothing under that either. It's already untucked, so would you like to check?" She followed that with another pout. "Soon 'Arold, I promise, but I had to come and give you a New Year kiss even if it's a bit chilly. Warm me up, 'Arold."

"Any time, Mercedes. Just remember that if you ever want to come inside, the gate is always unlocked for you." Harold stepped forward and Mercedes met him, not even hesitating before plastering herself against him. He got a good firm grip on her ass with both hands and pulled, while Mercedes wrapped her arms around Harold's neck.

"Search, not just hold, 'Arold." Mercedes licked her lips. Harold had just started stroking the tight denim when her soft, wet lips came up a bit and connected properly. Harold's arms tightened, but Mercedes had crushed herself against his front anyway. One hand left her jeans and came all the way up her back to her neck, under her blouse. The little noise Mercedes made into Harold's mouth burned out brain cells, as did the kiss itself.

Mercedes had very soft lips, her breath tasted slightly minty, and she slowly and thoroughly snogged Harold's brain into jelly. He badly needed a shot of Gayle's oxygen by the time Mercedes stepped back. As he did, his hand stroked slowly down her back and out onto her jeans. Mercedes glanced down at her blouse. "You checked, but round the back, idiot." Her delighted smile, when Harold realised that his hand hadn't found a bra strap, swept across to include the faces watching from Orchard Close. "That should keep us both going for a little bit longer." The silly sods on the wall actually gave her a cheer.

Harold watched that lovely sparkle in her eyes die as Mercedes stuffed it back into hiding, again. He wondered what would happen the day she couldn't, because this time Mercedes gave a little sigh. The Killer Queen wanted to abdicate. Mercedes turned and raised her hand in farewell. "I'll be back so keep it warm, lover-boy." After pointing at her ass to remind

Harold to watch it, Mercedes swaggered down the road to her motor. The Killer Queen waved and blew Caddi's watchers a kiss before climbing into the car and roaring off.

By now everyone knew the deal between Caddi and Mercedes. A good few, not all of them in Orchard Close, thought Harold should drag her into a bedroom and tell the Hot Rods to stuff it. Some knew him well enough to guess why Harold wouldn't, he didn't want friends to die when Caddi went ape. According to Liz, Mercedes was encouraging Caddi to wait, expecting her to come to him voluntarily under the deal. Liz, along with all the squad leaders, thought Mercedes would refuse.

Harold thought that whatever Mercedes suppressed during the Crash in order to survive had re-surfaced. When it broke free all hell would break loose. Some of the hell would be inside her head, as those happy eyes looked at what the Killer Queen had done to survive. He felt sure that when the Murphy war ended, Caddi would invite him to the Mansion to seal the deal. Mercedes would know that and have to run first, or kill Caddi and run. Harold, and the inner circle, believed she'd come here. Most thought that if Caddi died first, the Hot Rods might be too busy fighting for power to care.

None of them told Harold to turn Mercedes away, which gave him a real lump in his throat. Orchard Close usually tried to deflect any trouble, and not give any gang a reason to attack. Now even Tessa didn't recommend throwing Mercedes back. She still called Mercedes the bitch, but made it a joke. Maybe Sharyn had it right, and Tessa was content to wait and see what sort of train wreck ensued.

*   *   *

The watchers told Caddi about the visit, of course. Mercedes had blown a kiss to them on the way past to rub it in. Once Orchard Close reopened after New Year, the Hot Rod visitors arrived full of the gossip and the betting in the Mansion. The commando betting had eased off. The Hot Rods all reckoned the first confirmation would be Mercedes' underwear on Soldier Boy's carpet, or on the flagpole. Now the wagers were about if Mercedes would wait until Harold visited, if she'd wait until the war ended, and if anyone else would get a chance at her once Harold and Caddi had finished.

All that didn't help Harold's peace of mind, but sitting quietly fixing guns now and then did. Even then he had to put up with a bit of gentle teasing, about Tessa's job being in danger. Both jobs she reckoned, as Mercedes didn't look the sharing type, and if Harold cheated either way the bite marks or gun-oil stains would give the game away. They made more muskets, fixed guns, and loaded the brass for the new clips Dealer had supplied.

Harold still walked the wall each night, and meeting Casper gave him his chance. Harold kicked at the bricks. "This could do to be a bit thicker."

"Cripes, Harold, it's at least a metre thick, two metres at the bottom where the firing step backs it up." Casper stared at the bricks, then at Harold. "Where will you find another ten million bricks anyway?"

"There's plenty out there. Our people are still knocking down the ruins around the Farm. There'll be plenty left for walls around the new houses as well." Harold laughed and kicked the wall again. "These didn't take ten million bricks."

"They might have. I lost count." Casper stared out over the fields. "Are you worried about something ramming it? It would take a lorry to get through here."

Harold seized on the excuse. "Our tank is a small lorry under the steel. There have to be some wrecked lorries out there and someone like the General or Caddi could fix one up. If they stick a snowplough blade on the front it'll cut through the hump we left across the fields, and won't get stranded. Then ten or more tons, even moving slowly, might punch through. We should thicken up the ground floor walls of the guard houses as well, so nobody rams through them."

"They might, especially with a lorry." Casper looked along the line of bricks, towards the gates. "It'll be a hell of a job. Are you really worried?"

"Yes. Not all the walls, just those where a lorry might get a clear run at them." Harold didn't have to pretend to be worried because Dealer didn't give hints, normally. "You heard about the General hitting another enclave, a real bloodbath? According to a couple of the Barbie visitors it was someone called the SIMS, and they had proper walls and strongpoints. The General won so his men got through them somehow. Sooner or later he'll find a way to come for us and the Geeks, if only because of what happened to his men in that railway cutting, and he'll come prepared." Harold didn't mention his other worry, but Casper knew about Caddi anyway. "Top priority, Casper. I'll even let you use diesel to move bricks from the demolition to the gates."

"Cripes, that urgent? All right, I'll get on it." Casper put on a silly smile. "Building walls, ooh, that'll make a nice change."

* * *

Others made their own significant contribution to everyone's safety. Martha, one of the Demons and a trainee musketeer, suggested that the cheapest underskirts at the Mart might make bags for powder. She'd been disgusted with how thin they were, then realised the spark from the cap might burn through. A quick test using her underskirt had proved the theory. The shoppers bought a stack, which the sewing apprentices turned into tiny bags. Up to now the reloads varied from paper through a variety of cloths that had to be cut to make certain the powder ignited. Many had preferred putting the wads, ball and loose powder in, to be sure the weapon would fire. All the musketeers now spent some of their time creating pre-load bags with powder, wads and a ball. The musket volley from Orchard Close would go on, and on, and on.

At least sixty of the residents could now operate the hybrid musket, over twice as many as the number of weapons. That worked out well in the harsh reality of battle, when the shooter was more likely to be put out of action than the musket. Unfortunately, musket practice left tracks in the snow, while the noise of the firing couldn't be hidden. Hopefully, the watchers thought the Orchard Close musketeers were firing a few weapons a lot of times.

The second row of the Demons began practising with old spears, the less useful versions such as the knife blades on broom shafts, but only in the dark so no enemy had any warning. The ancient weapon enthusiasts finally agreed on a design for a proper spear head, so Liz and her strong shouldered assistant started making them. The new weapons totally outclassed the practice versions. The spear head consisted of a wide, leaf-shaped blade that would slice if it only got a glancing hit, while the sleeve went back half a metre up the shaft to stop someone chopping the head off. Harold certainly wouldn't want one jabbing in his face in a fight, or anywhere in his body at any time for that matter. The Demons and the fighters who would defend the walls were downright enthusiastic.

Liz produced the first copy of Harold's sword. He tested it, then Liz, Patty and Wamil tried his blade and the new one to compare how they felt and moved. The second sword Liz produced came in a lot closer to the original, near enough to use as a real weapon. Harold started proper sword training with four women and three men. Sword fighting, not fencing for touches, the style included an iron bar in the other hand and a kick in the crotch if the opportunity presented itself.

The trainees discovered how hard the sword could be hit without taking damage, and what the pointy bit could do. The iron bars improved when Liz filled the smallest bore steel tube with lead, before welding on a hardened sleeve to weight one end. The weapons were both robust and packed a hell of a wallop. Some were promptly paired with the swords, safely out of sight, while others replaced the plain bars other fighters already carried.

The sword wielders were to plug leaks, by killing any loners getting over the wall and avoiding the Demons. If possible, they would work in pairs with someone trained to use Wamil's knives, so hopefully two to one. Those training with Wamil and her knives sparred with those using swords, or fought alongside them, which gave both of them an idea of their partner's skills and weaknesses.

The Riot Squad wasn't a properly integrated force such as Ant had proposed, because of the variety of styles and weapons. At least letting everyone train in their preferred style meant the defenders were keen on practice, and were soon competent and pushing to get better. Harold tried to blend the lot into a system, to give them a chance at the enemy. He really hoped that when the moment came the trainees would take that chance and strike to kill, that nobody would freeze. His worst nightmares included the whole force breaking and running, leaving a few individuals to die.

*   *   *

Not everyone spent their time strengthening the defence. The scavengers resumed after the holiday with renewed enthusiasm. A cheering crowd pushed home a small touring caravan, found tucked away in what must have been a custom built garage. A falling wall had crushed the car inside the front but not the rest of the building. The scavengers broke into the intact rear for tools, but then spent half a day throwing bricks about to retrieve their prize. The triumphant group asked Harold where he wanted to go for his holidays.

Harold didn't have the heart to suggest cutting it down for a trailer, or for Liz to have the springs, but didn't know what the hell to do with it. Casper claimed a part of his initial connecting wall to the Annex needed rebuilding, as part of Harold's new fetish for better walls. Once he'd dismantled a short section, willing hands pushed the caravan inside to give them a garden shed. Casper and his apprentices rebuilt the wall, thicker as Harold had instructed. Once finished, the brickies went back to their long-term job, thickening the main Orchard Close walls by an extra half metre at least.

Despite all the work, none of the gardeners used the caravan as a shed, and Harold soon found out why. He'd stopped the unmarried couples getting a bit of privacy under the bypass, but now they had a love shack. Harold wondered how many others thought of the other use, an early warning system if someone did try to use those gardens as an attack route. He also wondered if Mercedes would like the caravan. After all, there'd be no kids or sister there.

Chapter 20:
New Year

Precinct Nineteen:

Deep under a hillside, on a raft in a dead-end canal, David the ex-policeman woke up after his own New Year celebration. No hangover, but he felt definitely dazed and still bedazzled. Beside him a low chuckle and a warm body brought a happy smile. "Good morning, and a very happy New Year."

David looked into brown eyes surrounded by tousled dreadlocks and some bedraggled feathers. Inga didn't need lamplight, even her bedhead looked damn sexy. "Happy New Year. I never realised mermaids were a New Year tradition." He started to gesture towards the water around them but the sleeping bag held them tight.

"It could be?" Inga yawned and stretched as much as possible, a startling but very pleasant experience for David. "I suppose we'd better sneak back home. Will you be drummed out of the barracks?"

David laughed gently and hugged her. "Possibly. I think we can safely say any hint of secrecy has gone."

"Hah, that big smirk gave the game away ages ago." Inga sighed, wriggling an arm out to snag her clothing. "But we ought to get back."

"I know, buffalo to milk, fish to feed, zebras to muck out." The pair got dressed, climbed into a small rowing boat and extinguished the small oil lamp.

* * *

As he rowed towards the entrance to the canal tunnel, David kept teasing Inga about the life of a Zookeeper, until her eyes opened wide and she put out a hand to shut him up. He turned to look over his shoulder, out of the entrance, and fumbled at his belt. Unfortunately he didn't have any firearms, and a machete wasn't going to stop the boat coming under the railway bridge. His first thought was that it would rip the net and let all the fish out, but that faded into insignificance when he took in the men with crossbows and the muzzles poking from loopholes!

"Quick!" Inga gestured. "To the side." David dug an oar in deep and she reached for the rope slung along the wall, stopping the rowboat before it reached the line of sunlight just inside the entrance.

David thumbed his radio, keeping his voice down. "Anyone, this is Six-One-Three. Armed boat in the fishpond. Out." The radio stayed silent so maybe the tons of rock above them had stopped the signal.

"I'll go." David turned at Inga's voice, ready to argue but he stopped, speechless. She'd pulled her jumper and shirt off and was dropping her jeans. "I can swim better in underwear. I'll use the buddleia on the wall, just there by the entrance, to climb up to the top of the bank. Then I'll let everyone know what's here. Don't say too much on that police radio because all the neighbours listen now."

David glanced at the distance, then back. "They'll see you. They might shoot, or catch you."

"But if they try to catch me they have to follow me, and you'll be waiting here in the dark with that machete. I'll dive back in if I'm spotted, deep so they can't shoot me." Inga put a foot in the water. "This water is freezing." She tried for a smile, but it looked more nervous than confident. "I'll need a rub down afterwards, to warm up?" Before David could answer she dived over the side, entering the water with barely a ripple. He grabbed onto the rope with both hands as the rowboat bobbed, trying to spot her. He knew Inga could reach that buddleia, she swam like a mermaid, but the next part worried him.

Sure enough, she'd barely got her feet clear of the water when a man pointed and two others aimed weapons. "You. Stay still! We can't miss from here. Who are you?"

"Inga." She'd abandoned the diving back in plan. The approaching canal boat had stopped, but much too close to risk a dash for safety.

"Let me see you. Hands empty."

"I'll fall if I let go." Inga showed her head, shoulder and an arm, her wet black skin in stark contrast to the bush and bricks. David eased the rowboat forward. If he showed himself and distracted them, just for a second, she'd have a chance.

"A woman?" The spokesman sounded baffled. "Swimming? In this weather? Where did you come from?"

"A good question." David sagged in relief as Sarge spoke up. "I'm more interested in where you came from, and who you are. Before you answer, I should mention there's three policemen pointing automatic weapons at you."

"Police? I've been looking for you. Are you Precinct Nineteen, the ones with the cows?" This voice, from inside the boat, laughed. "Or not cows, someone told me. It's all right lads, this is who we want." On deck the armed men, who had all crouched when Sarge spoke up, slowly straightened.

"You've got a very strange way of getting in touch. That canal leads under the motorway so how did you get past the Army?" Sarge wasn't relaxing.

A hatch clanged open and a tousled head came out. "There's people cutting holes in the wire and crossing all the time, ones and twos carrying a bit of meat or something similar to trade. It's easy if you wait for a gap in the patrols. That's no good for us but we've finally managed to clear a tunnel, one that starts and finishes out of sight of the Army. The government had welded big grills across it. We've got customers begging for real meat, if you'll sell wholesale?"

While the men shouted, David tried to get Inga's attention. She finally heard his low calls. "Come on, now. Quick, they aren't looking." Inga glanced at the tunnel, at the boat where the men were all looking at the banks or towards Sarge's voice, and took her chance.

"Hey!" The man stopped, staring at the widening ripples where Inga had disappeared under the water. "Bloody hell, is she a fish?"

"Nearly." This voice came from the other side of the canal. "I'm Teddy and I'm pretty sure I know exactly what Inga was doing. Now how about you put those weapons down and tie up this side." The sigh was loud enough for everyone to hear. "You'll see her again, and get the edge of her tongue when she has to mend the net."

"A net? Never mind. I'm Skipper and we run a frozen fish delivery service. We've traded with a couple of gangs for some of your meat, but I thought it would be more profitable to find the source." The man climbed out onto the deck. "Put the crossbows down, lads. I think this is a no fishing area."

Inside the tunnel Inga had surfaced beside the rowboat, her teeth chattering. "Give me a hand." David held onto the wall rope with one hand and her with the other and pulled her aboard. "Teddy can sod off." She could hardly talk for her teeth chattering, even when David wrapped his coat round her. "Or at least until I'm warm. Take me back to the towels so I can dry off and get back in that warm sleeping bag for a bit."

David would have argued but he didn't fancy facing Sarge and every-one else, not when it was obvious where he'd been with Inga. Not only that, but he'd just pulled Inga out the water clad only in wet underwear, and getting her dry and into the sleeping bag sounded like a terrific idea. As he sculled deeper into the darkness he could hear the newcomers intro-ducing themselves properly. Sarge and Teddy would be pleased with the new trade, a customer who had contacts elsewhere.

*   *   *

Sutton Park:

About sixteen miles away, the residents of Sutton Park were waking up to the consequences of their New Year party. "Wake up, dopy. That Nosy bloke tried to do a runner."

"Wha? Chelle? What's up?" Shiner, the leader of the Skins, skinheads, rubbed his eyes and peered up at his 'wife's' face. "My bloody head is kill-ing me."

"Serves you right. You just had to try everyone else's home brew. Now get your pants on because we might have a problem." Chelle, christened Michelle, nudged him with her foot. "Happy New Year, misery."

Shiner's eyes weren't tracking right but he finally managed to get dressed, even if Chelle had to lace his boots. When he finally picked up his baseball bat and opened the door, Shiner paused at the sight of all the bod-ies littering the floor. Not real ones, these were still breathing but might feel worse than he did once they woke up. He picked his way across to the kitchen, noticing in passing that Hangaku's idea had worked. The Yakuza leader had suggested a party with members of every gang, to break down some barriers.

The skinhead tangled with an Oriental and the two women, only one a Valkyrie, cuddled up in a corner, were obvious examples. Another met Shiner's eyes when he reached the kitchen because Odin, the big man lead-ing the Vikings, had an arm around a slim woman with a slit skirt, fishnets and long black hair. As Shiner stared a voice spoke behind him. "You'll need a wakeup, I'm guessing." Hangaku, an Oriental woman who always wore a Japanese sword sheathed across her back, pointed to the table. "Coffee. Hot, black, and stronger than Odin's willpower. I wonder if he actually learned any French."

"Doubtful." The Headmaster, boss of the Hard School, already sat sipping a drink. "Frenchie turned up well after the Crash. She said the school needed a French Mistress, but I'm not sure exactly what sort of lessons she gives." The woman in Odin's arm smirked.

"Now you're here, we can get started. After all, the asshole chose your gang." Odin raised his voice. "Bring him in, Asif." The door opened and a man with a big scar across his nose staggered in. He stopped as the man behind him, a middle-aged Asian, jerked on his collar.

"Nosy?" Shiner remembered what Chelle had said and his face hardened. "You were running?"

"No, I swear!"

"Asif?" Odin looked at the Asian man.

"I found him sneaking through the marsh towards the woods. There's no reason to go that way." Curious eyes centred on Asif. "One of the pregnant sheep didn't fancy using the barn. She'd snuck off into the wood so I went to fetch her back."

"What did he steal?" Shiner scowled at Nosy and raised his baseball bat. "Were you selling out to that Prophet bloke?"

"No, I swear. I didn't steal anything."

"He only had a pistol and blades." Asif put the knife, machete and firearm on the table.

"So where were you going?" Now everyone looked baffled, because those weren't enough to buy in anywhere.

Nosy opened his mouth three times and shut it again, looking around the assembled gangsters, before he took a deep breath. "I daren't say, just in case it gets back." He looked frightened, but not necessarily of the people present. "One of you could be a spy."

"If we are, you've already dropped yourself in the shite. A spy?" Hangaku frowned. "For who?"

"I'm not sure. I leave messages. Sometimes there's a message for me, asking for information about one of the gangs, or weapons, that sort of thing." Nosy had hunched right over, cringing in anticipation. The likes of Hangaku weren't noted for their restraint.

"Who pays you?" Chelle looked round the rest. "He has to know that."

"No pay." Nosy shut up again, until Shiner smacked his bat on the table. "If I don't do it, or I'm killed, my mother and sister go to the camps." A racking sigh followed. "They'll go there anyway if any of you are reporting as well, because I've told you."

"We're all gang leaders here, elite or whatever. I doubt we'll be selling out." A slow smile started on Hangaku's face. "We can send someone to watch this drop-off point, from a long way off. Better yet, we can feed whoever it is some shite information." She waved a hand at Nosy as he made an inarticulate noise. "Not shite enough to be obvious, or you're no good to us."

"Good thinking. Well done Asif. We'll take it from here." Odin nodded to Asif, who left. Shiner finally got his coffee, and everyone sat to find out what Nosy had been asked to find out. With luck, they'd figure out who wanted to know.

Just out of sight of the building, another of the erstwhile wildlife wardens, Jer, beckoned Asif behind a shed. "Well?"

"It's a mystery. He's a spy of some sort, but only because his family will go to the camps if he doesn't report." Asif shook his head in despair. "It's bad enough having to put up with this lot."

"They aren't too bad, and they're getting better. The camps sounds like government, maybe getting a read on all the gangs before the hammer comes down. Aren't you pleased we kept quiet about our hidden talents?" Jer smiled and clapped Asif on the shoulder. "We'll get the rest of the lads to keep an eye open, to see if there are any other leaks. Did you find out how he reports?" They walked off talking quietly, working out how to protect the gangsters without letting them know.

* * *

Conan:

The leader of the Barbarians had his own suspicions about where Sylvester got information and maybe sent reports, but it worked for him so he didn't actually care. Even so, Conan wasn't happy about the argument he'd just had with the spy. He ran it back through in his head. If it had been anyone else he'd have topped them, but Sylvester had become too useful. The trouble was the smartarse had started getting a bit too full of himself, trying to plan the campaign and choose targets. The nuns were working out well, but that sneaky fuck needed to realise he wasn't indispensable. The gang boss felt a little uneasy because that fucker hadn't been scared, he'd been ready if Conan had gone for him. Conan didn't, not just then, because he wasn't totally sure he'd win. Sylvester didn't look for trouble but he was too fast, almost professional when he had to fight.

After a little thought, Conan came up with another way to rub in who ran things. He would attack the next gang when he was good and ready, and it wouldn't be the one Sylvester suggested. Conan knew the perfect target, one that could be run over with lunatics and machetes. He fancied a bit of blood and mayhem instead of all this pansy planning and shit. No hurry, the blokes were all pissed or hung over, or playing with their women.

That brought a smile to Conan's face and he headed upstairs. He'd got some entertainment of his own, the Bitch. The smile faltered as the gang boss rubbed a long, partly-healed cut down his arm. Not all fun, she'd got to his knife when he dropped his jeans just a little bit too close. Still, after the beating he gave her for that she'd quietened down for a day or two. With a big grin he kicked open the bedroom door. "On your knees and drop your drawers, Bitch. I've got your New Year's present in my pants. Ready to suck it yet?"

A groan greeted him, then a low laugh. "Yeah, all right. Drop your pants and shove it between my teeth. I dare you."

"You'd like that. No chance. Though if you keep on biting, I might decide to knock the rest of your fucking teeth out." He'd already knocked a few teeth out, by mistake, but Conan didn't want to win that way. What he wanted was for her to give in like all the others.

She spat at him and made a gun hand, a finger out for the barrel. Sometimes Catherine felt tempted to give in, because she believed the bastard, about him letting her go after three days of total submission. It would be gross and humiliating but once she caved in she wouldn't be any fun for the sick shit. Then she'd remind herself why she kept going. The nasty bastard would pick on another woman, then another because he liked humiliating them. Well he couldn't do anything to her he hadn't already tried, and she'd survived it all. It was driving the perverted shit nuts. With a bit of luck one of the others would shoot the rabid bastard, or he'd get that frustrated he'd give her a clean chance with a gun or a knife. Catherine glared at Conan, eye to eye. "Come on then, limp-dick. Look, I'm terrified. Help, help."

* * *

The General:

Despite the Christmas break, too many Bloods were still healing for the General to make a move on Orchard Close. At least that gave the General time to rethink his plans, or refine them a little. Splitting the men had worked well, but Caddi was still dicking about with his war and the General didn't fancy taking Orchard Close without help. He tried another tack, telling Rhys to lean on the Pinkies harder. Maybe he could snip off those dykes first.

Just in case Caddi didn't play nice, the General also asked Rhys to ask around, try and find someone who would loan or hire him extra fighters.

* * *

The Professors:

It hadn't been long since they'd arrived, but the SIMS were already making a difference. Unlike the usual occasional refugee, lost souls fleeing some personal tragedy, the SIMS were still united. Better still, every one of them was determined that the next time the General came they were going to break him. To survive until then the SIMS needed housing and food, because they hadn't had room to bring bulk supplies. The convoy had brought every last coupon the SIMS had, and the more expensive Mart supplies, which helped them to pay their way. From the way the men and women set out to clear ground, they'd grow plenty of food next year, so the Professor dipped into the reserves to help out. Surprisingly, so did Benny's Boys.

According to Benny, the General had issued a warning about anyone helping the SIMS refugees. Since he hadn't broken his alliance with Prof, Benny would be on the shit list so he might as well go all the way. The General would be coming eventually so he wanted as many fighters as possible. From the rumours spreading about the casualties when the General took the SIMS compound, these were exactly the right sort. So far, Prof hadn't told Benny the other reason to be pleased the SIMS were here, just in case one of Benny's Boys had loose lips. The chemistry department had a new student, one who was teaching the professors a way to help them stop the General.

* * *

Reivers:

There wasn't anything quiet about New Year's morning far to the north, far enough for deep snow, as explosions tore apart several enclaves inside Inverness. Air raids hit first, quickly followed by smaller explosions as artillery and mortars added to the carnage. The inhabitants of Inverness, trying to cope with the sudden loss of their electricity and water, forgot about that as tanks smashed down their enclave walls. A full armoured assault drove into the city from the south. The news spread quickly, helped by the jets screaming overhead, the plumes of smoke, the thunder of explosions, and the non-combatants running north. There were plenty who didn't run, either trapped or just deciding to make a stand. In enclave after enclave, grim-faced men and women, some barely out of childhood, prepared to face the onslaught.

Most enclaves, or their leaders, had expected an attack sooner or later, but none were prepared for the sheer scale and ferocity. Despite knowing it wouldn't be enough, they sent out their fighters to harass the advance or launched their carefully constructed and hidden missiles. Tripwire and remote detonated bombs and other little surprises were put in place or activated, many created in case of an attack by neighbours. Gang wars were settled in minutes, as bitter enemies joined forces against the greater threat. Elsewhere, hate-crazed individuals hid in the ruins before launching themselves or vehicles at the attackers, intent on taking at least one with them. The shooters went out to try and kill officers, or artillery spotters, or anyone they could, but began to die almost immediately. The counter-sniping was heavy, and indiscriminate.

Despite every effort by the defenders, the attack ground its way into the city in an unbroken line. Along the northern perimeter of Inverness, those fleeing the fighting found the way wide open. The Army posts and the Marts were deserted. Refugees broke into the Marts, but the last 'supply' convoys had been removing stores so the warehouses were almost empty. Beyond the Marts, across the no-go zone, lay the deserted, snow-covered ruins of the suburbs and empty fields. Despite the lessons of Glasgow, the non-combatants had nowhere else to go.

Perhaps the fighters might have carried on longer, and made the invaders pay a higher price. Instead, when the flood of escapees were left unmolested, more and more turned from stubborn defence to a fighting retreat. Enough stayed to the last minute, or were trapped and died rather than surrender, to slow the clearance to a crawl. Those men and women passed back vital information before they died. The armour, and the troops supporting it, weren't British. They identified French, German, Spanish, Greek and Italian troops, passing on details of the equipment and unit flashes.

A few units of government paramilitary Specials joined the attack. Those were quickly targeted because of what the Specials did to Glasgow. The most suicidal of the loners made a point of heading for the Specials; they'd be the only part of the government anyone could reach. Despite their armour, casualties among the paramilitaries quickly escalated. After the first day the contractors held back, only moving in to round up survivors and process them. Even as the line of armour smashed deeper, the assault deteriorated into a series of small, vicious engagements.

* * *

An armoured half-track skidded to a halt at a junction. After inspecting the buildings and ruins, the rear doors opened for the soldiers to disembark, but the first ones out had to dive for cover as a line of flame shot out of a pile of rubble. The crude missile almost missed, but caught the door and ricocheted inside. Flame and smoke gouted from the vehicle as men stumbled out, screaming and beating at their clothes. Those already outside lashed the rubble with gunfire and advanced.

Pulling bricks aside exposed their attacker, a young teenager with tears still wet on a face frozen in a snarl. Beside him lay the crude tube used to launch the rocket, his only weapon. The soldiers turned back to try and save their vehicle and the injured men.

* * *

Three men, one with white hair, threw themselves from a first floor window into a squad of soldiers, lashing out with a hammer and kitchen knives. In seconds all three were dead, leaving two lightly injured soldiers to head back towards the medics. Inside the shelled house, everyone else was already dead.

* * *

A young woman, weeping bitterly, staggered out of a doorway. A squad of soldiers aimed weapons at her, because other women had been carrying explosives. This one held out a bundle, a baby, asking for help. As she came closer the corporal realised nothing could help the dead child, but by then nothing could save the soldiers as the bomb exploded.

* * *

A dozen ragged men leapt out of cover, swarming over the tank and tugging at the hatches. They smashed bottles over any possible vent or opening, bathing the vehicle in flames. Gunfire from the soldiers following the armour swept the attackers away. The tank rumbled forward, unharmed, while the flames flickered and died.

* * *

Three men burst into a room and looked at the two bodies. "Shite, they got them both. Both our bloody snipers."

The youngest picked up a rifle. "Then they won't be looking here, will they?" He glanced back. "I can't do the fancy stuff, but I'll shoot any officers or NCOs that I can hit until they get me. I've got nothing to lose, not now. Someone stay by the door and take the rifle away once I'm done." A savage grin split his face. "The Bruce will have a shooter who can use it properly."

"I'll take the other." The older man glanced at the third. "You're a crappy shot, so you get to take the Bruce his present." He laid down, snugging the second rifle into his shoulder. "Ready?" The two of them began to shoot as fast as possible. Sure enough, five minutes later both were dead but the advancing soldiers wouldn't get the weapons.

* * *

The tank pushed aside a barrier as the defenders fled, many of them going down in a hail of bullets. The armoured vehicle ground on down the street, until without warning a van reversed out of a shop window. It hit the tank and exploded, deluging the vehicle with burning liquid but without actually breaching the armour. With a roar, the stone-built building at the opposite side of the road came down over both. The shop building followed, the sheer weight of stone and brick trapping the armoured vehicle in with the intense fire. Soldiers began to tear at the rubble to free the tank crew, but gunfire swept them away.

By the time a second armoured vehicle and an air strike had been called up to clear the strongpoint ahead, a dull thud and crackling beneath the rubble announced the fate of the tank crew. Fifty-eight men and women died to kill them, but the defenders were willing to pay the price.

* * *

As the armour and the soldiers fought their way deeper into Inverness, any reluctance to target civilians died out. Time and again men and women threw themselves at the attackers, armed with everything from a kitchen knife to crude bombs. A few prisoners were taken and passed back, but the leading troops were now more inclined to shoot anything moving. A steady stream of wounded soldiers were picked up in armoured ambulances, or waited for the medics in the second wave. Not many vehicles were destroyed, but a slowly growing number were put out of action when crude rockets, mines, building collapses or pits damaged their weaponry or tracks.

Some small groups were coming out of shelter to surrender once the fighting had passed through. Others had no intention of surrendering, they were just hoping for softer targets. Soon even the second wave soldiers didn't always accept a white flag. Elsewhere, amateur booby traps that hadn't worked went off at the second or third attempt. Even as the flame and fury of the battle line moved north, fresh explosions and plumes of smoke grew in the 'liberated' areas.

At the rear the Specials collected prisoners, driving them into temporary camps. After cursory questioning, a few were segregated for further interrogation or a particular skill. Lorries were already waiting to ship the rest south, to a processing centre near Aberdeen.

* * *

"We can't help them Angus." The small band of Reivers stood watching as refugees flooded past. Columns of thick smoke rose over Inverness, while helicopters and jets dived to deliver their own contribution to the mayhem. "If we go into the city we'll get eaten up. That's battle armour and trained soldiers working in disciplined units, with close air support. We'd always expected the Army, but thought they'd respect non-combatants and be open to subversion. Christ knows what these have been offered, but it's enough for them to kill bairns."

"They're from the continent, and not the ones we've been fighting all year." Angus glared at Bruce and the rest. "If they come one step out of Inverness, it means they're driving these poor bastards tae another ambush. I'll not watch that happen."

"We agree, but there's no obvious place for them tae pen the civvies up for slaughter. Just tae make sure, we'd best split that column up so it's a smaller target, and aim them towards deserted towns and villages. At least they'll have cover from the weather." Bruce sighed, glancing both ways but the column stretched out of sight in both directions. "I've no idea how we'll feed them. Any reserves we put by will be eaten up long before spring."

A woman pushed through the fighters, offering a radio. "A relayed message from Maeve, for the Bruce. She wants you back there as soon as possible."

"About the food, nae doubt. Let her know I'm on the way." Bruce turned back to Angus and the other men. "Can I trust everyone tae at least think afore doing something stupid?"

"Aye, on one condition. Once we've got the refugees clear, I want tae take the best of our people hunting. It'll be a mess in those ruins, no proper front line. We haven't the weaponry tae stop them, but we can sting them." Angus's smile had even less warmth than the grey winter sky. "We should give the tourists a proper Highland welcome."

"With luck I'll be back tae help."

* * *

Two days later Bruce finally trudged down a valley to meet Maeve, the woman who acted as quartermaster since she lost an arm to a bullet. Half a dozen men and women waited with her, including one that Bruce recognised as a fisherman. "I doubt they'll catch enough fish tae help, Maeve."

The wan smile caught him by surprise, Maeve rarely smiled at all now. "But they can ferry a good few of yon refugees across the Minch. There's shelter over there, in the Hebrides, and plenty of sheep. Hardly any people, because the paramilitaries swept the islands clean, but not much damage and nobody went back tae loot." She opened a map showing red circles dotting the Hebridean Islands, just off the west coast of Scotland. "We've been setting it up in case the worst happened. If you'd been pushed back too far, we wanted tae give ye an escape."

"Why did ye no tell me?"

Maeve looked embarrassed. "'Twould have seemed disloyal somehow, as if we didnae believe in ye. We do, but we also know that war isn't all about quality."

"They've got quality as well now. Trained troops, foreigners with heavy armour and air support. Fully integrated units, not the mishmash of refugee soldiers sealing the line along Loch Ness." Bruce stretched wearily. "Let me have a brew and give me the details. Will there be enough?"

"I don't know. A lot depends on how many refugees there are, and how many can find food and shelter in the lowlands." Maeve turned towards a small croft. "I'll give ye the figures, but it's up tae God now. There'll be precious little cheer for anyone after this." As he followed her, Bruce felt more hopeful than he had since the radio told him Inverness had lost their water and electric. He wasn't sure why the government had spared all those people, but they had. With Maeve's help, most might survive the winter, a winter Bruce would spend training his new recruits. Then in the spring he'd use those extra recruits to break that front line, and turn the Reivers loose on these bloody foreigners.

* * *

The Cabal:

The Cabal were very pleased with the bloody foreigners. "That's what York needed." Vanna smiled happily. "Real armour to smash the scum."

"Not just real armour, but real soldiers. After all, your contractors have armour. How did they get on?" Joshua looked decidedly smug.

The scowl in reply just widened his smirk. "The scum concentrated on my people. Despite all the rubbish about Maurice keeping the news secret, the inhabitants knew exactly who they were." Embarrassment didn't suit Vanna. "I pulled them back to deal with processing any survivors."

"What about the aircraft? Were there any problems targeting non-combatants?" Owen, the chairman, leant forward. "No constructively disobeyed orders?"

"No, Owen." Faraz, the RAF liaison, smiled happily. "Better yet, they were more accurate because the pilots could get in close. There were a few attempts to shoot them down, but nothing like the Reivers' rockets." He glanced at his reports. "We could have thinned out that refugee column before it split up."

"No, we want them to eat the Reivers out of house and home. They'll all be starving before spring." The smile from Joshua had a lot of anticipation. "They'll have to assault experienced troops in fortified positions, just to get food. Once we've broken their fighters, we can roll over those caves and crofts with the women and children."

"When will Inverness go on the TV?" Ivy's smile faltered, as did others. "There will be an upsurge in trouble in the enclosures, especially at the Marts."

"So we don't tell them Inverness has been cleared. That way the British Army and RAF won't get curious about who did all the fighting." The youngest Cabal member, Gerard, shrugged. "They know we've got some foreign troops, but the numbers and armour might make some officers nervous."

"Good idea." Grace's aristocratic face twisted in a scowl. "The animals in my work camps would get stirred up, and I'd have to shoot some and recruit more. Leave all the mushrooms in peace, in the enclaves as well. Announce extra food in the Marts next Christmas after the Reivers are finally finished, available because the rebels are no longer stopping production. If I issue beer in the work camps the animals will get drunk and celebrate." Heads around the table nodded in agreement.

"What about London? Weren't we going to deal with that to free up troops?" Boris the diplomat looked through several papers. "I'm sure it came up, or am I thinking of Hull?"

"We might be better waiting until the Reivers are broken. Since these new troops seem to be working out so well, they can spearhead the drive in London as well." Vanna sneered at Joshua. "They're mercenaries, more like my people than your soldiers. That means they'll kill anyone we tell them to without insisting on rescuing babies and pensioners. We won't need them once they've done their job, so casualty numbers won't be a problem."

"Better yet." Joshua smiled broadly, completely unfazed. "The British Army can follow up if any attacks are driven back. That will harden their attitudes, because the scum in London won't be listening to reason by then. They'll be sending out children with bombs." He glared back at Vanna, a challenge in his voice. "I suppose the contractors will be holding back again, Vanna? You may as well send the armour back if it isn't going to be used."

Vanna narrowed her eyes. "I already have people holding strongpoints inside the city, including the comms centre in the Tower of London. Places where your precious professionals might see the wrong things and get a nasty attack of conscience. They'll have already started processing, long before your regulars are allowed in." She smiled sweetly, with a quick glance towards Ivy. "I'll send the armour back if you can spare the troops to guard the Mart convoys?"

Sure enough, Ivy jumped in. "Don't you dare mess up the convoy system, not now it's working!" Despite trying again, eventually Joshua gave up on the armour. He wasn't happy about how many real fighting vehicles the contractors now had. The number kept creeping up, but the Specials still didn't have anything like enough to stand a chance against the Army.

Joshua ignored the rest of the Cabal as they worked through the rest of today's business. He was deep in thought. Where had that idea come from, that the contractors couldn't take on the Army? There'd been no hint they'd rebel. Something had sparked the idea, something someone had said or done. Maybe the increasing numbers of contractors and the dwindling number of regulars. Some of the officers were definitely pro-Cabal, part of the conspiracy, and they were being pushed up through the ranks. Maybe he needed to drop a hint or two to a few old-style officers, about possible trouble from the contractors. A very careful hint so it couldn't be traced back. Joshua didn't fancy becoming another example like Nate, 'accidentally' exposed to an attack by gangsters. By the time the meeting broke up, Joshua had made one decision. He would replace his special protection squad with regular Army personnel, squaddies who weren't part of the conspiracy so they couldn't be bought.

* * *

Cyn Palace:

A few hundred miles south of Joshua, in London, hangovers were more of a problem than any conspiracy. An armed man opened the door into a room close to the old library and the fields. Preacher looked in at the two pale faces, and the way they held their heads. "The wages of sin."

"The rotgut came from one of your blokes." Sinner winced as he moved. "I hope he doesn't brew your communion wine, or your lot will be laid out if we need them on a Sunday."

"Our communion wine isn't exactly the right vintage, but it won't stop anyone doing the Lord's work come the day." The man wearing a clerical dog-collar, Preacher, patted his pocket. "I brought you something to make your New Year a little happier."

"Aspirin? Cyanide?"

"I'll take the cyanide." The woman, Sin, opened bleary eyes. "Why are you so cheerful? Did God nip down and smite the bloody cordon in the night?"

"No." Preacher put his hand in his pocket and brought out a metal ball, one with a pin and a handle on the side. "We've been contacted. There's a group trying to coordinate, and they've got resources. Some of the government's faithful guardians have jumped ship, and brought goodies." He tossed the grenade up and down a couple of times.

Sinner frowned, trying to focus on the grenade. "One, two, or a crate of those? We'll need a shitload to defend London."

"Not if we choose where and when to fight. This group want to work that out now, decide how to channel any attack, block roads, and plant mines." Preacher sat down and tested the coffee pot, then poured a mug. "If we start preparing now, we might get the Army to pull back and leave us be. It's not much of a life, but?" He raised the mug.

Sinner raised his mug in reply. "But it is a life, and better than the alternative." He glanced at Sin. "Well?"

"If they've got that sort of gear, I think it's time." Sin groaned and took a swig of her coffee. "You tell him."

Sinner turned back to Preacher and pointed at the grenade. "We've got our own stock of those, and an ex-soldier who came with his rifle, a shitload of ammo and a couple of other toys." The big man chuckled at the expression on Preacher's face. "Surprised? Wait until you find out why. Now when do we get to meet this group? We aren't handing everything over."

"Nor are we. They're more into organising what everyone's got to mesh them together, I think. The grenade is a sweetener because they want to look through that library of yours." Preacher looked at the hand bomb before gently placing it on the table. "Which sort of suits your librarian's style. For now, I'd rather not tell the rank and file, and I won't be spreading your bit of news to anyone. According to these blokes, there are government spies in London, embedded in some of the gangs." Even Sin managed to concentrate as the priest went on to explain what the visitors had told him, about men and women who'd killed themselves rather than talk. Not all the spies were so dedicated, or frightened, and what they'd given up wasn't encouraging. Time was running out for London.

Chapter 21:

Blood in the Snow

Any spy reporting on Orchard Close wouldn't have worried the Cabal, or anyone else very much right now. Not unless they were interested in the preparations for the January dance. All thought of dancing were abandoned when a woman on a cycle came hurtling down the slushy road and up to the gate. "Alarm! Raid!" Harold heard the shouting and then the clanging alarm while walking down the road from his house, and ran to the gates where Casper and Doll were shouting orders. He saw the cycles coming out and knew it must be serious. Forty-nine had been repaired and hidden, to provide transport in an emergency just like this. Better still, cycles could weave through the rubble-strewn streets without slowing down much, as Harold proved after shooting Jon the traitor.

Patty ran up the road carrying her baby in its disguise, and looking around, Harold saw others bringing carefully concealed rifles and muskets. Emmy arrived with her rifle under her coat and a question in her eyes, would Harold let her go this time? Harold shouted to Doll, in the doorway of the guardhouse. "Ring Tessa and ask her to bring my rifle and the two-two to the gate please." He turned to Casper to find out what was happening. It already looked like he'd need all the firepower he could find.

"Wait a minute, Harold. That might be the whole idea, to either pull you into the open for a sniper or just away from Orchard Close." Casper sounded serious. Even as he spoke Alfie limped towards them, tapping his coat to show he'd brought the old 303. Up the street Tessa could already be seen, bringing the two rifles as requested.

"The whole idea of what?" Harold still didn't know, but from their faces some people had been alerted over the phone.

"What's happened?" Ru carried the heavy rifle her accuracy had earned, well wrapped up, while Martha followed with the 308 Mad Max she'd been practicing with lately.

Casper raised his voice. "Our scavengers have been ambushed, by someone who must have killed or knocked out the lookouts. Thirty or so men with guns and crossbows surrounded our people. They've captured the whole party alive."

Harold tried again. "Who has?"

Casper pointed at a weeping woman. "We don't know. Penny said there were no gang colours, which is why this might be a feint."

Harold turned to her. "Penny? How come they missed you?"

The young woman sniffled and blew her nose, keeping her eyes on the ground. "I'm sorry. I went to the loo in a house while the rest moved on to scavenge the next ones. While I was stood out of the wind, fastening my coat back up, gangsters appeared from everywhere. There was one short burst of gunfire, then nothing but voices." She shuddered and glanced up at Harold, then back down again. "One came right past but didn't see me. I'm sorry, I'm armed but I just hid." A glance told Harold she meant a machete, not a firearm.

Harold patted her gently on the shoulder. "Well done. Exactly the right thing to do if the rest had to surrender. Who is getting ready?" The last was to Casper but the answer came from behind.

"I am, with mostly Demons and a few others. I've got twenty, including the ten best shooters. They've all brought their crossbows." All Patty's Demons made it a point of honour to be above average crossbow markswomen.

"I've got a score of the Riot Squad here from mine and Doll's squads, taken from the walls so they're already fully armed and ready to go. Casper has sent people to roust replacements." Alfie stood ready as well, including a spear slung across his back. Doll came up behind him, still strapping on her armoured vest.

Harold thought it might be too late for a reaction anyway. "Weren't they in motors?"

"It was very quiet out there, so we'd have heard them a long way away." Penny seemed certain, and that meant the captors and captives were on foot. The cycles could travel at three or maybe four times walking pace.

"They'll be headed for their motors." Harold said it but others were thinking the same from their eyes, and the surge to get on the cycles. The Orchard Close motors were kept outside the side wall but blocked in with a car that had no engine. That had to be heaved aside first, which took time. Even then, the engine noise would warn the attackers long before they got close, but the cycles wouldn't.

"We have to get moving." Patty already had a cycle and her Demons were mounting up behind her. "We'll radio after we start shooting, but not before. No point in warning the scroats." Harold gave Emmy his Blaser, so she passed her rifle on to another decent shooter. Ten of those with crossbows took a carefully wrapped musket each in case they got close enough.

"Doll, you take the other squad because Alfie's leg might slow him up." Harold shook his head as Alfie started to object. "Sorry, but I'd rather have you on the wall with a shotgun or musket. Logan will take your 303. I'll keep a two-two for emergencies." Harold wished everyone luck and got out of the way of the cyclists. As the gates closed he set into making sure that Orchard Close were ready for any unwanted visitors. While heading indoors to load muskets out of sight, Harold remembered the spies. "Caddi's watchers! They'll report the cycles to the Mansion, over the radio, so the kidnappers will hear."

Casper scowled, glancing in the direction of the spies. "We did this once before, remember. As soon as Penny arrives I send guards to see them. Caddi's blokes won't be harmed, not unless they object."

"I'll explain properly afterwards and give them a beer." Harold sighed. "I'll remind them it isn't actually Caddi's territory, hopefully without winding the bastard up again."

"I know the drill. Don't poke the animals too hard in case they bite. Burying them would be cheaper in beer." Harold stared after Casper as the big man went to organise the newly arrived guards, chewing over that last remark. Having to put up with the constant provocation annoyed the hell out of Harold, but now the watchers were bugging Casper as well. He'd better have a little chat, before someone nipped down there one night and disappeared Caddi's men on a whim.

Loading muskets didn't take long, which left Harold pacing up and down and waiting. The scavengers had been over a mile away by road, on the new strip by the water. The cyclists would be going flat out, following Penny's tracks in the snow, so they could be there in four or five minutes. It would have taken the same for Penny to get here, and then at least another five minutes to get everyone ready. Fifteen minutes at least so the attacker might have marched a mile. Probably less with unwilling captives, especially if any were injured. How near would the gang have risked vehicles? Harold noticed Penny, sat on the kerb with her head in her hands. "Penny?"

Two swollen eyes in a tearstained face lifted to look at him. "I ran away and left them, Harold. Those nasty sods could be doing anything. To my friends. We swore we'd never let them near us again."

"It's a raid into hostile territory. They won't touch your friends until they think they're safe. With the tracks in this bit of snow the Riot Squad will catch them before then." Penny wasn't believing him. "Come with me and have a cuppa. You tell me everything you can remember about it, while I explain exactly why your friends are safe."

Harold took her home, where he found that the talking helped him through the waiting as well. After he'd gone through the situation and timings over a cup of tea, Penny finally accepted that her friends weren't in immediate danger. Harold, Tessa and Sharyn tried to persuade Penny that she'd done the right thing, that the chances of catching the raiders were much better this way. Because she'd hidden and cycled like a maniac to bring the alarm, help would arrive in time. Penny still wasn't convinced. Harold hoped her friends survived, or it would destroy the young woman.

Harold also tried to work out who'd launched the raid because thirty men wasn't a feral gang, sneaking around in the fringes of the claimed areas. There were absolutely no clues in the appearance of the gangsters when he questioned Penny. At least talking about it distracted them both as the minutes ticked by without a message.

Casper came to the door, beckoning Harold outside. "Radio, but not ours. It just said 'clear, bring the motors' so I'm guessing it was them."

"Patty and Doll will have heard. They'll push it." Harold checked his watch and Patty had been gone ten minutes. "The cyclists can't be far away now, and engine noise will help our people zero in."

"But can they stop cars?" Casper dithered. "Maybe we could risk trying to reach Roy and his men on the radio? Get them to move in from the other side?"

"I doubt the radio would reach him, and we daren't try yet. Don't worry, if Patty sees their cars, she'll stop them." Harold smiled, or maybe snarled. "Patty has twenty full metal jackets for her baby. New ammo, not reloads, so they'll go clean through a car. There's special rounds with all the other rifles."

Casper bared his teeth as well, then frowned. "Cripes, how much did they cost?"

Harold glanced warningly back towards Penny. "Plenty, but I had extra credit after all that Christmas trading. If Doll's people get close enough to hit with a Mad Max .50 pistol, they've got a few jacketed rounds as well. Those might even break an engine block, I reckon."

Despite looking more confident, Casper still fretted. "So we wait for gunfire."

"We wait for gunfire." Harold went back inside to tell everyone there wasn't a problem.

*　*　*

Over a mile and a half from Orchard Close, the tracks here and there, where the thin snow hadn't melted, were clear enough for the cyclists to follow them at top speed. Patty slowed as the woman out front swerved sideways and waved frantically. Bethany peeked around the stump of a wall, but almost immediately scurried back towards the rest, keeping to the side of the road. Patty dismounted to meet her halfway. "A hundred metres, maybe a bit less. They've stopped but everyone I saw is looking the other way. A couple glanced towards us but luckily after I'd got into cover."

Patty scowled. "Waiting for the motors." They both listened. "Which aren't here yet. What about our people?"

"Johan is favouring one leg and sort of hunched over. Most of the rest are sat and some are laid." Bethany shrugged apologetically. "I didn't wait to count them."

"He probably objected to how they are treating the women, bless him. How are they being held?" Patty glanced back and beckoned to Doll. Those with rifles and muskets were already splitting from the rest.

Bethany waited for Doll to join them. "As far as I could see, they're in one big group with guards round them. Everyone's hands are behind them so probably tied or handcuffed, but I didn't see which. There's not many long guns in sight but some are shotguns and it's open rubble from here to there. Not even a decent garden wall so we'd lose half the squad getting to the prisoners."

"We have to get close enough for blades, or they'll just use our people as human shields." Doll looked in the direction of the captives. "How long have we got?"

Patty glanced the same way. "A few minutes yet. We can't hear motors."

"We'll move out that way, towards the GOFS border." Doll waved to include her squad and pointed. "If we cycle down a road the other side of those ruins, we can dismount and form up once we're past. We'll set up the shield line across their retreat. Get ready to give them a volley when I click the radio. With luck, they'll run into us. Then even if they've got hostages we'll be close enough to use steel."

"Take five of mine, make sure you've got enough to do the job." Patty pointed to five who, despite complaining, gave up their crossbows. The recipients promised not to waste the bolts.

One had a valid concern. "What if they click before Doll does?"

"They start dying earlier." Everyone who heard seemed happy with that.

Bethany still hesitated. "What if the cars arrive first?"

Patty called Logan over. "We'll be shooting at long range, so give Doll the Mad Max .50." She turned and looked over Doll's people. "Harold said they might stop an engine so let's find out. They've got a hell of a kick, but Henry for one has the wrists for it." Quick words followed while weapons were moved across to Doll's squad, including four more pistols and several spears. The shooters would be relying on long range this time, but had Rambos if it got messy.

As Doll's squad raced away on their bikes, Patty and fifteen shooters filtered into the ruins overlooking the open ground. One by one they found a concealed position with a clear view of the targets. Patty inspected the clump of dejected prisoners and their laughing, joking captors, then crawled down the line giving each shooter their target. Every enemy already holding a rifle or shotgun had to go down in the first volley. There were nine targets so Patty chose one for each of the eight with rifles. She chose a primary target for the five crossbows, to double up for the least accurate firearms, telling them to use their second crossbow on anyone with a long gun who didn't go down. That wouldn't include her target, the ninth man, nor Emmy's and Ru's at this range.

Ninety yards was borderline for real accuracy with a crossbow, but these women practiced relentlessly and were very good. The heavy, cranked crossbows could throw a bolt much further, but it took dedicated practice to hit a man at this range. Conversely, the same range meant point blank for the rifles, or at least for a chest shot. Patty took aim at the man with a double barrelled shotgun, just below his neck. She hoped to hit his spine so he didn't get off a reflex shot. Emmy and Ru would do the same.

Patty heard the motors approaching, but very faintly and she hesitated. Doll might want to let them into the trap. Not too bad if each vehicle only had one driver, but still a risky increase in the enemy numbers. A click sounded on her radio. Patty breathed, called "Shoot" without moving her eye, and stroked the trigger. The man dropped without a twitch as Patty jacked another round into the Winchester, swinging the barrel across to find someone aiming this way.

More men produced firearms but only the three rifles with magazines and the spare crossbows could respond. One's head exploded so Emmy had noticed him, and another went down with three feathered shafts in him. The big 303 roared again, throwing a kneeling gangster into the wall behind him. Patty dropped a man with a half-drawn pistol, a chest shot that knocked him over backwards. Some of the men who'd fallen were now trying to get into cover, only wounded. "Get down Johan, everyone!" Patty put another man down but ducked as return fire spat out. She fired twice at a man who had gone down, but recovered enough to pick up his rifle. He fell, and this time stayed still. Emmy would have emptied her clip by now but some of the single-shot rifles cracked a second time. More men staggered, wounded, or fell while others were scrambling into cover. Logan pinned those gangsters with a hail of heavy rounds from the 303, sacrificing accuracy for volume as he worked through the spare clips.

Patty thumbed in fresh rounds, her mouth curving into a smile as two loud cracks echoed from behind the kidnappers. A man raised his head to look backwards. Either Patty's shot or someone else made sure he never raised it again. Voices among the gangsters were shouting back and forth now, arguing, and some were definitely panicking. Those shooting at Patty's squad faltered as the crackle of pistol fire rang out behind them. Engines were gunned, suddenly and shockingly loud before one of the Mad Maxes sounded a second time, followed quickly by the other.

Shouting and screaming masked some of the engine noise now as a second volley of crossbow bolts lashed out. Patty's shooters tried to kill anyone with a firearm, but some were using the prisoners as cover. Then the engine noises started to move away! As their transport retreated most of the gangsters facing Patty panicked, breaking contact to chase them. Easy targets but the shooters had to deal with those still shooting back. The gunfire over towards the cars slowed, then stopped as the drivers pulled out of pistol range.

"Come on, Demons!" As the last of the men facing this way crumpled, Patty came to her feet and started running. She wanted to catch up with the fleeing gangsters because some still had crossbows or had snatched up firearms. Either would go through Doll's shields, especially at close range. Patty could see three still cranking crossbows, but most of the shooters came with her. There wasn't time to wait. A wounded man reared up from the ground as she ran closer, pistol raised. Patty fired from the hip, slamming him back down. Ahead, gunfire sounded briefly, followed by the clash of steel as the screaming and shouting started. Patty swerved to avoid a melee, seven or eight people with their hands tied were kicking or stamping on someone on a stretcher.

A bullet plucked at her jacket, clipping the metal plates. Patty staggered, fired again from the hip and kept going. Accuracy wasn't great like that, but it didn't matter at these ranges. The man doubled up, eyes wide in pain and shock but still alive so Patty shot him again and he spun away. She kept running, thumbing in rounds because she wasn't sure how many she'd fired. Ahead Patty saw a melee she daren't shoot into, spreading out across the road. One man looked back, saw the Demons coming, broke away from the crowd and ran. Patty stopped, slowed her breathing and nailed him. The man went to his hands and knees so she put a round through his chest, side to side, and he collapsed.

The gunfire from behind panicked the gangsters trying to break the shield wall. They faltered and tried to disengage, Dolls' fighters charged, and suddenly it was all over. Even as Patty thumbed more rounds into her rifle the last few gangsters scattered. They didn't get far as those with a crossbow bolt or round up the spout targeted them, ably assisted by any of Doll's squad who still had ammo in their pistol. Patty stopped where she was, reloading the Winchester, because her legs had gone. They felt like jelly and her arms were jumping and shaking. Cripes, she'd just shot at and maybe killed half a dozen people! Patty's stomach roiled and settled, and her head cleared.

It had been like that last time, all hell and damnation and then reaction to survival, but she'd recovered faster this time. Patty straightened, looking around. Three were being sick and a couple were dancing in a circle, arm in arm. Others just looked shocked, were crying, or were staring around a bit vacantly. Doll looked pale but raised a hand in greeting and managed a smile. Patty wasn't sure what her return attempt looked like. She felt her smile strengthen because they'd done it!

Victory wasn't without its cost. A cry of distress rang out behind, because not all of the erstwhile prisoners were getting up. Further back what had to be one of her Demons lay in a crumpled heap. Another sprawled nearby with a crossbow bolt right through her throat. Patty looked over at the Riot Squad again. Some of the still figures weren't gangsters. Bethany sat holding her bloody head, her helmet gone, while others were nursing wounds or hunched in pain.

Her radio clicked. Cripes, she'd forgotten! "Patty here. We got them, but we've taken casualties."

"We'll send help." Harold had answered personally, he'd probably heard the shots and would be having a kitten.

At least that thought made her smile a little. "No, it's not too bad." Patty looked around again. "There's nobody left to bother us." Tilly waved, pointing, and a car engine started. "We've captured transport for the badly wounded."

"Keep us notified. We'll have a squad ready." A pause followed before Harold continued, and Patty could imagine him bracing himself for the bad news. "Badly wounded? Are you all okay?" He had to mean alive.

Patty remembered the radios were very public. "Near enough. Tell you all about it in private."

"Good enough. Hurry home and thank everyone, please."

Everyone swung round as a rattle of gunfire sounded from the direction the cars had gone. Some pistols, but with four spaced rifle shots. Patty relaxed. "Roy, or maybe the GOFS sentries by the water."

"I might even kiss him, bloke or not, if he got one." Fergie didn't look at all kissable just now, spattered in blood with a big bruise coming up on her cheek, but at least she raised a couple of smiles.

"Celine will sort that out." This laughter seemed a bit less forced. Tilly whistled from the cars, beckoning for more drivers. Two of the stopped cars were leaking fluids, the front one and one that had started to move up alongside. The front door hung open on the second, with a hole through it and a body sprawled behind.

Doll gestured as Patty came closer. "Hiding behind the car door looks good in the films. The Mad Max went straight through." The five cars behind had broken headlights, starred windshields and one driver lay sprawled out of an open door. "The cars only had drivers, but I didn't want to risk letting them in. I didn't want them used as cover." Doll gave a short mirthless laugh. "Or not as it happens."

A quick glance round and Patty agreed. "Good call, it kept our casualties down. Any idea who it was? I don't think we took any prisoners back there."

"No, still no idea." Doll glanced back at the cluster of bodies. "I don't think anyone here will be answering questions. Some of this squad were a bit hesitant to start with, and then a few went the other way. Some of that is overkill." Her wan smile held a bit of embarrassment. "I went a bit Mad Max, never mind the gun, and then realised what I'd done." Patty noticed the amount of blood spatter on Doll's sabre and arm.

Emmy limped up, a rough bandage around her calf. She gestured to it. "The scroat was faking, only wounded. He tried to hamstring me. Terri is back there. She looks bad and Martha is dead with a crossbow bolt through her throat. One of the prisoners, Isla, is dead as well, and two are wounded. The wounded might be friendly fire but Isla had to be deliberate, she was laid down. At least we got whoever did it, because I can't see any survivors." Emmy's hands were trembling slightly as she wiped her machete on a gangster's jacket. "A few were killed several times, because I for one didn't take any chances after my leg. It's my first time hand to hand like this, with machetes instead of clubs. I'd like to get someplace to sit down."

"The same applies to most of us." Patty held up the radio. "Harold says to get home and then we can all talk. That might be a good idea. Nobody looks good." At least half were sitting down now, while others were wandering around in some sort of daze. Some were tending the wounded, but the rest needed something constructive to stop them dwelling on what they'd just done. "Is Ru all right?"

Emmy finally smiled properly. "Ru says she only had a knife the last time. A rifle makes killing the banchod much easier. She sent five people back with Logan to bring up our cycles but right now she's helping to bandage wounds." She glanced behind her, her grim expression back. "Johan reckons Karl died when the rest were captured. He wouldn't surrender. We'll pick him up on the way back, and the lookouts because they had to have been killed as well."

Doll grimaced, then pointed up the road. "Tilly has taken some of ours to check the motors and throw bodies out of those that still run. She's hurting from a slashed arm, but says work will take her mind off the pain." More engines started up, before two cars moved towards them. One stopped again until Henry's mace smashed the starred windscreen. Another windscreen shattered outwards as a third car started forward, leaving a body sprawled in the road. "Let's load up our people, and the weapons, and get home."

* * *

The rescued and rescuers drove, walked and cycled slowly home, with a detour to collect the dead lookouts and Karl's body. One of the leaky mo-tors, one hit by a Mad Max rifle round, only managed to get halfway before it seized up. The wounded were moved across to the other three vehicles, an estate car and two hatchbacks, which made it all the way to Orchard Close. The nine Orchard Close dead were laid across the roofs. That wasn't respectful but nobody wanted to leave them until later. The badly wounded needed the insides of the cars, while some with lesser wounds had to be pushed along on bikes.

Patty lost one Demon, Martha, and two of her wounded were serious. Three of Doll's squad were dead. The three scavenger squad sentries had been found with four crossbow bolts in each of them. Karl had been killed because he was a gunslinger. When the attackers appeared he'd reacted with a quick-draw, shooting three men before going down. He'd killed one, and another had been carried by the prisoners. The prisoners kicked their burden to death when they got the chance. Isla had been shot out of sheer bloody nastiness, or maybe because she'd been shouting for everyone to get down.

Patty and Doll walked by Emmy, pushing her on a bike because of the slash in her calf. Before long Patty stopped pushing, walking hunched over where the bullet had glanced from her vest and torn off two washers. There wasn't any blood, but the pain promised she'd have a hell of a bruise. The three of them chewed everything over on the slow hike home, mainly to keep themselves functioning. Patty's shooters had ruthlessly targeted any kidnapper with a gun or crossbow. The Gunslingers in Doll's squad had done the same with pistols, before the running gangsters could reply accu-rately. Despite that, all the dead and three out of four of Patty's wounded had been hit by either bullets or crossbow bolts. Doll's squad had nine wounded, but only four by blades or maces because nobody was counting bruises or even small cuts.

The Riot Squad shield line were hit by a hail of bullets, luckily an inac-curate hail as the drivers were more interested in escaping. The Gunslingers had emptied their guns at the cars and had to reload and retarget in a hurry when the rest arrived. Despite their inexperience, the formation had proved to be murderously efficient once metal met metal. The gangsters finally hitting the shields had bounced, more or less. Doll conceded the gangsters were panicking by then, and outnumbered.

Once the returning fighters came into sight of Orchard Close, a score of armed figures drove towards them, headed by Casper. They left their vehicles for the wounded, switching for cycles before setting off for the fight scene. Casper had explicit orders from Harold, to strip every corpse naked and slit its throat. Any fuel from the broken vehicles would be salvaged before torching them. Everything useful would come back to Orchard Close, the rest would go on the blaze. Harold wanted nothing left but dead meat, and they'd get round to burning that in time. Casper had a camera phone to take pictures, because Harold would be asking questions and sending a message to the neighbours.

When Casper came back, his party, many of them women, had cut the nuts and ears off the dead gangsters to send a better message. At least none of them had started a necklace. Casper reported that the rifle fire had been Roy and his men. They'd seen the shot-up vehicles fleeing towards the Barbies and opened up. Roy managed to shoot two drivers so they'd captured the cars, while the other men thought they'd hit cars at least. Unless Harold objected, Roy would keep one car as their taxi for weekends, at least until its fuel ran out. A few of the GOFS lookouts had taken pot-shots according to Roy, and he'd heard more shooting a bit later.

Patty, Doll and Emmy were quickly debriefed in the big house, before Harold, Tessa and Sharyn went to the canteen with them to talk to the rest of the fighters. Some of the fighters needed to talk more, some needed beer, and some needed a sleeping pill for a night or two. The worst affected of the women went to the Girl Club for serious sympathy and chocolate, while Harold dealt with the men. Casper complained nobody wanted a man-hug, which finally raised some smiles. Penny didn't smile, she blamed herself for Isla dying.

*   *   *

Harold couldn't work out who to blame. He'd like to pick on the Hot Rods, or Geeks, or the two combined. Within days the pictures Casper took were transferred to the neighbours' phones, using Bluetooth. Harold even offered a reward for identification, but none of the faces were recognised. Between that and the direction the cars retreated, towards the Barbies, Harold had to keep an open mind. That or he had to cross Barbies and Pink Panther territory to get at the General, not exactly practical.

Whoever it was had lost forty-one fighters or drivers and their weapons, including the two Roy killed, a serious setback to most gangs, but no rumours surfaced. The GOFS were pissed off because the cheeky sods had driven through back roads on their territory. Gofannon sent a message that he'd be talking to the Barbies to try and stop any repeats. He also thanked Roy, because his shooting diverted the escapees just far enough for the GOFS to nail three more. A message from Malibu let Harold know the Barbies were interested in the trespassers as well, lethally interested.

Those in the fight had a rough time but seemed to move on and past, helped in part by being successful. The wounded fighters were spoiled by the relieved ex-prisoners. Big Johan, in particular, cheered people up with juggling and awful jokes, the same ones he told the children. Penny had a bad time over Isla dying, but her friends had all made it and were very grateful. The smaller wounds soon healed, and Lenny confirmed the deeper ones would heal eventually.

One of the wounded died, while two Demons and two other fighters were partially crippled and retired from the Riot Squad. All four swore they could still stand on the wall and throw bombs if necessary. Six of the fighters asked to stand down. They'd load guns and throw bombs, even shoot muskets if necessary, but they couldn't handle hand to hand. Harold was agreeably surprised by how few felt that way. In contrast, he felt sure the eight prisoners who had kicked the wounded gangster to death were now blooded, at least enough to shoot a live person. Ten pyres burned one evening, and the ashes were scattered in the exclusion zone. This time the sergeant didn't raise any objections, and the Army squad from the guard post lined the edge of the overpass, standing at attention. The January dance proved to be a very subdued affair, more of a drawing together against the world than exuberant celebration.

Harold had a terse message from Caddi about kidnapping Hot Rods. Instead of telling him to get stuffed, which several people advised, Harold repeated the previous explanation and heard nothing more. A few of the Hot Rods, after a couple of beers, let slip there'd been a blazing argument between Caddi and Mercedes. Nobody dare go near enough to the house to hear what they said, but most Hot Rods assumed he'd stopped her visiting 'Arold. Harold wondered if she'd wanted to visit the hospital again.

Scavenger hunts recommenced, but with a stronger, heavily armed escort, and scouts were sent out before they moved to another section. As the actual horror receded a little, it was replaced by a quiet pride in their success, and a determination to do better next time. Riot Squad training redoubled, because when the evenings lightened, Caddi's spies would be able to see them so they would have to cut back. By then every fighter wanted to be ready for the next time. They all expected a next time, sooner or later.

* * *

Well to the north, the General didn't feel anything like pride. "You stupid fucking prick! Julius fucking Caesar? Dickhead wanker, more like. Forty-four fucking fighters, sensible ones, not Patton's fucking lunatics, and thirteen motors. Not to mention the wounded ones, and a shitload of weapons and ammo. Why shouldn't I stick your head on a pole outside the door as a hint to the others?"

The man standing at rigid attention looked pale but he didn't back off. "I did what you asked. You said you wanted to know how those pretty ranks stood up to a real fight, nose to nose, because you'd only seen them shooting on the TV." Julius gestured towards the third man in the room. "Rhys wanted a couple of Orchard Close residents to question. He told me about the scavenger parties, and sent a couple of men to watch them. Then we planned this. We still don't know how they did it, trapped our men."

"They shot the fuck out of the cars, and then presumably everyone else because all I've seen of them is this." The General tossed a phone onto the desk and Julius looked at the picture. He winced before passing it to Rhys.

Rhys took a longer look, flicking through them all. "Melee wounds as well as bullets and crossbows, before the mutilation I mean. That answers one question, they can fight up close. Our men weren't amateurs but my reports say Orchard Close only lost ten, five of them before their fighters arrived. The winner's wounded survive and the loser's don't, but even so that's impressive even from ambush. It means those pretty ranks didn't break." The spymaster looked grim as he shrugged. "I still don't know how the hell they managed to get enough people in position, not quietly enough to spring that bloody ambush. I will, but now I'd like more time to get information on Orchard Close. Judging by this, our ally Caddi has been a long way from truthful. I was never convinced they were all limp-wristed posers or girls pretending to be fighters, no good without their rifles, but now I'm worried. How long have I got?"

"As long as you need." The General had calmed down a bit. "We still need a couple of months for all the wounds to heal after the SIMS fight, and judging by that mess I'll need everyone fit when we hit Orchard Close. With luck, Caddi will have finished dicking about with the Murphies and can join us. Then we'll run right over them, pretty ranks or not."

"You've got the Pinkies and the Barbies? Christ, that's good news."

"No Julius, but the Pinkies have realised just who the scary bastard is around here, and that it isn't those dykes. Better still, that SIMS woman is well enough to build rockets now, or tell us how they're made and aimed. She won't give us the recipe for the propellant, which is smart of her, but she'll make the shit up if we give her the ingredients. I've persuaded her that's a better life than becoming a Bloods fuck-bitch." A nasty smile spread across the General's face. "Once we are ready to go, I reckon those rockets will persuade the Barbies to see reason. They'll also rip holes in that big brick wall around Orchard Close." He closed his hand as if crushing something. "Then I want a few minutes with that Soldier bastard."

"I'll find out what I can about the defences. It's bloody crazy. I could walk in there and have a pint in their pub, a pub for God's sake, but even the regular visitors can't work out how many can shoot, or who fights. I can see the wall, but can't get near it to see how strong the bloody thing is." A grin split Rhys's face. "Cadillac still reckons he's got a key to the front door."

"Make sure he doesn't use it, or not until I'm ready to walk through the gate with him." The General turned to Julius and let him off the hook. "All right Julius, I accept your idea had merit. A word of warning. Your next idea had better work, because merit isn't enough if all I get is that." He gestured at the phone. "No more adventures. The next time we put fighters in there, it's in force." Julius was smart enough to salute and leave without a word. Once out of sight he stopped and leant against a wall for a moment, heaving a big sigh of relief.

Rhys remained, producing a sheaf of reports to discuss with his boss. "If Cadillac won't play, I can maybe get you some more men. Real, experienced fighters, but there'll be a cost."

"Mercenaries? Maybe, if they're good ones. They can go in behind the bullet magnets, then Julius and his men can clean up." The General held his hand out for the notebook Rhys held. "How much?"

"Not coupons. This one wants a deal. He'll loan you up to a hundred and fifty real fighters, short-term. In return you loan him the same number for a similar time." Rhys braced himself because the General wouldn't like this bit. "He's called The Last Prophet, and his gang are the Children of Cain."

"A fucking loony-tune? I'm not teaming up with some bugshit bastard and his religious fanatics." The General stared at his spymaster, baffled.

"You should know better." Alarm flared in his eyes. "Shit, how near is he? The last thing I need is a religious enema while we're dealing with Orchard Close."

"Calm down. He's north of the motorway, and needs help to kick an alliance of gangs out of a big park. Maybe the bloke is bugshit, and his men are definitely fanatics, but more the Bloods type of fanatic than churchy. If they come here, lock up your daughters, goats, and probably your grandfather." Rhys laughed, deliberately, to calm the gang boss down a bit. "We can send our lunatics to help his once they've done their job, or keep his here. Patton would love them."

"I'll want a lot more information because I'm not keen. Religious nuts don't think like real people." The General handed the notebook back. "We'll want to know more anyway, because he could be a problem eventually."

* * *

Harold and Orchard Close would be better prepared to deal with violent problems after Dealer's visit on the tenth of February. This time Harold didn't buy much propellant, but might the next time. He'd have credit because Dealer produced another AK and a smaller automatic, apparently an Uzi, for repair, but warned they were the last of the urgent ones. There'd still be a steady trickle of repairs, but not automatics or poser weapons at inflated prices. Some of the shortfall could be made up by selling thick white rabbit fur, because once he'd seen some, Dealer wanted all he could get.

Harold took his payments this time in a new line of very expensive merchandise, antibiotics. The Barbies charged horrendous prices and never parted with very much at one time, so Orchard Close never had enough. Dealer only offered after Harold asked about inoculations for rabbits, and after some searching questions about the Orchard Close medic. Lenny's paramedic qualifications, and details on the level of trauma Orchard Close had handled, led to Dealer offering a limited range of medical supplies. Harold took a flier and asked about dental anaesthetics for Gayle, because she'd more or less run out. Once he'd confirmed that the dentist had real training, Dealer promised to source some but warned they would be expensive.

That prompted Harold to ask if Dealer's men needed treatment, because he hadn't heard of another dentist. Dealer assured him they'd got medical treatment organised, but he'd bear it in mind. David promptly offered to come to Orchard Close if he got a toothache, but only if Patty wore a nurse's uniform. Patty laughed and said she might once he'd been strapped into the chair. Then she laughed again when David made a big play of considering that before agreeing, providing she personally tied him down. On the way back up, Patty claimed she'd just had a bit of fun, because she knew the bloke wouldn't be allowed inside the gates. Harold had started wondering if Patty was getting serious, because Orchard Close would let any visitor in if he disarmed.

Lenny and Patricia were overjoyed with the antibiotics, and the possibility of other medical supplies, but Harold swore them to secrecy over the source. He'd got to the stage he didn't know who he'd sworn to secrecy over what and Doll was right, it had got out of hand. The fighters were supposed to keep some weapons concealed, but the last fight meant forty of them saw the Mad Maxes, sabres, all the shooters, and some saw the Winchester. People were relaxing around the Barbies and GOFS, so the visitors would probably pick up hints. Harold conceded, privately, that both those gangs probably had more idea of what went on than he liked.

The roads cleared again and business at The Pub picked up, mainly GOFS to start with. Within days several Barbies and then a few Hot Rods managed the trip. The GOFS pub visitors mentioned that the Hot Rods were buying machetes, big swords and crossbows again. Another flurry of work arrived from Caddi but none were captured weapons, so the Hot Rod boss was only getting his own firearms in tip top order.

Caddi bought more maces and Rambos and parted with coupons to do so, but Mercedes didn't visit. According to ET, Caddi had gone crazy about the New Year visit but not to her. Even ET didn't know what the later row had been about. Caddi definitely kept Mercedes busy, scouting around the edges of the Murphy lines and behind them if possible. The GOFS and Barbie visitors admitted their leaders were nervous in case Caddi switched targets. Despite that, both gangs were poised to grab a Murphy estate or two when the gang folded.

*　*　*

Early on Valentine's Day, the Hot Rods confirmed they were attacking someone. The squads scrambled to man the walls around Orchard Close when Caddi turned up with a big convoy, and hoped it wasn't them. Most relaxed when Mercedes climbed out of her Jeep, strolling through the slush to the gate while the rest turned their vehicles round. Harold went outside to greet her. Despite relaxing, the Orchard Close fighters still watched the convoy with crossbows and firearms ready. After all, Caddi might have picked a traditional time for a massacre.

Mercedes smiled happily when Harold came through the gate, and her eyes were warm and reassuring. If Caddi planned mischief then Mercedes didn't know. From the grins on the faces of the Hot Rods, Harold wondered if they would actually shoot with her in the line of fire. It would be terminally stupid of Caddi to shoot his Killer Queen just before a battle, painfully stupid if Mercedes survived. Harold relaxed as well.

Mercedes wore boots of course, but the rest hid under that long coat, fastened up to her collar again. As she slowly licked her lips before bending for the bottom fastener, Harold began to wonder just how little she might be wearing. Then he remembered the wall behind him, lined with interested spectators.

A lot of leg came into view as those nimble fingers worked upwards. Not as much leg as when Mercedes wore shorts, but the slightly flared black skirt definitely classed as mini. Her tight white blouse, with a row of tiny buttons up to the throat, broke her usual dress code. No bra games today. There again, the big red heart on a chain round the young woman's neck gave a definite message. Mercedes opened her coat wide before coming closer, almost close enough for contact.

"Happy Valentine's Day, 'Arold." Mercedes glanced down at her blouse and up at the gates and guards, before murmuring, "Not today." Harold looked over her shoulder and Caddi didn't see the joke any more. The warlord looked impatient, but Mercedes wasn't being hurried. "I don't think you need to ask any more, 'Arold." Her smile, and a little wriggle of her hips, were a clear indication of what Harold didn't need to ask.

Her coat opened wider than their shoulders at the moment, so his hands went inside and Harold got a firm hold of the back of her skirt. "Like this?"

Mercedes made a small, impatient noise. "Not on the skirt, 'Arold. What did you usually ask, back when you still had to?" While Harold processed that, Mercedes let go of the coat sides, slid her hands up round Harold's neck, squished herself up against him and her mouth came up.

She delivered another of those kisses. Long, slow and brain-melting and part of the effect was that it was just the same as the last one. Not a crushing, heavy, tongue down the throat job, but hot wet lips working very slowly and thoroughly. Even as Harold's brain turned to mush, he finished processing her last words. His hands went down a bit and up, because the question had always been if Harold could put his hands on her ass, not her clothes!

Even as soft, smooth skin slid under his hands, her lips pressed a little harder and Mercedes gave a little moan. Harold's mouth muffled the sound and the coat covered what Harold did, but the combination nuked Harold's brain. He wasn't sure if anything covered her long slow writhe against his front as both his hands found and stroked her thoroughly commando ass. Stroked for a long, long time, as far as his somewhat confused recollection could work out later.

Eventually they had to breathe, or at least Harold did, and very heavily once he had a chance. Mercedes also looked a bit breathless and very happy. As they parted Harold carefully slid his hands back down and up onto the miniskirt, which earned him a small pout. Harold nearly grabbed Mercedes again because she was the girl in the bathroom, with dancing eyes and mouth stretched in a triumphant smile. Instead, Mercedes sighed and the sparkle dimmed as she raised her voice, loud enough for the Hot Rods to hear. "Sorry about the buttons, 'Arold. Maybe you should have checked by hand." Harold looked at the blouse and back up.

He raised his voice as well. "When I check under there, the buttons are coming undone first!" A cheer sounded from behind him before Mercedes twirled so the gangsters could see the joke. Some ruder hilarity followed from the Hot Rods. Caddi looked pissed off now, and obviously wanted this over, but his men loved every minute so the warlord kept his mouth shut.

Mercedes held the coat closed and did a little shimmy. "Hmm, Soldier Boy went off the reservation a bit there." Harold watched the Killer Queen play them and it worked. The Hot Rods were now wondering how far Soldier Boy had wandered. "I think he's about ready."

Mercedes left another pause for the suggestions on what Soldier Boy might be ready for. Harold appreciated how nicely the ones from behind were put, in stark contrast to those coming from the Hot Rod convoy. "Don't worry boys, the commando betting will be settled next time. I don't think I can hold out any longer. I'll hang them out the window so you can all see what he's been ruffling." Mercedes did another shimmy as she pretended to get her underclothes straightened.

She turned back. "Got to go now, lover boy. Hang this over your bed and I'll come and get it when we're done." The chain with the red heart came off over her head and Mercedes took the two steps back to slip it over Harold's head. Her hands stayed behind Harold's head for long moments, but this kiss stopped too soon. Much too soon when a hot tongue gently licked Harold's lips as their kiss finished. "To keep the memory warm," probably wasn't loud enough to be heard elsewhere. Harold watched Mercedes walk back down the access road, one finger pointing out what he should be watching as it gave some extra wiggle.

Holding the coat closed with a hand, Mercedes reached into the jeep and came out with a bag. She headed for the nearest empty house, the ruined one used for trading with Dealer. "Now you know why I need to change before we go Spud-bashing." Caddi scowled because she obviously aimed the remark at him. A few minutes later Mercedes came out dressed to kill, literally this time.

Mercedes wore two handguns, one in a Tomb Raider thigh holster over her jeans, a Rambo, and two smaller pre-Crash sheath knives on her belt. A bandolier of shotgun shells hung over the shoulder of her short leather jacket and the thick plaid shirt beneath. The shotgun would be in her Jeep. Harold would bet on at least one more blade in one of her mid-shin boots, ones with low heels today. She bundled up the coat, throwing it into the Jeep before turning towards Harold. "So you can practice the buttons," she called, handing a small parcel to a youth. "Better get working on them. I'm in the mood to finish this quickly!"

A rousing cheer from the Hot Rods followed the youth as he trotted up the road to give it to Harold. He had to run even faster back down, because Caddi started the vehicles moving. The warlord shouldn't be scowling, because Mercedes had just done wonders for troop morale. She'd got every Hot Rod wound up, cheering and keen as mustard, and Orchard Close were cheering them as well!

Harold waved until the slim arm, stuck up out of the Jeep to say good-bye, went out of sight. He finally removed his stupid smile, turning round to meet a row of delighted faces. Sharyn took the bundle and unwrapped it a little to show both the skirt and blouse. "Do I need to check for knickers?" She laughed and continued quietly. "From your face probably not, or a bra. Mind you, it's chilly enough today for everyone to answer the bra question."

Tessa hooked an arm in Harold's. "Do I need to wear buttons so you can practice?" She prodded the clothing and sniggered. "I reckon she'd undo them herself anyway, if you asked." Harold didn't mind their teasing because it allowed him to get his head straight. It took some doing. Not just because of the kissing, but because now Harold had absolutely no doubts. Until now, despite everything, he'd harboured a tiny suspicion that Mercedes had been setting him up.

Telling him he could stick his hands up her skirt could still have been a come-on, a part of the relentless act. The reaction when he did meant Mercedes really did fancy Soldier Boy, or maybe 'Arold. Cripes, he'd better get spare pillows because judging by that, Mercedes would bite right through what he'd got. Unless she yelled instead. She'd suggested that once!

"Better get some new bedding." Harold stared because Sharyn appeared to be mind-reading. "If she bit you just practising, just think of the blood on the bed sheets after she visits!"

Tessa shook her head. "She means it, doesn't she?" Harold thought Tessa knew already, and just asked to get his take. "Women do look at a girl's eyes, dope."

"Yes, I wonder what happened to that sparkle." Sharyn must look at eyes as well.

"Who, most likely." Harold knew his voice showed he cared, and it didn't bother him with these two.

"What are you going to do?" Harold stared at Sharyn for a moment. What did she mean? Jump all over Mercedes wasn't the right reply to his sister. "After you bite off the buttons and Mercedes rips up the bed sheets, I mean, idiot. What if that smiling face doesn't keep the deal with Caddi, because she won't want to? That girl has found what she wants, though I'm sure I can't see why."

"Oh, he has his good points."

"Name one."

Harold tuned out the banter and tried to wrestle with it all again. It wasn't a certainty that Mercedes would break the deal. Yes it was, and Harold knew he didn't want her to keep it. A lot depended on Mercedes killing Caddi. An idea popped into Harold's head. What if he killed Caddi first? That shook him because Harold had never, ever, considered deliberately killing a man who wasn't a direct threat. Except Jon, who had already killed Sandy the carpenter and kidnapped Matti. Stalking a human and shooting him without warning, from ambush, didn't sit right. Harold had turned down a chance at sniper school just to avoid that.

Now he would, if it kept Mercedes safe. Two seconds thought told Harold he couldn't, not just now with the war on. He could shoot Caddi easily enough, from far enough away to escape afterwards, but every fighter in the Hot Rods knew Soldier Boy. Someone would recognise him while he tried to find Caddi in a war zone. Even if nobody saw him at the ambush, the sightings of Harold wandering about Hot Rod territory with a rifle would point the finger. Typical, he'd come up with the solution, but too late! The three of them were back in the house by now and Sharyn wanted to know what Harold's problem was, apart from hot lips? What the hell, Harold told her.

"Cripes. You mean that?" Sharyn looked a lot more shocked than Tessa, but then she knew about his reluctance to shoot people. "It would simplify things."

"I want to now I've finally thought of it, but I immediately realised it's impossible." Harold explained and the three of them sat for a long time with a mug of tea, chewing the situation over. Neither woman suggested throwing Mercedes to Caddi, or objected to cold-bloodedly killing the gangster. Somewhere along the line they'd both decided that whatever her other crimes and her public persona, Mercedes was at least partly a victim.

"Mercedes might kill Caddi. That would simplify things." Tessa wasn't even pretending to resent the 'other woman,' not any more. "She's smart enough to know that as well."

"So is Caddi." Harold scowled because Caddi's paranoia meant he'd kill her at the slightest hint of a double-cross. "I'm worried he'll strike first, but he'll leave it until the last minute. He's smart enough to want her killing Murphies and encouraging the Hot Rods as long as possible, because Mercedes is a psychological weapon." Harold paused, thinking about that. "Probably more that than killer now, because everyone will recognise her after parading through here so often. Any strange woman wandering around will be suspect, because every other gang knows how many Murphies she killed."

"Caddi won't care about how useful she is if he thinks Mercedes is ready to come here. From his display at the gate just now, the nasty shit won't wait until you've had your chance." Tessa sneered, but then looked more thoughtful. "Caddi trying to get his jollies might give her enough warning, or a chance at him. Mercedes won't need much."

Harold tried to work it out. "Mercedes will want the war over and won, so that the Hot Rods will fight over who controls the gang. She won't want the Hot Rods to choose a new leader quickly, in self-defence if the Murphies aren't finished. A strong leader might get full of himself, and think he had to avenge Caddi or some such bullshit."

"Maybe you'll have to take your rifle out anyway, to shoot Cooper, because he's the only one who will do that." Tessa raised her arms to mime shooting. "If Mercedes comes here, and Cooper turns up with the Hot Rods to demand her back, shoot the nasty little scroat right through the head. If Caddi arrives, shoot him and ask Patty or Emmy to shoot Cooper at the same time. The rest will probably go home."

"Patty already offered. She suggested shooting all the named ones in one volley. If it happened here, with Orchard Close lined up on our walls ready to fight, that might work. So until Mercedes turns up, I'd better get on with organising our defence." Harold smiled and stood up. "I'd better finish loading all the new brass, as soon as possible."

Tessa stood up and sighed. "An apprentice's work is never done." She brightened. "Unless someone else arrives and takes both my jobs?"

Sharyn had the last word. "Don't forget to practice buttons as well."

The rest of Orchard Close had got the message. The offers to walk Harold home after the Valentine's dance weren't even remotely serious, and Tessa toned the wench act right down. No kissing, a very chaste last dance, and she even suggested that Harold wore Mercedes' Valentine heart. That brought a lot of teasing, about inviting Mercedes to the next dance. Harold felt sure Sharyn and Tessa hadn't discussed it with anyone, but several men and women suggested shooting Caddi to break his deal.

In the following days Harold loaded ammunition, built muskets and taught sword fighting. The skirt and blouse were folded up in the chest of drawers in Harold's room. "Just in case you need to practice," according to Sharyn when she brought them in. The big red heart with 'Be My Valentine' went on Harold's wall, where he saw it when his eyes opened every morning. Harold had given up attempting to struggle, or even second guess.

* * *

Some chores couldn't be delayed, regardless of what else happened. Despite her limp, Emmy wielded her gardening whip. Trays of seeds, and small pots with green sprouts, spread through the conservatories as the gnomes swung into action. Hopefully there'd be enough clear space to plant them out to harden, despite Harold commandeering part of the protected garden. Within two days of the Hot Rod offensive, refugees began to pour in. Harold negotiated a score of big tents and forty sleeping bags from the Geeks and Barbies, and set them up in the enclosed area between the Annex and Orchard Close. The refugees were relatively safe there, but were occupying ground already prepared for seedlings.

The latest Hot Rods offensive turned into all-out, head-on war. Without Mercedes sneaking around at night, few people brought weapons. These refugees were running ahead of the final assault, bringing whatever they could snatch at the last minute. Not all of them had real instructions, just that a safe place lay to the east of the Murphies' northern border. The occasional runners with weapons always came across the fields, and those all had clear directions. A squad of GOFS brought a lost family, and Harold found out why the GOFS weren't stopping them. Gofannon had approached some and a few had accepted, but he didn't want anyone who wasn't willing. The rumours had been effective, most of the refugees were dead set on reaching Orchard Close.

Despite Mercedes' instructions, the gate guard had to send squads onto the neutral road to escort two obviously lost groups into Orchard Close. Caddi's watchers had been shepherding one group away towards the Mansion when Harold's squad arrived, so Harold had a chat to the gangsters. He reminded them that the road was neutral territory, so anyone coming up there should be let through. Otherwise, mishaps could happen to armed gangsters as well as unarmed refugees. For once Harold let the spies see how he really felt about them, and the message went home. Later refugee groups without precise instructions reached the gates unmolested, helped by the big signs at the traffic island saying 'Orchard Close' with an arrow. Another sign sat at the end of the access road.

Work accelerated on making the houses in the proposed new compound, the Farm, habitable. The work had to be finished before the seedlings came out of the cold frames and conservatories, so the tents could come out of the garden. Every inch of ground protected from rabbits would be needed for young plants, if Emmy was to grow enough food for the rising population. At least the myxomatosis had finally died back, and nobody had found a dead rabbit in the fields or ruins for over a month. According to Rabbit Bob, the remaining wild ones would be immune, but the tame ones still needed protecting.

Rob ran several connections from the nearest water main to the Farm, then started work on the small leaks that showed up inside the houses. Finn connected the electricity, but had to hook up the fourteen houses one at a time to stop the damp blowing the whole system out. At least they'd dried out a little over the winter, once the tiles had been fixed and blow heaters on extension leads installed. The joiners and willing assistants removed dry plasterboard from any ruin that still had some, to replace ruined internal walls. The few dehumidifiers in Orchard Close also spent the winter in the empty houses, with a rota set up for emptying them.

More bricks were brought in as the refugees cleared the surrounding land, and were placed in one big stack. Casper thought he still needed a few million more for a wall around the new complex, but until then he continued thickening the existing walls around Orchard Close. The guards in the boundary houses grumbled when he built a wall inside, because it narrowed the rooms by a metre. Casper and his bricky team laughed and told them to see Harold about his new fetish.

*　　*　　*

A regular stream of Barbies came to The Pub for the allegedly famous beer and soup. The women gangsters had mellowed further with more contact, and now they wanted to know if they could buy bulk beer to sell on to the Trainspotters and Pinkies. Beetch called by a couple of times, unofficially, without meeting with Harold. The rumour mill claimed she'd come for Logan to check her roots. Chandra didn't always visit to trade, sometimes she just visited Louise, while Ski bought Fergie a beer more often and started a campaign to be invited to a dance. Tessa thought it was the way Orchard Close treated them. The less manic Barbies could relax here, even if those three didn't quite class as less manic. Only their dress marked some of the other Barbies or GOFS out from local residents as they sat having their beer, chips or stew.

When Beetch and Ski visited officially, Harold assumed they'd come about beer, either bulk buying or training a brewer. Beetch arrived in the Embassy triumphant, because Casper had told Logan to search her. Ski wasn't as happy because neither Alfie nor Fergie were on duty, though that wasn't her first complaint. "How come madam here gets the invite to the posh house, and I only get this place?"

Harold smiled and shrugged. "Beetch came to breakfast. Maybe you could ask Fergie to invite you home for breakfast?"

"Would she?" Ski looked at the smiling faces and scowled. "She can't because she lives in a barracks." Her face lit up. "Could she visit me at Beth's? It would be cosier than the visitor's house here." Casper and Patty, with Louie and Tilly making up the guard numbers, all shrugged and tried not to smile too much.

Harold straightened his face. "What you actually came to ask is if we will train a Barbie to brew decent beer, pretty please, in return for another shopping trip."

Both looked surprised, then calculating. After a glance at each other, Beetch answered. "No, but if you'll consider it we'll throw another party at Beth's? Can we choose the guest list?" She glanced at Ski. "There's more than one who might offer breakfast."

"Maybe, possibly, not highly likely, and you'll have to promise not to sell anywhere else. After all, you'll stop spending your coupons here for starters."

"No we won't, or not all of us. There's side benefits, like The Pub. We couldn't open one, because as you know, we don't welcome visitors. We might open a very exclusive club, to persuade your army to invade again, as long as you stay for some pillage this time?" Beetch sounded totally serious, but Harold didn't think the top Barbies had mellowed that much. "Unfortunately, you might not be as keen to visit after we've finished our talk." Beetch looked at the guards. "No offence, but could we keep this to just you, Patty and Casper?"

"You can handcuff me to make everyone feel safer." Ski grinned at the groans.

"We can handcuff you anytime." Harold thought, but not for long. "Louie, Tilly, I'm sorry but what you don't know can't be let slip by mistake. Would you mind leaving us? Please stand in the corridor clear of the door to make sure nobody overhears."

"No problem boss." Tilly, still sporting a bandage from the last fight, beckoned to Louie and they left.

"Sorry, but we don't want to spread alarm and despondency and all that." Beetch hesitated, almost speaking a couple of times before shrugging. "What the hell, there's no nice way to dress this up. We think the Pink Panthers have signed up with the General. Maybe not completely voluntarily, but there's strangers over there now. Straight strangers, not gays."

"Cripes. He can strike straight at you, without any water in the way." Harold thought about what he'd seen of the outside of Beth's. "Can you hold him off?"

"We can hold Beth's for a long time, but we can't protect the estates. We've come here first, and we're calling on the GOFS on the way back. The Geeks will probably sit tight unless the GOFS and their flank are threatened. If we are attacked, will you help us?"

"Yes, that's the treaty. Get a message to us and we'll come with as much help as possible." Harold grimaced, because it wouldn't be as much help as he'd like. "But we can't strip this place too much because of Caddi. He might leave the rest of the Murphies to attack us, because we are definitely thetastier morsel." Both Ski and Beetch looked worried. "I'll come with our people, personally, so it won't be a token force." Both relaxed a little.

"Beth's will hold for several days, even if he throws the Pinkies in as bullet magnets with the Bloods right behind them. You saw how hard it is to get close, and with the height of the roof we can see exactly where an attack is going to hit. We can break the first one up earlier than expected and kill a shitload of them." Beetch hesitated, looking at Ski who smiled and nodded. "I don't suppose you'll be attacking us, not now you know how to open the door, so you may as well know. We've made three catapults. Nothing like as good as the Geeks version, but they're up on that roof so we've got a hell of a range." Her smile widened, definitely predatory. "After seeing the improved Geek version on the TV, we've been experimenting. Given a bit of time we'll make one like that."

It wasn't artillery that worried Harold. "Have you enough ammunition? We had to use a shovel to collect the empty brass after the Mart attack. What if the General ignores the catapults and just keeps throwing in more men?"

Beetch's smile turned downright savage. "Then you'll have no trouble wiping out what's left, because we'll slaughter them. There's not many ways into Beth's now, and we've got just the right people to heap bodies in those gaps. While they're milling around at the entrances, even bricks thrown from the roof will kill them." A little humour came back into her voice. "After your visit, we made a few improvements to the main entrance. Your threat to smash your way in wouldn't work now. The place looks the same, but if we see trouble coming?"

That didn't surprise Harold. "It only worked for me because we got so close first."

"As the actress said?" Beetch looked almost embarrassed, strange for a Barbie. "There's one other request, mainly for the GOFS. Will you let our tenants, the people on the estates, run for your borders?"

"I'll come with them, because allegedly I'm not as good at heaping bodies." Ski didn't look too happy with that.

"Good enough to earn a wig and name, and good enough to stop anyone messing with our tenants." Beetch turned back to Harold. "Ski will come to prove they aren't runners, or infiltrators, if that's all right?"

"I'm sorry, I truly am, but we can't house them. The place is full and I've already got refugees living in tents."

Sharyn butted in. "There's the Farm, the houses we're fixing up, but there's no heat or even electric in half the houses."

"They'll bring electric heaters, or sleeping bags and sleep outside if necessary. This is just so that bastard can't use them as human shields when his first assault bounces." Beetch hesitated again, very strange for a Barbie. "Bloody Cripes, we'll have no secrets left. The tenants will have plenty of warning because they all listen to Barbie Radio, and every estate has a transmitter to report strangers. That's why raiders always get caught. Everyone thinks we are nasty bitches who don't care if we kill our tenants, except you know better now, don't you?" Her humour dropped away again. "Believe me, we are definitely crazy and bloodthirsty in the right circumstances."

"Don't worry, I got that message." Harold glanced at Casper and Patty, who both nodded minutely. "Tell your tenants to move into anything with a roof and bring food. Hopefully it'll only be a few days, if the GOFS will join us and we hit the General from behind. I'll try to persuade Hawkins to come as well. I hope you'll come out to play, and not let us have all the fun?"

"We won't sit tight while you fight. If you hit them we'll join the party, then you'll see just why we got our reputation." Beetch relaxed, taking a long drink of her beer. "Thank God for that. Now if I could only be sure that bastard Caddi isn't planning to team up with the General. Hopefully they are both too bloody greedy."

"If Caddi gets too ambitious we've already got people waiting on the border. Not just for him, they're ready to snip a bit off the Murphies when they go down. They will stop any sneak attack if he comes for Beth's, and can retarget if he brings too many men this way. Oops, I shouldn't tell you that." Ski sniggered, completely unrepentant. "Except some of our idiots will have more or less told the barmaid or barman everything. It's sort of traditional. Speaking of which, can we take a brewer back in case it turns into a siege?"

"Naughty." Harold wagged a finger. "That needs a lot of thought, perhaps after Caddi gets done and all the dust has settled."

"Hah, you'll be too busy then, either screaming for mercy or pinning her down. Or both, she might go both ways. Want to borrow my handcuffs?" Ski grinned, putting a hand to her belt where she always carried them. "I'll ask Mercedes the same if I ever see her."

"No need, she's already got a ring through his nose." Patty shook her head in mock despair. "She seems as bad, so we're issuing earplugs and stocking up on bedding to replace the ripped stuff."

"Why don't you lovely ladies go and have a beer in The Pub? Then at least you can slander me in the traditional way, behind my back." Harold had started blushing, which just increased everyone else's fun.

"Good idea, then you can catch up on the gossip." Patty waved them towards the door. "I assume you'll let us know any developments with the Pinkies, or their new lord and master?"

"Oh yes, I'm sure we can convince someone to pop over." Ski smirked, heading for the door.

"Since Fergie is off duty, if you're quick you might catch her in The Pub." Patty smiled happily as Ski almost missed a step before walking a bit faster. Beetch paused to ask, with a gleam in her eye, when Logan came off duty. Casper promised to mention where she was having a pint.

While the Barbies relaxed, the squad leaders met with Liz in Harold's house to talk the whole situation through. Casper promised to hurry his wall thickening, in case the General left a holding force to pin the Barbies and GOFS and struck for Orchard Close with a lorry ram. They all agreed to leave telling the rest of Orchard Close until the Barbies had solid information. After some back and forth, everyone agreed Wellington would hit the General, but only if he went straight for Orchard Close. That would be from pure military necessity. Unfortunately, Beetch might be right about Hawkins not helping the Barbies out.

Within a week, Ski, Beetch and Chandra all called by on different days to confirm the General had taken over the Pinkies. A man called Rhys, who claimed to be his diplomat, had asked the Barbies to join as allies. He'd hinted at consequences if they didn't. The Barbies laughed at him, and explained that if he actually threatened them, only his picture would be going back to the General. They'd let him have pictures of some previous examples as a hint.

Chapter 22:
February

Precinct Nineteen:

While Orchard Close prepared to kill Bloods or Hot Rods, others were trying to save lives. The Zookeepers were rushed off their feet dealing with pregnant animals. They'd even got the boa pregnant at last, a bonus given the prices they'd been offered for snakeskin and the number of rats available to feed the young. Oddly enough, the nearby gangs were just as interested in the pregnant animals. None of them made the slightest move to interfere, which might have had to do with their future chances of both milk and meat. By now, the neighbours all knew the Zookeepers needed the animals to have young to keep the milk flowing, but couldn't raise all the piglets and calves. Most of them were saving coupons to buy a couple of young, something that could be fattened up.

* * *

Sutton Park:

The same type of work, and digging and planting, kept the allied gangs busy in Sutton Park. A little edge of worry ran through the leaders, because nobody had picked up any of Nosy's messages so there must be another spy. The leaders looked at their own people, and the neighbours, and finally concluded it wasn't one of the elite. After all, with one of them spying, the government—they all assumed it was the government—wouldn't have needed Nosy. Eventually the gang bosses concluded that whoever it was saw Nosy being captured by Asif. They kept their plans secret from the rank and file and relaxed. Relaxation became easier when the Last Prophet seemed to run out of steam. He'd stopped spreading, content to harass his neighbours now and then, and those neighbours were well away from Sutton Park.

Asif and his friends didn't relax at all, especially about the spy or spies.

One of their number had spent years in deep cover to break a terrorist organisation, so they knew what was possible.

* * *

Conan:

Elsewhere in the city, there wasn't any waiting or planning. Conan led his men over a barricade, coughing as he got a lung full of fumes. This was the second easy enclave, barely fortified and without properly trained fighters. He hadn't needed his spy or any fancy plans, the Barbarians had simply charged home under cover of a smoke screen. Conan's axe swung and a man spun away, blood arcing across the wall nearby. "Keep going, finish them now!" A figure dived out of a window and got a knife into the big, bearded figure, but he hammered the fist holding a pistol down on the bastard's head. The wound hurt like hell, but the plated jacket had stopped the knife before it did much damage. Conan plucked it out and blood gushed from the wound, too much blood! Conan stopped dead, trying to get his head round the fact some asshole had seriously injured him. Anger came to his rescue, got him back on balance. "I'll kill that fucking armourer."

Conan holstered his pistol and put a hand over the wound but blood trickled through his fingers. A man, a Barbarian, stared wide-eyed. "Keep going, kill any fucker that resists. It's just a scratch." The wound went much deeper than that, Conan knew, but he covered the blood and tried to hide the pain as he turned back from the battle. Where were the medics? He caught hold of a man as he ran past. "Where are the nuns?" The man pointed, wild-eyed, and Conan hoped the bloke actually understood the question. He strode quickly in the direction the hand had pointed, searching for the white van. He thought quickly. The men might panic if they thought he was down, or some twat might make a takeover bid while he was helpless. Conan called Garth on the radio, telling him to get to the medics but not mentioning a wound.

At least the ambulance stood out among the rubble and smoke, a bright white Luton van with big red crosses on the side. The nuns had sworn the defenders wouldn't shoot at it and they'd been right. The stupid bitches had wanted to keep close to the fighting, to save lives. Now Conan was pleased he'd agreed. He reached up, hammering on the back door until it opened. "Fix this, quickly."

The sister's face had tightened when she saw him, but now she pressed the control to raise the tail lift. "Come inside, quickly. Take off your jacket."

As the lift stopped for him to get off, Conan thought he saw a flash of calculation on the sister's face. He turned, looking for a Barbarian. "Hey, you!" The man stopped, staring at the blood on Conan's chest. "Get another three men, and be quick." The Barbarian nodded, turning and shouting to others. Conan took off his plated jacket while he waited, pointing at his chest while glaring at the nun. "Stop that for now. I'll lie down in a minute." She almost objected, then tore his shirt open, picked up a dressing and pressed it into place. The Barbarian leader turned back to the four armed men now standing just outside the van. "Watch her, and the others. If they do anything iffy to me, or if I die, take all the nuns from here and the hospital and give them to the men. Tell Garth when he gets here." He turned to the nun with a big smile. "That should encourage you."

* * *

Half an hour later Conan sat with his legs hanging out of the back of the ambulance, a big dressing taped across his bare chest. Garth had been back twice, probably hoping he'd been promoted to gang boss. Conan grabbed hold of a young novice and pulled her over onto his knee.

"Sir? I need all our staff to tend your wounded." Conan looked up at the sister, chuckling at her expression. The God-bothering bitch hated him but she stayed polite. Lamb of God or not, Conan reckoned she'd be first in line with a knife if she ever got the chance. Second in line, the Bitch would be first. Conan looked down at his wound, reassessing as he let the novice go back to her job. He'd better make sure he was out of danger before getting back to taming the Bitch. She'd stick her fingers in the wound and rip out his heart if she ever got the chance.

"Boss?" Conan looked up to find Garth waiting.

"Hard luck, I've survived." Conan looked beyond his second, out over the captured enclave. "Have they finished yet?"

"More or less. The fighting is done, or it is in here because they broke as soon as we got inside. Attila reckons some survivors have reached the next place. He wants to keep going, chase them, because there's fuck all defence facing this way. The place is like this one, easy meat, probably has no more than fifty or sixty fighters so it might be a good idea. Especially if we time it so our men are mixed in with runners from here?" Garth hesitated, because Conan sometimes reacted badly to anyone having an idea of their own. When the bearded man nodded, he pushed on. "If we force the serfs, especially women, to run in among our men it should work. The runners aren't stopping for searches but the defenders aren't shooting them."

"Tell him yes, but you are in charge." Conan beckoned, waiting until Garth bent close to him. "Tell Sylvester to shove his little pets in among them, and make sure some survivors escape to join the mob on at the other side." He laughed at Garth's curious look. "What you don't know you can't tell some bitch when you're pissed. Tell him, but not on the radio." Garth nodded, turning and trotting off to find the spy. He'd have to move fast to organise that because the Barbarians had to attack now, before the next enclave recovered. A little smile touched Garth's face. If it was rushed he'd get a chance to see who these spies were. Another of Conan's little secrets. One day, when he had enough of them....

* * *

When the time came, Garth didn't have any trouble spotting Sylvester's spies. A van had gone in almost with the fighters, pushing ahead of most of them, relying on the red crosses on the bonnet and sides. When Garth reached it the van only held a driver, one of Sylvester's men. By the time Garth fought his way across the enclave to the opposite wall, four nuns and a priest were running along among the rest of the survivors. He turned back to finish off the fighters, which let a few harmless-looking types get past him and escape. A few minutes later Garth cursed as he heard the radio. "Keep going, do it again. The runners are trampling the next lot of defenders. Come on, the twats can't shoot through the women."

"Attila, pull back. You haven't got the men. There's too many wounded and the rest are scattered all over." Even as he spoke Garth began to gather men, to try and stop the rest from following the idiot.

"Fuck off, you ain't the boss. He's out of action, and might be dying, so it's time for someone else to show how it's done. Come on boys, follow me. Three times the loot today!" Even from halfway across the captured enclave, Garth heard the cheer, so Attila had gathered enough to make a decent attempt. Garth switched to making sure this enclave was finished. There wasn't much point backing the lunatic up, then getting shot in the back.

* * *

Two hours later, Garth felt much happier about the time it took him to reorganise his men. By then it had been too late, even if he'd pulled them all away from killing and looting. Unfortunately, Garth knew that Conan might see it differently, and decide that enough extra men might have got the job done. Garth glanced at the others, the top Barbarians, and none of them looked at ease. Not all that surprising, considering the sight in front of them. Attila had been nailed to a roughly made cross and beaten to death by inches, starting with his fingers and toes. Personally, Garth thought the dumb fuck deserved it for coming back with the survivors instead of staying and dying in the fighting.

"What did I tell you dumb fucks?" Conan might still be pale from the wound, but his temper had recovered. "I said run some survivors into the next enclave. Not fucking attack them. Not give the fuckers a shitload of weapons. Not show everyone the Barbarians can be stopped. Now every spineless bastard out there will think they can do the same!" Spittle flew as he rounded on Garth. "You were supposed to be in fucking charge!"

Garth thought fast, because the wrong answer could get him nailed to another cross. No it wouldn't, he decided in a moment of cold clarity. If Conan told anyone to grab him, he'd empty his gun into the bastard and fuck the consequences. He fought back a smile at the thought that he should have loaded silver bullets. "I told Attila, and he told me to fuck off, said he'd show everyone how it's done. Everyone heard him on the radio." A few mutters of agreement from behind him surprised Garth, most Barbarians kept out of it when Conan started. He tried to pitch the explanation just right. Not an apology, because Conan pounced on any sign of weakness, but not a challenge. "I tried to get enough men together to stop him, but the stupid fucker attacked before I got the chance. We hadn't finished taking this place, so I daren't take everyone." Garth gave Conan time to actually think about it for a couple of seconds, then pushed on before the asshole could get wound up again. "Who the fuck are those wogs?"

"Not wogs, Sikhs. Indians with turbans and nasty fuckers in a fight." Garth tried not to heave a sigh of relief when the slim, fit-looking man stood just behind Conan interrupted. Sylvester might look cleaner and smarter than the other Barbarians, but he dressed as a fighter and he could handle himself. Better still, Conan usually listened to Sylvester. "That's why Conan wanted to push the spies in there. I'd heard rumours about how well they can fight. Now Attila's men have proved it."

Ivan, another of the top Barbarians, knew Conan's usual answer. "If we throw everyone at them, they'll go under."

"We'd lose too many men. There's too many wounded after taking two enclaves and we've lost another fifty following that stupid fucker." Conan hooked a thumb towards Attila's body. "We'll pick on someone else while Sylvester's spies get to work. I want to capture the Sikh women and kids, then those nasty fuckers can fight for me." The wounded gang boss turned to look back towards home, and hesitated.

Garth felt a moment's exultation. At last, the mad bastard was actually frightened of something! Not exactly frightened, but the Bitch had made him wary enough to leave her alone while he'd got a wound like that. With a little smile, Garth turned and beckoned. Two of his men dragged a couple of women forward and threw them on the ground in front of Conan. Both were struggling and kicking, even hobbled and gagged with their wrists tied together. "Here you go boss. Some entertainment in case you aren't up to travelling back home." The Barbarian didn't mention the Bitch, nobody did but everyone there knew Conan had sworn he'd break her before starting on another.

For a moment Conan hesitated, then he grinned, his mood switching in a moment. He eyed the women. "Two?" He took a long step forward and kicked one of them in the ribs, chuckling when she tried to kick back. "Yeah, why not. After that fucking mess I'm in just the right mood." He bent, tangling his fingers in her hair and set off dragging her towards an undamaged house. "Keep the other one handy."

As the door slammed behind Conan, Sylvester wandered casually over and paused as he passed Garth. "Nicely done." He paused for a moment, picking his words with care. Sylvester knew that Garth wasn't as volatile as Conan, but he wasn't exactly cuddly. "It might be best if nobody else knew exactly who those spies are."

Garth thought about his reply, a lot more carefully than he did when talking to anyone else but Conan. He couldn't quite figure out Sylvester's game, which worried Garth. Most of the Barbarians were in it for the killing, looting or rape, or all three, but Sylvester didn't get involved in anything but a bit of fighting. "I won't be telling, but the news might get out if I had a sudden fatal accident."

"That doesn't surprise me in the least, Garth. Just between us, if Conan ever does go down permanently, I've got your back." Sylvester wandered off, stopping for a couple of words with a few of the others and exchanging a couple of jokes. Garth didn't watch him, his eyes were on the house where Conan would be beating the fuck out of his latest toy. Was Sylvester suggesting it was time for Conan to go? Garth considered it carefully. Not yet. It would be best to wait until Conan finished off those Sikhs at least, because some of the men might not stay under a different leader. Then Garth knew exactly what to do. He'd make sure the Bitch found a gun, and he might put genuine silver bullets in the fucking thing. He wondered what the Bitch's name had been, but only for a moment because it didn't matter anymore.

*   *   *

The General:

The General could have told the inhabitants of Sutton Park exactly why the Last Prophet had eased off, he had another job for the Children of Cain. Bloodsuckers with crosses, or that's what Patton reported when he'd visited to check out if the fighters were worth hiring. Not exactly hiring, the man sat opposite the General had something more ambitious in mind. Rail thin, bald and dressed in a rough smock, he had a very modern hand gun and machete on his belt and an armoured vest. He spoke in a quiet, reasoned manner, but the General saw the occasional flash of bugnuts crazy in his eyes.

"How many men do you need?" The Last Prophet smiled quietly. "Temporarily, on loan. I have seen your men and an equal number of those will be an acceptable swap, when I need them."

"I'd like a hundred at least, maybe more if you can spare them. I assume you've got your own problem?" No harm in fishing a little, and the gentle nod didn't surprise the General one bit.

"Yes, but nobody who will take advantage while my men are gone. I am surprised your target is to the south. My messengers passed through an enclave to the north, not too far away, that could be a real threat to your rear." He leafed through a notebook, which meant the Prophet must have someone like Rhys gathering info. "The Professors. They seem to have several rare skills and some real engineers, and are drawing the neighbours into an alliance."

"I'll frighten Benny off when the time comes, then snap them up. Orchard Close is a much bigger prize than the Professors and led by a soldier, not an old school teacher." The General paused for effect, even though most of the detail had already been thrashed out by Rhys. Even so, he should dangle just a little carrot. "If this deal works out, we might do another when I go for the Professors. I'll let you know the date for this job three weeks in advance, so your men can filter through without anyone else realising how many are coming."

"I'd prefer that, just in case someone gets unexpectedly ambitious while my numbers are down." After finishing their drinks and a little more talk, the Last Prophet left.

As the visitors drove away, Patton moved closer to the General. He kept his voice low, so that Rhys didn't interfere until he'd got a straight answer. "Are you sure, sir? I'm okay with using someone else as cannon fodder, but a hundred of those Children of Cain will be a handful." Patton frowned after the small convoy. "His blokes think you two are going to combine to take over the whole city, along with some other fucking loony called Conan."

"We might, but my sort of alliance. After all, in a month or two I'll have a hundred blokes in his camp, more if I take a few more of his. He's right that if we combined the lot, and hardened them properly, we've got the men to take on the Army. The thing is, I can't see those spies in the sky letting us do it. If we tried, I reckon the RAF would drop by and we'd be the star turn in a barbecue. I just want to be big enough, and tough enough, so it's easier for the government to do a deal instead of losing men to kill us. They can give me and a few of my top men a nice little spot outside the wire, either a country retreat or bossing a few irregulars to help them mop up the rest." He turned towards Patton, his eyes narrowing. "I trust you with that thought, Patton, but don't let that shifty little fuck Rhys get any hints. I'm not sure, but he might be already working on his own deal."

"Got it, sir. So when do we send for the nutters?"

"Maybe never, unless Caddi keeps dicking about and we have to take Orchard Close without him. After what those women did to Julius's men, I'd rather someone else's people led the attack. If Caddi helps us crack Orchard Close, then we snap up the surviving Hot Rods, we might have enough for the Professors. Even then I still might do that deal, just to get my men into his camp." The General patted Patton on the back. "Look over your men. We'll need at least a hundred total lunatics who will stay loyal."

"On it, sir." Patton saluted and moved off, watched by the General.

That had been a mistake, letting the boss Bloodsucker know the master plan. Now he'd have to make sure Patton got a deal as well, or a fatal accident before then. He'd have to think about it, but long-term because Patton was the ideal man to turn a hundred or so Children of Cain into Bloodsuckers.

* * *

Professors:

This spring looked better for the ex-students than any previous ones. The SIMS had settled into untenanted ruins adjacent to the Mart, taking over a clump of habitable housing in the area captured with the help of Benny's Boys. The newcomers had set to with a will, spending the winter tearing down ruins to clear ground for their spring planting, renovating houses and building defences. A few SIMS spent long hours with the Professor and the faculty, designing a deterrent that couldn't be wiped out by one air strike. The rest hoped they'd have built up enough ammunition for the next round with the General, but practiced with crossbows just in case.

Three goats, one a Billy, were offered, in return for treating a lot of casualties. The Ringer's fighters had been injured when their neighbours tried to steal the animals, and now the gang had decided the milk wasn't worth the hassle. A steady stream of Benny's Boys came to see the animals, some with their families, just for the novelty. Benny himself conceded the Prof's compound was the safest place for livestock, providing the youngest children in his gang got a share of the milk. Now two and a half gangs waited to see if there'd be the clatter of tiny hooves.

Several heavily armed men, looking for the General and asking questions about the nearby enclaves, put everyone on alert but nothing came of it. Prof relaxed a little, but not completely. He thought the General would move this way sooner or later, unless he ran into someone as strong, which might not be an improvement. To prepare for whoever finally came after them, Prof let Benny's Boys have two trebuchets of their own. Some of Benny's women were training up on them, to avoid taking men from the front line. The SIMS already had a crew staying with the Professors, training while helping to build their own thrower.

* * *

Reivers:

Far to the north, in the ruins of Inverness, the watchword was stealth. Everyone knew the government had attacked, and won. Now the virtually deserted city had become a no-go zone, with a line of emplaced soldiers and armour sealing the southern borders. The ruins themselves had turned into a low-level killing zone of aggressive patrolling, squad actions and snipers. Oberfeldwebel Klaus Huber watched over the snow-swathed vista, careful to make sure his breath didn't show outside his cover. The wire from his spotter couldn't be hacked or overheard, a blessing because these so-called civilian rebels were more professional than any other mob he'd fought. "Klaus? I think this one is a messenger. She's a bit young for fighting, even here, but you know the orders."

"Nein." During the actual assault, the front line troops ended up killing anyone who moved, man, woman or child, but Klaus wasn't doing that in cold blood. He could understand what happened in the heat of battle, after all the suicide attacks and bombs, but a line had to be drawn somewhere. Otherwise he was just a murderer for hire.

A muffled crack sounded, and a curse came down the wire. "Someone else shot her." Neither said who, even if both of them were certain who'd fired the shot. The pale-faced, dead-eyed shooters brought in by the paramilitary troops weren't snipers, they were cold-blooded killers. Another shot sounded, but from ahead. "I think we've found him." After a brief pause the wire continued, "Or her." They'd seen fighters of both sexes now.

The quiet voice began to talk Klaus onto the target, hopefully before the sniper moved. He hoped this sniper was a man, or that at least he couldn't tell. He also hoped the rebel sniper had killed whoever shot the girl. If it wasn't for his daughters, he'd steal a boat and go back across the channel. Klaus cleared his mind, concentrating on doing his job and buying their safety. Maybe he really was a killer for hire, but on his own terms.

* * *

At one in the morning on the northern bank of Loch Ness, beneath an overhanging bush, the water bubbled, surged and then parted. Willing hands reached to help a black-clad figure ashore. A man poured hot coffee and brandy between her chattering teeth, then two men half-carried her through the trees to a well-hidden fire. Another man, wearing a uniform, waited. "How is she?"

One of those carrying the woman picked up a towel and blankets. "She'll make it. It's too cold by rights."

"Try telling her that. I'll not forbid it because we need the information, but I didnae ask."

The man with the towels snorted. "No need tae ask, Angus. Knowing you need the information is keeping her alive, or she'd push too hard and get killed. Now give us time tae thaw her out." The uniformed man retreated into the darkness, while the other two helped the woman out of her wetsuit before swaddling her in blankets and offering hot broth.

Half an hour later Angus, the uniformed man, looked up from the sheaf of hand-drawn maps. A heavily muffled figure came into the room. "How are ye, Lisa?"

"I'll do. Is that what you wanted?" She scowled, not easy with her features still stiff from the cold. "I passed up two good chances because you don't want anyone to know I'm over there. They were easy, drunk as skunks. When can I go back to killing them?"

"Soon, but not until we are ready." Angus repeated why, again, because otherwise Lisa might decide she'd waited too long. "You are our only trained diver, and have the only set of kit, so you're the only one who can get across there in this weather. I need this information without them knowing, so that we can break that line wide open. I promise you"—his smile had no humour but a lot of anticipation—"there'll be enough bodies to satisfy even you."

"No there won't." She turned to go and he barely caught the last bitter words. "There'll never be enough." Angus didn't argue, because he knew exactly how she felt, and why. Lisa had followed the lorries out of Inverness, to try and break her dad and little brother free. She'd lost track of their lorry, but there were plenty of them carrying prisoners so she'd found the destination. There'd be no prisoners coming back out of that place, dead or alive. Angus had made Lisa a solemn promise, in return for her promise to delay her vengeance until spring. If she helped him get enough fighters through the lines, he would make sure the last people to die there would be the Specials who ran it.

Angus checked through another file. On the east coast, a very peculiar boat neared completion. Other Reivers were going to deliver a special message for Easter, one demonstrating just how it felt to have their families targeted. Two other groups were training for suicide missions, Lisa wasn't the only one willing to die to get payback. Eventually, Angus packed everything up and headed back into the mountains. He had a lot of new recruits in training, men and women from Inverness who were every bit as bitter as Lisa. Bruce needed them ready for his army and time was running out.

*   *   *

Cabal:

Safe and warm, the Cabal were enjoying the thought of all those rebels freezing and starving in the snow. Everyone relaxed, enough so that for once Vanna and Joshua stopped sniping at each other about the relative merits of contractors versus regular Army. Apart from guarding convoys and Marts, and the sniper teams, Vanna's contractors in Scotland were in their barracks for the winter. Those were situated next to the tank repair shops in case the foreign troops became restless. The foreign troops were being rotated out of the front lines for R&R, the ones with families taking the opportunity to travel south to see them. Seeing their wives and children safe and sound reminded the soldiers and pilots why they had to do exactly what the controllers told them. The dependents of the foreign soldiers were housed in Rosyth, just north of Edinburgh and well within the range of several artillery emplacements and the guns of the naval vessels in the dockyard. Just as telling, troop transports were moored nearby where they could be used to transport the dependents back to Europe.

Across the UK, in the other cities, the gangs kept killing each other as planned. As Maurice and his agents built or destroyed alliances, one or two Cabal members started worrying about the size of some gangs. Both Vanna and Joshua scoffed, claiming that armour and air power would deal with them. Boris and Henry still thought the best of the enclaves should be saved, to help settle Europe once the big push started. They'd be loyal enough out of gratitude, because they'd seen the alternative, and because of all the fertile land they'd be given. Henry didn't push hard when others refused to even discuss it, but after some thought about what happened to Nate, he approached Joshua. The Army man seemed remarkably unsurprised by a request for regular Army bodyguards.

Henry wouldn't have time to worry about rescuing anyone, not for a month or two. He'd be too busy organising the planting of this year's crops.

*   *   *

Cyn Palace:

Oddly enough, the Sinners and their allies were also thinking about the benefits of armour and air power, and wanted to save at least some enclaves. Their problem was finding a way to stop the armour, then hopefully any saved enclaves could help them to spoil the rest of the government's plans. For now, however, these alleged gangsters would be busy with exactly the same job as Henry's work gangs. In their case, using manpower instead of machines to dig the fields wasn't to fool anyone, it was necessity.

Chapter 23:
Uninvited Guests

Outside the cities, especially in the Army, more and more people weren't being completely fooled. So far, none of them realised the whole truth. Even the most paranoid never imagined that the whole government, and a large part of the world, were now run by a small group of ruthless conspirators, but some were getting close. One evening, a few days after the Barbie visits, the loudhailer called Harold up to the bypass near Orchard Close. He spent the time walking up the access road wondering why. Maybe the flirting had begun interfering with the soldiers or some officer had found out, because the soup and chips party were all girls now. When Harold saw the Lieutenant, that seemed likely, especially when Harold was allowed through the sandbags and taken aside along with the sergeant. Sarge didn't seem too happy.

Harold realised that flirting wasn't the problem because neither the Lieutenant waiting to greet him, nor the Captain who'd just got out of a Land Rover, wore unit badges. That usually meant Special Forces, like the SAS. "Could I check your ID please?" Harold handed it over. "Good. Where were you stationed before demob?"

Harold gave his unit and glanced at Sarge, but the NCO looked worried and a little bit curious. "We were down in the Southeast, supposed to be getting a rest."

"Resting after what?" This was all in his records, but if this Lieutenant wanted to hear it?

"The Gulf. Kuwait, when the mad mullahs decided the locals were too cosy with the hated infidel."

The Lieutenant nodded, so he did know. "Was that your last action?"

"Depends on what you call action." The soldiers had been involved in some very bloody confrontations that didn't come under any normal military duties.

"Live firing. We all had to stand off rioters with bayonets at some time during that period." Sarge nodded, unconsciously, so he'd been in that sort of situation as well. The Lieutenant inspecting Harold's ID glanced up sharply. "Well?"

Harold sighed because he still didn't like remembering. "London estates and then the shit-fest in Calais."

"That was wrong. We should have made the Frogs sort the mess out." Harold stared, shocked. This was the first time he'd heard any officer admitting any mistake was made. "Do you have a stick?"

Harold's head spun for a moment until he made sense of the question. They were finally getting to the whole point of the visit. "Yes, it's down there."

"Still got the jewellery?" That had to mean the medal. Harold gestured to Orchard Close. "Could you bring the stick up, please? Just to confirm everything."

"Okay." Harold walked quickly because the Lieutenant had to be one of Stones's mob, SAS, and had been poking about in Harold's records. Harold tried to figure out why, and hoped they had word about the missing soldier. Despite claiming she'd got over Stones, he thought Tessa would want to know if he'd survived.

Working on that idea, as soon as he arrived back Harold asked the Lieutenant, "How is Stones? His son is down there." He pointed at Orchard Close. "Right under that Union Flag."

The Captain spoke up. "We both knew him, but he was still in Kuwait when contact was lost. Still, Stones is a resourceful sort so you never know. How are Tessa and Eddie managing?"

Harold's interest sharpened. The Captain probably knew Stones very well or at least had access to his records, very restricted records. Stones wasn't married so not too many knew the name of his son's mother, or even that he'd had a son. "Better now. They live with my sister and her two kids. Her husband, Freddie, didn't make it back from the Ukraine." These men wouldn't know Freddie but would know what Harold meant.

The Captain nodded in understanding. "A lot didn't, too many. May I?" He held out his hand so Harold handed over the stick. The officer held it with both hands, and Harold heard the click as the blade released. The Captain nodded to the Lieutenant, clicking the catch back in place and handing the stick back to Harold.

The Lieutenant turned to Harold. "You still practice?"

"Yes sir."

"Not sir now, you're a civvie." That was the Captain again, these two were a double act. "Word got around, and we thought we'd check if this chap we'd heard about was the right one. A few of us are making visits here and there before the regulars leave, and the Lieutenant and I thought we'd drop by for old time's sake. We'd like the right enclaves to survive until the Army get back." The Captain held out his hand for the Lieutenant to pass him a bag. "This is a bit naughty, but we prefer to pay our debts. I knew those lads in Kuwait, in the lorry. I thought this might help. Not much but I can't leave you a rifle and two thousand rounds, or a box of grenades."

When Harold took the small backpack, not an Army one, it had something very heavy inside so he had a look. Only a polished wooden box, nothing like big enough for the weight, so Harold rested the backpack on the sandbags to have a proper look. He opened the box lid and smiled at the revolver inside, though he still couldn't figure out why it weighed so much. The Captain shrugged in apology. "Only six rounds but the lads made sure it'll work. Keep it for when the bastards close in."

"I will, and thanks." The gun wasn't much compared to the weaponry already in Orchard Close, but it was a huge gesture and the officers had to be taking a big risk.

Both officers stiffened a bit. "Wear the jewellery in case it all goes wrong. Whoever takes it will wear it as a trophy, so we'll know which little gobshite to arrange a nasty accident for when we get back." The Captain glanced down at Harold's side. "The stick will help. We'll be sent in to teach the savages a bit of respect eventually. We'll look for hints like that, when deciding who would make a good object lesson."

"Will do, sir." Harold had never thought of that happening. He'd hidden the medal so no gangster ever found it, but if Stones's lot were going to take it personally? They were a bit wild off duty, but that wild? Harold let his smile show now. "Are the British Army head-hunting now?"

The Lieutenant's tone said probably. "Not officially, but some are still a bit wild at heart." The sergeant looked torn, probably because this would make a good story in the NAAFI but he shouldn't tell anyone. Harold hoped Sarge would at least keep his mouth shut until his unit moved away. A quick round of salutes and the officers left, but the sergeant had a million questions.

Harold explained the lorry ambush in Kuwait, the fight and his medal. "I don't like fighting." Harold thought Sarge would laugh out loud. "Seriously, I can only shoot because I used to be in a rifle club, and I sure as hell never stuck anyone with anything before. Then came London, and Calais. So, when Sis said she was on her own?" Harold shrugged. "I came here to help her."

"So all the bloody animals?"

"Think I'm Regiment or something similar because I had to do a couple of things. I gave them a shooting demonstration." Sarge's look sharpened, because that wouldn't mean pistols. "You know someone down there can shoot, but nothing has ever come near you or any other soldier up here." The sergeant nodded and relaxed again. "Look, if you're really worried about this?" Harold nodded towards the box, still inside the bag on the sandbags.

"It doesn't matter if I am. An officer gave you it so I'm golden. We all feel shitty about leaving the civvies to the animals, and even if the animals get it they'll never find more ammo for that thing. That .38 must be some officer's from the war." He chuckled at Harold's expression, puzzled because nobody had shown Sarge what was in the box. "I recognise that box. We took it off a toerag a couple of weeks ago. He'd probably found it in a ruin and tried to smuggle it along the bypass. I sent it off to gun heaven, but somebody got to it before the crusher." The sergeant glanced over at the guard post. "We appreciate the chips and soup, and the girls cheer the blokes up a bit. I tone down any reports of rifle fire, and ignore some of the training we see, but there's bugger all we can actually do to help."

"Just empty a few clips to cover the women's escape if someone attacks and breaches the walls. It'll take a lot of men, but a few gangs might combine because I'm letting in too many refugees." Harold nodded towards Orchard Close. "You've seen our refugees. A lot of them are just what the gangs are looking for." The large number of women were obvious from up here.

The sergeant nodded, briefly. "I'm sure there'll be a whole series of accidental discharges if the time comes, especially if the woman are running for the tunnel." Sarge looked embarrassed at the surprised look from Harold. "I never said this, but some of the Army is getting a little bit pissed off about things like treating ordinary men and women as the enemy. Or keeping them penned in the cage with the man-eaters. The offer still stands. Get the women and kids under the wire, and if you get warning, the men can come as well." He glanced towards the squaddies, safely out of earshot. "Our automatics will stop them following you across the zone, then we can blow the shites to pieces. Without collateral this time!" The sheer venom in the last part startled Harold, there had to be a very nasty story behind it. "Now sod off while I spin this lot some crap about back pay and personal kit you left behind." He looked significantly at the small backpack.

"Any chance of a hint about when you are leaving?" Harold half expected Sarge to deny it, even after the Captain said the regulars were going.

Sarge thought about it, then sighed and gave. "Just unconfirmed rumours you never heard of from me. Confirmed now that Captain accidentally let it slip." They exchanged wry looks; that wasn't a mistake. "We will be retraining over next winter, back with our units, in preparation for some mystery operation. You might hear something a bit more precise nearer the time. Now you'd better sod off before I cry and you kiss me better." Harold did as he'd been told.

* * *

After a bit of thought, Harold sewed a pocket on the side of the mattress on his bed, against the wall where it wasn't visible, and put the loaded .38 revolver in there. Harold had been thinking about how conveniently Paddy, the Murphy gang boss, had died just before Caddi attacked his gang. Other top Murphies had died mysteriously since then, and the Murphy stronghold had carelessly left their gate open. Mack had reckoned Caddi planned to go for the Ferdinands after the Murphies, and one of their top men had just bled out in Mercedes' bed, also more than just convenient. Harold didn't expect a midnight visit from Mercedes, or not for his ears, but Caddi might send someone else to remove an annoying Soldier Boy. That would be Caddi's style, a knife in the night. Now, if anyone unexpected disturbed Harold in his bed they'd get six .38 calibre shocks.

More than that, the weapon would be a backup for Tessa and Sharyn, because he showed them where he'd put it. Harold put the rest of the .38 pistol rounds from Caddi in his room as well. He didn't need them for the adapted shotgun now Dealer had sold him rifle rounds. Caddi might try to take hostages, but with both the pistol and the musket, Tessa and Sharyn should hold a few scroats at bay until help arrived. Tessa reckoned the pistol would come in handy anyway, for Harold to back off his other woman and get some sleep. Despite some teasing about that, both women ran through using and reloading the .38 until they were confident. Harold's bedroom stayed locked because of the kids, but Sharyn and Tessa already knew where he put the key.

When anyone asked about Harold's trip to the Army, it had been about the number of refugees arriving. Harold told Tessa and Sharyn, and the squad leaders, that the Army would be leaving before winter. He told the same people what else came in the wooden box, under the weapon. The box felt heavy, very heavy, a couple of stones at least, and looked much deeper than it needed to be. The original intent might have been to create a space to keep valuables, but not the sort it held now. When a curious Harold prised out the bed that held the pistol, he was greeted by lines of gleaming brass circles. The gift hadn't been anything like a token gesture.

His benefactors had filled the whole space with two layers of genuine, new, original 9 mm pistol rounds, twelve hundred of them. A thousand rounds were hollow point, the other two hundred were full metal jackets. All of it was better than almost any other ammunition in the city. The jacketed rounds would go clean through any of the homemade armour out there except Dealer's car. The hollow points with full original loads behind them would blow through most homemade personal protection. Even if they didn't penetrate, the recipient would feel as if he'd been hit by a sledgehammer.

The ammo stunned Harold because some of the British Army were well off the reservation, and their officers had joined them. Now Harold wondered how many other ex-squaddies were getting a quiet hand with stopping the Barbarians. The Captain said they were visiting here and there. Did that mean the Army were going to try and save some enclaves? Even if there weren't enough suitable gifts among confiscated weapons, some of the Special Forces had spare weapons stowed away, the sort without any records. Those like Stones had small private armouries, handy if Harold or Tessa had known where he'd kept them. Harold filled six clips with metal jackets and twelve with hollow point, then switched pistols about so each squad leader had a weapon that fired them, for emergencies. He'd ask Dealer for more clips to fill with the rest.

* * *

Harold didn't have much time to think about the Army, because the refugees kept coming until the number of residents topped three hundred. His fighters could read the signs, they pushed for more and more training. The new refugees were immediately put on the task of clearing the area around the Farm, the new housing, and working on the actual buildings themselves. Once the houses were habitable the walls would go up, but until people lived there, Harold wasn't creating a fortification that near to Orchard Close. Harold looked over the tents, the extension leads to give them light and heat, and the milling crowd of strangers, and finally voiced one big worry. "Caddi will try to put a spy in among them. Maybe he has already, but I can't turn the poor sods away."

Patty laughed out loud, but it had a bitter edge. "Six so far. Emmy wins the pool, because she reckoned with all these arriving so quickly you'd finally catch on."

"Six? What, spies? Who?" Harold looked closer at the crowd, but they all looked like innocents to him.

"Not here, we don't think." Patty patted him on the back. "Four women and two men so far. They are all under anonymous heaps of bricks out near the borders." She wasn't laughing now. "We've been watching from the beginning and the first two were easy. None of their supposed neighbours recognised them."

"What about the others?" Harold felt truly stupid now, because he should have guessed Caddi would put someone among the flood of new people.

A steely glint showed in Patty's eyes. "Caddi used their relatives to apply pressure. The refugees picked up on two of them. The others were a bit too desperate to get information. These refugees are as suspicious as we are, Harold. They watch each other, because under the Murphies they lived with informers."

It wasn't informers that shocked Harold. "You killed them in cold blood, even if Caddi forced them?"

"Yes. That's why we don't tell you. You'd give a weeping woman a pass, then she'd run off to Caddi and spill the lot." Patty looked him in the eye. "The scroats are not getting us that way and no, I won't tell you about the next one. You keep training us to defend the walls, we'll watch for the back-stabbers." She sighed, then plastered on a smile. "Now look happy and say hi to the latest three."

Harold thought about it, but didn't have the nerve to ask Sharyn if she knew. Patty had hit the nail firmly on the head; he'd always worried that Caddi could get a female spy past him if she looked like a refugee. Harold did as Patty told him and concentrated on defending everyone. To do that he needed even more of the high quality steel weapons, so whichever fighters were based in the Farm could arm and train any willing refugees.

Between arming the fighters and replacing the weapons Caddi took as payment for the forge, Liz had used up enough of the rail wagon springs to force Harold into launching his raid. It would have to be soon, before Caddi overran the location. To get his loot home, Harold had to let the GOFS into the source of the steel. Even if he could beg, steal or hire enough transport for this raid, he'd have to cross GOFS territory twice without a single sentry spotting him. Caddi's howl of rage when he found the robbed wagons would alert everyone afterwards, but hopefully too late. Harold sent word that he wanted a meeting with a senior GOFS to discuss steel, for mutual advantage.

Harold didn't expect Wayland, the GOFS smith, to come to Orchard Close the following day. The man asked if he could talk to Harold's blacksmith, or at least meet him, but Harold assured him that wasn't necessary. He'd tell the GOFS where the metal came from in return for help in getting more. Wayland promised to set up a meeting as soon as possible. With a laugh he admitted buying a Rambo to test it, and worrying Harold had found the Murphies' missing farrier or a real swordsmith. Wayland didn't stay overnight, though he asked again if he could meet the smith. From the little smile, Harold thought Wayland had guessed Liz's secret.

*　*　*

Gofannon didn't arrange anything, because the next GOFS convoy arrived at Orchard Close the following day with Vulcan aboard. Ogou visited now and then, and Wayland, but official business usually happened in GOFS territory. Harold made it to the gate in time to meet the GOFS party as they came through. "Welcome. This is a big surprise. I expected to be heading over to see you."

Vulcan nodded, with just a hint of mischief in his smile. "Yes, that would be the usual arrangement. The thing is we've been hearing stories from the likes of Cy, and second-hand from Barbies as well. We were definitely curious after your last visit. Your bodyguard was a bit unusual, and still is." He bowed a little towards Patty. "Still as decorative as ever, but a couple of the lads mentioned that your women weren't quite as genteel these days."

Harold answered cautiously, because that sounded like a complaint. "Depends on how they treat the woman."

"True, and both agreed it was their own fault and neither of the young women took permanent offence. The way my men were, well, I suppose chastised, intrigued me. One ended up on the ground being offered a hand up. The other ended up on his knees with his hand being held in a very painful manner." Vulcan laughed again, he seemed to be in a terrific mood. "He reckons he'd have knelt anyway if she'd asked him. They both apologised to me for causing trouble, so I think the message went home."

"I never heard a word. The girls usually deal with trouble themselves." Harold nodded towards Patty and her crossbow. "The couple of times things got serious, we retrieved the bolts and buried them. The last fatality inside the walls, except the one in The Pub, was over a year ago."

Vulcan had been frisked as they talked. Now, as they headed for the Embassy, the GOFS gestured to the men and women walking about. "This is what I wanted to see. In the past, anyone out of order found themselves surrounded by annoyed residents with, as you said, crossbows and a bad attitude. Recently the women have been dealing with it themselves, very efficiently. The only other women who do that are Barbies, but they tend to use a blade." His eyes sharpened as couple of people wearing bandages came past. "We know that Patty, and presumably other women, helped to carve up those visitors. Those pictures had a sort of Barbie flavour."

"I told them to cut up the bodies, as a message, and there were men as well as women in the fighting." Harold had worried about how far they'd gone, because some of the trainees were very, very intense and had got carried away. "You thought we'd got Barbies living here?" Maybe Vulcan thought Barbies had helped out and carved up the bodies, perhaps because there were some visiting most days.

"More that your women were turning into Barbies. Someone like her might pass as a Barbie fighter." Vulcan gestured to a woman on the wall nearby, fully armed for her sentry duty. "But the others definitely aren't, despite the Rambos and some bigger blades or pistols. Even that one on the wall hasn't got that manic edge." Vulcan smiled at Patty, bowing slightly. "Lovely as you are, having to fight you would be a little bit disturbing. The thought of fifty or a hundred like you, combined with the Barbies, could give a man sleepless nights."

"Not me. The Barbies keep offering me a job but I like it here. My boss gives me some lovely toys to play with, but I don't have to let anyone near my underwear. Unless I want to of course." Patty smiled back at Vulcan, giving him an obvious once-over. "You should come to one of the dances. We're always short of blokes for the last waltz."

Harold kept his face straight, because he wasn't actually sure if Patty was chatting Vulcan up or winding him up. Neither was Vulcan from the look on his face, then he laughed. "If you save me the last dance, I could be tempted to do just that."

"Oh no, that would depend on how you boogie. I never make promises because that stops them trying so hard." Patty wore a happy little smile now, but Harold still wasn't sure why.

"Having to work at getting a dance would be a novelty, but worth the effort I'm sure. I would love the chance to find out." The party went inside where Vulcan gravely greeted Sharyn and Tessa before sending Ogou to The Pub. Ogou looked puzzled, because as a top GOFS, he expected to attend. "I want to cut down on competition for the attention of all these lovely ladies." Vulcan had probably been a real smooth operator back in the day. The GOFS man looked to be mid-twenties, so possibly twenty during the Crash, and suddenly well-spoken to the women. Harold remembered Patty mentioning Vulcan's manner when she visited the GOFS.

When given the options, Vulcan asked for beer. "I have to fight for this at home." He sipped appreciatively. "The ladies truly are lovely, but I have other ulterior motives. I am alone in here so that we can talk about secrets. Will we?" Vulcan's eyes included all the people there in a discreet question. Could all these be trusted?

"All our top people know."

The secrecy part settled, Vulcan went straight to the point. "Wayland says the new weapons are down to the steel, rather than the smith, and you'll tell us where to get some of it. Why?"

There wasn't any point in Harold lying. "I need transport, and extra troops would be handy in case someone objects."

Vulcan looked a very happy boy. "If we supply transport and troops, we'll want sixty-forty."

Harold shook his head. "If we ask the Barbies they'll accept forty-sixty to get the steel. Then they'll sell the steel to you in exchange for good machetes and maces." He chuckled at the grimace on Vulcan's face.

"Ouch. True as well. If they had good, tempered steel we'd trade for some. So rather than arm the Barbies even better, how about fifty-fifty?"

That brought smiles from everyone here. "All I ever wanted. We'll bring some jacks, but the more the merrier. Your cutting gear is better than ours."

Vulcan frowned, not quite so happy with that. "Meaning we use our gas. In that case who supplies the diesel?"

"There's other plate steel, aluminium sheeting and some solid bar, and big hammers or cold chisels will be enough to remove some of it. You can keep any steel you cut loose so take extra vehicles. We will be raiding into Murphy territory but not the front lines, so how many troops?" Harold had no accurate count on how many soldiers the GOFS had, or could spare.

The extras seemed to settle any problems over gas or diesel usage. "The borders don't have more than a few sentries, because most of their men are tied up fighting Caddi. Forty of yours and forty of mine, properly armed with some firearms, should do it. Even the Barbies would think seriously before taking that on. How many extra vehicles should we take?" Vulcan realised he'd missed a vital bit of information. "How much steel is there? I assume we aren't raiding for half a dozen plates."

Harold tried hard to keep his face straight and voice off-hand. "Between eight and ten tons of spring steel plates, at a guess."

"F... Hellfire! Have you found a park? F... Cripes, it'll take forever to strip that many caravans!" Vulcan looked round at the smiling faces. "Hah. Got me, but I'll bet you already know about caravans."

"Yes, we have a few burned ones over the road. There aren't many about, nor wrecked pickups and SUVs." Liz had gleefully used the smaller leaf springs from some of those as well. "People might have caught on faster if there were." Harold frowned as he realised something. "You might be a tad annoyed when you find out where the steel comes from."

"Why?"

"You sold us the first lot. We found the plates among those houses." Harold hoped the GOFS didn't take that too badly.

Vulcan looked round the faces but it wasn't a windup. "Where was it?"

"When you see it you'll know." Harold shook his head. "I didn't know about the steel so you weren't stitched. It had been there since the Crash."

"I might still be annoyed, if you hadn't just offered me four or five tons of the stuff. Now it would be bloody ungrateful. Wayland will kick himself round our yard when he finds out." From Vulcan's smile, he'd be the one telling the smith. "We'll nip over the rubble across a corner of the Barbies' border, because ours doesn't quite meet the Murphies now Caddi has advanced. The Spuds will fight over that amount of steel, but we'll have enough men." He bowed towards Patty without getting up. "And women of course."

Nobody else looked worried. "The Spuds have no idea what they've got, so they won't defend it."

"Now I really am curious. I suppose I'll find out the day after tomorrow, which is the soonest I can get organised. Get to our border as early as possible, the usual place." Vulcan hesitated, calculating. "Four or five tons each? I'll make you a deal. We won't make Rambos if you don't make the big swords. They're a real money item for us and with four tons you could undercut. We will continue making our usual knives." Vulcan thought for a moment longer. "Open season on maces or we'll arrange a price with you, to avoid a price war? Maces aren't spring steel but yours are as good as ours. Wayland has had to pretty ours up to compete."

Harold didn't need Liz or anyone else to tell him that was a good deal, but he pushed for something a bit better. "We'll sort out a price list for all the weapons if you like. I'd assumed you'd keep making your usual knives and we won't make machetes. We won't make any blade more than two-thirds the weight of your big swords." Harold thought the new swords were less than half weight but wanted to leave a margin. Liz had been approached by a hobbyist with drawings of axes, but with narrow heads rather than the big double headed type.

"There's only you and the Barbies will use the smaller maces. All the men want the larger type." Vulcan's sour look wasn't completely convincing. "You'll probably get the Barbie custom anyway, because they still like you."

Harold smiled at a smirking Patty. "They still like Patty and her Demons."

"Yes, we listen to Barbie Radio as well. 'Walking the Demon,' 'Devil's Child,' 'Number of the Beast,' 'Beast and Harlot,' they do find some delightful love songs." Vulcan looked around the room, including everyone. "Have you found the Barbies a little bit less manic of late?"

Everyone looked at each other, not sure how to answer. The Barbies had never been completely manic in here, and several had struck up real friendships since the radio repair, but how much did Vulcan know? After a few moments, Patty answered. "The top lot are a bit full on, but we've never had real trouble. Maybe the Barbies just think the point has been made and they don't need to keep it up." That was what Harold and his advisors had decided.

"Unless some idiot raids them. We were invited to send someone to see those trophies." Vulcan pulled a face. "Until this war of Caddi's, that was the last raid on any local gang headquarters. I heard that the Murphy guards were dead and the gates unlocked when Caddi's men arrived. Was that your er, well, Mercedes?" Vulcan half-looked at Tessa, wondering if he'd just said the wrong thing.

Tessa sat on the arm of Harold's chair, but her legs weren't over his. Her jeans were new and tight as befitted a gang boss's woman, and she wore a tight blouse, but she no longer pulled his hand round her for the act. "Who the other woman is varies. Allegedly I'm the biting one, and have underwear." Vulcan looked a bit startled. "The other one only wears a knife as underwear, according to Harold. The lively is up for grabs at the moment, but I doubt I'll keep the title." Harold sat there trying not to blush.

Vulcan looked from him to Tessa, not sure if he should laugh or not. "What happens when Mercedes turns up and moves in?"

"I'm not sure, but I've asked Harold to teach me to shoot, just in case." Tessa gave a lovely smile, but right now Harold could also see real mischief in her eyes.

"I'm hoping to referee." Emmy had decided to rescue either Vulcan or Harold. "I'm taking a shotgun or I don't think they'll listen." She sniffed dismissively, then smiled at Vulcan. "I can't see what the fuss is, but then Sharyn has told me stories about when he wore nappies. She wasn't too surprised where he ended up, not after he got an Action Man."

The moment passed in jokes about what toys people had, and where they'd ended up. Vulcan asked again about more Country and Western sung by Jilli, so Harold promised to bring a couple of new CDs to the raid, as a bonus. As he left, Vulcan kissed the back of Tessa's fingers, then Emmy's. After a moment's hesitation, he asked Patty very formally if he could kiss hers.

"Yes, if you mean my fingers." Patty smiled and extended her hand. "But only my fingers, this time. If you come to a dance who knows what or who you might kiss?"

Vulcan laughed, kissing her fingers and producing a very overdone bow with a sweeping arm. "I can but dream, or perhaps lie awake lonely and heartbroken. Please send me an invitation, to the dance at least. Until we meet again, fair maid." As he left the house to collect his men from The Pub, with Alfie to keep an eye on him, Patty became the centre of a circle of enquiring eyes.

Emmy grinned as she repeated, "But only my fingers, this time?"

"Well it works for Mercedes, so I thought I'd try it out. What do you reckon? Is he interested?" Patty looked around. "What?"

Tessa managed to stop giggling long enough to speak. "He's a senior

GOFS. A gang boss?"

"So is Harold, but that doesn't stop impressionable women fluttering their eyelashes. Vulcan is a lovely strapping bloke, and I do like that beard. If he's at a dance here and he behaves, I might even consider a bit of ruffling." Patty thought about it a moment. "No more, not on a first date. Unless there's moonlight?"

Sharyn left Harold thinking hard with her final comment. "Maybe you could invite Mercedes to the Easter dance, and at least three Barbies would kill for the chance. Then Cy could come with Vulcan and Patty would have options?" Harold knew that promises about Easter burrows weren't helping him to be objective, so he kept quiet.

*　*　*

Orchard Close couldn't manage a very impressive convoy for the raid. Harold took his pickup, three transits, the three captured cars, Rabbit Bob's estate car, Roy and his men in their car, and the Tank. He left the battle bus, because towing that weight would slow him up too much. With all the pickups and SUVs the GOFS brought, thirty-seven vehicles carrying fighters brandishing firearms and sharp steel bounced slowly over the levelled rubble towards the Murphies. The GOFS graffiti on many of the vehicles, and the distinctive shape of the Tank, emphasised that the occupants were absolutely serious. The pair of Murphies watching their Barbie border ran for their lives.

Harold led the way in the Tank, and the only Murphy SUV they saw burned rubber getting clear. Vulcan and Harold set up a perimeter to make sure nobody could see what happened next. Wayland led a group to secure the actual wagons. When the smith saw them he almost drooled, stroking a couple of the top plates while pointing out they were already the right thickness for big swords. He promptly burst into the same sort of frenzy as Liz had, determined to get them away before anyone else had the chance. Wayland even issued the same sort of warnings about getting heat anywhere near his new steel. The GOFS smith had come prepared, he'd brought cold chisels and hammers to help cut the mystery metal free.

Both Vulcan and Wayland agreed with Harold, the exact purpose of the raid should be kept a secret if possible. The residents in the nearest street of habitable houses were escorted out of sight, after being promised their belongings were safe and they'd be back home tonight. As the last ones left, two Murphy SUVs full of gangsters came hurtling up the road. They screeched to a halt at the sight of forty heavily armed fighters running into position and taking cover.

Neither Harold nor Vulcan recognised the man climbing out. He kept his empty hands in plain view so they both showed their empty hands in reply. "Hello there. I'm Vulcan from the GOFS and this is Soldier Boy."

"Niall, and what the fuck are you doing? Have you teamed up with Caddi?" Which seemed a reasonable assumption.

"No, we'll be going home again before dark. Sorry about the trespassing, but there's some stuff we don't want Caddi getting hold of. If you just let us be, we won't even go into the houses." Vulcan waved a casual hand towards all the weaponry aimed at the Murphy. "Or you could attack and lose a lot of men? Then we might get annoyed and decide to keep those houses, and maybe a bigger bite?"

Niall took a good look at all the fighters, and the Tank. He could see more armed men further back even if he couldn't see the rail wagons. "What are you taking?"

"Steel, aluminium and plywood from the rail wagons." Harold patted the Rambo hung from his belt. "The GOFS always want more steel, and now we've gone into making weapons as well."

He didn't expect the curled lip and definite anger from the Murphy. "Yeah, we know all about those fucking Rambos. Especially the one you gave to that mad bitch of yours."

"Be careful what you call young ladies. There's quite a few in hearing, and I gave them all a Rambo." Harold made his smile as nasty as possible. "They're all looking for a chance to collect ears."

"Barbies! You've brought Barbies as well?" Niall looked carefully at the fighters pointing weapons at him from behind cover, some of them definitely female. The blonde hair showing from under Doll's helmet wouldn't be reassuring. "You must be bloody crazy to team up with those, er, women." Niall glanced each way before backing away towards his SUV. "I'm not promising anything. I'll take the message back." He might still look pissed off when he got back in the vehicle, but his driver looked relieved.

Harold watched the SUVs head off at speed. "Do you reckon they'll stand for it?"

"Especially now he thinks we've got Barbies as well. If they bring enough men to throw us out, it'll leave them sod all facing Caddi. Good thinking, telling him why we want steel. We'd better cut plenty off those wagons." Vulcan's grin had a lot of wicked in it. "When Caddi finally finds out what we did, I'd pay a lot of coupons for a video." His grin widened even further. "He might even be stupid enough to get stroppy in front of our cannon."

"We can but hope." They turned back towards the houses masking the actual work on the wagons. "We'll split the aluminium, but I'd rather take the plywood flooring and let you have all the steel apart from the springs."

"For the windows in that new enclave?" Vulcan didn't wait for a reply, he waved a negligent hand. "No problem. It's not much good to us."

To reinforce Harold's message all the wagons were dragged over, off their wheels, and Wayland made sure the GOFS cut off anything he could use. Harold's contingent took most of the plywood flooring, strapping that and sheets of aluminium to the tops of vehicles because the pickups and vans were loaded with spring steel. The coil springs under some wagons, apart from eight Harold kept, were scattered so a casual glance couldn't tell what had fitted where.

* * *

The small army left before dusk, cutting across the corner of Barbies territory again to get to GOFS territory. Harold wondered if he'd been too trusting, but the GOFS stuck to the bargain, sending the vehicles with Harold's springs on towards Orchard Close. When the convoy pulled up outside Orchard Close, Vulcan headed straight for Harold. "Those windows back there are being bricked up." He pointed at the sheets of plywood now being carried in through the gates. "So what do you actually want all that for?"

There wasn't much point in lying, because close inspection of the guards would give Vulcan the answer. "Our shields are plywood, under a thin skin of aluminium to cut down on splintering. The fancy paintwork is to cover the waterproofing." Harold kept his voice low. "It isn't exactly a secret, but I'd rather the first oik who tries to put his mace through a shield got a fatal shock."

"No problem. Is plywood that tough?" Vulcan looked closer at the Orchard Close guards. "I've always assumed the shields were aluminium, especially with the curve. I didn't realise plywood would bend like that, but now I'll have to experiment." His face broke into a big smile. "I could ask Demon if she'll let me check hers out."

"Try calling her Patty, we're not big on gang names. You never know your luck, you might get that invite to dance." It might be the buzz from the raid, but Harold made a snap decision. "We could be extending the guest list. A couple of Barbies are interested."

"Chandra?" Vulcan whistled softly, then his eyes narrowed. "Mercedes?" Harold shrugged but instead of the grin he expected, Vulcan looked totally serious. "You've got a real thing for her, haven't you?" The GOFS shrugged at Harold's sharp look. "You were a bit snarky when that Murphy called her your bitch."

"I never mentioned her." Harold tried to sound nonchalant and knew he'd failed.

Especially when Vulcan laughed. "Yeah, right, except I saw your hackles going up. From what our lads have been told, I reckon she'll be moving in as soon as this war of Caddi's is over." Vulcan glanced around and lowered his voice even more. "If she doesn't kill Caddi first, let us know. We'll watch for him getting his men together, then with luck we can catch him between a cannon and a hard place." He gave the wall around Orchard Close a significant look.

"Is it that obvious?" Harold was bloody horrified. Caddi would be on his guard, or even more than usual.

"Not quite, to most, but it's my job to notice things and prepare for the worst." Vulcan looked at the plywood again and smirked. "In which case I should check out these shields as soon as possible. Is Dem... Patty off duty now?"

Harold shook his head, laughed, and pointed at the gate. "Ask there while you're being searched."

"Has she got a bloke? You know, regular? I don't want to cause strife." Vulcan hesitated, his usual confidence definitely faltering. "Does she have a girlfriend?"

"Patty? I'm not stupid enough to ask about her love life." Harold tried to keep his face straight. "I'm sure she'll let you know one way or the other." He knew there'd be no girlfriend but wasn't sure about Patty's opinion of Vulcan, or Dealer's bodyguard for that matter. Harold smiled as Vulcan headed for the gate, because the GOFS looked downright nervous.

Vulcan wore a huge smile when he left. One of the guards told Harold the GOFS had carried Patty's shield while they walked to The Pub. Vulcan bought her a drink and they sat together talking and laughing for a good half hour, well past when his men were ready to leave. Patty came to find

Harold as soon as the GOFS left. "We're inviting Mercedes and Barbies to the next dance? When were you going to tell me?"

"Why, do you want to invite someone?" Harold held up a hand at her scowl and chuckled. "I had a rush of blood when we got back safe, and mentioned that we might open up the guest list."

"Mercedes? Caddi will go crazy." Patty suddenly looked very calculating. "He might have to suck it up if there's GOFS and Barbies here as well. Ah, right, I agreed that if a Hot Rod and Barbies were coming, we should invite a couple of GOFS. Vulcan will come to make sure they behave." She muttered the last part very quietly.

"Last dances and ruffling?"

Patty recovered from her temporary embarrassment. "You'll never know because you'll be busy playing grab-ass." Harold had no answer to that.

A couple of days later Ski complained to Harold about trespassers. Harold complained that someone kept nicking gear from his new houses near the Barbie borders. Ski had a beer and a laugh about all the naughty people running about. Harold took his opportunity, and offered her some gear he felt sure the Barbies had lost. He'd tripped over it while not trespassing.

Ski looked baffled by the big coil springs until Patty explained those were why the Geek catapults threw so far. Once she was certain it wasn't a windup, Ski 'remembered' losing them and went to get a barrow and some help to load them into a couple of Barbie cars. When she came to see Harold, to find out the price, he let Patty have the fun.

Ski cautiously agreed that there probably weren't enough partners for the women at Orchard Close dances. For a moment, when Patty wondered if there were any Barbies who might partner Fergie, Louise and Logan as a favour in return for the springs, Harold thought they'd both get a kiss. As the bubbly bewigged Barbie bounced out, she warned them if Harold changed his mind Beetch would probably come anyway.

*   *   *

Harold still had plenty of credit with the Barbie Girls for fixing their radio. Now it got a boost, even if nobody mentioned springs. Once the news spread about the dance, however, the attempts to get invites included personal dedications on Barbie Radio. They'd already played 'Je t'aime' again for Harold on Valentine's Day, and still dedicated 'The Trooper' to

Soldier Boy. Patty, Ru or the Riot Squad also had their fans, and dedications on the radio, as did those big strong men with their heavy metal weapons.

The Barbies also started broadcasting increasingly scandalous stories about Soldier Boy and Mercedes, mixed with inventive insults aimed at Hot Rods in general and Caddi in particular. Caddi already had the Barbies at the top of his shit list, but their latest broadcasts might move Harold up the rankings.

Meanwhile Liz had landed in heavy metal and light aluminium heaven. She smirked impressively about her new hammer man, while Henry seemed very happy in his new job and it showed as production ramped up. The quantity and quality of the weapons improved, especially the ones that weren't for sale. A good number weren't even on view, with only the gate and wall guards wearing their steel helmets where visitors could see them. With the paintwork, bright patterns to match the shields, they looked like a fancier version of Liz's first alloy attempts.

The Riot Squad members kept their weapons at home out of sight, including more muskets and live reloads, but Harold stocked three small armouries. He wanted extras to arm whoever finally moved into the Farm. Until then, in an emergency, any off-duty fighters could get to serious weaponry without going home. The spears, shields, helmets and a few maces and Rambos were kept in the three guardhouses, out of sight of visitors.

Despite some tension caused by overcrowding, most of the people living in the enclosed garden seemed to feel safe. Many were living with bad memories, still subdued by their narrow escape and new surroundings. So far they hadn't recovered enough to start volunteering as fighters. When more arrived, the sleeping bags ran out and some had to sleep on crude camp beds, wrapped in salvaged bedding. Emptying the composting toilets near the tents became a full-time job.

Meanwhile Emmy and Patricia came to see Harold, concerned about Elise, Trev's radio apprentice. Her withdrawal had gone on for nearly two years, and now seemed to be getting worse again. She barely spoke to anyone any more, except Thandia the mastiff. Harold tried talking to her but as usual Elise went almost monosyllabic, insisting all she wanted was to be useful and not cause trouble. That seemed to be a mantra, she wanted to be useful to pay everyone back for saving her. Despite Sharyn, Tessa, Liz and Patty all trying, she stayed completely withdrawn, even when working with Trev. Despite that, the repair man confirmed that Elise had learned quite a lot about radios. No wonder, the lass worked every hour she could and spent the rest of her time with Thandia.

The fallout from Caddi when he learned about the raid didn't amount to much. The warlord sent a message asking what the hell Soldier Boy and the bloody GOFS were doing poaching on Hot Rods turf. Harold told Charger, the messenger, that they hadn't touched any of Caddi's territory, nor had they given the Murphies anything in trade. Privately, in the Embassy, Charger admitted that Caddi wasn't that upset. The Hot Rod boss was too busy crowing, about the Trainspotters backing off, and promising not to interfere in the war with the Murphies. The message came just after Mercedes came back from a mystery trip.

Harold asked about Mercedes because it was expected, and anyway he actually wanted to know. The Killer Queen fought on the front line now, with the men, and her ear collection kept growing. The Hot Rod gangsters who came to The Pub, wounded fighters still recovering, were full of her exploits. Harold thought Caddi would have to be careful how he moved on Mercedes, because the Hot Rod troops loved her. Sex symbol and inclined towards bloody mayhem, she was a gangster's dream girl. Charger collected the real reason for his visit, the repaired muskets and pistols and a few repaired radios. He promised to let Mercedes know that Harold had asked about her.

Harold checked that Trev had made sure the Orchard Close listening post could tune in to the repaired radios. The listening post had a much better than standard directional receiver, a Trev special. In the right conditions, the listeners could hear Caddi's hand-held radios as far as the nearest sections of the front lines, four or five miles. Intercepted messages confirmed when Caddi finished off one half of the Murphies, with only scattered fighting as the victorious troops rooted out any survivors. The Ferdinands trimmed off a slice for themselves during the disruption, without any response from Caddi. According to the radio messages, Caddi had already started reorganising for a drive into the rest of the Murphy territory.

The numbers of refugees had dropped off while the Hot Rods were on the opposite side of the disputed territory, but there'd be another flood when he attacked the rest. Any who left it too late would find their route had become a battleground. Both the GOFS and the Barbies asked Harold, officially, if he wanted to come and carve a piece off the Murphies. He explained that territory the other side of another gang would be no good to him.

Orchard Close were fully occupied anyway, dealing with the territory and refugees they'd already got. Emmy's gnomes were in full gardening mode, commandeering a good third of the refugees to plant out seedlings. Almost all the rest of those fit to work were preparing the Farm, while Emmy chivvied Harold to get the tents moved. The experienced scavengers organised large groups of new arrivals. Instead of the previous piecemeal approach, the demolition teams methodically sorted out anything useful and cleared the rest. Bernie in particular kept telling the newcomers to look everywhere, look behind, look under and over and move things. Good finds were still turning up, like a half-buried builder's van with a ton of cement, still dry. A small electric trail bike and an electric quad joined the fleet of vehicles, both now in working order.

As Caddi closed in on the last of the Murphies, the number of refugees in tents topped seventy, bringing the population up to three hundred and twenty. Harold couldn't help feeling that time was running out.

*　　*　　*

Despite all the careful listening to radios and second guessing, the next development came a complete surprise. Four days before the end of March, just after nine in the evening, a radio call asked Harold to get over to the Annex quickly but not for an attack. Fergie met him, looking uncertain. "She just asks for you."

"Who?"

"Mercedes." Harold looked around. The guards stood on the walls, closed up and armed, at full alert, but no Mercedes. "Here, I'll take you."

Mercedes stood on the cleared ground outside the compound, lit up by a torch, and she wasn't posing or smiling. The torn rags the young woman wore were bloody, as were both of her hands, her face, everywhere. She gripped a Rambo in one fist, clotted with gore. Harold dropped over the wall even as Fergie put out a hand to stop him. "It isn't a trap. Get a bloody ladder!" Harold hurried over, and as he came near Mercedes swayed a bit and lifted her head.

"You came." Mercedes sighed and swayed again. "The bastard. Three of them. He set me up." Her other fist came forward and opened and lumps of skin and meat dropped. "They told me in the end." The first sob came with the next words, "Help me, 'Arold."

Harold caught her mid-crumple. Mercedes got an arm around Harold's neck, and as he picked her up he heard a clang behind him as the knife dropped. Now he could see she wore someone's slashed and gory jeans tied around her as a bra, and a torn shirt covered in bloody handprints as a skirt. As Mercedes put her head into Harold's chest the sobs started to come. Deep ones, racking her body.

"Pick up the knife someone, and clean it up will you? A hand up the steps please." Two people reached down to put an arm under Harold's armpits, steadying him up and over the wall. They did it again down the steps at the rear, where Ru asked what they should do. "Half and half on alert all night. I'll tell the rest and let you know more when I know."

All the way through the hastily opened gate, across the planks over the trenches and between the tents, Mercedes sobbed. She continued through the gate at the other end as Harold murmured quietly, telling her she was safe now. Mercedes probably never registered the actual words, lost in whatever had happened to her. Her sobs were quietening as Harold came up the path to the big house, where Tessa and Sharyn had the door open, ready.

"My room. Lots of hot water and some decent clothes please. Let the guard houses know, half and half on alert all night." Both shot back into the house. By the time Harold came in, Sharyn already had his bedroom door unlocked and open.

"What happened?"

"Don't know. Mercedes said 'him.' That might mean Caddi, in which case he's dead or coming after her." Harold went through the bedroom door carefully, trying not to knock his burden, and laid Mercedes gently on his bed. Her bloodied arms tightened as Harold tried to stand.

"No!" Then softer, "Don't leave 'Arold. Please?" She looked round and gave a huge sigh, relief he thought. Harold took the bowl Tessa had brought, catching her shocked stare as the room lights gave them all a proper look.

"Christ, Harold, what happened to her? Was it that bastard Caddi?" Tessa stopped when she realised there just wasn't time for questions. "I'll get more water, and towels. Padding and bandages."

"I don't know who hurt her, but they're dead men. So is Caddi." Harold got a grip, he could kill the bastards later. Right now he had to make sure Mercedes would survive while he went hunting. "I'll need clean bedding as well, please?" As Tessa turned to leave, Harold knelt to carefully wipe away the worst from Mercedes' face. He couldn't see a big wound, and started worrying about where so much blood could have come from? She was covered in it. Mercedes opened her eyes and they weren't dead now.

Harold flinched from the rage in there.

"Not you. Stay, please." Her hand came up to grab Harold's arm, but he had no intention of leaving. "I just need to rest a bit." Mercedes tried to sit up but gave up. "A lot. Sorry I went all soggy. It's just, well, I didn't expect to make it." Harold wiped some more and wiping wasn't working.

"Don't worry, you're safe now. I promise." He wiped some more but bowls and cloths weren't going to get the job done. "You need a shower or a bath." Mercedes opened her eyes wide in alarm. "Tessa and Sharyn will make sure you don't drown or something." From behind Harold, someone agreed.

Mercedes closed her eyes for a long moment. When they opened some of the rage had gone. "No, only 'Arold gets to see me. Or touch me. Only 'Arold." They closed again as Mercedes tried to move but gave up with a short exclamation of pain. The ghost of her old smile showed the next time her eyes opened. "Will you make sure I don't drown, 'Arold?"

"I haven't got a proper life-saving certificate, but I'll try." Harold kept it light, when what he wanted to do was get his rifle and see how high he could stack Hot Rods. He'd never felt like this, even when Holly died. Half of him wanted to kill someone, the other half wanted to stay here and look after Mercedes, to keep her safe forever. Not black despair, not this time, he was absolutely blazing mad and this time someone would definitely die. He heard Sharyn exit, then low talking on the stairs. Sharyn came back while Harold kept trying to clean Mercedes, or at least her face. The fresh blood from her split bottom lip didn't help.

"Tessa's running a bath. When Mercedes is clean there's clothes. You can put her in Eddie's bed. Eddie will sleep with Tessa and Wills with me." Sharyn looked past Harold at his bed. "The bedding's clean but don't worry if it gets messed up."

Mercedes had tensed up again, a bit of the wildness coming back into her eyes, "No! In here. I'll sleep in here, it's safe!" Her eyes went between them, then up to the red heart hung on the wall, and a faint hint of humour came back. "I belong in 'Arold's burrow. Please?"

"No problem. Now, can you make it if I give you an arm?" Harold smiled at her rather than punching the wall.

"No." This look was almost shy. "But if you carry me you can wash my back?"

"No deals, but I will carry you." The old Mercedes smile tried to bloom but it would be a long time before that came back, if ever. Mercedes didn't need to get her strength back to deal with Caddi. Harold would hunt the bastard down, and he didn't care who saw him. He'd just as soon shoot them as well. As Harold bent and slid his arms under Mercedes, her arms went round his neck and held on tight. Harold stood slowly but smoothly. Mercedes gasped as his arm tightened around her back, then rested her head on his shoulder with a little sigh.

Harold carried Mercedes carefully upstairs, where Tessa waited by the bathroom door. Sharyn pulled Tessa aside and spoke quietly as Harold went in, then pulled the bathroom door shut behind him. He lowered Mercedes carefully into the chair, and turned his back so she could get stripped and into the water. The little noise behind him might have been an attempt at a laugh.

"I told you 'Arold. You can look any time, and anyway"—she sighed—"I can't do it myself." Mercedes attempted another little laugh. "Sorry, no buttons."

Harold sighed as well and turned back. "Damn, and I'd practiced." If Mercedes wanted to deal with it this way, he'd go along. Mercedes bent forward so Harold could untie the jeans around her chest, giving a hiss of pain as the denim came free. A deep cut across her shoulder blade opened up again, explaining some of the blood. Harold hesitated, and once again Mercedes looked almost shy.

"Will you take all my clothes off please, 'Arold?" Harold wished he didn't like the sound of that, or the memories of other times Mercedes had promised he could. The comparison raised that red rage deep inside, but he fought it down again, for now. The ragged shirt came off and when he saw the blood, bruising and semen under it, Harold wanted to kill some bastard right now, again.

Mercedes stiffened a bit, sounding defensive now. "The first one was in me when I came round." Harold carefully picked the battered young woman up again. He lowered her into the water, which immediately turned bloody. "The other two held me down." Mercedes hissed as the water went into the cuts and abrasions. "I'd got a message, a problem."

"You needn't tell me." Because it had been bloody awful, and maybe she didn't want anyone knowing the details.

Mercedes passed Harold the sponge with a question in her eyes, so Harold took it and started to squeeze water over her. "Lada, Yugo and Truck, a new bloke. A big one. They came as an escort." Dirt and bits of leaf and grass came out of her hair with the blood as Harold began to use a jug to sluice it. "Truck got me from behind, chloroform or something. Lada said they threw my clothes out of the car windows." It came in a monotone and Harold let Mercedes get it out without interrupting, carefully sponging her arms and shoulders.

"They were bragging because they'd been paid for having fun. Told me they were to keep me a few days, break me to my new job." The first shampoo brought more red out of her hair and a hiss as some ran down over the other cuts. "The bastards kept hitting me. Why do men do that, punch women?" Harold could see the bruises where someone had punched her biceps and thighs repeatedly.

It wasn't a question Mercedes wanted an answer to just now, since her voice droned on. "I pretended to faint under Lada." Harold carefully rinsed the shampoo out of her hair, and gently mopped her bruised face. "That's the hardest thing I ever did, lying still while the bastard did what he wanted, but it worked. They let go." That was almost a whisper but with a snarl in it, animation coming as Harold gently sluiced her back, going round the knife wound on her shoulder blade. "When he started to get up I followed and grabbed the knife from his belt." The next bit had real venom in it. "And cut his dick off!"

Mercedes gave a little laugh that touched on hysterical. "The stupid prats froze just long enough. Maybe Lada screaming and spraying blood all over did it." The curl of her lips as Harold sponged down the front of her throat, and started on her arms again, was a mixture of grimace and snarl. "I rolled over until I could reach Truck with a swing, then hamstrung him. Yugo came at me but I grabbed his leg and pulled him down for a roll in the grass. I rolled onto his knife arm and he got an edge in my back."

Harold had started on the other arm and hand now, getting some of the dirt and blood from the cuts and abrasions and under her broken nails. "He got my point, and then I got his balls. I caught Truck crawling away. I asked him and Yugo some questions while Lada bled out." Mercedes sighed, a deep, racking one. "Then I came to find you, 'Arold, because Caddi will say I broke the Deal."

"It was rape!" Harold couldn't believe it but then realised yes, Mercedes was right. Caddi wouldn't care about Mercedes being willing or not, he'd want his turn.

"But Caddi will say I should have stopped them, because there were only three. I must have been willing, some such shit. Bugatti paid them but Caddi must have told him to." Mercedes laid back and let the water up around her. The shadow of the old Mercedes smile showed for a moment "I was almost ready. I wanted to be so clean and pretty for you, 'Arold. Now I'm all dirty and used and ruined again."

"Dirt washes off." Mercedes' eyes didn't believe him. "You can dip a diamond in shit, but if you wash the shit off it's still a diamond." Harold tried to show that he meant it, but it wasn't working. Maybe Mercedes wasn't looking at his eyes, or maybe Harold's eyes wanted to kill Bug and Caddi, for starters.

"Maybe, Harold. But you might not want to kiss it after it's been in shit." And maybe that was a sliver of hope in those swollen eyes.

"Maybe it depends on the diamond?" Harold put a hand behind Mercedes' head and very carefully, very gently, kissed her bruised and split lips. When Harold pulled his head back he saw the first bit of warmth in her eyes and a real smile, small as it was. Harold smiled right back. "Hey, I thought it was 'Arold? I sort of like it now, when you say it." It was the first time Harold had admitted that out loud, but he was done with pretence right now.

"In that case 'Arold, will you please wash the rest of the shit off? Because if I have to remember hands on me, I'd like them to be yours. I'd just got to like that and now it's all spoiled." She sighed, looking towards where her scraped knees jutted out of the bloody foam. "No point in stockings now. All that work gone to waste." That didn't make sense, so Harold let it slide.

"Wash you? Of course. It's the least I can do now I've got you in my burrow." Mercedes glanced up at that, a searching look, then relaxed and smiled a little at whatever she saw.

"I can't hop yet, and my fur is still a bit grubby?" Harold washed her until Mercedes felt clean and that took another bath, run while Mercedes sat in the chair wrapped in big fluffy towel. He lifted her out again and dried her hair, and then the rest of her because Mercedes refused to do it. It had to be 'Arold's hands, but now a hint of her wicked smile had come back when she said that. Harold opened the first aid box Tessa or Sharyn had placed near the chair. He put a big dressing over her shoulder blade, and several smaller ones and plasters over other cuts, then picked up the small heap of clothes.

When he tried to help Mercedes into knickers, she refused with a giggle. A real one which made Harold's heart skip a bit. "I don't need them under a nightie." Her face fell a little. "Not your Christmas present. Not yet."

"I'll ask Sharyn and Tessa."

"Haven't you got something that will fit? I'd like that."

Harold opened the door to find Sharyn waiting on the landing and explained. She went down to his room, coming back with one of what Harold called his posh shirts, one with a collar and buttons. "I remember what you said about nightwear on your visits." She glanced at the door, towards Mercedes. "How is she? Do we need Lenny?"

"Start with Patricia. She might not be keen on a bloke just now."

Sharyn's face tightened and she nodded once. "I'll get her."

Mercedes managed a smile when she saw the shirt and insisted that 'Arold did up the buttons. He had to practice for if he wanted to check the action in the night. When Harold carried Mercedes back downstairs, he found either Sharyn or Tessa had put on clean bedding. He laid her down gently, helping Mercedes to turn so she wasn't laid on her shoulder blade. With a sigh, Harold put on his Soldier Boy persona, explaining that he had to make sure that if any arsehole came for her it was fatal. He showed Mercedes the pistol. Her Killer Queen persona opened it to check the loads, testing the weight on the hammer and trigger. Her gentler, warmer eyes returned as the weapon went back in its pocket.

Mercedes had already dropped into a doze as Harold quietly exited. He told Sharyn and Tessa what had happened, enough so they weren't curious and didn't need to ask. Both women promised that one or the other would be outside the door, and nobody except Patricia would disturb Mercedes. Harold went out to make sure Orchard Close was ready, or, as it turned out, inspect and compliment what his lieutenants, friends or elite had done.

Chapter 24:
Thirty Pieces of Silver

The next few days were the tense calm before an expected storm. Harold told Caddi's watchers the ruins weren't safe, and they left. He told the visitors that Orchard Close would be closed until further notice. The solitary Geek in The Pub promised to pass the message. There weren't any Hot Rod visitors, but nobody had thought anything of it until now. The Barbies and GOFS knew or guessed that Mercedes had moved in, so maybe a resident had said something. The Barbies reckoned that if Caddi attacked Orchard Close, he'd be wide open for the Barbies to solve their Hot Rod problem once and for all. Harold wasn't sure of the official Barbie opinion, because none of the suggestions came from one wearing a blonde wig.

The following day Roy and his men arrived. "Vulcan said we were needed here. He said something about an iron ball and a hard place?"

"The Hot Rods might be coming." Harold explained, without gory details. "If Caddi decides to let it go, I'll go hunting for the bastard anyway. I should have done it a couple of years ago."

Roy lifted the rifle, which Vulcan must have let him keep. "You'll want someone watching your back." He glanced around. "Is there any place we can cram in together? If there's an attack we don't want to be scattered about sleeping on sofas." His glance towards Cherry Tree House, where Celine lived, was probably involuntary but Harold could take a hint that big. There were a few comments when the four men ended up in Celine's flat, but humour, not scandal. Celine offered, moving in with June and Janine next door.

Any humour came as a relief, because the whole place was on edge. Anyone properly trained carried their weapons, while others made sure they knew where to find serious armament in a hurry. Children were kept near to home and all work on the Farm stopped, as did scavenging. The newest refugees worked in the gardens around their tents, or carried in bricks that had already been stacked nearby for Casper to strengthen the walls. Despite Harold giving them all the option, only three families left to ask for refuge with the GOFS.

The muskets were still hidden, but were assembled and loaded, and the Riot Squad wore their full kit including the new helmets and spears. Doll wouldn't have so many secrets to keep after this. The covers over all the firing steps were put up, so the Army couldn't see any rifles and to deflect pipe bombs. The deep, narrow trenches behind them were uncovered, dug to catch any pipe bombs rolling down the sloping covers and contain the blast. Another bright idea from someone that just might make a difference. Orchard Close waited, as ready as they could be.

Mercedes slept, ate, and had more baths with the same criteria, only 'Arold's hands. The young woman's routine became sleep, eat, and then another bath. Mercedes could walk a few steps, but insisted that her feet hurt too much to get upstairs. That had to be partly true at first, because she'd walked barefoot across several miles of rubble to get to Orchard Close. Mercedes still claimed to be incapable of washing, drying or dressing herself, insisting on being carried up and down stairs, or lifted in and out of her bath.

Harold ignored the amused looks from Tessa and Sharyn, spending any spare time sat by her bed. They talked about what if, when she recovered, and Harold told her about the escape route if the General came with too many men. Caddi might wait to combine with him, and then Harold wanted Mercedes to leave with the women. She agreed but only if he came as well, then they could run away together to live in the wild. Harold could wear Army gear, but with all her bruises she wouldn't need camouflage.

The third day he carried her out to sit on the settee for a couple of hours, not an armchair because Mercedes needed 'Arold sitting next to her in case she fainted. Mercedes had real mischief in her voice now, and the warmth and even welcome in her eyes grew with every bath. Most of the time Mercedes' eyes showed neither hate nor the dead, flat stare. Unless someone mentioned Caddi or Hot Rods, when the Killer Queen appeared, primed and ready. Those names got the same reaction from Soldier Boy, Harold had never hated anyone so completely as he did Caddi.

They still hadn't kissed, apart from a gentle brushing of lips now and then. Harold didn't push at all, making sure to use the sponge, not his hands when bathing Mercedes. When she insisted, he began to wash her arms and shoulders by hand. She didn't make it a blatant sexual game, or tease. Mercedes just kept telling Harold that she wanted to remember his hands on her, because 'Arold was gentle. It was hard to say no to that. Harold didn't want to say no, because he'd been completely captivated.

The bright, sexy, dangerous Mercedes had been alluring enough, and her eyes and voice promised that version of Mercedes still lurked in wait. Harold still only expected a night, a week, maybe a month of wild sex and bitten shoulders and bedding. A wonderful memory he could hold onto, as Mercedes went off on whatever new path life had for the Killer Queen. Harold thought he'd have a few interesting scars from teeth or nails to go with the memories.

But Harold no longer wanted that. This quiet, gentle, abused but definitely not submissive Mercedes spoke to another part of Harold. The 'soft lad' part, as Sharyn and Tessa called it. The part that meant a younger Harold brought home stray cats and once a three legged dog. That part wanted to keep this latest stray, even if she bit him to the bone and every gangster in the city came for her. After five days Harold had progressed to washing her back, and her legs below her knees, by hand, and she'd started teasing about delectables. Mercedes warned him that since he'd got past the buttons so easily, his hopping had better be spectacular.

The soft lad wanted to kill someone first, but he couldn't go hunting because the rest of Orchard Close needed Soldier Boy here and visible. By now, Caddi had to know Mercedes had disappeared, and had probably found the bodies of his men. With the shutdown and sending the watchers home, he had to assume Mercedes came to Orchard Close. No messengers came, and no word on the radios except chatter about fighting the Murphies. The Hot Rods had won their war, concentrating on mopping up and consolidating their grip on the captured estates. More refugees arrived, replacing the ones that had left, and were put in tents with the rest after being carefully searched for weapons or radios. After six days, everyone began to wonder if Caddi had his hands full consolidating all his new territory, and had written Mercedes off.

* * *

Trev repaired more of Caddi's radios so Harold sent them to the Annex. Trev also finished a project. Just before Mercedes arrived the radio man had come up with something new. He'd managed an extra channel on the little handhelds, one that nobody else would be able to listen to. Now Trev called round Harold's house to say he needed a proper test. It was after ten, full dark outside especially with the low cloud covering the moon, but Trev never thought of time when he'd got some bee in his bonnet. Harold took the little radio down to the Annex as suggested, to try the new channel at a distance. He had a look round the walls when Ru insisted, but as far as Harold could see, the Demons had it covered.

The new radio channel sort of worked. It sounded very scratchy and cut out a bit but Trev said he knew what that was, bring it back. Harold picked his way back through the garden refugee camp, quietly because many had settled down for the night. He had to be careful because there weren't any outside lights, a garden didn't need them. Harold smiled to see light peeking from behind the caravan curtains; some couple were getting a bit of private time.

He spoke quietly to the pair of guards keeping a watch on the garden, then went through the gate. Trev met Harold before he reached the work-shop. He'd taken two adjusted versions to Harold's house, to save him the trip. Trev kept twitching but he always got excited over anything out of the ordinary, and the alert had to be winding him right up. He followed Harold through the door, chattering nervously about how useful the extra channel would be.

*   *   *

Half-blinded after coming in from the pitch dark, Harold started taking a step into the living room before the strained expression on Sharyn's face registered. He stopped, way too late as the washroom door in the hall behind him opened. Now he'd opened the door properly Harold could also see how many others were in the room, and one of them in particular. "Why hello Harry, nice of you to drop in."

Caddi! Something prodded Harold in the back. A man stepped out of the kitchen doorway behind Sharyn, Cooper with a big smile. He rested a Rambo on her shoulder, with the edge towards her throat. "Trev did it." Harold glanced down at Tessa, on the floor to the side of the door with some bloke wearing Army gear and carrying an SA80 Army rifle. Recognition hit him. Corporal 'Suggs' Young! From back in London and then Calais!

"Shut it. You need to learn manners, girly. I thought you'd been a sol-dier's bird? Twice?" Suggs half raised a hand from his rifle then put it back across the trigger, ready, when he saw Harold's look.

"Come in, Harry. I believe you have something of mine?" The warlord had a wide smile on his face but his glare looked bloody furious. "Didn't we talk about that?" Caddi gestured towards the study door. "One night, Harry, not a week."

Harold took three more steps, looking around as a hand came round him to remove his belt, pistol and knife. There were eleven Hot Rods in all, and the one behind him, and they'd somehow caught Patty, Casper and Elise as well as Sharyn and Tessa. Harold looked up the stairs as Pete came down with a smile on his face.

"Fantasia is looking after the kids and the dog." His smile disappeared as Harold got a snarl. "I've sold your ass this time, and now Fantasia is mine. Mr. Cadillac said so."

"Oh yes, we must reward the workers. He's paid all his debts off as well. You have been telling fibs, Soldier Boy." As Caddi sniggered, Harold tried to work out what the hell the little shit had done, how Pete had gotCaddi inside. Meanwhile Trev scuttled past to sit on a chair in the corner. One of the Hot Rods pushed Elise over and Trev pulled her onto his knee, then tried to kiss her. Elise looked horrified and tried to get away, but Trev had a firm grip.

"You need to learn how to reward the workers, Harry. Find out what they really want." Caddi tapped on the floor with Harold's stick. "Now, firstly, about your girlfriend." Harold's eyes went to Tessa. "Not that one. Ooh, this will be fun. My own Soldier Boy, my own gunsmith! Which woman will you build guns for, if you can only save one? After all, there's your sister as well. You are going to be a good little boy, Harry." Caddi beamed at everyone, savouring the moment. "Only one, because I've promised my new soldier an Army wife. But you can save the other."

Harold's head went around and around looking for an out, because he knew the little shit was lying. Caddi might make a deal to start with but he'd get bored. He'd take both women when it occurred to the arse that there were the kids. Caddi would use them to keep Harold and both the women obedient. "Now back to telling little porkies. What exactly did you do in the Army, big bad Soldier Boy?"

"You know and I never lied about it." Because Pete looked triumphant and Suggs started sneering. From Tessa's face she'd remembered what Harold had said would happen next, if the gangs found out about him being a clerk. He'd expected every nearby gang to combine and burn the whole enclave, then piss on the ashes. If Caddi had captured Orchard Close, he wouldn't burn it, but there'd still be plenty of nasty bastards wanting to get a piece of Soldier Boy.

"Pay clerk. Office weenie. Dipstick typist!" Caddi almost foamed at the mouth as he spat it out.

"Never said I wasn't, and I'm a crap typist." Two shotguns, two crossbows, and Cooper would have a hand gun as did at least two of the others. So would Caddi, so it would be a massacre. They all had machetes and knives, except Pete who only had a baseball bat and Trev with just a sheath knife. Casper had his hands tied together in front and a gag, and the Hot Rod behind him had a knife to the big man's throat. The man behind Patty had an arm round her waist, and his knife at her throat. Harold shrugged, playing for time. "You'll never make it back over the wall."

"I don't need to. Your guards around the gate are snoozing gently, because Trev took them all a lovely warm drink. Easy to do while you were off testing some imaginary piece of magic." Caddi preened, smirking at Harold's sudden comprehension. "By now they're already trussed up, ready for a bit of fun. Not yet, not until everyone else is under control." The warlord smiled broadly, a stark contrast to his rage only moments before. "I've already got another ninety men inside or coming over the wall by the gate, and there's more waiting to come at that Annex if they don't see sense."

Caddi pointed towards the gates. "We've got one armoury with those lovely new weapons, and your gun room once you give me the key. Meanwhile my men are stood on the walls near the gate tonight, wearing helmets and those armoured vests and skirts so everyone thinks it's all sweet. In a bit, when he's played with his new toy, Trev will take drinks round to more of the guards. We'll take the rest of the guardhouses and the people most likely to give trouble. When everyone wakes up in the morning, they'll be under new management." He eyed up Patty, smirking at her glare. "The most valuable experts, like brewers and bomb-makers, even the knitters, are all getting special visits. Soldier Boy's compound without a shot fired, and they all said it couldn't be done!"

"Yeah, well, thirty pieces of silver always was a problem." Pete winced but Trev didn't care, the radio man kept ferreting away under the blouse. Elise whimpered again, trying to pull away as Trev pushed her bra up to hang out of the front.

"Just sit yourself down a minute, Harry, where I can keep an eye on you." Harold looked where the casual wave indicated, picking a spot between a man with a single barrelled shotgun and one with a revolver in his hand. Harold knelt because hope never dies. Caddi and Cooper, ten Hot Rods, Pete and Trev, too many but if enough let their guard down he would go apeshit and see what happened. A fit, agile man could get to his feet faster from his knees than from sitting, especially if he didn't sink back on his haunches.

At least going apeshit would rouse Orchard Close. Gangs didn't arm serfs, so with luck, Caddi hadn't realised how many people had weapons in their homes. Trev had never been involved in the defence, because the radio man had always made it clear he wasn't a fighter. Caddi smiled happily. "On your knees? Getting the message?"

Cooper came in from the kitchen, pushing Sharyn towards an armchair. He sat down with Sharyn perched on the arm. The senior Hot Rod lieutenant held her wrist with one hand, laying the Rambo along his other leg, ready. "Just so you don't get ambitious, Harry." Cooper looked up, inspecting Sharyn. "Nice looking lass, so you wouldn't want her all scarred up. After all, that wouldn't stop the lads passing her round if you misbehave."

Caddi tapped Harold's stick on the floor to get everyone's attention. "I didn't need silver for bribery, Harry, I just gave a man what he wanted for the job. You actually sent him to me." Caddi sneered at an oblivious Trev. "I saw him eyeing the younger women on the first visit. I sent one to bring Trev drinks and help pull that crap apart, or at least that's what I told him." Several Hot Rods laughed. "Young but just about legal, when that mattered. She knew what was good for her, and made sure he got a good eyeful, and he was definitely interested but didn't bite." Caddi turned a little to look over at Sharyn. "You're lucky he likes some tit, or he'd be upstairs with your brat. I tried a brat, then a thirteen-year-old. He had her bent over in that garage full of radio bits within seconds of her flashing her panties and asking if he saw anything he fancied. I showed him the film afterwards." Caddi turned back towards Harold with a smug grin. "Then I fed him young playmates every visit, and filmed them all but by then he didn't care. After that it was just a case of choosing a time. I expected Mercedes to kill those three or die trying, but I'd have come after you either way."

Harold tried to hide his disgust, and get the subject off Trev's nasty habits. "Where did you find that piece of shit? He'll shoot you in the back given half a chance." He frowned, still looking at Suggs. "The silly sod does know that shooting that rifle will bring artillery?"

"Bullshit, Harry, not if they don't see it."

"Gospel, Caddi, the sound is distinctive. They'll turn Orchard Close into rubble, then search the bodies. The artillery is dialled in on any near-by enclave and on call twenty-four seven, just in case, so I hope you've got a tight rein on this idiot. He's not got enough brain cells to work it out himself." Harold nodded towards Suggs, who opened his mouth to answer.

Caddi cut him off. "Shut it Suggs. There's no need to risk it now, so don't pull that trigger." Suggs nodded, with a sharp look at Harold that promised payback. Caddi leant back against the wall with a little smile. "He can use it when I run over the GOFS, to shoot the fuckers clustered around that cannon. With the rifles and my own artillery, I'll take out the Barbies as well if that General doesn't get his thumb out of his arse. He expects me to share, stupid bastard." Caddi gave Patty a speculative look. "I might sell him this one, because he saw her on the TV and now he wants her more than ever. He wants the black bitch as well but I'd get a better price from Einstein. Einstein will offer a fortune, but he can't have her. With the kid to control her, Emmy can be my shooter one." Caddi turned quickly towards Harold, looking to see what reaction that got.

"You might not want to sell too many of the women, Caddi, or rough them up. You might be selling Shooters Three to Nine." Caddi's eyes jerked to Patty. "Yes, meet Shooter Three. I've got more shooters than rifles, and most are women."

Caddi relaxed, confident again. "I'll make them an offer they won't fancy refusing, not when they see what happens to the bitch in there." Caddi hooked a thumb at the bedroom. "Nor what happens to that blonde, Doll. The Marts have offered a reward, and they want her to be needing medical attention and grateful for being rescued. After what they paid for the first pictures, what do you reckon the local horny twats will pay for one wearing only her hat and boots? For the right price, they'll get to fuck her as well. Not too many, because she's got to be alive. Got you! That fucking got to you! Fuck, I've been trying for years."

"But I haven't lost it. Remember what happens if I do." Harold had to try and slow the bastard up before Caddi did get to him, and he blew. The longer they talked, the more chance someone out there would notice a problem or a strange face.

"You would have if Jon or that dick Spyke Pierce had brought a woman back. I told them any woman, but the blonde would have been a bonus. I was going to train up one of your bitches, then get her to come in naked on her hands and knees and offer to fuck any way you fancied. When you went for me I could have killed you inside the rules." Caddi laughed delightedly and pointed at Harold. "Again, I saw it in your eyes, I got you again!"

There wasn't any point in Harold denying it, because he was completely gobsmacked. "Back then? Why couldn't you just let me be, Caddi?"

In a split second all Caddi's humour evaporated. "You shot my men and fined them, and nobody gets away with that! Then you killed that fucker Jon in front of my gates, and threatened to kill me on my own doorstep! You caned my men, then fucking well executed one with the other gangs watching, you arrogant fucker! I tried for the black bitch and it cost me a quarter mile of housing. I even paid some arse up north for a sniper, but that just gave you another rifle. You threatened to cripple me, inside the Mansion, and I couldn't touch you! You snapped up all the women from the Murphies, and even got into Beth's and lived! My own fucking men think you're some sort of superman and that ice cold bitch in there crawls all over you. That chicken-shit fucker Mack wouldn't come after you! Told me no! You've been a bug up my arse ever since day one, you stuck-up, holier-than-thou bastard, and now they'll all see you crawl!" Caddi had nearly lost it, eyes wild and spittle flying as he spoke. With an obvious effort he got control.

Harold spoke up before Caddi started ranting again. "I'll repair guns if you leave my sister alone. You should think twice about giving Tessa to that fat, useless prat. She's my apprentice and you've got her kid, so she'll repair guns. Then if I lose it and you kill me, you've still got a repairer." Harold had to get Caddi believing he'd roll over, had to get him to relax. "You haven't seen my women fight. Give them the choice of being shock troops instead of giving them to your men. They'll run right over the Geeks for you, even without the threat. They'll be a hell of a shock for the Bloodsuckers if the General gives you too much shit, worse than Barbies."

"Not all of them. I've got to make a profit and Einstein has offered a small fortune for that Chink. If she's lucky she'll still be alive when we run over the Geeks." Caddi calmed a bit, calculating now. "Still trying to protect the women, Soldier Boy? Actually, you might be right, at least to start with. My blokes said half those who chopped up the General's men were women. That's why the General wants that bitch." Caddi pointed at Patty with Harold's stick. "An army on bicycles, who would have thought?"

Harold stared, caught out again. "He wants Patty for that?" Until the bit about bicycles, Harold had been thinking about the fight on the TV, at the railway cutting.

"You didn't know? He isn't a happy bunny about losing the men, or what she did to them." He glared at Patty then, volatile as ever, chuckled. "Ooh, I get all those bunnies as well, and your expert. Those experts are going to make me very, very rich, Soldier Boy. So will you, chained down on your knees in your workshop while you build new guns." Caddi scowled at Suggs. "Hard luck, you can pick another woman. Unless you've suddenly remembered you can repair muskets and pistols?" Suggs glared at Harold, then shook his head. "Right, enough yapping, time for fun." Caddi pushed off the wall and walked over to Cooper, handing him a pistol and a Rambo.

Cooper put the pistol in the back of his belt where Sharyn couldn't make a grab for it, and tucked the extra Rambo down the side of his leg. "Wouldn't want you tempted, dear." Harold glanced at Patty while Caddi was distracted. Patty's face looked calm, but set, and she flicked an eyelid. Movement caught Harold's eye as Patty flexed her hands, just a little, with the thumbs crooked ready for a Wamil move. Patty only needed half a chance and she'd go for the knife.

Caddi swaggered back to Harold's bedroom door, twirling the stick. He held it by the bottom and tapped the brass boss on the door. "Mercedes, dear, we're ready now." He glanced at the stick, then at Casper, and sneered. "This is a lot more solid than I thought, heavier. I might beat the fucking queer to death with it, to see just how tough they both are."

Casper sneered back at Caddi and moved backwards a bit, rubbing his ass on his guard. The man yelped and pushed him away. "Fucking queer! Did you see that?" He held the back of Casper's shirt in one hand and put the point of the Rambo against a kidney, keeping him at arm's length. "Try it again now, you fucking perv." Harold didn't smile, but Casper had just made himself a bit of room for whatever he'd got planned. Maybe when the door opened they'd get their chance.

Harold's bedroom door clicked and opened but Caddi didn't look, he watched Harold. The man with a crossbow standing opposite Harold raised it just a little. After a moment the warlord smirked. "Not springing to the rescue? Pity, because Samuel has been looking for a chance ever since you crippled his hand. I told him he can shoot you in the legs, because you can work without walking." In the open doorway the man just to the side of Mercedes, holding a double-barrelled shotgun, scowled at Harold. He pushed past her and stood beside the door, with his gun aimed at Harold's thighs.

Mercedes wore one of Harold's shirts, much too big for her even if it didn't bury her like the one at the Mansion. She insisted on sleeping in them until she healed up, and made 'Arold practice buttons at bath time. Her head was bowed, and when it came up Harold saw the Killer Queen's flat, dead eyes. His leg muscles flexed, ready, but Mercedes smiled at Caddi, a big bright smile. "Why Caddi, you only had to send word. I came here because I got knocked about a bit, and needed to get all cleaned up and pretty again for you."

"Bullshit, you've been banging his brains out, and we had a deal!"

"No, not even once. He left me to heal up. Oh well." Her eyes switched over. "Hard luck, lover boy, missed your chance." Caddi's suspicious gaze moved over so Harold shrugged.

"Stupid bastard. Like I said, a dying breed." Caddi looked back at Mercedes. "I don't mind if you're a bit banged up. I'm going to do some banging as well." A round of crude remarks from the Hot Rods suggested what might get banged and what with.

"In that case, come and get it, big boy." Mercedes turned on her heel, taking a step inside the room and pulling the shirt back to her shoulders so the front would be open. "Hurry if you want to win the commando bet, or I might just drop this and invite bids."

Caddi propped Harold's stick against the wall by the door. "Keep an eye on him, Samuel." He gestured towards Harold before looking around the room. "I'll be busy. I'm gonna ride a Mercedes hard enough to break the suspension." Caddi turned away from the laughter and walked through the door, kicking it shut behind him. The Hot Rods shouted various comments about leaving some for others, then watched Harold, Casper or the two women for a reaction. Trev didn't, he'd still got a hand up Elise's blouse, with the other around her stopping the teenager from getting away. He kept trying to kiss her while she whimpered and tried to avoid him.

"Here, let me look." Suggs gestured towards Harold's stick but Samuel ignored him. Harold realised his two-two bullet, just after the Crash, had permanently crippled Samuel's right hand. The gangster had his left hand on the trigger, with the other hand curled up in a claw that he used to support the shotgun barrels without gripping. The Hot Rod with the crossbow threw the stick along the floor but it bounced off the door nearby before Suggs caught it. The ex-soldier hefted it. "Fuck, it weighs a ton. No wonder you broke my fucking hand." His eyes narrowed and he rapped it on the floor. "Maybe Caddi will let me break your knees with it, since you won't need to walk."

"I'm surprised you had the balls to come near me after last time, even with a big rifle." Harold would settle for riling Suggs enough to get a break.

Suggs sneered, tapping the stick on the floor. "Caddi sent the word round for a soldier or civvie who knew your unit, since this dipstick told him where you served." The ex-soldier pointed the stick at Pete. "He wanted to check, in case the little arse just wanted to get out of debt."

An exclamation in the study and a smack, followed by a definitely feminine yelp, shut everyone up. Those who'd tensed up at the noise relaxed and laughed. More slaps and yelps, and a banging noise, led to more laughter, and comments about breaking the bed as well. Voices muttered, and a rhythmic banging came through the wall loud and clear. More muffled noises, wet smacks and short yells followed as the banging continued, for much too long. Harold tried to ignore those making comments about what he'd missed, because he knew the voice making the yelps of pain. They were from Mercedes, and in time with the thumping of the bed. But despite the jokes and laughter, none of the bastards relaxed enough for him to beat that shotgun and crossbow.

The noises finally stopped, followed by a long silence. Eventually the bed creaked and slow footsteps started towards the door. Harold worked his leg and arm muscles, pumping blood into them, because when Caddi opened the door and posed, everyone would look. Harold would take a flying leap at the bastard and drive him back into the study. They'd hesitate to shoot at Caddi, and if Harold could get to the pistol in the bed and stick in to the shit's ear they might all still get out alive.

When the bedroom door opened, Harold nearly went, but it wasn't Caddi! Everyone could collect on the commando bet, because Mercedes stood there full frontal stark naked if you didn't count the blood. A sheet of it spread from just above her left breast, other cuts had reopened, and more blood trickled down her leg where it looked as if Caddi had clawed her thigh. A spray of crimson and clotted hair covered her left shoulder, maybe from her ear, and she had a huge, livid bruise across her lower ribs on the opposite side. "One down." Mercedes paused, taking a couple of short, pained breaths, head still down but rising. "Does anyone else want some, because Caddi's finished?" Harold started moving.

Because her left hand held something bloody, and her right stayed out of sight behind the door jamb. As Mercedes raised her head far enough, Harold saw the sheer stark homicidal fury burning in her eyes. Not the rage when she'd first arrived in Orchard Close. That was just a kitty compared to this, the insane, blood-crazed berserker tigress. Her left hand came forward and opened, and every other eye followed what came out until it hit the floor with a sodden smack.

As her right hand moved and the gore-spattered .38 came into view, Harold had already pulled one knee up to plant his foot flat on the floor, reaching out sideways for the shotgun. He pulled the barrel down into the man's shin while his other hand went up, fumbling until his thumb found the man's finger. Harold pushed. A shriek followed on the heels of the roar as the weapon blew half the gangster's foot off.

Harold heard the .38 fire as he turned to his other guard, grabbed his pistol and yes, Mercedes had put the first one into him. When Harold used the man to lever himself up and forward, the gangster barely reacted except to bounce back off the wall from the impact of her bullet. Harold held the man's hand and forced his trigger finger back, aiming by holding the barrel with the other hand. Mercedes' .38 sounded again even as Harold shot Samuel, the shotgun man, using the gangster's revolver.

Samuel had reacted to the bloody handful hitting the floor by swinging his shotgun that way, towards Mercedes. He took vital seconds to react to the shotgun blast and the shriek, before trying to swing back towards Harold. His clawed hand lost its grip when Mercedes fired the .38 right beside him and he tried to change direction again. Harold gave Samuel two bullets to make sure, then ground his thumb between knuckles and wrenched the pistol free. He snapped off a shot at the man opposite him, already aiming his crossbow. The bolt went past Harold's ear when his bullet smashed the Hot Rod backwards. Harold made it to his feet now, elbowing the man he'd just taken the pistol from before starting down the room. Mercedes had both hands on the .38, leaning against the door frame as she aimed the opposite way towards Cooper.

Someone else started shooting but the .38 sounded again behind Harold, twice. By the door Tessa lay across Suggs as he yelled and thrashed, trying to shove her off his rifle. Meanwhile, Trev started screaming, oddly muffled because Elise had her face right in his. Blood dripped, and Trev kept trying to push her away, but Elise hung on with both her arms round the nasty little pervert's head. The hand Trev needed to get at his knife stayed trapped up her blouse, while the other couldn't reach around her far enough.

Casper had turned round. He must have nutted the bloke and grabbed his knife hand because he held it down behind the man's bruised head, while both Casper's arms were trying for a bear hug. He couldn't get one with his wrists still bound, not properly, and the Hot Rod still hung onto his knife. The pair wrestled back and forth, Casper unable to get in a proper head butt or apply full pressure, and the man unable to break free.

A Hot Rod had half-drawn his machete but Harold kicked him in the side of the knee and he stumbled, arms spread to catch himself on the wall. Harold left him because he had to stop Suggs first. "Tessa!" Tessa glanced round, rolling clear so Harold put the next two rounds into Suggs's chest. Two because the stupid shit had his finger on the trigger. If an SA80 opened up, the Army would level the place. Mercedes thought the same because an extra hole appeared at the same time.

Elise flew back, hitting the wall with a shriek. As she collapsed, Harold pointed the pistol and pulled the trigger. All six must have been loaded because it put a round right through Trev's hips, just his hips because Harold wanted to talk to Trev later. A spray of blood erupted as Trev tried to scream through the ruin of his nose and lip. Elise had finally given him mouth contact; she'd done her best to bite his face off.

The stick lay next to Suggs's crumpled form, so Harold dropped the empty pistol and scooped it up. One click and he swivelled, pulling the blade clear. The steel tube smacked a frozen Pete in the face as part of the same move, because Harold wanted a chat with that bastard as well. Casper's hands were still tied, and now the point of a crossbow bolt protruded from the back of one thigh. The Hot Rod had one eye swelling rapidly and his arms still pinned as Casper hugged him, and had dropped his Rambo. Unfortunately, the Hot Rod kept dodging further head butts and had twisted enough to avoid the knee trying for his groin. The man couldn't get his arms loose but had almost managed to wriggle his pistol free, twisting his body to try and aim it. Harold skewered his wrist and thigh, and the gun tumbled to the floor while the man stiffened and yelled. As he turned away Harold heard the wet smack as Casper took his chance to finally butt the bastard properly.

Harold started back down the room towards where Sharyn sprawled by the armchair. The Hot Rod next to Pete had now drawn his machete and he swung, but Harold caught the blade on his stick before following up with the sword through his heart. Harold wrenched the blade sideways to wreck his lung as well, because the instructor insisted. A stab could be survived, but that couldn't.

Another machete man rushed in but Harold smacked the upper part of the sword blade into his forearm, knocking the strike wide. Harold twisted his wrist to bring the point round, thrusting diagonally in beside the Adam's apple. As the point came out under the gangster's ear, another wrench tore out most of the man's throat. Even as the gangster crumpled, Harold caught a flicker of movement and ducked, but pain shot through his shoulder. He staggered but hung onto his stick despite the pain shooting down his arm. A Hot Rod with a bullet hole in his chest had hit him with an empty crossbow. Harold kicked at the man's kneecap, fending him off long enough to bring his sword hand up and over, driving the brass boss down on his opponent's head.

Patty had got her captor's knife, and from the blood, a piece of her man, but now he'd got a grip on her knife wrist. She held his other wrist as he tried to line up a pistol, snapping at his face and throat with her teeth. From the way he'd turned his body, she'd already tried to knee him. Her fingers and thumb dug in, Patty twisted her wrist, and with a short cry of pain the man dropped his gun. Patty's hand drove upwards, but he managed to block it and grabbed her wrist. Patty should get him now, eventually, but Harold didn't want to risk it. He daren't go for a killing stroke with them twisting about, but he ran the point deep into the bloke's buttocks. From experience that would hurt like hell. It hurt enough for Patty to wrench her knife hand free, immediately driving the blade up under his ribs. She turned towards the crossbow wielder Harold had shot, now dragging himself up the wall and groping for his machete.

When Harold's stick came down again, the man still shrieking over the ruin of his leg shut up. A Hot Rod, on his knees with a Mercedes bullet hole in him, fought to raise his single barrelled shotgun. Harold's sideways slash gave him an extra mouth beneath his chin and he crumpled.

Harold stopped his lunge at Cooper because it wasn't needed. As the Hot Rod's head fell sideways, Harold saw that Cooper had two .38 holes in his shirt. Something moved on the floor nearby, next to a dropped pistol. Sharyn, alive and staring up at her brother in some sort of shock. The room fell quiet except for the sounds of men in pain or dying. As Harold turned, shots rang out outside and the screaming and shouting started. Harold hesitated, but he had to concentrate on this mess first.

* * *

Casper half-sat against the wall, his leg bent awkwardly because of the crossbow bolt still through his thigh. His opponent lay very still with his head at an unhealthy angle. Patty rose from her second victim with a machete in her hand. She headed for Trev with murder in mind. "Not yet Patty. I want to talk to Trev first." Patty glanced back, nodding before using the machete on the unconscious man with a ruined leg. She headed for another one who wasn't dead yet. Trev wasn't going to enjoy the waiting when Patty finally got there.

Harold lost interest because he'd checked on Mercedes. She'd started sliding down the door jamb, the .38 tumbling to the floor. Harold dropped his sword and stick, leaping forward to catch her but her skin, slick with blood, slithered through his hands. He followed her down, keeping her half sat, while he looked for the wound. He missed it until Mercedes whispered "Ribs. Cooper." Another, slower look and the blood from above masked an innocent little 9 mm hole in her ribcage, just below her left breast. Harold tried to stem the flow from what he realised with a shock was a savage bite mark. Mercedes talked in between short, cautious breaths. "Had to. Shut him. Up." Harold moved her to see round the back but couldn't see an exit wound. He hoped the bullet hadn't broken up in there. "Sorry, 'Arold. All. Messed up. Again."

"Still a diamond." Mercedes tried to laugh and winced instead. From the huge bruise on her lower ribs opposite the bullet hole, they were cracked or broken. He had to get her to a doctor!

Mercedes' eyes came up to meet Harold's. They worried Harold more than anything else because they were calm, almost resigned. Then the steel showed. "Go on, 'Arold. Kill them." She grimaced. "All of them." Her eyes closed and Mercedes let go. Sharyn and Tessa were suddenly trying to take her, shouting in his ear.

"Go, get it sorted. It's old night and ruination out there. Sort it, Soldier Boy!" That jerked him up. Sharyn had only ever called him Soldier Boy once before! Harold raised his head and yes, muskets were in play so it wasn't one-sided.

"I'll reload that revolver, and we've got shotguns here. Don't worry about us." Tessa had already picked up Samuel's shotgun. "We'll take care of Mercedes and Elise."

Casper held out a hand for the shotgun. "Use the single barrels in here. I'll want a mace as well." He'd already snapped off the crossbow head. "And two pads and a bandage when this comes out."

Tessa stared at him. "You can't fight like that."

"I always stay behind when there's trouble, because I can't see far enough for a shooting fight. My job is to defend Orchard Close." Casper took a grip on the crossbow shaft. Patty hadn't argued, she'd wadded up two lumps of cloth and cut the sleeve off a gangster's shirt. "Well this time the bastards are inside the walls, so you're not leaving me behind again."

"I'll get some disinfectant." Sharyn turned towards the kitchen.

"Not now, I'll sort that out when we're done." Casper pulled. "Kerr-ripes!" He leant back while Patty and Harold bound the cloth on top of his jeans.

"Can you keep up?" Harold pulled him to his feet. He understood how Casper felt, the big man had always hated being left behind on guard.

"Don't run. If you do, wait now and then." Casper recovered his big machete and a Rambo, filling his pockets with shotgun shells. Harold went into his bedroom, avoiding the bloody mess on the bed to look down the road. He could see firearms flashing and moving figures.

"We'd best go out the back and pick up the girl club. The scroats are everywhere."

"Here." Patty gave Harold his belt with his Rambo and pistol, and as he fastened it stuck another two pistols in the back. He checked the clip and that the rest were still on his belt, then picked up his sword and stick. Patty picked up two more pistols and stuck them into the back of her belt, brandishing her recovered sabre and a pistol with a savage grin. "Let's go."

"Ready?" Casper nodded so Harold stuck the stick through his belt, drew a pistol, and the three of them headed out into the night.

* * *

Dawn was breaking as Harold limped up to Orchard Close. He stopped just inside the gates, looking slowly around with a sense of despair. How the hell would they get through this? Bodies, both gangsters and residents, still lay scattered in the street. Those, the bullet holes, the shattered doors and windows and the pools, trails and spatters of blood across the street, paths and walls, told a gruesome story. A story that had ended for too many of those calling Orchard Close their home.

Harold had left an hour before first light because one of the prisoners had talked. Loudly and repeatedly, and Harold would never know what his captors did to scare him. He didn't care much, or that the man probably died soon afterwards. Behind Harold a score of vehicles blocked the access road, while back where they'd been parked were a score of bodies. There had been no bloody assault and desperate fight. Harold's party snuck up on the shits and filled them with crossbow bolts, then went in quickly with blades while the wounded survivors were still screaming in shock.

Another Orchard Close survivor, with her arm in a sling, came past Harold and out of the front gate. She kept her pistol pointed at the two wounded Hot Rods carrying a limp figure on a door. They'd dump the Hot Rod body across the road on the potato field with the rest for now. Stretchers, moving slowly and gently, were taking the Orchard Close wounded to be cared for. Only Lenny and Patricia had the skills to deal with serious wounds, and some of these were well beyond their capabilities.

Eventually the stretcher bearers and medics would get round to enemy wounded, but Hot Rods were well down anyone's list. There wasn't enough in the way of dressings or antibiotics, or even disinfectant, to waste on the bastards who caused this. A hail from the bypass broke into Harold's thoughts. The Army wanted to talk, a relief because Harold had half expected a helicopter gunship and napalm to top off the chaos and gunfire in the darkness. He dumped his weapons, walked to the bottom of the road, did the twirl and limped up to the sandbags.

This time a lieutenant waited, one with unit badges showing he belonged to the sergeant and his men, or the other way round. "The only reason I didn't call in a strike was because the sergeant here kept insisting that you are decent people." The lieutenant's arm came up and pointed at the growing heap of bodies in the potato patch. "That doesn't look civilised."

"Suppose some bastard came into your house in the night, and stuck a knife in your sister or wife, and you managed to kill him. Would you care about his body while you were trying to stop up the bloody great hole in your sister?" Harold bit off the rest, about the bloody Army being useless if they let this happen. He wasn't in the mood for lectures.

"Those were inside your home? Your, er, enclave?" The lieutenant looked again and saw more men limping out carrying bodies, injured men escorted by heavily bandaged women pointing weapons. "Those are injured prisoners!"

"Those are the arseholes who injured those women. They're lucky to be alive. They can work or bleed out because I didn't ask them to come here." Harold pointed out over the city. "If you want decency and Geneva Conventions out there, do something about it. An armoured division and you could clean up the lot in a week."

The lieutenant drew himself up. "We are not allowed to interfere with the civilians. It is their..."

"That's the only human rights we have down there. The right to kill the bastards when they try to kill us." Harold managed to stop himself spitting. "You don't even allow us to do that properly."

"I was told you were a reasonable person. Not like the other lunatics." Beyond the officer Harold could see Sarge's eyes trying hard to say 'shut up' without speaking. Eventually the NCO actually mouthed it, silently.

Harold took a deep breath and shut his eyes for long moments. "My apologies for the tone. It has been a long and very hard night, and I have friends still dying down there."

The officer relaxed very slightly. "Still? I thought the fighting was over?"

"One of our human rights is to have no medical help. I would be truly grateful for an Army medic, just for the women?" Harold knew a bit of pleading crept into his voice.

The officer flinched slightly, then looked down at Orchard Close. "I am truly sorry but no, unless I call for ambulances to take them away?" Harold shook his head, which didn't seem to surprise the officer. "They attacked the women?"

"Those wounds aren't self-inflicted." Harold paused and moderated his tone again. "They came for me, but the women would have been an encouragement. Our women don't think that they are property so they fought. Use your glasses on the bodies in the street. The ones being laid out properly."

There was a long pause, then an obscenity. "Those are women. Girls! A child! They've been chopped to bits. They're bloody animals!" The officer whirled to look at the sergeant, who straightened his face. "Couldn't you have done anything?"

"Not allowed to go outside the zone, sir. When the shooting and screaming started it was all inside the compound, in the dark. We might have been able to help if the attack had been from outside or in daylight?" Sarge looked at Harold, not the officer, and Harold nodded that he understood. The Army simply couldn't help even if they wanted to.

"I damn well hope you do. If there's an attack on civilians from outside I mean." The lieutenant turned back to Harold. "So why did the anima... the intruders attack? I've been told this part is peaceful?"

"They found out who I was. The sergeant will explain. They came for an Army scalp."

"Then I'm damn pleased they didn't get it. There is still one problem, all the firearms that are apparently down there. You should hand them in." The officer's heart wasn't in that, because his eyes kept going back to the growing line of bodies. There were some very small shapes among the dead, where children had been caught in crossfire, especially in the tents.

"Then what happens when the bastards come again?" Harold paused to calm down again. "Most of it is small bore or old muskets. I'm hardly likely to start shooting at the Army, am I?"

"You really ought to hand any rifles in. How many have you got? You are ex-Army. What sort of rifles are they?" Suspicion had suddenly flared in the lieutenant's eyes.

"Not Army rifles. If I ever get one, I'll hand it over." Eventually, Harold added mentally. "I need at least one good rifle, in case another nutcase thinks it's funny to start shooting us from long range."

The officer thought for a moment, and then spoke to the sergeant. "Do you believe that?"

"Yes sir. This man can shoot, and I'd bet on him against any of the lunatics with a rifle. There was a very good rifleman shooting at the women in the fields some time ago, and this man killed him. It's in the old reports, sir, before your time." Harold thought that comment might be for him. Beware, newbie officer. "He's always been straight with us, and those are just ordinary girls down there. We see them up here sometimes. I hope they are all alive and well."

Harold answered the unspoken question. "The girls in the shopping party didn't all make it, sergeant, but they went down swinging. They all will if it comes to that." That part was true even if the girls weren't shoppers. All the girls bringing chips to the squaddies, the squadettes as they called themselves, were in the Riot Squad as well. Harold moved his attention back to the officer. "If that's all, I'd like to get back to my people. We need every pair of hands at the moment."

The lieutenant looked at the skinned knuckles, the plaster on Harold's cheek, the bandage showing through his slashed and bloody sleeve and the way he favoured one leg. "Yes. I've got all I need for the report." He hesitated. "I am truly sorry about the medic."

"I understand. No fraternisation." Harold pointed to the Union Flag over his house. "Even if we fight under the same flag."

The lieutenant had the grace to look embarrassed. "I suppose you are entitled to. I hope I don't need to come back, er, Soldier Boy?"

"Harold."

"Harold. Well goodbye Harold."

Harold got the hell out before he lost it again because that had to be a newbie. The lieutenant couldn't have been on the perimeter for long if he hadn't seen injured or dead women. Harold reckoned the lieutenant stayed about an hour, because after an hour and a quarter a squaddie came down the access road. That wasn't allowed, nor was leaving a conspicuous parcel in the road just outside the exclusion zone.

One of the surviving squadettes, Bethany, went to collect it. She blew the soldiers a kiss, the least they deserved for the First Aid supplies and wound dressings. The enclosed note actually apologised, pointing out that the dipstick was new. There were best wishes for the recovery of everyone down there. It wasn't signed.

By then a succession of people had pushed Harold towards his house. He should go and get cleaned up, see Mercedes, eat, drink and possibly sleep, while those who were fitter and less tired sorted some of this out. Then he could come back out and sort out the rest. One of those pushing, Doll, promised nobody would be going soft on the Hot Rods in the interim. Ever since gunfire had woken Doll up, laid in a guard house and tied hand and foot, she'd been looking for an excuse to kill someone. The rest who'd been given Trev's sleeping draught, apart from four, were also wide awake and in a foul humour. Two of the other four would never wake up again, while Gayle had been giving the last two oxygen and hoping for the best.

Sharyn spoke to Harold quickly and quietly as he came in, an update on Mercedes, Casper, the prisoners and the kids. His bed, the carpets and all the bodies had already been taken out, and a three-quarter bed had been brought from the girl's club for Mercedes. Harold took his food and drink through to his bedroom to sit with her. Mercedes seemed to be sleeping but he held her hand and talked quietly between bites, telling her what had happened. There were things he had to do, and he'd rest enough to get them done, but he promised to rest right here. Harold smiled as Mercedes opened her eyes. She tried to smile back, winced and slowly closed her eyes again.

Even as he smiled, Harold berated himself. He'd gone and done it again, let his guard down and cared for someone, and this time he'd actually thought she'd be safe. Worse, he really had given his heart to Mercedes, completely and utterly. He'd encouraged her and that had killed her. Sharyn had just told him that Lennie daren't even try to find out where the bits of bullet had gone, let alone dig them out. The paramedic didn't have the skills, and thought trying would just kill Mercedes quicker. Now Harold would spend as much time as possible with Mercedes, until she died. After that there'd be all the time in the world to sort out the other shit because he'd have no distractions, not ever again.

CHARACTERS IN MERCEDES FOR SOLDIER BOY

ORCHARD CLOSE ENCLAVE

Harold (Harry) Miller – aka Soldier Boy – 23 – ex corporal pay clerk CGC
Abigail – 25 – from the north.
Alfie – 18 – Probable orphan since his Mum disappeared. Living with Betty.
Alicia – 24 – small woman who retreats into herself.
Barry – 64 – Ex firefighter – ran from Geeks with granddaughters – designs bombs
Bernie – 29 – Bomb maker (under instruction) – Sal's 'Roger Rabbit'
Berry – 19 – daughter of Nigel. Taller, stronger, and also a brewer.
Bess – 22 – Ex- girlfriend of gangster, now Matthew's girlfriend
Bethany – 22 – Gnome Sweet Gnome
Betty – 62 – Oldest woman in the 'coven' – an original Orchard Close resident
Billy – 19 – resident of flats
Casper – 23 – big well-muscled gay man who becomes Harry's friend
Celine – 28 – slim redheaded typist. Shy – pre-Crash rape victim.
Charlie – 33 – home appliance (washing machine) repair man.
Chris – 29 – fighter – came with Roy
Christopher – 30 – Gnome on the Range
Conn – 25 – short skinny man, prematurely bald
Curtis – 27 – short and stout, amateur gardener – Emmy's bloke, wounded, taken by Army
Daisy – 7 – Harold's niece – hyperactive
Doll – Dolly – 22 – Barry's eldest grand daughter
Elise – 14 – reclusive, traumatised refugee from
Elizabeth – 37 – from north – Pricilla's mum – still grieving for her son
Emmy – 24 – Jamaican – tall, well-built woman – Curtis's gartered wench, Tammy's mum
Faith – 38 – short stout woman with light brown hair. Toby's Mum
Fergie – 21 – outgoing, teases men despite having a girlfriend
Finn – 51 – Electrician – 'Agent 002' because of his pistol shooting
Gayle – 21 – Dental trainee and now Orchard Close anaesthetist

George – 44 – rabbit breeder. Maryam's hubby – refugee from General

Georgina – 10 – Zach and Olive's daughter

Hazel – 17 – orphan, 'adopted' Harold as a sort of uncle

Henry – 26 – refugee – heavy hammer man

Hilda – 44 – ex clerical worker, loves collating lists. Switchboard operator

Isiah – 37 – reclusive – ex telephone engineer

Janine – 37 – ex laundry assistant, now coven member/teacher

Jeremy – 21- from north

Jilli – 15 – Jillian, 'bought' from gangsters – musical genius

Joey – 9 – Pippa and Robert's son

John's Pat – 38 – from north – Philip's mum – devout Christian – starts a church

June – 40 – ex-trophy wife, now coven member/teacher

Kerry – 35 – Shy – Isiah's wife – seamstress and embroiderer

Lenny – 28 – Nearly qualified paramedic – pacifist

Lillian – 22 – tall overweight woman lives with Conn

Liz – 24 – 5' 11" slim, very strong – ex-metal artiste – now the artistic smith – non-violent.

Louie – 21 – Refugee from north

Louise – 32 – quiet – ex-internet graphic designer – gay

Maryam – 42 – rabbit breeder. George's wife – refugee from General

Matthew – 27 – red haired ex traffic warden – weak arm after being wounded.

Matti – Matracia – 20 – Barry's younger granddaughter.

Max – 22 – Experienced fighter – General overran enclave – one of Roy's men

Millie – 6 – refugee from General

Nathan – 21 – Experienced fighter – General overran enclave – one of Roy's men

Nigel – 44 – brewer, widower, Berry's dad

Olive – 32 – Zach's wife, Georgina's Mum

Patricia Elliot – 29 – Trainee nurse. First refugee to join Harold's group

Pat's John – 39 – from north – devout Christian – starts a church

Patty – 27 – demon knitter, and a Demon with her outsized crossbow

Pippa – 28 – Genius baker – lost a hand when shot

Pricilla – 14 – from north – Elizabeth's daughter

Rabbit Bob – 36 – Rabbit breeder with buck, Rocket Man – refugee from General

Rob – 39 – Short and portly Plumber – Susan's bloke

Robert – 29 – Pippa's husband

Rory – 4 – Abigail's son

Roy – 32 – Experienced fighter driven from his home by the General – twice. Brings 4 other fighters

Sal – 29 – blonde woman – original resident – Bernie's Jessica Rabbit

Seth – 25 – trainee brewer – wooing Berry

Sharyn – 28 – Daisy and Wills mother, Harold's sister – widowed

Stewart – Mr Baumber – 59 – was caretaker in flats before Crash.

Sukie – 7 – Suzie's daughter.

Susan – 34 – Rob's gartered wench

Suzie – 24 – Sukie's single Mum – her sister died in fighting – Asian

Tammy – 0 – Emmy and Curtis's daughter, born after Curtis taken by Army

Theo – 28 – fighter with Roy, refugee from General

Tilly – 19 – refugee – 'Omeless Gnome-lass'

Tim – 25 – Refugee with nothing but his fiancée, Toyah

Toyah – 22 – Refugee with nothing but Tim

Trev – Trevor – 34 – Radio repair man – electrical engineer – terrified of Barbies

Umeko – 19 – Asian girl rescued from Geeks brothel

Veronica – 17 – daughter of Isiah and Kerry

Violet – 1 – Abigail's daughter – first child born in Orchard Close

Wade – 24 – refugee – amateur carpenter

William – 28 – amateur mechanic – refugee from General

Wills – 5 – Harold's nephew

Zach – 35 – ex-office manager

159 residents – March Year 4

Abraham – 53 – older refugee from Murphies

Ant – Anthony – 25 – refugee from Murphies and ancient weapons buff

Beverley – 17 – refugee from Murphies, lumberjill

Edward – 5 – Eddie – Little Ed – Tessa's son

Fredrick – 39 – from Murphies. Good amateur carpenter

Gulab – 4 – Ruhika's daughter

Johan – aka Big Johan – 42 – over six feet, well-built man – popular with the younger children because of his daft jokes, songs and juggling

Kathleen – 35 – Fredrick's wife, Rosalyn's mum

Logan – 26 – refugee – Hammer swinging candidate

Martha – 19 years – refugee from Murphies – Annex riot squad

Nate – 18 – refugee from Murphies, lumberjack

Rihannon – 17 – refugee – Riot squad

Rosalyn – 13 – Fredrick's daughter

Ru – Ruhika – 22 – small feisty Asian woman – Gulab's mum – refugee from Murphies – sometimes referred to as Aneka Myrtyua – many deaths

Sorcha – 19 – refugee with a talent for engraving, and an engraving kit

Stephan – 33 – Carpenter, refugee from Murphies

Terri – 17 – refugee from Murphies – Riot squad member

Tessa – 25 – 'Bought' from Hot Rods, Edward's mum, pre-Crash friend of Harold's

Wamil – 27 – tall, quiet Asian woman from Murphies – odd keep-fit techniques

Total residents March – Year 5
322 including 71 Murphy refugees in tents

One acre can theoretically feed eight people if meat is from elsewhere.

Potatoes are a very good crop – food value vs. space

Orchard Close fields are now a strip over 1,500 yds. long x 700 yds. wide – over 200 acres, plus all the gardens inside the walls. Will grow enough for 400 residents despite still being inefficient.

OTHERS

Private Lionel Vaughn – soldier on the bypass – Rihannon's boyfriend

Dealer – salesman
David – bodyguard

The Bunker
Owen -Chairman – tall, greying, confident, old money
Boris – Foreign Office – Small, slim, dark-haired, wants to recruit best of city enclaves

Faraz – RAF liaison, wiry, intense, Asian.

Gerard – Youngest of the dozen UK Cabal leaders – transport incl. distribution of food

Grace – tall spare aristocratic grey-haired woman dealing with work camps

Henry – Portly, thick black hair and beard, in charge of farms. Wants to recruit 'best' enclaves

Ivy – Stout middle-aged redhead in charge of food storage and sale

Joshua – Army liaison. Spare, balding man

Keris – Falklands operation

Maurice -Spymaster, bland, unassuming, mousy-haired and medium size and build.

Vanna – tall Asian woman dealing with special facilities and private military forces

Victor – Navy liaison, smart, impeccably groomed career navy man

IN THE CITY

Hot Rods – ex car thieves – neighbouring gang to the south of Orchard Close

Cadillac – Caddi – gang boss

Big Mack – Mack -7' bodyguard – named after trucks

Bug – Bugatti – full gang member

Cooper – Mini Cooper – second in command

Charger – full gang member

Chevy – full gang member

Dodge – full gang member

E-Type – ET -full gang member

Roller – full gang member

Samuel – man with shotgun and a crippled hand

Mercedes aka Killer Queen – 18 – only female who is a full gang member

Lada – probationary gang member

Yugo – probationary gang member

Truck – probationary gang member

Fantasia – 17 – woman forced to lure men into debt

Pete – 18 – Tessa's brother, sucked into debt

Spanky – ET's woman

Virginia – Roller's woman

GOFS – Gods of Fire and Steel – gang to the west
Gofannon – gang boss
Vulcan – senior gang member – warchief
Wayland – superb blacksmith
Hephaestus – Heff – senior gang member
Ogou – senior gang member
Cyclops – senior gang member wears goggles to protect spectacles
Cy – GOFS soldier
Brighid – GOFS woman
Henrietta – 'Head Girl' – Gofannon's woman

Geek Freeks – ex- shop assistants – gang to the north
Hawkins – gang boss – senior manager
Darwin – manager – (senior gang member)
Einstein – manager
Galileo – manager – inventive mechanic – creates superb crossbows and
   onagers
Marconi – manager – radio specialist
Nobel – manager – chemistry student
Tell – aka William Tell – gang bowyer & archer
Wellington – manager – warchief
Ly Thien or Thien – young Vietnamese woman now Wellington's com-
   panion
Mathias – Geek soldier

Barbie Girls – all-female gang beyond GOFS – based in 'Beth's' a shopping
   mall
Original gang were a group of prisoners who escaped during the Crash
Malibu – Senior Barbie leader – ex prisoner
Christie – Barbie leader – African ethnicity with big Afro and short blonde
   wig – ex prisoner
Ken – Barbie leader – Large and dresses as a man – warchief – ex prisoner
Chandra – Elite – Asian – wears two narrow curtains as a dress laced up
   sides – ex prisoner
Cherry Pie – Elite – Heavily tattooed – dresses as American farm girl – ex
   prisoner

Beach Beetch – Elite – genuine blonde (allegedly) – leather swimsuit – ex prisoner

Zahara – new Elite, mixed ethnicity – bright colours, big Afro, short blonde wig

Ski – 18 – new elite – wears a bobble hat and ski pants.

Vinnie – Barbie fighter, bought Splash

Splash – Staffy X bitch sold to Barbies

Maggie – Dobermann X bitch named after Maggie Thatcher

Fred and Ethel – only two gay men in Beth's

Pink Panthers – Male gay gang who wear pink underwear over their clothes as a 'uniform.' Based in a department store and a Victoria's Secrets lingerie shop.

Ferdinands – in American Football stadium – influenced by Mad Max films

Bull – leader – overweight – a bad look with skin tight pants.

Snoop – coach (lieutenant) – big muscular black youth

Slash – coach

Scarface – coach

Trainspotters – border the city centre with large park and trees. Wear anoraks

Franco – leader with red dreadlocks

Generals – Gang to the north across the flood. Allied with Bloods and MiB

The General – Leader – champion strategic games player. Ambitious.

Patton – big, burly, leads the General's fighters, gang boss of the Bloodsuckers, the Bloods

Hannibal – Patton's second in command of the Bloods

Julius (Caesar) – Patton's second in command of the more disciplined fighters

Rhys – spymaster, possibly a Cabal agent

Bloodsuckers – Bloods – Mixed race gang who file canines, notoriously savage assault fighters. Make up over half of The General's troops.

MIB – Men in Black – Elite wear black suits and shades. Salvaged a large number of Army police automatics and ammo from the City centre after the massacres.
Branson – Leader
Jones – senior MiB
Scrooge – senior MiB

Professors – mixed race and mixed sex leaders – originally from the University
Prof – Leader – old professor in a suit and robe
Celeste – Dance teacher
Chad – Rugby team captain, now leads fighters

Benny's Boys – gang next to the Professors, between them and the Mart
Benny – gang boss

Bargees – steel houseboats – surrounded by old canals. Have refrigerated van, sell fish
Skipper – gang leader
Smiley – senior member
Goldie – fighter

SIMs – democratic commune – use accurate short-range rockets for defence.
Bert, Julie, Maisie – rocket makers
Keith – fighter
Michelle – leader of the bug-out
Stevie – squad leader

Baggies – gang South of TesdaMart, ex-football hooligans. Wear black and white stripes.
Boing – leader
Throstle – elite

Murphies – wear a shamrock – gang west of Caddi
Paddy – dead leader
Niall – lieutenant, possibly the new leader

Precinct Nineteen – enclave led by ex-police – West of Motorway – use shortened ID numbers

Sarge – Three-Three – retired police sergeant – now the leader

Sergeant Koos – One-Five – senior fighter, ex police firearms squad

David – Six-One-Three – constable leading a squad of ten

Javed – Two-Two-Nine – constable leading a squad of ten

Simeon – Eight-One-Four – constable leading a squad of ten

Benny – Five-One-Eight – marksman

Sam – Two-Seven-Seven – marksman

Sue – Sarge's granddaughter

Barbarians – very violent gang to NW of city

Conan – leader. Physically very big and strong. Bearded, paranoid, abusive, keeps a 'slave.' Ambitious, wants to conquer the city

Garth – Warband leader

Sylvester – Conan's spymaster, possibly Cabal agent

Catherine – woman who remains defiant even after being, targeted and abused by Conan

Keepers – based in Dudley zoo – defend themselves with tranquilliser darts that kill

Teddy – ex manager of gift shop

Imogen – ex under-Keeper

Inga – Flamboyant ex tropical bird keeper

Stephanie – ex big cat keeper

Takato – refugee who brought firearms (ex big-game hunter)

Sutton Park Alliance – 9 gangs – based around big park in North of city

Odin – leads the Vikings

Angel – leads the Valkyries

Hangaku – leads the Yakuza

Headmaster – leads the Hard School

Shiner – leads the Skins

'Chelle – Shiner's 'wife'

Frenchy – 'French' mistress, Hard School

Jer and Asif – ex wildlife wardens in Park

Nosy – defeated gangster with long facial scar – given a chance to live because he protected women

The Last Prophet and the Children of Cain – rapidly growing gang of religious zealots, close to Sutton Park.

Cyn Palace – 5 gang alliance around school playing fields in NW of London

Sinner and Sin – Tall muscular blond man and redheaded woman who lead the Sinners. Based in a library, Sin Palace, controlling school fields, now a farm.

Preacher – leads enclave, C of E vicar – his services are now multi-denominational

Imam – leads enclave, genuine pre-Crash Islamic religious leader

Kermit – short, stocky, black leader of the Muppets

Eli – tall, thin white gang leader

Nita – The Sinner's librarian, a founder member

Marcie – ex prostitute, founder member of the Sinners

The Reivers – 278 survivors from the massacre of Glasgow

Bruce – leader – ex Black Watch

Angus – ex Black Watch – left a wife and three bairns dead in the snow

Maeve – one-armed woman who is quartermaster

Hamish – fisherman – trying to organise anti-aircraft defence

Lisa – vengeful wetsuit swimmer

Klaus – Oberfeldwebel Klaus Huber, sniper, ex German Army refugee who is earning a home for his daughter by fighting for the UK government (the Cabal)

Stilus gladio fortior – The Pen is mightier than the Sword
Si tamen habes in gladio? – But if you also have a Sword?

This ends Book Four of
The Fall of the Cities.

Find out what happens next!

**Book 5
will be available soon!**

VANCE HUXLEY

Vance Huxley lives out in the countryside in Lincolnshire, England. He has spent a busy life working in many different fields – including the building and rail industries, as a workshop manager, trouble-shooter for an engineering firm, accountancy, cafe proprietor, and graphic artist. He also spent time in other jobs, and is proud of never being dismissed, and only once made redundant.

Eventually he found his Noeline, but unfortunately she died much too young. To help with the aftermath, Vance tried writing though without any real structure. As an editor and beta readers explained the difference between words and books, he tried again.

Now he tries to type as often as possible in spite of the assistance of his cats, since his legs no longer work well enough to allow anything more strenuous. An avid reader of sci-fi, fantasy and adventure novels, his writing tends towards those genres.

www.ingramcontent.com/pod-product-compliance
Lightning Source LLC
Chambersburg PA
CBHW071329020726
47502CB00001B/20